FAR FROM MY
NATIVE SHORE

BY THE SAME AUTHOR

NOVELS
Bridles Lane (West Country Trilogy #1)
Hills of Silver (West Country Trilogy #2)
Wild Light (West Country Trilogy #3)
The Devil and the Deep Blue Sea

SHORT STORIES
Moonshine (West Country Trilogy Prequel)
Goldfields: A Ghost Story
The Dutchman
Afterlife

FAR FROM MY
NATIVE SHORE

A COLLECTION OF AUSTRALIAN HISTORICAL
NOVELS

JOHANNA CRAVEN

www.johannacraven.com

ISBN: 978-0-6451069-9-2

CONTENTS

ONE OF US BURIED   1

FORGOTTEN PLACES   265

PLAYING THE GHOST   503

ONE OF US
BURIED

PART ONE

I imagine I can still see the blood on my hands. Perhaps my fingers are forever stained.

I hide my hands in the folds of my skirts. Focus on the rhythmic clack of footsteps against stone.

I am surrounded by men, as I was the day I arrived in this place. And just like that day, there are soldiers in red coats, convicts, settlers. Englishmen, Irishmen and me, the lone woman. We all step into the courtroom together, though we are anything but equals.

My mind is on the distant sigh of the sea, on the pearly afternoon light, on the wall of birdsong that comes before evening. These things have been part of my world for the past two years, but only now, with my end approaching, am I coming to see their beauty.

They sent me to this place, this sun-bleached colony at the end of the world, to pay for my crimes; to weave cloth, to populate this land with my descendants.

But there will be no descendants. No more cloth, no more birdsong, no more light.

For there can be only one verdict. My bloodstained hands will see me to the gallows. How can I pretend to be surprised? I knew from the start I would never leave this place alive.

CHAPTER ONE

Penal Colony of New South Wales
1806

The land was a shadow breaking the horizon. An illusion, surely. I'd begun to believe the sea was without end.

Creaks and groans and rattles of the ship. I felt the shoulders of the other convict women bump up against mine.

The water came at me before I'd readied myself. Seamen upended buckets over our heads, to a grizzled chorus of cursing. I wrapped my arms around my chest as the water turned my thin shift transparent.

"That's it," laughed one of the sailors, as we tried to clean our grime-caked bodies with grime-caked hands. "Make yourselves presentable." And then more laughter, as though he, like the rest of us, knew any chance we had of making ourselves presentable was long gone.

I shivered. Here, on the outskirts of our new life, the wind was cold, though the air held a lingering warmth. The scratches Hannah Clapton had made on the bulkheads told us it was mid-April; autumn, apparently, here at the bottom of the earth.

I looked out across the sun-streaked water, watching the edges of that land sharpen. My lips parted and I tasted salt on my tongue.

Dire as conditions were on the *Norfolk*, they had become familiar. The fortnightly wash was not unexpected, nor was the speed with which we'd be shunted back into the convicts' quarters, or the beads of hot, black

1

pitch that seeped through the deck and dotted our bunks like remnants of plague. But the land awaiting us was utterly unknown.

Back down below, the stench swung at me; a soupy haze of bodies, and filth, and inescapable damp. The few minutes on deck had given me a chance to breathe. The iron grille slammed behind us, padlock closed tight. We elbowed and shoved our way to the pile of trunks against the bulkheads, hunting for our belongings amidst the dark roll of the sea. This was our chance, we knew, to escape the mythical factory for women and serve our time as housemaids, or cooks. Perhaps a settler's wife.

We'd been permitted to bring one small trunk on the voyage. And while many of the women had brought nothing but the clothes on their backs, I'd carted along my best worsted gown, along with woollen stockings and a pair of gloves I'd lost just days out of England.

On the ship we'd been given clothing for our new life: two sets of shifts and petticoats, a linen cap and apron each, matching gowns – one blue striped, the other the colour of milky tea.

I pulled my trunk out from the bottom of the pile. There was my apron, my striped dress, a shift that had become sweat-stained and worn.

My worsted gown was gone. I stared blankly into the trunk, as though I might will it to reappear.

"All right, Nell?" Hannah Clapton asked from behind me.

I nodded stiffly, though I felt anything but all right. The ship was lurching violently, and the world was lurching with it. The unknown land was approaching and I couldn't find my gown. I'd convinced myself it would be my ticket out of the factory. My way of making myself presentable. I felt a wave of deep panic.

Hannah gave me a wry smile. "We'll be off this cursed ship soon at least." She tucked lank, grey-streaked hair beneath her cap and tried to bash the creases from her skirts.

"And then what?" I asked, still staring into the trunk. The unfamiliarity of what was next was tying my stomach in knots. Somehow, having to face it without my gown made it worse.

Hannah had no answer for me. Not that I'd expected one.

I took the striped flannel dress and petticoats from the trunk and tied my underskirts over my wet shift, fighting the elbows of the other women. Like all the clothing the Navy Board had issued, the skirts only reached halfway down my shins. I was unsure if it was a deliberate attempt to shame us, or ignorance on the part of the Navy Board. I buttoned my dress with unsteady fingers.

In the pale, hatched light of the convicts' quarters, we were identical creatures: long, loose hair and striped skirts, skin so thick with dirt the seawater had done little to clean us.

"Would you look at us?" I said to Hannah. "No man could ever tell us apart. What does it matter which one of us they choose?"

A faint smile curved in Hannah's round cheeks. "They'll be able to tell you apart, Nell. Ain't no worry about that."

I smiled wryly. She was right, of course. My fiery hair had never allowed me to hide, nor had the inches of height I had on most women. Perhaps blending into a crowd was a little wishful thinking.

I shoved on my cloth bonnet. Seawater trickled down my neck, but my skin was still velvety with grime, hair stiff as tarred rope.

I could feel the ship slowing, turning, groaning. Heard the roar as the anchor slid from its hawser and rattled down to the sea floor.

Movement in the men's quarters on the other side of the bulkheads. Shouted orders from the sailors. And a barrage of footsteps as the male prisoners were corralled onto deck.

I stood bedside Hannah at the foot of the ladder, staring up at the thin streams of sunlight outlining the hatch. My gaze darted around for anyone wearing my gown. In spite of everything, I couldn't let the damn thing go.

And then I was on deck, my new home folded out before me, and all thoughts of the gown gone. New South Wales was vast and bright; cracked mudflats straining for the water beneath high clouds and a sky almost violently blue. The sea swept in between jagged nuggets of land, tiny islands dotting the bay. The harbour swarmed with movement; bodies darting in and out of harbour taverns, women in coloured gowns who looked like they'd been plucked directly from Mayfair. Men chained at the ankles to one another hauled wood along the mudflats, the scarlet coats of the soldiers stark against the prisoners' bleakness. Behind it all, untameable forest; brown and green and thick with shadow. Eighteen years of colonisation, it seemed, had made little more than a dent on the place. Warm wind blew my hair across my cheek, bringing with it peals of laughter, shouts of men. A scent of sea, of sweat, of a land that felt raw and rugged, caught halfway between horror and inescapable beauty.

A crowd of men was waiting on the docks; settlers, emancipists, soldiers. At the midshipman's signal they charged up the gangway onto the deck of the *Norfolk*, seeking cooks, seeking housemaids, seeking wives.

We stood in line, blue-striped skirts after blue-striped skirts, silently awaiting inspection.

"Officers first," barked the naval lieutenant who had overseen the fortnightly dunking. And the soldiers were upon us. *Click click* went their boots. Their eyes raked over us like we were stock in a shop window.

I understood. We were a precious commodity here. Precious and vital. Despite our grimy skin and light fingers, the colony would die out without us.

"Right here, sir," Hannah belted out, as a pink-cheeked soldier strode past her. "Whatever it is you're looking for, I got it, you'll see."

One of the sailors clipped the back of her head to silence her.

The men took their cooks, their housemaids, their wives.

They did not take me.

Though I did not want to be dragged from the ship and turned into a stranger's wife, I couldn't help a pang of bitterness. What was wrong with me? Was it my too-short skirts, or the crude colour of my hair? The freckles on my cheeks my governess had always urged me to cover with powder? Would things have been different if my gown had not been stolen? Perhaps.

Or perhaps somehow these men knew I was not well suited to being a housemaid. Even less suited to being a wife.

Us left-behind women were led from the ship and herded along the wharf that rose from the murky plane of the mudflats. Six months at sea and the ground was lurching beneath me. I felt unsteady on my legs as though I were a child just learning to walk.

We were led to a long log barge that knocked against the dock with each inhalation of the sea. A crooked shelter rose from the middle of the vessel like a misplaced turret.

I watched the waves spill over the edges of the barge. Such a thing was not seaworthy, surely. I had seen, had felt the power of the ocean; had witnessed the way it could toss ships and make men disappear. It would swallow a raft like that in one mouthful.

Hannah stopped at the front of the line, the rest of us dominoing into the back of her. "No," she said. "I ain't getting on that. I ain't. Not a chance."

The soldier at her side jabbed her in the shoulder with his rifle and she stumbled forward, landing on her knees on the barge. It seesawed on the surface, a swell of water gusting over it. One by one, we stepped on behind her. And before I could reconcile myself with the feel of solid earth beneath me, we were back on the water.

The barge, thankfully, did not take us to sea. Instead, the waterman guided it down a wide, dark river, where the water became coppery and trees hung above us like ghosts. Bronze light shafted through the branches, banks of thick wilderness swallowing the specks of civilisation scarring Sydney Cove.

I hugged my knees, watching coloured birds swoop down and ripple the river. The sound from the forest was unending; musical trills and discordant birdcalls, within the constant sighing of trees and water. My senses felt overloaded.

There were fifteen women crammed onto the raft, watched over by two marines and the burly, bearded waterman. But our humanity seemed insignificant. I felt as though we were the only people left on earth.

We were to be taken to the factory for women in Parramatta, I knew, but what was that but a name? It seemed impossible there could be any civilisation among this endless wild.

For the first time, I began to truly appreciate the abrupt turn my life had taken. Somehow, tucked away within the confines of the ship, I had managed to block out the reality of it. Perhaps a part of me had believed that when I finally set foot on solid ground again, I would be back at the docks in Woolwich. I'd never known any home but London, so how could my mind fathom this boundless forest and this quicksilver river and the impossible stretch of the sky?

When the last of the light was sliding away, the waterman tied the barge to a chalky tree trunk at the river's edge. He disappeared into the shelter in the middle of the vessel and returned carrying a flask of water and a loaf of bread. He passed them among us.

Surely we weren't to stay here the night. Not with trees all around us and nothing overhead by sky. The meagre shelter was barely big enough for a single person to stand.

In the corner of the barge, two women sat bundled in the thin grey blankets we had slept under on the *Norfolk*.

"Would you look at that?" Hannah said, jabbing a finger in their direction. "Don't I wish I were smart enough to have done the same."

I hugged my knees. The thought of bringing my blankets with me had never even crossed my mind. What kind of savage place was this, where we were not even to be given bedclothes? I forced down a mouthful of bread, the anxiety in my stomach leaving me with little appetite.

The waterman leaned back against the shelter, blowing a line of pipe smoke up into the darkening sky. The soldiers sat side by side on the riverbank, chuckling between themselves. One crunched on an apple and flung the core into the trees. The baby born on the voyage mewled in his mother's arms.

I wondered distantly at the time. The sun was slipping below the horizon, but in this strange place, I had no thought of whether that made it ten in the evening or three in the afternoon. Time seemed insignificant. A construct of men trying to tame an untameable world.

As the darkness thickened, a chaos of shrieking pressed against us. Birdsong, I told myself, but in this violent wall of sound, there was not the barest hint of musicality. The river lapped up against trees that seemed to grow within the water, their gnarled, bare branches eerie in the twilight.

And then there were stars; an endless brilliance lighting up a deep black and purple sky. I lay on my back with my spare clothing in a cloth bag beneath my head, staring up at the crescent moon that hung above the treetops. Lying there in the cradle of the river, I could give no form to the shape my life was to take. It hardly seemed to matter. Against the vastness of this place, what was I but an insignificant scrap? And with each minute I spent here, I was coming to see that, as a discarded woman bound for the factory, the shape my life would take mattered less than anything.

CHAPTER TWO

"It will readily be admitted by every impartial observer ... that there is no class of the community [that] calls more earnestly for the attention of the state than these unhappy objects, who have from various causes and temptations, departed from the paths of virtue and forfeited their civil liberty."

Rev. Samuel Marsden
A Few Observations on the Situation of the Female Convict in New South Wales
1808-1817

By dawn, the barge was carrying us back down the river. My back was aching from a night on the uneven logs, my skin a mosaic of insect bites. I'd managed a few hours of broken sleep, punctuated by images of creatures in the dark. I couldn't tell if they had come from my dreams or reality.

Bend after bend, the river swept onwards, the waterman's oar rising and falling, rising and falling. Just as I was beginning to believe it would go on forever, the wilderness broke.

A riverside tavern. A sailboat tied to a narrow jetty. And then a cluster of mud huts and farmland.

Parramatta.

A row of redcoats was waiting on the riverbank to meet us, rifles held across their chests. How many? Six? Eight? Ten soldiers with their weapons out, ready to greet a barge full of women. Their message was clear; we were prisoners. Step into line or come to regret it. But there was something oddly defensive about the soldiers' gesture. I couldn't help but feel as though those rifles offered them a little protection against everything that raft of women represented. Protection against allure, desire, temptation.

The redcoats peered at us as the raft bumped against the wharf, sizing us up like the men had when they'd climbed aboard the *Norfolk*. The look in their eyes told us we were both nothing and everything. A commodity to be coveted, bartered, perhaps even feared.

The tallest of the soldiers stepped up to the waterman, exchanging words I couldn't hear. He looked out across the barge at the new arrivals. I lowered my head, cowed by his presence, shame tugging my shoulders forward. I held my breath as I stepped past him onto the narrow wooden jetty.

I had not been expecting London, of course. But this place; what was this? Rusty plains of farmland pushed up against a tangled, grey-green forest, intercepted by a wide, dusty road that cut through the middle of the settlement. Huts dotted the farmland, presided over by the twin spires of the church. The morning sun was searing the tops of the trees, and I squinted in the brassy light.

Two of the soldiers strode past and I found myself taking a step closer to Hannah. She gave my wrist a squeeze as we followed the marines down the main street.

"Just keeping walking," she murmured.

And so I kept walking. For what else was there to do?

We were led to the government food store, a sandstone warehouse on the edge of the settlement. Soldiers turned through our indentation documents and scrawled our names on their ledgers. And here was our food for the week, wrapped into packages as small as our fists. I looked down at the bundle in my hand. I had little thought of what was inside it. But one look at its miserable size and my stomach was already rolling with hunger.

The factory was nothing more than two long warehouses above what

I would later learn was the men's jail. Up the stairs we went, herded by the soldiers who had lavished us with food.

It was the stench of the place that hit me first; the same filth and damp, and unbreathable air we had languished in on the prison ship. The floorboards were misshapen and dark, the blackened bricks above an unlit grate marking all there was of a kitchen. The place was a chaos of rattling looms and whirring wheels, punctuated by the shrieks of young children. Women hunched over spinning wheels, their babies in baskets, strapped to their backs, tottering across the muck and straw that carpeted the floor. The carding machines and looms sighed and thudded steadily, my muscles tensing as the jagged rhythm moved inside me.

Here came the superintendent, with his beak of a nose and cloud of white hair. Waistcoat straining against a puffed-out chest. He looked over us, clustered at the top of the stairs like lost sheep.

"Plenty of them," he said to the soldiers in a thick Scottish accent. "The men not like what they saw?"

One of the marines chuckled. "A bad bunch perhaps."

The superintendent led us into the second warehouse through a sea of blue-striped dresses. Some of the women peered at us, as though inspecting, calculating. Others kept their eyes on their spinning, seemingly oblivious to our arrival. What were we to these other women, I wondered? Potential friends? Rivals? Nothing more than an inconvenience?

The bad bunch of us was divided; some to the carding machines at the far side of the warehouse, others to the looms. I was shunted by the superintendent to an empty stool in front of a large spinning wheel, a sack of colourless wool dumped at my feet. I watched some beastly black insect crawl through the mass of it.

"See she knows what she's doing," the superintendent said to the woman next to me. Then his heavy footsteps clomped off towards the other new arrivals. I gave the young woman next to me little more than a glance.

"I know how to spin," I mumbled.

In truth, I'd had little cause to do such a thing in the past, but I didn't want to speak, or sit by that mangy sack of wool and be taught the ways of my new life. Tears were stabbing my throat, and I knew if I spoke again they would spill. For all its chaos, there was an empty, hollow feeling to this factory above the jail. A sadness that pressed down upon the place, wrought by the regret and grief of these striped-skirted women. I felt an ache deep within my chest that I was to exist in a place filled with such sorry creatures. And at the realisation that I was now one of them.

I shot a quick glance at the woman beside me, watching as she sat rolls of carded fleece on her lap and teased it onto the yarn that was gathering on her wheel. Yes, I thought, I remembered this from some long ago, barely accessible part of my childhood. An aunt's house. A spinning wheel in the parlour. I let the memory in my hands take over.

Slowly, I pedalled, then faster, eyes on the wheel to avoid even a glance at this horror that was now my life. At the feel of the wool sliding through my fingers, and the mesmerising cycle of the spokes before me, I felt my tears sink back below the surface.

An hour, perhaps two, and heavy footsteps sounded up the stairs, the rhythm a counterpoint to the clattering of the looms. Here was the soldier I had seen at the river. He strode across the factory floor towards the superintendent. Bent his head and spoke in a murmur.

His presence seemed to suck the air from the room. I felt my eyes pull towards him.

"No," hissed a voice beside me. "Don't even look at him."

The woman next to me at the spinning wheels was sharp-eyed and slender. A few years from thirty, I guessed; close to my own age. Strands of brown hair hung out the sides of her cap, the lines of her face precise and angular.

I frowned, taken aback by her brusqueness. "Who is he?"

"That's Lieutenant Blackwell." The woman's voice was dark, despite the gentle Irish contours of her speech. "He's the worst of all them lobster bastards. Full of hate."

Heat prickled my neck. But curiosity had me glancing back over my shoulder.

The lieutenant was somewhere between thirty and forty, I guessed. His hair was coffee-coloured and straight, slightly overgrown. A sculpted, faintly handsome face, but one that held neither kindness nor malice. There was a blankness to him. An emotionlessness. He looked too empty to be capable of hate.

His pale eyes shifted, catching mine. I looked away, my heart jolting. I pedalled the spinning wheel harder, focusing on the steady rhythm of the thing until the soldier's footsteps disappeared back down the stairs.

"I saw the raft come in this morning," the woman beside me said once my chaotic spinning had slowed. "Were your journey all right then? Did the most of you survive?"

I nodded. "The most of us, yes." We'd lost just four women on the journey; a number I knew enough to be grateful for. Their deaths had not been announced to us, nor were we allowed on deck for their burials. We'd just assumed them dead when they'd never returned from the surgeon's cabin.

"You're English," said the woman, making it sound like something of an insult. "Your ship come in from London then?"

I nodded.

She made a noise in the back of her throat. "What's your name?"

"It's Nell," I told her. "Nell Marling."

Her hazel eyes shifted, as though debating whether to trust me. "Lottie Byrne," she said finally, giving me a ghost of a smile. The warmth of the gesture filled me with relief. I hadn't realised how much I was craving kindness.

"You'll be all right, Nell," Lottie said, her eyes back on the wheel. "We do our best to look out for each other. There's no one else going to do that for us."

When dusk fell over the factory, bells rang and spinning wheels slowed. Women climbed from their stools and spread out around the edges of the room, claiming their belongings, their squares of floor, their children. Some, I saw, had brought their threadbare blankets from the prison ships. Others upended sacks of oily wool and curled up on them between the spinning wheels.

No beds in the factory, but room on the floor for perhaps thirty. Room for less than half the women whose hands were red and raw from weaving Parramatta cloth. No space for any of us who had just climbed off the barge. The superintendent herded us towards the stairwell.

"Where are we to go?" Hannah asked.

"I don't care. Find yourself lodgings somewhere in town."

A humourless laugh escaped me. This was a joke, surely. Find lodgings? With what money? All I had to my name were my shin-length skirts and a pair of old stockings.

I stepped blankly out of the factory, flanked by the other women from the *Norfolk*. I followed them over a rickety wooden bridge, back towards the main street. After the stench of the factory, the air smelled fragrant and clean. Birds shrieked, swooping and zigzagging through a pink and lilac sky.

I had been expecting bars and locked gates, like the cell I had languished in at Newgate. But my incarceration here was disguised as freedom. I saw then that there was little point in restraining us. In the fading daylight, the surrounding forest was a shadow. But I could see there was no end to it. The land was so vast it was dizzying. Only a madwoman would turn her back on the meagre security offered by the settlement.

I heard Lottie call my name. I spun around, achingly glad to see her.

"How do we go about finding lodgings?" I wrapped my arms around myself, wishing for a cloak or shawl.

She nodded to the street ahead of us. "They have lodgings."

Word of our arrival, it seemed, had reached the men of Parramatta. They stood on the edge of the street in clusters, reminding me of the men who had come trawling through the *Norfolk* in search of wives. But these were no well-dressed settlers, or soldiers with polished buttons. These men were grime-streaked and ragged, with scruffy beards and unwashed skin. Men, I knew with certainty, who had been sent here on His Majesty's pleasure. I recognised the dejected slope of their shoulders, the dulled anger in their eyes.

They called out to us. *Shelter and fire. Four shillings a week. Come on, lass, you can do no better.*

"We're to lodge with these men?" I coughed.

"Four shillings a week," Lottie said flatly. "For shelter and fire."

"Four shillings a week?" I repeated. "How am I to pay that?"

Lottie said nothing. My jaw tightened as the reality of the situation swung at me. We were that precious commodity of soft skin and curves. A novelty here in this land of men.

"They're willing to bargain," she said finally. "They'll give you a little coin as well as extra food and lodgings." She gave me a wry smile. "A fine deal."

"You do this?" I asked. "Sell yourself for a bed?"

She pressed her lips into a thin white line. I wondered if I had offended her with my sharpness.

I swallowed the sickness in my throat. "I'll sleep on the street."

"Don't be mad. You want to be torn to pieces by the savages?"

A hot ribbon of fear ran through me, but I pushed it away. I'd heard talk of the savages, of course; wild warriors who could throw four spears in the time it took to load a flintlock pistol. I'd convinced myself they were little more than a myth. The savages hiding in the dark was a fear I didn't have room for.

Head down, I began to walk. Away from the factory, away from the men. I had no thought of where I was going. I just needed to keep moving.

"Do as you like," Lottie called after me.

I closed my eyes, feeling a cold wind up against my cheeks. This place had taken my freedom. But it would not take my dignity. Not any more than it had already.

Huts of mud and bark lined the road, stretches of farmland behind them. I knew well I'd find nothing beyond the rim of the town but more of the trees and dark that had flanked us down the river.

"Where you off to, lass?"

I spun around to see a tall, dark-haired man standing a few yards behind me. His cheeks were pock-marked and leathery, thick stubble across his square jaw.

"You'll not find much out that way." His voice was rough and Irish. "Two hours to Toongabbie." He chuckled. "That's if the dragons don't get you."

I kept walking. "Leave me alone."

"I've a bed if you need it."

"No. I'm not interested."

He reached suddenly for my wrist and yanked me back towards him. "You think you're too good for us?" Breath stale against my cheek. "Look at yourself, lass. Just look where you are."

Fear shot through me and I pulled away. "Get away from me." I changed direction abruptly and strode towards the dark spires of the church. I heard the man's laughter behind me.

"You think a factory lass is welcome in a house of God?"

I began to walk faster. My cloth bag swung on one shoulder, carrying the creased mess of my spare dress. Animal sounds rose from the darkness; screeches, rasps, and the blessedly familiar lowing of cows.

In the falling dark, the church was empty. Through the narrow windows, I could see nothing but shadow. I pushed against the door, but it refused to move. Perhaps the man was right. Perhaps the factory lasses weren't welcome here. A locked door to keep out the lags.

I made my way around the back of the building, where shadows lay thick and allowed me to hide. The roof was slightly overhanging; perhaps half a foot of shelter. I leant wearily against the wall. Laughter floated out of a crooked hut I assumed was a tavern. The women from the *Norfolk* had disappeared, lured into houses for four shillings a week. I glanced into the street for the dark-haired man. Was glad to find him gone.

The sudden stillness struck me. When was the last time I had been alone? On the *Norfolk*, there had been not a scrap of privacy. In seven months, I'd not done so much as relieve myself without another woman watching. This sudden isolation felt disorienting.

My legs were aching, and my fingers stung from hours at the spinning wheel. Exhausted, I let myself sink to the ground.

The acrid stench of my food package hit me the moment I opened my cloth bag. I pulled it out warily, unwrapping the brown paper. The sliver of salt pork was discoloured and gnarled, the smell of it turning my stomach. I hurled it into the darkness. At the bottom of the package was a small cup of flour. Unspoiled, as far as I could tell. And what, I wondered, staring blankly down at my food rations, was I to do with a cup of flour and not so much as a candle flame to bake it into bread?

I wrapped up the package and set it back inside my bag. Curled up on my side and tried to find a little sleep.

CHAPTER THREE

"During the night these women spread themselves through all the town and neighbourhood of Parramatta, and [some] are glad to cohabit with any poor, wretched man who can give them shelter for the night."

Rev. Samuel Marsden
An Answer to Certain Calumnies
1826

At the spinning wheels the next morning, Lottie asked questions. Where did I go last night? Did I sleep? Who took me?

After rolling around in the dirt all night, I was too tired to speak. But her last question sparked something inside me. "No one took me," I said sharply. "I slept on the street is all."

"On the street?" she demanded. "What about the savages?"

"I didn't see any savages." I turned back to the spinning wheel. My eyes were stinging with exhaustion and Lottie's questions were getting under my skin. Hunger was gnawing deep into my stomach.

"So what then?" she said, after not nearly enough silence. "You going to spend your whole sentence sleeping in the street? Seven years without a roof over your head?"

I didn't answer. I couldn't contemplate the rest of my sentence. All I could think about was what I would do that night. That morning, I'd walked back up the stairs to the factory to find the door unlocked. Perhaps, I thought, I could creep inside at dawn and manage an hour of sleep on the staircase before the bells rang for the workday to start.

"What d'you do?" Lottie asked. "Thieving?"

I kept my eyes on the wool gliding though my fingers. "Yes. Thieving."

"And me," she said. "I asked a cobbler the price of a pair of shoes. He took one look at me and told me I couldn't afford them. So I pinched them."

I flashed her a smile. "Sounds as though he deserved it."

The superintendent stopped by the spinning wheel of a dark-haired woman in the corner of the room.

"Stand up," he said sharply.

The woman stood, arms held protectively around her swollen belly. The superintendent clicked his tongue in loud disapproval.

"Took him long enough," Lottie murmured. "Poor thing's about to drop right here on the factory floor."

"Who is the father of your child?" the superintendent asked.

The woman looked at him squarely. "Reverend Samuel Marsden, of course."

A snort of suppressed laughter went through the room. I felt a small smile on the edge of my lips.

Lottie caught my eye and chuckled. "Never in my life have I met a man with as many children as the good Reverend Marsden."

When I stepped out of the factory that evening, three soldiers were approaching the building. I recognised the tallest as Lieutenant Blackwell.

I put my head down and quickened my pace.

"You. Stop."

My chest tightened. I froze, looking ahead for Lottie, but she had disappeared. Two of the soldiers continued into the jail, but Blackwell took a few steps towards me, boots crunching on the road. Despite the dust, his uniform was immaculate, brass buttons gleaming and the braiding on his jacket inexplicably white. My heart began to speed.

"You came in on the *Norfolk*," he said. It was not a question. His voice was deeper than I had been expecting. I could feel it in my chest. "I passed

16

you this morning," he said. "Saw you sleeping behind the church. There's no need for that."

I felt a flush of embarrassment.

"I know the system here is not so easy for…" He hesitated. "New arrivals."

I almost laughed at that. Was he not part of the system, this polished officer in the New South Wales Corps? I kept my eyes on the ground, as though I might save myself from turning to stone by avoiding his eyes.

Somewhere between London and Parramatta, I had trained myself to not be afraid. I'd spent months in abject terror; a tearful mess in my Newgate cell, weak legged in the courtroom dock. I had no strength, because I'd come to believe it was my place to be weak. To let the men in my life carry me; to pick me up when I fell.

But one morning, in the dark and damp bowels of the prison ship, I came to see there was no one coming to rescue me. If I was to survive in this new life, I would have to find a way through my terror.

And so I steeled myself against my fear. Found some long-hidden part of me that vaguely resembled strength. The filth of the *Norfolk,* the mountains of ocean, whatever awaited me in New South Wales, I would find a way through it. Because my only other option was to die.

But standing in front of Lieutenant Blackwell, I felt that old fear returning. I felt unsteady around him, as though those expressionless eyes were prising away the wall I'd erected around myself to keep my terror at bay.

Full of hate, Lottie had said. But when I looked at Blackwell, I didn't see hate. I didn't see anger. I didn't see anything at all. And that, I realised, was what made me feel so damn unbalanced.

"I have shelter," he said after a moment.

I shook my head. "I know the price of shelter in this place."

"Four shillings a week," he said evenly.

"And what else?"

No response.

"I don't have four shillings a week." I put my head down and walked, making it clear our discussion was over.

That night, thunder rolled in across the mountains and the air thickened with approaching rain. Black clouds drained the colour from the sky.

I crouched with my back against the wall of the church. The awnings above my head were narrow and I knew they would do little to keep out the rain.

My stomach groaned. Hunger seemed to be seeping into every part of me, weakening my legs and tangling my thoughts. Tears pricked my eyes and I blinked them away. I couldn't find the energy to cry.

It was my empty stomach that led me to the tavern. Lamps flickered in the windows, and I could hear a muffled roar of laughter coming from inside. I had never been in such a place before, and I was dimly aware that I ought to have been nervous. But things had gone too far for that. What room was there for emotions as petty as nervousness when my life had been pared down to a thing of survival?

I pushed open the door. The place was cramped and noisy, bathed in hot orange light. Men in grimy shirtsleeves were clustered at the bar, and at the crooked tables dotted around the room. I spotted a few women among them; faces I'd seen at the spinning wheels that day.

I glanced around, my heart thudding.

What was I seeking? Money? Food? A man who would use my body as payment for shelter from the rain? I wasn't sure. I only knew that staying beneath the awnings of the church tonight would nudge me towards insanity.

I saw it then, on the edge of a table; a plate of roasted meat, two chunks of potato. A man sat with his back to it, howling with laughter, far too engrossed in the woman on his lap to bother with his supper. I edged towards the plate, as calmly as I could. Eyes down, cap pulled low. With my striped skirts and fiery hair, I knew I would draw attention. And before I could think, could hesitate, could judge myself, the potatoes were in my apron pocket.

The man whirled around at my movement. "Hey!"

He tipped the woman off his lap and made a grab for my wrist, but I was already darting towards the door. I clattered my way through chairs and bodies. Raced out into the street. I turned down the narrow alley beside the tavern and hurried into the thick darkness.

"Where the hell are you?" the man called. I could see the dark shape of him at the top of the alley. I pressed myself against the wall, holding my breath.

The sky opened suddenly, sending the man hurrying back into the tavern. I lifted my face upwards, grateful for the downpour. Water pelted the road, turning it to mud in seconds. I hurried back towards the church and pressed myself against the wall, trying to find shelter beneath the narrow awnings. Rivulets of water rolled from the roof and slid down the back of my neck. With each shard of lightning, pieces of Parramatta were lit up, picked out from the enormity of the surrounding forest. Rain drummed loudly against the earth, making the bush smell fresh and clean.

And then there was a figure a few yards from the church. Between the shafts of lightning, he was little more than a silhouette, but his height left no doubt as to who it was.

I turned away. I didn't want him here, with his *I have shelter* and his ludicrous pretence that I would not have to part with a piece of myself in order to claim it.

He came towards me slowly, footsteps sucking through the wet earth.

"I don't need shelter," I said, before he could speak. I gave an empty laugh; a laugh to keep myself from screaming. Rain ran down my cheeks. Ran down his cheeks. It pooled in the mud at our feet.

"And that is a humorous thing, is it?" he asked.

I didn't answer. In spite of his authority, I felt no need, or desire, to justify myself to this man. I took a step back, my shoulders pressing hard against the wall of the church.

He stood for a moment with his head tilted. He was still wearing his coat, but his head was bare and his gorget removed. Had he returned to his hut, then thought better of it, and headed out into the storm to rescue me? Why did the thought of that make me so uncomfortable?

"What is it that stops you from trusting me?" he asked. "Is it my uniform? Or is it the man inside it?"

"I don't have money to pay for lodgings," I said. I did not want to go into issues such as trust. I just wanted him gone.

"There are other ways to pay for lodgings," he said.

I gritted my teeth, shook my head. "Please leave."

He stood motionless, eyes fixed on me. "How can you sleep out here?"

"I'll manage," I said. But I was sure he hadn't heard me. The wild weather had carried my words away. A sense of complete and utter hopelessness pressed down on me. This storm, this land, this dark, it would swallow me.

Blackwell slid a hand around the top of my arm. "Come on now. You're being foolish."

My breath caught. "You're going to force me?"

But I walked with him, because what other choice was there? Take me to shelter. Take the last scrap of dignity I have left.

It had taken me less than two nights to crumble, to succumb to this twisted game Parramatta was playing.

For the first time since I arrived in this place, I let my tears fall.

CHAPTER FOUR

When we reached a small mud hut at the far end of the village, Blackwell let go of my arm. Beyond the building I could see nothing but darkness.

He opened the door and gestured for me to enter. I stood frozen in the doorway, wiping my eyes hurriedly with my wet sleeve. The lieutenant stepped awkwardly past me, his dark head inches from the roof.

"You're frightened," he said. "I'm sorry. I didn't mean to frighten you. I just wanted to get you inside. These storms are dangerous. They're far more wild than those in England. Last month a man was killed by a falling tree." He lit a lamp and turned to face me, his hollow cheeks darkened with stubble. Thick brown hair was plastered to his head, water dripping from the ends. The dancing light left shadows beneath his eyes.

I wondered distantly if he would chase me if I ran.

He took a step towards me and I inhaled sharply, but he just reached over my shoulder to close the door. I stood with my back pressed against it and glanced about the hut.

The sleeping pallet was narrow, pressed up against a wall, a wash basin beside it. A crooked brick chimney climbed into the thatched roof, a blackened pot hanging from a hook above the grate. Crooked shelves jutted out from one wall, lined with jars of potted meat and a bottle of liquor. A pile of books sat on the shelf below. A table was pressed into a corner of the room, the lamp flickering in the centre.

Water drizzled in through the cloth covering the small window, rain pattering in the puddles outside the hut. Thunder rumbled distantly. The storm was moving, I realised, drifting away from us, moving out towards the ocean. I could hear the faint burble of the river behind the hut.

"Please," I said huskily, "I don't want this." Every inch of my body felt taut. "Just let me go back out." When he didn't speak, I added, "The storm is passing."

Blackwell slid off his wet jacket and hung it over the back of a chair. "What's your name?"

I swallowed. "Eleanor Marling." I didn't know why I'd introduced myself that way. No one had called me Eleanor since my father had died.

Blackwell reached for the cloth that hung on a hook beside the table. He held it out to me. "Dry yourself."

I wiped my face and squeezed the water from my hair. I sat the damp lump of fabric on the table. It was streaked with the dirt I had wiped from my cheeks. Blackwell looked down at the bulge in my apron.

"What's in your pocket?"

Panic welled up inside me. Twice I'd broken the law. And twice I'd been caught.

I brought out the potatoes and sat them on the table.

"Where did you get those?"

I looked up at him. What point was there in lying? "I stole them from the tavern." I swallowed heavily. "My meat was rotten. And I've no way of making bread."

He nodded.

I gripped the edge of the table, my legs weak beneath me. Blackwell looked down at the potatoes.

"Eat them," he said. "You must be hungry."

I hesitated. Was I walking into a trap? Would he haul me to the cells the moment I took the first bite? But then my hunger got the better of me.

The lowest point of my life, I saw then, was not the moment I'd been arrested. Or sharing a shit bucket with fifty women at Newgate. It was this moment; here, now, eating a stolen potato, about to sell my body to the redcoats, with the filth of the factory clinging to my skin. I turned my face downwards as I ate, unable to look another person in the eye.

Blackwell took a loaf from the shelf and broke off the end. Held it out to me.

I chewed slowly, the dry bread sticking in my throat. But the food in my stomach took away an ache that had begun to consume me.

I could feel Blackwell's eyes on me. Could feel the heat rising from his body. I closed my eyes. I had eaten his bread now. The thing was done. I owed him compensation, and my only way of paying was to lie on my back and lift my skirts.

He opened a wooden storage chest beside the bed and took out a thin grey blanket. Laid it on the floor in front of the empty grate. "You'll sleep here."

I watched him smooth the edges of the blanket across the uneven dirt floor. What was this? If he was going to take me, I just wanted it over with.

But I went to it, that thin little blanket by the unlit fire. My sodden skirts tangled around my legs, dampening the blanket. I was barely warmer than I had been on the street. Blackwell crouched in front of the grate and laid a fire, despite the water drizzling down the chimney. I shuffled backwards and hugged my knees to avoid his arm brushing against mine.

The fire hissed and spat before taking. I watched a line of steam rise from my clothing. I was acutely aware of Blackwell's presence as he moved slowly around the edges of the hut, rearranging things that didn't need rearranging. The silence was thick and heavy. Rain pattered dully against the window.

He took a book from the shelf and carried it to his sleeping pallet. He slid off his boots and stretched out on his side, a blanket pulled to his waist and the book opened on the floor beside him.

A faint flicker of hope stirred inside me; perhaps he wouldn't come to me that night. But that scrap of hope felt too dangerous. I steeled myself against it.

I looked past him to the door. I could reach it without difficulty.

I could run.

But I didn't. What was keeping me there? Was it the warmth of the fire, or the roof over my head? Was it the faint flicker of curiosity I felt for this man? Perhaps I just wanted to see who would be first to break this silence.

I shivered hard and shuffled closer to the fire. Blackwell looked up from his book.

"Your clothes are wet," he said. "If you sleep in them you'll get ill."

His words were matter of fact. No threat, no lechery. But I understood them to be an order. I wrapped the blanket around myself and reached beneath it to unbutton my bodice, wriggling out of my dress and laying it beside the fire to dry.

Was he still watching me? I couldn't tell. I dared a glance over my shoulder. His eyes were on his book, but the muscles in his forearm were tense beneath his rolled-up shirtsleeves.

There were no more words. Just a thick, weighty silence and the crackle of the fire.

I see now, with painful clarity, that I should never have set foot inside that hut. I ought to have stayed beneath the awnings of the church and let the rain soak me through to my bones. But I didn't leave. Instead, I stayed with the blanket pulled to my chin, hardly daring to breathe. Waiting for footsteps to come towards me. Waiting for the moment that I lost a part of myself.

When I opened my eyes, dawn was flooding the hut and Lieutenant Blackwell's sleeping pallet was empty. I sat up, rolling the stiffness out of my shoulders.

I'd done my best to stay awake through the night, but exhaustion had finally pulled me down. It was a surprise to be woken by the morning light and not the lieutenant's breath on my skin.

I climbed to my feet and folded the blanket, hanging it over the back of a chair. My skirts were still damp and smelled of wet wool.

My eyes moved to the small wash basin sitting beside the storage chest. It was filled with clean water, a bar of soap and a washcloth resting on the rim. It was almost as though it had been placed there for me. I knew it foolish to think such a thing. I would likely be punished if Blackwell returned and discovered me splashing about in his washbin uninvited. But I didn't care. I could barely remember the last time my skin hadn't been caked in grime.

I plunged the washcloth into the water, scrubbing at my arms until they were red. I sloughed away at my face and neck, then lifted my skirts and worked the cloth up my legs, beneath my shift and across my stomach. I worked the soap suds over my body, inhaling their faintly sweet scent. Tears of gratitude overcame me. I had become so accustomed to the layer of filth on my skin, to my own stench of grime and sweat and saltwater. With soap suds gliding over my body, I felt fleetingly, preciously human again.

I looked back at the basin. I had left the water murky and brown. I carried it outside and emptied it into the vegetable patch behind the hut. Then I went to the river and refilled the basin, ready for Blackwell's return.

I stepped back out into the street, the door scraping loudly as I tugged it closed. Broken as my sleep had been, it was better than any I could remember. There was a clarity to my thoughts I'd not had for months.

I crossed the bridge and walked towards the factory, a wry smile on my lips. I tried to imagine the prisoners at Newgate walking obediently back down Giltspur Street to be let back into their cells.

As I reached the jail, I stopped abruptly. A man had a convict woman pinned up against the wall, driving into her with loud, rhythmic grunts. The woman caught my eye and I turned away hurriedly. I couldn't bear to look. Not at what was happening to her. And not at that haunted expression in her eyes.

On the *Norfolk*, I, like all the other women, had not been spared male attention.

A young ship's mate had ever so kindly chaperoned me back down below after we'd been let out to wash. Invited me to lift my skirts.

I shook my head, grabbing my dress from my bunk and holding it against my wet shift to shield myself. "Leave me alone." He could force me, yes, I knew that well. But why bother? There was nothing about me that warranted a fight. There were plenty of women who were willing. Talk rippled regularly through our quarters of girls who had earned a little extra favour by seeing to the sailors' needs. An hour of fresh air. A scrap of extra bread. A comfortable bed for the night.

"I can do things for you in return," the ship's mate said. "I'll call on your family in England. Give them news of you."

Later, I found out this ship's hand had promised to call on families from Glasgow to London with news of their wayward daughters.

I gave him a wry smile. "No one's waiting for news of me."

Foolishly, I'd imagined bartering with our bodies might end once we were back on solid ground. But I was quickly coming to learn the currency of this place. Coming to learn where the women in striped skirts fitted into the puzzle.

I hurried up the stairs, eyes down and my thoughts churning. I was acutely aware that I had not paid for my night on Blackwell's floor. Not in coin, not with my body. I couldn't fathom his intentions.

When the bells rang at the factory that night, what would I do? I'd been gifted a night of food and fire, and I knew myself lucky. Going back to that hut felt like I was tempting fate. But what was the alternative? Lottie was right; I could hardly spend my entire sentence sleeping in the street.

It was a decision for the evening, I told myself as I took my seat at the spinning wheel. I was coming to learn that the best way to survive here was to look no further than the moment I had in front of me.

Out the window that day I caught my first glimpse of the reverend. I'd heard talk of Samuel Marsden the day before; magistrate of Parramatta, assistant chaplain of the colony and, if the women in the factory were to be believed, father of every illegitimate child this side of Sydney.

Maggie Abbott, one of the most outspoken women in the factory, stuck up a finger as she filed past the window on her way to the carding machine. "Would you just look at that bastard? Strutting around with his chest puffed out like he were the king himself."

I glanced out the grime-streaked glass. I guessed Marsden close to forty; broad and flat-faced with pale, thinning hair. He swept past the factory, dark robes billowing, without a glance in our direction.

I took a sack of carded fleece from the corner of the room and carried it to my spinning wheel.

"Off he goes," Maggie sang as she made her way to the wheel beside me. "Potato on legs. And with all the mind of one too."

On the other side of her, Hannah gave a snort of laughter.

"Quiet, all of you," barked the superintendent. I hid a smile and tucked myself onto my stool.

Soft sobbing was coming from the woman behind me. I tried not to look at her. I wondered if Maggie's jabbering had been intended to block out the sound of the woman's grief.

I had become adept at ignoring another woman's tears. I'd been surrounded by crying women for the past year; tears in the cells at Newgate, in the convicts' quarters of the *Norfolk*, and now here at the factory.

Once, I had been empathetic by nature. Another's tears had tugged inside me. But here there was no place for empathy. Every one of us who'd been shipped out here was grieving; grieving for husbands, for children, for lovers left behind. Grieving for England, for Ireland, for the lives we'd had before. My own grief was striking enough, without taking on others' as well.

But this woman's tears were impossible to ignore. They turned into racking sobs I could feel deep inside my chest. When she got up to relieve herself, I turned to Maggie. "What happened to her?" I asked.

Maggie kept her eyes on her spinning. "Her little one got taken away today. Sent to the Orphan School in Sydney Town."

"A school? Is that so bad?"

Maggie looked at me as though I were half-witted. Her eyes were a brilliant blue, set deep in tanned, leathery cheeks. Dark corkscrew curls sprung out from beneath her cap. "Once a little one gets sent away, they got next to no chance of their mamas ever seeing them again." Her brassy voice dropped a little. I wondered if she were speaking from experience.

"Oh," I mumbled, not wanting to dig further. I felt an ache in my chest for the crying woman. Her plight reminded me why I had taught myself not to take on other people's pain. "How dreadful."

"Would you listen to you," Maggie crowed, "talking like a princess."

I said nothing. I could hear it, of course, the smoothed edges of my own speech up against the ragged phrases of the other women. I'd spent the six months of the voyage trying to roughen my words, but Maggie's comments reminded me I hadn't succeeded.

But I didn't want to stand out. Nor did I want to face the questions I knew would follow.

The woman's tears had dried by the time dark fell over the factory and we were sent back down the stairs. The air was thick and humid, and smelled of fragrant, passing rain.

I stiffened at the sight of Blackwell in the street outside the jail. Had he been waiting for me?

"You didn't eat this morning," he said, his voice low. "There was food for you on the table."

"I've no way of paying for food," I told him stiffly.

"You must be hungry."

I began to walk. My stomach was groaning with hunger, yes, but that was no business of his. I didn't want Lottie to see me talking to him. I couldn't bear for her to find out I had slept on his floor. I was surprised she'd not asked questions after I'd appeared at the factory with my skin scrubbed clean.

I could hear his footsteps behind me, sighing through the mud. "There's a bed for you, Eleanor."

I bristled at the sound of my name on his lips. Back in London, no man beside my husband would have dared call me by my Christian name. It was a cold reminder that I had sunk to the bottom of the pile. *Eleanor*, like some ash-streaked scullery maid.

I stopped walking. "What do you want for it?" I kept my head down, bracing myself for his answer.

"Housekeeping," he said after a moment.

A laugh escaped me. "Housekeeping?"

"Is that not to your liking?"

I swallowed, my gaze drifting over his shoulder to the crooked silhouette of his hut. Perhaps it was foolish to trust him. But how desperately I needed to believe I might earn myself a bed and fire just by sweeping a man's floor.

I hesitated. Blackwell stood beside me, silent and patient. I managed a faint nod.

"Good," he said shortly.

Inside the hut, the broom was resting beside the front door. I didn't remember it being there the previous night. Had he put it there in anticipation of my arrival? Had he known he could convince me to crawl back through his door? The thought made me inexplicably angry. But he had been right. Here I was.

Blackwell nodded towards the broom. "The floor needs sweeping.

And then please empty the grate."

I swept with my eyes down, losing myself in the rhythm of it. Sweeping an earth floor felt like a losing battle, but I was glad for something to put my mind to. Rainwater had seeped beneath the door, turning the floor at the front of the cottage to mud.

Blackwell hovered awkwardly in the corner for a few moments, his eyes following the rhythmic strokes of the broom. Then he stepped out into the night, giving me the space I craved.

Housekeeping, Nell? I imagined Lottie saying as I swept. *You believe he wants you for housekeeping?*

I was aware of my naivety, so perhaps that erased it. It was not blind optimism that had brought me to Blackwell's door, but desperation.

I swept that dirt floor, then scooped every last speck of ash from the grate. There was a part of me that believed if I worked hard enough, it might convince him that my shelter and fire had been duly paid for. Might prevent him from demanding more.

The dark was thick when the lieutenant returned. I wondered distantly where he had been. He looked at the swept floor, then at the empty grate.

"That's enough," he said. "You've been working all day." He nodded to the loaf of bread on the shelf. A monstrous ant was traversing the crust. "Take a little. Rest."

I broke off a small chunk of bread and hovered in front of the unlit fire, unsure what else to do. The hut felt too small for strangers. I chewed slowly, the bread coarse on my tongue. The crust was crisp and warm where I had sat it too close to the lamp.

I dared a glance at Blackwell. He was opening the jar of potted meat, his back to me. Would he come to my bed tonight, I wondered? There had to be more for him in this than a swept earthen floor that would become thick with dirt again before morning. The lid of the jar popped noisily.

I looked up at the sound of voices coming towards the hut. And then a sudden screech of fabric as a rock came flying through the cloth window. It thudded loudly against the bookshelf.

Blackwell snatched his rifle. "Get down."

I scrambled beneath the table.

"Did they hit you?" he asked.

"No." My voice came out breathless. "Who is it? The savages?"

"It's not the savages."

I heard yelling; mostly men, some women. Incoherent voices. English words? I couldn't tell.

Blackwell charged from the hut with the rifle poised. "Get the hell away from here," he hissed. His voice was taut and controlled, as though his anger, along with all his other emotions, was kept behind bars. I realised he'd not loaded the rifle.

"What'll you do, you *sasanaigh* murderer?" spat a gravelly Irish voice. "Shoot us in the street?" A cold laugh.

Terse, unintelligible words from Blackwell. He marched back inside and bolted the door.

I stepped out from beneath the table. "Who was that?" I asked shakily.

He leant the rifle up against the wall. Used his wrist to push a swathe of dark hair from his eyes. There was a moment of silence, as though he was debating whether to speak to me. "The rebels," he said finally.

"Who?"

He sighed heavily. "The Irish rebels. They rose up at Castle Hill in the north a few years ago. Tried to take Parramatta and Sydney Town. Overthrow the government and bring in Irish rule."

I wrapped my arms around myself, suddenly cold. "What was that they called you?"

Blackwell didn't look at me. "*Sasanaigh*," he repeated. "Englishman."

I nodded stiffly. But it was the other word that rang more heavily in my ears.

Murderer.

I looked down at the rock that lay beneath the shelf. "Why did they do this?"

Blackwell stared at it for several moments. "They're angry," he said. "They feel oppressed and abused. And I represent everything they hate." He picked up the rock and flung it out the torn window.

The muscles in my shoulders felt taut. It wasn't just Lottie who despised the lieutenant, I realised. Perhaps in my desperation I had been too dismissive of her warning. Perhaps I ought to have stayed beneath the awnings of the church.

"You can't leave," Blackwell said as I edged towards the door. "Not now. It's dangerous out there. The rebels are agitated. They'll likely go after you."

"Because of my English blood, or the fact I'm lodging with you?"

"Both."

I looked up at him, taking in his face up close for the first time. He was younger than I had first guessed. Little more than thirty, perhaps. I imagined that in England, his hair had been cut to his collar, trimmed within an inch of its life. But in this place, a raggedness had begun to creep over him, the way it had done to all of us. His hair tickled the top of his eyebrows, reached past his collar. His pale blue eyes were sharp and clear, but I couldn't see behind them. It made trusting him a difficult thing.

Outside, I heard loud laughter. I took a step away from the door. "And I'll be safer here with you?"

Blackwell held my gaze. "Do you think you won't be?"

I said nothing. Truly, I had no idea.

CHAPTER FIVE

"It would be a wise and prudent measure to bring up the rising generation in the Protestant religion, in order to remove that extreme ignorance and barbarism which constitute the natural character of all the lowest class of Irish Catholic convicts."

Rev. Samuel Marsden

A Few Observations on the Toleration of the Catholic Religion in New South Wales

1808-1817

I knew little of the atrocities taking place in Ireland, like I knew little of so many other things. My father had done his best to provide me with a sheltered upbringing; one in which I would be married to a gentleman and keep my eyes and ears closed to anything that might upturn my polished existence. Politics, my father liked to say, was no domain for a lady.

Nonetheless, I had caught word of the rebellion in Ireland some years back. I knew the Irish had allied with the French to overthrow the Englishmen who ruled their land. As an impressionable nineteen-year-old, I had panicked, sure the United Irishmen would gallivant across the seas and turn London upside down.

Father had laughed off my concerns. "This is why young ladies should not involve themselves in politics," he said, reaching across the supper table and topping up his glass with an enormous glug of wine. "Those witless fools have no mind to take London. I daresay their minds couldn't even fathom such a notion."

In London, I'd not known any Irish men or women. But sitting beside Lottie at the spinning wheels, I did not see a witless fool.

"I heard the rebels in the street last night," I said, careful to sidestep any mention of Blackwell.

Lottie made a noise in her throat, but she didn't look at me. I could tell she didn't want to discuss the matter.

"Do you know them?" I asked.

She shrugged, not taking her eyes off the spinning wheel. "Some of them."

"They want freedom," I said. "Is that it?"

Lottie looked at me then, her hazel eyes shining. "Aye," she said, with more sharpness than I had been expecting. "That's it. Freedom and respect."

"We all want those things," I said.

She snorted. "Your people have it."

I'd had no thought there might be an 'us' and 'them' between two lags sitting side by side at the factory. "Does it look like I have freedom?" I asked bitterly.

Lottie gave me a dismissive look that stung more than her sharpness. A look that said I wouldn't understand. A look that said I had no right to argue, or to have an opinion on the matter.

"They've taken everything from us," she said. "Even our God. You think we like spending our Sundays listening to your Protestant poison?"

"I'm sorry," I murmured, unsure of what else to say.

A part of me ached to ask her about the lieutenant. Ask her if she knew why the rebels had stormed his hut last night. Ask her what had happened at Castle Hill. The settlement was crawling with soldiers. Why was Blackwell the target of the rebels' rage? But then I would have to admit that I had crept through his door as his housekeeper. And that, I was becoming increasingly certain of, was something Lottie would not take well.

When dark fell and the spinning wheels stilled, we strolled out of our prison and wandered to the river. By now, I had come to understand that our punishment was transportation. Not incarceration.

There were plenty of men who came to join us at the river. Convicts, emancipists, free settlers, with liquor bottles in one hand and pipes in the other. They talked a lot, their shoulders pressed to ours and their bristly faces edging closer with each mouthful. Told us rum-scented stories about their farms and their houses and their hard-earned tickets of leave.

Just now need me a wife, they'd say.

It wasn't a difficult thing to find in this colony. Just that day, a settler had turned up at the factory with his marriage permit from Reverend Marsden. We'd lined up to be inspected, been given the chance to offer ourselves as wives.

The settler had left twenty minutes later, betrothed to Sally Quinn.

Being chosen as a convict wife, I'd learnt that day, was a thing to be celebrated. Once you'd signed yourself over to your husband-to-be, it marked the end of your time at the factory. Sally Quinn's settler was a loud-mouthed drunkard from what I could tell, but he'd saved her five more years of weaving Parramatta cloth. Tomorrow he'd be whisking her off to be mistress of a grand house in Sydney Town. Filthy and ragged though these men on the riverbank were, I was beginning to see they were the way to freedom.

The evening was warm, with parrots shrieking in the trees above us and bugs swarming the surface of the river. The sloping roof of Government House peeked out between the trees.

One of the wife-hunters climbed onto a log and squinted up at the row of dark windows.

"The governor in, Ned?" called Dan Brady, the man who had followed me on my first night in Parramatta.

Ned chuckled. "I think I see him there through the window. Eating his mutton with a finger raised to the poor croppies."

Brady leapt onto the log and bared his pasty white backside in the direction of the house. An unenthused chuckle rippled through the group.

I looked away, wishing for a mouthful of rum to dull my senses.

"Did you hear?" Maggie Abbott began brassily. "Tom Evans got caught stealing from the granary last night."

Lottie snorted. "Tom Evans is a bloody fool. How many times we seen him strung up for a flogging? He'll be off to the coal mines now, just you watch." She grabbed the rum bottle from the man sitting beside her. "He's a woman from the factory staying with him," she told me. "Only thing is he's got no way of paying her keep. Half the thieving in this place is lags stealing to pay their whores."

I hugged my knees, looking out across the darkening river. How precious us factory lasses were. Precious enough to steal for. Strange how something so precious could be treated with such disdain.

Lottie held the bottle out to me. I gulped down a mouthful, coughing as it seared my throat. The rum was terrible. Tasted like the sea had gotten through the barrel.

"Careful there," said the man beside Lottie. He was sharp-eyed and too handsome, with ragged, sand-coloured hair and a smile that wasn't entirely warm. Spoke with a liquored-up Irish lilt I had trouble understanding. "I'm yet to meet a *sasanaigh* that can hold their liquor." He reached over and took the bottle from my hands, to a chorus of laughter from the men around him. I felt my cheeks flush.

Maggie had introduced the man earlier as Patrick Owen, an emancipist who was seeking to sell his land for a plot in Sydney Town. He was loud spoken and sure of himself, with a constant flotilla of Irishmen around him, laughing at his questionable jokes.

Lottie's eyes followed him as he got up and strode towards the riverbank. He flung a stone into the river and sent water fountaining upwards. He looked over his shoulder and gave her a broad smile. She grinned.

"Patrick Owen?" I said witheringly. "Really?"

She shrugged.

"Sally's new husband is a free settler," I said. "You can do better than an emancipist."

"That's the thing, Nell," she said, watching Owen as he grabbed another stone and flung it into the water. "I'm not entirely sure I can." She gave me a wry smile. "Don't you know Irishwomen are as low as the blacks? So the good reverend says anyhow."

"Sally Quinn is Irish."

Lottie snorted. "Sally Quinn is all arse and tits. These things help." She traced a stick through the dirt. "Besides, it's not really about doing better now, is it. It's about getting out of the factory. I'd rather be an emancipist's wife than spend another four years weaving shirts for the lobsters." She looked back at Owen.

"It don't matter anyhow," she said. "Owen's got Maggie in his bed and she's got her claws in tight."

Dan Brady took his pipe out from between his teeth and blew a line of smoke down at me. "What did Blackwell want with you then?" he asked.

I stiffened. Felt Lottie's eyes pull towards me.

"I don't know what you're talking about."

"Saw you with him in the street yesterday," said Brady. "He after a bit of company was he? You tell him you're too good for him too?"

My cheeks flushed.

"If one of his kind were after my company, I'd give it to him," Maggie announced, planting a hand on her hip. "Earn myself a little sway over a powerful man. The Rum Corps controls everything in this place. Even the liquor."

I frowned. "What do you mean?"

Lottie tapped her fingernails against the side of the rum bottle. "The redcoats are the ones making all this. They got stills out behind the barracks. Their liquor's as good as coin in this place. Can buy yourself anything with it."

Maggie waved a finger at me. "That's what you want, girl. Believe me. An officer's attention. Ain't an easy thing to get. Most of them wouldn't dare let themselves be seen with our kind."

"Shut your mouth, Maggie," Lottie snapped. "She knows better than to go near that bastard Blackwell. Don't you, Nell?"

"Of course." I couldn't look at her.

Two soldiers marched past the river, heading towards the barracks.

"Fine work you're doing, lads," Owen sang, his words dripping with sarcasm.

His voice made the muscles in my neck tighten.

Sasanaigh murderer.

Suddenly I knew without a doubt that Patrick Owen had been at Blackwell's hut the previous night. Was he the one who had flung the rock through the window?

"Be quiet, Patrick," said Lottie. "We don't need you making trouble for us. Some of us still got to answer to the lobsters."

Owen chuckled, looking her up and down. "Who's making trouble?"

Lottie looked back at him for a long second. A smile flickered in the corner of his lips. And in swanned Maggie, scooping up Owen's arm and whisking him away from us in one smooth movement.

"Come on now, Patrick," she crooned. "Let's go, aye?"

For a moment, Owen kept his eyes on Lottie, despite Maggie's fingers crawling up his arm. He gave her one last hint of a smile and marched away from the water.

I stayed at the river until Lottie had disappeared into the hut of the man she was lodging with. I knew it only a matter of time before she realised I was no longer sleeping on the street. Only a matter of time before she began to ask questions.

When I stepped into the hut, Blackwell was sitting in a chair beside the crackling fire, a worn book in his hand. The scent of woodsmoke and eucalyptus was thick in the air.

He looked up as I entered.

"I'm sorry," I said. "I meant to be here before you returned, but…" I trailed off.

A faint frown creased the bridge of his nose. I could tell he was debating whether or not to reprimand me. This infant colony's idea of punishment was hazy. Neither of us knew the rules.

"There's meat for soup," he said finally, nodding to a bloodied paper package sitting on the table.

I nodded wordlessly, thankful he had not seen fit to punish me. I unwrapped the package and stared blankly down at the meat. I'd never cooked a thing in my life, and had little thought of how I might magic this slab of flesh into supper.

I hacked the meat into pieces and placed it in the pot with water and some limp carrots I'd discovered at the back of the shelf. I hung the pot carefully over the flames.

Blackwell stayed in his chair, reading. After the drunken chatter at the river, the wordlessness felt thick and heavy. I stirred slowly, eyes fixed on the pot, watching the meat darken as the liquid bubbled steadily. I was pleased to find it vaguely resembled soup.

"It's ready," I ventured, when much of the colour had drained from both the meat and vegetables. "May I eat some too?"

Blackwell put down his book and shifted his chair to face the table. "Of course."

I filled the bowls and set them on the table. Blackwell lowered his gaze and murmured a short prayer. I waited for him to begin eating before bringing my spoon to my lips.

The soup was watery and more than a little bland, but I felt my effort was admirable, given my complete lack of knowledge, and what I'd had to work with. I had no doubt I was eating an animal I had never even heard of.

Our wooden spoons tapped against the side of the bowls.

"There's no need to be afraid of me," Blackwell said finally.

"I'm not afraid of you." My voice came out softer than I had intended.

"Yes you are." He looked up at me for the first time. "Why? Because you fear I will come to you in the night?"

I swallowed hard, the meat sticking in my throat. That was a part of it, of course. But perhaps it was unfair to have such a fear. For three nights, he had not asked anything more of me than sweeping his floors and cooking his supper. Of that I was grateful.

"You're here as my housekeeper," he said evenly. "Nothing more."

It was the intimacy of this that frightened me, I realised then. For almost a year I had been crammed into jail cells and spinning rooms and the stinking convicts' quarters of the *Norfolk* with women on every side. These sparsely worded nights when it was just he and I alone felt foreign and hard to navigate.

But I didn't want to fear him. I wanted to believe Lottie's warning was misplaced. How much more manageable this place would seem if I had a safe haven to return to each night.

A sudden burst of wind made the cloth window drum and the roof rustle loudly.

"I ought to fix that," said Blackwell, as a triangle of bark glided down and landed in the middle of the table.

"Why do you not have convict workers?" I asked. "Men to tend to the garden and the like?"

"I prefer the solitude."

"Then why take me in?"

"Because you were sleeping in the street."

His answer made me feel strangely hollow. I didn't want him to have taken me in merely out of pity. I wanted him to see more in me than just another wretched lag. The thought was an uncomfortable one, and I was unsure where it had come from.

"I'm sure I'm not the only woman to have found herself sleeping in the street," I said.

He held my gaze. "I'm sure you're not. But as unfortunate as that is, I don't make a point of accommodating prisoners. I merely saw you as I passed by the church. You were clearly in need of shelter, and it seemed rather uncharitable not to offer it."

"I see." I hated being on the receiving end of his charity. Hated what I had been reduced to.

"If you are unhappy with this arrangement," he said, "you're free to leave anytime you wish."

I turned back to my bowl. I regretted raising the issue.

Blackwell took another mouthful of soup. "It's good," he said, after a moment of silence.

I managed a faint smile. Good, no, but I appreciated his kindness.

There was something about the civility of this; this act of sitting at a supper table, however crooked and rough-hewn, however foreign and ropey the meat. I couldn't remember the last time I had done something as refined as share a meal across the supper table.

Blackwell sipped the soup carefully from the edge of his spoon and I heard a laugh escape me.

"What's so amusing?"

"It's absurd," I said.

"What is?"

"This. Every bit of it. You, so careful with your manners; sipping your soup like you're at a gentleman's dinner party. And all the while we're sitting here in this mud hut with the roof falling down, eating heaven only knows what animal." I heard my voice get louder, bolstered by the awful liquor in my blood. "What point is there bothering with table manners when we're up to our knees in dirt like wild things? And," I said, dimly aware that I was making a scene, "you've never even thought to tell me your name. Am I worth so little I don't even warrant an introduction?"

He paused, his spoon hovering in mid-air. "I'm sorry," he said. "My name's Blackwell. Adam Blackwell."

I stuck a spoonful of soup in my mouth, embarrassed by my outburst. I couldn't remember ever speaking so openly, especially not in front of a man.

Finally, I dared to look up at him. And for a second it was as though the protective shell he hid behind had fallen away. I saw a flicker of a smile on his lips, a hint of warmth in his eyes. It caught me by surprise and I looked away hurriedly.

My eyes drifted to the book he had left on the edge of the table. "*The Vicar of Wakefield* was one of my father's favourites," I garbled, trying to take the conversation back to less hysterical grounds.

"You read?" he asked. There was a hint of surprise in his voice.

I nodded.

"If you wish," he said, "you may take it once I've finished. I know books are few and far between in this place."

His kindness emboldened me. "Why are you here?"

"Duty. Why else?"

"Well." I put down my spoon. "In London they used to say this place was an officer's dream. Land grants from the governor. Free labour. The freedom to choose a woman like we're fruit to be picked from a tree."

Blackwell raised his eyebrows.

"Isn't that why we were sent here?" I asked. "To keep all the lonely men company? To populate this place?"

He looked at me squarely. "You were sent here because you committed a crime."

I turned back to my soup. Found a chunk of gristle inside it. I scooped it out of the bowl and sat it on the table.

"This place could be better for you than England," Blackwell said.

I frowned. What did he know of my life in England? Who was he to make such judgments? I supposed he looked at me as the same as all the others. A street rat crawled from the Whitechapel slums. It was a fair assumption, I supposed. I'd heard all the stories, bleated out by those poor sorry girls I'd been crammed onto the *Norfolk* with.

A loaf of bread to feed my boys.

A cloak to keep out the snow.

Tales of pity.

But Blackwell knew I was a reader. And how many of those poor sorry girls from the slums had their letters? Perhaps my attempts to disguise my polished upbringing had been more successful than I'd believed.

Let him believe I too was a tale of pity. Bread pocketed from the market. A stolen cloak wrapped around my shoulders.

That was a far simpler story.

CHAPTER SIX

"Here," said Lottie as I made my way down the stairs into the jail yard behind the factory. She held out a small, misshapen pillow.

"What's this?" I sat beside her and Hannah on the patchy grass, a cannikin of lukewarm tea in my hand. The sun had vanished behind a cloud just in time for our afternoon break.

"Took it from old Bert's bed when he weren't looking," said Lottie. "Thought you could use it. Might make you a little more comfortable."

I shook my head, feeling a stab of guilt. After two weeks beneath Blackwell's roof, I'd still not found the courage to tell Lottie I was no longer sleeping on the street. "I couldn't."

She whacked me on the arm with it, making tea slop down the front of my dress. "Would you just take it, you madwoman? Bert won't even notice it's gone."

Maggie looked down at us from where she stood leaning against the wall of the jail. "Take it, Nell. She's right; old Bert's as blind as a bat. Everyone knows it."

"It's true," said Hannah, sipping her tea. "I saw him in the tavern last week asking some scrawny lobster for a dance." She winked at me. "The lad was quite pretty and all, but Bert would've got a right shock when he got him home."

Maggie laughed. "Look on the bright side, Lottie. Least he's too old and decrepit to get a child on you. When was the last time he managed to get it up?"

Lottie snorted. "Don't stop him from trying."

Maggie lifted her cannikin in a mock toast. "Good of you to take him off our hands, girl. You're to be applauded."

Lottie gave her a thin smile. "Ought to say the same to you. Must be hard keeping Patrick Owen under control with those wandering eyes of his."

"I will take the pillow," I said suddenly, desperate to steer the conversation away from their friction over Owen. "You're right, I'll be much more comfortable."

Lottie turned away from Maggie and tossed the pillow into my lap.

"Thank you," I said.

She flashed me a smile. "Of course. It's like I said, we look out for each other here."

I didn't reply. I wondered if that still held true where Patrick Owen was concerned.

With our break over, I went back upstairs to the carding machine, sitting on Lottie's pillow to keep it from the filthy floor. One day soon, I would tell her the truth. Return the pillow to her and admit I made Lieutenant Blackwell's supper each night. She would be angry, no doubt, at both my lies and my foolishness. Would likely speak to me in the same brusque tone she reserved for Maggie. I hated the prospect of that coldness. *We look out for each other* – and with each day I saw just how important that sisterhood was. With too much ease, the horrors of the factory were becoming commonplace – the settler taking a woman up against the factory wall, the girl sent back to the spinning wheels to birth her overseer's child. Talk of what the men did to their lodgers in the night. How were we to survive here without another to lean on?

Footsteps thudded up the stairs, two male convicts appearing in the warehouse, guarded by a marine. One of the men was a familiar face; most mornings when I returned to the factory he'd be gallivanting around the place with a kiss for any woman who'd let him near. He grinned at the young girl sitting closest to the door. Picked up one of the sacks of cloth that sat in the corner waiting to be taken to the government stores. He murmured to her in words I couldn't hear over the thudding of the looms. But the thump of the soldier's rifle I did hear, as it struck the man on the back of the skull. He pitched forward, dropping the sack and spitting out a line of cursing.

"Keep your mouth shut and do your job," the soldier barked. I turned my eyes away hurriedly. Found myself turning the handle of the carding machine faster, in time with my racing heart.

Footsteps again, as the marine and the convicts disappeared. My tea sat heavily in my stomach. I could hear the thud of the rifle blow echoing in my ears. I'd never known of a place in which the balance of power was so one-sided.

The thought made me turn the wheel faster, as though by throwing my energy into the carding machine, I might let some of it loose from my body. I fed the fleece into the whirring drums, eyes glazing over.

I thought of Blackwell. I'd not seen the same brutality inside him, but perhaps it was naïve to assume it wasn't there. I had made an active decision not to fear him. An active decision to trust him. But I knew there was every chance it might turn out to be a foolish choice. The men in red coats literally held our lives in their hands. Perhaps it was wiser to fear the hand that wielded the power. Grow too close and he could burn me alive.

I felt a sudden burst of pain in my fingertips. Heard myself cry out. And then a hand on my arm, yanking me backwards before my fingers were drawn into the teeth of the carding drum.

I toppled from my stool, landing heavily on the floor beside Maggie. I gasped for breath, gripping my stinging fingers with my other hand. Maggie put a hand to my shoulder.

"Careful, girl," she said, her face close to mine. "Careful. Got to keep your mind on the job."

I tried to reply, but my mouth just hung open. I opened my palm to see a rivulet of blood trickling down my fingers. Pain was pulsing through my hand, but I knew it could have been infinitely worse. I nodded at Maggie, unable to form words.

She got to her feet, picking up Lottie's pillow from where it had fallen beside me. She brushed the muck from the bottom and sat it back on my stool. Then she reached down and offered me a hand.

"Thank you," I murmured. And as I climbed shakily to my feet, my throbbing hand wrapped around hers, I couldn't help but stare at the chain of bruises reaching up her arm.

"Are you all right, Eleanor?" Blackwell asked as he came into the hut that night. I was rattling around the place in an attempt to make supper, unable to keep from trembling. All I could think about was what would have happened had Maggie not yanked me back from the carding machine. I reached for the frying pan and sent it crashing onto the floor.

I picked it up hurriedly and slapped a slab of meat into it. "I'm fine."

Blackwell hung up his jacket. "Has something happened?"

I shook my head, unwilling to speak of it. Thinking of my near accident made me feel as fragile as a bird. And fragility was something I could not afford to show in this place.

"Nothing happened." I took the frying pan to the hearth and sat it over the embers. I knelt on the floor and stared into it, watching the edges of the meat darken. The smell of the cooking flesh made my stomach turn.

I heard Blackwell at the washbin and kept my eyes fixed to the pan. For not the first time since I'd come to his hut, I was struck by the utter impropriety of our situation; of having a man who was not my husband so close upon me, washing, dressing, sleeping, breathing. In the fortnight we'd been sharing the hut, we'd fallen into an uneasy, wordless arrangement in which I'd dress beneath my blankets, and disappear into the garden while he washed and clothed himself each morning. In which he'd turn his back while I lifted my stockings and laced my stays.

On more than one occasion, the forced intimacy of the thing had felt too much. I'd thought to leave, to give him back the space he had so generously carved out for me. But each time, I arrived at the same conclusion. Without that scrap of space, I had not a single place to go.

I pressed the wooden spatula into the meat, watching as the juices ran clear. I carried the pan to the table and slid its contents onto Blackwell's plate. He looked down at the single slab of meat.

"You're not eating?"

I set the pan on the floor beside the door to cool. My bruised fingers throbbed in time with my heart.

"I'm not hungry." I took the bread from the shelf and sat it on the table for Blackwell. He stared up at me, a faint frown creasing the bridge of his nose. And that look, what was that? Something so close to concern that a part of me wanted to speak, to tell him of the foolish accident that had left me so rattled. But when I heard the words in my head, they sounded so petty, so inconsequential. Certainly nothing that would matter to a marine lieutenant. Just a thing that would reveal the delicacy I was trying so hard to outgrow. I nudged the bread towards him. "Here. It's still quite fresh."

Blackwell held my gaze for a long second, then slid around on his stool and reached for the rum bottle on the shelf. He filled a tin cup and placed it on the edge of the table.

"Drink it. It's quite dreadful, but it does settle the nerves somewhat."

I took the liquor and tossed it back, gasping as it seared my throat. I closed my eyes, feeling the drink slide through me, warming my insides and yes, somehow, faintly easing the nerves that were rattling through my body. A dangerous thing, I knew well, to find a little peace at the liquor stills of the Rum Corps.

When Blackwell was asleep, I pulled on my boots and slipped out of the hut. My mind and body were exhausted, but my thoughts were racing. I knew sleep was still hours away.

The air was cold and clean, a silver cloud of breath appearing in front of me as I strode away from the hut. Laughter from the main street hung in the air, and I turned towards the church to avoid the throng of men and women outside the tavern. I followed the curve of the river as it snaked through the trees, needing the stillness, the calming sigh of the water.

In the pale moonlight, I recognised Maggie's figure leaning against the railings of the bridge. She looked up as I approached.

"Don't often see you out at night," she said. She brought a clay pipe to her lips and blew a line of smoke upwards.

I stepped onto the bridge and stood beside her at the railing. In the darkness the water was hidden, but I could hear it churning beneath us.

"Couldn't sleep," I told her.

Maggie held the pipe out to me. I shook my head.

She nodded in the direction I had come. "That Blackwell's hut?"

I wrapped my arms around myself. Said nothing.

Maggie gave me a short smile. "Don't worry. I won't tell Lottie old Bert's pillow is snuggled up next to her favourite officer."

I let out my breath. "I feel dreadful. I shouldn't have taken it."

"It's just a pillow."

"It's not just a pillow. It's the principle of the thing. I've not told her the truth."

Maggie lifted the pipe. "You think too much. That's why you got yourself in trouble today."

I lowered my eyes. I knew she was right. "I'd appreciate it if you didn't tell anyone about… my sleeping arrangements," I managed.

She chuckled. "If I were curled up beside an officer in the night, I'd be letting everyone know."

I shifted uncomfortably. "I'm not *curled up* beside him."

Maggie shrugged. "Ain't nothing to be ashamed of."

"How can you say that?" Necessity or not, sleeping beside a man in the night made me feel as though I'd abandoned every scrap of my morality.

"It's smart," said Maggie. "Getting in with an officer. You do him a few favours and maybe he'll do the same for you. Make your time here a little easier."

"He's not asked for any favours. He says taking me in was an act of charity."

Maggie gave a short laugh. "It's coming. You just watch. This ain't a place of charity. There's no room for that here. Even men like Blackwell, they're just trying to find a way to survive in this wilderness."

I shook my head. "That's not true. This place might be about survival for us, but it's not for the men who carry the rifles."

She shrugged. "Maybe you'd be surprised." An echo of breaking glass sounded from the street, followed by wild laughter. Maggie looked back towards the tavern. "Fucking animals."

"Is Owen in the tavern?" I asked.

She nodded. "The man's a right bastard when he's in his cups. I managed to get out of there when he was looking the other way. I'll pay for it later though, I'm sure."

I thought of the mottled bruising on Maggie's arms. Felt rather certain

47

Patrick Owen was a bastard whether he was in his cups or not.

"Would you marry him?" I asked. "For a ticket of leave, like Sally Quinn got?"

"What other hope do I have? They ain't letting me out of this place til I'm dead."

My lips parted. "You're here for life?"

Maggie blew out a line of smoke. "Made one or two bad decisions in my time."

I gave her a small smile. "I know the feeling."

"Headed up a thieving ring back in London," she said. "Thought Lottie would have told you. The other girls ain't shy to remind me I'm the only lifer in the factory."

My fingers curled around the worn wooden rail of the bridge. Maggie was not the only lifer in the factory, but I couldn't bring myself to tell her. Couldn't admit to the shame of it. Speaking of it aloud was too brutal.

Instead, I asked, "How long have you been here?"

"Coming up on ten years. I were cleaning a man's house at first, til the old bastard turned over the perch."

I stared downwards, watching ripples emerge from the darkness. Who would I be after a decade in this place? Would I be desperate enough to chase a man like Patrick Owen? Seek some semblance of a future in the bed of any man who could offer it? This, I told myself, as my stomach turned over with dread, was why I could only bear to consider the moment I had before me. I felt a sudden, desperate need to return to Blackwell's hut.

CHAPTER SEVEN

Parramatta was still covered in golden dawn light as I made my way towards the factory. My boots sank into the mud as I walked. Cold wind whipped my hair against my cheeks and made my skirts dance around the top of my boots. Autumn was slowly becoming winter, though the trees were stubbornly green.

I stopped walking suddenly, my eyes drawn to the scrub on the side of the road. What had made me look? And as I realised what I was seeing, my breath caught in my throat.

I'd seen death before, of course. Seen my father, uncles, aunts laid out lifeless on the mourning table. But it was the unexpectedness of this that caused heat to wash over me. The presence of a body where a body should not have been. A white hand curled beneath the undergrowth; a thin wrist, a twisted arm, a motionless figure in a blue and white striped dress.

I stumbled backwards, my legs weakening. I felt as though the world was tilting around me. I lurched into the main street, whirling around in search of someone to tell. Felt a hand on my elbow.

"What's happened, Nell?" asked Hannah. "What's wrong?"

"A body," I managed. "A woman." I had trouble forming the words. "Where?"

I led her back to the white hand in the bushes. Bolstered by Hannah's company, I dared to look a little closer. The woman lay on her side among the undergrowth, her feet bare and her skirts tangled around her legs. I couldn't see her face, just the bundle of dark hair at her neck.

Hannah edged forward and touched the woman's shoulder. The body rolled over. I pressed a hand over my mouth to stifle my cry of shock. Maggie Abbott's blank eyes stared up into the trees. Her neck was dappled with red marks and bruising, her skin deathly pale against the darkness of her hair.

I swallowed a violent wall of sickness.

I realised we were not alone. People were gathering, clustered on the side of the road, trying for a look.

I felt a hand around my wrist. Lottie appeared beside me and stood with her shoulder pressed against mine, not releasing her grip on my forearm.

I stared at the bruises on Maggie's neck. "She was murdered," I said, more to myself than anyone else. My words seemed to ripple through the crowd.

She was murdered.

Lottie pulled me into her arms and squeezed tightly. And at last, here were the redcoats, elbowing their way towards the body. Blackwell was among them, his eyes skimming over me without showing a hint of recognition.

"Who found the body?" asked one of the soldiers.

"I did."

"This was how you found it?"

Her, I tried to say, but the word caught in my throat. I tried to swallow. "Yes," I managed. "I mean, no. She was on her side. We turned her to see who it was." I wrapped my arms around myself. "She was murdered," I said again.

Blackwell glanced at me, then back at Maggie's body. "Escort the women to the factory," he told the soldiers. "And take the body to the hospital."

And then we were back in the factory, spinning yarn as though nothing at all had happened. I sat dazedly on my stool and stared into the spokes of the motionless spinning wheel. The chalky smell of the fire thickened the air, making it hard to breathe. I felt as though I might fall at any moment. Lottie reached out and squeezed my hand. I squeezed back, grateful for her nearness.

Despite the wall of nervous chatter that filled the factory, I was acutely aware of Maggie's absence. The place felt empty without her. Quieter somehow, despite the constant thud and groan of the looms and carding drums. Each time I closed my eyes, I saw her blank face staring into mine.

The superintendent clipped me over the shoulder, barking about my laziness. I drew in my breath, trying to stop the tremor in my hands. I felt moments away from another accident. And today Maggie wasn't here to save me.

I turned to Lottie. "She was lodging with Patrick Owen," I said, though I knew she didn't need reminding.

For a moment, she didn't speak. "That doesn't mean anything." Her voice was thin.

I glared at her. Why was she defending him?

But in the back of my mind, I knew. She was defending him because there was a part of her that desperately hoped Maggie had not died with Owen's hands around her neck. That her body had not been so carelessly tossed into the scrub by one of the men we drank at the river with. There was a part of me that was hoping the same thing. But what was the alternative? I had seen the bruising on her neck. Had seen the bruising on her forearms the day she had saved me from crushing my hand in the carding machine. Still, I told myself, this was a wild land. Perhaps it was the doing of the savages, or some nameless creature that lived out there in the bush.

Maggie was dead, yes, but the horror of it was more manageable if she had not died at the hands of someone within the settlement.

Lottie turned away from me, pedalling rapidly in a sign our conversation was over.

I thought of Maggie's body. Hoped she was being treated with a little respect. I knew the hospital was without a mortuary; had heard tales of bodies being discarded in the passageways. Was she being examined? Or did the Rum Corps see no point?

We were precious, yes, us women at the spinning wheels. But so achingly replaceable. One of us buried would be replaced by another the moment the next ship came in.

A sense of unease hung thick in the air as we pedalled and spun. Restless murmuring rippled through the room. A baby began to shriek, the sound making the muscles in my neck tense.

Heads turned as heavy footsteps thudded up the stairs. Blackwell and one of the enlisted men appeared in the doorway of the warehouse. They made their way towards the superintendent.

One of the women at the spinning wheels leapt to her feet and strode towards the soldiers. "What you going to do about this then? Are you going to catch the bastard what done this to Maggie?"

"There'll be an investigation in due course," Blackwell said shortly.

"An investigation?" Hannah cried. "What need do you have for an investigation? Everyone knows it were Patrick Owen that killed her!" She stood abruptly, knocking over her stool. "Whatever you may think of us, we ain't bloody fools."

The younger soldier strode towards her. "Sit down and shut your mouth." He reached for Hannah's arm, but she pulled away violently. He grabbed her arms and forced her downwards, pinning her to the ground. Hannah screeched and kicked against him. And at once, the women were on their feet, crowding around her, trying to tear the soldier away. Another baby joined in the wailing. Children scrambled towards their mothers. I stood as well. Somehow, staying in my seat and obeying orders felt like a slight on Maggie. A slight on Hannah.

Blackwell dashed towards the fight.

I saw Lottie's eyes fall to him. Saw the hatred, the anger. And I saw her grab her stool by the legs and swing.

I had no thought of what I was doing. I was only aware of my body pitching instinctively towards Lottie, shoving her away from the lieutenant. And then of shock jolting through me as the full force of the wooden stool struck me instead.

It took a moment for the pain to hit, but when it did, it seared through my temple and brought me to my knees. Blood ran into my eye.

"Jesus, Nell," Lottie cried, crouching beside me and gripping my shoulder. "What in hell are you doing?" She shrieked as she was yanked to her feet by the superintendent.

I felt a hand around the top of my arm, helping me stand. Blackwell's imposing figure loomed over me.

"Get your hands off her, you corrupt bastard!" Lottie kicked against the superintendent. "Do you hear me?"

Blackwell handed me over to the other soldier. "Take her out to the yard. And find something to stop the bleeding."

I stumbled dizzily down the stairs, the soldier's hand clamped to my elbow. I swiped at the blood with the hem of my apron. It kept spilling from the gash in my forehead, soaking through the fabric and staining the skin on my wrist. The shouting from the factory grew steadily softer. The soldier led me out to the jail yard and planted me on the narrow wooden bench beside the door. Beads of blood slid from my chin, turning black in the striped flannel of my skirts. The soldier produced a handkerchief from his pocket and pressed it hard against the cut above my eye. Pain drummed steadily behind my forehead.

Blackwell appeared suddenly in the doorway, his footsteps crunching across the stone path. I was surprised to see him.

"Leave us," he told the soldier. "I need to speak with her about the incident." He took the bloodied handkerchief and knelt in front of me. He pressed it back against my forehead, then looked down at the crimson mess of my skirts. "Head wounds always bleed heavily," he said. "But it isn't deep. It looks worse than it is."

I gripped the edges of the bench, my teeth clenched against the ache of it.

Though his eyes were level with mine, Blackwell somehow managed not to look at me. Did he know, I wondered, that it was Lottie who had done this? Had he seen me step in front of her flying stool? Or had it all happened so quickly he had no thought of it?

I was glad he didn't ask for an explanation. I would not have been able to give it.

He lifted my hand and brought it to the handkerchief, gesturing for me to hold it in place. Then he disappeared into the jail for a moment, returning with a small bowl of water and a clean cloth.

He knelt opposite me again, dragging the cloth through the thin grey puddle at the bottom of the basin. Dabbed gently at the jewels of dried blood I could feel forming at my cheekbones.

"Maggie was murdered," I said. It wasn't fresh information to him, of course. I just needed him to know that I knew.

Blackwell's hand tightened around the cloth. Water drizzled onto the path and disappeared into the earth. "Yes. I'm sorry."

Sorry for what, I wondered?

I said, "It was Patrick Owen."

Blackwell didn't reply. Just slid the damp cloth over the side of my neck.

I waited for his questions, his interrogation. Wasn't that why he had marched down from the factory after me? I was the one to find the body.

But there were no questions. Just the rhythmic plinking as the water dripped from the cloth back into the basin. A crow glided across the jail yard and perched on top of the stair rail.

"Has it stopped bleeding?" I asked.

"Almost."

I got unsteadily to my feet, turning to face my reflection in the narrow window behind us. Lottie's attack had left a congealing red stripe above my eyebrow, but the cut was not as enormous as I had imagined it might be. The side of my eye was already cloudy with bruising.

I squinted at my reflection. It was the first time I'd dared to examine myself since I'd arrived in Parramatta. My hair hung in lank, coppery snarls, damp and darkened around my face. My cheeks were hollow, pink from the sun. But it was my eyes that caused my loud intake of breath. They were brighter and fiercer than I could ever remember, the flat grey planes of them alight with flecks of blue. There was my anger, my fear, my frustration. There was *four shillings*, and *I have shelter* and *who found the body?*

New South Wales had left a blaze inside me.

"I ought to go back upstairs," I said, "before the superintendent has me in the cells with Lottie and Hannah."

"You're to come with me to the courthouse," said Blackwell. "The magistrate wishes to speak to the person who found the body."

"So you were telling the truth. When you said there would be an investigation."

He looked me in the eye for the first time. "Why would you doubt that?"

I didn't answer.

We walked out of the jail towards the courthouse without speaking. I felt a faint flicker of nerves. The last time I'd been before a magistrate, I'd been transported upon the seas.

A few yards from the front door, Blackwell stopped walking. He looked down at me, eyes fixed to the cut streaking my forehead. "Eleanor," he said, his voice low, "you're not to put yourself in danger for me again. I don't require protecting."

He strode up the steps to the front door before I had a chance to respond.

CHAPTER EIGHT

I followed Blackwell into the courthouse, and down a long stone corridor with doors on either side. Our footsteps echoed in the stillness. He stopped at the door at the end of the passage and knocked loudly.

"Enter."

Blackwell opened the door to a small meeting room. A table took up most of the space, wooden chairs on both sides. White light filtered in from a window high on the wall. Inside, I could see the round-shouldered figure of Reverend Marsden, dressed in his customary black, along with two soldiers.

"Eleanor Marling, Reverend," said Blackwell. "She's the one who found the body."

The reverend walked slowly towards the door, rubbing a chin that disappeared into the mottled red folds of his neck. He looked me up and down, taking in the gash on my forehead, the blooms of blood on my Navy Board skirts. "You're a government woman." It was not a question. But I said:

"Yes, Father."

The bridge of his nose creased, then Marsden turned back to Blackwell. "It's not necessary for me to speak to her, Lieutenant. Please see her back to the factory."

Lottie and Hannah were put in solitary confinement for three days. A part of me was glad for the reprieve. I had no desire to try and explain my actions to Lottie. And I felt more than a hint of anger towards her over her attack. I knew Blackwell a target of the rebels, for reasons I didn't fully understand. And I knew Lottie was loyal to the Irish croppies. But surely that didn't warrant the whole stool-swinging debacle.

When she reappeared in the factory at the end of the week, she was uncharacteristically quiet. Shadows of exhaustion underlined her eyes, her hands discoloured with grime and the stale smell of the cells clinging to her skin.

For a long time, we sat beside each other without speaking. She glanced at the cut and bruising on the side of my face. I wondered if an apology would be forthcoming. But when she finally spoke, what she said was:

"Are you really sleeping on the street, Nell?"

I didn't look at her. "No," I said finally. I was surprised it had taken her so long to realise. I focused my gaze on my spinning.

Out of the corner of my eye, I could see her wheel was motionless.

"Tell me I'm wrong," she said. "Tell me you're not lodging with him."

I knew there was no need to reply. I had been expecting an outburst, but her silence was much more brutal.

"No," she said finally. "You've got to get out of there. Do you understand me?" She looked at me with an intensity in her eyes I had never seen before. "The street is safer. Risking the savages is safer."

Anger tightened my chest.

"Is this about what Maggie said?" she asked. "About having sway with a powerful man?"

I laughed coldly. "Power?" I repeated. "You think this about power? I was desperate, Lottie. I was sleeping outside the church. A person has to think of survival before they can think of power."

She shook her head. "Any man in this place would have taken you in. And yet you went with Blackwell."

"You're mistaken about him," I said, my voice coming out thin. I wasn't even sure she had heard me over the rattle of the looms. Her long silence suggested she hadn't. But then finally, she said:

"You trust him then? Is that why you... did what you did?"

I gritted my teeth. Why I did what I did? Had she not even the courage to say it aloud?

Why you stopped me from attacking him…

"Nell?" she pushed. "Do you trust him?"

I did trust him, I realised. And perhaps that made me a fool. But curling up on his floor made me feel fleetingly safe. That was not something I was willing to give up.

"He's giving me food and a fire in exchange for sweeping his floors," I said. "Tell me there's another man in the colony who would do that."

Lottie laughed coldly. "Sweeping floors. Is that really what you think he wants you for?"

I didn't answer. I wanted so desperately to believe in Blackwell's goodness. *Needed* to believe in it. I would not have Lottie and her anti-English sentiments ruin it for me.

She was wrong. She had to be. I had been sleeping on Blackwell's floor for more than three months, and not once had he even so much as brushed against me in the night.

"You're lucky I got in your way," I said sharply. "You could well have been facing the hangman if you'd struck an officer instead of a factory lass."

"Aye, well, it were grand of you to sacrifice yourself for me."

"Your attack was unwarranted," I said, not looking at her. I'd planned not to raise the issue. I knew we had all been rattled after Maggie's death. None of us had been thinking straight. But her comments had sparked something inside me.

Lottie snorted. "Just promise me one thing," she said bitterly. "When he gets a child on you, you name him as the father. Let the colony see who he is. Don't go pinning it on Marsden like the other women do."

We turned back to the spinning wheels. I found myself pedalling faster, letting the wool fly through my fingers. The wheel whirred and hummed.

"It's because of Castle Hill," I said. "That's why you despise him so."

Something passed over Lottie's eyes. "What do you know of Castle Hill?" She sounded angry I had spoken of it.

"Nothing," I admitted. "What happened? What did Blackwell do?"

"Why should I tell you? I warned you away from him once and I now I find out you're sleeping beside him in the night. I'm sure whatever I tell you you'll manage to see it with the eyes of an Englishwoman. You'll find a way to make him the hero."

"That's not true," I snapped. "I just want to know the truth."

Lottie snorted. "You want to know? Ask Lieutenant Blackwell."

Maggie was buried the next day while we were at the spinning wheels. I knew it was a deliberate attempt by Marsden and the Rum Corps to keep the factory lasses away.

An investigation into the murder had begun. Our information was hazy – mostly comprised of gossip from the men at the river – but in the factory that morning there was word Patrick Owen had been taken to the magistrate for questioning. Committed to prison to await trial.

I felt a faint flicker of optimism. Three months of Marsden's weekly sermons had shown me his hatred of the Irish. And if that hatred was what it took to send Owen to the hangman, then so be it. There was no doubt in my mind he had been the one to kill Maggie.

When work at the factory finished that night, we went to her grave; a meagre pile of earth at the back of the churchyard, with a crooked wooden cross shoved at the head. There was not even any mention of her name.

I tried not to imagine what her burial had been like. With all the women away at the factory there would have been few – if any – people to mourn her. I couldn't bear the thought of her being lowered into the earth with no one but the grave diggers to attend her.

Lottie and I stood at each other's side, not speaking, settled into an unspoken truce. One of the other women murmured a prayer.

As we were making our way out of the churchyard, several of the men approached. I wondered distantly why they had come. Were they here to pay their respects to Maggie? Far more likely, they'd come to persuade us to the river and talk some fertile young girls into becoming their wives.

In the half-light I could make out the tall figure of Dan Brady and several of the other rebels. They looked incomplete without Patrick Owen among them. Sheep without a leader. How many of those loyal croppies knew the man they followed was a killer? Did they, like Lottie, feel the need to push aside the truth?

Brady laid a stone beside Maggie's cross. "Patrick Owen sends his regards."

Anger bubbled inside me. "How dare you speak of him here."

Brady took a step towards me, eyes flashing. "You mean to send him to the hangman, Nellie?"

I turned away.

He grabbed my arm, yanking me back to face him. "Hey. We all heard how you got carted off to Marsden. What d'you say to him? Were you the one who led him to Owen?"

"I didn't say a thing," I hissed. "Marsden wouldn't even let me speak."

"And what about Blackwell? You open your mouth to him?" He snorted. "Word is you been opening your mouth to him a lot."

My cheeks blazed. "I didn't say a word to anyone," I snapped.

I could feel Lottie's eyes burning into the back of me.

"This true, Nell?" she asked. "You were taken to speak with the magistrate?"

"Yes," I said bitterly. "And it's also true that he wouldn't even let me speak. I had nothing to do with them going after Owen."

"Leave her alone, Dan," said Lottie. "She says she didn't speak to Marsden, then she didn't speak to Marsden. Patrick'll be back with us before you know it."

"You think Owen innocent?" I asked her.

She looked at me squarely. "What proof is there he's guilty?"

"Maggie was lodging with him," I said, aware it was an argument I was beginning to overuse. "And her arms were bruised. Just like her neck was."

And Dan Brady was up in my face, his nose inches from mine. "Watch yourself, Nellie," he said. "You hear me? No one wants to hear you mouthing off about what you think happened."

Lottie shoved him backwards. "I told you to leave her be."

I looked back at Brady, determined not to let him see how much he had rattled me. "What does it matter what I think?"

"You're right," he said. "It don't matter." He turned back to the other men. And then they were off down the main street, striding towards the jail.

I hurried back to Blackwell's hut, desperate for an escape. Through the cloth window, I could hear voices, footsteps, shouting in the street. Angry men, yelling in Irish.

With Blackwell on duty, the hut felt too quiet. I sat at the table, cutting up vegetables for soup while the clamour in the street grew louder. The chalky smell of a bonfire drifted beneath the door. I did my best to block out the noise. I needed that hut to feel safe. I realised I was craving Blackwell's company.

My stomach was groaning by the time he returned. I guessed it close to midnight. I spooned the soup into bowls and sat them on the table.

He looked surprised to see me awake. But not angry.

"I attended Maggie Abbott's burial," he told me as he took off his coat and hung it on the nail beside the door.

"You did?" I felt a sudden swell of gratitude. "Tell me about it."

He sat at the table and stirred his soup. "It was simple. Respectful. Reverend Marsden prayed over the coffin."

"Who else was there?" I dared to ask.

"Several of the officers. Parker and his wife from the tavern. A few others."

I was glad of it. "Thank you for attending."

He nodded. Somewhere in the distance, I heard glass shatter. Blackwell's eyes darted towards the door.

"Are you to sit on the jury in Owen's trial?" I asked.

"Yes."

"And do you think him guilty?" I felt it my duty to Maggie and the other factory lasses to prise out as much information as I could. I knew there were few other women in the colony who had the luxury of sitting opposite a solider and holding a civilised conversation.

Blackwell gave my boldness a ghost of a smile. "I can't discuss that with you, Eleanor. You know that."

"There were bruises on her arms," I said. "She—"

"Yes." Blackwell's tone darkened a little. "You told me that before. And as I told you, there's no proof Patrick Owen gave them to her." I could hear the impatience in his voice. Knew I was pushing the issue.

I was saved by a knock at the door. Blackwell pulled it open and noise flooded in from the street. Two young soldiers stood outside the hut.

"I'm sorry to disturb you, sir," said one. "Captain Daley has asked for you at the barracks."

Blackwell nodded. "Tell him I'm on my way." He closed the door on them, then grabbed his jacket from the nail. He slid on his gorget and buttoned his coat to his neck. He glanced at his pocket watch.

"Don't venture outside tonight," he told me.

"The rebels are angry," I said. "Because Owen has been arrested."

He didn't answer. But I didn't need the confirmation. I'd seen the anger in the eyes of Dan Brady and the other croppies. Knew they were fighting for justice for their leader. And I knew that in their eyes, Patrick Owen could do no wrong.

The hut felt cold and empty after Blackwell had left. I threw another log on the fire and scraped the last of our supper into the trough, setting the unwashed bowls on the edge of the table. I'd wait until morning to fetch water from the river.

I blew out the lamp and curled up on my sleeping pallet. The cut on my head was drumming.

I thought of the crude cross at the head of Maggie's grave. Thought of her sashaying about the riverbank on Patrick Owen's arm. Lottie was right of course; I had no proof it was Owen. But there was a certainty within me that he had wrung Maggie's throat. And I ached for him to be punished.

The person I had been in London would never have let herself get drawn into such matters. Would never have prodded a soldier for answers or churned through evidence in my mind. I would have stepped back, hidden my eyes, told myself the world was as it should be. After all, the person I was in London had no reason to fight. I had everything I needed. I knew, of course, of the inequality in the world, but saw it as an unavoidable part of life. Back in London, the injustices of the world had largely fallen in my favour.

My father, in his own starched and stilted way, had loved me. I'd never doubted that. My mother had died in her childbed, and my father's way through the loss was to lavish me with care and attention. I grew up with an endless parade of nurses and governesses, music teachers and tutors. A good head for arithmetic and a convincing French accent, I suppose Father assumed, would go some way to making up for my gaudy appearance.

I knew I was no great beauty, but I was confident in my intelligence. Father made sure I knew it a good substitute. He brought in master after master to train me in subjects far beyond the scope of most young women of my class. And each night, as we sat opposite each other at the supper table, he would quiz me on the things I had learned that day.

How might I ask for my supper in Italian, Eleanor? Or; *Tell me about Herschel's new planet...*

As a child, my life had been laid out for me; dutiful daughter and conscientious student, then I was to become a wife and mother. I'd never imagined I could be taken in any other direction. For all my studies of the skies and foreign phrases, my world was narrow. Though I could point to any city on a map, I had no thought of how life might be in any place but London. When, as a nine-year-old child, I heard of our ships landing in Botany Bay, the place seemed as distant as a dream. Never in the stretches of my imagination could I have perceived ever walking these shores. Especially not as a prisoner.

Jonathan Marling was an accounting client of my father's; an ambitious young man who shared ownership of a jeweller's on Theobolds Road. He'd come to our door one day with a valise full of papers, and while I waited for my father to return home, I kept him entertained with mindless small talk and a pot of Indian tea. At the sight of us laughing together in the parlour, my father's face lit up, and he set about arranging our betrothal with far too much enthusiasm.

A week later, Jonathan was back at the door to ask for my hand, no doubt buoyed by the sizeable dowry Father had dropped at his feet.

I'd held out no hope of marrying for love, of course, but accepting Jonathan's proposal left a hollowness inside me. I found reason after reason to delay my wedding; the need to be married in spring, our priest's runny nose, the unavailability of sky-blue satin for my bridal gown. I had nothing against my husband-to-be. I was just not ready to become a wife.

When Father fell ill with smallpox, I was still finding excuses not to marry.

But Jonathan was there beside me while my father's body was lowered into the earth. And he was there to accompany me home from the service, to manage Father's affairs on my behalf, to hold me when the grief broke inside me.

With Father gone, I felt the emptiness stretching out around me. As his only child, he had left me a good inheritance, but the thought of being alone in the world was terrifying. I felt utterly incapable of managing my own life. And so, three weeks after I had walked out of St James's behind my father's coffin, I was walking back down the aisle as Jonathan's wife.

I became the lady of a whitewashed townhouse in Clerkenwell, with a fortepiano in the parlour and a small garden in front.

My father would be proud of me, I told myself, as I managed our small staff and walked on Jonathan's arm to a parade of garden parties and banquets. Would have been proud of the well-respected young lady I had become.

But I knew he would not have pushed so hard for our marriage if he'd known I'd be a widow by the age of twenty-six. And he certainly would not have done so if he'd known that marrying Jonathan Marling would lead me onto a prison ship.

I lay awake for what felt like hours, listening as the yelling in the street continued. I could see the flare of the bonfire through the cloth window. Did the rebels plan to break Owen out of prison? Or was this chaos their way of announcing to the Rum Corps that they would not be kept down?

I got out of bed and lit the lamp, knowing there was little point trying to sleep. I went to the shelf and looked over the pile of books. Blackwell's collection was an eclectic one: a Bible interspersed with the novels of Goldsmith and Fielding, and an enormous brick on construction techniques that looked unbearably dull. I opened the novel at the top of the pile but it did little to hold my attention.

My gaze drifted to Blackwell's empty sleeping pallet, to the wooden storage chest beside it. I felt a sudden, desperate need to look inside. To learn just a little about this man I lay beside in the night. This man I had chosen to trust.

I picked up the lamp, my bare feet sighing against the dirt floor. I tiptoed towards the chest in which Blackwell kept a small piece of himself.

Guilt tugged inside me, but my curiosity won out.

I opened the lid and held up the lamp. The chest was filled with clothing; neatly folded shirts, trousers, a scarf and gloves. Beneath them, several more books and a large metal crucifix.

Tucked down the side, fallen between the books, was large oval locket. I clicked it open, holding it up to the lamp. A young woman peered back at me, pale hair falling in ringlets around a heart-shaped face. She had a delicate beauty, with large doe eyes and a smile at the edge of her lips. I remembered posing for a similar portrait in the year before my father's death.

Blackwell's wife, I wondered? I'd never been bold enough to take the conversation in that direction. I clicked the locket closed and tucked it back beneath the clothes.

I felt a hollowness inside me, though I couldn't fathom why. Guilt, perhaps? Or the inexplicable envy that his thoughts might have been on that curly-haired beauty while he was sitting at the supper table with me?

I regretted going through his things. I closed the lid and went back to my sleeping pallet, bringing my arms up over my ears to block out the chaos in the street.

CHAPTER NINE

"The Enemy hath so completely possessed himself of the minds of all ranks and orders here; that it is a matter of doubt with me, that His power will be ever seen in this place."

Letter from Rev. Samuel Marsden to Mary Stokes
October 1795

On Sunday morning, as I laced my boots for church, I said, "You're a man of God." My thoughts were with the Bible on the shelf. The crucifix within the chest. With a murmured prayer before each meal.

Blackwell buttoned his jacket. "Does that surprise you?"

I sat back on the chair, watching a tiny lizard dart under the door. "Sometimes it feels as though God has been forgotten here. At least within the factory walls."

He ran a comb through his hair and peered into his shaving mirror. "My father was the vicar of our parish," he told me finally. "So yes. I suppose I am a man of God."

I felt a faint warmth in my chest. It was the first time he had offered me a scrap of information about who he was.

I stood up and smoothed my skirts. "You go first," I told him. "I'll follow." I was always careful to distance myself from him when the colony was watching. I knew being seen with me would only bring him shame.

There was talk of course, whispered at the spinning wheels and hollered over rum at the river. Talk of the factory lass who'd found a bed beneath the roof of an officer. I refused to speak on the subject; refused to give any weight to the rumours. I was afraid that if the gossip came too close, Blackwell might see the error of his ways and send me back to the street.

I pulled the door closed and made my way to the church. And into formation us government men and women went, lining up like children before we were herded into the front pews. Redcoats stood at either end, rifles at the ready. Sunlight blazed through the windows, making dust motes dance above our heads.

Reverend Marsden strode to the pulpit. Though the morning was cold, his cheeks were pink with exertion. His thick fingers curled over the edge of the pulpit as he looked out over the congregation.

I wondered if Maggie would make it into his sermon. A prayer for the departed. An acknowledgement that a crime had been committed. An acknowledgement that Maggie Abbott, a rough-spoken factory lass, had existed.

If anyone was going to speak out against Patrick Owen, I knew it would be the reverend. If there was anything Marsden despised more than the factory lasses, it was the croppies.

Maggie did make it into the sermon that day.

A loose woman, the reverend called her. *A harlot*. His steely gaze moved along the front row where the factory lasses were sitting. He looked into our eyes as he spoke of the perils of carnal immorality. Of the way a woman's active sexuality threatened the very order of society. Upset the precious balance of masculine and feminine.

I stared back at him, forcing myself to hold his gaze. The person I was in London would have nodded along with Marsden. Yes, a sinner; a loose woman who deserved all that came to her. But the day I had stepped out of the factory with nowhere to sleep, I had come to see that there was not always a choice.

"The immorality of this colony is a thing you should all be ashamed of," he said. "The extent of which will become clearer in the coming days and weeks."

Murmurs rippled through the congregation.

I turned to Hannah, who was sitting beside me. "What do you suppose he means by that?"

She snorted. "Don't waste your time dwelling on it. When you ever heard anything but drivel come out his mouth?"

"Behave yourselves," a well-spoken man called down to the convicts.

"You behave yourself," a young woman snapped back. I hid a smile.

"1 Corinthians 14," the man boomed down at us, like he was trying to be the very voice of God Himself, "it is shameful for a woman to speak in church."

I returned to the hut before Blackwell, and gathered up my dirty clothes. I took the washboard down to the river and crouched on the edge in the pale winter sun. My boots sank into the muddy bank as I dipped my apron beneath the surface. For a moment, I just held it between my fingers, watching it float ghost-like through the bronze haze of the water.

I scrubbed my clothes along the washboard until my fingers were numb, hanging each piece from a tree; marking the forest with my fleeting scrap of civilisation. The washing helped take my mind off things. Helped take my mind off Maggie Abbott's blank eyes staring out from within the scrub. Helped me stop wondering what Marsden had meant by revealing the extent of the colony's immorality.

I bundled my wet clothes into my arms and went back to the hut, draping my shift and petticoats over the table, wet stockings spread out across a chair. I felt as though I was possessing the place, making it my own. Strewn about Blackwell's hut like this, my clothes felt almost as inconsonant as they had hung up among the wilderness.

His footsteps behind me made me start. I spun around to find him holding out the book he had been reading a few nights earlier. I'd not even heard him come in.

"I've finished if you'd care to read it," he said.

I murmured my thanks. There was something alluring about escaping into a fictitious world for a time. A precious thing here.

He glanced at the ghostly shapes of my washing. "It's the Lord's Day. You ought to be resting." He nodded to the book. "Read it. I think you will enjoy it."

I took the book and went back to the river. Followed it downstream a few yards to where the mangroves gave way to a battalion of broad trees.

There was a chill in the wind, but the sun was struggling through the clouds. I needed to be out in the daylight, not in the endless shadows of the hut.

I opened the book and stared at the first page. The words swam in front of my eyes. My mind refused to be drawn into the story. I had already been transported into another realm that I would have believed fictitious had I not been living it.

I became aware that Blackwell had joined me by the river. He had changed out of his uniform into dark trousers and a faded riding coat. There was a clay pipe in his hand. I'd not seen him smoke often. He looked upwards.

"These trees are very beautiful," he said. "Redgums."

I nodded.

"I come here sometimes," he told me. "For a little space."

"I'm sorry." I moved to stand. "I'll leave. I—"

He held up a hand to stop me. "I didn't mean for you to leave. I simply meant to say this place helps relax me."

"Why do you need help relaxing?" I knew it a foolish question. Maggie's murder. The Irish rebels. Owen's upcoming trial.

"You put me on edge," he said finally.

I looked up at him in surprise. "Why?"

"Well," he said after a moment, "there's the matter of my storage chest, to begin with."

I felt my cheeks colour with shame. How did he know I had gone through the chest? Had I not put things back neatly enough?

"I'm sorry," I said, meeting his eyes. "That was unacceptable."

His face was unreadable. He gestured with the pipe to the grass-flecked earth beside me. "May I?"

I nodded.

For several moments we sat in silence, Blackwell's long legs stretched out towards the river, mine folded neatly beneath me. Water burbled in the stillness.

After a moment, he gestured back to the redgums. "I used a little of this wood in the roof of the hut."

"You built it yourself?"

"Mostly," he said. "I learned a little construction when I was at school.

I've always found it most rewarding. A way of leaving your mark on a place." He chuckled lightly. "Although I can't imagine that hut lasting too many generations. Each time the sky opens I fear the rain will carry it away."

I ran my fingers over the faded leather cover of the book in my lap.

"You're not enjoying it?" he asked.

I lowered my eyes. "In his sermon today, Reverend Marsden spoke of revealing the colony's immorality. Do you know what he meant by it?"

"A muster," Blackwell said shortly. "Nothing more. The governor likes to keep track of who is holding land, how many colonial-born children have arrived. Which prisoners are on and off stores…"

"What does any of that have to do with immorality?"

He puffed a line of smoke towards the clouds. The pipe didn't suit him. He looked like a young man trying to whittle away the years. "Reverend Marsden is also to register the females in the colony. The service will take place next Sunday."

"Register us?" I repeated. "And? We are catalogued by our place of birth? Our ages? Our children?"

"Yes," said Blackwell. "Among other things." He jammed the pipe back between his teeth.

"What other things?" I looked at him through narrowed eyes. "How does the reverend catalogue us, Lieutenant Blackwell?"

"You are to be catalogued by your marital status," he said finally. "Wife or concubine."

He spoke the words carefully, gently, but I felt the sting of them. I was not a wife. So it left no doubt as to what I was in Reverend Marsden's eyes.

As to what I was in the colony's eyes.

Once I had been a wife. But my husband had died and his spilled blood had led me to New South Wales. Now I spent each night lying on the floor beside a member of His Majesty's Army.

Concubine.

"What do you think of this?" I asked, my voice hardening.

He shrugged. "It is what it is."

"That is not an answer."

"I'll not fight with you, Eleanor," Blackwell said calmly. "I'll not be a dumping ground for your anger."

"I don't want to fight. I just want to know what you think of this muster."

He lowered his pipe. "Reverend Marsden is doing what he thinks is best for the colony. And the women within it." His words sounded rehearsed.

"Is that what you truly believe?" I asked. "Or is that just what you think you ought to say to me?"

He looked taken aback by my boldness. "The reverend has been pushing for a women's barracks to be built. He believes the factory lasses' plight will be eased with a safe place to sleep each night. And he hopes the muster will support his cause."

"That may be so," I said, "but that's not what I asked. Do you think for yourself, Lieutenant? Or do you follow Reverend Marsden blindly?"

Blackwell's voice rose slightly. "What exactly do you mean by that?"

I gave a small shrug. My words had come spilling out half formed. But I was glad I had finally gotten a rise out of him. Glad I had finally seen a little emotion. I sat up on my knees so my eyes were level with his. "Do you believe us all immoral harlots, Lieutenant? Us factory women who curl up on your floors? You're a man of God. And the Bible says we must only do such a thing in the presence of our husbands. Is that what you're thinking each night I sleep beside you?"

Blackwell's neck reddened. And I saw then that my opinion mattered to him. What a strange thing, I thought distantly, that the views of a convict woman might hold such weight to a military officer. Perhaps I was not so insignificant. Perhaps none of us were.

"Reverend Marsden is not everything I believe in," Blackwell said shortly. He emptied his pipe into the river and disappeared inside the hut. I hugged my knees to my chest and watched the silver streaks of ash float away on the tide.

CHAPTER TEN

They blamed Maggie's murder on the blacks. Who could pretend to be surprised?

The verdict of Owen's trial had filtered through the factory that day. His version of events, which we had for days believed nothing but a garbled lie, had become the truth; Maggie had left his hut after supper the night of her death, with too much liquor under her skin. Wandered into the bush to be set upon by natives.

And perhaps that was all the Rum Corps believed she deserved.

"You don't know it a lie, Nell," said Lottie.

We were out in the prison yard, eating the slivers of bread we'd brought for mealtime. Clouds hung low, threatening rain.

"Her feet were bare when I found her," I said sharply. "Why would she have gone wandering into the bush without her boots?"

"She were a drinker," said Lottie. "You know that. She probably weren't thinking clearly."

"And what about the bruises on her arms?" I asked. "She didn't do that to herself." I wrapped my hand around my teacup, craving its warmth. I never felt Maggie's absence more acutely than when I was out in the jail yard with Lottie and Hannah. Without her brassy interjections, our conversations felt painfully incomplete.

"The bruises," said Lottie with a sigh. "I told you before, they don't prove anything."

"I know you and Maggie weren't the best of friends," I said. "But—"

"That doesn't mean I'm happy about what happened to her," Lottie said pointedly. "It sickens me as much as it does you. But Patrick has been found innocent."

I whacked the arm of Hannah, who was sitting on the bench beside me. "Would you make her see sense?"

Hannah jabbed the remains of her bread in Lottie's direction. "Ain't no making this one see sense."

I pulled my eyes away from Lottie's glare. I could feel our friendship beginning to strain under the weight of our disagreement. For the sake of our relationship, I knew I ought to keep my mouth shut. I had already lost one friend that month. I couldn't bear to lose another. But nor could I just sit back in acceptance while Patrick Owen walked free.

"I suppose it doesn't matter who killed her, does it," I said bitterly. "Because Maggie Abbott was nothing but a concubine."

"You still on about that damn muster?" Lottie asked. "It's just Marsden's blathering."

"It's not just Marsden's blathering. Lieutenant Blackwell says the register is to be sent back to England. Imagine what they'll think of us there."

Hannah gave a short laugh. "Sorry to say it, Nell, but whatever it is, I'm sure they're already thinking it."

Two days earlier, the women in the colony had been corralled outside the church before the service. We had presented ourselves to Reverend Marsden's secretary, and become nothing more than entries scrawled on a page. Name, age, marital status.

Widow, I'd said. But I knew when that register made its way back to England I would be listed upon it as *concubine*. I tried to tell myself it didn't matter. What difference did it make what men ten thousand miles away thought of us out here? But it mattered more than I wanted to admit. There was every chance the muster would be read by men who had known my father, known my husband. Men I had walked among at soirees and Christmas parties. The shame of being transported had been crushing enough. And now beside my label of *convict*, I would also be marked as a concubine.

I looked between Hannah and Lottie. "Doesn't this bother you?"

"Are you truly surprised by it?" asked Lottie, her mouth still half full of bread. "People like us, we're nothing. When are you going to realise that?"

Her words stung.

As a girl, I'd been led to believe I was a prize. Something to be awarded to the gentleman with the biggest income or the best family connections. I was preened and polished like a jewel, my dowry added to, my skills and etiquette smoothed until they shone.

But as we were herded back upstairs by a pimply soldier who looked half my age, I realised Lottie was right. We were nothing. Our names, our stories, our pasts; none of that was important. We were just marks on Marsden's register.

Concubine one.

Concubine two.

Three, four, five.

We could disappear, die at the hands of another, and who was there to care? We were just hands to weave the cloth. Wombs to carry the next generation. And there would always be more of us where we had come from.

"The blacks?" I demanded when I got back to the hut that night. Blackwell was dressed in full uniform, sitting on a chair and polishing his boots. I couldn't fathom why. They'd be caked in mud again the second he stepped outside. "You truly believe she was killed by the blacks?"

Blackwell didn't rise to my anger. It made me even more furious. I slammed my hand hard against the table, forcing him to look up. "Blame the blacks. Because it's easy. Isn't that right?"

"There was not enough evidence to charge Patrick Owen," Blackwell said, pressing the lid onto the pot of polish and setting it back on the shelf.

"Maggie was lodging with him."

"That's not evidence."

I paced back and forth, hot with anger. Anger at Owen's freedom, at Marsden's labelling of us. At Blackwell's calmness and his stupid need to polish his boots.

"Do you think him guilty?" I demanded.

Blackwell sighed as he stood up.

I planted my hands on my hips and glared as I waited for an answer.

Somewhere inside, I suppose I knew this wasn't his fault. At least, not entirely. But seeing him there in his lobster coat, all I could think of were the officers on the jury who had let Owen walk free. The skewed authority, the injustices. Everything that was wrong with this place. Besides, I had to take my anger out on him, because who else would listen?

"Of course," I said. "You've no opinion on the matter."

"I have an opinion," he said sharply. "I'm just not obliged to share it with you." He glanced down at his pocket watch, then grabbed his scarf from the back of the chair and wound it around his neck. "You would do well to remember your place, Eleanor."

My cheeks flushed with a mixture of anger and embarrassment.

"Where are you going?" I asked, following him to the door. I didn't want him to leave. I wanted him to stay here so I could unload my protests on him.

"I've a council meeting." He stopped at the door and looked back at me. "Can you sew?"

I blinked, caught off guard by the abrupt change of subject. "Sew?" I repeated. "Yes, of course."

"Good." He nodded towards the pile of shirts on the end of his sleeping pallet. "I've several pieces that need mending. I'll pay you a half crown apiece. I know it falls outside our arrangement."

I clenched my hand around the edge of the door in frustration. Damn Blackwell and his decency. I wanted to be angry with him. *Needed* to be.

"I thought the lobsters only traded in liquor," I said sharply.

"You ought to have some money of your own," he said, pushing past my comment. "And I'd hate to think you were resorting to… other means to earn yourself a little coin."

I felt my face colour violently. "No," I managed. "Of course I'm not."

Blackwell nodded. He looked away, as though embarrassed he had raised the subject. "Good," he said shortly.

I felt the loss of him as the door thumped shut. It was not just about needing to air my grievances, I realised. There was a part of me that wanted to be near him.

I hovered in the doorway for a moment, hot and disoriented by the realisation. Then I took the sewing tin from the shelf and carefully threaded a needle.

I heard voices outside the hut. Muffled, drunken laughter. I recognised Owen's drawl. I grabbed the lamp and stepped outside.

Owen and Brady were standing close to the door of the hut. There was something small and dark in Brady's hand. They were tying it to the post of the awnings with a length of rope. I squinted. Were they paws? And eyes?

"What in hell is that?" I demanded.

Owen looked unfazed at the sight of me. "A little gift for the lieutenant." He stepped back to admire his work. "Don't you go taking it down now, Nellie."

I realised they had hung the battered corpse of some poor creature from the edge of Blackwell's roof.

"This the best you can do with your freedom, Owen?" I hissed. But he and Brady were already walking away.

I went inside for a knife and sawed at the rope. The carcass fell to the earth with a dull thud. I picked the poor creature up by the legs and flung it into the bush.

CHAPTER ELEVEN

"[If Catholicism] were tolerated they would assemble together from every quarter, not so much from a desire of celebrating mass, as to recite the miseries and injustice of their banishment, the hardships they suffer, and to enflame one another's minds with some wild scheme of revenge."

Rev. Samuel Marsden
A Few Observations on the Toleration of the Catholic Religion in New South Wales
1806

"Wake up, Eleanor." Blackwell's voice was soft, and close to my ear. We had barely spoken since I'd confronted him about Owen's exoneration. I took his gentleness as a sign I was forgiven.

It was a Sunday. The bright morning light told me I had overslept. If Blackwell hadn't woken me I would have been late for church.

He was already at the door. "Meet me outside the hut after the service."

I pulled the blanket around my shoulders to cover myself. "Why? What do you need me to do?"

But he had slipped out the door before my question was fully formed.

When the service was over, I made my way back to the hut. Blackwell was already there waiting for me. He had changed out of his uniform into dark trousers and long black boots, his shirtsleeves rolled to his elbows. I wondered distantly if he meant it as a gesture; wanted me to see him as something other than a lobster who'd let Maggie's killer walk free. The neck cloth tied loosely at his throat made him look boyish and young. A small hessian sack was bunched into his hand.

He started to walk. "Come with me."

I had to skip to keep up with his long-legged strides. "Where are we going?"

"To find a little space."

My lips curled up slightly at his hazy response. I didn't press him. I was coming to recognise that the way to prise answers from Adam Blackwell was to not ask questions at all.

He led me down High Street and into a thick tangle of trees. Soon, any hint of the settlement had disappeared. I followed close, disoriented by the absence of a path. I could see the undergrowth had been trampled in places. By the savages, I wondered? My heart began to beat a little quicker.

I heard a murmured voice carried on the wind. At the sound of our footsteps, the words fell silent.

"This way." Blackwell gestured with his head for us to walk in the opposite direction.

I looked back over my shoulder. "Who was that?" I asked edgily. "All the way out here?"

"Father Dixon, I assume," said Blackwell. "Holding his Catholic mass."

"Out here?"

"Well," he said, "the Irish want his services. What choice does he have but to hold them in secret?"

"You're not going to stop them?"

Blackwell looked ahead, shading his eyes from the sun. "I've more important things to do today."

"Lottie says Father Dixon was allowed to hold mass before the Irish uprising," I said as we walked. I wanted to grasp the workings of this colony, however brutal things were. I felt as though understanding this place was the best way to survive it.

I knew my education was worth little here. What did it matter in this place that I could dance a minuet, or play a Bach fugue? They were meaningless skills when life was stripped down to its necessities. In this place, it was a different type of knowledge that would save me; an understanding of who held the power and who was about to fall.

"Dixon failed to talk the Irish down from attacking at Castle Hill," Blackwell told me. "The mass was taken away as punishment." He pushed aside an overhanging branch, holding it back for me to pass.

"Were you fighting in Ireland?" I asked. "During the first rebellion?"

He nodded.

"They say the fighting was particularly brutal."

He watched the ground as he walked. "Yes," he said finally. "But it's the life a man signs up for when he chooses to fight for the Crown." The undergrowth crackled loudly beneath his boots.

"Must be a strange thing," I said, "finding yourself fighting against the Irish again in this place."

"Not so strange. I feel I've spent my whole life fighting against the same men. And fighting with the same men, for that matter." He gave a short smile. "For a place so far from home, this colony certainly has its share of familiar faces."

I smiled wryly at that. I'd not seen any faces from my old circles trudging the riverbank of Parramatta.

Blackwell pointed suddenly to a small purple flower poking out of the undergrowth. "Here. Look." He knelt down, gesturing to me to join him. "The chocolate plant," he said. "They've just started flowering."

I smiled crookedly. "Chocolate plant?"

He nodded. "Smell it."

I bent forward, inhaling the scent of the flower. A rich chocolate and vanilla aroma that brought a smile to my face.

Blackwell dug into the earth and yanked out the root of the flower. "We roast these," he said. "Eat them with a little salt and butter. The taste is quite something." He put the tuber into the bag. "There ought to be plenty of them out here."

I smiled. "How did you learn to do this?"

"I watched the natives do it once."

My shoulders stiffened. For a fleeting moment, I had forgotten we were in a world of savages and sharp-toothed creatures.

Blackwell got to his feet and dusted the earth from his knees. "Come on. There's more over here."

In spite of my unease, I followed him through the undergrowth. Sprigs of purple leapt from within the carpet of green. I knelt down and began to tug the tubers from the earth. Dampness soaked through my skirts.

I inhaled deeply, drawing the clean, mint-scented air into my lungs. The bush rose up around me on all sides, the grey-green trees carpeting hills that rolled up towards mountains. A repetitive fragment of birdsong sounded above my head, its melody rising and falling. I sat back on my heels for a moment, trying to pick out the notes.

I felt suddenly, inexplicably calm. There was something about this vastness, this rugged beauty; the ability of this wild land to feel at once so empty and so alive. I had not imagined I would feel calm in such a place.

I allowed myself to get drawn into our search, hunting out the purple flowers from within the tangle of brown and green. I focused on the feel of my fingers buried in the damp earth; a foreign, raw sensation, but one I deeply enjoyed. My head felt pleasantly empty.

When Blackwell said, "That's enough," I found myself oddly disappointed. He swung the full bag over his shoulder. "Unless you want to carry some more back in your pockets."

I smiled, wiping muddy hands against my skirts. We began to walk back in the direction of the settlement.

The undergrowth rustled, and I heard the unmistakable crackle of twigs. Blackwell held up a hand, gesturing to me to stop walking.

My heart began to race. I felt myself edge closer to him.

Another hiss and snap of twigs. The sighing of branches. And the natives stepped out in front of us.

I heard my sharp inhalation. There was a part of me that had believed them a myth. A story told within the depths of the convict ships, like the two-headed monsters hiding in the bush.

But these were not the wild warriors of the stories I had heard. Three men stood either side of the group, two women in the middle, and children among them, ranging in age from perhaps twelve or thirteen to a baby pressed against its mother's hip. Each wore swathes of animal skin, reaching from their shoulders down to their bare feet.

The children stared up at us with wide, dark eyes. Clouds of black hair hung past their shoulders, their skin the colour of darkest coffee. My gaze lingered on the spear in one of the natives' hand; two heads taller than the man himself.

Blackwell stood close, reaching around me and pressing a hand to my shoulder to steady me. My chest tightened. Fear? Or the unexpected feel of his hand against my body? He put the sack at his feet and held up his free hand in a gesture of peace. Nodded to the natives in greeting. I could hear my heart thudding in my ears.

The tall man's hand shifted on his spear and I heard myself gasp. But then he gave us the faintest of nods. He murmured to the others in words I didn't understand, then they turned as one, disappearing back into the bush.

I felt my muscles sink in relief. The back of my shift was damp with sweat.

Blackwell's hand slid from my shoulder. "There's no need to be afraid," he said. "They'll not attack unless they're provoked."

"That's not what I've heard."

"The natives won't come any further east than Prospect," he said. "We've likely strayed into their land." He watched his feet as we stepped over a fallen tree. "It's the white men you ought to fear. Not the natives."

I didn't answer. What did he mean by such a comment? Was he speaking of himself? Or was he warning me away from Patrick Owen and the other Irish rebels?

He shoved aside a thicket of grass. "This way," he said, "I want to show you something."

The ground began to rise steeply, and I grappled at tangled tree branches to haul myself up the incline. And suddenly the trees cleared, the land opening out before us. I let out my breath at the sight. I could see out to a jagged mountain range, silhouetted in the late afternoon sun. It was achingly beautiful; the peaks dotted with snow beneath the harsh black of the rock. Golden winter light spilled over the hills, a stark contrast to the heavy gloom that pressed down upon England.

I sat on the hillside, hugging my knees to my chest. Let a sense of calm wash over me. I saw then that it had been a deliberate act, his bringing me here. He had known the mountains would be a tonic for my anger over Owen, over Marsden's register. He had known how much I needed it. I felt a sudden swell of gratitude.

I looked over my shoulder. He was standing several yards behind me, one hand shading his eyes from the sun. And for the first time, it was curiosity I felt about my new home, rather than terror. I thought again of the natives; of the mothers, the children, the tall man's nod of greeting.

I caught Blackwell looking at me.

"How long have you been out here?" I asked.

"Almost four years."

I imagined four years in this place must feel like a lifetime. The harshness of this land made time distort. My four months in New South Wales felt more like a decade.

"Do you miss home?" I asked.

"Sometimes."

I peered sideways at him, determined to eke out more than one-word answers. And then he sat beside me on the damp grass. I took it as a sign he was open to my questioning. I folded my legs beneath me, suddenly conscious of the shortness of my Navy Board issue skirts.

"Who is she?" I asked. "The lady in the portrait?"

Blackwell's dark hair streamed back in the wind. "My wife. Sophia."

"Where is she?"

I was expecting *dead*. Perhaps I was even hoping for *dead*.

But, after a brief moment of silence, he said, "London."

I heard a sound come from my throat. "Tell me about her."

He raised his eyebrows. "What do you wish to know?"

In truth, I wished to know nothing. The question had just fallen out in the surprise of finding her still living. I could tell from her portrait the kind of lady his wife was; polite, well-spoken, obedient. The kind of lady I was supposed to have been.

Blackwell had been four years away from his wife; four years, plus the length of the voyage. Had time apart made him long for her? Or had he pushed her to the back of his thoughts?

"Do you love her?" I asked boldly.

He didn't flinch. "Yes. She's my wife."

"A marriage does not necessarily equal love."

"No. But it did in our case." He shook his head. "It does." An afterthought.

"Children?" I asked.

"No."

And what was she doing now, I wondered, that lady in the portrait? Beautiful, curly-haired Sophia. Was she faithful to her husband, pining, praying, awaiting his return? Or had she long found someone to take his place?

"And you?" he asked. "Have you a husband?"

"No," I said. "He died." The words felt strange on my lips. It was the first time I had ever spoken of Jonathan's death, outside of the interrogation at least. I was surprised at the lack of emotion in my voice.

Blackwell said, "I'm sorry."

I nodded. Perhaps this was why I had never spoken of Jonathan. I didn't want the pity. Or the questions.

"You're not like the other women here," he said. "You did not commit a crime of desperation."

I gave a wry smile at that. His guess was not entirely accurate. My crime had been one of great desperation, just not desperation fuelled by an empty belly and starving children.

"Is this your way of asking how I came to be here, Lieutenant?"

"No." He got to his feet, slinging the sack over his shoulder again. "That's not for me to know."

CHAPTER TWELVE

The light had drained from the day by the time we returned to the settlement. Though I was warm from walking, the icy wind had made my cheeks and fingertips numb. I wished for the gloves I had lost on the voyage.

As we approached the main street, I held myself back, leaving space between myself and Blackwell. He looked over his shoulder at me, brow wrinkled in confusion. I wasn't sure if my gesture was for him or me. I did not want him to be seen in the company of a lag in mud-streaked skirts. And I did not want to fuel stories of me as his concubine.

As I approached the hut, I felt a stab of dread. The door was hanging open, the cloth on the window dangling by one corner.

Blackwell dropped the sack and strode towards the hut. The tubers spilled onto the road. I grabbed the sack and followed.

I let out my breath as I stepped through the door. The table had been knocked onto its side, the books flung from the shelves. Shards of glass jars were strewn over the floor between the remains of potted meat, and the wooden chest had been overturned. The place smelled of piss and spilled liquor. I hovered beside the grate.

"Why did they do this?" I dared to ask.

He ran a hand through his hair. "Because I'm a murdering bastard." His voice was low and dark. Was it sarcasm? Or self-disgust? I couldn't tell.

"A little gift from the croppies, Lieutenant," said a voice behind me. I whirled around to see Patrick Owen in the doorway. His arms were folded across his chest, and the grin on his face made me want to strike him.

Blackwell strode towards him and Owen backed out into the street. I put down the sack and followed.

Owen shoved against Blackwell's chest, making him stumble backwards. No retaliation. Blackwell had several inches of height on the Irishman, his shoulders broader, arms thicker. But he made no attempt to fight, or to reach for his weapon and threaten Owen into leaving. It made me nervous. I knew Owen was the kind of man who'd carry a pistol in his pocket. The lieutenant was in close range. If there was a shot, he'd not survive it.

I raced out into High Street, searching for the soldiers on patrol. I found them pacing the alleys close to Marsden's land. When they saw me charging towards them, their hands went instinctively to their rifles. But when I told them what was happening – *Patrick Owen* and *Lieutenant Blackwell* – they were off down the street without giving me another glance.

"Come on now, Blackwell," Owen was drawling when I raced back to the hut, "you can do better than that."

"I'm not going to fight you, Owen," he said. "Get the hell out of here."

Owen swung a wild fist. The blow landed on the side of Blackwell's jaw, knocking him backwards into the wall of the hut. I heard a cry of shock escape me. The two soldiers darted forward, each grabbing one of Owen's arms and yanking him away from the lieutenant.

"You all right, sir?" asked one.

Blackwell rubbed his jaw. "Fine. Just get rid of him."

One of the marines shoved Owen hard in the back, making him stumble into the street. "Get out of here, you mad bog-jumper."

Owen chuckled. He dug his hands into his pockets and began to walk in the direction of the tavern.

"What?" I demanded. "He's just to walk away after—"

"Eleanor," Blackwell snapped, silencing me.

One of the marines glanced at me, then at the lieutenant. "Shall I get rid of the lag too, sir?"

"No. That won't be necessary."

I stood with my arms wrapped around my body, watching as Owen disappeared around the corner.

And I realised it then. Realised why the blacks had been blamed for the death of Maggie Abbot, when so many fingers pointed to Patrick Owen. I turned to look at Blackwell. He was staring after Owen too, a hand pressed to the side of his jaw.

"Owen is untouchable," I said. "He can do as he likes and he'll never be punished. I'm right, aren't I?"

Blackwell didn't answer.

"Why?" I pushed.

But he had retreated to silence. I could tell it was up to me to put the pieces together. I bent down to pick up one of the tubers that had rolled into the road.

"Fetch some water from the river," Blackwell said tersely. "There's a lot of cleaning to do."

The next day was a visiting day; a day when the men crowded the factory floor and watched as we paraded ourselves as potential wives. A settler just arrived from Sydney Town had been given his marriage certificate.

"A wife is required for this man," the superintendent said, sounding as though he'd never been so bored in his whole damn life. "Those willing to be married, please step forward."

For a moment, I thought of it. Choose me. Take me away from this place. Make me *wife*. My label of *concubine* sat heavy on my shoulders.

But I had seen how this circus worked. And I knew there would be questions.

Have you ever been married before? Yes? What happened to your husband?

I didn't want my whole shameful story spilled out on the factory floor.

I stayed motionless, staring at my feet. Women from the *Norfolk* stepped forward, along with several others. The settler seeking a wife was young and handsome. A far better catch than most of the pock-faced scrubs who came traipsing through this place.

He chose a young girl from the *Norfolk*; a scrappy blonde thing who'd cried all the way to Gibraltar. Petite and birdlike, she made me feel like an ogre.

She gave the settler a tiny, shy smile, looking up at him with enormous blue eyes. I imagined her in her trial, weeping before the magistrate while telling a pitiful tale of a stolen cloak to keep out the snow.

"You ever been married before?" the settler asked her.

"No sir."

And I thought of Jonathan Marling with a bullet in his chest, sure I'd be at the factory forever.

We drank at the river in celebration of the tearful girl from the *Norfolk*. Within an hour of the settler's visit to the factory, she'd been hauled off to the church to sign her marriage papers. Now she was on her way to her new husband's farm with a ticket of leave in her pocket.

Lottie sat beside me on the log, and we passed the dregs of a rum bottle back and forth between us.

"I thought you would have put yourself forward," I told her. "Or did he not take your fancy?"

Lottie didn't return my smile. "You know it's not about that," she said. "Marriage is a necessity. It's the only chance I got of getting out of here. Getting out of old Bert's bed."

"So why did you not put yourself forward?"

Lottie hiccupped on the rum. "I've got to marry an Irishman, don't I. My poor da would be rolling in his grave if he knew his only daughter had married a *sasanaigh*."

I hugged my knees. The men had fashioned a cricket bat out of a fallen tree branch and were whacking a cloth ball across the riverbank.

"Do you truly want a lifetime shackled to some mindless croppy?" I asked. "It's not your only way out. They say good behaviour will get us a ticket of leave."

We all talked about the ticket of leave like it was the key to the greatest treasure in the land. A mythical treasure, for while we all knew someone who'd managed to get a ticket, there weren't one of us who had ever laid eyes on such a thing.

They said the magistrate handed out tickets whenever it suited him. There was no rhyme or reason to it, as far as any of us could tell. Stories were told of gentlemen convicts who'd stepped off the prison ship and had a ticket pressed into their hands. Others swore they could bribe their way to freedom. I knew several women who had climbed off the *Norfolk* with their liberty. I'd tried not to think of what they'd had to do to earn it.

"Is it true then?" I'd asked Blackwell one night. "We can bribe the magistrate for our freedom?"

True or not, I knew it was nothing but wishful thinking on my part. For the magistrate of Parramatta was the Reverend Samuel Marsden, and there was no way his fine, upstanding soul was getting bribed by a lowly concubine.

"A ticket of leave is a reward for good behaviour, not bribery," Blackwell had said, his face as impassive and even as ever.

Lottie snorted. "When did a factory lass ever get her ticket of leave without marrying for it first? And besides, what good is a ticket if you got no man to support you?" Her eyes were on Patrick Owen as he strutted over from the cricket match. The back of my neck prickled with anger.

Untouchable Patrick Owen. His eyes caught mine for a second and he gave me a ghost of a smile.

I stood abruptly. I couldn't just sit there across from him, sharing a drink like everything was all right. Lottie grabbed my arm and pulled me back down to the log.

"You've got to stop this," she said. "He's innocent."

I snorted. "You can't truly believe that."

"Yes," she said after a moment. "I do. The Rum Corps hates the Irish. If they could have put Owen on the scaffold, they would have. So aye, I believe he didn't do it."

I wrapped my arms around myself. She had things the wrong way around, I was sure. Owen's innocence – or lack of it – had little to do with anything.

The Rum Corps hated the Irish, yes, but they knew Owen was revered among the rebels. Send him to the scaffold, and who knew what chaos would be unleashed? The night of his arrest, the settlement had been in disarray.

The authorities were playing a dangerous game; letting a criminal loose among us to keep the croppies down. I knew with grim certainty that Owen had killed Maggie. Maybe such a thing simply didn't matter to the men who ran this place. What need was there for justice where the factory lasses were concerned? Perhaps it was far more crucial that a second Irish uprising was quelled.

Lottie planted the empty bottle in the dirt and stood, grabbing my arm and pulling me up beside her. "Come on. The drink's finished. We need to get more."

She looped her arm through mine as we walked towards the tavern.

"I wish you'd just give him a chance, Nell. That's all I'm asking. He's a good man. He's got a real passion in him. He's just doing what he thinks is best for his people."

I decided not to tell her about Owen's attack on Blackwell the night before. Nothing I said would make her change her mind, especially not where the lieutenant was involved. I knew it would only lead to conflict between us. And I didn't want that. Having a friend in this place was far too precious.

But my hatred for Owen was roiling inside me, pushing against my chest. That morning, the side of Blackwell's face had been purple with bruising after their altercation in the street. And one of the shelves Owen had kicked at had fallen in the night.

As we approached the tavern, I felt my stomach knot. I'd not set foot inside since the night I'd stolen the potatoes. Some foolish part of me was afraid I'd be recognised.

Lottie shoved open the door and we stepped inside through a curtain of pipe smoke. Men were clustered around the counter in mud-streaked shirts, cannikins of drink in grimy hands. I kept my eyes down as I followed Lottie to the bar. I recognised the woman serving as one of the convicts from the factory. Lottie reached into her pocket and handed over enough coin for the new rum bottle.

"Stay and keep us company, ginger," said one of the men at the bar, sliding a hand around my waist. I shoved him away, his friends' laughter ringing in my ears.

On the walk back to the river, Lottie was harping on about Owen and his cohorts again. My head was beginning to ache.

"Some of the croppies," she began, "they were sent here after the rebellion in Ireland without their convict records. They were only sentenced to seven years. But it's coming on eight now, and there's no word of them being freed." She turned to look at me, her hazel eyes shining. "Tell me you wouldn't be angry if you that were you."

I frowned. "I understand that, Lottie. But this is about Owen killing Maggie and leaving her body on the side of the road."

Her eyes hardened. "You don't understand," she said. "How could you? How could you have any idea? How could you have any idea what it's like to struggle and fight and not know where your next meal is coming from?"

I sat back on the log and began to trace a stick through the dirt. I'd not spoken a word to Lottie about my privileged upbringing – I'd not spoken a word about it to anyone. But I was beginning to see it was not a thing I could easily hide.

"You think I don't know, Nell?" Lottie pushed. "You think I can't hear it in the way you speak? And the way you bleat on about Marsden's register as though once you were actually worth something?"

I didn't reply. I felt chastened; an intruder in someone else's world.

"Why a toff like you was caught thieving I'll never know," said Lottie. Her tone suggested she was not interested in my answer.

I'd not been transported for thieving, as I'd told Lottie I had. I'd not needed coin, or food to fill my empty belly. But I'd craved security, nonetheless. Needed someone to show me how to live my own life. And so, when my husband had held out his hand and told me to follow him down the wrong path, I had done it without question.

I took the bottle from Lottie and gulped down a mouthful, coughing as the rum seared my throat.

Look at us!, I wanted to scream. Here we were side by side in matching slops, matching blisters on our fingers, the same rum bottle passed back and forth between our hands.

But I knew all the blisters in the world would not make me understand what it was like to grow up with nothing. I had no thought of what it was to struggle and fight because I'd never had to do it before.

Lottie stood suddenly, and made her way towards Owen and the other men. I rested my aching head against my arms, letting the drunken conversations wash over me.

I found myself longing for London; for the glittering, diamond and ruby world I had once known.

There was nothing for me to return to in England, of course. My husband and father were dead, and I would never be welcomed back into my old circles after leaving for this place on a prison ship. But I ached nonetheless for the cluttered grey skyline, the constant rattle of hooves and wheels, for the twists and turns of the river. Ached for a world I would never see again. Most of all, I wished for my own ignorance, for my ability to turn a blind eye. I wished for the naïve fool I had been when I had married Jonathan Marling.

I gulped down the rum, seeking drunkenness, seeking foolishness. I wanted my thoughts to still; wanted them to stop churning over Owen's exoneration and Maggie's blank eyes. But for better or for worse, I didn't know how to live in ignorance anymore.

My thoughts did not still. Instead, they crystallised. I wanted to speak to Reverend Marsden. Wanted that conversation I had been denied when he'd sent me on my way after seeing me at the courthouse in my bloodstained convict slops. At the back of my mind, I knew nothing I said would make a difference – Owen was free, Maggie was dead, and the female register was on its way across the seas. But just for a moment, I wanted to be seen. To be heard. To be more than an insignificant concubine. I would tell the reverend of the bruises on Maggie's arms. Tell him of the way she spent her nights by the river to escape Owen's fists. Pander to Marsden's hatred of the croppies and make him see that Patrick Owen deserved to be hanged.

Rum churning through my blood, I stood dizzily and strode towards the vast expanse of Marsden's land on the north-eastern edge of the settlement. I pressed my shoulders back and lifted my chin. I was a well-spoken woman from Clerkenwell who deserved to be taken seriously. Tonight I would make sure Reverend Marsden saw that.

As I approached the gates, a soldier came out of the blackness. "Where do you think you're going?"

I lifted my chin. "I wish to speak with Reverend Marsden," I said, trying my best to sound like an educated lady and not a lag filled up with rum. I wished I were wearing my worsted gown.

"Reverend Marsden don't have nothing to do with your kind," he said on a chuckle.

His dismissiveness made anger burn inside me. More than that, I hated that one look at me had told him I was a government woman. It was far too dark to see the tell-tale blue stripes on my skirts. What was it about me that told him I was not just the wife of a settler? Perhaps it was that bitterness in my words, or the fire in my eyes. Perhaps Hannah had been right when she'd claimed I couldn't blend into a place if I tried.

"It's very important," I said, continuing my march towards the house. It had never felt more pressing that I be permitted that conversation.

He grabbed my arm, fingers digging in hard. "Did you not hear me? The reverend don't have nothing to do with the factory whores."

Sudden anger tore through me. Before I knew what I was doing, I was swinging my arm, striking his nose and making blood spurt down the front of his coat. I stared open-mouthed, unable to believe I'd done such a thing. In a second he was on top of me, pinning me to the ground and wrenching my arms behind my back. Pain lanced through my shoulders. I felt hot drops of his blood against my ear. A shout into the night and two more soldiers came running. They yanked me to my feet, delivering me to the factory and the waiting hands of the superintendent.

CHAPTER THIRTEEN

"I would rather die than go out of my own country to be devoured by savages."

Convict Sarah Mills
Refusing transportation in favour of the death sentence
1789

They threw me into the cells on the bottom floor of the jail. Five days of solitary confinement. I'd not been given so much as a chance to explain myself, though I knew, even if I had, I'd have found no excuse for what I'd done. What did the Rum Corps care that I'd been mortally offended?

The cell was near lightless. Nothing to sleep on but the cold stone floor. I could only guess at the time of day by the clatter of footsteps up and down the staircase leading to the spinning room. Shivering in a corner, I drifted in and out of sleep, and soon lost any sense of whether the footsteps on the stairs made it morning, night, or somewhere in between. Once a day, a hunk of stale bread and a cannikin of water appeared inside the door, bringing with it a precious and fleeting gasp of light.

My anger at Marsden and Owen shifted into anger at myself. I was troubled by what I'd done. I'd been a criminal for some time, of course, but my crime had been carefully calculated. I had never acted so violently, so rashly in my life. I scared myself. My attack on the soldier had been rum fuelled, yes, but it had been a reaction to the injustices I saw in the world around me. I began to wonder what else I was capable of.

My dreams were vivid, filled with lags and blood and Jonathan. Time began to lose meaning, and I felt as though the whole rest of my life would be consumed by this dark cell.

I lost myself in my thoughts. My world was no longer Parramatta, populated by Owen, by Blackwell, by Hannah, by Lottie. Instead, I was back in a townhouse in Clerkenwell, with roses in the front garden and a fortepiano in the parlour.

I'd known from the first days of our marriage that Jonathan had secrets. There were many nights that he'd return home late, his explanations vague and insubstantial. I assumed he had taken a mistress, and like a dutiful wife, I did not ask questions. On the rare occasions we saw each other, he was affectionate and kind, full of questions about the books I was reading, the pieces of music I was learning, the ladies I had taken tea with.

It had never occurred to me that Jonathan might be bad with money. His jewellery business was flourishing; churning out fine pieces for ladies of our class and beyond. I had everything I needed; staff in the household, fine clothing in my wardrobe. Food and wine on the table and a bookshelf that reached the ceiling.

I had no idea that, with each day of our marriage, my dowry and inheritance were being frittered away in a string of bad business investments, and the occasional sorry night at the gambling halls.

A week after New Year, Jonathan took me to Hanover Square to hear a Handel cantata. A generous thing, I'd thought, for him to indulge my love for music, when I knew such a thing would bore him to tears.

As the carriage rattled its way back to Clerkenwell, he slid across the bench so his shoulder pressed against mine.

"Did you enjoy the evening?" he asked.

I smiled. "Very much. The music was magical."

"I'm glad." He took my hand and pressed it between both of his. "Nell," he said, "there's something I ought to tell you."

I was expecting to hear of the mistress. Couldn't believe he was planning to admit to it with my hand sandwiched between his. But Jonathan spoke in a tentative half voice, outlining the coining enterprise he and his business partner had been operating since the early days of our marriage.

The cellar of the jeweller's filled with silver, with copper, with scales, weights and crucibles. Moulds and tankards and bottle after bottle of aqua-fortis. For each gold necklace that had been finely crafted over the years, there was a pouch of counterfeit shillings and sixpences, put out to pay off gambling debts, or exchanged at the bank for legal white notes.

I forced a laugh. "I see." I waited for him to break into a smile. Waited for the confirmation that this was some wildly unamusing joke.

It didn't come.

"Is this what you do?" I asked. "When you're out late at night?"

Jonathan picked at a non-existent piece of lint on his greatcoat. "Mostly, yes."

I didn't know whether to be horrified, or relieved he had not spent our entire marriage in bed with other women.

I looked out across the coach, with its embroidered benches and gossamer curtains. Looked down at my silk gown, at the gold ring on my finger. How much of this had been paid for with counterfeit coin?

Jonathan's eyes were on me, waiting for my reaction. My insides were churning and my skin was hot. But I knew better than to unleash my anger on my husband. Paid for illegally or not, I knew how easily that coach, that gown, that ring could be taken away from me.

"And was this your idea?" I asked, careful to keep my voice level.

"No." As the glow of a streetlamp shafted through the window, I saw Jonathan had the good grace to look ashamed. "It was Wilder who proposed it in the beginning."

I shifted uncomfortably on the bench seat. Even the mention of Henry Wilder was enough to make my every muscle tense. I had met Jonathan's business partner several times in the past. An enormous man with a bald head and tiny, darting eyes, he would take my hand in his sweaty palms and press a kiss against it that made my stomach turn over. I had no difficulty imagining him in some shady cellar with a pile of counterfeit coins in front of him. Jonathan, however, was a different story.

I looked him up and down, taking in the neat contours of his face that were so familiar to me. In the half-light of the carriage, he felt suddenly like a stranger.

"Wilder asked you to be involved?"

"Yes." Jonathan picked at the stitching on the edge of the bench seat. "As he made clear, we have both the skills and the means to run such an enterprise. It seemed rather a logical progression for our business."

I let out my breath in disbelief. "A logical progression?"

Jonathan squeezed my fingers. "Don't get angry, Nell. It doesn't suit you."

I pulled my hand out from under his. "Why?" I asked.

He turned to look out at the passing street. Streetlights glittered through the glass, painting jewelled patterns on the carriage windows.

There were money issues, my husband told me then. Debts to be settled. Bills to be paid. He gave me a strained smile. "Perhaps you ought to have foreseen such things when you married a mere jeweller."

"Don't be so foolish," I said. "You're as fine a man as any." But I could hear the thinness to my words. For my kind and decent husband had just revealed himself to be entrenched in criminality.

"Wilder knew I owed money," he told me. "Said he could help me make what I needed. And plenty more."

I wished for my old ignorance. Wished to be sitting in Hanover Square with closed eyes, letting the lush arpeggios of the cantata wash over me.

"Why are you telling me this now?" I asked.

Jonathan reached for me again, covering my wrist with his long, thin fingers. "Because we need you to be involved."

An expansion of their business. Thanks to contacts Wilder had curated, he and Jonathan had a seemingly endless array of apprentices, servants and cashiers across London, all responsible for handling their superiors' money. Each would pay a fee for the counterfeit pieces, and exchange them for the genuine coins in their masters' coffers. Send the forgeries out with the business and keep the authentic coins for themselves. There was great wealth to be made, Jonathan assured me. Wealth that would ensure we lived a life of concert halls and diamonds until the day we died.

But with he and Wilder working long hours at the jeweller's, they needed a third person to run the coins to each business and manage the payments.

This, I realised then, was the reason for the evening at Hanover Square.

The reason my tone-deaf husband had sat through two hours of wailing sopranos. It was not just to please me. It was to make me agreeable.

"You've plenty of time on your hands, don't you, Nell." It was not a question. "It's not as though you've children to take care of."

His tone of voice said it all. During the five years of our marriage, Jonathan had watched his friends' wives produce child after child, while I had failed to give my husband an heir. Though he had never once said as much, I knew myself a failure as a wife. With each month, each year that passed, I became more and more certain he would find another woman who could give him the son he craved. Each night he returned home to me, I found myself almost surprised. I had no thought of what I would do if Jonathan left me. Running counterfeit coins across the city felt like the least I could do for the man who had saved me from facing the world alone.

And so when he looked me in the eye and said, "You'll do this for me, won't you, my darling?", I found myself agreeing.

For more than a year, I skulked across the city with coins in my reticule, liaising with the apprentices, the servants, the cashiers. Each of the clients had been groomed by Henry Wilder himself; men he knew would keep their mouths shut and their eyes down in exchange for a little wealth.

Though I knew, of course, that I was breaking the law, I pushed the reality of it to the back of my mind. I told myself I was doing no more than helping my husband, as a dutiful wife should. Making up for my failures, proving I was of use.

I'd had no thought the thief-takers were following until I got back to our townhouse. They accosted me at the front door and demanded to know why I was carrying a bag of coins, and the ledger recording the businesses I had received them from.

Jonathan had made sure I had a story prepared – *my husband has requested I assist with the banking* – but I told it in such a pathetic, trembling voice that even the densest of men would have known me lying. And with my husband away at the jeweller's, I could only stand and watch as the thief-takers tore the house apart, finding the counterfeit coins I was yet to bank hidden at the bottom of my husband's desk drawer. I had no thought of which of our clients had turned us in. But I knew it didn't matter.

With striking efficiency, I was escorted to the thief-takers' wagon, while our staff watched wide-eyed and murmured between themselves. My terror eclipsed any hint of shame I felt at the staff seeing me this way.

In front the magistrate, I admitted to it all. I told him how Jonathan had sat beside me in the carriage and outlined his plans. Admitted I had called at each of the businesses on the ledger that day, and had been doing so for the past year and half. Somewhere, at the back of my mind, I knew I was likely condemning both Jonathan and myself, but I had been raised believing my job was to appease the men around me, and I told the magistrate exactly what he wanted to hear. I was hoping for lenience, for mercy. Hoping blindly to return to that townhouse in Clerkenwell with little more than a slap on the wrist.

"Are you aware the crime of coining is considered high treason, Mrs Marling?"

I wasn't aware. Jonathan had played down the crime I was committing. I was nothing but a courier, he'd assured me, my hands clean of the silver dust and chemicals that saw the coins churned out into the world. And he had led me to believe we would not be caught. I had accepted it because I needed to.

"Are you aware of the punishment you will likely face for such a crime?"

In a hollow, expressionless voice, he told me how I would be drawn to Old Bailey Road to face the Newgate hangman.

I heard a laugh escape me. That same disbelieving, bordering-on-hysterical laugh I had given when Jonathan had first told me about his coining enterprise. I heard the sound of it hang in the still air of the interrogation room. My body went cold, then hot, and I saw the world swim.

"And my husband?" I managed.

But Jonathan was never to make it to the hangman. The day of my arrest, he took a bullet to the chest in the front garden of our townhouse. The constable delivered the news to me in such a blank, matter-of-fact tone that his words barely registered. I was far too shocked to feel anything; not grief, or anger, or regret. All I could make sense of was that I would not be returning to Clerkenwell, or Hanover Square. There would be no more townhouse, and no more fortepiano. No more roses in the garden where my husband's body had fallen.

My other realisation was that I knew who had killed him. There was no doubt in my mind that Henry Wilder had come after him to prevent Jonathan from speaking his name. Prevent him from revealing him as the architect of the enterprise.

But I stayed silent. I'd been taught never to speak out. Never to make waves. I told the magistrate I knew nothing of who the shooter might be. And with closed eyes and death hanging over me, I turned my back and let my husband's killer walk free.

Once, back in the blissful days of my ignorance, Jonathan and I had passed a prison hulk rotting on the banks of the Thames. We were returning by boat from two days at the seaside, and the sight of the sorry vessel beached in the mud at the low tide had yanked me back to reality. Men in ragged clothes moved about on deck and I could hear shouts and groans coming from within the lightless shell of the ship.

I found myself watching, unable to tear my eyes from these men who had been reduced to little more than animals. Stripped of dignity, of privacy, of freedom, a future.

"They'd be better off dead," Jonathan said, a hand to my shoulder ushering me away. I nodded along, forever in agreement.

And perhaps there were convicts on that hulk who wished they had faced the hangman. But when I was sent to New South Wales for the term of my natural life, I found myself sobbing with relief.

I kept to myself as the *Norfolk* slid down the Thames and into the English Channel. At least as best as I could with elbows in my face and women on every side of me. I couldn't fathom that this was my life now. Somehow, engaging with the chatter, the gambling, the out-of-tune singing made my new life far too real.

I'd managed the seasickness well enough in the early days of the voyage, when the *Norfolk* traced the coast of Europe and slid smoothly into the Bay of Gibraltar. But in the open ocean, the ship was seized, and down in those airless, lightless quarters, we lost all sense of up and down.

Water poured in through the hatches and the sea was thunder against the hull. Most of us were too sick to stand, to speak, to do anything except huddle in our own mess, and the pool of seawater gathering at our feet. I shivered and retched, and clung to the edge of a bunk until my fingers were raw. I tried to close my eyes, but that only made things worse. I had no idea of how many days and nights had passed. All I knew was that, there in the bowels of the ship with months at sea ahead of us, I wanted to die.

With my eyes half closed, I was dimly aware of a woman weaving her way through the bunks and groaning bodies. Hannah Clapton. I couldn't fathom how she was on her feet.

And then she was standing over me, offering me a gentle smile.

She held out a small hunk of bread. "Here, love. You ought to eat something."

I shook my head.

"You'll feel better for it. Trust me."

I took the bread. Forced down a mouthful. It wasn't like I could feel any worse.

"That's it," she said with a small smile. "It'll help. Take a little more."

She watched me like an anxious mother as I took another minuscule bite.

"Why are you not sick?" I asked. My throat was burning, and my mouth felt horribly dry.

Hannah shrugged. "Spent half my childhood on my pa's fishing boat. Seems I still got my sea legs after all these years." She tilted her head to look at me, chuckling to herself. "And here I were thinking you couldn't speak."

I leaned my head wearily against the edge of the bunk. "What are you talking about?"

"You've not said a word to any of us since we boarded," she said. "Me and some of the others were wondering about whether you was soft in the head."

I would have been insulted had I not been too sick to care. I felt shame wash over me then. Shame that came not from hunching in a corner of a convict ship with half my insides on my skirts. But from looking down upon these women crammed below decks with me.

Hannah was right; I'd hardly spoken a word since London. I'd told myself I was above them; all those dirt-encrusted women I shared a shit bucket with. I had been raised to look down on people of their kind. But with each day, my old life grew more distant, and I began to see things as they really were. What place did I have to look down on these women? What separated us other than the fact that they had stolen to feed their families, while I had carted counterfeit coins around the city? That didn't make me better than them. It made me a fool.

When the door of the cell finally creaked open, I started at the sound. I cowered in the corner, squinting into the shaft of light from the soldier's lamp.

"What day is it?" I asked, my voice husky from disuse. "Am I to be released?"

The soldier chuckled. "Unless you fancy another night in here."

With a hand pressed to the wall for balance, I made my way out of the cell and into the street. I stood outside the jail for a moment, inhaling deep lungfuls of the clean, fragrant air. I stretched my arms above my head, and rolled my shoulders, my whole body aching.

It was night, but after the blackness of the cell, the lamp above the jail door made it feel as bright as morning. I walked across the bridge towards High Street. A peal of laughter rose from a group of men outside the tavern. And in that moment, Henry Wilder and Jonathan were gone. I was relieved to have escaped the dark, and the past it had pulled me into.

I walked slowly back towards the hut. It wouldn't have surprised me if Blackwell wanted me to leave. After all, I'd struck one of his fellow soldiers.

I could see the lamp flickering through the window. It made me realise how much I did not want him to send me away.

I stood outside the door for a moment, debating whether to knock. I decided against it. That little mud hut was the closest thing I had to a home. I wanted it to feel that way.

Blackwell was stooping by the fire, stirring the embers to life. A pot hung on the hook above the grate. He looked at me for a long second, his eyes giving nothing away.

Suddenly, I was acutely aware of the grime on my skin and the blood on my hands. Aware of the stench of the cells that had followed me back to the hut. Without speaking, I went to my little pile of clothing in the corner. Took my clean dress and shift, and hurried outside, making my way to the river. I could hear the water sighing in the dark.

I took off my boots and stepped into the river. The iciness of it stole my breath, making me gasp aloud. But there was something exhilarating about the feel of the water against my skin.

With the river lit only by the moon, I stripped myself naked and stepped deeper into the water. The tide was high, and I could feel the swell trying to tug me towards the sea. I kept my feet firmly planted in the mud as I scrubbed at my skin. Above my head, an owl let out its husky, jagged cry. I lifted my face to the sky, inhaling the clean air. I plunged my head beneath the surface and the sounds of the world around me fell away, leaving only a deep, sighing silence. I felt the water move around my face, the cold making my blood pump hard. I emerged breathless and shivering, but blessedly clean.

I stepped out of the river and pulled on my clean clothes. I squeezed the water from my hair and let it hang wet down my back.

When I returned to the hut, Blackwell had placed a bowl of soup on the table. He nodded towards it. "Sit down. You must be hungry."

I paused. "What about you?"

"I've eaten already. I wasn't sure if you were to be released today. But there's enough left for another bowl."

I perched on the edge of the chair, looking up at him. "Will you sit with me?" I asked. "I'd appreciate the company."

Blackwell sat. Pretended not to watch while I spooned the soup into my mouth. It was thin and flavourless, but its warmth was achingly welcome after five days of bread and water. After only a few mouthfuls, my stomach felt full and slightly unsettled.

"You're lucky you didn't hang," said Blackwell. "It's a serious crime to strike an officer."

I nodded, eyes down. I knew that well, of course. Knew who held the power in this place.

I wanted to speak; to put into words that desperate need to be seen I'd felt the night I'd gone to Marsden's property. To be more than just a discarded convict, sent to New South Wales to be forgotten. And I wanted to speak of the wild anger that had torn through me when the soldier had looked me up and down and called me *whore*.

When I looked up at Blackwell, his eyes were on me, intense and dark in the candlelight. I felt seen. Unforgotten. And in that moment it was enough to be sitting at the table with another human being, feeling warm soup sliding down my throat.

"You're right," Blackwell said after a moment. "About Patrick Owen being untouchable."

I stopped eating suddenly, the spoon halfway to my mouth.

He said no more, as though he knew he had crossed a line. Told me something he shouldn't have. "I think there's a little bread," he said, sliding back on his chair to search the shelf. "Would you like some?"

I pushed past his question. It was too late to pretend he hadn't spoken. "And what's to be done about it?" I asked.

Blackwell sighed. He met my eyes with a dark, pointed look. Yes, I understood. This conversation was never to go further than this table.

"Nothing," he said tautly. "It's the way things have to be. Or else more people will die."

CHAPTER FOURTEEN

"Many of the Irish Convicts are well acquainted with the art of war, and all the secret intrigues that can work on the minds of the ignorant and unwary."

Rev. Samuel Marsden

A Few Observations on the Toleration of the Catholic Religion in New South Wales

1806

And so it was; the way things had to be. Around the other women, I steered my conversations away from the rebels, from Castle Hill, from Blackwell. Away from anything that might disrupt the sense of solidarity I felt at the spinning wheels. I needed my friendship with Lottie. I would not let Owen take that from us. But at Blackwell's supper table, I asked questions.

"Why is he untouchable?"

Sometimes the lieutenant kept his thoughts to himself. Other times, he seemed to want to speak.

"The government fears another uprising is imminent," he told me one night, tossing a log onto the fire. "They fear that if the rebels see their leader strung up it will incite them to violence."

I felt a flicker of self-satisfaction that things were as I had imagined. That I was beginning to develop an understanding of the world around me.

"And what of Maggie?" I asked, at the table with a cannikin of tea in my hand. "Does she not deserve for her killer to be punished?"

I was careful to keep my voice even, controlled. Though he had stood on

Owen's jury, Blackwell was being open with me now. Allow myself to let my anger loose and I would destroy this precious chance at knowledge.

"Yes. She does." He jabbed the poker into the fire and made a log break noisily in the grate.

I thought of Jonathan and Henry Wilder. For all his faults, my husband deserved justice just like Maggie did. Deserved for his killer to face the gallows. And yet I had kept silent out of fear. Let Henry Wilder walk free. I knew my guilt over doing so had fuelled my desire to see Owen punished.

"But it's like I said," Blackwell continued, taking the teacup I had nudged across the table, "if Owen is hanged and the rebels retaliate, far more people will die."

It was the closest I'd come to hearing him acknowledge Owen's guilt. I wasn't sure if it felt like a victory or a defeat.

But I was acutely aware that he was sharing far more with me than he ought to. I knew as a factory lass I had no place knowing these things. But sometimes, with the fire burning and cups in our hands, Blackwell and I felt oddly like equals. Strange that we might seem to be standing on such even ground when we were at different ends of the scale of power. It was not just the information about Owen, but the small pieces of himself he would toss out into conversation.

I always dreamt of seeing this place.

My mother died when I was twelve.

I much prefer coffee to tea.

I feared the moment would come when he would realise he had let me too close. Allowed me to step onto ground on which a factory lass was forbidden to stand.

"And what of you?" I asked. "Owen is untouchable. Are you not afraid he'll come after you again? With a pistol this time?"

Blackwell turned the cup around in his hands. "His immunity goes only so far."

"So his immunity doesn't stretch to killing an officer. But it does stretch to killing a factory lass."

Blackwell took a sip of tea, meeting my eyes. A wordless response. But the words did not need to be said.

"If Owen dares come after me, the other officers will have him on the scaffold," he told me. But I could hear the uncertainty in his voice.

After church that Sunday, I set out for the market. I lifted my face to the sky, letting the spring sun warm my cheeks. The rain had stopped for the first time in days, a dazzling blue emerging from within the clouds. The surrounding bush smelled clean and damp.

I filled my basket with meat and vegetables from the farmers' stalls set up in the backs of wagons. As I passed the clothes stand, I stopped, my eyes falling on a swathe of violet fabric on the racks of gowns and cloaks.

That colour, I knew it well. I pushed aside the cloaks to reveal my worsted gown. There was the neat pleating at the waist, the single brass button, the delicate scoop of the neckline. Whoever had stolen it from the ship must have sold it for a few pennies.

I ran my finger over the skirts. They were as soft as I remembered, despite their months at sea and subsequent kidnapping by some nameless woman on the ship.

The stall owner caught me looking. "Yours for a crown," she said. I felt for the coins in my pocket. I knew it was foolish to spend what little I had on something I would never even wear. I could hardly strut into the factory in a pleated gown. But I needed it back. It was my last piece of a life I thought had gone forever.

I handed the coins over before I could change my mind.

I was glad to find the hut empty. The fire was still crackling mutedly from the bread I had baked that morning, and the air was thick and humid. With the fire still lit, I knew Blackwell couldn't have gone far.

I pulled off my dress and stepped into the gown, fastening the hooks and closing the single button below my throat. I felt the weight of the skirts around my ankles.

I took Blackwell's small shaving mirror and peered into it. My hair had come loose from its plait and hung over my shoulders. With my free hand I bundled it into a knot on my neck, searching out the gentleman's wife I had once been.

I could not find her. The eyes that looked back at me were hardened. The eyes of a woman who did not belong in a worsted gown.

I put down the mirror. I didn't want to see my reflection. I didn't want that reminder of who I'd once been, of all I'd squandered with my terrible choices. Nor did I want Blackwell to return and see me in the dress. Perhaps for a fleeting moment, a part of me had wanted him to see that I had once been more than just a factory lass. But that lady in the worsted gown was nothing to be proud of. What pride was there to be felt when I'd let that life unravel so dramatically?

I undid the hooks and let the gown slide from my shoulders. I stood for a moment with it in a pool around my feet, before stepping out of it and tossing it into the fire. It caught with a burst of orange light, and I sat back on my heels to watch. I felt the blaze warm my cheeks.

The door creaked open and I leapt to my feet, suddenly aware I was standing there in searing daylight in nothing but my underskirts.

My eyes caught Blackwell's for a second and I grabbed my striped dress, holding it to my body. He disappeared again before I could speak.

I dressed hurriedly and stepped out into the street, feeling the need to apologise. It had been wrong for me to strut around the hut indecently in the middle of the afternoon. I couldn't bear for Blackwell to think I had been parading myself for his benefit.

I called after him, but he didn't respond; just kept striding out towards the edge of the settlement.

I followed. I wanted to explain myself. But I also wanted to know where he was going.

We climbed into the hills, along a narrow track beaten into the scrub. I stayed some distance behind, not wanting him to know I was following, but close enough to keep track of him as he wove through the trees.

We walked for over an hour, perhaps closer to two. Sun streaked through the trees, insects dancing in the needles of light.

I could see a clearing up ahead. I hung back, hiding myself among the trees.

I peered out between the gnarled white trunks. Rows of graves, each marked with a crude cross, like Maggie Abbott's.

Blackwell walked slowly among them, eyes fixed to the crosses. I stood motionless, barely daring to breathe.

My heart lurched. Why had he come here? Who lay beneath his earth?

I darted into the undergrowth so he wouldn't see me. Held my breath as he walked past, back onto the narrow path.

Once his footsteps had disappeared, I stepped out into the makeshift cemetery. A heaviness hung over the place. A coldness, despite the warmth of the air. There were shallow engravings on the wooden crosses and I bent closer to read them. No names appeared in the inscriptions, but there were snatches of Gaelic, carved in a rough hand. And then English words that made my breath catch.

Castle Hill 1804

Had the battle taken place among these trees? I had learned from some of the men at the river that the site of the main conflict lay further to the north, where the Rum Corps had surrounded the rebels and brought them to their knees. But I also knew there had been men killed in the uprising from Toongabbie to Sydney Town; days of underhand warfare following the main attempted rebellion. I imagined the redcoats storming through these trees, imagined rifle fire shattering the stillness.

How many of these men had been sent to their graves by Blackwell's bullet? Was it guilt that had brought him here?

Surely it was no easy thing to be a soldier; to shoot to kill on another's bidding. Could a man still be haunted if he were acting in the name of duty?

I stood suddenly, unable to bear the oppressive atmosphere of the cemetery. I turned back the way I'd come, seeking out the narrow path that snaked back towards civilisation.

When I returned to Parramatta, I detoured to the river so Blackwell wouldn't ask about my absence.

"Oh," I said, in the world's worst attempt at feigning ignorance, "you're back. Collecting the chocolate flowers?" I set the bucket of water on the ground beside the hearth.

He returned my smile, but it didn't reach his eyes. "Something like that."

I had hoped, of course, I might nudge him into speaking of the burial ground. But I could tell today he was to be tight-lipped.

"I'm sorry about earlier," I said. "I didn't mean for you to see me that way. I dirtied my dress and I…"

Blackwell shook his head dismissively. "It's no matter." He slid the Bible from the shelf and sat at the table, opening the book in front of him.

His message was clear: conversation over.

The weight pressing down on him was almost a physical thing. A part of me longed to ask him outright about the cemetery. I couldn't bear the thought of him locking all that regret away to be passed over.

"I saw you come from the north," I said clumsily. "What's out there?"

Blackwell eyed me. I could tell, even without him saying a word, that he knew I had followed him.

Beneath the table, I saw something slide through the shadows. I shrieked, and bounded onto the empty chair. "Snake!" I yelled, pointing wildly.

Blackwell stood, his chair toppling. He reached down to pick it up.

"Be careful!" I cried. "Did you not hear me? A *snake!*"

His lips curled into a smile. "I heard you, yes."

My eyes widened as he bent to straighten the chair. I watched the creature slither out from beneath the table. I couldn't pull my eyes from it. There was something horribly entrancing about the way it glided across the floor. I glared at Blackwell. "Do something!"

"Stop yelling, Eleanor," he said, with a calmness I found unfathomable. He took his rifle from where it rested beside the shelf.

"You're going to shoot it?" I demanded.

He laughed. Brought the butt of the rifle down on the snake, mashing its head into the floor. He picked up its limp body and carried it outside. I found myself peering frantically around the hut, searching for other intruders.

I was still teetering on the chair when Blackwell returned.

"You can come down now," he said, offering me his hand. I climbed down carefully, before beginning a thorough search of my sleeping pallet. I heard him chuckle.

"It's not funny," I said. "What if it had gotten into the blankets?"

"I didn't imagine you to be afraid of snakes," he said, sitting at the table and opening the Bible again.

"What kind of madman would not be afraid of snakes? Did not you see the way it moves? It's completely unnatural."

Blackwell laughed again, eyes on the book as he turned the page. I straightened my blanket and tried to catch my breath. My heart was still beating fast. But I was glad I had made him smile.

In the morning, I awoke to find the brass button from my worsted gown on the floor beside my head. Had Blackwell found it in the fireplace? I stared at it for a long time; that fire-tarnished piece of my old life I couldn't burn away. His message was clear; I had my past and he had his. They weren't for each other to know.

I took the button from beside my bed. Stepped out of the hut in the early morning and buried it beside the river.

CHAPTER FIFTEEN

On Christmas Day there was no spinning.

After Marsden's service, we were given the day to ourselves. While the scent of roasting lamb floated from settlers' houses, we gathered at the river with slabs of mutton and pork, and enough rum to drown a whale.

The men set a bonfire roaring on the riverbank and soon had the meat roasting over the embers.

The sun blazed through the trees, painting long shadows across the earth. Insects swarmed the surface of the water as we languished in the sultry heat that lay over the land.

Two of the factory lasses hacked up the meat and shared it among us; on plates, in wooden bowls, or into bare hands. The men stretched out shirtless on the edge of the water, women with their feet dipped into the swell. The convicts and emancipists took turns telling stories as they passed the liquor bottles between them.

"Helped myself to a side of pork like this from my master's kitchen," said one of the lags who worked Marsden's land. "Woulda got away with it too if it weren't for the dog. Bloody thing were only six inches high, but it had a bark like pistol fire. Held me up by the back gate."

An enormous roar of laughter.

"You've got a tale or two for us, don't you, Nell?" asked Lottie, nudging my shoulder with hers. "You can tell us a little about how the toffs live." There was a playful smile on her face.

I whacked at the giant ant crawling up my ankle. "Nothing as interesting as being held up by a dog."

Lottie passed me the rum bottle. She'd seemed to have made peace with who I was – or rather, who I had been. I was glad of it.

I ate until my stomach was straining against my bodice; a long-ago, forgotten sensation. I sat with my back up against the great white trunk of a gum tree, a pleasant liquor haze pressing down on me. I could feel the embers of the bonfire warming my cheek.

"Well," said Hannah, wiping greasy hands on her skirt, "this is a damn sight better than last year, ain't it."

I smiled. Our last Christmas had been spent in the depths of the *Norfolk*. We'd not even been sure of the date until we'd been pulled out onto deck for the church service.

As the afternoon stretched into evening, the gathering grew. Settlers emerged from their meat-scented houses and men I recognised as soldiers sat among us in shirtsleeves. Dark clouds rolled across a blazing sky, the air thick and humid, and scented with rain.

Someone arrived with a fiddle, and Owen, who'd been drinking since before noon, struck up a jagged beat on an empty crate. The music drowned out the birdsong and the constant burble of the river. Songs in Gaelic burst up around us, and everyone was dancing. I felt a smile on my lips. It had been far too long since I'd heard music. Lottie grabbed my hand and yanked me to my feet.

"I don't know the steps," I said on a laugh.

"It's easy," said Lottie, whirling around and pulling us into a circle of other dancers. "Like this. The Fairy Reel… Watch, Nell… *Watch!*… No, like this, other way!"

I gave up, whirling around in the circle and making up my own steps. I shrieked with laughter as we galloped around the uneven riverbank. I danced until I was breathless and a line of sweat ran down my back. Some blessed soul hurled Owen's drum crate onto the bonfire.

As the sun slipped away, the fire drew everyone towards it, making cheeks sweat and hair curl. It was no weather for a fire, of course, but this was all we knew. Fire was the centre of the Christmas celebration, no matter if snow was falling or the land was cracked and dry.

I thought of childhood Christmases spent behind ice-speckled windows, candles lighting our dinner table. Father and I working our way through roast meat and pudding, or gingerbread by the fire. For a moment, I missed him deeply.

I looked out towards the water. Patrick Owen had an arm slung around Lottie's shoulder, as they sat close together on the ground beside the river. I watched her laugh at something I was sure wasn't funny. I tried to catch her eye across the flames. I hated seeing them together. Lottie turned her back, avoiding my eyes.

I slipped away from the gathering. Stumbled down the road towards Blackwell's hut. The shrieking cicadas began to take over, pushing the raucous sounds of the party to the background.

I peeked through the gap in the door. I could see the lieutenant at the table, a quill in hand.

Writing to his wife, perhaps? Good wishes for Christmas, dear Sophia, that she would receive some time next September. There was something about him sitting there alone on Christmas night, hunched over his ink pot while the rest of us drank and danced. Something that made my chest ache.

I pushed open the door, making it squeal noisily against the floor. He looked up from his letter in surprise.

I sidled up to the table with what, in my drunken state, I assumed was an alluring strut. I peered down at the letter, not even pretending to be discreet.

'Dear Father,' it read.

"What are you doing?" I asked stupidly.

"Writing to my father." His sleeves were rolled up against the heat, his shirt open at the neck. I could see the sparse curls of hair at the top of his chest.

I leant over his shoulder to look at the letter.

'Governor Bligh has earned himself no favour with his order to destroy the liquor stills. The colony is still so short of currency – can he truly be against trading liquor for a sack of grain? It galls me that a naval officer might stride into this place and interfere with military order.'

I said, "There's a party going on."

"Yes," said Blackwell, his quill hovering above the page, "I can smell it on you." Ink dripped from the edge of the nib and splattered onto his letter. Insects flickered around the lamp.

"You ought to come," I told him. "It ain't right to be alone at Christmas." Sometimes the drink made me enunciate like a queen. Other times, I spoke as though I'd been hauled out of Whitechapel with a bottle of gin in my hand. "The other soldiers are there," I said. "Ensign Cooper and that one with the nose hair."

A smile played on the edge of Blackwell's lips. He tilted his head, considering me. He leant back in his chair, his arm brushing against my hip. "Go back to the party, Eleanor," he said after a moment. He dipped his quill back in the ink and continued writing, without looking at me again.

Dejectedly, I strode back towards the river.

"Where d'you go?" Lottie drawled when I returned. I was glad she had dislodged herself from Owen's claws.

"Just a walk is all." I slid my hand around her arm. "Let's have another drink."

"Fine idea," she said, looking around for someone with a bottle for us to steal.

I needed it. Needed to forget my childhood Christmases and the sight of Owen with his arm around Lottie. Needed to drown the emptiness that had come when Blackwell had sent me away.

Dan Brady was strumming a fiddle like a lute. He spoke to Lottie in Irish, though his eyes were fixed on me. Lottie looped her arm through mine. "You leave her alone now, Dan," she said in overenunciated English. "She's all right. Aren't you, Nell?"

Brady's eyes cut into me.

"Watch yourself, Johnny," Hannah hollered to some farmhand who was wading shirtless into the river. "Them eels will get you and pull you all the way to China."

I looked past her at the towering figure of Blackwell striding towards the river. I felt a smile on my lips. He went to the cluster of soldiers on one side of the fire. If he was going to stay with his own kind all night, so be it. I was just glad he was out of the hut. Glad he'd finished that dizzyingly dull letter.

Lottie followed my gaze. She looked back at me with fire in her eyes.

I ignored her. What place did she have being angry at my seeking out Blackwell when she was swanning around the place on Patrick Owen's arm?

I sauntered over to the soldiers with a bottle in my hand. I recognised one of the men who had sent Owen on his way the day he had attacked Blackwell. Even out of their uniforms, the Rum Corps exuded authority. One of the officers, an older man with a thick grey moustache, looked me up and down. Disapproval on his face, but something else beneath. I had already watched several of the enlisted men disappear into the bushes with factory lags attached to them.

Blackwell was on his feet before the man with the moustache could get his pipe out of his mouth.

"I learned the Fairy Reel," I announced. "I'm going to teach you."

A faint smile passed over his face. "No you're not."

I held out the rum bottle. "This will change your mind."

Blackwell laughed. His face lightened, giving him a sudden and unexpected beauty. If he was irritated at my storming his side of the party, he didn't show it. He took a gulp of rum, his nose crinkling in distaste.

"That's awful," he said.

"Bought it for a sack of grain," I told him. "Though Governor Bligh didn't like it."

He gave a short chuckle. "I see you managed an eyeful of my letter."

"Well," I said, "we must make a stand against those who dare interfere with military order."

He failed to hold back a smile.

I took the bottle, my fingers grazing his. "The Fairy Reel?" I asked. I was acting inappropriately; a part of me was well aware. I was also well aware that I'd never been so drunk in my entire life. It was a blissful, liberating feeling.

"No," he laughed. "Still no Fairy Reel." He nodded to where Hannah and Lottie were chatting by the edge of the water, heads bent towards each other, their brows creased in deep concentration. "Looks as though they're solving all the colony's ills. Perhaps you ought to join them."

I nodded, knowing even in my drunken state it was his polite way of telling me to disappear.

Blackwell returned to the marines, and I went and sat with Lottie and

Hannah. As I'd guessed, the only thing they were solving was who'd drunk more of the liquor. The party was going to pot quickly. Bodies were dozing around the fire, upturned bottles scattered across the riverbank. Hannah disappeared into the trees with some mud-coated scrub, and Lottie made her way to the remnants of the bonfire, hands all over Patrick Owen. Sounds of pleasure drifted out from between the trees.

The first time I had heard such a thing on the *Norfolk*, I had been horrified. I'd been taught that my wifely duties were never to be spoken of, an act that took place behind locked doors. I had always been silent in the bedroom out of fear the staff might hear. I couldn't bear the thought of anyone knowing what we were doing.

But I had come to understand it was different here. For the women, such a thing was not a duty, but an act of survival. And it didn't matter who witnessed it.

Sitting alone on the log, I felt a tug of loneliness. And in spite of everything I knew was decent and right, I found myself wishing I were one of those women sitting beside the river with a man's arms around her. I longed to forget myself, to forget where we were, and what my life entailed now. Until the morning at least.

A distant roll of thunder and the air seemed to grow thicker.

I felt the log shift beside me as someone took the place left empty by Hannah. The man's words were garbled. But his hand on my knee left no doubt as to his intentions.

I let that hand move up my thigh. Let him bend over and kiss my neck. Let myself sink into the warmth of another's touch. I could let it go no further, of course, but in that fleeting moment, I relished the company.

"Fetch me a drink," I said.

And he got to his feet unsteadily, giving me a smile. I felt a tangled mix of disgust and desire. And a tug of guilt at having let him think I was offering more than I was. I watched him saunter over to the bottles that sat ridiculously close to the bonfire.

"Don't." A voice close to my ear. "He's not a good man."

I opened my mouth to speak, my words dying in my throat when I turned my head and saw Blackwell's eyes inches from mine.

I watched him for a moment, trying to make sense of what I was feeling. Anger at his intrusion? Or flattery? The liquor was tangling my thoughts.

"Why do you care who I spend my time with?" I asked.

"I just don't want to see you get yourself in trouble."

"Why are you looking out for me?"

He frowned slightly. "Why do you need to ask that?"

Because I was lulling myself into the belief I might be worth caring for. That the safety of a convict woman might matter to a lieutenant in the Rum Corps. And I knew they were dangerous beliefs.

Lottie turned back from the bonfire and her eyes met Blackwell's. Then she glared at me. I looked away.

Thunder rumbled again, closer this time. Raindrops the size of marbles began to pelt the dry earth, sending wisps of steam spiralling up from the fire. With the arrival of the rain, the oppressive heat vanished, and I drew down a long breath, lifting my face to the sky.

My suitor returned with a fresh bottle, confusion wrinkling his face when he saw me with Blackwell. I could tell he was trying to remember which woman he'd been after.

Blackwell stood suddenly, as though he had only just become aware of how close he was to me. "I'm going back to the hut," he said.

He began to walk. For a moment, I sat motionless, unsure if his words had been an invitation to join him. He glanced back over his shoulder and I got to my feet. Hurried after him.

He opened the door and lit the lamp. His letter and inkpot were still spread out across the table.

I sank to the ground, not quite making it to my sleeping pallet. The earthen floor felt soft beneath me. My skirts and boots were splattered with mud.

Blackwell sat beside me on the floor, his long legs stretched out in front of him and his knee knocking against mine.

"Your letter," I said. "It's very boring."

He chuckled. "Yes, I know. My father is not the most vibrant of men. I'm playing to my audience." I could smell the liquor on his breath.

I made some sort of response, halfway between an acknowledgement and a groan. I rolled onto my side, my back to him. I closed my eyes against the violent tilting of the world.

"You shouldn't spend your time with men like that," he said after a long silence.

I didn't answer at once. His comment felt intrusive. Who was he to demand such things? Who was he to care?

I opened my eyes a crack, watching the flame dance inside the lamp. "Sometimes this place just feels overwhelmingly lonely," I said finally.

"Yes," said Blackwell. "It does." And I felt his body curl around mine, his big hand gripping my wrist as water drizzled in from the roof and put the candle out.

CHAPTER SIXTEEN

"The poor girl who yields to a misplaced passion, no matter how her ruin has been effected ... is immediately fallen. She has passed the threshold over which there is no return."

Thomas Beggs
An Inquiry into the Extent and Causes of Juvenile Depravity
1849

On the twelfth night, the officers gathered at Government House for a celebratory dinner. I watched Blackwell peer into the shaving mirror and glide his razor along his cheeks.

He had been distant since Christmas night. I could tell he regretted the way he had acted. But which part of it, I wondered? His drunkenness? Or the fact he had let himself get close to me?

The morning after Christmas, I'd woken alone on the floor beside the hearth. Blackwell had been back on his sleeping pallet on the other side of the hut. No doubt when the liquor had faded he had seen the gross impropriety of curling up beside me in the night. I had seen it too, of course. But it had not felt like impropriety at the time. It had felt far too natural. Far too easy. A thing both of us had needed.

After he left for Government House, I sat at the table staring into the spluttering candle. I was exhausted, having sat hunched over the carding machine all day, but I felt too alert to sleep.

I took Blackwell's shirt from the back of the chair, where I had hung it for mending. I had little doubt he was hacking at his hems on purpose. A reason to put coins in my hands and keep me from selling my body.

Threading a needle by candlelight, I stitched the torn hem carefully, the rough linen warm in my hands. The Parramatta cloth was thick and coarse. I wondered how many of Blackwell's shirts had been woven by my own hands. His musky scent infused the linen. Made me feel close to him. Closer than I, as a mere convict woman, ought to be.

These thoughts felt sinful in so many ways. There was Sophia, of course, and the ghost of Jonathan, not long enough in his grave for me to be thinking of another man.

It was improper, my governess had taught me, for a lady to feel desire. Only a loose woman, a harlot, a *concubine*, would let her heart quicken in the presence of a man.

There was regret in me that I had let Blackwell see my desire. I knew as a military man, he was expected to look down on a factory lass like me. To see me as the loose woman the female register painted me as. But I knew my attraction was not one-sided. On Christmas night, while rain pelted the roof, I had felt his body slide closer to mine. Felt the warmth of his hand against my bare forearm. That night, as I had laid my cards on the table, Blackwell had also laid his.

I finished the sewing, folding the mended shirt and placing it on the end of his sleeping pallet. I undressed and blew out the lamp, curling up on my blanket beside the unlit hearth. The air was thick and humid, frogs clicking loudly in the river.

Voices came towards the hut, along with a spear of light. I sighed inwardly, wondering what gift Owen and the other rebels had for the lieutenant this evening. I glanced across the hut to where the rifle was leaning against the wall. If I burst out the door and threatened the rebels with it, would they be afraid? I smiled wryly to myself. Do such a thing and I'd find myself celebrating the twelfth night back in solitary confinement.

I grabbed my shawl and threw it over my shoulders, yanking open the door to confront them. "Get the hell out of here," I hissed. Owen and

Brady charged towards me. I stumbled back into the hut. Felt hands around the tops of my arms. I thrashed against them. "Get your damn hands off me!"

"You're coming with us," said Owen. "It's important."

My heart thundered, Maggie Abbott's blank stare flashing through my mind. I tried to scream, but Owen clamped a hand over my mouth before the sound could form.

"Keep your bloody mouth shut. We can't have that lobster of yours coming running."

They yanked me back towards the door. "My dress," I spluttered. "And my boots." If I was going to be found in the undergrowth like Maggie, I at least wanted to have a little decency about me.

After a moment, Owen nodded reluctantly. He and Brady released their grip. I yanked my dress on over my head. As I bent to lace my boots, I felt a pang of regret. If I were found with my dress and boots on, it would look as though I had left the hut on my own accord.

But it was too late. Owen's hand was back around the top of my arm and I was being marched out towards the river.

"What's this about?" I demanded. Fear lurched inside me. Was I to be the next body found in the scrub? Did the croppies still believe me responsible for turning Owen over to the authorities? Or had they some twisted idea that they could punish Blackwell by harming me?

When we reached the river, I found Lottie pacing back and forth across the bank, arms wrapped around herself. Wind was rippling the surface of the water.

"Lottie?" I demanded, shaking myself free of Owen and Brady's grip. "You knew about this?"

"I'm sorry, Nell," she said. "I told them to bring you here. There are things you ought to know. Things between you and Blackwell have gone too far."

"What do you mean 'things between me and Blackwell'?"

Lottie sighed. "Come on, Nell. I'm no fool. We all saw the two of you together on Christmas night. Breathing on each other's necks. You mean to tell me there's nothing between you?"

"I clean the lieutenant's house," I snapped. "Nothing more."

Lottie took my arm and led me towards the log. She sat, tugging me down beside her.

"Are you truly warning me away from Blackwell?" I hissed. "When you're spending your time around Patrick Owen? He terrified me, charging into the hut like that! I thought I was going to end up like Maggie!" I knew Owen could hear me. I didn't care.

"I'm sorry," said Lottie. "I didn't mean for you to be afraid."

"And what exactly did you imagine I might feel?" I glared at her, then looked up at Owen and Brady. "What's this all about?"

Lottie looked up at the two men.

"You ever heard of Castle Hill?" asked Brady.

I felt the muscles in my neck tense. "Yes," I said tersely. "I know of the uprising." I couldn't help feeling a tiny flicker of self-satisfaction. The men had clearly been hoping to catch me unaware. I got to my feet, needing to face them. I was eye to eye with Owen, but Brady still towered over me.

"He told you then?" said Owen. "The things he did?"

My silence brought a smirk to his face.

"Thought not." He took a step closer, his breath hot and stale against my nose. I wrapped my arms around myself tightly.

"That lieutenant of yours is a murderer."

I kept my gaze steady. "He's a solider," I said. "Of course he's killed."

A cold laugh from Brady. Lottie looked up from the log, her eyes darting between me and the men. Above our heads, the trees rustled in the hot wind.

"We just wanted freedom," said Owen. "A ship to take us home. There weren't no one needed to die. But the lobsters marched up from Parramatta and surrounded us at Rouse Hill. Told us they were willing to parley. But when our leader come down the hill to speak with them, Major Johnson put a damn pistol to his head. Ordered his men to open fire."

"What were you expecting?" I hissed. "That the army would just stand by and allow prisoners to sail out of this place?"

I turned to leave, but Owen grabbed my arm, yanking me back.

"The lobsters were sent out into the bush," he told me, his nose close to mine. "To hunt down those of us who got away. Hunt us down like animals. All throughout the settlement. Just like they did in Ireland."

I stiffened, unable to look at him.

"Lieutenant Blackwell, he went downriver. Three of my cousins lived out near Squires' inn, all of them sent out together after the rebellion in Ireland. Two of them weren't even at Castle Hill. But Blackwell, he just saw croppies and pulled the trigger. Charged into their hut and shot the three of them without asking no questions."

His words hung in the stillness for a second. I held his gaze.

"I don't believe you," I said. "I know him. He wouldn't do such a thing."

"He's telling the truth," Lottie hissed, getting to her feet.

"Is he? And how do you know that? Were you there?" I turned back to Owen and Brady. "Were any of you there?"

"I was there," Owen spat. "I went out after the fight to check on my cousins. Bullets in their chests. Point-blank range." He leaned close to me. "My cousin's wife was hiding in the woods. She saw it all. I went out into the bush after I found the bodies. Saw Blackwell riding off. Too far away for me to shoot."

I started charging away. Lottie called my name. Her footsteps crunched behind me and she snatched my arm. I yanked away.

"Let go of me."

"Listen to them, Nell." Her voice was pleading.

"Listen to them?" I repeated. "Listen to these lies they're spouting? Do you actually believe this?"

"Yes," she said. "I do."

I shook my head in frustration. "You've been blinded by Owen. All of you, you think he's your way to freedom, but you're wrong. Following a man like him is going to destroy you."

"You've no idea what you're on about," Lottie hissed. "You're the one who's been blinded. You're so desperate to believe you got someone who cares about you that you're refusing to accept the things he's done."

I kept striding back to the hut.

"Nell," called Lottie. "I told Owen to come for you because you need to know this. I'm scared for you. Blackwell; he's dangerous."

I whirled around to face her. "All the while you're spending your time with the man who killed Maggie?"

Lottie didn't answer.

"Stay away from me," I hissed. "And tell those bastards to stay away from Blackwell."

I paced back and forth across the empty hut, anger bubbling inside me. With too much energy and no thought of what to do with it, I went back to the river to fill a bucket for cleaning. Water sloshing over the sides, I took it back to the hut and unloaded everything from the shelves, dumping it onto the table. There was the locket containing Sophia's portrait, tucked in between the books. I wondered when Blackwell had taken it from the chest.

I scrubbed violently at the dusty shelves, rage at Owen shooting through me. There was rage at Lottie too. For the first time since I'd sat beside her at the spinning wheels, we were not sisters. We were Irish rebel and *sasanaigh*. The reality of it stung.

I was still scrubbing when Blackwell shoved open the door. His hair was windblown and I could smell tobacco on him. He eyed me, and then the contents of the shelves I had upended across the table. Books and candles and soap and razors were piled high.

"You're still awake," he said sharply. "Why are you still awake?"

I raised my eyebrows, hand planted on my hip. "I'm cleaning the shelves."

"I didn't ask you to do that." He slid off his jacket and hung it on the nail beside the door. "I hoped you'd be asleep."

I tossed the cloth back in the bucket of muddy water. I didn't deserve this sharpness. I had not dragged him to the Christmas party. I had not poured the liquor down his throat, or forced him to fall asleep on the floor with his body pressed to mine.

"I'm here as your housekeeper," I snapped. "And you are to reprimand me for cleaning your house?" My words came out drenched with my best high society inflections. Blackwell looked taken aback.

For a moment I thought to tell him of the way I had been dragged from the hut by Owen and Brady. Something to shift his anger from me to the rebels. But no. I did not want him to know what tales were being told of him.

He took the rum bottle from the table and poured himself a cup. Sank heavily into a chair and brought his drink to his lips.

I hovered beside the bucket of water, twisting the cloth between my hands.

Blackwell filled a second cannikin and set it on the edge of the table. The chair creaked noisily as I sat beside him. In the centre of the table, the candle hissed and spluttered. I wrapped my hand around the cup, but didn't drink.

He lifted Sophia's portrait from the top of the pile. With one hand, he clicked it open, then closed it again quickly.

"Do you miss her?" I asked.

"Sometimes."

I ran my finger around the rim of the cup. "Just sometimes?"

He didn't speak at once. "It's as though she belongs to another life," he said finally. "Another world."

His eyes were down as he spoke. Was he ashamed of the distance he felt from his wife? Or was he feeling the inappropriateness of sharing all this with a mere convict woman? He sat the portrait back on the table and took a mouthful of rum.

"Forgive my coldness," he said after a moment. "It was not about you."

I nodded, though I did not believe him. I knew this had plenty to do with me.

"How were the celebrations?" I asked.

He scooped back the dark liquid of his hair, his shoulders relaxing visibly. "Captain Daley's wife singed her eyelashes playing Snapdragon."

I smiled. "I almost did the same as a child once. My father was horrified. He told me it was most inappropriate for a young lady to set herself on fire."

And so there it was; my admission that I was not a pitiable story of stolen eggs and squalid slums. I was a long-ago lady who'd fallen from a world of twelfth night balls. It felt right to tell him, after his brief moment of openness.

He peered at me, turning his cannikin around in his hands. I could tell there was much he wanted to ask. Could tell he desperately wanted to break that unwritten rule and ask me what had led me to my prison ship. Instead, he said:

"And how did you spend your Christmas once the Snapdragon was forbidden?"

I smiled. "Father had me play carols on the fortepiano."

It seemed impossible that such things had happened on the same earth as this. Blackwell was right; it was as though our old lives belonged to another world.

"You play the piano?" he asked.

I nodded faintly. "At least, I used to." I was quite certain I would never do such a thing again.

"Captain Macarthur's wife owns a fortepiano," he said. "Downriver."

"Really?" I heard the light in my voice. While I knew, of course, that a lag like me would never get her hands to it, it filled me with inexplicable joy that the instrument had made it to this outpost of the world. It made me feel less like I were living on the wildest edge of the planet.

"I had a lesson or two when I was a boy," said Blackwell. "My mother used to play. But I rather think I gave my tutor nightmares."

A laugh escaped me. It hung in the stillness of the hut. Brought a crooked smile to Blackwell's face. I found it oddly easy to imagine him as a boy, bashing at the keys of his mother's piano.

A smile moved across his face. A smile of reminiscence? Or was he simply enjoying the present moment? I wished I could see inside his head, if just for a second.

He emptied his glass, chuckling to himself. "I must say, Eleanor, of all the strange things I've seen in this place, you are by far the most surprising."

I raised my eyebrows. "I'm not sure how I ought to take that."

"You ought to take it as it was intended. As a compliment. A sign I value your company."

Stillness hung between us, half pleasant, half terrifying. I wanted to scream to break the silence, wanted to hold it forever. Wanted to step towards him, wanted to run away.

Lottie had warned me away from him. But my trust in Lottie had splintered. She had been standing there at Patrick Owen's side, spouting tales so vicious they could only be lies.

I was no fool. Blackwell was a soldier. I knew there was blood on his hands. And I knew much of that blood had likely come from the rebel uprising at Castle Hill. But how could I believe the word of Patrick Owen, who had wrung Maggie's throat and left her lifeless in the undergrowth?

How could I let Owen stain my image of this man who had been so good to me? Perhaps Lottie was right; I had been blinded. But I didn't want my sight returned.

I pushed Patrick Owen from my mind. I didn't want him in the hut with us.

Blackwell reached for my hand and held it in both of his. He turned it over in the lamplight as though it were the most fragile of specimens. The contact made my heart thunder. He looked at my hand closely, the faintest of frowns on his forehead, as though he had never seen a woman's fingers up so close before.

Had he ever seen his wife's body, I found myself wondering? Had he ever cast his eyes over the female form in its entirety? In my head, Sophia Blackwell was the kind of meek and submissive lover who hid beneath the covers and slid her shift to her hips. Sophia Blackwell, if she were here, would be labelled *wife.*

I wanted to challenge him. Wanted to break through that cursed shield he hid behind. I wanted to see how far I could push him, how much power I had. Here, in this lamplight, with lust in a man's eyes, was the only place a woman had the upper hand. Playing on his desires was the only way to make a man weak. I had to take control any way I could.

I rose to my feet, bringing Blackwell with me. Slowly, I unbuttoned my dress and stepped out of it, letting it fall to the floor with a sigh. I stood before him in my underskirts, my shoulders ghostly white in the candlelight. I could feel his eyes moving over every inch of me.

He took a step closer. Pressed his palm to the top of my arm. I heard myself inhale, sharp and loud. His hand felt rough against my skin. The hut rustled and creaked around us.

I tilted my head, offering him the bare white slope of my neck. Up his fingers went, over the protrusion of my collarbone, over my throat, pushing aside the flaming snarls of hair, tracing the constellation of freckles on my cheeks. His other hand went to my hip, feeling the shape of me.

Fingers slid along my collarbone, pausing at the top of my stays. I heard his breath. Fast. Shallow. Or perhaps it was my own.

At the feel of him against me, it went past my need for power. Now it was about my need for him. I was burning beneath his touch.

His hand was motionless, his thumb resting on the laces of my stays, and two fingers held against the place my heart was beating. He breathed heavily, caught in hesitation.

"No one would ever know," I said, trying to wrestle this back to a thing of power. But my skin was hot and my heart was beating between my legs. Blackwell had the control now, and I cursed myself for it.

But even as I spoke, I knew it was not a matter of who in the colony would see. God would know; would see him break his marriage vows; would see him lie with a woman who was not his wife. He would become an adulterer. And I would become a concubine.

I stepped away, leaving Blackwell's hand hovering in the dark space between us. I felt cold and hollow. But I could not be what Reverend Marsden had accused us of being. I picked up my dress and held it tight against me. I felt ashamed of my boldness, of all I had tried to do.

"I'm sorry," he said, his voice little more than a whisper. I wondered why he was the one apologising.

Blackwell moved quietly across the hut. He blew out the candle, leaving me standing alone in the blackness.

PART TWO

CHAPTER SEVENTEEN

"Nell Marling," the superintendent barked. I looked up from the spinning wheel. "You're to go with Corporal Anderson." He nodded towards the sunburned young soldier dithering at the top of the stairs. "You're being assigned. Housekeeper to Mr Robert Leaver. You'll be escorted to his property shortly. He has a room ready for you."

I swallowed. "A room?"

The superintendent chuckled. "I trust that's to your liking."

I traipsed down the stairs behind the soldier, feeling stupidly unsteady. Had Blackwell had a hand in this? I couldn't tell.

I looked back over my shoulder as I climbed down the staircase from the factory. A place that, for all its horrors, had become strangely comfortable in its familiarity. The life I had scratched together here – days at the spinning wheels, nights on Blackwell's floor – was something I knew I could cope with. But here I was facing the unknown again.

It was almost a relief to be leaving the stool beside Lottie. In the three days since Owen had manhandled me to the river, we had barely exchanged a word. Each night as I'd left the factory and walked back towards Blackwell's hut, I could feel her eyes on me. Once, I'd thought to call out to her, make some attempt at resurrecting our friendship. But it felt like the time for that had passed. It had disappeared the night Owen had dragged me from the hut and told me lies about Castle Hill.

Or perhaps it had disappeared on Christmas night when I had shown the colony the way my heart sped for Adam Blackwell.

My new overseer, Robert Leaver, was waiting outside the factory. The soldier escorting me squinted as he read from the crumpled paper in his hand.

"Eleanor Marling, sir. Twenty-eight, childless, healthy."

Leaver was a short man with a wide, sun-streaked forehead and pale tufts of hair that reminded me of tussock grass. Forty perhaps. Maybe younger. I knew this place had a way of ageing you. He looked me up and down.

"She'll do."

Leaver was building himself a farmhouse on the eastern end of the settlement, downriver from the military barracks. As he led me wordlessly down the front path, I saw a number of what I assumed were government men, constructing the walls of the house from large sandstone bricks. Beyond the skeletal outlines of the new rooms, two wide paddocks had been hacked out of the forest. Sheep and cows dotted the patchy brown grass.

Leaver deposited me in the main house with little more than a nod, abandoning me to his tiny, blonde-haired wife. Mrs Leaver was much younger than her husband, with a soft, doll-like face and dimpled cheeks. I guessed her little more than twenty. She glided around the house with a curly-haired child pinned to her hip.

"It's good to have you, Eleanor," she said in a girlish voice. "We've just had our last government woman finish her sentence." She set off down the hallway, gesturing for me to follow. "Quite a shame, I have to say. She were a good worker and all. But never mind. I'm sure you'll fill her shoes just nicely." She launched into a rapid tour, waving a hand at each room as we passed. The parlour, the dining room, and this will be my husband's smoking room... "The place is only half finished, I'm afraid. But we've room enough for you to have a little space of your own." She led me down a small set of stairs off the kitchen, the child squirming out of her arms and barrelling down the hallway like a wild rabbit. Mrs Leaver pushed open a door and nodded at the tiny room. A narrow bed sat against one wall, with a wash basin and chair beside it. "This will be your lodgings. I trust it has everything you need."

I murmured my thanks. The last time I'd slept in a proper bed, I'd been lying beside Jonathan in Clerkenwell.

"You've belongings?" she asked.

I thought of my old stockings and spare dress, tucked into my cloth bag beside my sleeping pallet. I would go for them later that night, when Blackwell was on duty. "Yes," I managed. "I can fetch them this evening." It would be far easier, I knew, if I was just to grab my belongings and disappear from his life. Pretend not a thing had passed between us. After all, nothing could come of it. If I hadn't known that before, I certainly did now.

"Very well." Mrs Leaver lurched for the child as he made a grab for the candlestick on the nightstand. She swung him back onto her hip. "The windows are due to be cleaned today," she said. "I trust you can see to that now, please? The polishing rags are in the kitchen. The cook will help you find them."

Her request was polite and achingly reasonable, but I bristled as I went to the kitchen for the rags. Once I had been the young wife, directing the staff to clean the windows. And now here I was with the polishing cloth in my hand.

My own bitterness infuriated me. How had I managed to dig up a scrap of my old spoiled self when I'd just been hauled from the spinning wheels? I knew women considered themselves lucky when they were chosen to leave the factory. As housemaids and cooks, the hours were better, the food better, the lodgings better. But I'd not had the experience of the other women, had I? I'd not had to sell my body to eat. I'd not taken men behind the factory to pay for a roof over my head.

In the back of my mind, I knew what this grief was really about. That tonight when I slept, I would not hear Blackwell breathing beside me. I hated that I could not control my attraction to him – that in his own quiet, underhand way, he had exerted his power over me.

It was better this way, I told myself, as I wiped acres of dust from the Leavers' windowsills. Best that I tried to forget.

But that night, when I crawled into my bed, feeling the softness of a mattress beneath me for the first time in two years, I felt nothing but sadness pressing down upon my shoulders.

My days became filled with laundry and bed-making, dusting and polishing, and the constant thud of hammers as the Leavers' house grew up around us.

While Leaver employed a small army of convict farmhands, there were just three of us inside the house; a pink-faced cook who had come over as a free settler and young housemaid, Amy, who broke glasses with disturbing regularity.

One morning, Amy and I made our way into town with an endless list of errands. A thick heat haze drifted up from the land, and the track into town crunched beneath our feet. The tuneless hum of insects rose from the grass.

Amy walked with her eyes down, twisting the corner of her apron around her finger. In the month I'd been at the Leavers', I'd barely heard a word from her.

"You come over on the *Norfolk*, didn't you," she said as we walked. "You was friends with Hannah." Her voice was tiny and bell-like.

I felt a tug of guilt then; I'd not had any thought that we'd travelled to this place together, lost in my own thoughts as I'd been for much of the voyage. But yes, with the reminder, I remembered shy, soft-spoken Amy. She'd been one of the youngest convicts on our ship. I guessed her little more than thirteen.

I swatted the flies from my face. "Have you been working for Leaver all this time?"

She nodded. "He took me off the ship. The place weren't no more than a few tents on his land when I first got here."

"And how do you find him? Has he treated you well?"

She shrugged, looking back at her feet. She barely reached my shoulder. "Could be worse. Could have been sent to the factory."

I smelled the butcher's stall long before we reached it. The acrid stench of flesh floated on the hot wind, making my stomach roll.

"You go for the fruit and vegetables," I offered, pressing the list into Amy's hand. "I'll fetch the meat."

And I stopped walking abruptly, caught off guard by the figure of Blackwell striding out of the government stores. Since I'd begun working for the Leavers, I'd barely seen more than glimpses of him; sometimes at Marsden's services, sometimes here at the market, or on his way to the courthouse. I'd been careful to hide myself. What point was there in speaking? We both knew what had passed between us on the twelfth night had been a mistake. I had crossed a line that should never have been crossed.

But today, he had seen me. I knew I could not turn away without appearing petty and childish. Amy glanced at me expectantly, but I said nothing, just watched frozen as Blackwell strode towards us. He offered something vaguely resembling a smile.

"Good morning, Eleanor."

I hated the formality in his voice. Hated that the wall around him I had spent eight months chipping away at had so quickly been rebuilt. I gave a short nod. "Lieutenant."

Amy's eyes were fixed to the ground. She chewed her lip, knotting her fingers together in front of her chest. Blackwell towered over her.

A strained silence hovered between us, punctuated by the clatter of leg irons coming from the chain gang across the street. A wagon full of vegetables rattled past.

Blackwell's stiltedness left me in no doubt he had been the one behind my going to the Leavers'. Was it a punishment, I wondered? My penance for luring him to break his marriage vows? For daring to bring shame to his door? Perhaps I deserved what came to me.

I value your company, he had told me that night, as I'd reached up to unbutton my dress. And I had been foolish enough to believe his words. Had been foolish enough to believe I mattered.

"How are you getting on with Leaver?" he asked finally.

My hand tensed around the handle of the basket. "Fine, thank you."

He nodded. "I've heard him a decent man."

I looked up at him then. "Have you?" My voice came out sharper than I intended.

Blackwell made a noise in his throat and I regretted my outburst. Because standing there by the market, caught between a chain gang and the shadow of the courthouse, I saw the two of us as what we really were. Government lag and military officer. I saw I had no place to question him, to speak back to him, to stand in the lamplight and slide my dress from my shoulders. If he wanted me gone from his hut, who was I to fight it? I swallowed.

"And you?" I asked stiffly. "Are you well?" My skin felt damp beneath my shift.

"I'm well, yes. Thank you."

I wanted to ask him more; whether he'd had any trouble with Owen and Brady. What book he was reading now. If he had any shirts that needed mending. But I knew it was no longer my place to do so. Perhaps it never had been.

He glanced down at my empty basket, then back at me. "I'll let you get on with your business." And then he was gone.

Amy dared to look up, staring after Blackwell as he disappeared around the corner. Threads of blonde hair blew across her eyes. "Do you know him?" she asked in an awed half-voice.

My jaw tightened. "Barely." I felt longing, felt anger. Felt like a worthless lag who'd been slapped down to where she belonged.

I put a hand to Amy's shoulder, ushering her towards the fruit stall. "Come on. Let's get the food. It's far too hot to be out here."

At the end of February, Leaver put in a good word with the magistrate and one of his farmhands was given his ticket of leave.

When we had finished serving dinner to the family, I joined the other workers out by the barn for a farewell drink to the lucky man. The night was hot and still, cicadas shrieking in the paddocks and the musky smell of animals thick in the air.

Amy sighed heavily as we sat beside each other on the brown grass. "Wish it were me leaving this place." She stretched her legs out in front of her and began rubbing at a stain on her skirt.

I nodded. I knew we were all thinking the same. All wished we were the one with the ticket of leave being pressed into our hand. I picked up a twig and dug it listlessly into the earth.

Was I being foolish to imagine I might get such a chance? I knew with my life sentence and a stay in solitary confinement, there was not much to pin my hopes on. I had little to do with Leaver beyond his gruff orders for more food, but his young wife had taken a liking to me. Perhaps with a few well-placed words in her husband's ear, such a thing would become possible.

I had to believe it so. I couldn't spend the rest of my life scraping out another woman's hearths. I knew I would never see England again, but I didn't want to die in chains.

But even with a ticket of leave, what prospects would I have? I knew if I were to have any chance at a decent life, I would have to put myself forward at the marriage market. I would have to speak of my past; of my first husband's death, and hope the wife hunters saw only the obedience that had led me to New South Wales.

I left the celebration early and crawled off to bed, hanging my dust-streaked skirts over the chair in the corner of the room. I'd grown used to my tiny, silent bedroom; to the feel of waking alone each morning. I closed my eyes, my body aching with exhaustion. I craved the escape of my dreams.

From the back of the property I could hear the distant laughter of the farmhands. The steady wail of the cicadas. I shifted on the mattress, the air hot and stifling. And as I waited for sleep to pull me down, I heard another sound. Rhythmic footsteps, like an army in motion. Approaching, passing, fading away.

CHAPTER EIGHTEEN

"Our servant burst into the parlour pale and violent in agitation … he told us that the croppies had risen … we then learnt that Castle Hill was in flames. The fire was discernible from Parramatta. It was recommended that as many ladies as chose should go to Sydney, as constant intelligence was brought into the barracks of the near approach of the Irishmen."

Elizabeth Macarthur
1804

I was on my way to the apothecary for Mrs Leaver when the chain gang shuffled out into the street, arms laden with hammers and saws. With chaotic footsteps, and leg irons rattling, they edged towards a building site close to Government House. Two soldiers marched beside them. I recognised one of them as Ensign Cooper, who had sent Owen away the day he had attacked Blackwell.

I stood watching for a moment, the empty basket held against my chest. New South Wales had left its mark on me – the scar above my eyebrow, the calluses on my hands, the restlessness in my heart – but at that moment I was grateful for the hand I had been dealt since I'd stepped off the *Norfolk*. And perhaps I was even grateful to be a woman. My ankles were not scarred from chains, and my back was not flayed when I stepped out of line. I did not spend my days breaking rocks and building the government's houses. But gratitude felt like a dangerous thing. A thing that could so easily be taken away.

One of the convicts glanced at me and I turned away, unable to bear the sorrow in his eyes.

"What did you say?" I heard Cooper roar, his voice coming from nowhere and making me start. He loomed over two men at the back of the chain gang. Jabbed one in the side with the nose of his rifle. "What d'you say, bog-trotter?"

The man looked up at him with blank, frightened eyes.

"He don't speak no English, sir," the man behind him ventured. Cooper slammed the butt of the rifle into his nose. The man crumpled, blood spurting down the front of his shirt.

Several of the convicts began to shout in protest, others kept their eyes down. People appeared from inside the shops and taverns, watching as the convict's blood vanished into the mud. I pressed my back against the wall of the apothecary.

Here came more soldiers, marching in step, their coats stark against the muted earth and green.

"They're plotters, sir," I heard Cooper say to the captain striding towards him. "Bloody Irish rebels." The captain bent down and unlocked the shackles of the beaten man, along with the prisoner who had defended him.

"Take them to the cells. Find out what they're planning."

I hurried back to the farmhouse with the tonics for Mrs Leaver.
Plotters.
Take them to the cells.
Did the soldiers truly believe the men were planning another uprising? Or was this just a show of strength? A warning to the wayward Irish?

I found Mrs Leaver sitting up in bed, blankets piled up over her knees. With her second child on the way, she was pale and weak with nausea.

I placed the tonics on the table beside her bed. "The apothecary said these will help. Shall I boil up the ginger? Make you some tea?"

"Yes," she said. "Thank you." She sat her book on the nightstand and looked up at me. "Are you all right, Eleanor? You look a little out of sorts. Has something happened I ought to know about?"

I shook my head, smoothing her blankets and collecting the empty tea tray from the side table. "Nothing you ought to bother yourself with."

And why, I wondered, was I so bothered by it myself? Why had the mistreatment of two Irish lags made me so unsettled? Was I afraid of a second rebellion? Afraid for Blackwell's safety? Yes, but I was coming to see it was more than that. In the abuse of those croppies, I saw every injustice in the colony; the women with no place to sleep, the rations of rotted meat, Maggie's murder and Owen's freedom.

Since I'd made the choice to be ignorant no longer, I felt as though I were absorbing everything; the fear, the anger, the grief of the people I shared this place with. Everywhere I looked, I saw a thing to spark my anger; a thing that made me rail against my complete and utter powerlessness. I knew one day soon I would no longer be able to keep that rage inside.

The cup rattled against its saucer as I carried the tray towards the door. I looked back at Mrs Leaver and forced a smile. "I'll fetch you that tea."

After supper that night, Amy knocked on the door of my room. I was sitting cross-legged on the bed, mending the hem of my striped gown.

"There's a woman here for you. Says she knows you from the factory. She's waiting for you out back."

I put down my sewing and grabbed my shawl, murmuring my thanks as I headed for the door.

I found Hannah waiting for me outside the farmhouse, a blanket wrapped around her shoulders to keep out the icy wind. I was glad to see her. It had been many weeks since I'd sat at the river and drunk with the factory lasses. There was too much coldness between Lottie and me. Too much hatred in me at Owen. Too much sadness and anger over Maggie.

In the flickering lamplight, I could see Hannah's smile was strained. "All right, Nell? How they treating you?"

Wind tunnelled across the paddocks and I tugged my shawl around me tighter. "Can't complain." I looked at her expectantly. I knew this more than a visit to see how I was faring. "Has something happened?"

Hannah knotted her gnarled fingers. "Patrick Owen came to the factory today. With his marriage certificate."

I closed my eyes. "Lottie."

Hannah nodded.

"No. She can't have. She can't." What in hell was she doing? Surely she couldn't think this was the only way.

"Were there others who were willing?" I asked.

"One or two," said Hannah. "Far less than normally put themselves forward. But Owen didn't even look at the others. He wanted Lottie. It were obvious from the start."

I wondered sickly whether the two of them had discussed this earlier. Had he spoken to her of his plans to marry one night while we were drinking at the river? Had she known he was about to strut into the factory with his marriage permit in his hand?

"They're saying he got himself land in Sydney Town," said Hannah. "He's planning on taking her down there."

I began to march down the side path and out into the street. "I've got to speak to her."

I went to the hut of old Bert, the ex-convict Lottie was lodging with. Did he know, I wondered, that his concubine had betrothed herself that afternoon?

The hut was tucked away at the end of Back Lane, in a darkness so thick I could barely see the edge of the street. I walked towards the faint light shafting beneath the door. Unlike Blackwell's mudbrick home, Bert's hut was made almost entirely of wood, and it leaned dramatically to one side. A thin line of smoke curled up from the chimney. When I knocked on the door, it was Lottie herself who answered.

She sighed resignedly. "Had a feeling you'd show up tonight."

Peering over her shoulder, I could see no sign of Bert, just a small firelit hovel with a crooked table and a single, narrow sleeping pallet.

"You can't marry Owen," I said bluntly.

"No word of congratulations, Nell?" Her words were thick with sarcasm.

"Why are you doing this?" I asked.

She folded her arms across her chest. "You know why I'm doing this. Because I got more than three years of my sentence left and I don't want to spend them weaving cloth and sleeping beside an old man."

I softened my voice. "Is lodging with Bert truly so bad you'd risk your

141

life by marrying Owen?" I wanted our old friendship, our old closeness. But Lottie had her guard up.

She laughed coldly. "Lodging with him? Is that what you imagine this is? Just lodging with the man?"

The bitterness in her words chilled me.

"And do you imagine things with Owen will be any better?" I asked.

Lottie held my gaze for a moment, her eyes narrowing. "The thing is done," she said finally. "The papers have been signed. We're to be married on Thursday. Leaving for Sydney on Friday. It's too late for any of this."

I heard the soldiers marching again that night. Crunch and thud from the direction of the barracks. This time I was wide awake; thoughts of Lottie and Owen keeping me from sleep.

I slipped out of bed and peeked through the curtain. My window looked out over the front of the farm, but I could see little in the darkness. I pulled on my dress and boots and slipped out of the house.

One of Leaver's farmhands was leaning against the stone fence at the front of the property, blowing a line of silver pipe smoke up into the dark. I stood beside him and watched in silence as a parade of redcoats strode out into the wilderness.

"Is there trouble?" I squinted into the night, trying to pick out Blackwell's figure.

The farmhand took his pipe out from between his teeth. "Just a drill, I'd say."

"A drill?"

"The Rum Corps likes to be prepared."

"Prepared for what?" I asked. "Another rebel uprising?"

He nodded.

I frowned. This had to be a new development. When I'd been staying with Blackwell, I'd never known him to leave in the middle of the night. I was a light sleeper. I was sure I would have heard.

"The governor fears another rebellion?" I asked. I thought of the Irishman in the chain gang, his blood disappearing into the mud. "Has something happened?"

The farmhand shrugged. "He's been fearing another rebellion since Castle Hill."

I pulled my shawl tighter around me. I realised I was fearing another rebellion too. "Were you here in Parramatta?" I asked. "During the uprising?"

He nodded.

"What was it like?"

He took a long draw on his pipe. "Phil Cunningham raised an army of croppies at Castle Hill. Went from farm to farm recruiting men, taking weapons. There were a mad panic here when we heard it were happening." He chuckled. "Reverend Marsden jumped in a boat and fled the place like a scared cat."

I felt a small smile in the corner of my lips.

"Croppies had no chance though," the farmhand said. "The redcoats marched out to meet them and the battle only lasted a few minutes. Could hear gunshots for days, mind you, what with the lobsters sent out to find all the rebels who got away."

I felt a sudden tightness in my throat. Owen's story about what had happened at his family's cottage echoed at the back of my mind.

I went out into the street, staring through the darkness the soldiers had disappeared into. I wrapped my arms around myself and shivered.

It felt as though this fragile colony was teetering. I had little doubt the army would quell another rebel uprising as quickly as they had the first. But I knew they would not do so without blood being shed. And I knew if the croppies rose up in battle, Blackwell would be a target. Would likely be the first to die.

I whirled around at the sound of footsteps. Found Dan Brady standing in the road behind me. Had he been watching the soldiers too?

I felt the sudden urge to hurry back to the farmhouse. But I didn't want to give him the satisfaction of knowing he unnerved me.

"I thought you'd be out there pounding down the jail doors," I said. "Trying to free those two croppies they locked up. Or are they not as important to you as Patrick Owen?"

Brady chuckled humourlessly. "If we rose up every time a croppy were mistreated there'd be none of us left."

"I know," I said. "It's not right. I was there when it happened. Any

143

fool could see they were just speaking their own language."

Brady tilted his head, considering me. I could tell he was surprised by my agreement.

"And yet here you are," he said, "staring out into the night after your lieutenant."

I felt my cheeks burn. Was grateful for the darkness.

I didn't reply. Admitting to it made me feel like a fool.

Brady jabbed his pipe in the direction the soldiers had disappeared. "You think this is right, *sasanaigh*? The redcoats out training to take us all down? So Blackwell can take more innocent lives?"

I clenched my teeth, forcing my anger away. "Instead we're all just to sit back and let the croppies take over the colony? Do you truly think that's what's best for this place?"

Brady chuckled. "What does a factory lass know about what's best for this place?"

I said nothing. He was right, of course. What did I know?

"I know how it feels to be powerless," I told him. "Just like you do."

"That's right," said Brady. "You do." He took a step closer, pointing a long finger at me. "But here's the difference between us, Nellie. Us croppies fight for what we want. The factory lasses just sit back and accept things the way they are."

CHAPTER NINETEEN

"A light punishment for rebellion will excite revenge, not terror … Transport all prisoners in the gaols and give full power to the generals."

Advice from England to Undersecretary Cooke, Dublin
The Rebellion Papers
12th March 1797

The next day, the Irishmen from the chain gang were dragged from the cells for a flogging. Robert Leaver, the most patriotic of Englishmen, herded us all from the farmhouse to watch. A crowd had gathered, the murmur of voices thick in the air. Soldiers lined the edges of Jail Green, rifles held at the ready. Reverend Marsden paced in front of the triangle, thick arms folded across his chest.

The two prisoners were dressed in grimy shirtsleeves and breeches that reached just past their knees. They were led out to the green, a mess of bloodied faces and swollen eyes.

I thought of untouchable Patrick Owen, merely sent on his way after striking an officer. Protected from punishment by his position as the rebels' leader.

Was this the government's way of striking back against the Irish? Flogging two lowly convicts for speaking their native language? Surely no one truly believed them capable of inciting another uprising. These were simply men they could punish without fearing backlash. Or was I just being naïve?

The first of the prisoners was shoved towards the triangle, shirt yanked from his body and his arms bound to the structure, high above his head.

I glanced around the crowd for Blackwell. There was no sign of him. No doubt he had marched off on last night's drill. I wondered stiffly what he would think of all this.

No. I knew what he would think of this, and the thought was an uncomfortable one. Blackwell was a lieutenant in the New South Wales Corps. He had fought in the Castle Hill uprising. Had fought in the rebellion in Ireland. Hardly a man who would sympathise with a couple of lowly croppies. I pushed the thought aside. What difference did it make? The only one of Blackwell's thoughts that mattered was his decision to send me away.

The first crack of the whip made my shoulders tighten. The prisoner cried out as it tore through his bare skin. Beside me, Amy murmured and turned away.

The flogger hurled the cat again. The prisoner tried to swallow his cry.

"This isn't right," I said, to no one in particular. "These men aren't plotters."

On the other side of me, Leaver's farmhand chuckled, taking the pipe out from between his teeth. "I hadn't picked you as a rebel sympathiser."

"I'm not a rebel sympathiser," I said. "Those men just didn't understand what was being asked of them. Any fool could see that."

"Aye." He took a long draw on his pipe. "It's politics. It weren't about their crimes. It were just about the government making a point."

I clenched my teeth. There hadn't seemed to be a point to make when Owen had his hands around Maggie's throat.

I felt horribly on edge. Each crack of the whip rattled through me, as though the cat were striking my own body. I felt my muscles tighten, my stomach turn over. My thoughts were storming; with Maggie, with Lottie, with Owen. With *wife* and *concubine* and these blood-streaked convicts.

The officer overseeing the flogging stepped close to one of the prisoners, their noses inches apart. "What are you planning?" he hissed.

The prisoner groaned out a line of Irish.

"Give him another hundred," said the soldier. A murmur rippled through the crowd.

Afraid as I was for Blackwell, I understood then why the Irish felt the need to rise up, to fight against the hand they'd been given. I thought of what Dan Brady had told me the night the Rum Corps had left on their drill.

The factory lasses just sit back and accept things…

There'd been anger among us the day of Maggie's murder. But how quickly we'd been put back into our place. How easy we were to tug back into line. While the croppies plotted and planned rebellions, we just lifted our skirts so we might have a place to sleep. Bared our skin in the lamplight so we might have a little sway. We were weak and voiceless.

"This isn't right," I said again.

I felt a firm fingers digging into the top of my arm. Turned to see Leaver inches behind me.

"Shut your mouth," he hissed, breath hot against my cheek. "Just who do you think you are?"

I clenched my teeth, closing my eyes as the whip fired again. I felt as though an enormous weight was pressing down on me.

Tonight those prisoners would sleep with flayed backs because they had dared speak their own language. Marsden's register was on its way around London, painting us as concubines. And now Owen, the man who had taken Maggie from us, was to take Lottie as well.

For the rest of the day, I went about my chores in a daze. I felt hot and disoriented. Unable to see clearly. I spoke to Amy and the cook in terse, one-word answers. And when the house grew dark, I went to the kitchen and pulled a knife from the drawer.

I felt oddly outside myself as I made my way across the farm and stepped into the street. My thoughts were hazy. Likely, there was a part of my brain preventing me from thinking too clearly in case I saw the foolishness of my behaviour.

I strode towards Owen's hut, my hand tight around the handle of the knife. I felt a surge of determination.

Once, I'd blindly followed my husband, believing I had no other choice. But I saw now that I had had a choice, and I'd made the wrong one. I'd made the choice to believe myself powerless; to let circumstances carry me away like the tide. And now, in this place, where I felt more powerless than ever, I'd made the decision to be powerless no more.

My hand tightened around the knife handle. I would die for this, of course; some distant part of me knew that. But it didn't matter. It was hard to value my own life when no one else did. I would face the hangman, but Owen would finally have his punishment. Maggie would have justice and Lottie would be safe. And men would learn they would not get away with murdering a factory lass.

The darkness was thick and cold, just a few stars straining through the cloud bank. I could feel the emptiness all around us. A day by barge to Sydney Town. Half a lifetime to the existence I had once known. The place felt inescapable.

I stood several feet from the door of Owen's hut, feeling the smooth bone handle of the knife between my fingers.

How would it be, I wondered? Was there someone in the hut with him? Someone who would witness his death? Was Lottie in there?

A part of me hoped so. She would see the things I was willing to do to save her. She would see that, even though we had grown distant, I still loved her like a sister.

How would I do it? A blade through the heart? Or perhaps the throat. The thought caused me to inhale sharply. When had I become a woman who could do such a thing? It was a natural progression, I supposed; obedient daughter to obedient wife, convict to murderess.

I felt capable. And I felt ready.

Here were the footsteps again. Distant, dreamlike. The soldiers returning. They would drag me to trial, put a rope around my neck. But not before Owen was dead.

"Eleanor. What are you doing?"

It took a moment for me to register that Blackwell's voice had not come from inside my head.

I turned to look at him. He stood a foot behind me, dressed in full uniform, his rifle slung across his back. I slipped the knife into my pocket, keeping my fingers wrapped around the handle.

Blackwell looked at the shack, then back at me. "This is Patrick Owen's hut."

I squeezed my eyes closed. "Go away."

"What are you doing?" he asked again.

I turned back towards Leaver's farm, unsure what else to do. Blackwell took my arm gently, preventing me from leaving. "What's happened?"

I felt tears threatening. No, this was all wrong. I was not supposed to fall apart. I was supposed to charge into Owen's home and deliver the justice he had so far escaped. But instead, Blackwell was leading me towards his hut, his hand around my wrist, and I was going without hesitation.

Inside the hut, everything was just as I remembered, except for the bare space on the floor where my sleeping pallet had been. I wanted to leave. But his hand was still firm around my wrist and I couldn't find the strength to pull away.

I shifted my fingers on the handle of the knife to stop it falling from my pocket. Blackwell lifted my hand in his, bringing the blade out into the light.

He looked down at the knife, then back at me. "What were you doing at Owen's hut?"

"He's to marry Lottie," I said, not looking at him.

"And so you will kill him?"

"He deserves to die," I said. "He murdered Maggie."

Blackwell stood motionless for a long second. "You don't want to kill him," he said evenly.

"And how do you know that?"

He stepped closer, pushing gently against my shoulder, urging me to face him.

No, I didn't want to look at him. Didn't want him to see this darkest side of me. I felt tears spring up behind my eyes.

"Because once you kill another, it never leaves you." His voice was low. "The look in their eyes, it stays with you forever. It's a stain you will never be rid of."

I thought of Blackwell hunching beside the rebels' graves. Thought of the heaviness that had hung about him when he had returned to the hut that day. How many ghosts haunted Adam Blackwell, I wondered? Whose invisible eyes watched him at night?

But he was wrong. There was a part of me that did want to kill Owen. To hell with the consequences and the ghosts and the unerasable stain. I wanted to look into Owen's eyes and see fear. See the realisation that a woman held the power.

For those few precious moments I would be more than *concubine*. I would hold life and death in my hands.

"You don't have it in you," he said.

"Is that what you think?"

But I knew he was right. I had walked that path from obedient daughter to convict, but *murderess* was still beyond me.

Blackwell wrapped his fingers around mine, his hand dwarfing my own. "Please, Eleanor," he said, "put the knife down."

My fingers tensed around the handle. I couldn't release my grip on it. What I would do with it now, I didn't know, but it felt like all the power I had in the world. How could I let that go?

"Lottie's going to die," I coughed. "Just like Maggie. She's going to die and no one will think twice on it. They'll blame her death on the blacks and Owen will walk, just as he always does."

Blackwell looked down at the knife. "So you will sacrifice yourself for her? Send yourself to the hangman?"

I felt my shoulders sink, as though the earth was tugging me down. I let him take the knife from my hand. He placed it on the ground between our feet. He slid the rifle from his shoulders and opened the chamber, setting the balls and cartridge on the table.

Inexplicably, the gesture made rage flare inside me. I thought of all the dominance, all the strength, men like him had over the rest of us, casually taking the shells from his weapon with a practised ease. And all I could see was him standing on the jury and letting Patrick Owen walk.

I swung at him suddenly, my blows pounding his chest, his shoulders, his arms. For several moments, he stood still, letting me take my anger out on him. But when I bent to pick up the knife, he grabbed my wrists, pulling me up to him and forcing me into stillness. His nose grazed mine.

"Wave that knife around and you'll hang for it," he hissed. "It doesn't matter if you kill Owen or not. You're a factory lass. Just carrying it will be enough to put you on the scaffold."

I shook my head. "I don't care."

His hands tightened around my wrists. "*I* care."

My tears spilled suddenly; tears of grief, of exhaustion, of frustration.

And his arms were around me, holding me tightly.

I closed my eyes, feeling myself sink against him. I buried my head against his broad chest, so he couldn't see me cry.

He slid his hand over my hair, holding me close. I could feel the warmth of his palm against my neck. Could feel his body rising and falling with breath. A little of the distress inside me began to still.

I wished for my old sleeping pallet beside the hearth. I wished for the sound of him breathing beside me in the night. Nothing more. Just that reassurance that someone was there to know, to care if this place swallowed me whole. I felt my fingers tighten around the edge of his coat. And with the gesture, he pulled away, his hand ghosting over the plait that hung down my back.

"I'm sorry, Eleanor," he said huskily, "you need to go back to the farm."

On Thursday, I made it a point not to step off Leaver's property for a minute. I couldn't bear to be out in a world in which Lottie was marrying Owen.

The next day I woke before dawn, lighting the fires and laying the table. Then I slipped out of the house and made my way to the river, desperate to catch Lottie before she sailed away on the morning barge.

I found her waiting on the riverbank beside Owen, a few other travellers clustered by the jetty. She stood with her arms wrapped around herself, staring across the murky plane of the water. Owen was pacing back and forth across the riverbank, hands dug into his pockets to keep out the cold.

He looked up, his face breaking into a grin. "Nice of you to come see us off, Nellie."

There was a positive to their leaving of course; no more dead animals hung from Blackwell's hut, no more rocks through his window. Perhaps in Sydney Town, Owen would learn to forget the anger he held towards the lieutenant. And perhaps with Owen gone, Blackwell could move out from beneath the shadow of Castle Hill.

But with Owen gone, Lottie would be gone too. And the thought of it made me ache.

I made my way towards her. I wanted to plead with her one final time, but I knew there was no point. The marriage permit had been signed, the ceremony complete. Instead, I just pulled her into my arms and held her tightly. I couldn't shake the fear that the next grave I would be standing at would be hers. Her arms slid around me, pulling me close.

And here came the barge, gliding up the river, ready to carry her away. Ready to carry her to a life as Patrick Owen's wife.

"Be safe," I managed, my voice coming out broken.

When I stepped back, Lottie's eyes were glistening. "And you, Nell," she said. "He's not who you think he is."

CHAPTER TWENTY

I opened my eyes to thick darkness, aware something had jolted me awake. It had been several months since Owen had left Parramatta, and I thought constantly of Lottie. Thought constantly of Blackwell and the redcoats out on their midnight drills.

To still my thoughts, I'd thrown myself into my work. As Mrs Leaver's confinement approached, I'd become something of a lady's maid to her, running to answer the ringing of her bell throughout the day and night. My devotion to her earned me the occasional smile from Leaver, who was clearly besotted with his young and pretty wife.

I sat up in bed, listening for Mrs Leaver's bell.

No. That was not what had woken me.

Murmurs were coming from Amy's room. Male grunts of exertion.

I climbed out of bed. Had one of the farmhands crept into her room? Had he been invited?

I stood outside her door, debating whether to intervene.

A muffled cry came, followed by another grunt, this time one of aggression. I darted instinctively into the room.

In the shafts of moonlight streaming through the gap in the curtains, I could see the square figure of Leaver on the bed, trousers around his knees and Amy struggling beneath him.

I snatched the candleholder, the only meagre weapon I could find.

"Get away from her," I hissed.

Leaver whirled around and stumbled from the bed, yanking up his trousers and buttoning them hurriedly.

Amy was watching open-mouthed, her blonde hair ruffled, eyes wide with fear. Her nightshift was tangled around her knees.

"Go," I told her.

She scrambled off the bed and disappeared out of the room.

Leaver came towards me, forcing me backwards. His face was darkened with shadow, his untucked shirt hanging around his knees. "Who the hell do you think you are?" he demanded, voice thin. Beneath his miserable attempt at forcefulness, I could hear the uncertainty, the embarrassment.

I held the candleholder out in front of me. "She's just a child."

"She's my lag. I can do with her what I like." He tucked in his shirt, looking at me with flashing eyes. "What will you do? Go to the Rum Corps? You think they'll give a shit?"

"The Rum Corps won't care," I said. "But I'm sure Mrs Leaver will."

I watched a look of horror pass over his round face. What a weakness it was, I thought distantly, for a man to care what his wife thought. He pointed a finger at me. I could see it trembling. "One word to my wife and I'll kill you."

I smiled thinly. My time in this place had shown me the difference between men who could kill and men who just talked. Robert Leaver was a man who just talked.

"You'll not kill me," I said.

He looked taken aback by my boldness. "What do you want?" he hissed.

I faltered. Let out a short laugh. "Are you trying to bargain with me?"

He clenched his jaw. "I said, what do you want?"

And I saw it then. I had power. For the first time since I had stepped onto these shores, I had the upper hand.

I thought of Lottie, wed to Patrick Owen, carted off to Sydney Town. And I said, "I want my ticket of leave."

I signed my name and the paperwork was handed to me.

'It is His Excellency the Governor's pleasure to dispense with the attendance at

government work of Eleanor Marling...'

Below it was a detailed account of my appearance, my voyage on the *Norfolk*, and my trial at the Old Bailey. But it was the last line that had my attention:

'Permitted to employ herself in any lawful occupation within the district of Parramatta.'

No. I couldn't be imprisoned here in this settlement. Not while Lottie was in Sydney.

I stared down at the page. Demanding Leaver go to the magistrate on my account had been selfish. I ought to have bargained with him for Amy's freedom. Not my own. I had done as I had out of a desperate need to help Lottie. But this would not help anyone.

I bought myself a room at the lodging house on High Street. At the market, I found two poplin dresses for sixpence each. They were threadbare and their prints faded, but with a little rehemming, they both blessedly reached my ankles. I stood in front of the mirror in my room at the lodging house and fastened the hooks to my neck. For the first time in almost two years, I was not dressed the same as every second woman in Parramatta. Nor was I the lady I had been when I had last stood in front of a mirror like this and fastened a lace collar at my throat. The relentless sun had darkened my skin and lightened my hair, almost two years of labour scarring my hands with callouses. But I knew the changes this place had wrought on the inside were far greater. Parramatta had stolen my ignorance, my ability to turn away. Twenty months in New South Wales and I was a woman who walked with a knife in her hand.

I looked down at my papers I had laid across the bed. Though I had little else, I had freedom of sorts. The enormity of that was not lost on me, despite the underhand way it had come about. I felt little guilt at having blackmailed Robert Leaver. Twenty months in New South Wales had also taught me there was little place here for decency.

I combed and pinned my hair, scrubbed my skin clean. And when dark had fallen thick across the street, I went to Lieutenant Blackwell.

I stood outside the hut and knocked, my heart pounding harder than it had the night he had first brought me here.

The door groaned as it opened.

He stooped in the doorway, looking at me without speaking. His eyes glided over the floral print of my skirts, my neatly pinned hair, the hint of lace at my neck. Beneath the calluses and the second-hand dress, I had conjured up a little of my old refinement. Chin lifted, shoulders back; a way I'd not carried myself in many months. Last time Blackwell and I had spoken, I'd been a chaotic mess with a knife in my hand. I needed him to see I was stronger than that. Capable. I needed to him to do as I asked.

I held out my paperwork. I knew one glance at the page would tell him I was here for life. But as he glanced over it, his face gave nothing away.

"You have your freedom," he said finally, passing the papers back to me. "That's wonderful."

I shook my head. "It's not wonderful. I can't leave Parramatta. And I need to get to Lottie in Sydney Town."

Finally, Blackwell took a step back, gesturing for me to step inside the hut.

"I'm sorry, Eleanor," he said, "this is the way things are. But do things right and perhaps one day it will become a pardon."

I couldn't wait for a pardon. Not while Lottie was lying beside Patrick Owen in the night.

I looked up at him. "You could persuade the magistrate on my behalf," I said. I knew there was little point dancing around the issue.

Blackwell scooped back his hair, exhaling. "This is highly inappropriate."

"Yes. I know." I looked him in the eye. And I kept my distance. Perhaps there were ways I could have persuaded him. Gentle fingers down his arm, lips on his neck.

Concubine.

I stayed fixed to the floor, my papers held out in front of me. "Please," I said. "Lottie is in danger."

"Danger you plan to walk right into."

He cared for me; yes, I saw that. And a part of me was grateful. But I didn't want to be cared for right then. I wanted – *needed* – that extra gasp of freedom.

"You were the one who arranged for me to work for Leaver," I said suddenly.

"Yes."

I swallowed, taken aback by his blunt admission. "Why?"

156

His eyes shifted. "You know why."

"I want to hear you say it."

"Because when I'm around you, I fear I will be unfaithful to my wife."

The words fell heavily into the silence. They did not bring me nearly as much satisfaction as I had expected.

"I thought it better for both of us," he said. "I know working in the factory is difficult."

Perhaps he was right. Perhaps it was better for both of us. But that didn't stop me from feeling as though I'd been discarded.

My hand tightened, crumpling my papers. "Patrick Owen should never have been allowed to walk free," I said. "We both know that."

I saw his jaw tense.

"I need to get Lottie away from him."

"How?"

"I don't know," I admitted. I only knew it was not something I could do from the depths of Parramatta. "Please," I said. "You know how important this is to me."

Blackwell rubbed his stubbled chin, exhaling deeply. Finally, he reached for the papers. "Let me speak to the magistrate."

The following day, the factory burned. Flames roared up from the warehouses above the jail, a cloud of smoke drifting across the sun.

We all stood by the river, watching flames pour out the side of the building. The smoke stung my eyes and made my throat burn.

The women from the spinning wheels milled about in the street, staring up the fire. They chattered among themselves, some with children clamped to their hips. The men from the prison below the factory stood lined up in their shackles, guarded by a row of soldiers. Convicts and enlisted men formed a line from the river, passing buckets of water up the chain to be flung onto the blaze.

I sought out Hannah, who was standing among the women. I could feel their eyes on me, taking in my floral skirts, my straw bonnet. I felt myself shrink under their scrutiny. For so many months, I had longed to be more than a miserable factory lass. But now I felt painfully disconnected. Caught between two worlds.

"What's this about then?" asked Hannah, gesturing to my dress.

I shook my head dismissively. "Had a little spare coin is all." I couldn't bring myself to tell her I'd wrangled a ticket of leave.

I stared up at the factory, imagining the spinning wheels ablaze. "What happened?"

"Started in the kitchen," she told me. "Some logs come out of the grate and landed on the girls' blankets."

Fitting, I thought, that that dreadful place might turn to ash. It deserved little more. But I feared what it would mean for the women and children who spent each night on its floor.

I edged away from Hannah and the other women, feeling an inexplicable tug of guilt. Guilt that I had escaped the factory. And guilt that fate had fallen in my favour and led me to Blackwell's door.

I felt his presence before I saw him. He stood at my side and pressed a piece of paper into my hand.

I unfolded it, heart pounding. My ticket of leave.

And there, at the bottom of the page, was the thing I had longed for: *'Permitted to employ herself in any lawful occupation within the district of Sydney.'*

I looked up at him with gratitude in my eyes. I was going to find Lottie. And then?

I couldn't bring myself to think that far ahead. I was terrified of what I might find.

"Thank you," I murmured. He was standing close; close enough for me to see the dark blue flecks in his eyes. At the back of the crowd we were hidden; Parramatta's eyes on the burning jail.

"Be careful," he said huskily. He bent his head and kissed the salty skin on the side of my neck.

Before I could reply, he was gone.

PART THREE

The courtroom is hot and cramped. I stand pressed between the other prisoners, their shoulders hard against mine. I can sense their racing hearts, can smell the sweat on their skin, feel as though I'm drowning in their fear.

Our trials are cursory, and we are given little chance to speak. The magistrate metes out punishments like a dull schoolroom recitation.

Assault of an overseer: to the coal mines in Newcastle.

Theft of government stores: remainder of sentence at Toongabbie.

And then I am brought forward; my name spoken, my charges read out.

I am given the chance to speak, but I know nothing I say will save me. I am a factory lass who has robbed a man of his life. I have taken that final step: murderess. *I am to be made an example of; a cautionary tale of a woman who took the wrong path. A warning to the other factory lasses to be quiet, be moral, be obedient. I grip the railing of the dock, praying my legs will hold me when the inevitable verdict comes.*

The magistrate's words are no surprise.

For the murder of Adam Blackwell, you are sentenced to hang by the neck until you are dead.

CHAPTER TWENTY-ONE

With my ticket of leave in my pocket, I climbed back onto the barge. The morning was hot and hazy, eels wrestling beneath the surface of the river. I watched over my shoulder as Parramatta and the charred shell of its factory vanished behind a wall of forest.

I felt focused as we wound along the river, my eyes fixed on the road of coppery water. I had no plans beyond finding Lottie, no thought of what shape my life would take now. But my days as a Parramatta lag were behind me. I had more freedom than I had ever imagined I would have again.

The sun was sinking when the barge bumped against its moorings in Sydney Cove. In my twenty months away in Parramatta, Sydney Town had grown. I saw hints of London in its neatly carved stone and the church spires that interrupted the vastness of the sky. Rows of jetties had sprung up out of the mudflats and the sprawl of huts and cottages had begun to take over the forest. And the people; more people than I'd seen since England. Sailors and soldiers, ladies and lags, filling the streets with chatter, with colour; overwhelming in their sheer number.

How was I to find Lottie among the expanse of this place?

Hastily built taverns teetered on the waterfront, men clustered outside them, roaring with laughter. I dared a glance through the window of one, and saw hordes of sailors at bare wooden tables, some stumbling drunkenly into one another. I kept walking. On the corner of the road weaving inland from the harbour, I found a smaller tavern without the men gathered out the front. A wooden sign squeaked above the door, announcing my arrival at the Whaler's Arms.

I stepped inside. The bar was small, with dark wooden panelling, barrels and bottles lined up neatly behind the counter. Round tables were dotted about the room.

"Close the door behind you, lass," called the man behind the bar. "Flies'll take over the place if you let them."

The door groaned loudly as I yanked it shut.

"I'm looking for a man named Patrick Owen," I told the barman. "Do you know him?"

The man was big and bearlike, with a dark beard that reached halfway down his chest. "Never heard of him."

"Irishman," I said. "Fair hair, handsome."

The barman chuckled. "Taken your fancy has he? Sorry lass, afraid I can't help you."

As I made my way towards the door, I heard a tangle of Gaelic. I stopped walking. The voices came from a group of older men, crowded around a table in the corner of the bar. I had little doubt that Owen had caused as much of a stir among the Irish in Sydney as he had in Parramatta. I made my way towards the table.

"Patrick Owen," I said. "Do you know him?"

One of the men blew a long line of smoke in my direction. "Who's asking?"

I hesitated. "I'm a friend of his wife."

And a gnarled brown finger was pointing in the direction of the street. "Owns a place out past the cemetery. Not too far from here."

By the time I stepped out of the inn, the last of the sunlight was draining away. The sea slapped rhythmically against the docks, interspersed with horse hooves and the crunch of cartwheels against stone.

I followed the directions the man had given. Owen's property was small and simple; a stone cottage at the front of few square paddocks. A lamp flickered at the front of the house, but it scooped out little of the darkness.

I made my way up the narrow path and knocked on the door, heart pounding. Was I scared of Owen, or scared of how Lottie might react when she saw me? Perhaps a little of both. Most of all, I was scared I would be too late.

A young woman in a mobcap opened the door. She looked me up and down. "Yes?"

I faltered. I hadn't expected Owen to have a housekeeper.

"I'm looking for Lottie." I swallowed. "For Mrs Owen."

The girl knotted her apron around her finger. "Mrs Owen ain't here no more."

My stomach clenched. "What happened to her?"

"I heard she went to the Rocks."

I frowned, not understanding. Still no wiser as to whether Lottie was alive or dead.

"The Rocks," she said again. "Down by the cove."

I let out a sigh of relief. "Why is she there?" I asked.

The girl chewed her lip, avoiding my gaze. Mothwings pattered into the glass of the lantern.

I gave up. It didn't matter why. "Down by the cove," I repeated.

She nodded. "But best you don't go there yourself, Miss. It ain't a good place to be venturing at night."

The knot in my stomach tightened. "I've no choice."

CHAPTER TWENTY-TWO

"I observe that [when they are let out of the barracks on a Sunday, the convicts] run immediately to the part of the town called the Rocks, where every species of debauchery and villainy is practised."

Major Henry Druitt
Chief Engineer of New South Wales
27th October 1819

The Rocks was a noisy, narrow, London kind of chaos. Mudbrick and sandstone jostled each other for space, houses climbing up rock terraces and threatening to topple into the alleys below. Clothes lines were strung across the streets, hung with linen and stained shirts. Men and women gathered outside houses, laughing, drinking, blowing pipe smoke into the sky. Two children barrelled past me, knocking into my hip.

I thought of the slums of Whitechapel, a place I'd only ever heard stories of. A humid haze hung over the place, and I could smell the stench of human waste, of unwashed bodies, of food gone sour in the sun. Beneath it all, the salty breath of the ocean.

I peered down one of the narrow alleys that snaked off the main thoroughfare. Two women were sitting side by side on the street, babies squirming in their arms. One of the children stared after me until I reached the end of the lane.

Down another alley, another, another. The streets felt circular and maze-like. Another turn and I was at the sea. I drew in a long breath, filling my lungs with the clean, salty air. I looked out over the dark plain of the ocean, listening to the water clop between the rocks. I could see the faint flicker of a lamp glowing on an island in the bay.

My feet were aching, my body weighted with exhaustion. I knew I ought to find myself a bed. But I couldn't bear to leave without finding Lottie. Not now I was so close.

I turned and walked back down the alley. And here were men coming towards me; all rolled up shirtsleeves and puffed out chests. Three of them. No, four.

I realised I'd made myself a target. A foolish target who had learned barely a scrap of street sense in her time in Parramatta.

I put my head down and walked faster, but I had lost all sense of my bearings.

"Don't leave us, darling," called one of the men, making the others roar with laughter. I suppressed the urge to run, sure it would make them chase me. But as one of the men reached for my arm, I grabbed my skirts in my fist and darted around the corner, deeper into the narrow warrens of the Rocks.

When I felt another hand at my wrist, I swung away wildly.

"Nell," said the familiar voice. "It is you."

I stopped running and gulped down my breath.

"Saw some lunatic charging by," Lottie said, before I could speak. "What in hell are you doing here?"

I threw my arms around her, overcome with relief. "I came looking for you. I…"

She looked at me with questions in her eyes – and yes, I knew there were many questions. A firm hand around my arm, she led me back down the alley I had run through. A narrow doorway led into what looked to be a dimly lit kitchen. The room was crammed with women in ragged clothing; some huddled on the floor, others herding children, a couple bustling around a cooking pot hung over the fire. The heat was stifling.

"Where are we?" I asked.

"A woman named Mary owns the house," said Lottie. "She made her fortune once her sentence were up. Helps out those of us with no place

166

to go. Gives us a place to sleep."

Still holding my wrist, she led me to a corner of the room where a filthy grey blanket was spread out over the flagstones. A straw basket sat beside it. Inside was a sleeping baby.

My stomach knotted. I had many questions for Lottie too, of course.

"What happened?" I asked. "Why are you here?"

She shrugged. "Got sick of me, didn't he." She was trying for lightness, but the tremor in her voice betrayed her. As did the vicious streak of anger. "Threw me out."

She didn't look me in the eyes. Afraid, perhaps of *I told you so*.

On the other side of the room, a child began to wail.

I felt anger roiling inside me. This place was crammed full of women and children. Had they all been as carelessly discarded as Lottie?

I sat beside her on the blanket. The stench of hot bodies was making my stomach turn.

"Who are all these women?" I asked. "Where did they come from?" I was dimly aware that I sounded like a naïve young lady from Clerkenwell.

Lottie shrugged. "Some finished their sentences and couldn't find nowhere else. Or their husbands had enough of them. Decided they could do better."

I didn't answer. I couldn't find the words.

"So what then?" she asked. "You a runaway? Or that lieutenant of yours get you a pardon?"

I hugged my knees. "I've a ticket of leave," I said simply, not wanting to venture into details.

Lottie made a noise in her throat. I could tell she didn't want details either.

A throaty wail came from the basket beside her. She bent over to scoop up the baby.

"How old is he?" I asked. "She?"

"He's four months," she answered, her eyes meeting mine for the briefest of moments.

Four months. I realised then that Lottie had been with child long before she had left Parramatta. Long before she and Owen had married.

I swallowed. "Why didn't you tell me?"

I knew the answer of course. She and I had barely spoken in the months before she had left. And even if I had known, what would I have had to offer her but another diatribe of abuse towards Owen? What good would any of it have done?

She unbuttoned her bodice with one hand and wrangled the baby onto her breast.

"Is he Owen's?" I asked.

She nodded, not looking at me.

"Did he force you?"

Lottie let out her breath. "What do you want, Nell? To prove you were right and I was wrong? To show me how well you've done for yourself? Is that why you've come?"

"Of course not," I said. "I was worried about you. I worried for you every day. I just want to help you."

She shook her head. "You ought to have stayed in Parramatta with your lobster. How d'you even get here? You have him swing things for you? Persuade him to get you a little more freedom?"

I clenched my teeth. Said nothing.

"You left him," Lottie said after a moment. "I didn't think you would."

I lowered my eyes. "There was nothing to leave." Heat flushed the back of my neck. I knew myself lying. But I couldn't let Lottie know how far things had gone between Blackwell and me.

I stood up. "I'll leave you then. If that's what you want."

Lottie rubbed her eyes with her free hand. "Where will you go?"

"I don't know," I admitted, heading for the door.

She sighed. "Come back, Nell. It's not safe to go wandering about out there with no place to go. You're better off here. Safety in numbers and all that." She spoke without looking at me. "I'll deal with you in the morning."

As the salty smell of broth seeped across the kitchen, the women made their way towards the fire. A young girl at the cooking pot brought a stack of bowls from the shelf, and ladled a thin puddle of soup into each. One by one, the women filed their way towards the table in the centre of the room and took the soup bowls back to their own corners. A well-practised routine. I wondered how long some of them had been here.

"Make yourself useful," Lottie told me, wiping the baby's mouth with the hem of her dress. "Fetch us some supper."

I took two bowls from the table and carried them carefully back to Lottie. We huddled together in the corner, angled towards the wall so we might block out the world around us. Lottie bent over her bowl to scoop a spoonful into her mouth, the baby fidgeting in the crook of her arm.

I ate in silence, unsure what to say. Whatever was to come out of my mouth, I felt certain she wouldn't be interested in hearing it. She attempted another mouthful of broth, swatting the spoon out of the baby's grasp.

"Let me take him," I said, as I swallowed my last mouthful. She dumped the child in my lap and picked up her bowl to drink from it.

I peered down at the baby. Tiny pink fingers were darting in and out of his mouth. He felt small and fragile in my arms.

Patrick Owen's child. And Lottie's.

"What's his name?" I asked.

She gulped down a mouthful. "Willie. After my da."

He wriggled in my arms and began to whine.

"How long have you been here?" I asked, rubbing his back.

She didn't look at me. "Half a year maybe."

I said nothing. Half a year. I wondered if Patrick Owen had ever laid eyes on his son.

"I know what you're thinking. But he did what I wanted. He got me out of the factory." She lifted her bowl to her lips to drain it, then sat it on the floor beside her, pulling Willie from my arms.

"It's good to see you," I said finally. Both an understatement and a lie. I was inexpressibly glad I had found her alive. But my heart ached to see where she had ended up.

"It's good to see you too," Lottie said, giving me a ghost of a smile.

I leant wearily back against the wall. There was so much more I wanted to ask, but I had learned a precious skill in my time around Blackwell. There was nothing so good as silence to encourage an answer.

"Things were good," she said. "At first. He was kind to me. Decent."

"Why did Owen come to Sydney?" I asked. "Why not stay upriver? He had it good in Parramatta."

"He served his time there," said Lottie. "Can you blame him for wanting a fresh start?"

"I suppose not." I hugged my knees, watching a women steer a barefooted child away from the fire. "And the rebels?" I asked. "Is he involved with them here in Sydney?"

Lottie eyed me. "I suppose so. Dan Brady came down here not long after we did. And there was croppies at the farmhouse all the time. Talking among themselves. But I never heard what they were saying."

"Are they planning another rebellion?"

She sighed. "How would I know that? Look where I am." And she turned her eyes away, making it clear the conversation was over.

That night I slept curled up beside Lottie on the floor of the kitchen. The flagstones beneath my head were cold, despite the thick, wet heat pressing down on us. I kept my knees pulled to my chest to avoid kicking the women around me.

Before I had closed my eyes, Lottie had lifted the corner of Willie's blanket to reveal a pistol tucked into the basket.

"Here," she said. "In case anyone troubles you. Door don't lock so good. We have visitors in the night sometimes."

I stared down at the pistol, feeling an inexplicable tug of dread. "Where did you get that?"

"Stole it from Patrick."

"Does he know you have it?"

"Course not."

I closed my eyes and tried to breathe. Far from reassuring me, the sight of the pistol was unnerving. *Visitors in the night. Door don't lock so good…*

This was what I wanted, I reminded myself. This was what I had cajoled Blackwell to get. The freedom to come to Sydney Town and find Lottie, in whatever state she might be in. The freedom to get her out of it.

I wanted to believe there was hope for us. For me. For Lottie. For her son. I wanted to believe we could cobble together a decent life from the wreckage of our mistakes.

My sleep was broken and shallow, interrupted by footsteps and dreams and Willie's midnight shrieking. I was glad when the first hint of morning strained down the alley.

But I was nervous about the day ahead. And every other day after that. My only plan had been to find Lottie, and now my life stretched out hazy and uncertain. I needed to find work. Somewhere to live. But I had little idea how to go about doing either. Every day of my life, I had been told where to sleep. At least until my ticket of leave had been pressed into my hands.

"Come with me," I told Lottie, as I tried to smooth the creases from my skirts. After a night on the floor of the kitchen, they were in dire need of a wash.

"Come with you where? I've a child. I can't take him out into the world with nowhere to go."

"You can no more keep him in this place." My words came out sharper than I'd intended. I had offended her, I could tell. But surely she could see this was no place to raise a child.

"Get out of here, Nell," she said. "A ticket of leave lass can do far better."

I shook my head. "Not without you."

"If you stay, it's just another person I've got to look out for. Another person I got to worry over. I'm walking around with another man's child on my hip – no one's even going to look at me." Her eyes met mine, and her tone changed suddenly. "But you got a chance. You can make a go of things." She pressed a hand to my wrist and gave it a gentle squeeze. "Don't waste it."

I trudged out towards High Street. I wasn't abandoning Lottie, I told myself. Getting out of the Rocks and finding a way to earn some money was the best way to help her and her son. It was the best thing for all of us.

I had no thought of where I was to go from here. I was a free woman. Free for the first time in almost three years. It was a lost, shipwrecked feeling.

Here I was without a thing to anchor me. No Father. No Jonathan. No Blackwell. My entire life I had been shaped into what men wanted me to be. How was I to craft a life on my own? I felt horribly, sickeningly free. A concubine let loose in the streets of New South Wales.

A lodging house, I supposed was the logical first step. I had a few coins left in my pouch, courtesy of Blackwell's incessantly unhemmed shirts. Enough for a bed for a few nights at least.

I went back to the Whaler's Arms where I had asked after Owen.

"I need a room," I told the barman. I could hear the tremor of uncertainty in my voice and I cursed myself for it. After all I had been through, was it truly asking for a room that had my nerves rattling?

"Pound a night," he said.

I reached into my coin pouch and handed over enough to cover me until the end of the week.

For three days I traipsed through the colony, calling at houses and shopfronts in a desperate search for work. But a ticket of leave lass, I was quickly coming to learn, was no great commodity. Why would a man pay a woman to wash his laundry, clean his house, make his supper, when he could pull a lag from a prison ship and put her to work for far less cost? In a fleeting burst of optimism, I'd even called on a wealthy couple seeking a governess for their daughter. Outlined my education and my bank of unused knowledge. There had been enthusiasm in their eyes until I'd laid my ticket of leave on the table.

I slunk back to my room and perched on the bed, hands folded in my lap. My head and heart were thudding with anxiety. My coin pouch was close to empty, and I'd paid for just two more days at the Whaler's Arms. It felt like only a matter of time before I'd be on the floor of that kitchen beside Lottie.

I pulled the end from the loaf of bread I'd bought and chewed on it, short of anything else to do. I longed for a drink. Craved a few mouthfuls of the Rum Corps' dreadful liquor. When had I become a person who relied on moonshine to get me through the day?

I swallowed another mouthful of bread, trying to push the thought from my mind. Sashaying alone down to the tavern and ordering a glass of rum would be wildly inappropriate. I could barely believe I was even considering it.

But considering it I was, and before I could stop myself, I was tiptoeing down the stairs into the tavern. I peeked through the crack in the door that led to the bar. In the late afternoon the place was almost empty, just a couple of older men drinking by the window. I stepped inside before I changed my mind.

The innkeeper was leaning on the bar with account books opened in front of him. I hoped he would be too engrossed in his paperwork to judge me.

"Rum," I said, my voice impossibly small. "Or whisky, or... whatever it is you have." I dug a coin out of my pocket and sat it on the bar. A humoured smile flickered within his beard.

He filled a tin cup and sat it on the bar in front of me. "Only our finest for you, lass."

I snatched it up and scurried into a corner, trying to disappear into the long shadows that lay over the tavern. I took a gulp of the liquor. It was as dreadful as it had been in Parramatta, but I felt a hint of tension begin to slide from my shoulders. When I dared to look up, the barman was peering across the room at me.

"I don't bite," he chuckled, nodding to the row of empty stools in front of him. I hesitated. I didn't want to be judged. But I was beginning to drown in my own chaotic thoughts. I knew the company would do me good. I carried my drink over to the bar and slid onto one of the stools.

The barman sat his pencil in the fold of his account book. "You find the fellow you were looking for then? Mr Owen?"

I sipped my drink. "I did. For all the good that did me."

"What you doing here?" he asked.

"Looking for work."

"His Majesty send you over?"

I felt my cheeks colour. I knew well I did not need to answer – what would I be doing here if I hadn't been hauled out on a prison ship? As a convict woman I was barely a novelty, of course. But I couldn't shake the shame of it.

Avoiding the barman's eyes, my gaze drifted over the scrawled numbers on his ledger. I pointed to one of the sums at the bottom of the page.

"That's wrong."

He chuckled. "You'll forgive me if I don't trust a lag to do my books."

I straightened my shoulders indignantly. "You've not carried the two," I told him. "You're out by twenty pounds."

With a look of reluctance, he glanced down at the page. Irritation flickered across his eyes as he scrawled the correction on his ledger. "I was never one for arithmetic," he said, cheeks reddening beneath his beard.

I couldn't help a smile of self-satisfaction.

In the morning, he found me in the kitchen of the tavern. I was hovering by the fire, waiting for the kettle to boil.

He folded his thick arms across his chest. "Papers?"

I raised my eyebrows. "Pardon?"

"Your paperwork," he said impatiently. "I need to see it. Make sure you ain't a runaway."

I pulled out my ticket of leave and shoved it into his hand. "Why've you decided now that I'm a runaway?" I asked. "Because you're annoyed I corrected your arithmetic?"

He said nothing, just skimmed over my paperwork. He folded it messily and held it back out to me. Gave a half-satisfied grunt.

"Can you pour a drink?" he asked.

I hesitated. Was he offering me work? "I can do your books," I ventured boldly.

He snorted. "I already told you, I don't want no government lass rifling around in my accounts. I said, can you pour a drink?"

I allowed myself a smile. It had been worth a try. I thought of the woman from the factory who had poured drinks at the tavern in Parramatta. Never in my life had I imagined myself doing such a thing. But how hard could it be?

"Of course I can," I said.

The barman nodded. "Good," he said gruffly. "A lass behind the bar gets men through the door." He turned to leave, then looked back at me. "Name's Charlie," he said. "I don't like laziness and I keep things clean. And I don't need no help doing my books. You can start tonight."

I smiled to myself as I lifted the kettle. Hoped Charlie's accounting errors would fall in my favour.

CHAPTER TWENTY-THREE

"He is under no obligation to maintain her longer than she suits his inclination. There arises a very heavy national expense, as these women with their children are constantly likely to be turned out of doors; poor, friendless and forsaken."

Rev. Samuel Marsden
A Few Observations on the Situation of the Female Convict in New South Wales
1808-1817

The next morning, I went straight to the Rocks. I'd spent the evening behind the bar at the Whaler's Arms, learning my way around barrels of the Rum Corps' finest, and pouring ale that looked remarkably like dishwater. I'd not made it to bed until long after midnight.

But I'd woken with the dawn, eager to tell Lottie of the position I'd secured. To tell her she and Willie were welcome to stay with me for as long as they needed it. Tell her she had a chance at a life outside that filthy kitchen. Somehow, I would see to it that we both survived this place.

I found her on the street outside the kitchen, dunking her shift in a washtub. She was barefoot in dirt-streaked skirts, brown hair hanging loose on her shoulders. Willie was bleating in the basket beside her. At the sight of me, she stood up from the tub and wiped her hands on her apron.

"I've found work," I told her. "A place to stay. There's room enough for you and Willie. You ought to—"

"Don't be mad," she cut in. "I'll not think of it."

"Why not?" I'd not for a second imagined she might refuse.

She planted a hand on her hip. Her eyes held nothing but bitterness.

"What am I to do all day?" she demanded, swatting a platoon of flies away from her face. "Sit around in your room while you earn a living?" She shook her head. "No. I'm not a cause for your charity. However much you might think it."

I stood in the middle of the alley, clenching my teeth at her stubbornness. I debated whether to argue.

Think of your son, I wanted to say. But I held my words. In spite of, or perhaps because of all life had thrown at her, Lottie had a pride about her. A pride, I saw then, that would not let her accept charity from a *sasanaigh*. No matter how well meaning.

"And you'll not change your mind?"

"No, Nell," she said, hand on her hip. "I'll not change my mind."

Dejected as I was, a part of me understood. Being a cause for Blackwell's charity had stung. I'd not stopped to think I might be cutting Lottie as deeply. And what could I do but give a nod of understanding and head back towards the tavern?

Sydney Town was refreshing. In Parramatta, I'd seen the same stale faces walk the streets each day, added to only once or twice, when a new shipment of convicts had come crawling up the river.

But Sydney reminded me there was more to this world than the sand and stone of New South Wales. The Whaler's Arms was full of merchants, of sailors, of settlers with big dreams. They spoke of their new homes and their old, raged against the governor, the Rum Corps, the English, the Irish. I listened in on as many conversations as I could as I wiped tables and refilled glasses.

Did you hear young Bobby's been pardoned?

Can't get a thing to grow in this soil.

Bligh's behaving like God himself…

Soldiers and farmers, and emancipists celebrating with one too many ales. Sailors with hands that felt like tree bark when they pressed their coins into my palm.

I knew what the sailors were after, of course. Their eyes would gleam as they leaned across the bar to order their drinks, hands lingering against mine when I passed them their change. I was always quick to let them know I was no good for anything but putting a drink in their hands. But sometimes, when the tavern was quiet, I would listen to them speak. Hear them tell tale after tale of their travels. I needed to hear of that faraway world. Needed that reminder that we weren't all alone out here.

"London," I said to one. "Have you been to London?"

The sailor was older, with grey streaks dashed through his dark hair. Had a round, rough voice that spoke of coasts and cliffs and wrecks. He said:

"Aye. Of course. Was in London not a year ago."

"Tell me of it," I said wistfully, as though the place were paradise and not the hell I'd sailed out of with blood on my boots. I rested my chin in my palm and listened as he told me of strikes against the wars in Europe. Of the gas lights that had lit up Pall Mall as though it were morning.

"And this place?" I dared to ask. "What do they think of us back home?"

The sailor chuckled. "Every hot-blooded man has a mind to visit. They say them factory lasses are a good thing."

As I had learned in Parramatta, we lived in a deeply divided colony. The Whaler's Arms saw its fair share of croppies, who huddled in the back corners and murmured beneath clouds of pipe smoke. Though I never saw Owen or Brady among them, I was constantly on edge at the prospect of another uprising. I'd sidle past tables in hope of catching fragments of English. The murmured Gaelic made it all too easy to imagine them plotting their next rebellion. I felt a pang of shame as I thought back to the two croppies in Parramatta. Tied to the triangle for speaking their own tongue.

But while the croppies kept to themselves, the tension among the Englishmen was no less stark. Most evenings, the Whaler's rang with terse voices as the farmers and enlisted men argued the way forward.

"Would you listen to them?" Charlie snorted, passing a glass of rum to the older gentleman sitting at the bar. "Harping on like fishwives."

I peered over at the throng of men. Tonight there was plenty of them; half in their lobster coats, the others in the faded shirts and breeches of the men who worked the land. "What are they arguing about?"

"Love for Governor Bligh," said Charlie. "Or lack of it. Redcoats are losing their mind cos he's taking away their liquor stills." He looked over at the gentleman he had just served. "What do you make of all this, Flynn?"

The older man chuckled. "Heaven forbid we stop trading in liquor like savages and use the grain for bread instead."

I'd grown to like Arthur Flynn, with his neat frock coats and polished boots, a far cry from the mud-caked lags who usually tramped through the tavern. In the three weeks since I'd begun working at the Whaler's, he'd appeared on several occasions, always with a kind word for me.

Charlie nodded at the glass in Flynn's hand. "Didn't see you coming in here and ordering a loaf of bread."

Flynn chuckled. "Quite right. But all things in moderation."

"Get rid of the rum stills like Bligh wants and this place'll fall apart," said Charlie. "We're in a colony of drunkards."

Flynn lifted his glass. "Exactly. And if we're to flourish, that must change. Bligh's done damn fine work here, if you ask me. Half of us holding land would have lost everything we had if it weren't for him. The Rum Corps would have bought all our land for pennies and ended up with this entire place to their name."

"My business is flourishing just nicely, thank you very much," said Charlie. "It's all those fine drunkards that are keeping me in business."

I smiled.

Flynn turned, catching me listening. He gave me a warm smile. "Good evening, Miss Marling."

I'd never bothered to correct him; to tell him I was no *Miss*; that I carried my dead husband's name, as well as his guilt. There seemed little point.

He nodded to the corner of the bar where one of the men was gesturing wildly. A fat cloud of cigar smoke hung over his head. "Have you ever seen such a pitiful display? Those men ought to be ashamed of themselves, behaving this way in front of a woman."

"I think she quite likes these pitiful displays," said Charlie. "Always with her ear to the ground, ain't you, Nell? Always keen to know what's happening." He winked at me. "She thinks we don't notice."

Flynn chuckled. "Is that so?"

"Here." Charlie took a fresh ash tray from beneath the counter and handed it to me. "You want to catch an earful you can take this over to them."

I took the ashtray and set it on the men's table, collecting the old one with its overflowing cigar butts, and as many empty cannikins as I could bundle into my arms. Oblivious to my arrival, the men continued talking over one another.

"Watch your damn mouth, boy," one of the soldiers was hissing. "Or you'll be at the coalmines before you know it and that farm of yours'll be nothing but dust."

"It's as it always is," I said, as I returned to the bar and dumped the empty cannikins in the trough. "The Rum Corps are the ones with the power. The rest of us just go where they lead us."

Flynn emptied his glass and took his top hat from the counter, pressing it on over his thick grey hair. "They'll be pulled into line soon enough. Bligh's cut from far too strong a cloth to let them keep up their run of the place." He bobbed his head at me as he made his way towards the door. "Take care, my dear. Keep that ear to the ground. You never know what you might hear."

I smiled, turning back to the trough to scrub out the empty glasses. The door creaked and thudded as several of the men left, a momentary quiet falling over the bar.

"I remember you," said a voice behind me. I whirled around to see a young soldier sliding onto a bar stool. "You're a Parramatta lass. Blackwell's lodger."

The words made heat blaze through me. I both did and didn't want to be Blackwell's.

"How d'you get down here then?" he asked.

"I have my paperwork." I reached into my pocket. "If you wish to see it, I—"

He waved a hand dismissively. "'S'all right. I was just making conversation." He slid off his jacket. "Ale, if you please."

I poured him a glass and sat it on the counter. The soldier's face had a faint familiarity to it. I remembered him standing on the edge of the green while the two Irishmen from the chain gang were flogged. "Lieutenant Harper," I said.

He nodded. "That's right."

"You're a long way from Parramatta."

"I've come downriver with the fishing party," he said. "We're to head back up north in the morning."

"And you managed a decent haul?"

"There's fine kingfish in Sydney Cove," he said, gulping down his ale. "Government stores'll be well stocked when we return."

There was far more I wanted to ask him about, of course. The rebels and their uprising. The rebuilding of the burned-out factory, and whether the women from the spinning wheels had roofs above their heads. Above all, I wanted to ask him about Blackwell.

My missing him was a deep ache inside me.

I opened my mouth to speak; nothing but casual questions of course. *Is he well? Will you pass on my regards?*

But it felt dangerous. Felt as though speaking of him would stoke a fire that needed to burn out. Perhaps even then, hidden somewhere at the back of my mind, I knew that having Blackwell in my life would destroy me.

Later that week I went back to the Rocks. It had been almost a fortnight since I'd last seen Lottie, and each night I fell asleep thinking of her crammed into that squalid kitchen with her baby in the basket beside her.

I made my way down the alley and peeked through the door into the kitchen. Lottie was sitting on the floor with her back to the wall, Willie held to her breast. Healthy, as far as I could tell. As safe as could be hoped for.

I hurried away before she could catch sight of me, and wove through the alleys towards the market. Carts were crammed into the streets, loaded with potatoes, with cabbages, with hessian bags of grain. An enormous brown horse nudged my shoulder as I passed.

I bought a loaf of bread and hunk of cheese, and tucked them into my basket.

A faint tug on my skirt. I whirled around and caught a small hand reaching into my pocket. I grabbed the wrist of the young, dark-haired girl. I guessed her no more than nine or ten. Her eyes widened as I tightened my grip.

"I didn't take nothing," she said hurriedly. "I swear it. Not a thing." She spoke with a forced confidence but I could see the fear in her wide blue eyes. I loosened my grip a little.

"What do you need the money for?" I asked. "Food?"

She nodded.

I let go of her wrist and reached into my coin pouch. Handed her a couple of shillings and a little of the bread.

She crammed the food into her pocket and tightened her fist around the coins. Gave me a tiny smile of thanks.

"Wait," I said, pressing a hand to her shoulder before she could dart away. "Do you have somewhere to sleep? Someone to take care of you?" I couldn't shake the fear that when night came, she would disappear into the maze of the Rocks with all the forgotten women.

She chewed her lip, as though debating whether to talk. Dark, tangled curls blew loose around her cheeks. "I lost my ma," she said.

"Where did you last see her?"

The girl didn't speak for a few moments. "Well," she said carefully. "I don't really remember." She looked down at her scuffed boots. "They took me to the Orphan School when I was little."

I let out my breath. I had heard far too many stories of the Orphan School around the spinning wheels.

I thought of the crying woman I had sat beside in my first week in Parramatta, tears falling for the child she would never see again. I thought of all the women in the factory sleeping beside their babies in the night, knowing it was only a matter of time before they were taken away. And I thought of the lifeless body I had found in the scrub on the side of the road. Because when I looked down at the young girl with my coins in her hand, I saw Maggie Abbott's stark blue eyes staring back at me.

CHAPTER TWENTY-FOUR

This runaway from the Orphan School would not find her mother; of that I was certain.

I swallowed heavily. "What's your name?"

She looked over her shoulder, then back up at me. "Kate," she said finally. "Kate Abbott."

My heart was beating fast. "You've got to go back to the Orphan School, Kate. This is not a safe place to be."

She shook her head. "I finished at the school now. Got my Bible and everything. Only they sent me to work for some toff up in George Street. And he were real nasty... He... Well, he..." She faded out, her eyes back on the ground. "I don't want to say."

Something twisted in my chest. "You ran away?"

A faint nod.

My heart lurched then, for this child, traipsing through Sydney Town, looking for the mother she could barely have remembered. Walking the streets and waiting for a woman to claim her.

"All right," I said, churning through my mind for a way to tell her of Maggie's death. I had to take her back to the tavern with me. I could hardly tell her the truth standing here in the street with Sydney Town heaving around us. Who was I but a stranger with the worst of news to give her?

"Come with me," I said carefully. "I've a room at the Whaler's Arms. You can rest there. Have some food and—"

Kate whirled around suddenly and started to run. I looked over my shoulder to see what had startled her, coming face to face with a soldier. Kate's pockets, I guessed, were full of stolen coins.

I grabbed a handful of my skirts and ran in the direction she had disappeared. I wove past the market and into the narrow streets of the Rocks, my basket bumping against my hip.

I called after her, my voice bouncing between the walls of the alleys. I turned corners, climbed terraces, peered into shops and houses. But Maggie's daughter had disappeared.

By the time I made it back to the tavern, I was a dishevelled, sweaty mess. I was also late for work.

Charlie glared at me as he heaved a fresh rum barrel onto the shelf. "Don't make me regret hiring a lag."

"I'm sorry," I mumbled. I tossed my basket into the kitchen and hurried back to the bar. My stomach groaned loudly and I realised I hadn't managed to eat.

Charlie flung a dish cloth at me. "Get to work."

I poured ales and rum with my head full of Kate Abbott. I couldn't bear the thought of her roaming the streets of the Rocks, searching for her dead mother.

A part of me wished I could return to the state I had been in when I'd first been shipped out to this place; that state of pushing others' predicaments to the back of my mind. Of emptying myself of empathy.

But I couldn't do it. I ached for Lottie, for Willie, for Kate. I felt the weight of it all upon my shoulders. I felt the loneliness of the men and women shipped away from their loved ones; of men like Blackwell who had left their wives in the name of duty. I ached for the croppies tied to the triangle, and for the women sleeping between the spinning wheels on piles of tick-infested wool.

I felt suddenly exhausted. This was my life now, I realised. Even if I were somehow to obtain that magical pardon, and see the shores of England again, I knew I could never go back to my old ignorance. Couldn't turn my back while men were flogged and women died, and pretend the world was as it should be. I was powerless, yes, but I was no longer unaware. This place had changed me irrevocably.

I cringed at the sight of Arthur Flynn strolling into the bar in his top hat. I knew I looked a right mess, after tearing through the streets in search of Kate. Loose strands of hair clung to my cheeks, my plait hanging limply down my back. I knew my face had caught the sun. But at least with Flynn, I would be guaranteed an intelligent conversation, whether I looked a right mess or not. Something to take my mind off Kate and Lottie, and all the others who were pushing their way into my thoughts.

"This heat is quite dreadful, don't you think?" he said, as I poured him his customary liquor. "Although my farmhands tell me the corn crop is flourishing in this weather."

"Well," I said, pushing the cork back into the bottle. "Perhaps you ought to wish for more hot weather. I hear there are many farmers not lucky enough to have their crops flourishing."

"That's very true." He smiled. "You've a sharp mind. I like that." Flynn climbed awkwardly onto a stool at the bar. "Are you a free settler, Miss Marling?" he asked suddenly.

"No, sir," I said, cheeks colouring with shame. "I have my ticket of leave."

His gaze didn't falter. "I see." He slipped a tobacco box from his pocket and filled his pipe.

"I'm seeking a wife," he said matter-of-factly.

Short of a more astute response, I said, "Is that so?"

He used his little finger to tamp the tobacco into the pipe. "Perhaps you might consider it?"

That night, I found myself considering it.

I lay on my back, staring up at the crooked beams of the ceiling. The room was near lightless but I could hear laughter and the clop of horse hooves rising up from the street.

What would it mean for me, this elevation from concubine to wife? As I'd stood dazedly behind the bar, caught off guard by Flynn's proposal, he had outlined his credentials while puffing on his pipe. A house overlooking the sea. Fifty acres of farmland. A small household staff and eight convict workers.

I didn't love Arthur Flynn, of course. I barely knew the man. But who married for love in this place? Who married for love anywhere? Flynn was kind and studious, with a large property and a successful business. As a husband, he would be far more than I could ever have dared hope for when I'd been sent to the factory as one of the left-behind women.

As proud as I had been of finding work, I knew without a man beside me I had no security. No way of getting ahead in the world. Marrying was the only hope I had of a stable, protected life. It had been true in London and it was even more true here. Without a husband I had no way of getting ahead in the world, or of doing anything to help people like Lottie and Kate. Without a husband, I saw with grim certainty, I was nothing but a candle trying to outlast a gale.

CHAPTER TWENTY-FIVE

When Flynn returned to the Whaler's Arms two days later, I pulled my hands from the wash trough, wiped them on my apron and told him I would be most happy to become his wife. He took my water-creased hand in his, planting a small kiss on my knuckles.

"I'm very glad of it, my dear. I'm certain we will have a happy life together."

The following morning I met him outside the Whaler's, to begin a backwards courtship. Despite the heat, Flynn was dressed in a neat black frock coat, a pale blue scarf at his throat. Beneath his top hat, his grey hair was combed neatly.

Waiting beside him was an older woman in a dark dress and mobcap. She stood with her eyes down, hands folded in front of her. I smiled to myself that Flynn had thought to bring a chaperone. I had come to believe such traditions outdated after I'd been reduced to dressing under a blanket while lying on Blackwell's floor.

Though the woman's face was half hidden by her cap, I recognised her at once. Ann and I had made the journey to New South Wales together, crammed into the convict's quarters of the *Norfolk*. She'd been taken from the ship the day we arrived. Taken, I saw now, by Arthur Flynn.

Ann's eyes flickered with recognition. And resentment. She bobbed her head in greeting, but didn't say a word. I wondered if my husband-to-be knew he had walked right past me on the deck of the *Norfolk* and not looked twice.

Flynn smiled, broad and genuine, the creases beside his eyes deepening. "I'm very pleased to see you," he told me. "I thought perhaps a walk this morning? There are fine views to be had from Point Maskelyne." And off along the waterfront we went, my hand folded into my betrothed's arm, and Ann clomping along sulkily behind us.

We followed the curve of the sea up to a small stone structure on the headland. It looked out across the glistening puzzle of coves to where the Parramatta River spilled into the open ocean.

"Here now," said Flynn. "Dawes' observatory."

I peeked out from beneath my bonnet. "An observatory? How wonderful."

I thought of the astronomy lessons I'd had as a child, in which my tutor had painted a faraway world of comets and stars and planets that circled the sun. Against the limitlessness of the universe, England didn't feel quite so far away. I was surprised to find myself thinking such things. When I'd first climbed onto the *Norfolk*, New South Wales had felt more distant than the moon.

Flynn smiled as I shared my thoughts. "Well of course it feels that way," he said, as he squinted out over the ocean. "After all, one can see the moon from the streets of London. But they cannot see New South Wales."

I felt comfortable with the man, I realised. Certainly more comfortable than I had when I'd first been betrothed to Jonathan as a mindless scrap of twenty. Back then, I'd been terrified of putting a foot wrong. I'd answered questions the way I thought he wanted them answered, and kept the less agreeable parts of my personality well hidden. But Arthur Flynn knew I had put enough feet wrong to be thrown onto a prison ship and he still wanted me as his wife.

"Where is home?" he asked me. And, "Have you ever been betrothed before?"

I told him then, in vague, broad strokes, about my marriage to Jonathan. About my inability to provide him with an heir.

Instead of the displeasure I was expecting, Flynn ventured a small smile. "Well," he said, with a shyness that was almost endearing, "perhaps you and I will have more luck."

I felt emboldened enough then to ask that that had been rolling around in the back of my mind since I'd agreed to become this man's wife.

"There's a woman I was at the factory with," I said carefully. "Her husband threw her out and she's fallen upon hard times. I wondered if perhaps there might be a position for her in your household."

A flicker of disappointment passed over Flynn's eyes. Disappointment that I'd brought my convict past to the table so early in our courtship.

He watched his feet as he walked. "I've no need for more staff."

"Please," I said, feeling my fingers tighten involuntarily around his arm. I knew, of course, that the hand I'd been dealt here in New South Wales, as in London, was better than most. And I needed to use that. But I knew Lottie was far more likely to take up my offer if it involved her working, rather than relying on charity. "She's sleeping on the floor of someone's kitchen, all crammed together with other women and children. She's—"

"You're not to go to such places," Flynn said, his voice hardening suddenly. "I'll not have my wife seen in such an area. Do you understand?"

I gritted my teeth. "Please. And I'll never ask anything of you again." I stopped walking and looked into his eyes. "It's very important to me. If you could find a way to do this one thing, I would be forever grateful."

Flynn rubbed his eyes, and for a moment, he looked an old man. He sighed, then finally gave a slight nod. "Very well. Just this once."

I slid my fingers down his arm to cover his leathery hand with mine. "Thank you."

He gave my hand a quick squeeze, managing something close to a smile.

Lottie was sleeping when I arrived at the kitchen that afternoon. She lay on her side, knees pulled to her chest and her body curled around Willie's basket. I rocked her shoulder gently.

She opened her eyes. "What are you doing here?" She got slowly to her feet, twisting the stiffness out of her shoulders.

"I'm to be married," I told her. I knew there was little point sidestepping the issue.

"Are you now?"

I pushed past her coldness. "There's a place for you," I said. "At my husband's farmhouse. Work. Shelter."

Lottie planted a hand on her hip. "I've told you before, Nell. I'm not one to accept charity. When are you going to get that into your head?"

"This is not charity," I argued. "There's work for you." I let out my breath in frustration. "I just want you and Willie to be safe."

"You got to prove yourself, don't you?" Lottie demanded. "You got to make sure everyone knows how well you've done for yourself."

"You truly think that's what this is about?"

"Isn't it?" A cold laugh. "You fell down to our level for a time, but you just got to show us all how much better than us you are." She stared at me for a long, wordless moment before turning away and shaking her head. Frustration burned through me.

"If you change your mind," I said tersely, "Mr Flynn's farm is at the top end of Bridge Street. Out behind the new Government House. We're to be married next Wednesday."

Lottie cut me with cold eyes. I turned at the sound of footsteps behind me. Heard my sharp intake of breath. Patrick Owen stood in the doorway, arms folded across his chest. His sharp blue eyes bore into me.

"Well, well. Nellie *na sasanaigh*. Dan'll be pleased to hear you're floating around." He turned to Lottie. "What in hell is she doing here?"

"She's leaving," said Lottie, not looking at me.

Owen took a step towards me, without even a glance at his sleeping son. "How's Lieutenant Blackwell faring?"

"I've no idea," I said stiffly. I hated the sound of Blackwell's name on his lips. "I've had nothing to do with him since I left Parramatta."

Owen looked me up and down, as though trying to determine whether I was lying. I held his gaze, despite the hot shiver it sent through me.

"You've a new life here," I said. "Why not leave the past where it is?"

He took a step closer. "Is that all the lives of a few bog-trotters is worth to you, Nellie? You think we ought to just forget?"

I said nothing.

Finally, he turned away and spoke to Lottie in Irish. She picked up the baby and turned to follow Owen out of the kitchen. I grabbed her arm.

"Where is he taking you?"

"Back to his farm."

"He's taking you home?"

"For a time."

"What do you mean 'for a time'? What does he want?"

Lottie looked at me witheringly. "What do you think he wants?"

"And when he's finished with you? He sends you back here?"

Lottie didn't reply. Owen called her name.

"You can't go," I said, not releasing my grip on her wrist.

"Jesus Nell, would you mind your own damn business? What do you know about any of this?" She sighed, then lowered her voice. "He's the only chance I got of a little security. One day he's going to realise he was wrong to have let us go."

I could hear the uncertainty in her words.

"He is not your only chance," I hissed. "Flynn has work for you."

Her eyes flashed with impatience.

"All right," I said hurriedly, before she could speak. "Don't take the position. But please don't go with Owen."

"I have to," she said. "You wouldn't understand."

Lottie was wrong. I understood. I knew what it was to follow a man down the murkiest of paths for the sake of a little security.

And so, standing there in the kitchen, with Patrick Owen in the doorway, I told her of Jonathan's coining business and the way my desperate need to please my husband had almost led me to the gallows.

Something passed across Lottie's eyes. It was the first time I had told anyone I was not just a tale of stolen bread. The first time I had admitted I had been sent here for life.

Lottie's lips parted. Then she looked up and down at my neatly stitched skirts. At the leather boots buckled at my ankles.

"Seven years," she said bitterly. "You told me you got seven years for thieving. And now I learn you're a lifer."

"I'm sorry," I said. I knew there was no excuse for my lies. I'd just been too embarrassed to tell the truth.

Lottie snorted. "And yet you seem to be doing just fine for yourself now."

She pulled free of my grip and followed Owen down the alley, leaving me standing alone in the corner of the kitchen.

CHAPTER TWENTY-SIX

On our second tramp around the settlement, Flynn asked, "What was your crime?"

The question was put simply, as though he were asking about the weather. But there was enough forced casualness in it for me to know he had been trying to bring himself to spit out the words.

I couldn't blame him, of course. He was to sleep beside me in the night. For all he knew, I'd been shipped out here for murder.

As I told my sorry tale, I heard myself return to a victim, coerced into counterfeiting by my scheming husband. I felt oddly outside myself. When I'd first told this story to the magistrate in London, I'd clung to my victimhood, to my belief I'd been so grossly wronged by the world around me. Now the memory of my naivety just made me angry.

But I also knew what a precious thing it was to find a good man to marry here, and I felt instinctively that that naivety would tug at the sensibilities of fine upstanding Arthur Flynn. If I had to be a victim in order to please my betrothed, then that was what I would do.

I looked up at Flynn with wide eyes. "I was a fool," I told him. "And I was too afraid to turn my back on my husband."

He gave me a small smile. "We all make mistakes. Besides, what hope did you have with a man like that in your life?"

And I nodded along, *yes, indeed, a hardened criminal, the worst of men*, feeling more than a small pull of guilt for my murdered husband lying in his grave.

Flynn covered my hand with his. "I'd very much like you to see my property," he said, and I felt my shoulders sink with relief at the change of subject. "I could show you around the place. You could see your rooms. With Ann in attendance of course."

I smiled. "I'd like that very much."

Flynn beamed, patting my hand again. "Excellent. Tomorrow then. I'll have one of my workers come to collect you with the trap."

And he steered me back in the direction of the Whaler's Arms, Ann wheeling around to follow.

When I stepped through the door of the tavern, I froze. Lieutenant Blackwell was sitting at the table closest to the door. I felt a jolt in my chest. His hair was slightly overgrown beneath his cocked hat, the arctic blue of his eyes stark against his tanned skin.

At the sight of me, he stood, his face giving nothing away.

Flynn glanced at Blackwell, then back at me. "Is there trouble?" he asked the lieutenant.

"There's no trouble," I garbled. "Lieutenant Blackwell is… He was kind enough to offer me lodgings in Parramatta." I felt my cheeks blaze. "Lieutenant, this is my betrothed, Arthur Flynn."

"You're to be married?" A flicker of surprise passed over Blackwell's eyes, but he blinked it away quickly.

"I am," I managed. "Yes." My mouth felt impossibly dry.

Blackwell's jaw tightened as the men shook hands. I could tell from Flynn's welcoming smile he had no thought of what a man usually demanded of his lodger in Parramatta.

Blackwell turned away from Flynn and looked me square in the eyes. "It's good to see you, Eleanor."

I tried to swallow. I wasn't sure the emotions roiling inside me could be described as good. "Lieutenant Harper told you how to find me?"

He nodded.

A stilted silence hung between us, punctuated by Charlie thumping a liquor barrel onto the shelf.

"Well then," Flynn said brassily. "A drink then perhaps? What do you say, Lieutenant?"

Before either of us could reply, Flynn was herding us towards a larger table in the centre of the tavern. Ann followed his lead, plopping neatly into a chair between Blackwell and me.

Flynn hovered over me. "Tea for you, my dear?"

"This is a tavern," I reminded him. "Tea isn't on offer." If I was going to stumble my way through this debacle I was going to need something far more mind-numbing than tea.

He waved a dismissive hand. "Nonsense. I'm sure Charlie will be quite happy to boil up a kettle for you. Won't you, Charlie?"

He grinned. "I've heard your wife-to-be has a liking for things a little stronger."

I shot him a glare.

Flynn smiled thinly at Charlie. "Tea will be just fine."

With my betrothed at the bar, I turned to Blackwell. "Why are you in Sydney?" My voice was low and far more conspiratorial than I had intended. Ann's eyes darted between us.

"I've completed my term of duty," he told me. "I'm entitled to a discharge."

In spite of myself, my stomach plunged. "You're going back to England."

He had brought me a sense of security, I realised then. Even with the Parramatta River between us, it had been reassuring to know Blackwell was in the colony with me. Reassuring to know I had the eye of such a powerful man.

I knew I was being foolish. I was to become another man's wife. Blackwell was another woman's husband. Neither of us had a place in the other's thoughts.

I forced a smile. "Your wife will be very pleased to see you, I'm sure."

No response.

"So you've come to say goodbye."

He looked at me with that infuriating expressionlessness I had come to know so well. I felt a flicker of annoyance. Why had he bothered coming to see me if he was to be so closed up?

"Yes," he said finally, as though sensing my irritation. "I suppose I have."

"When will you leave?" I tried to keep my voice light.

"I believe the next ship leaves in a fortnight."

"A fortnight?" I repeated. "And why did you come to see me now?"

His lips parted, as though caught off guard by my question. "Because I wished to see you," he said finally. "Forgive me. It was out of place. I—"

He stopped abruptly as Flynn reappeared at the table, two cannikins of rum in his hand. He set one in front of Blackwell, then slid into the chair beside me.

Flynn lifted his cup. "Well then, a toast perhaps? To this fair colony."

Blackwell smiled thinly. "And to your happy marriage." He gave me a sideways glance.

I suddenly had no idea what to do with my hands. I willed Charlie to hurry the hell up so I could at least hold my teacup.

Flynn beamed. "Indeed." He tossed back a mouthful of liquor.

Blackwell set his cannikin back on the table. His presence seemed to fill the room, and squeeze the air from my lungs.

"You're stationed in Parramatta then?" Flynn asked, crossing one leg over the other.

"I was," said Blackwell. "For the past five years."

"And do you have many women from the factory lodge with you?"

"No." Blackwell held his gaze. "Very few." He looked too tall for the chair.

Flynn took another mouthful. "I see."

"Lieutenant Blackwell is to return to England in a fortnight," I said, far too loudly.

Flynn's face lit up. "Really? How wonderful." I could tell his excitement came mostly from having found a conversation topic that did not revolve around my time in Parramatta. Out came a barrage of questions that felt as though he had prepared them in advance. Which ship was he travelling on? Which route was to be taken? Was he to be deployed to Europe on his return? Blackwell answered them all as though he were being quizzed by a magistrate.

"Tea for you, Nell," Charlie bellowed across the bar. Clumsily, I made to stand, but Flynn pressed a hand to my wrist, keeping me in place.

"Ann will fetch it," he said.

His housekeeper shuffled to the bar and returned with a tin cup filled with lukewarm tea. She slapped it down in front of me. I peered at it in disinterest.

"And you've a place to stay in the meantime, Lieutenant?" asked Flynn. "I assume you've somewhere more appropriate than this fine establishment."

Blackwell gave a thin smile. "I've lodgings at the home of a colleague. He and his wife are due to leave for Van Diemen's Land shortly."

"Ah," said Flynn, his face lighting with recognition. "Captain Grant's house perhaps?"

"That's right."

He chuckled. "I've been hearing about this little jaunt from Grant over cards for months now. At these very tables, in fact. He says the farmland's better down that way. I told him his wife would take one look at the settlement and curl up in horror. I've heard this place feels like Paris compared to how primitive things are down there."

I turned my teacup around in my hands. Ann shifted on her chair, making it squeak loudly. I wondered if I ought to offer her my tea.

"Give Captain Grant my regards," Flynn continued. "I regret that he's to miss our wedding celebrations."

"Of course." Blackwell tossed back the last of his liquor and stood a little too abruptly. "I'll not keep you. I only came to say goodbye." His eyes met mine. "And to wish you all the best."

My throat tightened.

What was I to say? How did you farewell a person you knew you were never going to see again? I couldn't bear the finality of it. I looked up at him. It felt as though Flynn and Ann were watching me, every nuance of my face under scrutiny.

"Have a safe journey home," I managed, my voice sounding hollow and completely unlike myself.

"Thank you." Blackwell opened his mouth to say more, then stopped. I could tell he too had no thought of how to proceed. "Take care."

I swallowed heavily, forcing down a sudden swell of tears. "And you."

Blackwell gave a short nod. And then he was gone.

The hollowness of it stayed with me into the afternoon. When Flynn and Ann returned to the farmhouse, I took a broom up to my room, biding time until work started that evening. I tried to focus on my cleaning, tried to let the rhythm of the sweeping still the commotion of my thoughts. I knew I was being foolish. How lucky I was to have a man like Arthur Flynn as my husband-to-be. But I couldn't help feeling empty.

I leant the broom up against the wall and picked up my empty wash basin for refilling. I trudged out of the tavern and headed for Tank Stream, waving wildly at the flies as they circled my face. The heat was making my skin itch beneath my stays and I felt inexplicably close to tears.

As I stepped onto the muddy bank of the stream, an arm grabbed me from behind. I thrashed against my captor and whirled around, coming face to face with Patrick Owen and Dan Brady. My washbin thudded dully into the mud.

I knew it no coincidence they had appeared the same day as Blackwell. Had they seen him at the tavern? Or had they simply caught word he was in Sydney? Assumed they might find him with me? I had little doubt Lottie had told Owen where I was living.

I knew what they wanted, of course. A chance to go after Blackwell without the rest of the Rum Corps around. A clean shot out of the confines of Parramatta. I was sure even Owen knew his immunity didn't stretch to the murder of an officer.

"He's not here," I said, before they could speak. Instantly, I regretted my words. I ought to have feigned ignorance, given them no hint that I knew anything of the lieutenant.

"Where is he?" asked Owen.

"Do you honestly imagine I would tell you?"

He took a step towards me and I stumbled back towards the water, the edge of the stream licking my boots. I forced myself to hold Owen's gaze. My heart was thundering. But I knew he intended to scare the information out of me and I refused to let him win.

"How dare you lay a hand on me," I hissed.

Owen gave a short chuckle. "Would you listen to her ordering us around?" He turned back to me, eyes close to mine. "Have you forgotten who you are, Nellie? You're nothing but a factory lag."

"Leave me alone," I said, my voice rattling.

Owen grabbed my arm again. I heard myself gasp as his fingers dug into my flesh.

"Blackwell does not just get to walk away," he hissed. "Not after what he did to my family. Tell me where he is."

I yanked out of his grip. "I've no idea where he is."

I grabbed my empty washbin and hurried back to the tavern.

Back in my room, I paced.

A fortnight until Blackwell's ship left. And the rebels knew he was here. In the anonymity of Sydney Town, it would be all too easy for Owen to pull the trigger. All too easy for him to emerge unscathed from yet another murder.

Lieutenant Blackwell does not just get to walk away.

I had to warn him.

CHAPTER TWENTY-SEVEN

"I snuck a little rum in that tea for you," said Charlie when I came down to the bar. "But you didn't even drink it. Highly ungrateful if you ask me."

"Do you know how to find Captain Grant?" I asked, pushing past his jibe. I prayed he hadn't overheard our conversation in the tavern earlier. Prayed he didn't know I was seeking out Blackwell.

Charlie frowned. "You all right, Nell? Something upset you?"

"Captain Grant," I pushed. "He plays cards here with Arthur Flynn. Do you know where he lives?"

"I know where everyone lives."

I raised my eyebrows. "Except Patrick Owen."

Charlie chuckled. "I know where everyone important lives."

I managed a small smile at that. Nodded impatiently as he rattled off directions, and then I was out of the tavern before he could ask questions.

Grant's property was not far from the Whaler's; the house guarded by a high wooden fence with a gate cut into one corner. I stood for a moment, hesitating. Would it be wildly inappropriate to just knock on the door? I was beginning to lose sense of what was right and wrong in this place. All the lines I knew had been blurred.

I clicked open the gate and stepped into a neatly manicured garden. Saplings surrounded a small, circular pond, grass hemmed with roses that had withered and browned in the heat.

And there was Blackwell, leaning against the house and lifting a pipe to his lips. He was without his jacket and waistcoat, shirtsleeves rolled to his elbows. His dark hair hung over one eye. He turned suddenly, catching sight of me. And at once he was striding towards me, the pipe left smoking on the garden path. The deliberateness of his movements made my heart jump into my throat.

"I know I shouldn't be here," I said. "I just—"

He grabbed my hand and led me around the side of the house, where the fence was covered with white-flowering vines. We slipped through the door and wove through empty servants' quarters, before climbing a wooden staircase to the second floor. Blackwell led me into the guestroom and locked the door behind us.

Before I could speak, he reached out and pulled me into a tight embrace. I felt myself sink against him, my arms sliding around his waist.

I stepped back, my hands tight around his bare forearms. "Captain Grant and his wife have left?"

"No. Not until tonight." His voice was low. "But they're in the front wing. They needn't know you're here."

I nodded. Standing there before the tall, wide bulk of him, the idea that the rebels could touch him seemed almost laughable.

"Patrick Owen found me at Tank Stream," I said. "He must have caught word you'd visited me. Followed me from the tavern."

Blackwell's eyes darkened. "Did he hurt you?"

I shook my head. "No. But I'm worried he'll come after you." I swallowed. "I know he wants you dead." The words caught in my throat. Speaking them aloud made the brutality of it sting.

I needed to know the truth, I realised then. I needed to hear Blackwell's version of what had happened in that little hut near Squires' inn. In two weeks' time, he was to disappear on the sea, and all I would be left with would be Owen's tall tales.

"Patrick Owen says you killed his family," I said. "In their kitchen. After the uprising at Castle Hill."

I saw something pass over Blackwell's eyes.

"I told him I knew it was a lie."

But right then, I questioned it. Had I allowed myself to love a man who had done such things? For that was the other realisation that swung towards me as I stood there holding his gaze: that I was irrevocably in love with Adam Blackwell. I felt like a fool. I had no place to love such a man. All it would do was break me.

His lips parted. "You think it a lie?"

I stepped away from him and stared at the polished floorboards. Blackwell moved towards the bed, the floorboards groaning loudly beneath his weight. He sat on the edge. Laced his fingers together and looked up to meet my eyes.

His story of the uprising was not the same as Owen's. There were no heroes; not the rebels, nor the Rum Corps. Just an impassive retelling of the rebels' attack on the government farm at Castle Hill, and of the way they had beaten down their overseers. Of their advance towards Parramatta, and the way the army had so quickly responded. A midnight march to meet the Irishmen. The surrounding of the rebels at nearby Rouse Hill. Firing lines formed to cut the croppies down.

His story emotionless, a thing of duty.

I thought of the rows of crosses in the clearing outside Parramatta. That day, I had seen emotion in Blackwell's eyes. When he had thought no one was looking, he had let it slip above the surface.

"And afterwards?" I asked.

"We were sent out to hunt down the rebels who got away." He spoke calmly, evenly. "We were told to find every one of them. Told that if we let them live, they'd overturn the order we'd created here. Undo everything we'd worked for.

"I found the Owens' hut out behind Squires' inn. Three of them were hiding there. I saw the stolen muskets up against the wall."

"You killed them."

"Yes," he said. "I did."

I closed my eyes for a moment. It was not surprise I was feeling. Not shock. Just a quiet acceptance that I had known this all along. I had seen the guilt within him the day I had followed him to the rebels' graveyard.

"You speak of it so calmly," I said finally.

Blackwell looked up at me. "How would you have me speak of it?"

I tilted my head, trying to see behind his eyes. "Do you regret what you did?"

"I was doing my job. Doing as I'd been instructed."

"That's not what I asked you."

For the first time, I understood Owen's hatred. But I also understood my own love. It was deep and unyielding. Unmoved by the blood on Blackwell's hands. And this, I realised, was my biggest betrayal of Lottie. I saw then how right she was to have refused to share things with me.

I would never see things from her point of view. How could I? Not only was I an Englishwoman of a far higher class, I would give my life for the man who had pulled the trigger.

There was regret in him; I could hear it in his voice, could see it in his eyes. But perhaps it showed too much weakness for him to speak of it, especially in front of a government lass. Perhaps it went against everything he had committed to when he had taken on his commission. Went against everything this place expected of him.

"I saw you at the graveyard outside Parramatta," I said. "Do you go there often?"

He let out his breath and ran his fingers through his hair. "You ask a lot of questions."

"What of the Owens' cottage? Do you ever go there? To pay your respects?"

Something flickered across Blackwell's face. The look in his eyes told me I was right; that he had returned to that cottage, as he had returned to the rebels' graves. Seeking what? Forgiveness? Absolution? The thought of it filled me with dread. If Owen or any of his remaining family were to discover the lieutenant alone at the cottage, he would likely not return.

I took a step towards him. Placed my hands on the broad plane of his shoulders and looked down to meet his eyes. He reached up, tracing gentle fingers along my bare forearm. I shivered.

"It's best that you leave," he said, but his hand slid around me as he spoke. Came to rest on the small of my back. A gentle pressure, guiding me closer.

His body felt heavy against mine, at once both weighted down and liberated at having spoken of the cottage. I wanted to give him a little in return.

I drew in a breath and sat beside him on the bed. "I was transported for high treason," I said. "I ran counterfeit coins across London."

I made no mention of Jonathan. I wanted to claim my crimes, just as Blackwell had done.

He said nothing. Just gave a nod that made my guilt fall away. He tucked a strand of hair behind my ear and ran his thumb along my cheek.

And then his lips were on mine. This was not what I had come for, I told myself. I had come to warn him about Owen. But a part of me knew that a lie. I had also come for that goodbye I had been deprived of at the tavern.

My mouth opened beneath his, deepening the kiss. My hands in his hair, pulling him towards me.

For all his urgency, Blackwell was hesitant, uncertain, his fingers sliding to the hooks at the front of my bodice, then pausing there, as if awaiting permission. I reached down to pull apart the first hook, sighing against his lips as his fingers slid beneath.

I pulled his shirt up over his head with a fervour I didn't recognise. Perhaps this place had corrupted me. Perhaps I had grown to fit the label the colony had saddled me with.

I didn't care. At least not there in the humid, sea-scented air, with Blackwell's breath on my skin.

It was me who loosened the last laces of my stays and let them ghost against the floor. Me who lay back on the bed, pulling him down over me. My hands slid up and down his back, over his shoulders, the backs of his thighs. I could feel the tension draining from his body, replaced with something far more urgent, more temporal.

"I missed you," he said, close to my ear. "I missed having you in my home. I missed seeing you each morning."

In the half-light, he pulled my shift up over my head, his lips moving over the pale skin of my shoulders, coarse fingers finding the warmth between my legs. I heard myself murmur, and pulled him down over me so he might trap the sound within his lips.

Was I marking myself as a loose woman? Perhaps. But the rest of the world couldn't see inside this room. The only man who knew this side of me was to disappear on the seas. I dug my fingers into the hot skin on the back of his neck, wanting to mark him as I was marking myself.

And his broad, tanned body was over mine; covering me, consuming me, filling me. I felt that barrier around him splinter as he groaned into my ear, worked his lips along my neck. Felt his control slipping and shattering as we moved together in the hatched sunlight spilling across the bed. The shame was there at the back of my mind. But I felt far too alive to care.

I lay in the shadows, feeling his heart beating against my ear. His arms were warm against my bare skin. I felt like all the things Reverend Marsden had accused us of being.

And I thought of her then, beautiful Sophia, with her doe eyes and her perfect curls, and I felt her husband's body shift beneath me.

Look what I had become.

I was always doomed to fail. I had been playing opposing games – on one hand, challenging myself not to give in, not to fall for him, not to succumb and be that weak, indecent concubine the female register had labelled me as. And at the same time, I had sought power. Tempted Blackwell to forget his wife, his God, his morality. Somewhere along the line I had fallen in love.

A losing game.

Blackwell's breathing grew steady and rhythmic, his chest rising and falling beneath my head.

I watched him in his sleep. I wanted to hold him, love him, take away the guilt and regret he refused to speak of. Take away the memories of that bloodstained cottage near Squire's inn. Perhaps that made me as bad as him. Perhaps those men who had fallen deserved more than for the memory of them to be taken away.

I climbed from the bed, careful not to wake him. I had to leave. I was due back at the tavern. And I needed to leave Grant's house before anyone realised I was here.

I took my shift from the floor and slid it over my head. I had left a thread of coppery hair on Blackwell's pillow. I stared at it as I laced my stays.

I felt an emptiness inside me. Now the line had been crossed, what did we have left for each other? He had Sophia, I had Arthur Flynn. I felt certain that when I stepped out of that room, I would never see him again.

I crossed the room, each step carefully placed to avoid the creak of the floorboards. I slipped out into the hall without looking back, that coil of red hair stark upon his pillow.

CHAPTER TWENTY-EIGHT

I crept down the stairs, each footstep carefully placed to avoid making a sound. Eyes down, I headed towards the empty servants' quarters. But as I stepped into the hallway, I came face to face with a tall, well-built man, whose grey eyes flickered in surprise. A regular fixture at the Whaler's Arms.

We stared at each other for a long second. I knew there was no need for questions. He had seen me come down from Blackwell's room.

There was a silent understanding between us that this was to remain wordless. Unspoken. I turned abruptly and disappeared out of the house.

The shame gathered over me as I made my way back to the tavern. I had been caught as a concubine. Caught behaving as what Marsden's register had made me out to be.

But beneath the shame, there was a hint of relief. The afternoon I had spent with Blackwell would allow me to move on. Allow us both to. He, back to England where Sophia was waiting. And I could marry Arthur Flynn, without feeling caught in an unfinished chapter. I knew such a marriage was the only way I would ever have a future.

The next afternoon, I went to see that future. Flynn had sent one of his farmhands to collect me in the trap and I sat in the back of the wagon, winding up towards the edge of Bridge Street where the colony met the wilderness.

Flynn's home was a great sandstone monolith that seemed to grow from the paddocks, the distant turquoise of the sea visible beyond the hill.

Behind the house, a patchwork of fencing outlined the sheep-dotted farmland. There was a barren, eerie beauty to the place, with its oceanic fields glittering in the heat haze, gnarled skeletons of trees stark against the fierce blue of the sky. I felt a flicker of nerves at becoming the lady of such a vast and unfamiliar property. But for the first time since I had climbed off the *Norfolk*, I was able to see a future that did not make me cower at its misery.

The farmhand offered me his hand to help me out of the trap and I climbed down, my boots crunching on the brittle brown grass. Ann was waiting outside the house to meet me.

"Mr Flynn's asked me to bring you into the parlour."

I followed her across a wide veranda and across the dark polished floorboards of Flynn's entrance hall. She knocked lightly on the parlour door and I entered at Flynn's invitation. As I stepped into the room, he put down his teacup and rose from his armchair. He turned to look at Ann.

"Please leave us."

She bobbed a quick curtsey and pulled the door closed behind her. It clicked loudly in the stillness. My eyes pulled towards the vast stretch of glass that filled one wall of the parlour. I could see out to the rusty fields of the farm, and a landscape so predominantly sky.

I hesitated, waiting for the invitation to sit. The offer of tea. Perhaps Flynn wished to show me around the farm first. I wondered whether I ought to remove my bonnet. "The property is beautiful," I said. "This view is quite something."

"Yes. It is." He did not return my smile.

And as I looked in his eyes, I realised. He knew. There could be no doubt.

I felt something sink inside me.

Was I to speak first? Find some petty explanation? Assure him such a thing would never happen again?

"Captain Grant and I are good friends," said Flynn, before I could find the words.

At the back of my mind, I had known that, yes. Had known it when I had stared Grant down in the middle of his hallway. Foolishly, I had believed – or at least hoped – our meeting might go by unacknowledged.

Flynn rubbed his shorn chin and stared out the window. I wondered distantly if this was the end. I knew there were many men in this colony who would look past such things. But I felt instinctively that Arthur Flynn was not one of them.

He came towards me slowly, his boots clicking on the floorboards.

"I chose to look past what they say about your kind," he said. "Because I believed you were different. But I see now how wrong I was to do so."

"I'm sorry," I said. And I was; truly, deeply. Flynn had been achingly decent to me. He had been willing to see beyond my convict stain and make me *wife*. I felt a striking guilt at having hurt him. But I also knew that, had I the chance, I would do the same again and again.

My throat tightened. "I was a fool."

Flynn stood close. I could see the green flecks in his eyes. "No," he said. "I'm the one who has been a fool. To have let myself be shamed by a government lass. Any man with half a mind knows better than to try and find a little decency in a woman so unspeakably impure."

I waited for him to strike me. Closed my eyes and braced for the impact. But instead he swept a wild hand across the table, sending his teacup flying across the room. It shattered noisily against the hearth, making my heart leap into my throat.

Flynn turned away, folding his arms across his chest. "You need to leave."

I trudged back into town, having refused his stilted offer of the trap. This hot, dusty trek was what I deserved, I told myself, as I swatted furiously at the relentless onslaught of flies. Craving the bliss of drunkenness, I stopped at the first tavern I came to and bought a flask of the Rum Corps' finest. I didn't care who saw me. I had already been irretrievably shamed.

I carried the liquor up to my room and took a long mouthful. As it seared my throat, a barrage of tears spilled, and I pushed them away hurriedly. I couldn't bear to sit here in self-pity. Everything that had happened to me I had brought on myself.

I tucked the bottle beneath the bed and trudged down to the tavern with my apron in my hand. I wasn't due to start work for another hour.

"You're early," said Charlie, as he strode in from the kitchen.

"I know. I need the distraction. You don't have to pay me." I knotted my apron around my waist. I could smell the dust and sweat on my skin. Could feel my hair frizzing wildly around my cheeks. A lass behind the bar might bring men through the door, but one look at me and they'd walk right back out again.

"What's happened?" asked Charlie.

"Nothing." I couldn't bear to speak of it. Couldn't bear to think of it. Of any of it. I couldn't think of the hurt in Flynn's eyes, or of Blackwell sailing home to his wife. I couldn't think of Kate Abbott running through the streets picking pockets, or Lottie on the floor of that squalid kitchen. Couldn't think, couldn't think, couldn't think.

The tavern filled quickly and I was grateful for it. Exhaustion was pressing down on me, but I kept myself charging through the bar, wiping tables, and serving drinks.

When I knocked a glass of rum from the counter, sending it exploding on the floor, Charlie took the dish cloth from my hand.

"Go upstairs, Nell. Go and rest."

I shook my head. "I'm fine."

"You're not fine. Any fool can see that."

"I've got to clean it," I said, pointing to the shards of glass lying in the pool of liquor. Inexplicably, the sight of it made my tears spill.

Charlie pointed to the stairwell. "Upstairs," he said. "That's an order."

I trudged up to my room. Rain was beginning to patter against the windows. I sat on my bed, trying to swallow my tears.

I pulled the bottle out from under my bed and gulped down a mouthful. And then another. And one more for good measure.

I had never felt more alone in my life. Never felt so directionless, or so empty. I stared at the window with glazed eyes, watching lines of water snake down the glass.

I knew that just a few blocks away, Blackwell would be alone in Captain Grant's house. I longed to go to him. To curl up against him and disappear from the world. But I couldn't do that to Sophia. Or to him.

And I couldn't do it to myself.

But nor could I stay here, drowning in rum and sadness. I got shakily to my feet and headed out towards the Rocks.

CHAPTER TWENTY-NINE

The sky ripped open as I walked, the drizzle growing into marbles of water that turned the roads to mud. The rain brought cool air with it, and I shivered as droplets ran down my bare arms. I put my head down and quickened my pace towards the kitchen.

I knew Lottie would not want a thing to do with me. Perhaps she would send me away. Or perhaps she would not even be here. Perhaps Owen had decided he wanted her for the night again.

The alleyways of the Rocks were near empty, rain pounding against roofs, and water trickling from the gutters. A few sailors were sheltering beneath dripping awnings with pipes in their hands. One of them called out to me as I stumbled past, but didn't bother following. I squinted in the darkness. Which way to Lottie?

I stumbled through the maze of cottages and shacks until I found the narrow door leading to the kitchen. I knocked loudly. Tripped slightly on the doorstep as an old woman let me inside. Lottie pushed her way towards me.

"Nell," she said. "What are you doing here?"

I felt myself swaying slightly. "I'm worried for you," I said. "I thought Owen…" The lie spilled out without me having a thought of it. Why couldn't I admit that I needed her? Why did I feel the urge to appear in control, even when I was soaked to the skin and my steps were crooked with liquor? Perhaps Lottie was right. Perhaps I did need to show her how well I'd done for myself.

"Are you drunk?" she demanded.

"A little." Water trickled down the back of my neck.

Her hand was suddenly around my arm, leading me to the corner of the room where Willie's basket was tucked away. Water dripped from the ceiling and ran down the wall, but the kitchen was marginally drier than the alley.

"Christ," Lottie said, unwrapping her shawl and draping it over my shoulders. "What happened to you?"

Suddenly, I wanted to tell her everything. The breaking of my betrothal, and being thrown from Flynn's house, and all that had happened between Blackwell and me. I wanted to tell her of the chaos of guilt and love that roiled inside me. But instead, I said:

"Has Owen been back for you?"

Lottie sighed. "Would you forget about Patrick for one damn minute? What's happened to you?" She slid an arm around my shoulder and I felt myself break. Deep sobs racked my body and I buried my head against her shoulder. She held me tightly.

My words came out in a tangle. "Flynn broke off our betrothal. I ruined everything. And Blackwell…" I knew I ought to stop; knew I shouldn't speak of him in front of Lottie. But I couldn't stop myself. "He's leaving," I sobbed. "Going back to England. To his wife."

Her arms tightened around me. "It's for the best, Nell. You know that. You know how the Rum Corps sees women like us. We're the lowest of the low. They can't look past our convict stain."

I wiped my eyes with the back of my hand. "Blackwell's in Sydney. Staying with a colleague. Flynn found out I went to him… To his room…" Perhaps it was a foolish confession. But with the words, I felt a weight lift from my chest.

"I see," Lottie said after a long silence. Outside the window, rain poured from the edge of the roof and thundered into the street.

A part of me wanted to tell her about the conversation I'd had with Blackwell about what had happened at the Owens' cottage after the rebellion. Tell her I understood her hatred, Owen's hatred. And I wanted to tell her of the remorse I could sense in Blackwell's words. Tell her of the way he saw the world through a guilty man's eyes.

But I did none of that. It felt like a conversation I was not permitted to have. She would know I still saw the story from Blackwell's side. How could she not, after all I'd just confessed?

I wiped my eyes. "I'm sorry," I coughed. "I didn't mean to burden you."

"Don't be a fool, Nell. You're not a burden." She leant her head against mine. I was so glad for her closeness, for the friendship I'd feared had been washed away completely.

In the basket beside us, Willie gave a weak cry. He rubbed his eyes and squirmed beneath his blankets.

I frowned. "Is he unwell?"

"A fever," said Lottie, scooping him into her arms. "Came on last night. Neither of us have had a wink of sleep."

"Come back to the Whaler's with me," I said. "Stay in my room. It'll be quieter there. And drier." I could see her hesitation. "Please. I could use the company."

Lottie glanced at the baby, then back to me. "All right," she said finally. "But just for the night."

The rain was beginning to ease as we made our way back to the tavern. Lottie held Willie tightly to her chest, while I carried his empty basket, drawing in lungfuls of air to clear my liquored-up thoughts.

As we passed Captain Grant's house, I lowered my eyes and began to walk faster. Lottie jogged to keep up with me.

"What's this about then?"

"Nothing," I said. "I just—"

Oh." She peered up at the house with knowing eyes. "This where you paid the lieutenant a visit?"

I felt my cheeks burn with shame.

Lottie glanced back over her shoulder, then gave me a crooked smile. "House is dark," she said. "No need to rush by with your tail between your legs."

"The family's left for Van Diemen's Land," I mumbled. "But I'm sure Blackwell's still there." I turned the corner hurriedly, glad when the Whaler's Arms came into view. I stopped in surprise at the small figure standing outside the tavern. "Kate."

She offered me a sheepish smile, twisting a strand of dark hair around her finger. "You said you had a room here."

I smiled. "I do. Yes."

Her clothes were grimy and torn, her wet hair hanging loose on her shoulders. Had she been sleeping on the streets since I'd found her all those weeks ago?

"Where have you been?" I asked.

She chewed her lip, avoiding my eyes. "Just about."

I nodded. Wherever she'd been, whoever she'd been with, it didn't matter. I was just glad she was here now. I put a hand to her shoulder, ushering her inside. "Come on. Come and get yourself dry."

I led her and Lottie into the alley behind the tavern and used my key to unlock the back door. I ushered them up the stairs to my room.

As Kate hurried inside, Lottie reached for my arm, holding me back. "Who is she?"

I kept my voice low. "She's Maggie's daughter. I found her in the street."

Something flickered behind Lottie's eyes. "Does she know what happened to her mother?"

I shook my head. Kate turned back to us and I forced a smile, stepping inside and locking the door. I had no thought of where we would all sleep in my little snuff box of a room.

I went to the table by the bedside and lit the lamp. Lottie took the baby's basket from me and laid Willie inside it. She sat it on the floor and knelt beside him. I took my cloak from the hook beside the door and tucked it around the baby.

"He's sleeping at least," I said. "That's good. We can take him to the physician tomorrow."

Lottie gave an incredulous laugh. "You've no idea, do you, Nell? Two years in this place and you've not learned a thing. There's no physician who'll look at him once they learn he belongs to a factory lass."

"That's not true," I said. "It can't be."

Lottie looked at me witheringly, shaking her head. A reminder that my time at the spinning wheels had not washed away all my naivety.

She chewed her thumbnail. "He needs his father. Patrick would know what to do."

I glared at her. She couldn't speak his name. Not in front of Maggie's daughter.

Kate was hovering at the foot of the bed, chewing her hair and peering down at the baby.

"Is he going to die?" she asked.

"Of course not." I ushered her away from Willie's basket.

Lottie let out her breath. "I see she's got the same gift with words as her mother."

My stomach plunged. Kate's lips parted, and she looked up at me with wide eyes.

"Take off your dress and hang it up," I said hurriedly. "You'll catch a chill."

She slid her smock over her head, not taking her eyes off mine. "Do you know my mother?"

I glared at Lottie, willing her to speak. But she was kneeling over Willie with her head down, refusing to meet my eyes. Making it clear Kate was my responsibility. The girl was a fragile figure in her thin wet shift, with skeletal white arms and a face dwarfed by wild, wet curls.

"Your mother is dead, Kate," I said. "I'm sorry." I clenched my fist behind my back, trying to force away my anger at Lottie. A drop of water slid from the end of my hair and beaded on the floorboards.

Kate's mouth opened, then closed. She perched on the bottom of the bed, her feet dangling inches from the floor. "Oh," she said. "Oh."

I sat beside her, my wet skirts tangling around my legs. "Lottie and I both knew her. At the factory in Parramatta." I opened my mouth to say more, but could find few words. My most vivid memories of Maggie were of her lying lifeless on the side of the road. But Kate was looking up at me, expectant. I knew I had to give her more. "She was a kind woman," I managed. "She always spoke her mind. And she loved you very much."

I remembered the tremor in Maggie's voice when she'd spoken of the Orphan School. I had no doubt her head had been full of her daughter at the time.

Kate began to gnaw on her thumbnail. I waited for her reaction. Tears? Anger? There was none of that. Just a silent acceptance. I put my hand to her shoulder and gave it a gentle squeeze.

"Come on. We ought to sleep. If we squeeze up we can all fit." I looked over at Lottie. She was sitting on her knees with her back to me, a protective hand on the edge of Willie's basket.

"Lottie," I said, "there's room for you on the bed." In spite of my anger, I hated the thought of her spending yet another night on the floor.

"There's no room for three," she said. "I'll stay here." The divide that had sprung up between us felt almost a physical thing.

Kate stayed planted on the edge of the bed, staring into the lamp. "How did she die?" she asked suddenly.

I hesitated. Was I to lie? Cobble together some more manageable version of the truth?

"She stopped breathing," I said finally. I stared at Lottie, willing her to turn around. Willing her to face the reality of who her husband was. What good would it do her; this blind hope that one day Owen would take her back? That impossible dream of having a family. I understood her need for security, of course. But surely she would do better if she let her faith in Owen die.

Kate stared at me with her mother's deep-set blue eyes. "What do you mean she stopped breathing? How?" I knew she'd spent too much time on the street for my all-too-gentle truths.

And I was thinking of Lottie and Owen when I said, "Someone killed her."

CHAPTER THIRTY

"Killed her?" Kate repeated. "Who killed her? Why?"

"She was killed by the savages," Lottie said, before I could answer. "She had too much to drink and wandered out into the bush." Her voice was cold. Empty of emotion. And suddenly she was on her feet, grabbing Willie's basket and making for the door.

I chased her out into the hallway, letting the door slam behind me. "Where are you going?"

"It was a mistake to come here." She strode towards the stairwell. I grabbed her arm.

"Please don't leave."

She pulled free of my grasp. "Instead I'm to stay here and listen to you spout lies about my husband?" She shook her head. "I ought to have known you'd do something like this. You turn up at my door, filthy drunk because you lifted your skirts to your lobster, and you're still doing all you can to show me how much better you've done than me."

"That's not what I'm trying to do," I hissed. "Kate deserves to know the truth."

"And that's what I told her. That Maggie was killed by the savages."

I let out my breath. "You can't truly believe that."

Lottie shook her head. "No," she said. "We're not going back here, Nell. Not after all this time. We're not having this conversation again."

I closed my eyes for a moment. "You're right." I dared to take a step towards her. Dared to press a hand to her forearm. I was relieved when she didn't pull away.

"I'm sorry," I said. "I never meant to look down on you. I just want you to be safe. That's all I've ever wanted."

Lottie sighed, but she didn't walk away. A burst of drunken laughter floated up from the tavern.

"We look out for each other," I said. "Isn't that what you always told me?" I squeezed her wrist. "And it goes both ways, Lottie. I need you to look out for me just as much. You saw the mess I was in tonight. I'm barely stumbling my way through this place."

Finally, she looked up to meet my eyes.

"Please come inside," I said. "Willie needs to be warm and dry. You know that." I flashed her a tentative smile. "I'll not speak of Owen again. I promise."

When I woke, I was alone in the bed. Pale dawn light was filtering into the room. Kate was at the window, peering through the curtains. I sat up, frowning. "Where's Lottie?"

Kate looked back over her shoulder at me, a thread of dark hair clinging to her lip. "She left."

"What do you mean? Where did she go?"

She shrugged. "I just saw her leave."

"When?" I tried to rein in my impatience.

"Don't know. But it was still dark. And then I went back to sleep."

A knot of panic tightened in my stomach. Had something happened to Willie in the night? Or had Lottie gone to Owen? Was she making another attempt at getting him to take her back?

If she had, who was I to stop her? Perhaps I had done all I could. Perhaps the time had come for me to accept that. To let her live her own life and make her own mistakes.

I pushed the thought aside. I knew I would never be able to do such a thing. Owen had wrung Maggie's throat and left her body at the side of the road. I would fight until I died to stop the same thing happening to Lottie.

I grabbed my damp dress from the chair and slid it over my head. "Stay here," I told Kate, fastening the hooks with unsteady fingers. "There's bread on the shelf. And you can go to the kitchen and make some tea. Charlie will help you."

"Where are you going?"

"I need to find Lottie."

I climbed downstairs and out through the empty tavern, locking the door behind me. In the early morning, the air was cool and still. Empty barrels were stacked up against the wall of the tavern, flies swarming and the smell of stale liquor thick in the air.

I began to walk. I would go to Owen's farm first, and if there was no sign of Lottie, I would try at the Rocks. The streets were close to empty, just a few sailors stumbling from the taverns. At least if Lottie was roaming the alleys, I would have a chance of finding her.

I passed the Dog and Duck tavern, and hurried along the street that wound around past Captain Grant's house. Kept my eyes firmly on the ground.

The sound of footsteps made me look up. There was Lottie, rounding the bend, flanked by Owen and Brady. Willie was strapped to her chest. They were striding down the narrow street from the direction of Owen's farm, heading for Captain Grant's house. A pistol peeked out of Brady's fist.

At once I knew exactly why Lottie had left the tavern in the night. To lead Patrick Owen to the man he despised. To give him a chance at Blackwell without the Rum Corps watching.

Heat flooded me. Lottie's betrayal burned under my skin. But it was the fear that caused my heart to race. Fear that Blackwell would never set foot on that ship back to England. That he might die by the rebels' bullet and never again see his wife.

I darted down the side of a neighbouring house and stood with my back pressed against the wall. By now, Grant and his family would have left for Van Diemen's Land. The house would be near empty. If Owen and Brady made it inside, they would have a clear shot at Blackwell, with not a single witness.

I would not make it to the Grants' without being seen. But I had to warn Blackwell the men were coming.

At the sound of my footfalls, Lottie turned to look behind her. Our eyes met. I stared at her, hot with fury. I'd never felt more betrayed. I knew, of course, that at its core, this conflict was about Owen and Blackwell and all that had happened in that cottage after the uprising. But at that moment, it felt intensely personal. Felt as though it were between her and I alone.

The baby whined against her chest. She turned away, refusing to hold my gaze. And I saw the end. Saw that, for all I had tried to make it otherwise, the two of us were to go no further. Saw that an Irishwoman and a *sasanaigh* could not build a friendship strong enough to withstand what a woman would do to survive this place.

Owen turned, catching sight of me, and I raced towards the Grants' gate, calling Blackwell's name. A firm hand grabbed my arm, yanking me backwards. Brady clamped his grimy hand over my mouth.

"Let her go," said Owen on a laugh. "Let her bring him out here. Save us from breaking in."

I shook free of Brady's grasp and whirled around for something to use as a weapon. I grabbed a scrap of wood lying on the side of the road. I held it out in front of me, backing towards the gate.

"Get out of the way, Nell," said Lottie, a waver in her voice.

I didn't look at her. She had no say in this.

I heard a movement in the Grants' garden behind me, and felt a sudden weakness in my legs. I wished I hadn't called for Blackwell. For all I ached for him to run and hide, I knew he would come for me, come for the rebels; come to see an end to this thing that had poisoned both him and Owen for the past four years. If Owen got through this gate, there would be shots fired. And someone would die.

Suddenly Brady was coming at me, wrestling the wood from my hand. He flung it onto the ground. I kicked hard, connecting with his shins. He slammed me back against the gate. My vision swam and pain jolted down my spine.

"Please, Nell," I heard Lottie say again, "just get out of the way. Please." Her voice was tearful.

Brady came at me again and I drove my knee upward into his groin. I was dimly aware of Owen reaching for the plank of wood. Dimly aware of Lottie shrieking.

As Brady stumbled backwards, I lurched at him, my fingers grazing the cold metal of the pistol in his hands. I wrenched hard, trying to seize the weapon. A sudden pain to the side of my head and the world around me was gone.

When I opened my eyes, I was alone. The back of my head was thumping, the ground rough and cold beneath my cheek. I tried to sit, but dizziness was pressing down on me. And then I remembered. Owen. Brady. Lottie.

Blackwell.

Everything was quiet. Too quiet.

A pistol was lying beside my head. And as I looked past it, I saw the Grants' gate swinging open. Panic overtook me, pushing through the dizziness. I climbed to my feet, swallowing a violent wave of nausea. I swiped at the thin line of blood trickling down the side of my face. I turned. I stepped. And then I saw it.

The body lay just a few feet in front of me, a pool of blood creeping steadily towards my boots.

I stumbled, terrified to approach.

I took one step. Then another. Horror welled up inside me.

I had been expecting a gunshot wound, but the entire figure was a mess of crimson. The limbs were thrashed and misshapen, the face a chaos of slashes. The red coat was blackened with blood, buttons opened to reveal a maze of knife wounds. And there, below the ribs, the entry point of a single ball. I stared at it for several moments, my vision swimming. Flies darted around the wounds. My gaze drifted up to the neat white braiding on the jacket, the stark yellow facings. And to the glimmer of gold poking from the coat pocket. I bent, breathless, and looped a finger around the chain of the pocket watch. It thudded dully into mud, a drop of blood sliding over Sophia's engraved dedication. I stumbled, landing heavily on my knees, and vomited beside the body.

CHAPTER THIRTY-ONE

I stayed on my hands and knees, gulping down my breath. My body began to shake. A desperate sob escaped me.

And so Patrick Owen had gotten what he wanted, in the most vicious way imaginable. Repayment for that blood-streaked shack in the bush behind Squires' inn. Repayment for the lives taken in the aftermath of the uprising.

Had the rebels killed Blackwell inside the house, and then brought his body down into the alley? Laid him here beside me so I might see what my actions had brought about? Or had the lieutenant heard me calling him? Had he come down to help me? Had my own actions led to his death? The thought brought another sob from deep inside me.

I stared at the blood seeping into the gaps between the cobbles. Tears blurred my vision and I let them slide unhindered from my cheeks. I couldn't bear to look at Blackwell's body. And I couldn't bear to look away.

I was distantly aware of footsteps coming towards me. Distantly aware of soldiers approaching. Standing over the body. Standing over me.

I looked down. My floral dress was covered in blood. So were my hands. A pistol on the ground beside me. And as they hauled me to my feet, I couldn't find a single word.

My thoughts were blank as they shoved me into the back of the police wagon. We began to rattle along the streets, the wheels sighing as they slid through the remnants of the downpour.

The journey was a short one, and I wondered distantly why they had felt the need to put me in the carriage. Hands around the tops of my arms, and I was led into a vast sandstone building. Led down a narrow corridor into an empty room. A table with three stools sat in the middle. A tiny window above the table let in a spear of sunlight. The soldiers shoved me onto a stool. And there I sat in my bloodstained skirts, clasping my bloodstained hands.

For a long time, I was left alone on that stool, in front of that table, with the morning light building as it streamed through that tiny window. A guard stood at the door, rifle across his chest, not saying a word. I felt an old terror. The terror I had felt when I had heard *high treason* and *death by hanging*.

Finally; two marines. A captain. An ensign. They asked me my name. Asked me my status. I pulled my ticket of leave from the pocket of my dress, and sat it on the table. The edges were stained in blood.

The captain leant forward and placed the pocket watch on the table. "Who does this belong to?"

I swallowed hard. "It belongs to Adam Blackwell." I looked down at the blood on my hands, feeling sickness rise in my throat. Feeling a little hysteria rise with it. "Let me wash. Please. I need to wash."

"You're not going anywhere."

I squeezed my eyes closed and tried to breathe deeply. I felt as though I were trapped in the worst of my nightmares. "I didn't kill him," I said. "It was Patrick Owen."

A moment of silence. I kept my eyes on my knotted fingers. I couldn't look at that watch. Couldn't look at the stains on the edge of my ticket of leave. I thought of Blackwell handing it to me as smoke poured from the factory above the jail. Thought of the fleeting kiss he had pressed into my neck. I blinked back my tears.

"Tell me what happened," said the captain.

But of course, I knew nothing of what had happened. Nothing beyond the moment Owen had struck me with the plank of wood.

I garbled through a tangled tale of finding the rebels outside Captain Grant's house. Of my altercation with Brady. Of Lottie's cries and Owen's laughter and the blow to my head that had left me unconscious in the street. "The next I knew," I said, "Lieutenant Blackwell's body was beside me."

"You did not see Mr Owen kill Lieutenant Blackwell."

A question? Or was he painting a picture of my guilt?

And then I told them, as slowly and calmly as I could, of the way I had taken Lottie back to my room at the Whaler's Arms. Of the way she had disappeared in the night and gone for Owen. Told him of the lieutenant's whereabouts.

I spoke of the events that had taken place at the Owens' cottage after the Castle Hill rebellion. And I spoke of Patrick Owen's need for revenge.

"How did you come to know Lieutenant Blackwell?" asked the captain.

I knotted my fingers together. "I met him in Parramatta. He… offered me a bed."

"Ah." And that one word was all it took for me to know my story had been taken for fiction. I was a concubine from the factory above the jail. As striking an admission of guilt as there could ever be.

Do you know why Lieutenant Blackwell was in Sydney?

Yes. He was returning to England to see his wife.

That must have angered you I'm sure. Perhaps enough to kill?

My body shook with anger, fear, grief. But I clenched my fists and pressed my shoulders back. I would not fit neatly into their story. I was not a jealous government lass driven to murder.

I used a clean patch of skin on my wrist to wipe my eyes. "It was Patrick Owen," I said again. But I had no proof. I could not even claim to be a witness. "The body," I coughed. "It was… defaced. How do you imagine I might have done such a thing? With what weapon?"

But the look the captain gave me said he knew the weapon would be found. And he knew that I was capable.

The guard led me down the passage and unlocked the door to a narrow stone cell. He followed me inside and locked the door behind us. Shoved me hard against the cold stone wall. Pain jolted down my spine.

"Blackwell was a friend," he said. "A schoolmate."

I heard a sudden, hysterical laugh escaped me. Because of course he was. Because this place was ruled by redcoats who had studied together,

221

trained together, fought together. And they would band together to see that everyone below them fell into line.

And when I laughed, I also cried; sobs that came from deep inside me and stole my breath. I turned away from the guard and crumpled to the floor, my head pressed to my knees.

I waited to be thrown against the wall again. Waited to be struck, or for some fierce interrogation. But the guard didn't speak again. Engulfed in tears, I did not hear him leave. Did not hear the door open, or close, or lock. All I knew was when I finally looked up in an attempt to catch my breath, the dark was thick and I was alone.

That night, I huddled in the corner of the cell, shivering in spite of the thick, wet heat. In fleeting moments of clarity, I told myself I would fight. I would make sure the world knew Patrick Owen had been the one to pull the trigger. But my resolve was without determination. My will to fight was swamped by grief.

Every time I closed my eyes, I saw Blackwell's beaten body, stained in blood, his face unrecognisable, the uniform he had always worn so neatly hanging open at his sides.

I heard myself inhale.

The jacket unbuttoned.

In all the time I had known him, Blackwell had never worn his jacket unbuttoned.

I hugged my legs, pressing my eyes hard against my knees. A trivial detail. Owen had likely caught Blackwell unaware. Or he had heard me calling for him. Had raced out of the house to help me.

But the thought gnawed at the back of my mind.

The jacket unbuttoned.

And in the darkness I was back there again; in the street outside the Grants' house, with Brady's hands on my shoulders and my fingers reaching for his pistol. I felt the metal, felt my hand slide around the stock. And then? I dug into my memories, into that fragment of a second before I had been struck. Had there been the sound of a gunshot? Had I pulled the trigger?

I heard myself breathe louder, faster. Dan Brady, lurching in front of me as I thrust my knee into his groin. Dan Brady stumbling, my hand on his weapon. Had I put a bullet in his chest?

Brady was tall like Blackwell. Dark-haired and broad-shouldered. The two men could easily be mistaken from a distance.

And at once I was on my feet, pacing back and forth across the lightless cell, my feverish mind grappling at the possibility. Was it was Dan Brady's body that had been lying at my feet?

I knew I was walking a straighter path to the hangman. But the next morning, I told the captain I had pulled the trigger on Dan Brady. Told him the body had been defaced. Made to look like Blackwell.

I knew the bloodstained ticket of leave in my pocket would send me to the gallows, no matter what I said in that interrogation room. But I needed the truth to be known.

Was Owen seeking to punish me? Had he broken into the house and gone to Blackwell's room to find it empty but for his belongings? Had he defaced Brady's body to disguise his identity? Put him in Blackwell's uniform and left him lying at my feet?

I felt deathly certain of it. Knew Owen had done this so I might believe he had killed the man I loved.

I told my story again, of the altercation outside the tavern, ending with my new and firm belief that I had pulled the trigger on Brady before I had been knocked out. But there was nothing but my word to support my story. Nothing beyond my desperate belief to suggest the body did not belong to Blackwell.

"If the lieutenant was not killed, as you claim, why has he not come forward?"

I closed my eyes. It almost felt as though the soldiers wanted the dead man to be Blackwell. What an example they could make of me then; the factory lass who had murdered a soldier. My body would hang in a gibbet over Pinchgut Island, to greet the ships as they bucked their way into the harbour.

"Perhaps Owen found him," I said. "Perhaps he's harmed him." This, of course, was the other reason I was so adamant that the body was proven to be Brady's. Because I knew there was every chance Blackwell was in danger. And I needed him to be found.

The captain was quick to remind me there were no witnesses to the shooting. Nothing but my word to go on. The rest did not need to be said. *The word of a factory lass found covered in blood with a pistol beside her.*

"What of Dan Brady?" I asked. "You've not found him, have you." But I knew hunting down Brady, an emancipist with no fixed address, was not something the redcoats were willing to entertain.

Back in my cell, I paced. My heart was racing and my skin was damp with sweat. I was overflowing with fear. But the fear, I realised, was no longer for myself. I was a factory lass with blood on my hands. I'd escaped the hangman once, but I knew I would not do so again. Somehow, knowing I had no chance to win made it easier to push away the terror.

But my fear for Blackwell was consuming. Now I had let myself believe he was alive, I couldn't bear to go back to the alternative. But there had been no sign of him since the morning of Brady's death. Had he fallen into the hands of the rebels? If he were still in Sydney Town, he would surely have been sighted. I would not be being held for his murder.

I had no answers, of course. Just a desperate hope he still lived. The optimism felt dangerous. A thing that could all too easily be torn away.

Two and a half years ago I had stood in a courtroom dock at the Old Bailey and listened to the judge sentence me to a lifetime in New South Wales.

It had felt like a reprieve. I had been expecting a walk to the gallows.

I'd learned later that a literate, well-mannered woman like me was never destined for the hangman. I was a desirable thing for this new colony.

Now here I was with the murder of a soldier to my name. I knew well my education would not save me.

The trial was short. A foregone conclusion. Beside me, the other prisoners shifted in the dock; sent to the coalmines, sent to Toongabbie. Two hundred lashes, three days on Pinchgut Island.

I let my mind escape. I thought of birdsong and pearly light and the distant sigh of the sea. Thought of the rugged beauty of this place I had not learned to truly appreciate until now, when it was far too late.

Though I could not claim to be surprised by it, the verdict still weakened my knees.

"For the murder of Adam Blackwell, you are sentenced to hang by the neck until you are dead."

PART FOUR

CHAPTER THIRTY-TWO

And so tomorrow morning I am to die in the orange light of New South Wales. I always knew, as I felt the ship buck its way down the Thames, that I would never be returning to the land of my birth. But I did not expect the end to come so abruptly. I will not see my thirtieth birthday.

In the dim light of my cell, I look down at my hands. I can still see the bloodstains; can still see where the skin is discoloured, darker than the rest. For all my astronomy lessons and garden parties, for all the scales my fingers have churned through on the piano, I will go to my death with blood on my hands.

I don't sleep. Though I want to escape the violent chaos of my thoughts, I know I will have this escape soon enough. The darkness is almost impenetrable, and the hours are blank. At once both interminably long and painfully fast.

I am terrified for Blackwell. Wherever he is, I know he is not safe. Perhaps Owen has already killed him. Perhaps the rebel leader has gotten the revenge he so desperately sought. And I am the one who will swing for Blackwell's death.

Untouchable Owen.

Faint birdsong breaks through the dark and it makes sickness rise in my throat. Throughout the night, I felt a sense of cold resignation, but with the light, I am terrified. Today I am to die.

The sunlight comes, brighter and brighter, straining beneath the door, through the keyhole. My entire body shakes as I wait for the footsteps of

229

the men who will take me to my death.

I wait.

And I wait. I alternate between pacing the cell and huddling in the corner with my knees to my chest. At times I want this horror to be over; I crave stillness in my pounding chest. The next moment, I want time to freeze, so I might catch hold of every last thread of my waning life.

I hear footsteps, murmurs, but they do not come to my cell.

And then it is afternoon. And then the pink light of evening. My thoughts knock together, jumping around my memories. Twelfth night balls, the stained bulkheads of the *Norfolk*. Counterfeit coins in my reticule, Blackwell's hands in my hair.

Another night comes and I am still alive. I am dizzy, sweat-soaked, disoriented. I don't know what to do. I was not supposed to be here, not supposed to see this hour. And so I keep sitting. Keep pacing. Keep waiting.

It is the next morning when the footsteps finally come. I am unprepared. I readied myself for my death and the moment passed. I even fell into an exhausted sleep.

The door clicks open and I hear a cry of fear escape me.

"This way," says the guard. His voice is cold and empty.

My legs feel weak beneath me. The world swims and my mouth goes dry. I grapple at the stone wall, searching for something to steady myself. My legs give way and I fall to my knees.

The guard looks at me with something close to pity, and for some reason, this is worse than his coldness.

I follow him out of my cell and down a long stone corridor. We stop in front of the door leading to the room I had first been interrogated in. The guard knocks.

"Enter," says the voice on the other side.

When we step into the room, I see the captain and ensign who placed this murder at my feet. They gesture to a chair in front of the table.

I crumple into the seat, my legs barely able to hold me. My vision is swimming. I don't understand what is happening. I was expecting to be led to the gallows.

The captain folds his hands on the table in front of him. He says:

"Another woman has come forth and confessed to the murder."

For a long time, I don't speak. There is so much wrong with this. I was the one to pull the trigger. The memories are there; hazy, but they are there. I made myself certain of them. But if I am wrong about this, perhaps I am also wrong about the body being Dan Brady's.

"No," I hear myself say.

They tell me of a trial that took place while I was waiting out my last day on earth. They tell me of the woman who came forth and spoke of the altercation outside Captain Grant's home. Spoke of the ball she put in the chest of Dan Brady.

Dan Brady, says the voice in my head.

Dan Brady.

Dan Brady.

I don't understand why Lottie has done this; I only know it can be no one else.

I don't move. I don't speak. I can't deny this story, of course. I was unconscious at the time.

Even if I could deny it, the trial has taken place. Lottie has already condemned herself to the hangman. And in doing so, she has freed me.

"Please," I say. "Let me see her."

The guard takes me to Lottie's cell, two doors down from where I was held for the past five days. She is sitting in the corner with her knees to her chest. She barely looks up as I enter. I glance over my shoulder at the guard.

"Will you let us speak?"

A faint nod. He pulls the door closed, locking us in.

I kneel beside Lottie in the filthy straw and press my hand to her arm. Her skin is cold. I am still blazing from my aborted date with the hangman. Even at the touch of my hand, she doesn't shift her gaze.

"Lottie," I say. Finally, she looks up at me. Her eyes are dry, almost expressionless. Her hair hangs in pieces around her hollow cheeks.

"Why are you doing this?" I ask.

"Because I was the one who killed Dan Brady."

"No. You're lying."

Lottie looks at me squarely. "Why would I do that?"

231

"Why would you kill Brady?"

"Because you were struggling with him. He was going to shoot you."

She is lying. I remember the feel of my finger on the trigger. Don't I?

"How did you kill him?" I ask.

"With the pistol I stole from Patrick. The one I kept in Willie's basket. I took it with me everywhere."

I shake my head. "Owen would have killed you for it."

"For harming Brady?" She lets out a cold laugh. "Patrick don't care what happens to anyone but himself. All he cares about is his revenge."

I wrap my arms around myself, suddenly cold. "What about Willie?" I ask. "What is he to do without you, if—"

I stop speaking as Lottie shakes her head. And then her tears come. "The fever," she says, "he couldn't fight it off. He was too weak. Too small."

I let out my breath, pulling her into me "I'm sorry," I cough. "I'm so sorry." She feels limp and fragile in my arms, as though all the fight has drained out of her. After a moment, I sit back, trying to find her eyes. "Is that why you're doing this? Because you lost Willie?"

She winds her bootlace listlessly around her finger. I hear the guard's footsteps thud back and forth outside the door.

"The whole of it was my fault," she says after a while. "I was the one who brought Patrick to the house. I thought if I led him to Blackwell he might see I was worth something. See I was of use." She swipes at her tears. "I thought he might take me and Willie back to the farm. For good this time. Not just for the night. I thought we could make another go of things. Be a family."

My throat tightens, my own tears threatening. I want to feel anger, but all I feel is sorrow.

"Where is Blackwell?" I dare to ask.

Lottie sniffs. "I don't know. After Dan… was killed, Patrick broke into the house looking for the lieutenant. He came back with his coat. Said the whole place was empty. He was furious about it."

"You've not seen Blackwell since?"

She shakes her head.

My thoughts race. And they go to a tiny hut near Squires' inn where Patrick Owen's family died.

232

Has Blackwell been driven there by the ghosts he is haunted by? The ghosts he refuses to speak of?

I want to go to him. But I don't want to leave Lottie.

"Was it Owen's idea to do what he did to the body? To make me think it were Blackwell?"

Lottie nods faintly. "He took the coat from Blackwell's room. Defaced Dan's body so you'd think…" She coughs down her tears. "That was it for me, Nell. When I saw him do that to Dan… His friend… Just to punish you for prying into our business… I couldn't have nothing more to do with him."

I swallow hard. Her realisation has come far too late.

"I asked him why he killed Maggie," Lottie says suddenly.

For a moment I don't speak. "I thought you believed him innocent."

"That's what I needed to believe."

I nod slowly. I understand, of course. How many times did I tell myself Blackwell did not pull the trigger on Owen's family? In the end, the truth did not matter for me. But I know it matters to Lottie.

"He was my way out of the factory," she says, looking at her hands. "I couldn't have managed three more years of weaving cloth and lying with old Bert. I had to get out. You must think me such a fool."

I shake my head faintly. "I understand," I say. "I know you don't believe it, but I do. I know how desperate the factory can make you."

Lottie wipes her eyes with the back of her hand. "Phil Cunningham was the leader of the croppies before they rose up at Castle Hill," she tells me. "He'd come to Parramatta sometimes and drink with us at the river. Tell us of how things would be different after the Irish were in charge. We all believed him. He gave us hope. There weren't one of us who thought things would end like they did. There weren't one of us who thought Phil wouldn't come back that day." She stares blankly ahead, her eyes glazed.

"After Castle Hill, Patrick took his place. Tried to keep our spirits high. I was so taken by him, Nell. I was drawn to him right from the day I first met him. But he were a different kind of man to Phil. He weren't interested in freedom. Not once did he ever try and rouse the croppies to rise up again. He were only interested in revenge. In making Blackwell pay for what he did to his family.

"I'd convinced myself it were the savages that killed Maggie," she says. "But after I saw Patrick do what he did to Dan's body… I weren't so sure." She turns to face me then, her eyes round and glistening. "He couldn't even find a reason. Just told me she had it coming." She takes a deep breath. "I know that being Irish makes him feel weak. Powerless. He needs to prove how strong he is."

A knot tightens in my stomach. Killing a mere factory lass will not have given Owen the power he craves. That will only come with killing Blackwell.

"Does he know you've turned yourself in?" I ask.

Lottie shakes her head, tears sliding down her cheeks. "The day Dan died," she says, "Patrick sent me back to the Rocks. But I didn't go. I went to his farmhouse and I stood there with his pistol in my hand." She looks me in the eye. "I wanted to do it, Nell. I wanted to break back into the house and kill him. Retribution for Maggie. And Dan. And you. But I couldn't do it." For a long time, she doesn't speak. "He needs to be stopped," she says. "The Rum Corps won't do it. They had the chance after Maggie, but they're too afraid of another uprising."

I nod silently.

"And the croppies," she says, "they're blinded by him. They can't see the kind of man he truly is. The colony would be better off without him. And the Irish need to follow a better man." Her eyes plead with mine. "He needs to be stopped," she says again.

I open my mouth to speak, but can't find the words. "I couldn't," I say finally.

"Of course you could. You despise him. And he wants Blackwell dead. You're strong enough to do it, Nell. I'm not."

I think of myself, tearful and pleading when I was first hauled away by the thief-takers in London. How have I become the strong one?

I think of the night I stood outside Owen's hut with the knife in my hand. And I think of Dan Brady's body, lying lifeless in the alley. I have already become a killer. Or is Lottie telling the truth? I have no thought of it. All I know is that now she is the one who will be taken to the gallows. And I am the one who is to live.

"You must," says Lottie. "Or else more of us will die. More croppies. And more of the factory lasses."

She has given her life for me. And so what can I do but agree?

The guard escorts me down the corridor, towards the heavy wooden doors that lead to the outside world. A part of me is oddly reluctant to step through them; to do so is to acknowledge completely this sacrifice Lottie has made for me. Acknowledge she will be sent to the scaffold in my place. And acknowledge that she is sending me out into the world to end Patrick Owen's life.

Before I step into the street, I look back at the guard. "Lieutenant Blackwell's family," I say. "Have there been letters sent informing them of his death?"

I think of Blackwell's father. I think of Sophia. The next ship to England leaves in days' time. And I have no idea whether Blackwell will be aboard. But word of his death must not leave the harbour. If news of the murder is sent on the ship, it could be years before his family learns the truth.

"The situation has been rectified," says the guard. He has been stiltedly polite to me since he learned I did not kill his schoolmate. "The letter informing his father of the murder has been recalled."

"And his wife?" I ask.

"The lieutenant has no wife."

"He does," I say. "Sophia."

The guard looks at me curiously. "Sophia died years ago in London. Long before Blackwell came out here."

I feel suddenly hot and unsteady. "Are you certain?"

"Certain as anything," says the guard. "I was at her burial."

CHAPTER THIRTY-THREE

The weight of it all cows me. Sophia's burial and Lottie's sacrifice and this great overwhelming relief that I am standing here; living, breathing. Sydney Town is searing in its brightness and I hunch for long moments in the street outside the jail, wearing the grey flannel smock I expected to die in. My heart is thundering in my chest, a stark reminder that I have survived.

I fill my lungs with air, trying to steady myself. I was not supposed to see this world again. I have no idea how to act within it.

My head is full of Lottie, of Owen, of Blackwell. Of beautiful curly-haired Sophia lying lifeless in her grave.

I push the thought of her away. There is no room in my mind to grapple with the reason for Blackwell's lies.

I know he has gone to the Owens' cottage. I know he is in danger. And I know that, for all his painful untruths, I have no choice but to find him.

By afternoon, I am walking a narrow track out of Sydney Town, following the river into tangled wilderness. One pocket is stuffed with bread, the other with an apple I took from the Whaler's kitchen.

"You sure about this, Nell?" Charlie asked, when I went to him for directions. Kate clung to my wrist as I filled a flask of water. "It's a hell of a walk."

I am terrified, but sure. I know this is where I must go to find Blackwell. And only once I have done such a thing can I turn my thoughts to what Lottie has asked of me.

I trudge along the riverbank, following the narrow path along the water. Trees hang low, trying to reclaim the wilderness. Thin walking tracks are beaten into the bush, interlocking paths carved by the boots of twenty years of settlers. Flies swarm about my face, clouds of mosquitoes rising from the mangroves.

I keep walking, my skirts in my fist and my eyes darting. My shift is damp with sweat, and my hair curls and clings to my cheeks.

I will see James Squires' inn at Kissing Point, Charlie has told me. And from there I must turn in towards the forest to find that hut belonging to the Owens.

I feel certain Blackwell will not find the absolution he is looking for. Instead, he will stand on that doorstep and make himself a target. If he comes face to face with the woman who watched him kill her family, it will not be forgiveness he receives. It will likely be a ball to the chest.

As I walk and walk, my thoughts turn to Sophia. To all the lies Blackwell told me. Lies, I see clearly, that were constructed to keep me at a distance.

I understand. I despise it, but I understand. For all my twelfth night balls and worsted gowns, I am still a convict woman. It is a stain I will never wash away. I understand the great shame it would bring to a military officer, a man of God, to give his heart to a factory lass. A concubine.

A part of me loathes myself for this unshakable love I feel, after all the lies he has told. I want to turn my back. But I know I will never be able to. Because as hard as I tried to be the one with the power, I am well aware of the pull he has over me. Instead of the anger I want to feel, I am gripped with terror that I will find him dead.

There is Squires' inn; square and white at the water's edge. Row boats are tied to the jetty, men sitting on the riverbank with pipes in their hands. The sinking sun sears off the water.

I turn away from the river to face the thick wall of bushland. I push my way through branches and step over tangled knots of ferns.

Is that an overgrown path beneath my feet? Impossible to tell. I follow it anyway, deeper into the shadowed wilderness, pushing away thoughts of natives' spears, and of the monsters that hide in the bush. Ancient trees reach forever upwards, barely moved by a breath of hot wind.

And then I stop walking. Because I see a crooked stone chimney peering out from between the trees.

The thin path leading up to the cottage is almost lost beneath the undergrowth. Exhaustion pressing down on me, I take slow, careful steps, holding my skirts above my ankles. With each step, the twigs beneath my feet crackle loudly. Birds flee as I approach; flashes of colour in the fading light.

I can tell from a distance the place is abandoned. The bush has started to reclaim the house, vines growing up one wall and a tree branch curling through a window. The door hangs open on its hinges.

I step inside. Remnants of old lives are still here; the table in the corner, the iron fingers of the grate, jar lids scattered between fallen leaves. And there on the wooden walls are the bloodstains; wine-dark shadows that have barely begun to fade. But at the back of the house, a rotting patch of wall has been replaced, the new planks of wood stark and white against the old. They seem out of place, out of time.

I stare at the bloodstains. And I imagine Blackwell pulling the trigger. Imagine Owen's cousins falling. The images don't make sense to me; they don't feel right. A part of my brain refuses to accept that Blackwell is capable of doing such a thing. But I have learnt better than to succumb to my naivety.

He has killed. And he has lied. But none of that changes the worry that is heaving in my chest.

I call his name. It feels wrong to do so; to disrupt this silence with the name of the man who pulled the trigger. My voice vanishes. And I turn abruptly, unable to bear being in the place any longer.

I call again.

Still, there is silence. I keep walking.

A hundred yards from the hut, I see a swathe of grey fabric hanging from a tree. Old curtains, I realise. Taken from the cottage. They have been hung from low branches to create a crude shelter.

In front of the tent is a burned-out campfire, and beside it, a pile of tools; a hammer and saw, a wood plane lying on its side. I walk towards them, holding my breath.

Blackwell steps out from beneath the shelter.

A sob of relief escapes me and I throw my arms around him. For a fleeting moment, I don't care about his lies, or the blood staining the wall of the cottage. I am just glad he is alive. Glad I am alive. The odds of us both standing here breathing seem impossibly high.

His arms slide around me. And I could break. But I step back, out of his embrace. He grips my shoulders, eyes full of questions.

"What are you doing here, Eleanor?"

"I came to find you. I was worried for you. I was so afraid that…" I glance around. "Are you alone? You've not been followed? Owen…"

"Owen's not here," he says. "No one is here."

That doesn't feel true. There are ghosts from the past here. Spectres of Owen's family, of Blackwell's unspoken guilt.

"Why have you come out here?" I ask, though I feel I already know the answer. If he leaves this place without absolution, those ghosts will follow him all the way to England.

"When I came to this cottage after the uprising," he says, "there was a woman here. One of the men's wives perhaps. She was hiding in the bush outside the house. She must have seen me coming." He sighs deeply. "I didn't see her until after the men were dead. I looked into her eyes and all I saw was hate."

"I came back here to tell her how much I regret what I did." His voice is low, and as unsteady as I've ever heard it. "But she's gone. There's no one left."

I stare through the trees at the outline of the house. Look back at the makeshift shelter he has erected. A cockatoo swoops; a ghostly flash of white.

"Why such guilt over this above all the other conflict you've seen?" I don't mean to excuse this bloodstained cottage. Just to understand.

"Because this was no battlefield," says Blackwell. "This was a man's home."

"You were doing as you were instructed."

"Yes. Without question." I hear that expressionlessness I saw so often in that hut in Parramatta. An emptiness, I see now, for his guilt to hide behind. Is this the cost of power, I wonder? A haunting guilt? Perhaps power is something that ought not be so fiercely sought.

"You must have been here for days," I say, thinking of all the blurred sunrises and sunsets I was locked in my prison cell. My eyes drift to the tools scattered beside the firepit. And I think back to the day we sat beside the Parramatta River and stared up at the towering redgums.

I learned a little construction when I was at school, he said. *A way of leaving your mark on a place.*

"You're the one who made the repairs to the house," I say. "A way of leaving your mark."

He doesn't speak at once, just turns to look at the cottage, silhouetted in the twilight. "Well," he says finally, "perhaps in this case it is more about undoing the mark I have left on the place."

"The cottage is empty. Why have you continued? Fixing the house will not change what happened inside it."

"No," he says. "It won't. But mending this cottage was to be an act of decency. Perhaps in some small way it still can."

I hear the fragility in his voice; the guilt hiding beneath the surface that is pushing its way out.

"Maggie's trial?" I say huskily. "Is that why you let Owen walk free? Because of all that happened at this cottage?"

Blackwell's eyes are on the cracked windows of the house. "How could I send another member of this family to his death?"

I let out my breath in a sharp exhalation. I need to walk away. I can't stand here speaking to the man who has lied to me from the beginning. The man who let Maggie's killer walk free.

I stride out past the tent, past the cottage, past the remains of the campfire, yanking on my skirts as they entangle themselves on branches. I have no thought of which direction I'm walking, or what I will find. A part of me wants to walk all the way back to Sydney Town, but if I set out in the dark, the forest will swallow me. I turn in a circle. I cannot have walked more than a mile from Squires' inn. But in which direction?

I hear footsteps behind me, the undergrowth crackling. Blackwell calls my name. I hear confusion in his voice. Why am I running away?

He reaches for my arm, but I yank away.

"You lied," I say. "About your wife."

Something passes across his eyes. What is he to attempt? An apology? An explanation? How can any of that be sufficient?

"Yes," he says finally. "I did."

A part of me is glad for his bluntness – glad he has attempted neither apology nor explanation. I don't need him to explain. I know what I am.

I know why he did what he did. I arrived on his doorstep in blue-striped skirts.

Wind rustles the bush, making me shiver. The light is draining quickly. The shadows are thickening and the birds shrieking in the trees.

"You can't stay out here," Blackwell says finally. "It's getting dark." He turns back to look at the tent. "I have shelter."

I let out a humourless laugh, because at those words I am back on the streets of Parramatta, standing in the rain outside Reverend Marsden's church. Where would I be right now if I had chosen not to follow Blackwell back to his hut? A pointless question, of course. Because we both know well there can be no changing the past.

And just like I did that stormy night, I walk with him back to his shelter, because I have no place else to go.

I take the food from my pockets and sit it on the edge of the blanket. Despite all the walking, I'm not hungry. All I want is to sleep. To forget this most confronting, draining of days; a day I was never supposed to even see.

I curl up on the edge of the blanket Blackwell has laid across the ground. The wool smells stale and damp. And I watch the last of the light give way to the dark. My thoughts are churning. I think of Lottie alone in her cell, awaiting death. Waiting for me to take Owen's life; to bring about the justice I have been so desperately craving since I found Maggie's body on the side of the road. I think of Blackwell's lies and the ghosts in the cottage that have kept him unable to leave this place.

I lie there in the dark, listening to him breathe. I know he is awake. I imagine he is staring into the darkness, eyes open, thoughts whirring as quickly as my own.

I feel his hand slide over my shoulder. I can't bring myself to look at him, even through the thick dark. Moonlight shafts through the trees, painting shadows on the roof of the tent.

"A God-fearing soldier like you is not supposed to love a woman who sits at the spinning wheels in the factory," I say. "That's why you lied, isn't it." It is not a question.

He lets out a deep breath. "I was led to believe certain things about this place. About the Irish. And about the convicts. Especially the women. And I never questioned any of it.

"I was taught to think of the Irish as animals. I didn't question that before I came out here to the Owens' cottage. And I pulled the trigger on innocent men." His fingers tighten around the top of my arm. "And when I took in a factory lass from the street, I was not expecting you. I was expecting what I had been told I would see."

"Immorality," I say. "A loose woman."

I know that, had I not been the one in convict slops, I would have seen this place in the same way. I would have watched the women from the factory crawl into bed with their settlers and soldiers, and I would have called them whores.

"And so? Your lie was protection against temptation?"

"Yes," he says. "I suppose that's what it was."

Protection against the shame of falling for a factory lass.

I can't bring myself to speak – to do so would be to either voice my anger or relinquish it. And I can do neither.

The silence between us is thick; heavier than it had been the night I first lay beside him in the night. Did he decide then to lie to me about his wife? Erect that barrier that would keep me distanced? Or did that decision come later?

"For whatever it's worth," he says, "I feel a great anger at myself."

"Because of me? Because I caused you to sin?" I hear my own bitterness.

"Because of you," he says. "But not because you caused me to sin. Because I lost you. To my own foolishness. And my own lies."

I roll over. I can barely see more than his outline, but I know I am looking into his eyes.

"You're a good person, Eleanor," he says. "You deserve far better than what you've been given in this place."

I let out a cold laugh. I'm unsure if his words are an understatement, or the greatest of untruths. I don't feel like a good person. I'm not sure I ever have.

"Captain Grant told Flynn you and I were together," I tell him. "He broke off our betrothal."

For a long time, Blackwell doesn't speak. "I'm sorry," he says finally. "I truly am."

His words have left an ache inside me. For the first time, there is no

242

barrier between us; no Flynn, no Sophia, no colony watching. No barrier but my own anger, my own reluctance to let him near me after all he has done.

His hand tightens around my arm. Does he mean to hold on to me? Do so and he will likely drown. I am barely able to hold my head above water.

"My entire world," he says finally, "it's been upturned since I came to this place. I've found myself questioning everything I thought I knew. And that has shown me very clearly that I should not have blindly accepted the things I was taught. I ought to have thought for myself."

How well I know that feeling. *I ought to have thought for myself*, as I carted counterfeit coins around the city. *I ought to have thought for myself* as the thief-takers led me from Jonathan's townhouse.

"This place changes you," I say.

"No. Not the place. The people in it." His thumb moves against my shoulder.

"I was to die," I say. "For your murder."

He sits up suddenly. "What?"

And I tell him it all; of the rebels coming to the Grants', and the body in the street. I tell him of how I slid out of the hangman's grasp and how Lottie is to die.

Blackwell lets out his breath. He shuffles across the blanket, pressing his forehead against mine. His hands are tangled tightly in my hair. He pulls me hard against him, his nose brushing against mine. "I'm sorry," he breathes. "I'm sorry I wasn't there. I'm sorry for everything."

I let him hold me. I need him to do it. My anger has not faded, but I need something to steady myself. The relief of escaping the gallows is so fierce I can barely fathom it. Coupled with grief over Lottie and the pain of Blackwell's betrayal, I feel as though I am falling.

"In the morning," I say, "we go back to Sydney. You've only days until your ship leaves. And nothing you do here is going to change the past."

Each of us here must live with our mistakes; live with the crimes that sent us into this new world. Why should Blackwell be any different? But in spite of myself I curl up against his chest, trying to memorise the feel of him beneath my fingers before he disappears from my life forever.

I hear noise outside and sit up quickly. A crackle of twigs. It is not the sound of an animal. It is the sound of footsteps.

Natives? My heart speeds.

Blackwell climbs out from beneath the shelter. On my knees behind him, I look into the darkness. I can make out the shapes of the trees in the moonlight.

"Who's there?" says Blackwell. The old authority is back in his voice. The sound of it is swallowed quickly by the dark. He reaches for the tinderbox and lights the lamp. He holds it up, shining it over the thick pillars of the trees. The orange glow picks out a small face between the gnarled trunks.

"Kate?" I can't make sense of her being here.

Blackwell looks at me for an explanation, but I just stumble through the darkness towards the girl.

"What are you doing here? You came all this way on your own?"

She throws her arms around my waist. "A man came to the tavern," she coughs. "He made me tell him where you were." Her voice is wavering, cheeks stained with tears.

My stomach tightens. "Did he hurt you?"

She shakes her head, but keeps it pressed hard against my chest. "He's here," she says. "He came for you." She looks past me at Blackwell. "And him."

I catch Blackwell's glance, then look hurriedly back at Kate. "Did he force you to come out here?"

She shakes her head. "I followed him." Her voice is trembling. "I thought he was going to hurt you. I had to find you. Tell you he was coming."

I close my eyes and pull Kate close again. "You must be exhausted." I feel a tug in my chest that she might put herself in danger on my account. "Where is Owen now?" I whisper. And her gaze drifts past me to the inky outline of the cottage.

Blackwell steps out into the night.

"No," I say. "Please don't."

I know that somehow, this has to end. But Blackwell is walking towards Owen without a weapon. And I see that this can only end one way.

CHAPTER THIRTY-FOUR

"Now my boys, liberty or death."

Philip Cunningham,
Leader of Castle Hill rebellion
Sunday 4 March 1804

Faint light appears in the window of the cottage. Blackwell walks towards it, his steps almost soundless against the undergrowth.

I crawl back into the shelter, feeling my way through the flickering light for his pack. A water flask. A husk of bread. Jar of potted meat. I find no weapon.

I let out my breath in frustration and crawl back out of the shelter. Hand the lamp to Kate.

"Stay here," I tell her, putting my hand to her back to usher her inside. She crawls onto the blanket and sits up on her knees. "Rest," I say, though her eyes are wide and bright. Lamplight flickers on her cheeks, and for a second I see her mother.

The cottage door is hanging open. I can see Owen at the table. Blackwell sits opposite him, on chairs they have reclaimed from the wilderness. There is a pistol in the centre of the table, Owen's hand splayed over it.

"You're not welcome in this place, Lieutenant," he is saying. "You shouldn't have come." He shifts in his chair, making it creak loudly.

Blackwell nods slowly. "I understand. And if you wish to kill me now, I understand that too."

Owen falters. A response he was not expecting. He glances out the door. "Where's Nell? I know she's here."

"Your business is with me," says Blackwell. "Not with her."

But Blackwell knows nothing of the silent promise I made to Lottie as we knelt together in her jail cell. My business with Patrick Owen goes far deeper than either of these men know.

You're strong enough to do it, Nell. I didn't believe her words then and I don't believe them now. But I want to.

Owen's hand tightens around the pistol and I clench my teeth to keep from crying out. If I force myself to look at this from his perspective, I can see the perfection of Blackwell dying in this place. Of catching him here so his blood might be added to that he spilled.

Owen turns the pistol over and shuffles in his chair. It scrapes noisily against the earthen floor. Opposite him, Blackwell is motionless. His hands are curled around his knees, chest open as though awaiting the shot. Taller, broader; he is the more dominant of the men, without even trying.

He faces Owen, waiting. Waiting for him to do as he has been invited, and pull the trigger.

I see then that Blackwell's invitation has taken the power out of this moment. Maggie's murder was a way for Owen to prove his dominance, Lottie said. He kills to be powerful, to be strong. But where is the power in this?

"Where is Nell?" he asks again.

"I'm here," I say, stepping inside the hut. Blackwell glances at me. My eyes go to the pistol on the table, then I look back at Owen, expectant.

"The girl," he says. "Who is she?"

"You know who she is."

His jaw tightens.

What does he see when he looks at Kate? Does he see her mother writhing beneath his hands as he crushed the life from her? Or does he just see something to be discarded, like Maggie, like Lottie, like his son?

His breathing grows louder. Is he rattled by the sight of Kate Abbott, with her mother's eyes, her mother's face? Is he haunted by his own ghosts, just as Blackwell is? Have the women of the factory somehow crawled beneath his skin?

"Does she make you feel guilty, Owen?" I ask. "Does she make you think of her mother?"

"Guilty?" he repeats, his humourless laugh sounding hollow in the stillness. "Why would I feel guilty? They're just worthless lags."

In a flash of rage, I snatch the gun from the table. Hold it out, Owen in my line of sight. And in a second, Blackwell is on his feet. I feel his hands on my shoulders, easing my arms down. And then he stops. Steps back.

He is giving me the choice, I realise. He is letting me make my own decision.

Untouchable Owen. If I pull the trigger here, with only Blackwell as a witness, I know I would avoid the hangman. My thoughts are far clearer than they were the night I walked towards Owen's hut with a kitchen knife in my hand.

I couldn't do it then, but perhaps I can do it now.

For a moment, I see it; Owen's body slumping as I fire into his chest. The look of shock on his face as he falls; surprise that he might be taken out by a factory lass. I imagine the sense of satisfaction I will feel to know I have done as Lottie asked. To know there is some tiny flicker of justice in this place.

And then I see the Irish rebels, gathering, rising at the death of their leader, inspired to seek revenge. Placing the blame for Owen's murder at Lieutenant Blackwell's feet.

And it won't be satisfaction I feel; not really. It will be that awful sickness I felt when I saw Dan Brady's body sprawled across the alley. And it will be terror at the thought that there are still days until Blackwell's ship leaves for England and the croppies may ensure he does not see them out.

I keep the pistol held out in front of me. Still, I don't know what my decision will be. Perhaps Owen's death will let me feel some hollow sense of justice. Perhaps it will still the constant churning in my chest. Or perhaps taking his life will haunt me forever.

Owen's eyes meet mine for a moment. In the flickering lamplight, they are glazed and expectant. Fearful. The sight of his terror brings a rush of satisfaction.

I hear my heart thudding in my ears. An animal shrieks in the bush beyond the hut. The sound seems both close and far away. The world feels unsteady, as though I am being tossed upon the seas.

The next sound I hear is footsteps. Soft footfalls against the floor of the cottage. Owen is walking. He has decided I will not shoot. Has decided I am too weak.

I tighten my hands around the stock of the pistol, feeling my finger on the trigger. And then I feel Blackwell's hand against my shoulder. I lower the pistol and set it on the table as I hear Owen's footsteps disappearing into the bush. Let him walk, I think, as he is swallowed by the darkness. Let him carry his guilt, and his shame, just as the rest of us must.

CHAPTER THIRTY-FIVE

A swarm of people has gathered in George Street, waiting for the gates of the jail yard to open. A woman's execution always draws a crowd.

People are chatting excitedly, laughing, children leaping over puddles. I want to scream; want to shake them. How can there be chatter, laughter, leaping, when Lottie is to die?

My eyes dart, searching for Owen. I pray he will stay away. I don't want Lottie to know I have failed to do as she asked. And I don't want him to be the last thing she sees before she dies.

I don't see Owen, but I do see Blackwell. As the gates creak open and the crowd funnels through, our eyes meet. I look away quickly.

At the sight of the hangman standing upon the gallows, I am breathless. I have never seen a person put to death. And just a few days earlier, the noose was tied for me. I want to rush from the jail yard. Close my eyes and pretend this isn't happening. Pretend that when I next step into the Rocks I will find Lottie in the kitchen with a baby's basket at her feet. I try to breathe. And against every thread of instinct I have, I push my way to the front of the crowd. I need Lottie to see me. I need her to know that today she is not alone.

Though my eyes are on the noose dancing in the hot wind, I'm aware of Blackwell making his way towards me. Always, I'm aware of him.

He pushes his way through the crowd and stands behind me. Puts a hand to my shoulder. And yes, this simple gesture is a big thing, a part of me sees that. Him with his red coat and me with my convict stain, and anyone in the colony who could see us. But it is not enough to undo two years of lies.

In spite of myself, a part of me wants to step closer. Let him hold me while I watch Lottie die. But I don't want to be comforted by him. I don't want to need him. I've already needed him far too much. I take a step away.

Out Lottie comes from the jail; a soldier in front of her, behind her; a rifle at her back. Her chin is lifted defiantly and her eyes are sharp. She has conjured up her pride, her confidence, her brassiness, and I am glad of it. This is the way I want to remember her, not as the tearful mess she was the last time we spoke. She looks strikingly, painfully alive.

I think of that tiny smile she gave me the day I first arrived in Parramatta; a smile that did so much to calm me, to reassure me, to show me this place had some humanity in it.

I think of drinking with her by the river, and of dancing on Christmas night. And I think of standing outside her hut the day she was betrothed to Owen, begging her to stay. What if I had found kinder words? Or had not turned away from her when she had the men tell me of Blackwell's crimes? Could I have tried harder to keep her from marrying? Tears well up behind my eyes – I know it is far too late for any of these questions.

She climbs the scaffold on steady legs. My throat is tight and my heart is fast. I look up at her. I want her to see how grateful I am that she came forward, gave herself up to save me. Still, I have no thought of whether she is telling the truth about Dan Brady's death. Perhaps I never will. There are no more words I can say to her, of course, but I meet her gaze; thank her, forgive her for leading Owen to Blackwell. Hope the look in my eyes tells her how much I love her.

As the hangman slides the noose over her head, I feel my body grow hot, begin to shake. I keep my feet planted in the dust of the jail yard, praying my legs will support me. I hold my breath and clench my jaw, as though trying to preserve this last fleeting second of Lottie's life.

A knock of the trapdoor and she is gone. A quick death, but one that feels all too easy. As though it is nothing but a trifle to take a factory lass from the world.

I stumble out of the jail. There is a strange energy to the place. Perhaps it's just my imagination; I am dizzy and unsettled as I try to navigate this world of which Lottie is no longer a part.

Soldiers are gathering in the street, murmuring among themselves. Blackwell passes me and his eyes meet mine. Then he leaves the jail with the other soldiers. Crunch and thud go the boots, in flawless formation.

For a moment, I stand motionless, watching after them; that vibrant wash of colour against the muted earth and sandstone of Sydney Town. The Rum Corps dominates this land in every way.

On my walk back to the tavern, a dam opens inside me. The tears I have been holding back cascade down my cheeks. I cry messy, racking sobs as I walk, ignoring the stares of passers-by. I cry for Lottie, for Willie, for both my inability to kill Owen and out of gratitude for the fact I found the strength to let him go free. I cry over Blackwell's lies, and for the convict stain I will never wash away. I cry because tomorrow he will be gone.

When I get back to the Whaler's, my eyes are swollen and my cheeks are hot.

Charlie goes to the counter and pours a shallow cannikin of rum. Presses it into my hand without a word.

I manage a faint smile. "Thank you, Charlie. You're good to me."

"Ain't hard," he says with a smile. "Mouthful of liquor and you're tame as a kitten." He nods to the cup. "Drink up. It'll help."

I toss back the rum, relishing the warmth in my throat. "Where's Kate?"

"Upstairs. Sweeping the hallway." He gives me a pointed look. "She's a good worker. But I can't spare another room."

I nod. "She can stay with me."

"You sure?"

"Of course." It feels like the least I can do for Maggie, and for all the women still weaving cloth in Parramatta.

Charlie takes a glass from the shelf and pours his own drink. "How was it?" he asks, elbows on the counter. "It happen quickly?"

I nod, my throat tightening. Two fresh tears slide down my face.

He reaches across the bar and squeezes my shoulder. "That's all you can hope for."

I turn the cannikin around in my hands. "It ought to have been me."

Charlie tosses back his drink in one mouthful. "You remember killing that man?"

I shake my head. "I don't remember anything except—"

"Well then," he cuts in, "how do you know it ought to have been you?"

I appreciate his attempt to relieve me of my guilt. But I know the sight of Dan Brady with a bullet in his chest will haunt me until I die.

By evening, the tavern is busy, full of curious chatter. Soldiers march past the windows, people clustered to the sides of the street, cheering, hooting, booing as they pass.

Kate stands with her forehead pressed to the glass. "What's happening, Nell?"

"I don't know." I look over her shoulder. A military band struts past the window, the pompous brass melody muted behind the glass. I usher Kate away. "Go and wipe those tables in the back."

The gossip filters in later in the evening, the story told by men with shining eyes, the tale growing more theatrical with each cannikin of rum.

Captain Macarthur, the governor's most prominent opponent, refused to stand trial over unpaid fines.

"They say the judge owed Macarthur money," one man tells me, jabbing his pipe in my face for emphasis. "Can't hardly blame him for not wanting to be tried by such a man, now can you."

Macarthur, another man announces, was supported by the Corps officers presiding over the trial. And in response Governor Bligh brought charges of treason upon the soldiers. Demanded they present themselves at Government House.

"Them officers, they didn't go to Bligh," says the man with the pipe. "They went to Johnson, their commanding officer. Then they all marched their way to Government House and overthrew the governor." He slams his empty cup on the bar. "Another, lass. Fill it to the top this time."

The conversation in the tavern becomes louder, more heated. There are those who support the Rum Corps' coup. Others who are wary of the military's power.

"They say Macarthur planned the whole thing from his prison cell."

"Heard Bligh was hiding under his bed when the redcoats came."

"What hope we got now the lobsters are in charge?"

And so this is the rebellion that has been brewing throughout my time in New South Wales. I imagined it would be the croppies who would rise. Imagined the Irish rebels would be the ones to turn this place on its head. But I can't be surprised by this. Can't be surprised it is the Rum Corps that has marched forth with guns out to take what they want. The power has been with them all along.

Much later, when the tales have become muted and all heard before, Blackwell slips into the tavern. His uniform makes him a beacon, and men and women surround him, asking questions, demanding answers. I can tell from his flushed cheeks and slightly dishevelled hair that there is liquor in him. Can tell he was among the men who descended on Governor Bligh. Though the tavern is heaving, the patrons clear a table for him to sit at in the corner of the room. One man, who's already told five conflicting stories, waves a hand in the air, trying to get my attention.

"A drink for the lieutenant, lass! Quick now!"

I can feel Blackwell trying to catch my eye through the crowd. I turn away, filling a glass and handing it to Kate.

"Take this to the lieutenant."

She weaves her way through the people, returning with a sassy smile on her lips that makes me think of Maggie. "He wants to speak with you."

"I'm busy," I say, well aware of my own pettiness. And I sail up and down the bar, finding glasses to polish and shelves to tidy. But I am acutely aware of his presence. Unable to keep from looking at him. And finally, I give in, taking his empty glass from his table with as much nonchalance as I can muster.

He holds out a penny. "May I have another?"

I take the money and slide it into my apron. "Two in an hour. That's not like you."

"Well," he says, eyes meeting mine, "I've to do something while I sit here hoping you'll eventually speak to me."

I say nothing. I want him to leave. But I also want him to stay. Stay in the tavern. Stay in the colony. But it's far too late for any of that.

"I was a fool," he says. His words should feel like a victory, but they don't. Because I know he was not being a fool. He was acting in line with beliefs that have been ingrained in him since he first pulled on his uniform.

I shake my head. "You're no fool. You knew exactly what you were doing."

"Yes," he says. "I knew what I was doing. I was doing as I was taught to do. And that's what makes me a fool."

I close my eyes for a moment. A dark strand of hair hangs over his cheek and it takes all my resolve not to reach out and touch it.

"Meet me at the wharf tomorrow morning," he says. "Please. Nine o'clock."

I fold my arms; a gesture of self-preservation. "Your ship is due to leave tomorrow."

"Yes," says Blackwell. "In the evening. So give me the day. And then you never need have anything to do with me again."

I hesitate. But then I find myself nodding.

I see the faintest of smiles on Blackwell's lips. "Thank you," he says. He stands. "I don't need that second drink."

He is out the door before I can give him back his penny.

CHAPTER THIRTY-SIX

In the morning, I sit at a table in the corner of the tavern and write a carefully worded letter. I fold it, seal it, and slip it into my pocket. And then I make my way to the wharf.

Blackwell is waiting for me on the edge of the water, coat buttoned to his neck and boots gleaming. At the sight of me, a tentative smile breaks across his face. "I'm glad to see you. I wasn't sure you'd come."

A small, single-masted boat is bobbing on the swell, its sail furled against the hot wind. A seaman sits by the tiller, legs stretched out in front of him, awaiting our arrival.

I raise my eyebrows. "Where are we going?"

"You'll see."

Blackwell offers me his hand and helps me step into the boat. I fold myself neatly onto the bench seat and look out over the glittering sea. An enormous three-masted ship lies at anchor beside the dock, men swarming up the gangway with crates in their arms. Tonight it will set sail for England.

Soon, our boat is flying down the river, the hot wind billowing the sail. When last I made this journey, from the silver swell of Sydney Harbour, inland towards Parramatta, I was bound for the factory above the jail. The enormous shadows of the trees, the animal shrieks within the bush, the inky darkness that cloaked the land; every part of it filled me with terror. But today the golden water feels different. I lift my face upwards, enjoying the warmth on my cheeks. This sun-bleached land will be my life forever, but I am achingly grateful to be living it.

For a moment I imagine I am the one with the ticket for England in my hand. The one with the freedom to leave this place at will. Would I climb onto that ship if I had the chance? The woman I am now has no place in London.

And is there a place for me here, on the edge of this vast wilderness? I have been gifted the life I thought I was to lose, and I want to believe there is something for me in it beyond the misery of the factory. A purpose beyond mere survival.

I can feel Blackwell's eyes on me. He peers beneath the brim of my straw bonnet, trying to catch my gaze. I'm acutely aware I've barely spoken a word to him as the hot morning has stretched towards afternoon.

I reach into my pocket for the letter. Hold it out to him. "When you go back to England, I need you to deliver this."

He frowns. "What is it?"

That morning, I penned a letter to the magistrate who sent me across the seas. I outlined the role Henry Wilder played in my husband's coining venture. And I outlined my firm belief that he murdered Jonathan Marling in order to keep his involvement a secret.

Perhaps Wilder will not be found guilty. Perhaps I am too late in finding my voice. But I can no longer stay silent. There is already far too much injustice in the world.

Blackwell slides the letter into his pocket. "Is this the reason you came today? To see that the letter got back to London?"

I hesitate. Would I be here otherwise? I don't know. But here I am.

The boat knocks against a narrow jetty. Ahead of us, the trees part to reveal manicured farmland, the outline of a large brick cottage in the distance. I frown.

"Who lives here?"

"Captain Macarthur and his wife." Blackwell climbs to his feet, helping me out of the boat. I stay planted on the jetty, swatting at the flies that are circling my face.

"Why have you brought me here?"

"I'll show you." He puts a gentle hand to my elbow, ushering me up the path from the jetty and across a wide brown lawn towards the house. Fledgling trees waver on either side of the path.

My nerves are roiling. Once upon a time I could have held my own against people like this. Dined on jellies and drunk champagne. But I am wearing threadbare skirts from Parramatta market, my stained convict papers tucked in my pocket. I don't belong in this world any longer.

I look edgily at Blackwell. Is this an attempt to parade me on his arm? To show me he has found a way past his shame?

But then I see it is more than that. Because after stilted introductions, Mrs Macarthur leads me into a drawing room where a fortepiano is sitting against one wall.

"Lieutenant Blackwell tells me you play," she says.

I stare at the piano, hardly able to believe the sight of it pressed up against the wall. "Yes," I manage. "At least, I used to."

"A surgeon on the First Fleet brought it over with him," says Mrs Macarthur. "When he returned to England he had no mind to take it back. The dear man left it for me." She gestures to the instrument. "Please."

For a long time, I don't play. I just sit at the bench and stare down at the keys. I have left behind so much of who I once was, a part of me feels lost and unsure. I was a lady when I last sat at the keyboard. I don't want my skills to have left me.

From somewhere deep in the house, I hear the ringing of servants' bells, footsteps, children's laughter. I feel almost unbearably small. I know well that following last night's coup, Captain Macarthur has taken joint control of the colony. I am a factory lass sitting in the drawing room of the most powerful man in New South Wales.

I bring my hands to the keys. Lower my fingers into a deep, resonant chord. The sound feels oddly out of place with the forest encroaching on the window. But it brings a smile to my face. Brings a warmth to my entire body.

My fingers move, uncertain and imprecise, as they begin to remember this part of me. Faster they go, churning through preludes and fugues, and neat, rippling sonatas. And then a freeing improvisation that goes some way to easing the grief pressing down on my chest.

Blackwell enters the room. He sits beside me on the piano bench and watches my fingers move.

I stop playing, letting the silence settle. And I turn to face him. "Thank you. This means more to me than you could know."

A nod. "Of course." He puts a hand to my wrist. "We ought to leave if I'm to get this letter back to the ship in time."

When we are gliding back down the river, I say, "Are you not to leave New South Wales?" Blackwell's farewell with Mrs Macarthur was casual, brief. Not the farewell of a man leaving for the other side of the world.

His eyes drift towards the bushland on the edge of the river. The Owens' hut is there somewhere, with its bloodstained walls, being slowly devoured by the forest. Then he looks back to face me.

"Eleanor," he says carefully, "I didn't come to Sydney to find a ship back to England. I came to find you. To tell you the truth about Sophia. In hope that you might find some way to forgive me."

I open my mouth to speak, but find nothing but silence. I never questioned the fact that Blackwell was to leave. But did he ever say as much? Or did I draw the conclusion on my own?

"That day at the Whaler's Arms, you told me your ship was leaving in a fortnight."

He looks at me pointedly. "And you told me you were to be married."

"Oh," I say. "I…" My unformed sentence trails off. The sailor leans on the tiller, easing the boat through the mangroves encroaching on the centre of the river. If he has heard our murmured conversation, his face gives nothing away.

Blackwell shifts forward on the bench, so his knees are inches from mine. "I know I will never make things right with Owen. It's something I must live with." He looks up to meet my gaze. "But perhaps I might begin to make things right with you?"

There is apprehension in his eyes; a certain shyness completely mismatched with the ruby-gold brilliance of his uniform. That shyness makes my breath catch. Because for the first time, I see without doubt that I matter. That a factory lass with a bloodstained ticket of leave might be the difference between this officer staying in this place or sailing away.

But I also realise that I do not want that power.

I feel an unbidden happiness at the thought of him staying. But the lies he told me are still there, not so far beneath the surface. Still I don't know if I will be able to look past them.

"That choice must be yours," I tell him. "I can make no promises."

He nods. "Of course." But the tiny smile that passes between us makes something warm in my chest.

Last night, I trudged upstairs long after midnight. Crawled into bed beside Kate and stared out into the darkness. Something felt different about the place; an energy in the air, brought about by the governor's demise.

I know that, in the aftermath of the Rum Corps' coup, little will change for those of us at the bottom of the pile. The overthrowing of the governor was all for the benefit of the men at the top.

But things have been shaken, tipped from their axis. And if things can change at the top, perhaps one day they might also change at the bottom. Perhaps an officer and a factory lass might find a way to share a life.

And perhaps when the next barge of women comes gliding up the Parramatta River, they might find a safe place to sleep. Perhaps the next Irish lag to open his mouth will not be tied to the triangle and flogged until his back is raw.

Perhaps if we continue to speak, one day we may be heard.

HISTORICAL NOTE

Reverend Samuel Marsden's "female register" was created in 1806, classing all women in the colony, with the exception of some non-convict widows, as either "wife" or "concubine". Only Church of England marriages were recognised as legitimate; any woman married in Catholic or Jewish services was automatically considered a concubine. The document reached influential circles in London and led to the perception of Australian women being sexually immoral; a view which survived long into the 20th century.

But the female register was not entirely without benefit. Samuel Marsden was acutely conscious of overcrowding at the "factory above the jail", and well aware that many women were turning to prostitution in order to secure lodgings, particularly after the fire that destroyed much of the factory in December 1807. The register was part of Marsden's ongoing attempt to have suitable housing built for the ever-growing number of female convicts. In 1818, he was finally successful, with work beginning on the colony's second female factory, which would operate from 1821 to 1848. While overcrowding, limited rations, and an unsanitary work environment were still major problems at the new Parramatta factory, the women were at least provided with a place to sleep each night.

The Castle Hill Irish rebellion became known as "Australia's Vinegar

Hill", named after a major battle in the 1798 rebellion in Ireland. While the Castle Hill uprising of 1804 was swiftly quashed by the Rum Corps, its ideals of freedom and justice later served as inspiration for one of Australia's most famous rebellions. In the Eureka Stockade of 1854, in which gold miners protested against over-policing and unfair laws, rebels used the password "Vinegar Hill".

In 1793, the trading vessel *Hope* arrived in New South Wales from America carrying much-needed supplies – along with 7,500 gallons of rum. The *Hope's* captain stubbornly announced that he would not sell a scrap of his supplies until every ounce of liquor was first purchased. A group of officers from the New South Wales Corps banded together to purchase all the *Hope's* cargo without competition. New South Wales, like many British colonies, was short on coins, and rum (a catch-all term for all liquor) soon became an accepted form of currency, with its value largely controlled by the military. The newly nicknamed Rum Corps soon began importing stills, exchanging the liquor produced for food and labour at extremely favourable rates.

In 1806, William Bligh became governor of New South Wales. He found himself in charge of a colony with a severe shortage of food, largely due to the fact that so much of the grain produced was being used to make liquor, rather than bread.

Bligh had been ordered to control the use of alcohol as currency, and put an end to the Rum Corps' monopoly on trade. Almost immediately upon his arrival in New South Wales, Bligh clashed with Captain John Macarthur, a prominent landowner, politician and former military officer who held great sway over both the Rum Corps and the colony at large. Bligh was an iron-willed disciplinarian, a trait that had contributed to his infamous mutiny on the *Bounty,* and was again to be his undoing in New South Wales.

In January 1808, Macarthur was due to face trial over an unpaid fine, however refused to be tried by the judge, Richard Atkins, on the basis that Atkins owed him money. Macarthur received the support of the six Rum Corps officers presiding over the trial.

The following morning, Bligh requested the officers present themselves at Government House to face charges of treason. Rather than doing so, the soldiers called for their commanding officer, Major George Johnson. After almost two years of tension between Bligh and the military, Major Johnson appointed himself lieutenant governor of New South Wales, despite there being no legal grounds for him to do so.

On the evening of the 26th of January 1808, the twentieth anniversary of the First Fleet's arrival in Sydney Cove, almost the entire New South Wales Corps marched on Government House to arrest Bligh. He and his daughter remained under house arrest for more than a year, with Major Johnson and Captain Macarthur taking control of the colony. The rumour that Bligh was cowering under the bed when the soldiers arrived was almost certainly started by the Rum Corps themselves.

The colony's first piano was brought to New South Wales by First Fleet surgeon George Wogan, and gifted to Elizabeth Macarthur several years later. After many years in the custody of Edith Cowan university in Perth, Western Australia, the piano was returned to the UK in 2019, to be restored in Bath.

FORGOTTEN PLACES

PART ONE

DERWENT VALLEY, VAN DIEMEN'S LAND

AUSTRALIAN COLONIES

CHAPTER ONE

There were ghosts in this forest. Perhaps she was already one of them.

She lay on her back, tangled in a faded tartan cloak. Her skin was pale, almost translucent. Shadows beneath her eyes.

Yes, thought Dalton. *Dead.* The forest had done the job for him.

He peered down at her. Long, spidery fingers, veins stark on the backs of her hands. Her hair was a mess of jagged brown curls that barely reached her shoulders; tufty and uneven as though they'd been hacked at with blunt scissors. Some clung to her cheeks and neck. Others sprung from her head like piglets' tails. A blood-flecked hand lay beside her chin.

The first white person he'd seen in almost eleven years.

He saw it then; a faint rise and fall of her chest. He knelt, one hand tight around the legs of the possum he'd pulled from the trap, the other gripping the handle of his knife.

No one could know of this place. Of him. No one could know he hadn't died when he was supposed to: eleven years ago in the heart of this wilderness. Out here, the trees were legs of giants; the ferns knitted together like brambles. Rivers carved the cliffs and the earth fell away without warning. This was a place of thick darkness, a straining moon. Soupy fog and rain that thundered down the sides of mountains.

No place for a woman in a faded tartan cloak.

Perhaps the woods were shrinking, hacked away by convict axes. Attacked from the east. He'd come from the west. Knew there wasn't an axe in the world that could penetrate the bush of the western highlands.

Dalton put the possum down beside her head. Its glassy pink eyes caught the last threads of daylight.

He had a free hand now. He could shake her, wake her. Food and water and *thank you*. Or he could press the blade into that milky skin beneath her chin and never have his world invaded again.

Grace's eyes flew open. A scream caught in her throat. She scrambled out from beneath the wild creature and the knife hovering above her neck.

She spun around. Where was Violet?

"Where are you, angel? Violet! Are you hiding?"

The girl was crouching behind a tree several yards away, the hem of her pinny in her mouth and tears rolling down her cheeks. Grace ran to her. "I'm so sorry, angel. I don't know what happened. I just meant to rest. I— "

Violet grabbed a fistful of Grace's skirts and stared at the man. Stared at his knife.

"Stay away from us." Grace's voice was tiny. Dizziness coursed through her and made the forest twirl. She gripped the tree trunk.

A tall man. Hunched and bearded.

A savage? No. The skin on his bare chest was grimy and tanned, but she could tell it had once been white.

He picked up the dead possum and walked, his bare feet soundless on the faintly worn path.

And he was gone. Grace drew in her breath and tried to slow her racing heart.

The smell of wood smoke began to filter through the bush. And then, cooking meat. Her stomach lurched with hunger. She reached into the pocket of her cloak. A few oats clung to her fingertips. The last of their food.

She gripped Violet's hand. Followed the threads of smoke.

The man looked up from the fire as they approached. The knife lay across his knees. Blood on the blade now. Fur was scattered beside a chopping block. He had skewered the meat on two thin branches and laid them across smoking coals. Behind him was a crude bark and clay hut. Crooked and box-like. Barely tall enough for a person to stand.

A madman, surely. Who else could live in a place so devoid of humanity?

She ought to run. But they were five days' walk from Hobart Town. Miles and mountains from the last settlements. Grace's steps were crooked and her pockets empty.

She swallowed hard. "Perhaps you might help us. We're ever so hungry. And my girl, she's, well, as you can see, she needs a rest and…"

He looked past Violet. Stared at Grace.

"We'll be no bother," she managed. "I swear it."

He backed away from the fire and stood at the edge of the clearing. Grace glanced at the skewered meat. She reached out and carefully lifted a piece from the coals.

The food slid hot down her throat. Her stomach turned over at the forgotten sensation.

When she looked up, the man was gone. She glanced at the hut.

A little piece of inside.

It felt easier to face the forest at night with walls around them, however flimsy they were. Walls offered at least the illusion of security against the spiders and snakes, the devil dogs with razor teeth, the savages who roamed this land like shadows.

She pushed aside the bark door. Inside was dark and windowless. The floor was damp earth, one wall filled with a rough wooden hearth and chimney.

The man sat on a stool beside a crooked table. A rifle leant against the wall behind him.

"Are we to stay here?" Violet asked in a tiny voice.

Grace glanced at the man, searching for some reaction. His face remained unmoved.

"We need to stay here tonight," she said, loudly, clearly. "With you."

He slid back on his stool until his spine was hard against the wall.

Grace ushered Violet into a corner of the hut and laid her cloak across the floor. "Lie down here, angel. Good girl." She glanced at the man, waiting for him to stop them. He stayed motionless, avoiding her eyes. Grace curled up on the floor and wrapped herself around Violet's body. The man leapt up suddenly and grabbed the rifle. He disappeared into the purple dusk.

271

Grace heard herself breathe, loud and fast.

A sudden gunshot, echoing across the forest. Birds shrieked. And then stillness as night crept over the sprawling woods.

She closed her eyes and tried to slow her pounding heart. Stay, and death at the hands of this man was a possibility. Leave, and death in the forest became a certainty.

CHAPTER TWO

He heard breathing that was not his own. He sat, yanked from his dreams with a thumping heart.

The marines come to hang him.

Greenhill with his blood-slick axe.

But then he remembered.

Her.

Pale morning light pushed beneath the door. She lay on her side, chest rising and falling. He stared at her. More than thirteen years since he'd watched a woman sleep. A part of him longed to reach out and touch her. Instead, he drew the rifle close to his body. A little security. He was as afraid of her as she was him.

He was suddenly conscious of the animal blood on his toes, the mat of hair down his back. Aware of his ragged clothes and the stink of him. He pressed a hand into the wiry expanse of his beard and felt his leathery, dirt-encrusted cheek. Felt the hollows beneath his eyes. He was a terrifying and inhuman sight, surely. Only the most desperate of situations could have led her to ask for his help.

Dalton stood and pulled on a yellowing linen shirt. The woman opened her eyes. She sat, face foggy with sleep, and glanced at the hunk of bread on the table.

"May I?"

He nodded. She snatched the remains of the loaf and tore at it hungrily. Chewed slow and loud, savouring the sensation of food on her tongue.

Yes, I know. An incredible feeling.

273

"Thank you." Her voice was husky. She placed the last piece back on the table, nodding towards the girl. "For Violet." She frowned at him. "You don't speak. Why don't you speak? You know English then? You understand me?"

Dalton turned away.

"There ought to be settlements here. Hamilton. Bothwell. Have we gone in the wrong direction?" She began to pace. Her shawl slipped from her shoulders and tangled around her ankle. She kicked it away and tugged at her hair, making white beads of her knuckles. "Are we at least close to civilisation?" She clenched her jaw at his silence. "Get up and put your boots on, Violet."

She'd come too far west. Walked for days in the wrong direction onto the fringe of near-impenetrable bush. Four days or more to Hamilton and her limbs were twigs. No path, just brutal wet mountains laced with natives' spears.

She'd never make it. He could barely believe she'd gotten this far. Leave this hut and a hunger the likes of which she'd never known would take her over. A hunger that quickly became madness. Her only hope of survival was to stay in that hut with him.

But he wanted her gone. This life wasn't made to share with others.

She held out her hand for the girl. "Well," she said, the brassiness in her voice doing little to disguise her fear, "thank you and all. Can you at least show us in the right direction?"

He pointed northeast and handed her a few strips of smoked meat. She nodded her thanks. Dalton turned away to face the emptiness in his hut. But, once she'd left, he stood in the doorway and watched until her grey skirts had vanished into the settling mist.

Before her, his thoughts were simple.

Cold. Tired. Hungry. Afraid.

A life without words, for what words were to be had in this nothingness?

The world Dalton couldn't see had stopped existing. For all he knew, Britain had turned its back on this place, leaving creepers to swallow the huts and gallows. Downpours to wash away the white man's footprints.

The emptiness of the land was beautiful. Never silent, of course; there was always the howl of the wind, the devils' grunts, the patter of rain, of ice against the thatches of his roof. Carolling birds as the sun rose and set. But devoid of words.

If he were to pick up a pencil, would the language he had once known come back? Would he remember the words he had used when he was among the living? Remember that once he had laughed and whispered and shouted the abuse that would see him thrown onto a prison ship?

In the afternoon, he thought to make more bread. Something to keep himself busy after the woman had set his mind rattling.

First, a fire. It had drizzled throughout the day and the undergrowth was damp. He whittled away the wet bark to find the dry hearts of the branches. He set a pile of twigs flickering on last night's ashes, inhaling the scent of wood smoke and damp eucalyptus. He carried the flour into the clearing and poured in the water from the pot he kept beside the woodpile. Stirred it slowly with a stick.

Had he impressed her with all this? The way he could make something from nothing? Bread from crushed seeds and river water. A fire from rain-soaked branches. House from a fallen tree.

Stay out here long enough and the bush begins to give up its secrets. Eat this berry, crush this pod. Dig here, lay a trap there. Instinct, they call it. Like the animals have.

Instinctive animals have no need for language, of course. But as he stirred the dough, words circled through his mind.

Cold. Tired. Hungry. Afraid.

He lifted the stick from the pot and ran its pointed end through the dirt, tracing letters beneath the bluegum.

Greenhill.

He stared at the word for a long time.

"That your name?" she asked. "Greenhill?"

He wasn't surprised to see her. Just surprised it had taken her so long to come back. How far did she get before she realised they were truly surrounded by nothing? Dalton stood and stamped out the writing. His throat felt dry and tight. Why of all the words for all the things on this earth was it *his* name he'd chosen to scribble first?

"No?" She chewed her thumbnail. "Then what?"

For near on eleven years he'd been a ghost, a dead man. Nameless and invisible. He didn't know if he could go back to being real.

He carved a careful 'A'.

Paused. Should he hide himself? Use another man's name? But perhaps if he gave himself his identity back, he could pull together some other pieces of his life he thought were gone forever.

A dreamless night.

His voice.

Careful letters. *Alexander.*

The woman gave a tentative smile. Those hacked curls danced around her cheeks. Dalton saw a sudden beauty that had not been there when her face was twisted in fear.

She took the stick. "Grace," she said, carving her name in childlike letters below his.

And for a moment, they were children in the schoolyard. Lovers carving their names in a tree.

"We've nowhere else to go," she said. "I can't take Violet out into the open again. There ain't nothing out there. Just miles and miles of forest."

Dalton heard a grunt from the back of his throat.

"You've been most kind to us, Alexander. Violet and I are very grateful."

Such a strange thing to hear his name spoken aloud after so much time. How had she found some lingering scrap of *Alexander* within this wild animal? He glanced down at the scribbles.

Alexander and Grace.

Above it, his angry footprints where he had scrubbed out that name.

"Who's Greenhill?" asked Grace.

With a sudden swipe of Dalton's boot, the writing disappeared. He felt a dull ache in his chest. The ache of being Alexander Dalton again.

CHAPTER THREE

Colonial Times, Hobart Town
Tuesday 11ᵗʰ December 1832

'*Ship News*
Dec. 7: Arrived the barque Duckenfield, *from England.*'

"Carry me," said Violet. She clutched a grimy rag doll beneath her chin, its one beady eye peering up at Grace. The stitching of its mouth had come loose and left it with a permanent look of bewilderment.

Grace pulled Violet into her arms, her legs and back aching. Last night's hot supper had brought back little of her strength. Violet wrapped her legs around Grace's hips.

"You're getting too big for this, angel." She walked slowly to the edge of the clearing, drowning under Violet's weight. Alexander disappeared towards the river.

Had she angered him by returning? Those grey eyes were hard to read. She'd eaten the last of his bread. Interrupted his silence. But surely he knew she had no choice. Surely he knew she couldn't take a little girl any further into the open forest.

Five days, she and Violet had been out here. Five days since she'd escaped. She'd swallowed half a pot of paint so they'd take her to the hospital wing where the windows were unbolted for ventilation. They'd fed her castor oil and laudanum. Scrawled in her record. She'd made it out the window and over the gate before emptying her stomach on the edge of the Hobart Road.

There was a fogginess to her memories; the details lost in a drug-induced haze. She remembered little but the walking. The crunch of boots on earth. Back to Harris's house in Hobart Town where she'd plucked Violet from her bed. They'd buried deeper into the woods until the lights of the settlements had disappeared. Grace had woken to an otherworldly pink dawn, Violet curled up beside her.

She looked down at the pot of dough Alexander had abandoned. Should she put it to the fire? Did she need to wait for coals? She'd never been much of a cook.

Violet chewed the end of her blonde plait. "I'm thirsty."

Grace set her down and ushered her inside. Took the canteen from the table and handed it to Violet. She dragged a stool across the hut and used it to prop the door open. A rat darted out from beneath the table. Daylight flooded the room, making stars of the dust motes.

A crooked shelf was hammered high on one wall. Along it sat hunks of wood, finely whittled into human forms. Some were whole bodies; lanky legs, sunken chests. Others just smooth wooden busts, their features meticulously detailed. Eyebrows. Lashes. Buttonholes and ribboned bonnets.

Grace stood close, taken aback by their beauty. She reached out and ran her finger over a dimple in a woman's cheek. Her tiny, motionless eyes stared over Grace's shoulder. Beside her sat an old man with deep wrinkles and a crooked smile.

An exquisite talent. How could a man speak in grunts and go about filthy and half-naked, yet whittle such life into chunks of wood? Grace could sense the personalities of the people who lined the shelf. The seductive woman. Grumpy child. Cheeky old man. Such detail carved by those meaty black paws.

And then, at the very back of the shelf: seven wooden men. Each with beards and long, unkempt hair. Wide haunted eyes. Each so real she expected their chests to rise and fall with breath. Their tortured faces stared into her. She saw coldness, desperation. A little of herself.

"Grace," said Violet, making her start. "I want to go home."

Grace's throat tightened. She ran a hand across Violet's downy hair and kissed the side of her head. Her skin was pale and grimy.

"Papa will be mad when we get home so late," said Violet.

Harris would be looking for them, of course. Perhaps lost in the forest was the safest place for them to be.

Violet stared at the carvings and gnawed the edge of her finger. "I don't like the wooden men."

Grace squeezed her tightly to ward off her own sudden chills.

"I want to go home to the blue house. I want to go and see the sideshow again. I don't like it here."

Tears pricked Grace's eyes and she blinked them away. *No, my darling, I don't like it here either.*

They had stepped onto this foreign soil beneath a blazing, exposed sun. Had sailed out of a wet London summer and watched the sea turn grey, then black, then become green and full of light. As they crossed the equator, seamen dressed as Neptune danced shirtless in the hot evening. And then down they went. Down, down, down to the bottom of the world. Down to the land where her country sent its most unwanted. To the bottom of this prison colony with its roaring oceans and inland sea, neighboured by the great frozen world of the Antarctic. At the end of the earth, Grace was expecting ice and snow.

But when they stepped off the *Duckenfield* that hazy December afternoon – she and the twins and Harris, gripping hold of each other like they were trying to salvage some sense of family – she breathed the air and thought her lungs would turn to fire.

They were marched off the rocky outcrop of Hunter Island to a lodging house in Market Place, Violet clinging to Grace's hand; her sister, Nora, to their father's. All the migrants wore a slightly vacant expression as though they were trying to remember what bizarre twist of fate had led them to this place.

The wharf was lined with warehouses and taverns spilling dishevelled men onto the street. Half-built boats and whaling pots peeked out of workshops. Red-coated marines lined the docks, rifles across their backs. A Union Jack dangled from a flagpole, lolling in the hot wind. But this was no England. Here, the clouds were high and the sky was a vivid, cornflower blue. Men walked the streets with rolled-up shirtsleeves and bare feet. Sunburned foreheads, peeling cheeks. Smells of sea and sweat and the minty fragrance of the great grey-green trees.

Grace squeezed Violet's hand. The motionless earth beneath her feet made her stomach turn. That same awful churning she'd felt as the *Duckenfield* slid out the mouth of the Thames. The hot wind swirled, blowing dust onto her damp cheeks. She swatted at the flies until she grew weary of it and let them settle in clusters on her back.

They queued for two hours outside the lodging house before being herded into a pen of a room with peeling plaster walls. The beds were sagging and covered in stained sheets. Mice scuttled across the floor. Grace wondered if those sent here on His Majesty's pleasure were being treated to the same luxuries as the free settlers.

She didn't sleep that night. Just sat up in bed, hugging her knees. There were no curtains in the lodging house and an orange glow from the street lamps lit the room. Beside her, Harris lay on his back, snoring in a deep, sweaty sleep. Violet and Nora were curled up at his feet in thin cotton nightgowns; their matching mouths open, matching eyelids fluttering. A fly crawled across Nora's cheek.

On either side of them were two more beds, each filled with people. The room stank of breath and hot bodies. Grace got up and wove through the maze of beds, stepping over drawers stuffed with sleeping babies. Below them, the street was almost empty. A policeman on horseback paced through the dust and a dog pressed its nose beneath a warehouse door. Through the open window, Grace heard the faint clop of hooves. An owl hooting. The sea slapping the docks. And between these frail sounds of life was a great, overwhelming emptiness.

What she would have given for sooty skies and dung-filled streets. For street vendors and Bow Bells and clunks and hollers and shrieks and the filthy all-night-ness of London.

This will be a great adventure for us, Harris had said, striding down the hallway of his house in Covent Garden and shaking the tickets in the air. Grace had been drawn in by his excitement, the way she was drawn in by everything else about him. There was a foolishness in her she hadn't been able to see until it was illuminated by Hobart Town's orange light. A need to rise above herself, which had sucked her towards Harris like riptide.

Across the room, a bed creaked.

"What's the matter, Gracie?" Harris was leaning up on one elbow, his nightshirt sliding off his shoulder. The waves of his pale brown hair hung about his cheeks. He climbed out of bed and stood behind her at the window. Wrapped one arm around her middle and traced his fingers down her arm. She shivered and pressed herself against him, needing his familiarity. He pushed aside her long brown plait and kissed her neck.

"Come to bed. You need to sleep. Everything will seem better in the morning."

She closed her eyes at the feel of his lips against her skin. "You're right." She reached behind her and ran her fingers through his salt-hardened hair. "A great adventure."

She felt Harris's lips turn up against her neck. "That's my girl."

She looked out at the vast, foreign sky, glittering with unfamiliar stars. A thin peal of laughter rose from the drunkards by the docks. Grace leaned out the window, straining, straining towards that fragile sound of happiness.

CHAPTER FOUR

As the sun drooped towards the horizon, Grace began to wonder if Alexander had left.

Don't panic, she told herself. She had the gun, the hut, the fire. Still, she felt a surge of relief when his footsteps crackled up to the clearing. He had hacked off the length of his hair and it lay sleek and jagged against his neck. His skin had been scrubbed free of the film of black filth. A tattered linen shirt clung to his wet shoulders, dark coils of hair escaping out the open neck.

A dead creature dangled from his fist – something rat-like, but larger, with the tiny front paws and pointed snout of a kangaroo. He flopped the furry body onto the chopping block.

"You caught that? Without the gun?"

He slid a knife down the animal's belly.

"You got traps set up out there?"

He nodded without looking at her.

"I was afraid you weren't coming back."

He pulled out a trail of intestines and flung them into the scrub.

Grace chewed her thumbnail. "You're wondering, no doubt, what in hell I'm doing out here with a six-year-old girl."

Alexander didn't take his eyes off the animal. If he truly had been wondering about her, he was damn good at hiding it. Grace watched for some reaction from him. A flicker of the eyes, a movement of his lips beneath that dense black and silver beard. Nothing. His expressions hidden, age hidden. Could have been anywhere between twenty-five and fifty.

He smacked the knife into the tree stump and took the head off the animal. His silence made Grace's voice seem louder, garish with its east London vowels, cutting through the slop, slop of his slaughtering.

"It was right foolish of me to come out here, I know it. But I had to run away. It's Violet's father, you see, in Hobart Town. He's treated me awful bad and I was so afraid of what he would do to the girls that I didn't think this through. I suppose I thought we'd come across the northern settlements if we kept walking. Somewhere I could keep Violet safe, then go back for her sister."

In her head, the escape had been the only hard part. She'd spent weeks memorising the attendants' schedules, committing the layout of the compound to her mind's eye. She'd given little thought to what would happen once she made it out that window. Surely it would be no more than a day's walk to the next settlement. With no money, she'd have relied on charity when they arrived, but she felt certain they'd find someone willing to give a bed to lost women and children.

But what was in her head was much different to the reality. She'd avoided the main road, so she wouldn't be caught. Had no thought it might be the only road. The lights of the next settlement hadn't appeared when they were supposed to. The earth had risen. The undergrowth thickened and tangled. And the sun had dipped below the horizon leaving her and Violet lost in the dark with nothing but a pocket of stolen oats and flint. Her first night in Hobart Town, Grace had feared the wildness of this land, but tucked up safe in the settlement, well that was nothing. This unclaimed forest was a place from a dark fairy-tale. A world of ghosts and shadows and nameless creatures beyond the reaches of her imagination. She'd made up names for them to try and keep Violet calm.

"That's just a curly bear. A golden goose. A wriggly worm."

One night became two, then three, four, five. Days of crawling through mud and clambering over the monstrous mossy corpses of fallen trees. Days of torn, bloody hands and aching feet. Hysterical tears and desperate prayers. They spent hours traversing what could barely have been a mile. With each day came the slow dawning of the expanse of this place. As the pile of oats grew smaller and their stomachs shrank with emptiness, Grace saw that they would die out here. Her own foolishness would bring about Violet's death.

"I don't understand how there can be nothing out here," she told Alexander, pacing in front of the chopping block. "Where I come from you can't walk more than half a day without reaching another village. When I was a girl my sister and me once walked from Stepney to Cheshunt and back to fetch a flour grinder off my aunt. You been to London? Never? What are you, some country dandy? An Irishman? Took us all day to get there, mind. Got chatting with some lad who reckoned he knew our ma, but it turned out he were just trying to get up our skirts.

"Anyway, I'm damn glad me and Violet came across you when we did, what with your fire and your traps and all. We was nearly out of oats and then Lord knows what we would have done."

She forced a smile, but he didn't look at her. He just peeled the skin off that creature like he was turning a coat inside out. Grace pulled her cloak tighter around her shoulders.

"This land, it ain't like nothing I ever seen before. So wild, like even God never been here. You're the first person we've seen in four days. When I was a girl there were eight of us living in one room. Couldn't scratch yourself without getting an elbow in your face. I never imagined there was a place on this earth you could walk for four days and not see another soul."

She glanced at Violet, who was sitting in the doorway making her doll dance on her knees. She swallowed hard. "These girls, they mean more to me than you could ever know. I love them like they're my own. I loved their mother too, and I promised her on her death bed I'd do all I could to keep her babies safe." She felt a stabbing in her throat as she thought of Nora back in Hobart with her father and the convict workers. "I couldn't get her sister out. Their father came home before I could get her out of bed. But I'll go back for her. I'll find some place safe for Violet and go back for Nora. I'll go back for her if it kills me."

Still nothing from Alexander. Suddenly she despised him; so cold and silent while she wrenched her heart open in front of that stupid slab of dead rat.

"Nothing then? Not even a nod? A cough?" She wanted suddenly to strike him, tear words from his lips. Her fists flew into his arm, pounding, pounding, trying to shake out an answer. He dropped the knife and grabbed her wrists. Grace struggled against his grip, then gave up, stilled. His grey eyes looked past her.

"I'm sorry," she coughed. "I'm sorry."

His grip tightened, then he released her suddenly, picking up the knife and turning back to the meat. Grace stumbled backwards, her breath short. She held out her hand to Violet.

"Perhaps we should leave you a while. Have a walk or something. Won't we, angel."

And so they walked, her and Violet, hand in hand along the narrow path worn through the scrub. Threads of late afternoon sun shone through the trees. The evening chorus of birds was beginning; a great wall of trills and shrieks and bells. The river roared to their left.

"Not the river," said Violet, her hand tensing in Grace's.

They turned and began to walk in the opposite direction.

"We going home now, Nanny Grace?"

She thought of Harris's vast rolling paddocks in Hobart Town; a place she'd never call home. He had bought the land before they'd left London. For two thousand pounds he'd put his name to fifteen hundred acres of the finest farming land on the edge of the settlement.

"Fifteen hundred acres, Gracie," he'd announced, the day he came home with the deeds in his valise. "All mine. Can you imagine?"

Now how could she imagine such a thing? Fifteen hundred acres? The words meant nothing to her. He opened the papers with a flourish.

Fifteen hundred acres. Covent Garden to Whitechapel.

How was it possible that a man who wasn't the king could own so much land? Even the richest men in London had houses jostling their neighbours' for space on the street.

That was the allure for Harris, of course, all that property to his name. Heard of it from a friend emigrated to Sydney Town. Fortunes to be made in wool, in wheat, in land ownership. He spoke of it like it was a paradise across the water.

But when they came to that precious land, it was just miles and miles of coarse brown grass and tangled, wiry scrub. The forest pushed onto the western edge of their land; a vast bank of ancient, gnarled tress they were too afraid to venture into. On the edge of the property, close to the dirt road, Harris strung a sheet of canvas from a tree and hammered three edges into the earth.

Home.

Grace had grown up drinking from the drains in Stepney and had never had such miserable lodgings.

"Well," she said, too brightly, one girl attached to each hand. "There sure is plenty of space." She didn't know what she had been expecting. But it wasn't this.

They spent the first three nights bathed in dust while the girls screeched themselves silly at the depth of the darkness. Grace took them outside to the rolling black expanse of their father's land. Behind them, the mountain rose solid and lightless. Mosquitoes hummed around their ears. Grace looked upwards. An eruption of silver light.

"Look," she said. "It ain't darkness. Did you ever see so many stars?" No clouds for them to hide behind. No lamps to dim their brilliance. They sat with their necks craned, trying to count the things until she felt the girls go heavy in her arms. On the fourth night they found a snake under Nora's pillow and Grace demanded Harris take them back to the lodging house until his palace had a floor.

She never saw much of that floor, in the end. He had her sent away before the house even had walls.

She'd gotten far too close to him. She saw that with such clarity now.

She was seventeen when she became his wife's lady's maid; the most coveted position in the household that Grace, with no experience, had little right to step into. She didn't know a tiara from a turban, and the only curling tongs she'd ever seen were the ones she'd dug out of the Thames in the mudlarking days of her childhood. For the mop fair, she borrowed a dress from the woman in the room above them who bragged she'd once been on the stage. It was a ridiculous pink powder puff of a thing with rosette sleeves that made Grace look like a wedding cake. It was inches too long and so tight around the shoulders she could barely lift her arms. Her mother laughed as she sucked on her pipe.

"What you playing at? You think anyone's going to hire you looking like that?" She gave a loud, wet cough. "God made a place for everyone. And I'm sorry to say it, my treasure, but you're stuck down here with your old ma."

Grace said nothing. She'd argue with her mother after she'd proved her wrong. She went into the street and peered at her reflection in a shop window. Crammed her hair beneath a ratty straw bonnet and practiced the smile a man had once told her had made him forget where he was going.

She'd settle for washerwoman, be overjoyed with scullery maid. Anything that might get her out of the leaky lodging house and the bed crawling with her sisters' snotty fingers. Anything to prove God had a damn better place in mind for her than this.

She stood among the other job seekers with their pressed aprons and *how do you do, my lady*s. Watched them thrust glowing references into the hands of wealthy employers. She'd be going home to Stepney tonight for certain. Back to stale bread and the sticky-handed monster God had deemed she share a bed with.

But then, there he was, Mr James Harris, the young customs attorney after a lady's maid for his new wife. He had a jawline like a Roman statue and eyes that shone like pebbles in the rain. He wore a dark blue frock coat and a tie of silver silk. Grace flashed her most disorienting smile. Harris took off his top hat and rubbed his freshly shaved cheek.

"You have experience?"

"Oh yes, sir. Of course."

His lips turned up. "Are you lying?"

"Yes sir, I am. Whatever gave it away?"

Harris laughed and looked her up and down. His grin widened as he took in the pink monstrosity of her gown. Grace's cheeks flushed. Her eyes hardened.

"I got no experience, sir, but you'll not find anyone who wants to work as much as I do. And you'll not find anyone who'll learn half as fast as me."

Harris tilted his head. His eyes met hers and something passed between them. "You'll be good for my wife," he said with a gentle smile. "She has a knack of taking life a little too seriously."

Gratitude flooded over her. She curtseyed low. "Thank you, sir. Thank you. You ain't going to regret it."

It wasn't until the first night of her new position, when a plate of mutton was set in front of her, that Grace realised she'd spent the rest of her life hungry. The gnawing in her belly had been such a fixture she'd ceased to notice it. As she felt her stomach press against her bodice for the first time in her life, she vowed she'd never go wanting again.

The Harrises' lives were filled with silk dresses, red wine and Beethoven. A great three-storey terrace house on Maiden Lane with pale blue walls that made Grace think of the sea. Wind chimes in the entrance hall sang when a breeze moved through the house. Though Grace was lacing the gowns instead of wearing them, and carrying the wine glasses instead of drinking from them, she was besotted with the luxury of her new home.

The lady of the house, Charlotte, was a great porcelain-doll beauty: fair and fragile, polite and sweet. She moved in willowy whispers of pink and blue silk. Next to her, Grace felt like a mess scraped off the bottom of someone's shoe.

But when the twins claimed their mother's life, Grace took her place indecently quickly.

Harris, lonely, full of brandy. Grace, lovestruck at nineteen with no prospects of marriage. He called her beautiful and poured her a drink. Waited until the rest of the staff were asleep and led her upstairs by the hand. Oh, she kept the promise she'd made to Charlotte and looked after those babies like they were her own. But she was in her husband's bed before the girls were crawling. Kept on as the twins' nurse, her pay bumped up to thirty pounds a year. Enough to buy her silence.

"We shan't tell anyone about us, shall we," Harris whispered, panting into her ear. And she smiling, nodding, unbuttoning. Pretending the secret was to protect the beauty of their love and not a gentleman's reputation. She told herself she pitied him; this generous man widowed at just twenty-five. But there was far more lust and greed than pity in her. She'd seen James Harris as her step out of poverty since the day he'd plucked her from the mop fair. As his mistress, she saw an even greater chance. Soon she'd be the one in silk dresses, drinking wine from crystal goblets. The shadow of herself stealing from the markets to survive began to fade away.

He bought her silk petticoats that sighed when she walked. Sometimes she'd go without drawers to feel them slither against her skin. When there was no one around, he'd help her practice her letters, taught her to play *Home, Sweet Home* on the piano. She'd sit beside him on the bench, his shoulder pressing against hers. She'd play with the flattest hands you ever saw, so he'd lift them in his own and curl her fingers over the keys. He sang along in a syrupy voice, pausing patiently when she found the wrong chords.

Mid pleasures and palaces though we may roam
Be it ever so humble, there's no place like home.

Harris was a gambling man; a frequenter of the Whist tables at White's gentleman's club. He prided himself on being a winner; on parading his overflowing pockets in front of his adoring mistress.

But then, a dispute, he said. Came home in morning sunlight with his shirt untucked and his top hat bent. One cheek was red and swollen. The girls, near on five, sat either side of Grace at the breakfast table, kneeling up in their chairs and chasing slivers of egg around their plates. Thank the Lord they barely noticed their father stumbling in like a vagrant.

A dispute. Harris had accused the Earl of Wilton of cheating. Refused to pay the fifty pounds owed. Fist to the jaw.

"Just pay the man, James," said Grace. "Swallow your pride and pay him quick smart. Get him out of your life." She'd never stood up to him before. Never argued, never questioned. But even she knew fifty pounds wasn't worth another thrashing for a man as wealthy as James Harris.

He flung his hat onto the table. He stank of sweat and cigar smoke. Violet cowered in her seat as he strode past.

"It's not about the money," he said. "It's the principle of the thing." The goddamn principle of the thing.

The next night they came to the house; the Earl of Wilton and his footmen. They pushed past Ann at the front door and charged into the parlour. Harris leapt from his armchair. Grace and the girls were reading by the fire. Nora leapt into Grace's lap. Violet hovered at her shoulder, tugging at her shawl. The men shouted all at once, like they were ever going to come to any agreement like that.

One of the earl's men threw a wild punch. Harris ducked, cursed and swung at the man. He called for his valet and footmen. Grace tried to stand. Nora's arms were clamped around her neck, Violet dangling from her back.

"Get the girls out, Grace, for God's sake," hissed Harris. "Now!"

The men stumbled towards them, all curses and wild arms. A stray fist flew into the crystal vase on the mantel above their heads. Nora shrieked and down the thing came, crashing onto her sister's head. Grace felt the shards explode against her cheek. Blood poured from a gash on Violet's forehead and ran into her fluttering eyes. Harris pulled off his cravat and pressed it to Violet's head.

"Why didn't you get them out?" he demanded.

Grace felt rage bubble inside her. She left the door open as the surgeon stitched closed Violet's tiny forehead. Let Harris hear his daughter scream. She flung the bloodied cravat onto his bed sheets.

See what you have done. You and your goddamn pride.

She saw regret behind his eyes.

Harris was an intensely private man. He kept his emotions walled-up behind polished manners and a deep honeyed voice. After the incident with Violet, he said little, but vanished to White's more often than before. *To ease the guilt,* he said, when Grace finally pried an explanation from him. To help him forget how he had failed his daughter.

He came home at midnight and climbed up to Grace's attic room; slid into her bed and pressed himself against her.

He was jittery and restless. He pulled his arms around her tightly. "I don't blame you for what happened to Violet," he breathed. And then, for the first and only time, said, "I love you, Grace."

She held her breath. James Harris had been her path to security. She'd not meant to fall in love with him. And yet love had found her, with an intensity that made her ache. She'd never spoken of it, sure it would never be reciprocated. She was a product of the Stepney slums, he a handsome lawyer of the gentry. She had no right to love him, or expect love in return.

His declaration hung in the dark. Grace was afraid to speak, as though any words from her might scare his away. Instead, she pressed her lips hard against his and breathed in his heady scent of rosewater and brandy.

She woke to an empty bed. Harris stood up from the breakfast table when she arrived downstairs clutching Nora's hand. He looked at her with distant eyes. Eyes that knew he'd made a terrible mistake. Eyes that said: *you are not their mother. You are not my wife.*

He cleared his throat. "The nursery washbin needs emptying, Miss

Ashwell."

They slid back into their roles as employer and employee with alarming speed. Grace was sure she'd be out of a job soon. She starting asking around. Signed herself up for the next mop fair. Glanced at the job pages of Harris's newspapers.

But then he came home early one day, all serious and glowing about the eyes. He called Grace down from the nursery. She was sure he was about to let her go. Instead, he sat beside her on the sofa and took her hand. She felt a fluttering in her chest.

And how his eyes lit up when he talked about that place. His Majesty's Australian Colonies. The land and the wheat and the opportunities, all those damn opportunities.

"A prison colony," Grace said, for her cousin had been sent out there for stealing a pair of shoes.

"Not just a prison colony. Not anymore. We've been there forty years or more now. Made a real civilisation of it." Harris filled a glass and brought it to his lips. "New land has come up for sale on the southern island. Van Diemen's Land. They say it's the best farming land in the colony."

"You don't know nothing about farming."

He smiled. "My friend Richard in Sydney Town has told me all about it. He's got himself a fine wheat crop. Thinks I could do the same. Get myself a few convicted men to do the toughest jobs. They say they're good workers. Happy to do anything after they've been spared the rope. I'm sure I've it in me to do this. And the change will do us the world of good."

Grace saw he had his mind made up. Couldn't say a thing to change it. She felt something in her throat clamp up. "I'll miss you then," she said.

Harris gave a gentle laugh. He squeezed her hand. "Gracie," he said, "I want you to come with us."

She lifted the glass from his hand and took a long gulp. "Bloody hell."

Her world went as far as the marshes in Cheshunt. A day's walk. That day, the earth had seemed to go on forever. Harris's friend in Sydney Town and her thieving cousin, they'd just been shipped around the river bend, hadn't they? It was impossible to imagine the world going further than the snaking brown mire of the Thames.

Harris slid across the sofa so his knee pressed against hers. "It will be a great adventure. In a new world."

Grace managed a brandy-warmed smile.

Harris squeezed her knee. "You know, Gracie, in Hobart Town no one will think to bat an eyelid at you and me. We'll not have to hide any longer. Who we are, where we're from; it won't matter. We can live as husband and wife. Be a real family."

That was the clincher, of course. She saw herself in silks and lacy bonnets, walking on Harris's arm through his forest of wheat. No longer just the nurse. No longer just the mistress. The allure of it was intense. That great open land with all its opportunity.

He leaned in and kissed her, his tongue hot with brandy. "Think on it," he said.

But she didn't need to think.

Until they left London, it was all make-believe. They'd packed up the house, said their farewells, but they'd be back soon, wouldn't they? London was all Grace knew. How could it not be a part of her life?

But then, there they were in the cab to the docks, all their worldly goods packed into wooden trunks. The dome of Saint Paul's grew smaller and smaller until it disappeared into the bank of cloud. Out of the soupy sky, three skeletal masts appeared.

Duckenfield.

The weight of it swung at her suddenly. They weren't just going around the river bend. Her neck prickled. She tried to gulp down more air, her lungs straining against her corset.

Harris put a hand over hers. "A great adventure, Gracie. What we need."

Her heart banged against her ribs.

Turn around. Please. I can't do this.

She couldn't get the words out. What would he think of her? A coward, that's what. No sense of adventure. No seizing the bloody opportunity. He'd probably throw open the carriage and kick her out without even bothering to slow down. And then she'd be forced to crawl back to Stepney with her tail between her legs while the loves of her life sailed off the edge of the earth. She couldn't bear to lose them. Couldn't bear to lose her life of pianos and red wine. Without Harris she'd be back at

Leadenhall Market, pawning her petticoats and sliding stolen eggs beneath her shawl.

And so she got on that ship. Watched everything she knew fade into a white haze. Harris stood behind her at the gunwale and said, "I'm going to marry you in Hobart Town."

Grace concentrated on counting her breaths to stop herself from collapsing.

On and on Harris bleated about his *great adventure* between those hideous bouts of seasickness. When the ocean grew so big Grace thought it would swallow them whole.

Harris had unrolled the world map ceremoniously across the dining table and traced a finger along their route. Hugging South America, rounding the Cape, across that vast stretch of unbroken sea. Atlantic Ocean. Indian Ocean. Southern Ocean.

Well, all those bloody oceans look the same when you got your head between your knees coughing your kidneys into a bucket. She never imagined the world could go on so long. Never imagined they could travel so many days and nights and still have nothing around them but sea.

For four months they lived in a cabin smaller than Grace's attic room. Slept in bunks with raised edges that kept the sea from spitting them out in the night. They ate cabbage and pickled fish. Salted meat and suet. At night, Grace lay awake listening to the ship groan. She could hear the coughs and snores of fifty other migrants through the paper-thin bulkheads.

She longed to walk down the Strand and hear the chimes of Saint Mary's. Longed to sit in their parlour in Covent Garden with the girls squeezed onto her lap, books in hand. But with each watery mile, that life grew further away. The blue house drifted to the furthest edge of the world.

A great adventure.

She ought to have known how easy it would be for him to be rid of her. Even in an upside-down world where the land baked at Christmas, a man still wielded the power. A woman could only argue her point so many times before she found herself a prisoner.

Grace and Violet returned tentatively to the hut. Alexander was crouched by the fire, holding two skewered slabs of meat over the coals. The rest of the carcass sat in pieces on the chopping block.

"I'm sorry for my outburst. It's just that… well, I'm afraid."

He looked up.

"I thought it would be easier. Find the northern settlements and earn some money. Make enough to get me and the twins back to London."

Creases appeared in the corners of his eyes. A smile?

"What?" she snapped. "You think I'm mad for trying to protect my girls?"

He turned the meat.

"Well, I don't care what you think." She clenched her jaw. She did care. Greatly. She knew what happened when people thought you mad. "I know now it won't be easy. I'm sure there are people looking for us. And I know what the forest is like. But somehow, I'll get us back to England. I swear it. Just you watch." She tilted her head and watched Alexander curiously. "You can speak, can't you? You's just choosing not to. Why? You afraid of what will come out if you open your mouth?"

He lowered his eyes.

Violet was snuffling around in the ferns beside the hut. Grace watched her pull the narrow leaves from the fern fronds and carry them in her pinny. The rag doll was stuffed beneath her arm, eye gazing at the clouds.

"I'm making a bed for Rosie," Violet announced. "A bed of leaves, like ours. Nice and warm cos she don't got no coat."

Grace smiled.

'She *does not have a coat*, Violet,' she imagined Harris sighing. She liked it when a little of the east rolled off the girls' polished West End tongues.

She stood, feeling useless. An intruder. "Perhaps I can do something to help, Alexander? Perhaps I can cook that for you?" She leaned towards him, but he held up a dirt-streaked palm, blocking her way. "Water," she said. "I can collect us some more water. Shall I fill the pot then? From the river?" She snatched the heavy iron pot from beside the woodpile. Violet looked up from the ferns.

"I'm going to the river to fetch more water, angel," said Grace. "Do you want to come with me?" Violet's forehead crinkled. She crammed her pinny in her mouth, the leaves scattering at her feet.

"She's afraid of the river," Grace told Alexander. "She don't like how fast the water moves. Will you watch her? Just for a moment?"

He paused. Gave a slight nod. Violet's eyes widened.

"I'll not be long, angel. I promise. You stay here."

Violet stared at the swarthy figure hunched over the fire. She picked up her doll and hugged it to her chest.

When Grace returned, lugging the pot up the path, Violet was still watching Alexander like a hawk. She ran up the path and flung her arms around Grace's waist, Rosie tossed face down in the dirt.

Alexander lifted the meat off the fire and held it out to Grace.

"You don't got no plates?"

He scratched his beard, his forehead creasing in thought. He laid the meat back against the coals and wandered into the bush, returning with two small sheets of bark. Grace smiled slightly.

"There's three of us."

He marched back into the bush and returned with a third, smaller piece of bark. Grace laid the meat on the three wooden plates. The largest serving for Alexander. Smallest for Violet.

She looked up and he was watching; eyes right on her. For a second she saw behind them. Saw pity, compassion, the soul of a man. He turned away hurriedly.

CHAPTER FIVE

Conduct Record of Convicts Arriving in Van Diemen's Land 1804-1830

Alexander Dalton, Caledonia *1820*
May 22ⁿᵈ, 1821: Assault and beating his overseer in Oxley. Fifty lashes and gaol
gang labour for three months and to be confined at nights.

He followed her to the river. Several yards behind so he might stay hidden. She bent to unlace her boots, slide off her stockings. White knees, stick-thin calves.

She began to unbutton her dress. Dalton realised he was holding his breath. There was something about the way her fingers pulled at that row of buttons down her chest that made him need to watch.

Curiosity, that was all. Just curiosity.

A woman's dress was such a novelty to him. A woman's fingers. A woman's skin. He'd forgotten these things.

He felt a sudden urge to touch. He tensed his fingers against the tree he was leaning on. Bark crumbled into his palm.

She'd been here a week. No, closer to two. Had built herself a bed where he could hear her breathe in the night. She had him eating off plates and writing his name. Had left his fingers tingling where their skin had touched. Fingers he thought too hardened to feel any sensation again.

This wasn't meant to happen. He was the only person in the world.

She stood knee deep in the coppery water, her shift pooling around her like a lily. She pounded her petticoats against the rock with fragile white arms. Her grey dress lay on the bank. She had not chosen to wear such a dress. He felt this instinctively. Someone had given it to her; forced her into it perhaps. She was not a wearer of grey. She was pinks and blues and yellows. *Why the grey dress?*, he wondered, listening to the *thwack, thwack* of linen against stone. She stepped out of the water, her underclothes clinging to the narrow curves of her legs. What would she do, he wondered, if he came from the trees and put his hand to her face, or her arm, or the protrusion of her hips? Would she believe it if he said, *I just want to remember? I just want to remember how it feels to be human.*

"What are you doing, angel?" Grace sang suddenly, seeking the girl out over her shoulder. She squeezed the water from her shift and stepped into her dress. She flung her wet petticoats over the mossy branches of a gumtree that arched over the river. Laughter. "You trying to dig your way to China?" She ran into the forest after the girl and Dalton was alone.

Her wet skirts fluttered in the breeze like sail cloth. The mud hadn't all washed out. They were becoming the colour of tea. Had they once been white?

White petticoats, he thought, and suddenly there was a girl attached to them. Blonde hair, with freckled skin and firm breasts. Maggie? Sally? Her name was lost to him. All he remembered was the velvety feel of her, his hands exploring every inch of skin. Her breath against his ear, the soft sigh of muslin when the petticoats dropped to the floor. Yes, once he'd been just like any other man.

Grace's petticoats danced in the wind like there were legs inside them. Dalton stepped closer. Touched. He felt the coarse thread of them; saw the crooked stitching on the hems. Stains that couldn't be washed away. The grey of river muck, rusty bloodstains, great green streaks where the bush had left its mark. He felt hot and disoriented.

"What in hell do you think you're doing?" She yanked the skirts from the tree and bundled them into her arms. "In case you didn't know, it ain't the done thing to go about playing with women's underclothes."

He was vaguely aware what he'd done was wrong. Vaguely aware of these social outlines. He wanted to explain the way the rest of the world dropped away once you left it. Away, with its rules and codes and finely whittled etiquette.

"How long you been there?" she asked icily. "Come to watch, did you?"

Yes, come to watch. The pull towards humanity, towards her, was intoxicating. Terrifying.

He had to put an end to it.

Grace ran into the forest with the petticoats in her arms. "Look Violet," he heard her say. "Let's take this branch. We can sweep the floor with it, like we done in Hobart... This one's a pretty colour. Why don't you put it in your hair? All right, angel, you pick one for me too. Mind the bugs now."

Dalton walked back to the hut and sat at the table. The nose of his rifle stuck out from beneath his sleeping pallet. He stared at it.

Look at her and her helpless predicament. He'd be doing her a favour, putting an end to her hopeless life.

He crawled towards his locker and opened the cartridge box. Five balls. His supplies were getting low. Powder flask; far too close to empty. He poured powder into the rifle and slid in the ball. Slowly, carefully. He was out of practice.

Three rounds a minute, he thought suddenly. Something heaved itself up from deep in his memory. Once, he could fire three rounds a minute. And suddenly he was back in Gibraltar with sunburned cheeks and a rifle across his shoulder, beating rhythmic footsteps in tight-fitting boots.

He'd joined the army out of necessity. What love did a pauper from Kilkenny have for England? His dead mother surely rolled over in her devout Catholic grave, spitting *curse of God on you, Alexander. How can you risk your life for that vagrant King George?*

Well, sorry, Ma, but a man's got to eat.

He'd been the son of a fleshmonger in Ireland, but as a military private, he was at the very bottom of the pile. He couldn't stand the state of this world where men were ranked like horses.

Yes, sir. No, sir. He'd never been much good at yes, sir; no, sir. Eat, sleep, shit when you're told.

"What am I, sir, your fucking dog?"

They had him pegged as a troublemaker from the beginning.

"Do we have a problem, Mr Dalton?"

"Aye, sir. A big problem."

Knocked out the captain's teeth with the butt of his rifle.

From the sun-bleached cliffs of Gibraltar to the battered shores of Van Diemen's Land.

It is therefore adjudged by this court that you be transported upon the seas…

The bush had let Dalton forget he was ever a soldier. A fat, grim chunk of the past he'd managed to bury. But yes, he felt very comfortable with a rifle in his hands.

He heard Grace's voice floating on the wind. "Look, Violet, see that bird? Ain't he a colourful one!"

He imagined putting her in the earth. He'd give her a proper grave, a proper burial. After all, it wasn't really her that was the problem. She'd just gotten in his way. Stepped into a space that was only made for one. Crowded him into the corner of this vast, empty land. And when there was another person about, well then there was that human desire to share. To say, *all right then, Grace, you've told me your story. Are you ready for mine?*

Three rounds a minute.

He'd find her a nice spot by the river. Lay her out with her shawl beneath her head like she was just in the deepest of sleeps. Then he'd sit all night in the clearing and listen to the silence. Let himself sink back into a solitary stillness where his memories turned to dust.

He stood. The gun felt heavy in his hand. He wished he'd done it the moment he'd found her. Then, she was just a body. Now she was a real woman, with a story behind her. It was harder this way.

Her head and shoulders rose above the green explosion of tree ferns.

He never fired the gun if he could help it. Who knew how far the sound would travel? Who knew who could be listening? Only if the traps were empty and there was no flour and the wild berries were staved off by ice. Or if he'd ceased to be the world's only living inhabitant.

The night she'd arrived, he'd pulled the trigger and sent the bullet into the sky so he'd not be tempted to use it. The echo had coursed through his body. Shaken him to the core.

He'd not gone far enough into the bush. He saw that now. The settlers were pressing themselves up against the edges of the forest. Red-coated marines and overseers with their bullwhips. He ought to have gone deeper, higher, further. West. But in the west, the forest rose and darkened. No possums stirred the trees. The birdcalls were few and distant. He'd seen that western bush and it was full of death.

A place man did not survive.

Grace watched him bring the rifle to his shoulder. One eye closed, the other squinting down the barrel. *Must be possums in that tree*, she told herself. Up there in those twisted grey branches.

She knew nothing about this man, she realised. Not a thing. A madman? Murderer? Or just a self-sufficient hunter?

"Violet," she whispered. "I want you to lie on the ground. Be as still as you can."

"Like the Mary statue?"

"That's right, angel, just like the Mary statue."

She sucked in her breath and stood. "Alexander? Are you hunting?"

He didn't move. He stood several yards away, poised liked a soldier in battle.

"Nothing in the traps then?" She glanced upwards. "What will you shoot? A possum?"

He opened his eye. Kept the rifle resting against his shoulder.

"Did you not see Violet and me down there?" She tried to push the tremor from her voice. "Let us get back safe to the hut and then you shoot, all right?" She stepped towards him until she was inches from the barrel. She swallowed hard and looked him in the eye. "You want to kill me, you'll have to do it to my face." She reached out and touched the cold metal. Pushed it downwards. Alexander jerked the rifle and fired into the scrub where Violet was lying. Grace shrieked and dove towards the girl. Violet lay motionless, her eyes wide, fingers clinging to the ferns. Grace pulled her from the ground and squeezed her to her chest. Her hands trembled violently.

"You animal! Why do you want to hurt her? She's just a little girl!"

Alexander looked towards Grace's feet. She glanced down too. A thick seam of blood was edging towards her boots. She held Violet out in front of her, searching frantically for any injury. Alexander reached down and lifted the carcass of a wallaby from the scrub. He gripped it in his fist and stepped back over the tangled undergrowth. Violet watched wordlessly, clinging to Grace's neck. Blood from the dead animal dripped over the ferns.

"We've nowhere to go," Grace called shakily. "I'd leave you, but we ain't got nowhere else to go." Tears threatened to spill down her cheeks. "I'm begging you. Please don't hurt my girl."

Alexander looked over his shoulder and met her eyes. She looked back into them. The cinder grey of storm clouds. His cheeks and chin were covered in so much woolly black hair she could see little skin. But deep into those eyes she saw. There was loss in them, and suffering and shame.

He walked back towards the hut, the wallaby carcass in his fist and the rifle bumping against his thigh. Grace kept her eyes on him until he disappeared. She and Violet clung to one another.

"Are you all right, angel?" she asked finally, her voice husky.

"I don't like him," Violet whispered. "I don't like the bear man."

Grace carried her to the edge of the clearing, afraid to venture too deep into the forest; afraid to be close to Alexander. She heard him skin the wallaby. Smelled the meat smoking on the fire.

Night fell quickly; cold and solid. Violet lay in Grace's arms, blinking wearily. A blanket of clouds had drifted over the moon. Grace shivered. Early May. The edge of winter in this upside-down land.

She stroked Violet's hair. It was greasy and tangled beneath her fingers.

My little angel. I'm sorry for all I've done to you.

She kissed her forehead at the place the vase had struck her, feeling the dent of the scar beneath her lips.

"Nanny Grace?" Violet's voice was thick with sleep. "Do you remember the sideshow? By the river?"

"Yes, angel."

"What was your favourite thing?"

"My favourite thing?" She hesitated. Truly, she remembered little of the sideshow. The Palace of Curiosities had come to London the day after the earl had sent the vase crashing onto Violet's head. Grace remembered little but her blinding fury at Harris, her need to get the girls out of the house. She had vague memories of the twins in fur-trimmed coats, their mittened hands in hers. A trail of coloured flags, hairy men and tattooed women. The details were blurred by anger. And then, her own guilt: Violet complaining her head ached and Grace knowing she ought to have been home in bed.

That night, Harris had ranted and screamed, all red-cheeked and brandy breath.

"What were you doing taking her out, Grace? What in hell were you thinking?"

"My favourite thing was the mermaid lady," said Violet. "I liked her long hair."

Grace was glad she remembered the sideshow fondly. "Perhaps when we go back to London we can visit her again."

Violet fell asleep, limp and heavy in Grace's lap. She wrapped the girl in her cloak and laid her on the mossy ground. She rolled her tired shoulders, stretched her neck. Violet was too big, too heavy. Grace couldn't carry her much longer.

She could hear Alexander clattering about in his wooden chest.

The hut was too small for three of them. Shelter for three, food for three. A much different sum than food and shelter for one. They were a burden to be shot at like wild dogs. But where could they go? She'd be locked up if she went back to Hobart Town. And heaven only knew how many more days until the forest cleared and showed the next settlement.

She'd wait out here until Alexander slept. Give him a little of his solitude back.

With each crackle of the undergrowth, her heart sped. The darkness was terrifying. She kept her eyes on the few flimsy stars, trying to drink in their light.

It must have been close to midnight when Alexander strode from the hut, his boots missing Violet's head by an inch.

"Christ! Be careful!"

Violet woke at Grace's screeching and crawled into her lap. She watched Alexander with distrusting eyes. He stared at the patch of earth where the girl had been sleeping.

Grace swallowed hard. "I'm sure it ain't easy for you to be sharing your home. And, truly, I appreciate all you done for us. Soon as I figure out what to do we'll be gone. I promise."

He held out two pieces of smoked meat.

"We ain't hungry."

Alexander nodded towards the hut. Beneath the door, Grace could see the fire's orange glow.

"You want us to come in?"

He nodded.

Grace held Violet to her chest. "Did you mean to shoot us?"

Alexander gestured to the hut again. Grace hesitated. A throaty grunt echoed from the trees beyond the woodpile. She stood slowly, Violet's feet dangling down past her waist. Followed Alexander inside. The rifle leaned against the wall. She paused in the doorway.

"Tell me you ain't going to shoot us in the night. Tell me I can trust you. Just one word. Please."

He opened the chamber of the rifle and pulled out the ball. He had reloaded while she had been outside, Grace realised sickly. He pressed the bullet into her palm.

She managed a faint smile. "Thank you." Hesitantly, she laid Violet onto their sleeping pallet and curled up beside her. "I'll not say a word," she promised. "Quiet as a mouse, I swear it."

Her hand around the bullet, she closed her eyes and tried to push her breathing into the same sleepy rhythm as Violet's. She heard Alexander poke the fire.

A shallow trust, but what choice did she have? Take away that shallow trust and she was completely alone.

CHAPTER SIX

Standing Orders from Lt-Gov William Sorrell to Lt John Cutherbertson,
Commandant of Macquarie Harbour
Saturday 8th December 1821

'You will consider that the active, unremitting employment of every individual in very hard labour is the grand and main design of your settlement. They must dread the very idea of being sent there. ... You must find work and labour, even if it consists in opening cavities and filling them up again. ... Prisoners on trial declared they would rather suffer death than be sent back to Macquarie Harbour. It is this feeling I am most anxious to be kept alive.'

"Violet?" Grace burst outside, tugging on an ankle boot. Dalton watched from where he sat on the tree stump, cannikin of tea in hand.

"Violet? Where are you, angel?" She circled the hut. "When I woke this morning she weren't in her bed. Have you seen her?"

Dalton shook his head.

"You didn't think to wake me when you saw she weren't here?" Urgency rose in her voice. "Where is she?" She strode around the tiny hut again as if she could possibly have missed her the last time.

"Violet!"

The calls turned to shrieks. Dalton looked down at the mud and the trails of prints leading out of the hut.

Grace's footprints. His footprints. No little girl's footprints.

Grace's eyes followed his to the trails of prints. She grabbed his collar and shook. Tea slopped across his trousers.

"You carried her! You took her!" She shoved him hard. "What have you done with her? I never should have trusted you!"

He let her punch and shriek; her arms, skirts, hair, all wild and flying. She ran into the bush.

"Violet!"

The shouting grew distant.

Dalton followed. Didn't know why. He wanted his silence back, but curse of God on her, his legs wanted to follow. They walked, then ran towards *Violet, Violet.*

When he caught up to her, her eyes had overflowed with messy tears. "She wanted to go back to Hobart. She thought her father would be angry at us for being late home. I'm so afraid she tried to find her way back." A deep, gasping breath. "She's just a baby. She ain't going to last a minute out there on her own."

Her suspicion of him gone.

Did she truly believe he hadn't carried her out of the hut and cut her throat? Of course, it was easier to convince herself he was just an irresponsible bastard who'd turned a blind eye as a girl lost herself in the wilderness. The alternative was to believe she was alone with a madman who had her child's blood on his hands. He'd have chosen to believe the easier option too, if he hadn't seen what men were capable of. Now choosing the easier option was just naivety.

They searched the entire day, following the river as it narrowed and swelled. Grace beat the brush with a long stick, scouring the land for any sign, any clue. Dalton followed wearily, sure they'd not find a thing.

"She's afraid of the river," Grace kept saying. "She wouldn't have come this way." But she kept along the edge of the water, thrashing at the reeds, calling her name.

When the light turned orange, Dalton stopped walking and pointed towards the hut. His stomach growled. No point them spending the night out there. Grace's tears had stopped several hours ago, but at the suggestion of turning back, another great sob welled up from her chest.

"She's gone, Alexander, just gone."

Yes, gone like a ghost. Left no trace; not a bootlace, or a button, or a thread of hair. But nor had she left a drop of blood, or scrabbled finger marks, or any cause for Grace to lose hope that she'd stumble back to them, disoriented, hungry and stained with tears.

Dalton pointed again.

"No. I can't give up on her."

He began to walk. What, did she think he was going to do the chivalrous thing and follow her to the end of the earth?

"Alexander," she said. "Please."

He kept on towards the hut, knowing how quickly the light would disappear.

Grace called his name. She ran towards him, staying close to his heels.

Her shoulders sank when they arrived back at the hut to find it empty. She paced, tugged at her hair. Dalton lit a fire in the hearth, though he was still hot from all the walking.

"I got to go back out," Grace kept saying. But it was dark by then and he was sure she knew it was no use. She chewed fingernails. Alternated between heaving, messy sobs and single, silent tears. Dalton lifted a small stump of wood from the pile beside the hearth and sat on his stool. He began to carve. Grace stopped pacing. Dalton could feel her eyes on the knife; on its rapid back-and-forth *scrape, scrape, scrape*. Shavings settled at his feet. He began to forget himself in the monotony. He imagined the features on the wood as though they were already there. The determined eyes, narrow nose. Bird's nest of curls. Then Grace said loudly:

"We ought to be out there looking for Violet. Instead, you're sitting here carving dolls."

He put down the knife. Looked up at her. That's what she wanted, wasn't it? Some attention?

She gnawed the side of her thumb. "Your chimney. It's made of wood."

Yes, pine.

"A wooden chimney? That's the most ridiculous thing I ever heard."

He tore a hunk off the loaf of bread on the table, flicked away the ants and held it out to her. She shook her head. He gestured again, insistent.

"No," she said sharply. "How could I eat?"

Dalton tore the bread in half and chewed slowly on his piece. He

306

placed Grace's share on the table.

"She must be so hungry. She'll not sleep out there without me. What will she do? It's so late. Must be eight or nine at least. Not that that means anything to you, I'm sure. Have you any idea what day it is? Do you even know the year?"

Stay out here long enough and she'd realise the hours and the days were meaningless. Just names. A way of measuring the immeasurable.

He had kept track for a while; counting the days after they ran from Macquarie Harbour.

Escaped on a Friday.

Reached the river on a Monday.

He had left the other men on a Sunday.

After that, there had seemed to be little point counting.

He had walked alone through land that twisted into caves and mountains. His stomach was empty, his legs like lead. His heart weary and hopeless. Each night, he had closed his eyes and waited for the end. A big part of him wanted to die. What was there to live for when he'd been thrown from society like a rabid dog? But the part of him that wanted to live was stronger. It kept him walking, kept him seeking out the lights of those mythical eastern settlements. Kept him placing unknown berries and roots on his tongue, gambling with his life for a meagre supper. A slab of kangaroo meat stolen from a natives' camp. The discovery of the purple berries. And each morning, another rising sun. Another reprieve. His body refused to give up. Dalton felt he'd been cheated out of death when he found the cattle duffers.

Delirious with hunger, he stumbled into the camp of a cattle-raiding ring on the Fat Doe River. They poured water down his throat and stuffed his mouth with salted pork until he could sit up and look at them. Six men; bolters and crooked emancipists who'd not lost the taste for crime. They took one look at Dalton's convict slops and decided he was the perfect man to join them.

Livestock plucked from the settlements, driven down the coast and sold in New Norfolk and Hobart Town. In their plans they saw riches, the wealth they had been denied in England. Dalton saw a ticket back to Macquarie Harbour.

So this is how a man makes his own world:

While the duffers are plucking cows from the paddocks, he takes other things from the farmhouses. A rifle and cartridge box, powder flask, knife and saw. An axe, twine for the traps. He uses his own resources. While the men are snoring, he wraps up their boiler and cups in the shirt they gave him. He raids a farmer's shed in the middle of a thunderstorm. No-one will see him and even if they could, would they bother braving the rain for a hammer and a tin of nails?

Dalton left the duffers' camp in the middle of the night, stolen goods in a pack over his shoulder. He walked in the fragile light of the moon. The bush became a labyrinth of purple and green. The beginning of his own world.

So no, he couldn't have told Grace what day it was. The sun and stars kept time for him, beyond the restraints of ticking clocks and calendars. The colour of the sky and the changing winds told him of each year's passing. Eleven summers. Eleven autumns. Made this a cold night in the year eighteen hundred and thirty-three. The eleventh winter was on its way. Sit a little closer to the fire.

Grace rubbed her eyes. "She got Rosie with her at least. Her doll. I didn't find it nowhere. Least she got Rosie." She pushed her tears away with her palm. "What is it you're making?"

Dalton held it out to her. He had barely begun; one edge of the branch still rugged and dark, the other smoothed down to its soft white flesh. He'd begun to whittle her narrow chin, her long, graceful neck. Could she tell it was her? Soon he'd have her sitting on the shelf with the others. He'd put her at the front, beside the farmer from Oxley who had given him a pair of boots in exchange for digging a ditch.

Carving was the one piece of his old life he'd allowed himself to keep. He'd not let himself think of the things he didn't have. They'd just stopped existing. Sugar. Tea. Whisky. *Good morning.* Over the years, his mind had stilled and, before long, it was enough to spend his days hunting, stripping bark, making flour. Watching the light change and the land swell and wither with the passing seasons.

But, over time, familiar faces had begun to appear from amongst his woodpile. The commandant of Macquarie Harbour with his dead slug smile and *fifty lashes.* That bastard of an overseer at Dalton's first convict post in Oxley. And there at the back were Pearce and Bodenham and the others. He'd carved them years ago in the hope that giving them some form might drive them from his mind. All seven of them, in the order Pearce claimed they had died. Bodenham first, then Mather, the weak fuck. Greenhill with madness in his wooden eyes.

Grace stared into the glowing remnants of the fire. She felt the carved faces watching her. Judging.

How could you lose her?

"I got to go back to Hobart Town," she said. "Bring a search party."

Alexander's breathing was deep and even with sleep. He didn't stir.

Five days to Hobart Town. Five days back, if she could ever find the hut again. Ten days at least, then she'd be thrown back into New Norfolk for her troubles. Violet couldn't last out there for ten days. She had to stay here and find her herself.

She stepped outside and pulled her cloak tight against the cold. She couldn't just stand still and hope. But where to even start? Perhaps if she were Violet's mother, she'd have been able to find her. Perhaps if she were Violet's mother she'd never have lost her to begin with.

She'd had her chance to be a mother. Life had stirred inside her before the twins were a year old. There was a woman, Harris had said, in Seven Dials, who could take care of such things discreetly. Grace had left the blue house in tears and walked all the way to the lodging house in Stepney. She sat on a stool and cried while her mother puffed on her pipe. The house smelled of tobacco and piss and her childhood.

"And here I was thinking you had a few brains in that skull of yours." Her mother coughed loudly.

Grace had been bringing her mother a crown each week since she'd begun working for Harris. She knew it went mostly on booze and not the coal she'd intended it for. Grace always left Stepney with a quiet satisfaction that she'd crawled her way out. That she'd have walked the shit off her boots by the time she returned to Covent Garden. But now, as she sat opposite her mother and stared through the rag-patched window, she saw how easily her charmed life could topple.

"I love him," she said. And in spite of herself, she loved the unborn child they'd created. Couldn't bear the thought of losing it at the hands of some witch in Seven Dials.

Her mother snorted. "You love him. You think that matters one scrap? He's a gentleman. You ain't never going to be a thing to him but a good time."

Grace cried harder. She knew these things happened all too often; the man of the house making a stitch with the help. For all she wanted to believe things were different, she knew a girl who'd crawled out of these shit-infested slums would never be clean enough for a man like James Harris.

Her mother leant forward and grabbed Grace's chin in her hand.

"Stop that weeping. You want to end up on the streets with some snotty-nosed chavy hanging off your hip?"

Grace shook her head.

"Course you don't. So if your Mr Harris says he'll take care of it, you let him take care of it. Plenty more than most girls in your position could hope for. Don't know how lucky you are."

She returned to the blue house after midnight. Harris was pacing across the parlour, shirt untucked and waistcoat unbuttoned.

"Gracie," he said, "I was afraid you'd left."

The next day, he sent her off with a pouch of silver to take away the shame.

The second time, six months later, the pennyroyal potion hadn't worked. Harris's woman had taken to Grace with a bowie knife and the resulting torrent of blood ensured she never need worry about bastard children again.

Losing her phantom babies was a dull ache compared to the desperate pain of Violet. She longed for that little voice singing along to her lullabies, the sticky hands at her skirts. Of course, she had no choice but to think of Violet safe in a bed of moss like a fairy. Couldn't let herself consider the alternative.

Violet had left no footprints. Had Alexander truly carried her out? Or had the previous night's sprinkling of rain been enough to wash away any trace of her? How desperately she wanted to trust him. But perhaps Violet was safer out there than she was in the hut with him. A gnawing fear sat in her stomach. Only two sets of footprints. The thought circled through her mind until she was convinced he was about to bury her beside Violet.

She ought to run. But what if she was wrong? What if Violet found her way back to the hut and Grace wasn't there? As much as she knew Alexander wanted his silence back, she had to stay.

She sat on the tree stump, shivering in the drizzle. Moonlight spilled across the tree ferns. She squinted, trying to make out shapes in the dark. The more her eyes strained, the more the shadows blurred and shifted. A moving branch? A native? Perhaps nothing at all.

She heard rustling in the bushes. Saw a flash of glowing eyes. Two devils pushed through the scrub. Grace drew her knees to her chest, balancing on the stump. They came closer, drawn to the smell of meat. She ran into the hut and curled up on her side. Beside her, Alexander lay with his coat pulled to his waist. In the dim glow of the fire, she saw the interwoven trails of the cat splayed across his back. The white whip scars stood out against his brown skin the way a dewy spider web glows in the sun. She tried to count the lashes, but they ran together, curled, meshed. She had an odd urge to touch them. Instead, she stared into the mess of it until the first hint of sun slid beneath the door.

CHAPTER SEVEN

Confession of Alexander Pearce

As recounted to Lieutenant John Cutherbertson, Commandant of Macquarie Harbour

1824

'I was working with a gang at Kelly's Basin, under Overseer Loggins. On the 20th September 1822 ... we made up our minds to seize a boat and proceed to Hobart Town.'

He found the bones poking from the mud. A skull, backbone, a few other scattered pieces. They were aged and yellow.

Human.

He'd kept her away from the cliffs the previous day, knowing she'd want to search them. He sure as hell didn't want to climb down there.

But by the second morning, Grace had found them herself. She must have gone looking again at dawn, because when she shook Dalton's shoulder to wake him, the light in the hut was still grey and pale. He rolled over. Grace's eyes were shadowy from sleeplessness, her skin blotchy with tears.

"We need to go down the cliff. What if she's fallen?"

Dalton stood wearily. He'd not slept much either. Had found himself worrying she would run into the darkness and try to find the girl.

He laced his boots and took a chunk of bread from the table. He turned to offer some to Grace, but she had already sprinted away.

He caught up with her on the edge of the escarpment. She knelt, peering over the edge into the hazy valley. Beneath her, the cliff fell away in columns like the pipes of a church organ. Dalton pointed west. Further around the ridge, the rocks opened out into an incline. Steep, but climbable. He turned up the collar of his coat as they walked. The back of his neck, having been covered in hair for the best part of a decade, was feeling the chill.

Grace tucked her skirts up and began to climb. She moved quickly, streams of pebbles shooting out from beneath her boots. Twice, she lost her footing and cried out. Perhaps she'd fall. Dalton hoped it would be a swift death. Skull against rock. Not a broken ankle or something that would have him shooting her like a lame horse.

He reached the bottom first and began to beat his way through the web of creepers. The bush was wetter down here. Water trickled beneath his collar and soaked through the holes in his boots. He could hear the dull thunder of a waterfall.

And there, poking out of the ferns were the bones.

Dalton picked up the skull. Turned it over. A gaping hole at the back.

A fall down the escarpment?

Axe to the head?

Flit flit said a bird above his head.

"Alexander? Where are you?"

He dropped the skull and kicked the bones into the undergrowth.

"What have you found?" Her eyes were wide with fear.

He shook his head.

Nothing at all.

They walked along the base of the cliff. One end to the other, until their path was blocked by a great curtain of water. No Violet.

Grace's steps were crooked with weariness. He'd not seen her eat in days, Dalton realised. She turned her eyes to the steep, mossy slope and sank to the ground, skirts pooling around her like tar.

"I got to rest a moment."

Dalton pulled a handful of berries from a bush and handed them to her.

"To eat?"

He nodded.

"Not poisonous?"

He took one, swallowed. Grace placed one cautiously on her tongue. She winced with the bitterness and flung the rest onto the ground.

Dalton plucked them from the scrub and held them out to her. Food. A gift.

Don't you know what happens when it runs out?

He stood with his hand outstretched, the berries like flecks of blood on his palm. Finally, Grace took them, crammed them into her mouth and swallowed.

"Now can we go?"

He nodded.

Up she went, her long fingers curling around the rocks. Sometimes she would pause and look back over her shoulder at him. Dalton would point: *this way, that way,* and up they went like this until they both collapsed at the top of the escarpment.

Grace stumbled back to the hut and fell asleep at once, her skirts still tucked up and one bootlace undone.

Dalton paced back and forth across the clearing, thoughts banging against his head.

Bones in the gully.

The skeleton of a black? No.

Once he had heard their songs drifting through the bush and had followed the sound for half a mile. He peered out from behind a tree and watched them shroud a dead man's bones in a hollow log. Their chants and sung prayers reverberated inside him. Human life at one with the wilderness. If the blacks could survive out here, so could he.

That burial was a thing of beauty, of respect. They'd never leave a man to rot at the bottom of a cliff. That was the domain of the Macquarie Harbour bolters.

Eleven years this September since they had run from the harbour. The timing, the decomposition was right. The place? After the first death, Dalton had run north. Perhaps the others had continued this way, southeast past the lakes and into the valley. That gaping hole at the back of the skull, well that was Greenhill all over.

Could be anyone.

But there was no one else out here.

In eleven years, he'd seen no one but a few blacks.

Likelihood of it being one of those seven men? High.

So what? Whoever it was was dead. It mattered little if Dalton had known him or not.

His thoughts knocked together until he wanted to cry out.

He didn't want the bones near his hut. He'd done his best to forget those men. Forget what the worst of humans were capable of. How could he do it with a beaten skull lying at the bottom of the cliff?

Next he knew, he was standing in the gully with the axe in his hand. He swung the blunt end into the skull. Bone splinters shot into the sky. He swung at the arms, the rib cage. And then with the blade, hacking at the legs, the spine. With each swing, he felt anger rising within him.

There was a beauty to being the only person in the world. When there was no one to judge, a man stopped judging himself. When there was no one judging a man's past, the past ceased to be. A man could kill another and learn to forget it, as long as there was no one there to hold him accountable. What do the trees and the birds know? What do they remember?

A beauty, wouldn't you agree? You see now what you took from me when you thundered into my life?

He swung again, again. Finally, he dropped the axe. He had reduced the skeleton to a pile of brown fragments. Could be bark now, or dried leaves. It would wash away with the next rain.

It had been many years since he'd thought of the world he'd left behind. Grace had brought a little of it with her. Started his thoughts churning again. Forced him to remember that once there had been an alternative to living like an animal. Forced him to remember what he'd done to end up here. His thoughts were forming with increasing complexity. Now there was no longer just *cold, tired, hungry, afraid.* Now there were stories, histories, guilt and self-loathing. A reminder of his own dark capabilities. He hated her for it.

He swung the axe. *Thunk* into that tree trunk. Into that mud bank. Into that burrow.

Anger at her, at himself. Why hadn't he been able to pull the trigger?

315

In that second, as her chatter had stopped and she'd stared at the rifle, he had felt himself drowning in the silence. Found himself longing for another word from her. More garbled instructions to the girl. He hated the way she'd crawled beneath his skin.

His world had begun to feel small and empty, inhabited by dead men's bones.

With each swing of the axe, he imagined he was able to silence her. Her endless babble and burnt bread and her little vanishing Violet.

Animal rage. He welcomed the familiarity of it. Nothing of the past weeks had been familiar. He charged up the escarpment, wild sprays of rock flying from his boots. Beads of animal blood dripped from the axe blade. He scrambled over the top of the cliff and ran towards the hut. *One swing of the axe*, he thought. All it would take. He thought of her sprawled across her sleeping pallet, passed out with exhaustion and grief. She'd never even see him coming. Never have a chance to be afraid.

She opened her eyes as the axe arced above his head. She scrambled from the sleeping pallet, her scream sticking in her throat. He swung the blade into the table and felt the vibration charge through his body. He released the handle and kicked the table leg. Grace pressed her back against the wall. She glanced at the rifle leaning beside the door. She would need to pass him to reach it. Dalton yanked the axe from the table and tossed it into the clearing. It left a cavernous slash in the wooden surface. He hated himself for not being able to do it. Hated himself for considering doing it. He was afraid of how much he'd remember if she stayed, shaking his mind out of its decade-long hibernation. He upended the flour pot over the table and traced a finger through the mess, carving letters in the scattered black seeds.

Leave.

Grace kept her back pressed to the wall. Dalton smacked the table hard.

"I can't leave. What if Violet finds her way back? Why do you want me to leave? Why now? I thought we was all right." He grabbed a fistful of her shawl and yanked her towards him. He felt heat rising from her body. Her face was inches from his. There were details that hadn't been there before. Faint pores, freckles. A fleck of wattle clinging to an eyebrow. Tiny white scar on her chin.

His lips quivered.

"What?" She leant forward.

Leave. Go before I hurt you.

He heard the words in his head. Felt them rising in his throat. He exhaled loudly, hoping the words might escape on his breath. Grace pressed a hand against his fist. His skin tingled beneath hers.

"Tell me, Alexander. Whatever it is. Just say it."

Dalton let go of her shawl and shoved her away. He swept his hand over the table, scattering the flour. The roof creaked and rustled.

"I can't leave," coughed Grace. "Not without Violet. If you want me gone, you'd best kill me too."

CHAPTER EIGHT

Colonial Times
Thursday 29th October, 1863

'It is ... very generally acknowledged that the New Norfolk Asylum stands pre-eminent throughout the colonies for ... the admirable mode of its management.'

The rain began. Grace went out to search in the grey dawn, the hood of her cloak pulled over her head. She shoved her way through banks of dripping ferns and trunks running with silver water.

Violet, Violet.

But each call was answered only by the patter and drizzle of rain. She heard hopelessness creep into her voice.

By the third day, the forest was a great expanse of mud, the land beyond the river near inaccessible. Grace paced the clearing until her boots and cloak were soaked through, calling out into the shimmering mist. Finally, Alexander pushed open the door and took her wrist. Led her back inside the hut and gestured to the fire.

When, on the fourth day, the rain finally eased, she carried their dirty clothes and cooking pots to the river. The sky had cleared to a fierce blue. The water roared as rapids charged towards the falls.

Grace crouched in the mud at the river's edge and beat Alexander's shirt against the rocks.

Was she trying to prove herself indispensable, she wondered? Show him he couldn't survive without her? Prevent him from swinging the axe again?

She looked up edgily. He was stripping sheets of bark from the bluegums with his whittling knife; a replacement for the wet, curling wood of the door. Snowflakes of gold wattle clung to his chest.

Grace turned away and scrubbed the grimy sleeves, laying the wet shirt over a log to dry. She stopped suddenly.

A swirl of blonde hair in the river.

Her stomach plunged. She leapt into the water, her feet sliding through the pebbles on the bottom of the river. She dove towards the swirling mass.

Not blonde hair, she realised sickly, but a thatch of yellow reeds. She grabbed them anyway. Fell to her knees in the water and lay her cheek against them. She felt their dampness, cold like the skin of the dead. A sob welled up from her stomach.

Her teeth began to knock together, arms trembling with cold. And suddenly she was back at the asylum in New Norfolk, strapped to a chair beneath streams of freezing water.

Be a good girl now. You'll feel much better after this, I promise.

The river snatched her. She clutched at the reeds, but they snapped in her fists. She was pulled along, down, under. White water, brown water. Leaves and branches and sharp twigs. She tried to stand, but her feet tangled in her skirts. Ahead, a low branch stretched across the water. She clutched at it desperately and managed to lift her head and shoulders out of the rapids.

She was following Violet's path. She knew it. Could sense her flying, terrified through the swells. Could sense the water closing in over her little head.

Grace felt an arm around her waist. Alexander pulled her tight against his body. She could feel his heart thumping.

"Is this where you brought her? She was here. I can feel it." Her legs flailed, tangled in her petticoats. "Let go of me. I can walk."

He kept his arm tight around her waist and dragged her upstream. And then a dip in the floor of the river. Alexander stumbled, losing his grip on her. Water rushed over Grace's head. She saw her then, little Violet, blonde hair floating around her face like a halo. Grace opened her mouth in a silent scream and the river rushed down her throat. And suddenly she was pulled through the surface, coughing, gulping air, more air, feeling herself go limp in Alexander's arms.

He hauled her onto the bank. Water streamed from her dress.

"She's here," she sobbed. "I saw her. I saw Violet." Her throat seized with tears. Alexander picked up his greatcoat from the riverbank and slid it over Grace's shoulders.

"She's in the water." She moved to stand, but Alexander pushed her back to the bank with such force she didn't dare argue. He stepped into the water. The river hissed around his knees.

"There." Grace pointed to the place where the branch hung low. "That's where I saw her."

Alexander dived beneath the surface. Grace held her breath. She could see his hazy shadow moving along the bottom of the river. She felt dizzy with fear, terrified that he both would and wouldn't find her. He resurfaced, empty handed, his hair slick. He dived under again, again. Grace held her breath in the same rhythm as he; filling her lungs to bursting as he plunged beneath the surface. Each time he came up with nothing and each time she let herself breathe. Eventually, he waded out of the river and shook his head.

I'm sorry, said his eyes.

Grace wondered, *Sorry for which part?*

He shook the water from his hair like a dog, picked up the clothes and pots and tucked the bark sheets beneath his arm. He began to walk, dripping, back to the hut. Grace followed slowly, his coat around her shoulders. Violet's watery face flickered through her mind.

It was all too easy to see things in this forest. Things that weren't there. She grappled with the image of that little face as the memory threatened to lose its sharpness. By the time she reached the hut, she was unsure whether Violet had ever been there at all.

She sat by the fire with the coat around her, watching steam rise from the wet petticoats that clung to her legs. They'd drunk cups of wattle tea, cooked a possum they'd caught in one of the traps. Grace had sat her share on the floor and stared at it until Alexander picked it up and swallowed it in one mouthful. He sat at the table, knife in hand and a hunk of wood in his lap.

"She's gone, isn't she."

Alexander met her eyes.

"I can't bear to think how Nora will cope. The two of them were so close. How is she to go from being a sister her whole life to being an only child?" She smiled slightly. "They were so different, you know. Violet's the shy one. Nora's always doing the talking for the two of them. She's a bossy little thing. A real chatterbox. Suppose she picked that up from me, right, Alexander?" She pressed her chin to her knees. "They were so different, but looked so alike. Both even got a freckle in the same place near their nose. It's awful hard to tell them apart when they got their bonnets on."

Alexander ran his palm over the chunk of wood in his lap. A tiny version of Grace watched them from the shelf now, beside a man with weathered cheeks.

"Will you carve Violet?" she asked.

Alexander raised his eyebrows. Shook his head.

"Please."

He sat for a moment with the knife motionless in his hand. Then he began to carve.

Selective absence of speech. An intriguing project for Doctor Barnes at New Norfolk, Grace was sure.

There were fifteen women on the ward in the asylum. Forty or more men on the other side of the compound. Convicts and free settlers thrown in together, labelled insane. The cell to Grace's left belonged to Molly Finton, who'd been plucked screaming from the Cascades Female Factory. On the right, a woman transported for life who'd slit her wrists in grief for the husband and son in England lost to her forever.

New Norfolk Insane Asylum. Twenty miles from Hobart so those on the outside could forget.

The building was a few years old at most, built by the government when the streets of Hobart Town became a gauntlet of madmen. A government asylum for government men and women. But always willing to take the money of a free settler with a troublesome mistress he wished to dispose of.

While Harris had watched his convict workers lay the foundation stones of his house, Grace had tried to make a game of it for the girls; tried to make their miserable tent liveable.

The palace, they called it. And the flap of canvas sheltering their convict workers: *the summer house.* Tree branches became brooms, their pit fire a marble hearth. They hung great swaths of bluegum across their sleeping pallets so they could pretend they had bed curtains.

Yes, yes, they were just playing house. All a game.

"Why not go into town?" said Harris, like the fool hadn't seen the whores plying the docks or the bloodied backs of the men tied to the triangle. Grace had been at the wharf with the girls one day when a ship arrived full of female convicts; dirty, sorry creatures with bare feet and swollen bellies. Wrists and ankles bleeding from their shackles. Violet and Nora pressed themselves against Grace and peered at the women from behind her skirts. They watched silently as the prisoners were herded into a wagon bound for the Female Factory. Grace imagined she was the one in leg irons. Seven years' transportation for theft of an egg.

Slowly, slowly, the house grew up around them. And with it, the tension that had begun to build in London.

Mrs Harris they'd called her on the voyage. Who was there to argue? They were heading to a colony without parents or pasts. A few well-spoken lies could make a man and woman husband and wife.

But fifteen thousand miles of sea had not changed James Harris. He was the same starchy man in Hobart Town he had been in London. His promise of marriage withered and vanished. He found the Whist tables in Wapping before their first fortnight was through. Came home bragging about his winnings. And when the owner of the neighbouring farm came to introduce himself, Harris was deliberate in keeping him out of the hut. God forbid anyone lay eyes on his rough-spoken, frazzle-haired mistress.

She'd let herself believe things would be different. That here in Hobart Town she'd no longer be a source of embarrassment. That *I love you, Grace* might become more than just a drunken mistake.

Van Diemen's Land, it turned out, was populated by half of London. Hobart Town was full of familiar faces. There was Harris's school friend William Bell, who ran the apothecary on Collins Street. The Allens from Islington who'd bought land out in New Town. Bloody Archie Tyler who they'd run into their first week in town. He may have been digging a ditch in leg irons, but it didn't stop him grabbing his crotch and yelling, "Over here, Grace Ashwell, I'd know them tits anywhere."

And then there were the Wintermans; clients of Harris's from London. When they'd crossed paths leaving church one morning, Harris had turned white.

Mr Winterman clapped him on the back.

James, my boy, small world, blah blah blah.

His wife peered over her fan at Grace and the girls, who were fidgeting in the heat. Violet had been moaning for weeks. Desperate to go home.

The blue house.

The river.

The sideshow.

Grace tugged her hand to make her stand up straight. "Stop your bleating this second." She hurried towards Harris, pulling the girls behind her. Waited to be introduced.

My wife, Grace...

"I'm dreadfully sorry, James," said Mr Winterman. "You've had a rough time of things haven't you. You'll let us know if you need anything."

Harris smiled thinly. "Very kind of you, but we're managing just fine."

Violet erupted into an epic tantrum, arms and bonnet flying. Harris grabbed Nora's hand, leaving Grace struggling with the screeching Violet. He nodded hurriedly to the Wintermans and marched back to their waiting carriage.

"He's dreadfully sorry?" Grace climbed into the seat opposite him and hauled Violet onto her lap. "Sorry about what?"

"Nothing."

"Sorry about what, James?"

Harris looked out the window, avoiding her glance.

"He's dreadfully sorry you're stuck with a woman like me? Dreadfully sorry you couldn't find no one better to come out here with you?"

Harris sighed. "Of course not. It doesn't mean anything. Just an old mess at work, that's all."

"You're lying."

He glanced at Nora, who was making handprints on the window. "Let's not have this conversation now."

When the girls were asleep, Grace stormed up to the table where Harris was reading by candlelight. She slammed the book closed. "You're ashamed of me."

"That's ridiculous."

"You didn't even introduce me to those people. Couldn't wait to get me away from them. How am I supposed to take that? You think I don't know shame when I see it?"

"Keep your voice down," he hissed. "The workers will hear you." He stood and marched across the single, dirty room of their new home. Reaching the other end of the tent, where the girls were curled up on their sleeping pallet, he turned, striding back and shoving Grace out of the way. He'd never lived in a place so small, she realised.

"You can't walk away from me here," she said with a bitter smile. "Fancy that. You carted us out here for all the bloody space, but look where we've ended up. Crammed together like pigs in a sty." She picked his top hat up off the table and flung it across the tent. It thudded against the wall and dropped onto their sleeping pallet. What was he trying to prove, dressing up like some cursed dandy in a place like this? His silk waistcoats were dulled with dust, shirts stained with sweat. She glared at him. "Your daughters hate it too."

Harris rubbed his eyes. "Grace, please…"

"It's true. You heard how much Violet's been whining. She hates it here. You just ask her."

"Grace, stop it." His voice began to rise. "Now!"

Violet sat up in bed and began to cry. "Nanny Grace?"

She forced a smile. "It's all right, angel. Everything's all right."

Harris sighed noisily. Violet cried harder.

"Look at her!" Grace gestured wildly. "Look how miserable she is! Tell Papa, Violet. Tell him what you told me. Tell him how you want to go home. Tell him how you want to see the sideshow again."

Harris whirled around. A sudden flash of white-hot pain as his palm struck her face. Grace stumbled backwards, blood blooming inside her mouth where her teeth had dug into her cheek. She glared fiercely. She had grown up dodging her father's fists, and when he'd died, she had sworn she'd never take such a thing again.

"Good Lord, Grace, I'm sorry. This tent and that damn couple and this blasted mess with Violet… It's just more than I can take."

Violet's sobs turned to shrieks. Harris swore under his breath and marched towards the girls' bed. He clenched his fist. Grace's heart leapt into her throat. She lurched at him suddenly and yanked his arm back.

"Don't you dare! You lay a hand on those girls and I'll break your damn neck!"

Harris whirled around, his cheeks flushed. He looked back at the girls, chest rising and falling with rapid breath. Violet's shrieks became terrified murmurs. Harris rubbed his eyes.

"I'm not— " he began. "I— " He reached for Grace's arm.

She shoved him away. Her cheek throbbed and she tasted blood. "Don't you touch me! Don't you even bloody look at me, you bastard!"

"How dare you speak to me this way?"

"I'll speak to you however the hell I like! I ain't your wife, as I know you're so damn happy about!"

His eyes flashed and Grace wondered if he was about to strike her again. She planted her hands on her hips, daring him. Harris glowered for a moment, then gave up and sank back into his chair. "To hell with you, Grace. Can't you see that all I've done has been for your own good?"

"My own good? You lay a hand on me and tell me it's for my own good?" She'd not spend her life with a violent man. Wouldn't let the twins be raised by one. Wouldn't let them grow up as she had.

She crammed into the girls' bed and stroked Violet's hair until her tears stopped. Flies pattered against the inside wall of the tent. She could smell the salty remains of the pork she'd cooked for supper. Cicadas shrieked in the paddocks.

What a mistake she'd made by coming here. Believing Harris would give her the life of security she craved. She vowed then and there she'd see London again.

Harris's sleeping mat rustled. "Come on, Gracie. Come back over here. Please."

The thought of lying next to his hot body made her stomach turn.

"Come on. I've told you again and again how sorry I am. It won't happen again, I swear."

Grace snorted. She'd heard the same line from her father more times than she could remember. She'd stood for it then because it was all she had known how to do. But she was a woman now. She had the girls to protect. She would give her life to make sure they never knew the pain of their father's fists.

"I know things have been hard for you," said Harris. "Believe me, they've not been easy for me either. But we need to do this together."

"Together?" Grace spat. "You couldn't wait to hide me away from the Wintermans."

"I'm sorry. I wasn't expecting to see them."

"I thought we'd left our old life behind. But you'll always be ashamed of me, won't you." She rolled over and curled around Violet's body. "You needn't worry no more. I'll make sure everyone in this colony knows you're just a beard splitter who docked with his children's nurse. And who uses his fists when things don't go his way."

Harris sat up suddenly. "Grace. Please— "

She laughed coldly. "Don't worry. I'm sure such a scandal will make you well popular around the gambling tables."

Two days later, Harris rode into town and returned with a carriage. The girls ran out excitedly to meet him.

"We're going for a trip." His smile was forced.

Grace folded her arms. "We'll stay here if it's all the same to you."

"No!" whined Nora, grabbing Harris's hand. "I don't want to stay! I want to go in the carriage!"

Grace gritted her teeth. She was thankful Nora had slept through the whole ordeal, but her adoration of her father felt like a betrayal.

"You must come," said Harris. "I insist. It will do us all good to get out for the day."

Violet gripped Grace's arm and peered warily at Harris.

"Come on!" sighed Nora. "We have to go! Tell her, Papa!"

Harris smiled stiffly. "You heard the girl."

Grace sighed and climbed into the carriage. She sat with Violet on her lap while Nora scrambled across the bench and knelt with her head pressed against the glass. The carriage crawled past brown potato-sack hills.

"Where are we going?" Grace asked finally.

"New Norfolk," said Harris. "The next town to the north."

326

They rolled into a sleepy settlement, cottages dotting patchwork fields. Purple mountains rose in the haze behind the town. Men reclined shirtless on the riverbank.

The coach turned off the main road. It rolled towards a long sandstone building that rose from the sun-bleached plains.

Grace stiffened. "James." Her voice was throaty. "Where are we going?"

He avoided her eyes. "I'm sorry, Grace. This is for the best."

The carriage pulled into the gates and came to a stop beside the long verandah.

"Stay here," Harris told the girls sharply. He took Grace's arm and pulled her from the bench.

"James? What in hell is this?" She gripped the door of the carriage, but he took her by the waist and pulled her down the coach steps. "A hospital?" The realisation squeezed her chest. "A *madhouse*?" She felt suddenly hot and breathless. Harris tightened his grip and led her up the gravel path towards the entrance.

"Please don't make a scene," he whispered.

"Don't make a scene?" Anger flared inside her. She glared at their convict worker, Samuel, who was driving the carriage. "Are you just going to sit by and watch while he does this? Help me!"

Harris jabbed a finger at his convict. "Stay where you are. This is none of your business."

Grace thrashed against his arms. "Why are you doing this? Because I won't whore myself to you any longer?"

"You know things can't go on the way they have. It's not fair on any of us."

"Then let me go! Give me my earnings and let me go back to England."

A man in glasses and a shiny brown frockcoat came out the front door, trailed by a woman in a nurse's apron.

"Good afternoon, Mr Harris." The man smoothed his moustache. He nodded at Grace. "Mrs Harris."

"It's Miss Ashwell," she spat. "He don't have no power to put me in here!"

"Her things are in the carriage," said Harris. Grace whirled around to see Samuel hauling her trunk from the back of the coach. When in hell had they packed her things?

Harris stepped close. "You're to stay here with Doctor Barnes a while." His voice was thin and controlled. "It's important you remember the way of things."

"The way of things? You think you can bring me here and turn me into a woman who'll just sit by and let you treat her as you please? Don't know what in hell I were thinking coming to this place with you!"

Barnes rubbed his chin. "You were right to bring her here, Mr Harris. She is quite hysterical."

Grace stared at Harris with glacial eyes. "You're trying to turn me into Charlotte."

His eyes hardened. He stepped back and pursed his lips. "Take her," he said, his voice stiff and empty of emotion. "Goodbye, Grace."

A cell the size of a cupboard. Force-fed castor oil to purge the madness from her body. Tied in a freezing bath to ease her sadness.

Your husband has your best interests at heart.

Once a week, Doctor Barnes would take her to his office, sit her in the leather armchair opposite his desk and speak in a honeyed voice Grace assumed was supposed to be calming.

"Tell me about London," he would say, puffing on his pipe.

Tell me about London, Miss Ashwell. Or: *Let's start at the beginning.* In her four months of incarceration, they never seemed to get past the beginning.

"You were a nurse to Mr Harris's twin daughters."

"I was more than their nurse. I was the only mother those girls ever known. Was I just to stand there and watch when he became violent? You think I'd let the bastard put a finger on them?"

Barnes made a noise from deep in his throat. In a fleeting moment of optimism, Grace imagined him unlocking the door to her cell.

Forgive me, Miss Ashwell, we've made a terrible mistake.

"All right." She sighed. "I ain't stupid. What is it that Harris wants? Does he want me out of the way so he can hunt down another hedge whore at the gambling halls? Or does he want me in his fancy new house as a well-behaved little wife? Come on, Barnes! You're taking his money!

He must have told you what he's after. Why don't you just tell me and then I at least know what I need to do to get out of here. Then we can put an end to this stupid game."

"I can't do that."

"Of course you can't. Because then he'd stop paying you. You know as good as I do that Harris and I ain't married. He's got no right to put me in here." Her voice began to rise. "But you don't care, do you. Sixty pounds per year in your pocket. That's the sum, ain't it? It's nothing to Harris. Spare coin!"

Barnes took off his grimy glasses and wiped them with an enormous handkerchief. "Calm down, Miss Ashwell, or there'll be consequences."

"Shove your consequences! You expect me to be calm when Harris has me locked up like a criminal?" She sat back in her chair defeatedly. "The men with the money always have the power, don't they. The rest of us can just bloody well curl up and die."

The next day an attendant led Grace into a room covered in murky white tiles. In the centre, a chair sat beneath a series of narrow pipes. Doctor Barnes stood with his back pressed against the wall. He smiled warmly.

"You'll feel much better after this, I promise you. Much calmer."

Grace stood shivering in her shift. Her heart sped. Nausea tightened her stomach. She tried to imagine which part of this might possibly make her feel calmer.

The attendant sat her on the chair and buckled straps around her waist and chest. Fastened her wrists to the arms of the chair. Fear shot through her.

"Let me up. I'll be calm, I swear it."

Doctor Barnes said nothing. Grace squeezed her eyes closed and tried to will herself away. The whir and groan of the pipes began from somewhere deep within the building. The sound moved through the walls and up above Grace's head.

And then the water. A thin, icy stream. Her hands clenched around the arms of the chair, shocked at the coldness and the intensity of the pressure.

Just water, she told herself. How could such a thing hurt her? But down it poured, stealing her breath, freezing and relentless, like chiselled shards of ice. Against her head, the water felt like needles, then nails, knives. She tried to move, but the straps kept her pinned to the chair.

She gritted her teeth. She wouldn't cry. Wouldn't scream. Wouldn't give them any reason to think her hysterical, or weak.

Behind her eyes she saw a great expanse of stars. The room was washed away into blackness.

Molly Finton was playing the game the other way around. Weighed up life as a convict at the Female Factory and a life at New Norfolk asylum. Decided she could play the part of a lunatic.

"Sometimes you got to choose the lesser of two evils, you know." She looked at Grace across the sewing table. Spoke in a hushed tone so the attendants couldn't hear. "You know what I'm talking about, don't you, girl. You got more wits about you than the rest of the rabble in here put together. You don't belong in this place anymore than I do."

"You think this were my own doing?" Grace snorted, pushing a needle through the chemise she was hemming. "No sir. Just got mixed up with a man who thought he could put a hand to me and his girls. When I didn't sit down and take it he threw me in here."

"Fucking men," said Molly. She leant across the table. Molly was twenty-five like Grace, but her skin was as leathery and wrinkled as an old woman's. "The bastards at the factory put me in solitary for a whole week. Left me in the dark and fed me nought but bread and water. When I come out, I pretended I was seeing ghosts. Started screaming in the night and keeping all the girls awake. When I waked up all the babies in the nursery one night they had enough and threw me in here."

"You got out of the factory," Grace said. "Do you have to keep up the act so good?" She'd been yanked from sleep many a night by Molly's howling. Hated being dragged from the bliss of unconsciousness.

"Got to keep it up, don't I? Or they'll think I come good and send me back to the factory."

Grace heard London in Molly's words and was hit with a bolt of homesickness. She'd kept away from Molly at first, the way she'd kept away from all the others. She wanted Doctor Barnes to see her apart from all the dribblers and shriekers and think, *well that Grace don't belong in here, do she?* But then Molly asked her for the cotton across the sewing table one day and Grace's loneliness got the better of her.

It turned out Molly Finton had grown up in the slums of Whitechapel, a mile from the room where Grace's family had lived. At seventeen, Grace had gone west to the mop fair and Harris's grand blue palace. Molly, east, into a world of pickpocketing in Rotherhithe where she found an undercover policeman and seven years' transportation. Grace knew Molly's fate could easily have been hers. A step to the left instead of the right and she'd have been hauled out to this place on a convict ship. But what did it matter now? She and Molly; free settler and convict, and here they were side by side at the sewing table. Here they were with matching grey dresses and matching shorn hair, a matching wild anger that simmered beneath their skin.

"Sometimes I think you truly are mad," Grace told Molly. "Choosing the hell of this place."

"See this." Molly leant forward so Grace could see the thick brown scar on her neck. "At the factory they had me six weeks in an iron collar. Trussed up like a dog." She tossed her head indignantly.

"What d'you do? How come they put you in solitary?" But Molly wasn't answering. She just ran a hand through her unevenly cropped hair.

How fitting it was they'd hacked at Grace's hair here, her pride and joy. Curls she'd been growing to her waist since she was a girl. Harris had loved to wrap them around his fists and pull her into him. She'd never plaited her hair when she was in bed with him; just let it loose all over his pillow. Once, his hands in her hair was the best feeling in the world.

"My beautiful Gracie," he would say.

When she sat in that chair at New Norfolk, there was a cold satisfaction to watching those curls pile up at her feet.

"This will cool your mind," the attendant told her as the scissors squeaked around her ears. But her short hair made Grace hot with anger.

Look what you've lost, James Harris. Look what you'll never have again.

Grace lay on her side and pulled Alexander's greatcoat around her. Sometimes she wondered if this hut was real at all. What if she'd passed out beneath the water pipes with shackles at her wrists and this strange silent man was nothing but a dream? She shuffled closer to the flames. No, the heat was too real for this to be a water-induced fantasy.

She watched the silver blade dart across the wood, tiny in Alexander's hand. A frown of concentration creased his forehead. Wood shavings clung to his bare feet.

He placed the figure of Violet by Grace's head. Its wooden eyes were level with hers. She squinted. The cheeks were too round. The hair too short. Eyes too close together. It had none of the personality of the other carvings. This was cold, empty.

"That ain't Violet. It don't look nothing like her."

Alexander's lips twitched. He flung it into the fire. They sat watching as the flames closed in around the carefully whittled face.

CHAPTER NINE

Mist hung over the bush. Dalton could smell rain in the air. He sat on the tree stump and opened the chamber of the rifle. Electricity gathered in the sky.

He tied a piece of cloth to a bootlace and fed it into the gun for cleaning. He pulled slowly, carefully. When he was a young man, he had loved the feel of a weapon in his hands. It gave him a feeling of power. That ability to control life and death. His captain could holler at him all he wanted, but if he pulled the trigger, the bastard would die.

Dalton had trained at Gibraltar among men who'd fought in Spain, across America. Men who'd been at Waterloo. They'd speak of their adventures while they puffed on pipes and watched the sun sink into the water. Great men, great soldiers. Dalton, he had a great anger in him. The great anger of the poor and oppressed. The great anger of the Irish.

The sky tore open. Globes of water pelted into the mud of the clearing. Dalton lifted his face and felt rain explode against his skin. He was dimly aware the soaked rifle would be useless for days, but he didn't care. He couldn't leave the energy of the storm. He shrugged off his coat and shirt. Tiny rivers ran down his chest. He opened his mouth and tasted the water. So clean and cold. Christ, he felt alive. The bush smelled fresh and clean, as though the storm was washing away the terrors that had taken place among these trees.

Grace ran out of the hut and laid the pot and cups on the chopping block to catch the water. She was barefoot in her shift and cloak, her dress hanging from a tree branch after being washed that morning. There was a routine to her cleaning, Dalton had noticed. One session she would wash her dress, the next her petticoats, then her shift and stockings. She'd come to him with nothing but the clothes on her back, but did her best to stay clean. There were always clothes hanging up at the hut now, flapping in the trees in fine weather, or thrown over the chairs where they cast shadows that made him jump in the night.

Her decency made him behave less like the rabid dog he'd become out here on his own. With Grace about, he kept himself washed, dug a hole to relieve himself in, drank from a cannikin instead of burning his lips on the boiler. With Grace, he ate at the table like a human being, instead of gnawing at bones while he paced through the bush.

She pulled her dress from the tree branch. Dalton grabbed her wrist. *Stay.*

She had to experience this storm. Had to see the thickness of this sky, the great forks of gold lightning. She glanced down in surprise at the hand he had clamped over her wrist. Unlaced her cloak and tossed it and her dress inside. She lifted her head and smiled, but her eyes didn't reach him. A private smile. What was she thinking? It was the first time he had seen her smile since the girl had disappeared. Her first acceptance there could be life after Violet.

Thunder rolled across the sky and a flock of blood-red birds shot screeching from the trees.

Dalton watched the water run over Grace's eyelids and cheeks, through her hair. The skin on her upper arms was the colour of milk, a contrast to the tan on her wrists and hands. A contrast to his own leathery brown skin.

He moved towards her, but she turned away. She lifted the pieces of the gun and carried them inside.

Rain had made its way down the chimney and soaked the ashes. No fire tonight. Their wet feet and the seeping rain were turning the floor to mud. They ate hunks of bread and drank the rainwater, sitting opposite each other at the table. Around them: the smell of soaked linen, wool, and the clean mint fragrance of the wet bush. Rain pattered rhythmically in the doorway. Rivulets of water drizzled onto the shelf and bathed the carved faces.

Grace in her petticoats, Dalton bare-chested. He was dimly aware he ought to have been cold, but felt lit up inside. He breathed deeply, enjoying the coarseness of the bread on his tongue.

"You got two stools," said Grace. "Why? Were you expecting me all along?"

Why two stools? He had wondered that as he hammered together the second so many years ago. Maybe a part of him *was* expecting her.

She wrapped her fist around the handle of the knife they had used to cut the bread. Something tightened in Dalton's chest. He stood. His stool toppled and thumped against the dirt floor.

"Sit." Grace clutched the knife. He reached down and lifted the stool upright. Sat. She stood over him, droplets of rain falling from the ends of her hair. The bare skin on her neck and arms glistened. She slid the blade of the knife beneath Dalton's chin and used it to tilt his face upwards. His eyes to hers. When was the last time someone had looked at him so closely? He couldn't turn away.

She held his chin between her thumb and forefinger. Human contact. A precious thing.

Could she begin to imagine the coldness, the sense of isolation that comes over you when you go eleven years without touching another soul? When the only life you ever feel is an animal thrashing in your hands before you break its neck?

She pushed the knife into the wiry hair beneath his chin. Dalton held his breath. What was she doing? That blade, it was far too close to his throat. Was she after retribution for Violet? For the first time in years, he felt a flicker of panic at the thought of death. He couldn't die now. He'd only just come back to life.

She slid the blade across his cheek. Whorls of black hair fluttered to the ground. Dalton saw it had become flecked in grey. He was beginning to grow old. What a gift. To sprout a grey hair had seemed so unachievable when he was waist deep in water hauling pines at Kelly's Basin. He was sure he'd be dead by twenty-five.

The blade moved over his chin. Dalton sat motionless, heart thumping, entranced by the touch of Grace's hands on his face and the wet white skin at the top of her shift.

He watched the hair fall from his cheeks. What would he hide behind now? Did he want to hide any longer? He was afraid of what Grace might see.

He flinched at the thought and the blade caught on his skin. A flash of pain. Grace pushed her finger against the cut. A bead of blood hung on her fingertip.

Dalton touched his cheek. The skin felt silky, raw, like a gum that had just lost a tooth. The remains of his beard were scattered around his bare feet. Grace smiled faintly. Wet hair clung to her cheeks and a thick, ropey strand had worked its way into the corner of her mouth. Dalton thought of reaching out and lifting it off her skin. He played that simple action out in his head.

His finger curling around her hair. His skin to her skin. A gentle pull. And she would say *thank you, Alexander.*

You're welcome, he would reply.

But when he raised his hand, her smile disappeared and the strand of hair came free. Her eyes fell to their sleeping pallets, which were soaked in black mud.

"Oh," she said. "Alexander…"

He wanted her hands against his cheeks again. There was so much life in her. He wanted to feel it. And so he said, "You missed a little."

Grace stared at him. The knife teetered in her fist.

Dalton was surprised by the pitch of his voice. Didn't sound like him. And that odd vibration in his throat, he'd forgotten that.

Eleven years since he'd last used his voice.

Go n-éirí leat, mo chairde. Coughed out to Kennerly and Brown, as they crawled their way back to Macquarie Harbour.

Good luck to you, my friends.

Grace kept staring, her mouth opening and closing around unformed words, as though he'd passed his voicelessness onto her. Suddenly he wanted his silence back. She'd ask questions, expect answers.

He stumbled out into the orange dusk. He paced across the clearing with his hands behind his head. The rain was cold against his cheeks and reminded him of their nakedness.

"You missed a little," he repeated, listening to the words slide off his tongue. His voice sounded tiny against the slapping rain. And then he tried, "Greenhill."

For those men were pushing hard inside his head, begging for attention. She could never know of them.

He came back inside. Grace was scooping the pieces of the sleeping pallets from the floor. The hem of her shift was covered in threads of brown fern, her toes black with mud. Dalton sat at the table and said, "Grace."

"Grace," he said again, as though testing his voice.

"Yes?" she said. "Yes, Alexander?"

She thought, *I see you now. You ain't no old man.*

Thirty-five, perhaps. She saw the sharp angle of his jaw, the wideness of his cheeks. His eyes seemed bigger, darker, dominating a face that still held the last flush and smoothness of youth.

His hand went again to his chin, feeling, feeling, reminding himself of what was there. He used his wet shirt to wipe away the stray bristles. Rain slapped into the mud outside the door. He pulled the shirt on and it clung to his chest. Grace's heart beat hard, desperate for answers, yet afraid to hear them. Her thumbnail went to her mouth.

"Don't know where we going to sleep tonight. The sleeping pallets all fell to bits. All this rain we had lately. Maybe we can take turns sleeping on the table. Won't be much comfortable but be drier at least. I suppose you're used to this. Where do you sleep when it gets so wet?"

Alexander's eyes fell to the mess of leaves and grass she'd strewn around the hut. Somehow she'd managed to make more of a mess than before.

She sucked in her breath. "Why you out here? You hiding?"

Nothing.

"You're a government man."

He nodded.

"No, speak to me."

So he said, "Yes."

"What d'you do?"

"Struck my army captain."

Grace reached tensely for her cloak and hooked it around her shoulders. She sat at the table and folded her icy feet beneath her. "Well," she said finally, "you done your time then?"

He shook his head.

Oh. I see. So we hide.

"How long you been out here? You got any idea?"

He answered in a rusty Irish lilt. "Eleven years."

Surely she'd misheard. "You been out here alone for eleven years? I don't believe you. You would never have survived." But as she spoke, she began to see the possibility of it. Water from the river. Berries from the trees. Meat from the traps.

She began to see a possibility for herself. A life in which she might never be forced back beneath the water pipes at the New Norfolk asylum. A life free of James Harris. If Alexander could escape and survive, then she could too. Yes, she believed him. She believed him because she had to.

"No-one has ever found you? Before me and Violet?"

Alexander shook his head. He pulled on his coat and climbed onto the table. When Grace thought she'd get no more from him, he mumbled, "No-one goes searching for a dead man." His voice was thin and hollow. Told her to ask no more.

CHAPTER TEN

Conduct Record of Convicts Arriving in Van Diemen's Land 1804-1830

Alexander Dalton, Caledonia *1820*
July 6th 1822: Wilful and corrupt perjury. One hundred lashes and remainder of sentence to Macquarie Harbour.

As hard as Dalton tried, there were fragments of the past that refused to be forgotten. A human brain, he'd come to realise, needed madness to truly forget. And so, with another living person in his life, the story had begun to slip out.

Prologue.

Convicted for assault at Gibraltar Court Martial. Fourteen years' transportation.

Grace had thought nothing of it, surely. In Hobart Town this was every second man.

Fourteen years. At twenty-three, it was almost two thirds of his life. But then there were the stories of those lucky bastards who'd made their fortune in this new land. Cast off their leg irons for early pardons and ended up rolling in gold. He'd be one of those men, he'd told himself. Turn up back in Kilkenny and buy the whole bloody town a drink.

If he'd stayed with his first overseer in Oxley, perhaps he'd have made it through his sentence. Managed a ticket of leave. But he saw the stain of authority in that overseer and took him down with his fists.

He was sent to Hobart Town to work in the chain gangs, carve this new colony with his bare hands. A miserable existence to be sure, but in Hobart, the convicts still felt part of the world. A working week. Church on Sundays. They had coins in their pockets, rum in their bellies. Friends to laugh with and women to ogle. Yes, their ankles were scarred from the shackles, but they walked the streets with felons who'd been pardoned and rewarded with land. For the convicts of Van Diemen's Land, Hobart Town brought a speck of hope that they could salvage something from their lives.

But then: an Englishman shuffling along in front of Dalton in the chain gang. A staunch royalist with a hatred for the Irish.

Michael Flannagan, with a mouth like a fucking moocher.

Dalton's ticket to the great green hell of Macquarie Harbour.

While they stood waiting for the chains to be locked, Matthew Brown whispered to Dalton that he was going to rob a man and buy his way off Van Diemen's Land.

"You'll swing for it," said Dalton.

"Aye, perhaps I'll swing. But then I'll be in God's kingdom instead of this Englishman's hell."

"I saw it all," said Dalton, when the police came searching for the thief. "I saw Michael Flannagan rob that man. Said he planned to buy his way off Van Diemen's Land."

They said all men had a chance of making it in this new land. Said even the Irish could rise above the lowliness of their birth. But when forced to choose between the guilt of the English and the Irish, it was always the bog-jumper who would swing.

Flannagan watched with a grin as Matthew Brown was led to the scaffold. Dalton to Macquarie Harbour with a flayed back and a certainty that any God he may have known did not exist in this backwater of the planet.

Dalton knew his lies, like all his crimes, had been foolish. He had never set out to live the life of a criminal. He'd just been cursed with a need to see his own perverted sense of justice done. Cursed with an anger that took away all sense and reason. Even back when he was marching in the king's colours, he felt he belonged somewhere far from civilised men.

Hell's Gates, they called the wild swells at the mouth of Macquarie

Harbour. And when the ship bucked its way through the whirlpooling sea, Dalton felt the devil at his shoulder. He'd spent five weeks at sea without a hammock or coat, curled up on the ballast with thirty other men. The ship ploughed through winds that howled between the rigging and somehow managed to penetrate the hold. Days passed where they seemed to make no progress, the ship plunging left to right, up and down, but never forwards towards their destination.

Macquarie Harbour, for reoffenders. The most secure of all the colonies' penal settlements. At Sarah Island Penitentiary, the pounding heart of the harbour, great purple swells heaved themselves out of the Southern Ocean and made whirlpools of the cove. The rocks were bald and glistening, the bush thick as castle walls. Rivers poisoned with salt and decay. A prison perfected by nature.

When Dalton stepped onto Sarah Island and felt sleet sting his cheeks, any speck of hope he'd had in Hobart Town was gone. His new world was grey and brown, coloured only by rust-streaked rocks that rose jagged from the water. On one side, a chain of mountains. On the other, a screaming ocean. This was it, Dalton realised. This was where he belonged; living on an island even God had forgotten, among people who were slowly turning wild.

Most of the prisoners were normal men when they arrived on Sarah Island. There was some rage in them, some bad decisions, but they were able to laugh a little, tell a good story from home.

From Bill Kennerly, a poteen still that could blow your very eyes out.

From Tom Bodenham, a girl with tits the size of melons.

John Mather was a married man with three sons in Edinburgh. He relayed their entire lives to the men while they hacked away at the pines.

But the stories didn't last long. Hauling logs back to the boats like they were oxen sucked away the chatter.

One morning, Dalton swam out to the boats with Pearce. Shivering beneath sheets of rain, they waited to be rowed to the logging station. Pearce turned his eyes to the grey sea.

"*Cad atá cearr leat*, Pearce?" What are you thinking?

"Leave him be, Dalton," said Greenhill. "He's due a flogging for breaking his axe. Don't feel like hearing your blathering, do he?"

Pearce's silence fell over the rest. Their thoughts turned from women and grog to escape or death. Suddenly that was all there was.

Escape or death.

Dalton had not been at the harbour two months and he knew his sentence would kill him. In a way, it already had.

Eyes would meet across bowls of porridge and in each man's glance was a dream of leaving Van Diemen's Land for a paradise across the water. They'd cursed at the rest of the world before they came to Macquarie Harbour. The poverty in London, politics in Ireland, tyrannical leaders in Gibraltar. But suddenly those places were heaven.

"The boat," said Greenhill, "gets left unattended." And then he was too careful to say more. The men's eyes went back to their porridge. Hands in bowls, bread chewed with open mouths.

Look at us.

Turning into animals long before they escaped.

Is it really any wonder we did what we did?

A drizzly day at Kelly's Basin. Eight desperate men waist-deep in water, arms aching from hauling pines. The boat unattended outside the coal miners' hut.

They eyed each other silently.

A chance.

Greenhill motioned for them to wade ashore. He used his axe to crack open the miners' chest. Sacks of pots, boilers, flint. Bread and flour. Salted meat.

"Take it all," said Greenhill. He emptied the boiler over the fire to prevent the miners from making a signal. Smoke hissed and plumed. Dalton slung a sack over his shoulder. The food was heavy in his arms. He felt a burst of optimism he'd not experienced in years. A boat would get him off Sarah Island, past Hobart Town. Hell, if he rowed far enough, a boat would get him back to Ireland.

A rustle in the trees.

"Go!" Greenhill shouted. "Hurry!" Eight men leapt into the boat, water cascading over the gunwale. Bodenham grabbed one oar, Pearce the other. The boat crawled along the rocky coast; Sarah Island disappearing behind a wall of trees.

Columns of smoke began to spiral up along the waterline. The miners had built new signal fires, alerting the settlement of escapees. Dalton began to laugh. They were playing with death and it made him feel dazzlingly alive. Greenhill grabbed Dalton's slops and wrenched them hard around his neck.

"Shut your fucking mouth, flogger. You want them to hear us?"

Dalton swung furiously, but Bill Kennerly grabbed his arm before he could make contact. Greenhill stumbled and the boat seesawed wildly. Dalton glanced over his shoulder. A cutter was approaching from the harbour. Marines. Dogs. Rifles.

"Leave the boat," Greenhill said suddenly. He grabbed the oar from Bodenham and began to pull furiously towards the shore.

"You lost your mind?" spat Kennerly.

"We can't out-row them. I ain't letting the bastards put a rope around my neck."

"Where do you plan to go? There's nothing out there."

Greenhill pointed to the tallest of the purple mountains that cut into the horizon. "That there is Table Mountain. Other side is Hobart Town."

Dalton stood and felt the boat pitch. Five weeks at sea between the town and Macquarie Harbour. Surely Greenhill was mistaken. "He's wrong," he said.

Kennerly nodded.

But Greenhill and Pearce had thrown down the oars and were splashing their way to shore. Dalton swung the pack from the boat and followed Greenhill into the bush. Behind him, Kennerly's aging legs slipped in the ankle-deep mud. Dalton grabbed his arm and pulled him to his feet.

"Madness," hissed Kennerly. "You hear me, Alexander? This is madness."

As far as Dalton could tell, no one came after them. No one wasted their time. This was wilderness in which few could survive. Certainly not eight foreigners for whom the land was an unreadable maze.

Leave the fools to fight the forest and the darkness that lies within themselves.

CHAPTER ELEVEN

She started making plans. The other girl. Nora.

Christ Almighty. He'd forgotten there was another one.

He woke to find her beating the dust from her cloak with a stick. Her petticoats were laid out in the clearing, drying in the bright morning sun. The boiler and canteen had been filled and a fire was crackling in the pit. Two loaves of bread lay baking in the coals.

There was something about the way she carried herself that morning. Her shoulders had straightened. Her head was up. There was a newness about her.

"I made a decision," she said. "I got to go back to Hobart Town for Nora."

Dalton raised his eyebrows. *Back?*

"I can't stay here forever. I'll go mad." She slapped the stick rhythmically against her cloak. "This forest does things to your mind, don't it. The way the light gets trapped, it makes you imagine things that ain't there. I imagined three or four times now I seen Violet coming out of the trees. But there's never anyone there." She stopped beating. "Don't know how you done it, Alexander. Lived out here so long. Don't know how you ain't barking at your own shadow."

He saw it then; what life would be like without her. Empty. Silent. Full of death instead of life. Just him, the bush and memories of dead men.

"You can't go," he said.

She raised her eyebrows. "I thought you'd be glad to be rid of me."

Did she not remember the walls of trees and the freezing rain and the

344

earth that sank and rose with each step? Did she not remember the hunger? The pain in every muscle of her body? He had to admire her optimism, he supposed. Thinking she could flit across this savage island like she was crossing the street. But he couldn't let her go.

She didn't look at him. Perhaps she could see the foolishness of her plan. Perhaps she was afraid his eyes would reflect it back at her.

His voice was husky. "Where will you take her?"

She hesitated. "I'll try again for the northern settlements. I know now I came too far west. I'll not make the same mistake." She swallowed hard. "I know you're thinking I'm mad to try again. But you don't know her father. He's become a violent man. I can't bear to imagine how he's treating Nora without Violet and me there." She traced the stick through the mud, her confidence gone. "I tried to get them both out. I tried so hard. Violet, she weren't sleeping. She hated Hobart Town. When I came to get them, she was already awake. Had her pinny on quick smart. But I couldn't get Nora out of bed. Harris came back from the gambling houses early. Me and Violet had to run or none of us would have got away."

Dalton sat on the tree stump and poked at the fire. "Is that really what happened, Grace? You just left one of your precious girls behind?"

Her blue eyes flashed. "You wasn't there, Alexander! You don't know!" She bent the stick between her hands. It snapped loudly and she hurled the pieces into the scrub. "He threw me into New Norfolk. Do you know what that is? Do you? No? An asylum for the insane. He told them I was mad. And for what? For daring to stand up to him when he became violent! For not standing by and letting a man treat me however he wishes!"

Dalton said nothing. He was too out of practice with conversation to think of anything that might calm her.

"You can't imagine the things they done to me in that place. The cells and the water pipes and the oil forced down my throat til I was sick. I know how lucky I was to have gotten out without being caught. If Harris had found me in the house that night he would have thrown me straight back in. The colony thinks us married, so he has ultimate power over me. Any man can have his wife committed if he got enough money. I tried to tell them the truth at New Norfolk but the bastard just told them it was part of my affliction. I saw the true side of him when we came to this place. I got to go back and get Nora away from him."

She'd be lost in an hour. Dead in a week.

"You don't even have any oats left," said Dalton.

"You'll give me food and water won't you? And I've thought it through. This river leads to the Derwent, don't it? I can follow it back to Hobart Town."

His chest began to shake with humourless laughter.

"You think this funny?"

"The Derwent will lead you straight into New Norfolk. You want to be thrown back in the asylum? Although if you ask me, if you think you can get back to England with a pocket of bread, the madhouse is where you belong."

Grace glared at him. "I didn't ask you, did I?" She folded her arms. "I preferred you when you were silent."

Dalton batted the two charred loaves out of the fire. How many times did he have to tell her not to put it on the flames?

She kicked furiously at one of the burned loaves. There was such desperation in her eyes, he thought she'd charge back to Hobart then and there. He held her shoulders.

"They'll catch you if you follow the river. And if they get you back in the madhouse, they'll never let you out."

She shrugged out of his grip and charged down the path towards the river.

Don't be like that, now. I gave you a chance to leave. You ought to have taken it.

He was sure somewhere deep inside, she always knew the girl wasn't coming back.

CHAPTER TWELVE

Hobart Town Gazette
Friday 6th August 1824

"Pearce is desirous to state that this party, which consisted of himself, Matthew Travers, Robert Greenhill, Bill Kennerly, Alexander Dalton, John Mather and two more named Bodenham and Brown, escaped from Macquarie Harbour ... taking with them provisions which afforded each man about two ounces of food per day, for a week. Afterwards they lived eight or nine days on the tops of tea-tree and peppermint, which they boiled in tin pots to extract the juice. Having ascended a hill, in sight of Macquarie Harbour, they struck a light and made two fires. Kennerly, Brown and Dalton placed themselves at one fire, the rest of the party at the other; those three separated, privately, from the party on account of Greenhill having already said that lots must be cast for someone to be put to death."

She walked to the river.

Violet? Are you there, angel?

How could she stop hoping for a miracle?

A bird chirruped above her head. She sat on the riverbank. Another five days walk through the mountains. Her stomach turned at the thought. It would be different this time, she told herself. Easier. She'd have food and water. No one chasing her.

No one to carry.

She felt an awful sense that she was abandoning Violet. Leaving her lost in this wild land, so far from everything she knew.

A flicker of white in the river. Grace stood. A piece of leather. Not Violet's. Her heart lurched with sadness. She'd take anything; a torn piece of dress, a thread of hair. Any clue, any fragment of Violet. Any meagre reminder that she'd once been here.

The belt had snagged itself on a rock. Grace picked up a thin branch and lay on her front to pull it from the water. It swung, dripping, on the end of the stick like a resigned, weary fish. She ran her fingertips along the stiff leather. An ammunition belt? She'd never seen Alexander wear this. Had someone else been here? Perhaps Alexander wasn't as hidden as he believed. He would be furious if he knew another person had been here. She had seen that anger. The enormous gash down the middle of the table was a constant reminder. Still, it was best he knew. She rolled up the belt and carried it in her fist.

When she arrived back at the hut, Alexander had laid strips of smoked meat on the table. Steam was rising from the boiler.

"You're going back?" he asked.

She nodded.

"When?"

"I'll leave in the morning."

"And you'll not change your mind."

"No."

"Eat then. You'll need strength." He poured the boiling water into two cannikins filled with wattle seeds. Passed one to Grace. She wrapped a hand around it, the other clinging to the belt in her lap. Alexander sat opposite her.

"And you?" she said finally. "You'll stay here forever? Die alone in your hut and vanish into the earth?"

He nodded at the strips of meat. "Eat. I'll not let you go if you've nothing in your stomach."

She bit off a mouthful of meat. It was tough and tasteless. She washed it down with a mouthful of tea. "You don't wish for a little more from your life than to grow old and die out in the wilderness?"

"That's more than I could have hoped for. Once, I thought I'd die out here as a young man."

"Well," said Grace, "I think you want more, but you'll not admit it. Just surviving ain't enough for a person. They got to have a purpose."

"Perhaps surviving is my purpose. Perhaps we don't all have great dreams of revenge."

"Revenge?"

"That's why you want the other girl, aye? To take revenge against her father for throwing you in the madhouse?"

Grace stared into her tea. "No," she said finally. But she felt an ache of truth to Alexander's words. She squeezed the damp belt, desperate to change the subject. "At the river, I..." She put down her cup. A faint blurriness on the edge of her vision. She blinked hard.

"You what? Are you well, Grace?"

"I don't feel right." A sharp pain seized her stomach. Sweat prickled her face. She threw down the belt, rushed outside and vomited in the clearing. Alexander followed, holding out the canteen. She pushed it away, gasping. "What d'you give me? What was in that tea?"

"Nothing. It was the same tea you've been drinking since you came to me. You must have eaten some bad meat."

"We've been eating the same meat. Why ain't you sick?"

"I've been out here longer. My body's used to it."

"You poisoned me." Another violent pain in her stomach. She dropped to her knees in the kaleidoscope sunlight.

"Drink some water." Alexander knelt beside her and pressed the canteen to her lips. Water drizzled down her throat. She coughed it back up, along with what was left inside her. Her heart raced.

"What d'you give me? Am I going to die?"

"Of course not. It's a little bad meat, is all." His voice was distorted and distant.

"This ain't bad meat." She tried to stand, but her legs gave way beneath her. Trees swung in front of her eyes. Alexander carried her into the hut and laid her on his sleeping pallet. The heat of the fire was unbearable. She felt his fingers at the buttons down her chest. She thrashed her arms. "No! Stop! Get away from me!" She tried to force away the heaviness in her eyelids.

Alexander placed his hands on her cheeks. "Grace, calm down now. You messed up your dress. I just want to clean it for you."

The softness of his voice, his lilting accent made her muscles heavy again. She dropped her arms and felt him open the buttons of her dress, sliding her out of it. She shivered in her shift, though her skin was damp with sweat and her cheeks burned.

"I got to go. Nora…"

"Not today," Alexander said gently. "Not today."

Grace felt her cloak being laid over her body. A damp cloth against her face. The chalky smell of the fire, the hiss of his breathing. In and out. In and out.

Pink gill mushrooms.

You ought to have been more careful, Grace. We live in a vicious land, where nature is against us and the men are animals.

He knew of those mushrooms and the way they messed with your body as well as your head. He'd swallowed some early on, gambling with his survival on the edge of starvation. Had spent the afternoon curled up beside the river, puking out his insides and dreaming he was chained at the legs to a string of men.

Where were they taking her? Back to the asylum? Her eyelids were fluttering as she rolled about, pulling the sleeping pallet to shreds, groaning, clutching her stomach.

Yes, I know. I'm sorry. The pain will pass.

In a moment of lucidity, she opened her eyes and said, "I know you put something in my tea, Alexander. Why?"

She could have come up with a thousand reasons if she'd tried hard enough. Let her mind wander and think of how he did it to save her from Harris, from New Norfolk, the bush. Or did it out of jealousy, or love, as if he were capable of such things, any more than a dog that wags its tail and slobbers over the hand that feeds it.

"Why kill me?" she said.

Oh no, she had it so wrong. He didn't do it to rid himself of her; he did it so he'd never lose her. So he'd never be alone again.

She tossed and groaned and wretched into the pot he had placed beside her bed. Then she fell still, lying on her back with her cloak tangled around her legs. Dalton dampened the cloth and ran it over her face. He slid it down her neck and across her white shoulders. One, two, three buttons at the top of her shift. He undid them carefully and drew the cloth over her chest. He rested his palm between her breasts, feeling her heart beat beneath his hand. Feeling her rib cage rise and fall. Feeling her life flood into him.

As night closed in, he crawled across the hut and threw a log on the fire. He noticed something white lying beneath the table. A bandoleer. He had worn one himself many times. His heart quickened.

"Grace," he hissed, shaking her shoulder. "Where did you find this?"

She rolled onto her side, mumbled a stream of rubbish and batted him away. The belt was damp. Had she found it in the river? The rivers flowed downstream to Hobart Town. This could not have come from the settlements. The bastards must have been here. Searching. For which one of them?

He stepped into the clearing and squinted in the dark for any signs of life. The bush was still. He could hear the river hissing in the distance. Could hear his own breath.

He took a step, then froze as twigs crackled beneath his boots. The noise seemed to radiate across the forest. He felt a pang of deep loneliness. He peered through the door at Grace, but she was asleep on her side, her flushed face lit by the fire.

Was there someone out there to see their light? To see the glow of silver smoke? Dalton pushed aside the bed of leaves on the floor of the clearing and dug up a handful of earth. He hurried inside and tossed it on the fire.

Blackness. Silence. The kind of stillness that falls over a place touched by death. From deep in his memories, Dalton heard Pearce's mournful lilt, singing to break the silence. So real he could swear the men were sitting in his clearing.

Ma'am dear, I remember
When the summer time was past and gone
When coming through the meadow,
Sure she swore I was the only one
That ever she could love

The saddest, most desolate sound he ever heard. A lone man's voice

351

in the middle of an empty world.

Dalton wrapped himself around Grace's limp body. He let the blackness engulf him.

On the edge of sleep, he saw them. Seven men in convict slops, their faces as strained and desperate as they had been the last time Dalton had seen them. Hovering in his hut where the fireplace should have been. He scrabbled into sitting, yanked back to consciousness. His breath was hard and fast. He fumbled in the darkness for the flint and lit the end of a log. Had he been dreaming?

He felt watched. He stood and whirled around in the flickering light, half expecting to see a little girl with plaits and a dirty pinny. But no. There was a heaviness here that did not come from a ghost girl.

A dream. Just a dream. A memory crawled from the wilds of his subconscious.

His ma, she'd believed in these fantasy tales, God rest her soul. Fairies and ghosts and otherworlds. But not Dalton. He didn't believe in anything anymore.

Suddenly he wanted to be anywhere but this forest. Tie him to the triangle. Throw him in chains into the stinking hold of the *Caledonia*. Anywhere but here, where the past hung so thick in the air.

For eleven years, he'd managed to block out the things that had gone on in this forest. But Grace was right. There was something about this place. The threads of gold light, the cavernous shadows, they trapped memories. Imprinted whispers and screams in the atmosphere.

His hut felt unfamiliar. The table he had carved with his own hand was suddenly strange, deformed. That sound? What in hell was that sound? And the grotesque shadows made by the firelight; how had he never noticed those before?

He blew out the flame and curled up close to Grace.

You wouldn't leave me, would you? Not alone with these men.

But oh the false and cruel one,
For all that, she's left me
Here alone for to die.

CHAPTER THIRTEEN

Hobart Town Gazette
Friday 6th August 1824

"Pearce does not know, personally, what became of Kennerly, Brown and Dalton. He heard that Kennerly and Brown reached Macquarie Harbour, where they soon died, and that Dalton perished on his return to that settlement."

It was two days before Grace managed to crawl from her sleeping pallet. The sky was vast and colourless, the bush dripping. Winter had descended on them while she was curled up with her fevered thoughts. Her eyes were cloudy and her back ached from days on the sleeping pallet. When she stepped onto the wet undergrowth, her feet turned to ice. Alexander was staring into the fire, the flames hissing and spluttering. He stood when he saw her and hurried to her side.

Grace pulled her cloak around her tightly. "I need to wash. What have you done with my clothes?"

"I packed them away for you. In the locker." He hurried inside and returned with a bundle of grey and white in his arms. "I'm glad you're well. I was lonely without you. Stay here by the fire. I'll bring you some water."

"No. I can walk." She snatched her clothes and set off towards the river, her feet sinking into the damp earth.

Alexander reached for her elbow.

"I don't have the strength to leave," she said bitterly, "if that's what you're worried about. Go away. I don't want you near me."

She walked to the river on unsteady legs. Untied her cloak and placed it on a mossy log with her dress and petticoats. She stepped carefully into the shallows and splashed her face, her arms, trying to wash away the grime of sickness. She plunged her head into the icy brown water and felt suddenly awake, alive again. From now on she would make her own tea, cook her own food. And when her strength returned, she would go for Nora.

She'd become a game to Alexander.

Leave now. No, stay forever.

Was Violet part of the game too?

She hurriedly pushed away such thoughts. How could she bear to think them when she was stranded alone in the forest with him?

A loud crackle from the woods.

"I told you to leave me alone." Grace climbed from the river and stepped into her dress, glancing edgily over her shoulder. She pulled on her shawl and cloak. Glimpsed a shock of red through the trees. A tall, broad-shouldered marine pushed his way towards her. Grace stumbled backwards. The soldier held a hand out in front of him, as though she were a wild animal he was trying to tame.

"Miss Ashwell? I'll not hurt you. Everything's all right. Just come with me."

Grace turned and ran, her bare feet slipping on the muddy undergrowth. She heard the soldier calling out. A second voice.

Their footsteps grew closer. The mud beneath her feet gave way and she slipped into the shallows of the river. She scrambled out desperately, wet skirts tangling around her legs. A rough hand grabbed her wrist.

"Let go of me!" She made a wild swing for the man's face, but he forced her to the ground. She thrashed beneath his arms, shrieking and cursing.

"Calm down," the soldier grunted. "We're not here to hurt you."

And a second pair of hands was on her, pinning her ankles to the ground. She kicked hard.

"Get off me!" she shrieked. "You ain't taking me back to that hell! I ain't no lunatic!"

A sudden crack and the first man fell sideways, the stock of Alexander's rifle flying into the side of his head. Before the second marine could react, Alexander had pulled the trigger. A man trained to fight. The soldier fell across Grace's legs. She scrambled out breathlessly from beneath the bloodied body.

The two men lay on their backs amongst the undergrowth. One stared into the white sky, blood gushing from the side of his head and running into the river. The second looked to Grace with fluttering eyes. A dark stain crept across his middle. Blood was blooming from his mouth. Grace pulled off her shawl and pressed it hard against the bullet wound below the man's ribs.

"What are you doing?" Alexander emptied the balls from the dead marine's cartridge box and shoved them in his coat pocket. He picked up their guns.

"He's still alive."

He yanked Grace to her feet. "Get up. He'll be dead in a minute."

She looked up. The man she saw terrified her. His eyes were dark and soulless. His stubbled jaw was clenched and splattered with blood. For weeks she had tried to convince herself Alexander was incapable of murder. Convince herself of his innocence. But in the glassy eyes of the soldiers, she felt herself take a step closer to the most dreaded of possibilities: that he had the blood of her little girl on his hands.

"You wanted them to take you back?" he puffed. "Is that what you wanted?"

She shook her head stiffly, afraid of the dark in his eyes.

Alexander charged back to the hut. Grace followed hesitantly.

"There may be others." He threw open the lid of the wooden chest, pulled out the cartridge box and powder. He snatched the boiler and canteen from the table and wrapped them in a shirt. Into the bundle he crammed the last of their bread and smoked meat, along with his whittling knife. He tied the sleeves into a square package. "Get your boots."

Grace grabbed her shoes and stockings, too afraid to argue. She pulled them over her muddy feet and tied the laces with shaking fingers. Alexander shoved one of the rifles into her hands.

"Take this. You might need it."

She shook her head. He cursed under his breath and grabbed the axe from the chest. "Then at least take this." He thrust it towards her. The stained blade stopped inches from her hands.

She wrapped her shaking fist around the handle. "What are we doing?"

Alexander slung the package over his shoulder. He tucked his rifle beneath his arm and marched back out to where the soldiers lay. "We have to bury the bodies."

Choose to believe him or not, but before those soldiers, Dalton had never shot another man.

He'd spent two years marching up and down the training base, but they never saw him fit to be placed in the line of fire. He was buzzing with the feel of it. But the echo of the gunshot had shaken him. How far had the sound travelled? How many ears had heard?

The ground was wet and soft at the foot of the mossy pine tree. Dalton used his hands, tearing through the knots of ferns and roots. Grace dug with the boiler. The marines' blood was on them both; on wrists and hands and clothes. Dalton had laid them face down so the bastards couldn't look at them.

Grace didn't speak. Just knelt down and dug. Now Dalton had gotten his voice back, he couldn't bear this stillness where there ought to have been words.

Finally she said icily, "Is it deep enough?"

"No. More." It was deep enough, yes. But he didn't know where they went from here. They couldn't go back to the hut. It wouldn't be long before more soldiers came looking for the missing. They'd come for him. For them. So for now, he'd just keep digging.

A few minutes more and Grace flung down the pot. She threw her bloodstained shawl into the hole. "Just do it, for God's sake. I can't bear the sight of them lying there no more. Bury them and be done with it."

Dalton dragged the bodies by the legs and rolled them into the muddy graves.

Grace chewed her thumbnail. "Ought we say something?"

He kicked a spray of dirt over the bodies. "Say what?"

"I don't know. A prayer perhaps."

He snorted. Grabbed the pot and began to bury them. Pack the earth tight or they'd be sniffed out by the tigers.

"I never saw a man killed before," said Grace. The fingers in her mouth were shaking.

They stood on the damp soil of the graves. "We can't go back to the hut," said Dalton. "There'll be more of them."

Grace shook her head. "I want to stay."

"They'll find you if you stay. They'll find you and they'll find the blood on the track and what do you think they'll do then?" Anger flared inside him. "Eleven years I've been out here and not a peep from the authorities. Then you turn up and bring half the fucking cavalry with you! They were out here looking for their little escaped lunatic!"

"I ain't a lunatic!" she hissed.

"Then I did you a favour."

Grace wrapped her arms around herself. "I ain't going anywhere with you. So if you're planning to kill me, you'd best do it now."

Dalton laughed without humour. Such paranoia. Perhaps he should have tried to calm her, reassure her. But he was hot and wild with anger. "If I were to kill you, don't you think I would have done it when I killed Violet? That's what you think, aye? That I tossed her in the river and let her float back to Hobart Town?"

At the mention of Violet's name, deep sobs began to well up inside her. She curled into a ball beside the graves, hugging her knees, burying her eyes in her muddy skirts. Dalton felt full of resentment. He knew those marines had been sent to look for her. Sent by Harris and the New Norfolk police.

Find her. She's in danger.

And the only men who had ever come looking for him were the ones who wanted his back flayed and his neck broken.

"Here's how it is, Grace. I can't go back to the hut. I can't take the chance now the marines are in the area. So you either come with me into the bush, or you go back to the hut alone. They'll find you there and they'll take you back to your Mr Harris. They all think you're mad. Remember, he threw you in the asylum because you dared stand up to him." He picked up the pack. "So unless you want to go back there, you're just going to have to trust me."

Grace's jaw tightened as she stood. "Where will we go?"

"We'll head northeast. Without the traps we'll struggle to find food this time of year. We'll have to get closer to the settlements. Steal from the farms, or the drovers on the Hobart road."

"Settlements?" A flicker of light in her voice.

They'd need to build a new shelter. With what? His blunt axe could cut little but bark and vine, his saw was long rusted. The ropes of his traps were fraying and his boots worn through.

"We can make Bothwell or Hamilton in four days," he said. "Get supplies from the farms. And then build somewhere new to live where the law won't find us." He thought of his hut with its thatched roof and crooked bark door. Six months of cutting, hauling and hammering. That patch of earth was his world.

He started walking, away from his world. Clouds hung grey and low, an Irish sky. He shoved the rifle into the pack and took the axe from Grace, using it to hack away the tangled branches in front of them. Beating a path towards civilisation. Not an easy path, he was sure of it. There were mountains this way. Roaring rivers, glassy lakes. He told himself he'd follow the stars, like Greenhill had done.

But look where Greenhill had led them.

In the falling shadows, he imagined them; Greenhill at the front, whispering with Travers and Pearce. Kennerly and Brown hunched together, plotting their escape. Mather and Bodenham in the middle; doomed men.

Dalton was alert to every crackle and hiss, every popping twig. The bush itself was breathing. He saw this dark forest for what it was; a great living entity that kept secrets and took lives. How insignificant man became when pitted against it. These woods had the power to turn men against each other. To send cohorts running in the night with bloodstained axes. And yet, there was a savage beauty to this place Dalton was sure existed nowhere else on earth.

They walked for two hours or more without a word. When Grace said, "Slow down, Alexander," it made his heart bound into his throat.

She started to sing. Keeping herself calm, he supposed. He wanted to tell her to stop – *what if there are soldiers about to hear you?* – but the sound of her voice made those dead men disappear. He glanced over his shoulder at her. Her head was drooped, her singing flat and tired.

Here, give me your hand. Lean on me a little.

But he couldn't dig out the words.

"We can't make a fire," said Alexander. "In case someone should see the smoke."

They'd made it into the foothills on the fringe of the mountains. The ground had risen and the temperature plunged. Thick dark was falling over the forest. Grace's breath made a silver cloud. She stumbled over a log and fell forward; her hands sinking into the mud.

"Stop," said Alexander. And like that, down he sat, right in the middle of the path they'd beaten. No shelter but the thick canopy of trees. No warmth. No light. At least she'd managed a fire on those dreadful first nights with Violet.

She sat several feet from him, needing her distance. But he shuffled closer to her, his hand brushing the edge of her skirt.

"Your dress," he said. "It's soaked."

She hugged her knees. "The soldiers chased me through the river."

Alexander paused, breathing heavily. "I'll light the fire," he said finally.

"No. No one can find us. I ain't going back to the asylum. I'd rather freeze."

He took off his coat and slid it over her shoulders. She buttoned it over the top of her cloak, pushing her chin against its coarseness. Heat from Alexander's body infused the rough wool.

He untied the pack and broke an end off the stale loaf of bread. Grace struggled to swallow. The thing was too tough and tasted of charcoal. When she reached out to put it back in the pack, she realised she couldn't see her hand in front of her. The darkness was absolute. She tried to slow her breathing.

It's just darkness. That's all. Just darkness.

"We'll take turns keeping guard," said Alexander. "Listening for them."

Grace cradled her knees. She was far too agitated to sleep. Far too cold. Far too afraid. Her legs were wet and achy, her eyes stinging from old, dry tears. She wanted nothing to do with Alexander. But nor could she bear to be alone. She sat close enough to hear his breathing. A little assurance the forest had not taken him the way it had taken Violet.

A horrid, throaty scream echoed across the bush. Alexander moved suddenly, clattering the pots at his feet.

"It's just the devils," said Grace, swallowing hard. "You know that. You've heard it a thousand times."

He rustled the ground. Mumbled in Irish.

"What? What did you say?" She heard him leap to his feet. Footsteps passed back and forth in front of her as he paced like a dog in a thunderstorm. "The soldiers ain't here, Alexander. No one's followed us." She lay back and closed her eyes. Tried to convince herself there would be light around her when she opened them. Convince herself the darkness was a choice.

"What are you doing, Grace? Don't go to sleep. Please don't go to sleep."

"I ain't going to sleep."

"Leave!" he yelled suddenly.

"Who's there?" She leapt up. "The marines?"

Alexander's voice dropped. "Get the hell out of my head." His words disappeared into the night, leaving only the hiss of the bush. An owl struck up with a pale coo.

Grace touched his wrist. His skin was hot, despite the bitter cold. "Alexander, tell me what happened out here."

"You don't need to know."

"Yes I do. You're scaring me. I need to know what's in your head."

He stood beside her, silent for a long time. Finally, he said, "We escaped from Macquarie Harbour. Eight of us. Me and Pearce and Greenhill and some others."

"No one escapes Macquarie Harbour."

"Well, we did. We were fools. But we had to try. The place was hell. We laboured like animals. Lived in wet clothes, shared our beds with rats. So crammed together we had to sleep on our sides. I had twelve more years til I was a free man. I'd never have made it. I'd have taken my own life." He sighed heavily. "We stole a boat. Greenhill was a sailor. Said he'd get us off Van Diemen's Land. But the marines came after us. We had to run into the bush instead.

"Greenhill, he got us lost. Took us round in circles. Into the heart of the island."

Grace saw them then, in her mind's eye. Eight convicted men. She and Alexander were walking in their shadows. She waited for him to continue, but no more words came. "And then?" she said finally.

"There was no food. No shelter. Men died. Bodenham first, then the rest. It's like you said, no one escapes Macquarie Harbour."

"Except you."

"Aye, well. Guess I was the lucky one."

The lucky one. She'd always believed a person made their own luck.

Seven dead men and one survivor?

In her mind's eye, she saw the rifle arc through the air. Saw the marines crumple. Was it possible these bolters had fallen at Alexander's hand too?

She couldn't bear to be near him. She walked with arms out in front of her, feeling her way like a blind man along the narrow path they had beaten. Without sight, her other senses were heightened. The screaming devil, the sigh of the wind. Wet leaves grazed her cheek. The ground dipped suddenly and she stumbled on her skirt. The earth felt unsteady. The blackness turned everything on its head. She looked upwards. Where were the stars? The moon? Suddenly being alone was more terrifying than the possibilities of what Alexander may have done.

"Where are you?" she called, panic rising.

"I'm here."

She heard him shuffle towards her.

"You asked," he said. "You wanted to know."

"What happened to the other men? How did they die?"

"I told you. There was no food. You think the land here is harsh? It's nothing compared to what's in the west."

Grace could hear the bush move. She imagined it closing in around her, circling, entrapping. "Why did it spare you?"

"I found a native camp. Found the berries. Found a ring of cattle duffers who fed me til I was strong again." He paused. "You doubt me."

There were soldiers about. Her best chance was to go back to the hut and try and get herself found. Shriek until those men pushed through the trees. They'd take her back to Harris and New Norfolk. But she couldn't stay here in this restless forest with a man who left a trail of death behind him.

She began to walk again. Quicker this time. The ground was slippery and uneven. She pushed through wiry branches and felt them whip back in her face. Her shoulders bumped against tree trunks.

"Grace?"

She began to run, ploughing through the mud and ferns like she was knee deep in snow. She'd lost the path. She hunched low and kept running; pulling her skirts up over her thighs. A sharp branch stabbed her cheek. She reeled backwards with the shock of it, thudded against a tree trunk and fell to her knees. Pain shot through her shoulder.

She heard the strike of flint, saw a flicker of light. Alexander came towards her, holding a flaming branch out in front of him.

"You can't leave," he said. "I have the food and the water and the gun." He lowered the branch so it was close to her cheek. "If you leave, you'll die."

Grace squinted in the hot light. Alexander pressed the cuff of his shirt against the cut beneath her eye. He took her arm and helped her stand.

"I know you don't want to be near me," he said. "But it'll get near freezing tonight. If we don't stay close, we'll likely not survive."

Grace could hear his teeth knocking together. She took off his coat and pushed it back into his hands. He dropped the branch and stamped out the flame. The darkness seemed thicker than before. If such a thing were possible. His hand tightly around her wrist, Alexander led her back to the path, navigating the dark forest like he was following their scent. Grace's foot slammed into the boiler and she knew they had returned to their camp.

She curled up on her side, cradling her aching shoulder. Alexander wrapped his arm over her, then his leg, encircling them both in his coat. His breath ruffled her hair. Grace tensed, both repulsed by and craving his nearness. "Where?" she said. "Where did they die?"

"Forget them. Stop talking about them." His voice was taut.

She squeezed her eyes closed and tried to sleep away the darkness. "You can't forget them. So why should I?"

PART TWO

HAMILTON

CHAPTER FOURTEEN

Bathurst Free Press and Mining Journal
Wednesday 28th Jan 1857
Derived from the *Hobart Town Gazette*, 1824

"Constant moisture from heavy rains renders travelling unpleasant in such a region under any circumstances. If, with a good commissariat and all available comforts, Sir John Franklin's overland expedition to the harbour from the capital proved so laborious and trying that several men never recovered from the hardships and sufferings they then endured, we may readily imagine the wretched prospect before the eight wanderers in the pine woods."

In the morning, she wouldn't look at him. She kept her eyes down, as though he were a wild animal she didn't want to provoke.

They were up with the blue dawn. The winter night had seemed endless as Dalton lay shivering at her side. With the first hint of light, he'd unbuttoned the coat wrapped around them. Grace was on her feet first. Eager to get moving or eager to get away from him?

East, they walked, into the rising sun. Dalton hacked a path through the trees, sending twigs and leaves flying. He looked over his shoulder. Grace was cradling the gun. Yesterday she wouldn't touch the thing. With her other hand she held her skirts bunched above her knees. The tears of yesterday had dried and hardened inside her. A stripe of dried blood along one cheek.

The ground rose in a chain of mossy mountains. Dalton had been this way before. He had traipsed west from the Fat Doe River with all his worldly goods on his back, over the mountain range to disappear into memory. The last time, the days had been long and warm. Now there was ice in the air and their breath made clouds.

Settlements to the northeast. He hoped the map in his head was accurate. They had bread and smoked meat for a week at most. There were few animals in these mountains. And many days in this cold would kill them.

Clatter, clatter of the pots on his back. The rhythmic crunch of their footsteps. And the invisible presence of dead men.

Dalton hated this new silence. He reached into the pack and handed Grace a sliver of smoked meat, hoping for *thank you*. She glanced at his hand, still stained with the blood of the marines. Waited for him to eat his share before swallowing hers.

When she finally spoke, what she said was: "Did you kill Violet?"

Dalton didn't answer. He wanted her to trust him, though he knew he'd given her little reason. What would she have done had he said, *Yes, Grace, I killed her?* What choice did she have but to keep walking beside him?

When the ground became too steep, they crawled on hands and knees. Mud squelched between their fingers. Dalton's ears and nose stung with cold, but his back was damp with sweat.

She didn't speak of Violet again. Made up her own mind, he supposed.

The earth rose and fell. Dalton tossed the pack and axe onto a rocky ledge and hauled himself up. He reached a hand towards Grace.

"Pass me the gun. Let me help you."

She stood beneath the ledge, hesitating. He understood. That rifle was a little security for her. Reluctantly, she passed it to him. He took her hand and helped her up the cliff, her boots scrabbling against the slippery rock. She pulled away quickly.

Dalton said, "Your tea, Grace. I put poison mushrooms in it." He said, "I didn't want you to try and get back to Hobart Town alone. You would've died. That's why I did such a thing."

She started to laugh, a sound like threads of ice. "The tea. Believe me,

Alexander, I ain't thinking about the bloody tea no more."

She didn't look at him. Just step, step, step, like she was trying to walk everything away.

On the third night, the air dropped below freezing. Leaves hardened with ice. With each breath of wind, the trees tinkled like bells. Before the sun had disappeared, Dalton had looked back at where they'd come from. He could still see the fat brown trail of the Derwent River.

He scratched together some bark and fern fronds to cover them against the cold. Built a fire that hissed and spat before succumbing to the wind. He shuffled across the rock and pulled Grace into him, feeling her shiver hard against his chest.

They woke to clouds closing in around the mountains. Banks of mist blew towards them from above and below, leaving them suspended in a great sea of white. Beads of rain exploded against Dalton's cheeks. He began to walk in the direction he hoped was east. The fog made flecks of gold and black dance in front of his eyes.

The rain grew heavier. Tiny rivers rushed through the crevices in the rock. The trees thinned and the ground became slippery like sheets of black marble.

"Why were you at Macquarie Harbour?" asked Grace.

He told her every bit so the silence might not return. The tale of Matthew Brown and Flannagan and how he'd tried to frame the Englishman for robbery. Told tall stories with his hand upon the Bible.

"Oh," said Grace. "So you're a liar then too."

Dalton felt the rock give way to sodden earth. He waded through the sludge without speaking. Mud clung to his ankles, his shins, his knees. Behind him, he could hear Grace's heavy breathing, her murmurs of exertion.

When the earth grew solid again, he sat and watched Grace edge her way out of the mud. "Would you rather I'd let them take you back to the madhouse?"

She sat a distance away and hugged her knees. "I just never seen a man act so vicious before."

"I did it for you."

She met his eyes for the first time in days. A cautious, sideways glance.

"Do you want me to leave you?" he asked finally.

She squinted through the rain to the carpet of treetops, unbroken but for the copper threads where the rivers pushed into each other.

She shivered. "It's like you said, ain't it. Got to stay together or we'll die."

There were always parts of a man a woman tried to ignore. With Harris, it was the way he chewed his meat so damn loud. The way he'd change the subject whenever Grace tried to talk about her life in Stepney. To make any relationship function, there had to be a certain amount of ignorance.

And so it was with Alexander. With each step, she pushed those murdered marines further and further from her mind. Pushed out the dead bolters and the nightmares of Macquarie Harbour until they were nothing but the stuff of legends.

The land itself made it hard to block out the horror. Grace stood upon on a ridge and breathed air that smelled of mint and honey. Looked out over her toes at a beautiful green and purple land, haunting in its isolation.

But beneath the ridge was the darkness. Trees swallowed the sunlight in one mouthful, and those brutal settlements came to life. Down there, where branches blocked out the light and the tiger dogs tore at their prey, was where the crack of the whip still echoed. Where the men with bloodied backs had vanished into the bush. Where the last cries of the dying hung on the wind. It took every inch of Grace's willpower to keep those stories silent.

But that man who had given her shelter, who had saved her from drowning, well he wasn't capable of killing his seven fellow convicts, now was he? And he sure as hell wasn't capable of killing a little girl. Ah yes, there was a great simplicity to ignorance. A great comfort. A great skill to choose to forget.

On the fourth night, she dared to ask, "Are we lost?" They lay on the rock, wrapped in their damp coats. After a day and night, the rain had stopped, leaving a vast, wet forest. Alexander had crouched over the kindling for an hour, whittling waterlogged bark and attacking the flint. The sparks had refused to take.

"Lost? No, we're not lost. The stars, they show me the way."

Grace curled into a ball, her clothing stiff with mud and ice. Her shivering was violent, uncontrollable. She rolled onto her back and stared at the glittering sky. She could see colours behind the blackness, whirlpools of purple and blue. Its beauty was breathtaking. "How?" she asked.

Alexander pointed upwards. "The five bright ones, they call it the Southern Cross. You see? Now draw a line through that cross in your mind. Imagine it extending out four times the length of those stars. Now drop that line down to the horizon. There's south."

"You making this up?"

He gave a short chuckle. "No, I'm not making it up." He paused. "Greenhill said that's the way they do it here. There's no polestar, so they use the cross."

Grace hugged herself. "I don't think this Greenhill were the best of navigators, Alexander."

She gazed up at the cross until she saw that line pointing to the south. Until the sky wasn't so damn foreign. Until the stars began to light the way.

And that moon, she thought, *that's the moon that makes the Thames rise and fall. We might be sitting on the edge of the Antarctic, but that's the moon that shone through my window in the blue house.*

She watched the sky until the clouds blew in. Until she could see no stars, just a shower of white crystals that fluttered down and blanketed the earth. She slid her arms beneath Alexander's coat, searching for body heat. Her stiff fingers clutched at his chest, clung to the sparse curls of hair. He unbuttoned the coat and pulled it over their heads.

She woke to sunlight glowing red through the threadbare fabric. She sat and squinted in the white light. Not piss-stained, London slush, but brilliant sheets of clear ice that lit up the landscape. The whiteness changed everything. Which way had they come? Which way to the settlements? To think was too exhausting. All she wanted was to lie back down and sleep until the cold went away.

Alexander turned in a slow circle, taking in the glittering landscape.

"We're close to the settled districts." His voice sounded far away. "I came this way before." He reached into the snow-spattered pack and broke the smoked meat in two. Handed her the larger piece.

Grace sat with the food in her fist, unable to find the energy to lift it to her mouth. Melting ice dripped from her hair and ran down the back of her neck. She stared into the cloud-streaked valley. Everything she knew felt so far away, like she was trapped in a dream she couldn't wake from.

"Grace? Why aren't you eating?"

She looked up at Alexander. His face was blurred, unfocused. She blinked hard. He dropped to his knees and gripped her shoulder. Held the meat to her lips. "Eat. Come on now." Panic in his voice.

"I got to rest some more."

"No. No more resting. Get up." He pulled her to her feet with sudden urgency. She stumbled into him. "We're almost out of the mountains. Won't be so cold." He slid his arm around her waist. "Keep walking. Just got to keep walking."

CHAPTER FIFTEEN

At the foot of the mountains, the land opened out into a maze of rivers and creeks. When last here, eleven years ago, Dalton had managed to wade across them, the water barely at his hips. But now they were crawling through a long, wet winter. The roar of the rivers was ever present.

Grace's steps were dizzy and crooked. He had to get her out of her wet clothes and into some warmth. Where he would find such a thing, he had no clue, but the thought of it kept him moving, one arm around her waist, the other clutching the weapons, pots clattering on his back. He felt an undercurrent of terror at the approaching settlements. Towns held police and soldiers and people who could put a rope around his neck. But the thought of losing Grace terrified him more than the gallows. And so he kept walking. Dry clothes and warmth.

The river lay before them, dappled with faint rain. Dalton paced with his hands behind his head. The water looked to be two hundred yards wide or more. His body ached with cold and exhaustion. He'd not swum in years. But what choice did he have?

He pulled off his coat and shirt. "Take off your cloak," he told Grace. "And your dress."

She squinted up at him from the bank. He unhooked her cloak, then fumbled with the buttons down her chest, his fingers frozen and ineffective. He rolled their clothing into a tight bundle and tied it to the pack. He grabbed Grace's chin and she opened her eyes begrudgingly.

371

"The water's deep," he told her. "You got to hold tight to me, you understand?" He tugged her to her feet and stepped into the water. He pulled her onto his back with one hand, the other holding the pack above his head. Water swelled around his chest. "The settlements," he said. "They're on the other side of this river."

"And then what?"

And then what?

He'd planned to wait on the edge of the village until night, sneak onto the farms and gather what they needed to build a new hut. But Grace wouldn't survive another a night in the open. "We'll make a fire," he said. "Get ourselves warm."

Another step and the ground dropped away, leaving his legs flailing. He kicked hard. Grace's arms tightened around his neck.

He stumbled out of the water and carried her onto the grass beside the river. He pulled her out of her wet shift and slipped the damp dress over her head. Covered her with the cloak and greatcoat. He hurried into the bush, searching for anything that would burn. Hacked away at some branches until he'd managed a pile of kindling. He pulled the flint from the pack and poked and puffed at the fire until tiny flames began to lick the wood. Grace opened her eyes.

"That's it," he said. "Lie close now." He held his hands to the fire and felt the heat bring life back to his fingers. He fumbled in the pack for the boiler and filled it from the river. Sat it on the flames until a thin thread of steam began to rise. Lifting Grace's head, he poured the warm water into her mouth. A thin drizzle trickled down her throat, the rest pooling on the leaves beneath her cheek.

She looked at him with vague, glassy eyes. "Where's Violet?"

Dalton stood. "Violet's not here."

"Where is she?"

"I don't know." He paced, shivering hard. She urgently needed dry clothes. Blankets. They both did. They couldn't have been more than a mile or two from the first settlement. He sucked in his breath and crouched at Grace's side. Her breathing was shallow, eyelids fluttering on the edge of consciousness. He pressed his fingers to her neck. A faint pulse. He tucked his coat tightly over her and left the rifle at her side.

The land was vivid green between patches of snow. From a distance, Dalton could make out tiny forms dotting the plains. Cattle, he realised as he drew closer. Kangaroos lolloped on the fringe of the pasture, drinking from the creek. At the back of the paddock was a farmhouse. Smoke poured from the chimney.

Civilisation.

Dalton felt suddenly lightheaded. He grabbed a fistful of the wire fence. Sickness rose in his throat. In the neighbouring paddock, two men were turning the earth with shovels. He fought the urge to leave. Logic told him he was well hidden by time. If the cattle duffers were to be believed, the reports of Alexander Pearce had led the world to believe Dalton was dead. But his fear was stronger than logic. He pictured men lined up on the edge of the settlement, rifles raised, awaiting his return. A scaffold in the town square. Bodenham himself, defaced and dead, yet somehow resurrected.

Look what he did to me.

Dalton doubled over and vomited at the corner of the fence. Then he kept walking.

"Can I have a blanket?" he practised. "I need a blanket."

Can I have a blanket? He repeated it under his breath, forcing his footsteps to keep pace with his rhythmic words. *I need a blanket.*

On the other side of the paddocks was a smaller cottage. Uneven wattle and daub walls with a thatched roof that reminded him of his hut. He stumbled through the long grass towards the house. A washing line stood in front of the cottage, yellowing underclothes fluttering like sailcloth. Dalton pulled off the wooden pegs and bundled the petticoats beneath his arm. He opened the door and stepped inside. A range stood against one wall, table in the centre. A simmering pot, spitting fire. Smells of cooking meat, pipe smoke and misplaced earth. A sideboard sat opposite the fire, cluttered with rusty cannikins, rolls of twine and a half drunk bottle of whisky. At the back sat a woven Irish belt. Dalton had not seen one since his father was alive. Never seen one outside of Ireland.

He stepped close and ran his fingers across the red and blue weaving, over the delicate tassels on the ends. For a fleeting moment, the years fell away. He was a boy on his father's lap, letting the tassels slide through pudgy fingers. Watching features emerge on the carving in his father's hands.

"What the bloody hell do you want?" A woman appeared in the doorway, a shovel raised above her head, poised to strike. She looked about Dalton's age, her wide shoulders jarring with a narrow, bird-like face. Pale strands of hair peeked out from beneath a mobcap. She looked up and down at Dalton's mud-caked clothes.

"*Blaincéad*," he said.

"You'll not find any blankets in there." The woman lowered the shovel and looked him up and down. "What d'you need a blanket for? And what in hell are you doing with my underclothes?"

His heart was racing. "My... A woman... She's all cold and wet... Dying..."

"I see. Where is she?"

"I made a fire..."

"You left her out there?"

Dalton nodded.

"Christ. There's no accounting for stupidity, is there. Bring her here."

He paused. "I just need a blanket."

"You're not taking my blankets out there. They'll get ruined. If there's truly a woman needing help, you go and get her. Otherwise you bugger off out of my house and leave my things alone."

Dalton nodded finally. "I'll get her."

The woman folded her arms. "Leave my petticoats on the table."

He rocked Grace's shoulder. "There's a woman. Told me to bring you to her house. She's got dry clothes for you."

Grace lifted her head. "A house?"

"Aye. You got to get yourself warm and dry. Come on now." He took her hand and helped her climb shakily to her feet.

"You went to a house?"

Dalton threw a handful of dirt on the burning embers.

"You said you was going to steal from the settlements."

"Aye. Well." He tied the pack around the axe and gun and slung them over one shoulder. "You need dry clothes, don't you." He wrapped an arm around her waist. "Hear that? That's a boo hoo bird. Only lives where the people do."

"A boo hoo bird? No it ain't."

"Aye, it is. Listen. *Boo hoo.*"

"You're making that up," said Grace. But he saw a smile on the edge of her lips.

"You're not bringing that gun in here." The woman marched out the front door and took Grace's arm. "Give her to me. You want to come in, you get rid of that first."

Grace looked sideways at Dalton. He let his arm fall from around her waist and trudged out across the plains.

He used the boiler to dig a hole beneath a tree and threw in the gun and axe. Tore a strip of fabric from his fraying shirt and knotted it around a branch as a marker.

He let himself back into the house. Voices came muffled from one of the rooms. He followed the sound. The woman stepped from the bedroom and closed the door.

"Grace," said Dalton.

"That her name? I got her out of those wet clothes and into bed."

"Is she going to die?" Dalton asked in Irish.

"Wouldn't think so. But I'm not God, am I."

He tried to step past her into the bedroom, but she blocked his way.

"Leave her. She needs to rest." She marched into the next room and brought out a shirt and pair of brown corduroy trousers. "Here. They belong to my Jack." She nodded to her bedroom. "Get yourself out of those wet things. I don't fancy disposing of you if you freeze to death in my kitchen."

Dalton changed, then carried his wet clothes out to the living area. The clean shirt hung loose on his shoulders, the trousers cinched at the waist with a length of rope. The woman pulled a mug from its hanger above the hearth and filled it with broth from the pot. She handed it to him.

"I got some of this into her. You best have some too."

Dalton nodded his thanks.

Nothing felt real. Not the heady smell of wood smoke, or the hot, salty broth sliding down his throat. Not the noisy breathing of the stranger in front of him. All an illusion, surely.

He sat inches from the blaze. He'd forgotten such heat existed. Illusion or not, he craved the warmth against his skin.

"What's your name?" she asked.

Dalton tugged his shirt towards his neck to cover his scarred shoulders. "Don't think you ought to know that."

She snorted. "Look at you, all precious with your secrets." She smiled crookedly. "A bolter then. I'd have done the same if I could have managed it." She threw another log on the fire. "I'm Annie. She your wife?"

Dalton shook his head.

"Didn't think so." She hooked a finger around the rim of his mug and pulled it towards her to check its congealing contents. "The soup is rubbish, aye?" She pulled the whisky bottle from the sideboard and filled two cannikins. Handed one to Dalton. "This is far better."

He smiled faintly and brought the cup to his lips. The smell was overpowering. The whisky slid hot down his throat, warming his belly. Hell, he'd missed this above all things. He took another long drink and felt his thoughts knock together. *Out of practice*, he thought wryly.

Annie watched him curiously. "Where you from then?"

Dalton said nothing.

She sighed. "Look. I'm not asking questions I don't want to hear the answer to. Don't want to know what in hell the two of you were doing in the mountains. Just saw you looking at my belt earlier. I'm wondering where home is."

"Kilkenny," he said finally.

"My pa was from Kilkenny. Went to visit when I was a girl. Were a beautiful old church with a tower that reached to the sky."

Dalton smiled crookedly.

"You remember it, aye? Windows made of glass a thousand colours. Feels like another lifetime, those windows. Might as well be too, with all the chance we got of seeing it again." She smiled faintly. "It's nought but a fairy land now, is Ireland. Somewhere we're best off forgetting."

Dalton nodded. He wished Grace could see home in the same way. A distant memory. Unobtainable.

Annie reached onto the sideboard for the belt. She tossed it to Dalton. "Take it. I've another."

He ran his fingers across its rough stitching. "Thank you." His chest tightened with an unexpected rush of emotion. He stood abruptly. "I need to see Grace." His legs felt weak with whisky.

"She's sleeping."

"I'll not wake her."

The belt in his fist, he let himself into the bedroom. Grace lay on a narrow mattress beneath a mountain of grey blankets. A fat curl lay across her cheek. He pressed his fingers to the side of her face. Her skin was warming; not that deathly cold it had been in the mountains. Her breath tickled his thumb. Life. The relief that washed through him was so intense, it brought a murmur from his throat.

He sat on the edge of the bed. Grace shifted in her sleep. She reached an arm out of the blankets and felt for him, as she had done those cold nights in the mountains. Her eyes fluttered open. She clutched a fistful of his shirt and weakly tugged him forward.

"I dreamt I was watching the sun set over the Tower." She smiled sleepily. "If you stand on the hill at just the right time, the walls turn gold. I'll show you one day." She closed her eyes against the sunlight. "What you going to show me, then?"

"Grace," said Dalton. "Can I lie beside you?"

She mumbled sleepily and shuffled across the mattress. He slid beneath the blankets and laid his head against hers, her curls tickling his nose.

Once, before Van Diemen's Land, he imagined he'd live the life of a normal man. Wife, children. Lying here with his body pressed against Grace's, he saw a flicker of what could have been. It was as though he'd managed to catch hold of a thread of the life that had passed him by. The life stolen from him by his own bad choices. There was no normalcy for a man like him. No wife or children. No one holding him in the dark. This was the best he could hope for. A few stolen moments of intimacy with a woman too delirious to fight, while he waited for the world to hunt him down. He wrapped his arm around Grace's chest. Warmth. She would live. He closed his heavy eyes. Today those stolen moments were enough.

When he opened his eyes again, it was dark. Grace lay on her side, breathing deeply. What had woken him? A creak of the floor. Voices. Dalton peered through the darkness, hot and disoriented.

The night is for the dead, his ma used to say. *Off to bed with you and leave the house for the spirits.*

His hand tensed around Grace's shoulder until reality returned to him. Tonight he slept among the living.

CHAPTER SIXTEEN

Grace woke to a room filled with pale grey light. Alexander lay beside her, his breaths long and slow.

She'd come close to dying, she knew. Would be frozen on top of the mountains if it weren't for him. How to reconcile that with the man who had aimed the rifle at her and Violet? The man who had killed two marines with a single bullet.

In sleep, there was a vulnerability to him, a childishness. Lying with the blankets pulled to his neck, he looked an ordinary man. Had he left a family behind? Grace knew nothing of his life before this place. Had he loved, been loved? Had children of his own? Who had he been before Van Diemen's Land had turned him wild? Strange it had taken a night in civilisation for her to consider such things.

She climbed out of bed. She felt drained and heavy, but more alert than she had in days. Clean flannel petticoats and a blue woollen dress were draped over the end of the bed. Grace had vague recollections of the woman in the mobcap bringing them to her. She searched her blurred memories for the woman's name. Annie?

She washed, buttoned herself into the clean dress and walked slowly into the kitchen. She stopped abruptly. A tall man stood at the table, pouring a mug of tea. His skin was the colour of caramel, his face with the wide, flat features of the blacks. Grace stepped backwards, her spine pressing hard against the wall.

He looked up and smiled wryly. "A black man with a tea cup in his hand. Whatever is the world coming to?"

"I'm sorry," Grace spluttered. "I didn't mean no offense. I … Where's Annie?"

He nodded to the garden. Poured a second mug of tea and placed it on the table. "Here. You're still down on your strength, I imagine."

She nodded her thanks and picked up the cup, eying him curiously.

Annie shouldered open the door and tossed a handful of carrots on the table. She kicked off her muddy boots and wiped her hands on her apron. "I see you met my Jack," she said, pouring herself a mug of tea. "How are you feeling?"

"Better," said Grace. "Much better. Thank you. For everything."

Annie shrugged. "We help each other as we can out here. Still finding our way, aren't we. And Lord knows Jack and me have seen our share of trouble."

"What kind of trouble?"

She gave a humourless laugh. "Irishwoman and a man with black blood in him? You think the rest of the village likes having us around? No sir." She gulped down her tea. "Dogs, the lot of them."

Grace waited for Annie to continue, but she just reached for a knife and began to hack the tops off the muddy carrots.

"Well," said Grace. "Dogs or not, I got to find work. I got to earn some money to get back to Hobart Town. You know of anyone hiring?"

"You ought to head up to the Porters'," said Jack. "I heard they just had three of their lags got freed."

Annie snorted. "Bill Porter's the worst of the lot." She attacked the carrots without looking up.

"Course he is. But she needs money. And Porter's got money." Jack motioned to Grace. "I'll show you which is their house. You can see it from here."

She followed him into the paddock at the front of the cottage. The morning was misty and grey, the sun a perfect circle behind the cloud. Jack pointed to a hill behind the village. A sprawling white house sat on the slope.

"Up there. Bill Porter's. He's a bastard of a man, but he's desperate for workers."

Grace nodded. "What they do to you, then?"

Jack ran a hand through his thick black hair. "Killed our cattle, dug up the crops. Did their best to drive us out."

"But you stayed."

"Where else were we to go? This place is all we got." He smiled to himself. "They underestimated Annie's stubbornness. Takes more than a few dead cows to force that woman from her home."

Grace looked back towards the mountains. Snow glittered on the peaks. "I'm lucky you were here."

Jack followed her gaze. "Men went up there during the black wars. Tried to flush out the natives. There were plenty didn't make it back." He smiled wryly. "Bloody fools come out from the cities. Never seen a mountain in their lives. They think they can take on this land and come out on top."

Grace wrapped her arms around herself, hearing her own foolishness in Jack's words. She shivered. "Alexander, he sees things out there. Ghosts, like. At first I thought it was just his imagination. But there's something about this place, ain't there. It's like the land... remembers." She laughed humourlessly. "You must think me a complete fool."

Jack dug his hands into his pockets. "My ma, she always said the land is alive. It has a spirit. A soul. Perhaps that's what you felt." He began to walk back towards the cottage. Annie was back in the vegetable garden with a shovel in her hand. "Perhaps if the rest of these colonists could feel it, they might respect the place a little more." He touched Grace's shoulder. "You're no fool. I promise you."

She smiled faintly. Suddenly Jack's arm was ripped away.

"Get your hands off her," Alexander hissed. Jack whirled around and shoved hard against his chest. Annie threw down her shovel and charged out of the garden.

"Alexander!" cried Grace. "What in hell?"

He paced in a circle, his hands behind his head. "Get your things," he told her.

Annie hurled out a torrent of bitter Irish. Alexander glared at her.

Grace's eyes darted between them. "What did you say to him?"

Annie planted her hands on her hips and snorted. "Said he's a mad bastard. Ought to have let him freeze."

Grace shoved Dalton into the bedroom. "What the bloody hell's the matter with you?" she cried. "He weren't doing nothing but helping me! And why've you got that filthy shirt on again? You stink like a dead goat." She watched with cold eyes as he pulled off the old shirt and slipped the fresh one over his head. "What's this about then?" she demanded. "You want me all to yourself? Christ Almighty."

Dalton marched into the kitchen to fetch his damp clothes. She chased him through the house.

"You can't go about behaving like this! You're in the real world now! And these people have been nothing but good to us!"

Dalton shoved his dirty trousers into the pack and charged back into the bedroom. The walls of the house seemed to have closed in on him in the night. He'd never meant to stay this long.

"Get your things," he said again.

Grace shook her head. "I ain't going back into the forest."

"Of course you are."

"No. You were right about me going back to Hobart Town. I can't take Nora with no place to go. I'm going to Mr Porter's at the top of the hill. He's looking for help. I got to earn some money so I can make a decent life for the two of us. And then I'll go back for her."

Dalton's insides felt hollow. For a strange, fleeting moment, he saw his isolation for what it had been: a desperate attempt not to face his own shame. A self-imposed purgatory as he waited out the rest of his sorry life. "What will you tell them?" he mumbled.

"I'll tell them the truth. I'm a free settler who fled a violent master in Hobart Town. They don't need to know nothing about New Norfolk."

"They'll take you for a bolter."

"Me? A bolter?" She laughed, then swallowed it abruptly. "They've no proof."

"They don't need proof! This place is corrupt as hell! There are police running around who are lags themselves! Men who'll do anything for that ticket of leave. They'll lock you up for being a bolter until you can prove otherwise. That's the way things work here, Grace. Guilty until proven innocent."

She chewed her thumbnail. She looked different in her blue-striped skirts. Young and clean. Her hair was pinned neatly at the base of her neck. He could smell soap. So this was Grace in the real world.

"I got to do this for Nora. I got to take that risk. Besides, many more nights rolling in the mud, I truly will become mad. I'm going over there soon as I packed my things."

"You can't. You need to rest. You're not well enough to go looking for work."

She smiled out the corner of her mouth. "But I'm well enough to go back into the forest with you, is that right? I'm fine. Just a little tired. I got to do this, Alexander. You know I do."

She gathered her muddy clothes from the end of the bed and folded them neatly. Dalton searched for an argument that might keep her from going. But he saw the determination in her. Determined, he supposed, to move on from the loss of Violet and do something right for the other girl. Determined to shake off the title of *lunatic* she'd been shackled with in Hobart. He felt ill.

Grace turned to him. "Tell me," she said suddenly, "about your life in Ireland."

"What?"

"Who is waiting for you? A wife? A child? I'm sorry, I don't know why I never thought to ask before."

Dalton let out his breath and looked away.

"There was a woman in New Norfolk what saw ghosts," Grace said after a moment. "One night she couldn't bear it no more and hung herself with her bed sheets."

Dalton clenched his teeth. "Why are you telling me this?"

"Because I can see such a thing happening to you. I can see your memories driving you to your death. You're a human being. It ain't right for you to be so alone. No one here knows who you are. You said yourself, the world thinks Alexander Dalton is dead."

"Then why shatter their illusions?"

"I worry for you," said Grace.

"Why?"

She laughed a little. "What you mean, why?"

"Why should you care?"

"Because I can see a decent man in you."

"Is that what you were thinking when we were burying those soldiers?"

"Well. It's like you said, ain't it." She straightened the bedclothes. "You did that for me."

Dalton pulled the blanket from her hands. "I buried the gun behind Annie's house. Marked it with a strip of my shirt so we could find it. We'll dig it up and shoot a couple of kangaroos. Or those cows we passed. And they've got a garden full of carrots. We can take those too."

Grace glared at him. "How dare you even think it after all they've done for us!" She sighed. "Go if you must. I understand." She ran a finger along one of the thick white scars that snaked over to his collarbone. He shivered. She pulled at the lacing of the shirt, closing the linen over the scars and tying it tightly at his neck. She placed her hands on his shoulders and looked into his eyes.

"You saved my life," she said. "Thank you." The front door slammed and she pulled away.

Grace trudged out of the cottage and crossed the rickety bridge into town. She couldn't bear to think what would become of Alexander. More silence, more loneliness. A life lived in the shadow of the dead.

In spite of herself, she'd come to care for him, perhaps more deeply than he deserved. She knew he'd be forever in her thoughts as he hid, waiting out the rest of his life. She felt an ache in her chest. Isolation wasn't what he truly wanted, she was sure. He'd not buried his human need for companionship so deeply.

The Hamilton settlement was little more than a couple of streets, narrow alleys shooting off like fine veins. The roads were thick with muck, but the clean smell of the bush pervaded the stench of civilisation. Grace walked the length of the high street towards the house on the hill. Sandstone cottages were nestled together between bakers and butchers, an apothecary and a looming two-storey inn. Here, a grand private house. There, a crooked shack with drunken men spilling onto the street. A woman passed with a rickety baby carriage. Two men rode horses down the middle of the road, scattering a flock of disoriented chickens.

The place was a speck on London, but after months in the forest, it seemed bustling. Grace drank in the buzz of humanity. She felt alive. Motivated. Like she might begin to rise above the grief that darkened each of her days. She had to do right by Nora now. Find work. Get them out of this filthy colony.

The Porters' was a grand two-storey house like the one Harris had been building in Hobart Town. Grace stood at the edge of the property, her fingers tensing around the fence.

They'll take you for a bolter.

She'd laughed at the thought until she realised that was exactly what she was.

She strode up to the front door and knocked loudly, trying to conjure up her courage. She was shown inside by an old woman in a food-stained apron and instructed to wait in the hall.

She paced in a nervous circle, listening to an ornate wall clock tick away the seconds. Back where she belonged, she realised. Grovelling to the upper class so she might scratch together a living.

God made a place for everyone...

But when the woman returned to lead her into the drawing room, the couple waiting were without the frock coats and finery of the gentry. The man of the house was slouched in an armchair, the sleeves of his linen shirt rolled above his elbows, stockinged feet stretched out in front of him. He was a broad-shouldered man with flat features and a balding head. His wife perched on the edge of the couch, wearing an apron and dark woollen dress, mud streaked along the hem. A younger man with a patchy blonde beard and pocked cheeks hovered behind them. Working-class people, Grace realised. And yet here they were in this grand house with workers of their own. An upside-down colony, for certain, where society's rules were twisted and bent. And Harris had still been ashamed of her.

She managed a curtsey. "Heard you had your convicts freed and was after some new workers."

Porter sat his teacup on the side table. "Where've you come from?"

"London. I mean, Hobart Town. Had to leave. My master was trouble."

"Your master were trouble, or you were trouble?"

Grace chewed her lip.

"I suppose you ain't got no references then."

"No, sir."

"And nothing to prove you ain't a runaway."

She was silent.

Porter cracked his toes. "You got no references, you got no nothing. I ought to have the police check you out. See if the Female Factory's missing any curly-haired Londoners."

Grace's heart sped. "I'm a free settler, sir, I swear it. *Duckenfield,* 1832. London to Hobart Town. Me and Mr Harris and the girls and— "

Porter folded his arms.

"I'll work for half rates," she spluttered. "Give me a trial. Please. One week. I'll be the best worker you ever saw, just you wait. Be twice as good as them lags just got freed."

Porter looked to his wife, who shrugged nonchalantly. "One week trial," he said. "Without no pay. Then we'll see. Agreed?"

"Yes sir." Grace dropped a hurried curtsey. "Thank you ever so much."

Dalton had stood on the edge of the farmland and watched until her silhouetted figure had disappeared.

He dug up the weapons, and trudged towards the mountains. Shot a kangaroo and carried the carcass into the woods. He'd go back to the farms when night fell. Steal what he needed to build a new hut.

He skinned the animal, drained its blood into the river and watched the water turn pink.

What would he need? Ammunition. Powder cartridge. Saw. Boots.

He'd made the same plan by the cattle duffers' fire. Back then, he had craved solitude, stillness. But now, it was the stillness that got to him first. The prattle of the birds. The endless sigh of the river. Sounds so embedded in the landscape, they turned into silence as the night wore on.

Wordlessness had been his sanctuary. Out here, where there was no one to speak, the story of Tom Bodenham's death could never be told. It was the thing Dalton feared more than death: someone looking him in the eye and knowing the crimes he had committed in order to survive.

Whilst he had sat around the fire with the cattle duffers, he'd heard that that madman, Pearce, had made it to Hobart Town. Told their horror story to anyone who would listen. Pearce was sent back to Macquarie Harbour and their story was plastered across the newspapers. Eight names, a hideous crime. The people of Van Diemen's Land urged to keep a watchful eye for the missing convicts. Six of the men, Dalton was sure were dead. Just himself and Pearce left.

Tales from Dalton's own life were relayed back to him by the cattle duffers. Tales of the bolters from Macquarie Harbour who had done the inhuman. Tales of their gruesome deaths. Of his own death. A strange thing to hear, of course.

Greenhill had killed him. Or was it Pearce?

He had run away and died of exhaustion in the forests outside the harbour.

They all still lived and roamed as bushrangers.

That was the thing when a story got passed around. The truth got lost in no time at all. Make it up, tell your own tale. The bloodier, the better.

As he heard these conflicting stories, beer-fuelled gossip told with glowing eyes, it crossed Dalton's mind to say, *Dead? Me?* just to see the looks on the duffers' faces. But of course, then he'd have to face the shame of the crime. So he kept silent. Silence was easy.

He lay beside the fire, listening to the duffers argue the truth of Alexander Dalton and the other missing men. He never wanted to hear those stories again. Never wanted to hear his name spoken as part of such an inhuman horror. Let Alexander Dalton die. Let him live the lonely life of a nameless man.

But he could do this no longer; this *cold, tired, hungry, afraid*. Pretending he could forget his sins by retreating into silence. He hadn't forgotten, had he? Hadn't forgotten Greenhill's flying axe and the sight of Bodenham's mutilated body. The sickness that had lasted long after his stomach was empty.

Perhaps Grace was right. Perhaps the way to make the past fade was to build a new life. Perhaps he truly could do more than hide in the woods and wait for death to find him.

The door to the Porters' kitchen was unlocked. Coals glowed behind the fire screen. Dalton walked into the parlour. A sofa faced the tiled fireplace. Heavy blue curtains, porcelain lamps. A calendar hung on the mantel.

Well, look at that now. The month of August, 1833.

Beside it sat a pair of bronze candleholders and a hideous marble bust of the king. A velvet armchair. Felt like a horse's flank when he rubbed his hands across it.

Upstairs, the hallway was thick with the oily scent of extinguished lamps, the darkness filled with snores and coughs. Three closed doors on either side on the hallway. Where was Grace?

He eased open the first door. Inside, he could make out the shape of a double bed with a couple sleeping inside. In the next room, three beds were laid out like army cots. The children snuffled and sighed in their sleep. All this life around him. Dalton felt dizzy, like he'd overdosed on a drug.

The floor creaked. He froze, not daring to take a step until the silence had thickened. Finally, he turned the handle of a narrow door that opened onto a timber staircase. He felt his way downstairs. The servants' quarters, he was sure of it.

Inside the first room, a single bed and washstand were crammed into narrow confines. And there she was, asleep on her back, the fingers of one hand curled beside her cheek.

He crept to her bedside and shook her shoulder, clamping a hand over her mouth to muffle her gasp. Her eyes widened. His nose was inches from hers. "The castle."

"What in hell?" she hissed.

"You asked me what I'd show you. I'll show you Kilkenny Castle. Six hundred years old and right on the river."

She scrambled out from beneath him. "Leave! This second! You got any idea what will happen if someone catches you here?"

"I had to see you. To tell you about the castle."

She threw her dress on over her shift. Shoved him from the bedroom and out into the yard. A pink dawn was pushing against the bottom of the sky.

"You're a bloody madman, Alexander. Get out of here. If I lose this job because of you, I'll never forgive you."

He grabbed her arm impulsively and squeezed.

"Let go. You're hurting me."

"London, Grace. You want to go back to London, we'll go. We'll get away from this place. This forest. This goddamn prison."

"London?" she repeated. "You want to come to London with me? You think I want my Nora around a man who sneaks into women's bedrooms at night?"

Nora. There'd been no Nora in the London of Dalton's mind. Just he and Grace.

"There's no one," he told her, "in Ireland. No wife or child waiting for me." His grip on her arm tightened. "There's just you in all the world."

Her eyes caught his for a second. She swallowed hard. "Let go of me like I asked. Please."

Dalton heard fear in her voice. He let his hand fall. "This house is a goldmine. There are candleholders on the mantel that'll see us to London."

Grace closed her eyes. "I want you to go. And I don't want to see you again."

He frowned. "Grace—"

"This, Alexander… Breaking in here like this, threatening Jack… it ain't right. Can't you see that? It frightens me. You frighten me. Now please, just leave. The family will be up soon and I got to lay the fires." She gathered an armful of wood from the pile beside the door. Dalton grabbed at her and the logs thudded to the porch. Her eyes flashed as she bent to pick them up. The door creaked.

"Is there a problem, Miss Ashwell?" A balding man stood over her, arms folded against his thick stomach. He wore a muddy greatcoat over his nightshirt.

She stood. "I beg your pardon, sir. I—"

The master looked Dalton up and down. "Who the hell are you?"

Dalton opened his mouth. He looked at Grace, her eyes unforgiving.

She'd turn him in. Now they were out of the bush, she had no need to trust him. They'd haul him down to the police station and Alexander Dalton would be brought back to life just long enough to be led to the scaffold.

"My friend here's come to see you about some work," she announced brassily. "He heard you's looking for help on the farm. He's saving to get to London. I told him how you were so good as to give me a chance and he said he'd be willing to work for half wages too."

Dalton clenched his jaw. He realised he wasn't breathing.

"Told him to come see you first thing in the morning. Didn't think he'd take it quite so literally, coming at this hour. Must be his enthusiasm."

The master scratched his beard. "Half wages? This true?"

Dalton thought of running. His legs would crumble beneath him, he was sure of it. "Aye," he mumbled.

The master looked him up and down. "What's your name?"

Dalton scrabbled through his memories. "Brown," he said. "Matthew Brown."

Porter nodded. "Wait here. I want a word with my son about this first." He strode inside, letting the door slam.

Grace gathered the firewood and shot Dalton a glare. "Where are the weapons?"

"In the paddock."

"Bury them," she said. "And stay away from me. Come to me in the night like that again and I'll tell Porter who you really are."

CHAPTER SEVENTEEN

Conduct Record of Convicts Arriving in Van Diemen's Land 1804-1830

Alexander Dalton, Caledonia *1820*
December 12th, 1820: Drunk and disorderly.
Fourteen days labour for the government in his own time

It turned out the great man of the house, Bill Porter, was hauled out from England in 1803. One of the first government men to do his time in the desolate hell of Van Diemen's Land. But the authorities, they just loved old Porter. No black marks on his conduct record. Life sentence whittled down to a pardon within five years. Five fucking years.

At his ma's insistence, Bill's son Edward took Dalton out to show him the farm and spent the whole time rabbiting on about how his pa was a petty thief come good.

"And now look," he said, waving an arm at the acres of land, "all this is ours. A gift from the lieutenant governor himself."

Dalton saw what he could have had if he'd kept his fists to himself. Bill Porter, he realised, got all this by bowing down to the authorities. By licking his overseer's arse and doing what he was told.

Edward was nineteen or twenty, with the flaccid shoulders of a farmer who liked to dish out his work to other men. Too much blond hair on his head and not enough on his chin. Spoke with the wide vowels of the currency lads and lasses. Brown skin that had never known the bitterness of a European winter.

At dusk, the workers were herded into the kitchen where the cook had laid out a spread of food Dalton had not seen since he was a convict worker in Oxley.

Mutton and vegetables, gravy, measures of watered-down rum. Of course, in Oxley he was eating stale bread while the smell of mutton drifted beneath the door. He couldn't remember the last time such a meal was cooked for him.

There were five of them around that table. The elderly cook and the children's governess, an older woman with hair so thin and pale her scalp showed through. The stable-hand; his muscular arms bursting out of rolled-up shirtsleeves. And there was Grace, dishing out polite smiles, trying to hide her excitement that she was about to eat something that hadn't been dangling in their traps all afternoon.

Each turned to Dalton with chirpy introductions and polite nods. How to fit in? To seem a normal man? To behave as though he weren't about to piss himself in fear? He took a long gulp of his rum.

The cook shuffled round the table with her gravy pot and slopped a spoonful onto each slab of meat.

"Lumps again, Ellen," the stable-hand grinned. "Just the way I like it."

She whacked him on the knuckles with her serving spoon. "Got a nice pot of porridge on the stove you can have if you got a problem with my gravy. Plenty left now we only got two lags to feed."

Dalton snorted to himself. The convicts were eating gruel and here he was with a plate full of mutton. He picked up a slice of carrot and popped it in his mouth. Grace glared at him, gesturing to her knife and fork.

For Christ's sake. He grabbed the fork in his fist and stabbed the slab of meat, brought it whole to his lips and began to chew. At least with his mouth full he couldn't be expected to speak. The stable-hand snorted with laughter, but Grace's eyes were black.

"This is ever so good," she said, slicing off a miniscule piece of mutton. Wasn't she a little social butterfly with her manners and breathy compliments. A few nights ago, Dalton had watched her drop a piece of smoked meat in the mud, wipe it on her front and swallow it whole.

The cook winked at Grace. "Nice to have some appreciation. Can tell you're a city girl." She pointed a fat finger at the stable-hand. "Better manners than this country hick here. London, you said?"

And then Grace was off. A great torrent of jabber about Stepney and blue houses and a sideshow with a mermaid. Dalton refilled his rum.

The stable-hand, it seemed, had seen a sideshow too when he was a lad. Blathered on about conjoined twins while Grace giggled and fluttered her lashes like something had flown into her eye.

Dalton despised the Grace of civilisation. All flirty eyes and exaggerated hand gestures. Sickening. Did she learn this performance from the toff emporium of Mr James Harris? Wondered if a little of her London charm might earn her an extra sliver of mutton? He liked her better when she smelled of river muck.

He lay awake that night, squeezed onto a sleeping pallet beside the stable-hand. So close, Dalton could feel the heat of his body. Would have thought himself back at Macquarie Harbour if it were gruel on the stable-hand's breath and not roast meat. Head swimming from the rum, he took his coat and blanket and carried them out to the barn.

He came into the house before dawn. He would sneak back to the servants' quarters and no one would know he'd spent the night with the animals.

A fine layer of frost lay over the land. They'd be up and about soon, these farmers. Dalton would have a master again. He felt an old tension return to his shoulders.

The back door opened into the kitchen. He took a match from the box above the range and lit a candle, carrying it into the parlour.

Here it was. The life he could have chosen.

A government man with a velvet armchair. Wasn't that just the best thing you ever bloody well heard?

These fucking colonists, he thought. Trying to turn this godforsaken prison into a civilised land.

Don't you know the things that have happened out there?

On the other side of this island, men were pulled from the triangle and sent to the logging stations with their shoes full of their own blood. Here, these bastards sat in velvet chairs and lay jewels upon their mantels. Could none of them feel the darkness in the forest? Or sense the ghosts hiding in the shadows? Could none of them see the monsters this system had created?

He held the candle up to the stone features of the sculpture on the mantel. He thought of his wooden carvings. Imagined them staring across the empty hut, creepers growing up the wall and swallowing them whole. Above the statue was an enormous gilded mirror. Dalton lifted the candle and, for the first time in more than a decade, looked into his own eyes.

God Almighty, who was this man? His skin was brown and weathered, his beard wiry. A permanent scowl creased the bridge of his nose. He brought a hand to his chin to make sure it was really him.

The last time he'd seen his reflection, he was a young man of twenty-three. An insignificant lag. He'd never seen Macquarie Harbour. Never met Robert Greenhill or Alexander Pearce or wretched Tom Bodenham. Had never considered the lengths he'd go to in order to ensure his own survival.

Once, he'd been vaguely handsome. There'd been women – flings, games, Maggies and Sallies. Never love. But now: such darkness in his eyes. He felt like all the horrors of his life were etched into his face. What had these colonists seen when he'd sat amongst them at the dinner table?

He turned his shoulders, checking those tell-tale scars were hidden beneath his coat. White streaks showed above his neck cloth. He wished he hadn't cut his hair. Wished he'd let himself hide.

After breakfast, Dalton traipsed out to the farm with Edward Porter and the two remaining convict workers, short stocky men with scowls and hunched shoulders. One was Dalton's age, with a shock of orange hair on his head and chin. The other was older, greyer. Sunken and weary.

Frost crunched beneath their boots. There were fences to rebuild and their arms were loaded with axes and saws. The redhead looked over his shoulder and gave Dalton a twisted half-smile.

"All this is ours," Edward announced. "Right up to the creek."

Yes, thought Dalton, *you told me that already.*

The four of them got to work in the wood yard, sawing and planing tree trunks into fence posts. Dalton let himself get lost in the physicality of it, the way he used to do hauling pines at Sarah Island. Feel the burn in his arms instead of the ache in his chest. Don't think further than the next swing of the axe.

They'd not been at it a half-hour, when Edward wiped his brow with his shirtsleeve and wandered across the wood yard. Following his lead, the redheaded convict released the saw and let it rest in the log.

"Keep at it, Howell," shot Edward. "You got a whole forest to get through after that one." He nodded at Dalton. "Why you still got that coat on, bog-trotter?"

Dalton kept his eyes on the log. "There's ice in the air."

"Ice in the air. You're pouring sweat, you mad bugger."

Dalton tried to lose himself in the rhythm of the plane against the wood. *Shah. Shah.*

"Take it off. I'm hot at the sight of you."

Dalton looked over his shoulder at Edward. "I'm not one of your convict slaves."

Edward cleared his throat and spat into the grass. He leant against the barn and watched the men work.

Dalton snorted. "Lazy fucking narrow-back."

Howell grinned.

"You say something?" Edward demanded.

"No, sir. Not a word." He lost himself in the beat of it. *Shah, shah, shah.*

CHAPTER EIGHTEEN

Hobart Town Gazette
Friday 25th June, 1824

"The Learned Gentlemen then proceeded to detail certain confessions made by the prisoner [Alexander Pearce], before ... Lieutenant Cutherbertson – commandant at Macquarie Harbour – and to the Reverend Robert Knopwood. Confessions which, although in some respects inconsistent, would yet, when coupled with all the facts, merit the most serious attention."

The bastards hired them. Called Dalton and Grace into the parlour on Friday morning and said they'd have them on at half rates, three shillings a week. Three shillings.

Did you do the sums, Grace?

Four years or more of sweeping the floor until she got two tickets back to London. Good thing she'd lost Violet, or she'd have had to earn enough for three.

They stood side by side in the Porters' parlour. Grace was gushing with curtseys and thank yous, pretending Dalton wasn't there.

He'd proved himself good with a saw. Convinced the Porters to hire him and made that Edward look like a right pansy in the process. He'd thought she'd have been pleased with him.

He followed her into the kitchen. Brought his muddy boots from the doorstep and sat at the table. He slid his feet into them slowly, not taking his eyes off her. She had a faraway look about her. "I thought you'd be happy," he said.

"I am happy."

"You don't seem it." He followed her gaze. Through the window, he saw the Porters' two daughters rolling a hoop across the lawn.

Grace went to the cupboard for the broom.

"You miss your girls," said Dalton.

She attacked the floor with violent, noisy scrapes. The broom shot out and collected his ankle. "Don't you got work to do?"

Dalton snatched the broom.

"Alexander—"

"Speak to me," he said. "Please."

She sighed. "They know you're sleeping in the barn. People are talking. Porter's only kept you on because he ain't going to find no-one else who'll work as cheap." She folded her arms. "Why are you out there?"

"I don't want people around me."

"You've had me around you for months."

"But these people… They're not like you."

Grace took the broom. "Please, just come inside. Try to fit in. Whatever you've come to believe, you belong in here, not out with the animals."

Dalton bent to lace his boots.

"Alexander? Will you try? Please?"

He nodded.

Grace smiled faintly. "Thank you."

A week, and then a rifle shot in the cold morning. Bill Porter stood on the edge of the cattle paddock with the gun in his hand. Beside him, Edward peered into the scrub. They stalked back towards the wood yard where the convict workers hovered, watching with disinterested eyes. Dalton stood beside them with his arms folded.

Mrs Porter stepped onto the porch and squinted. "Catch them, Bill?"

Porter spat in the grass. "Fucking animals ran off like dogs. You—" He held the rifle out to Dalton. "You a good shot?"

Dalton nodded.

Porter tossed him the gun and powder. "Couple of blacks come out of the bush and nicked my boots. Go find them. Take Howell with you."

Dalton slid a ball into the chamber. The click was loud in the cold morning. He wove through the cattle paddock and out into the thin blue-grey scrub on the fringe of the plains.

Howell trotted behind him. "We going to shoot these bastards then?"

"Why would I want to do that?" Dalton looked down. No flattened foliage here. If there truly had been blacks at the farm, they'd not come this way. He kept walking anyway.

Howell began to whistle. A tuneless thing with two flat notes. *Tuu, haa.* "Heard a story once. They say some bolters got themselves lost in these woods."

Tuu, haa.

Dalton felt something twist inside him.

"Done some real bad things. Inhuman things." Howell stomped through the scrub. "You heard those stories too?"

Dalton shook his head. Began to walk faster.

"I think you have." Howell combed two fingers through his rust-coloured beard. "Porter'll find you out, you know. Sooner or later."

Dalton kept his eyes down. "Don't know what you're talking about."

"Aye, you do. A man stumbles out of the bush half dead, you tend to remember him."

And Dalton realised it sickly. He'd seen that bushel of orange hair before. Seen this man in a cattle duffing ring on the Fat Doe River. Howell smiled, like he'd seen the flicker of recognition in Dalton's eyes. He stopped walking.

"A silent man. A man that don't speak because he don't want no one to know his secrets." He laughed long and low. "Can't imagine the Porters would take it too well to find they'd hired a bolter. Especially one with a horror story behind him."

Dalton stared him down. "I'm no bolter."

Howell grinned. "I seen you come out of the bush, mate. Convict slops hanging off your shoulders. That canary yellow they dish out at Macquarie Harbour. I gave you my coat and a double ration of salted pork. Half carried you to the fire. You'd be dead if it weren't for me." He stepped close and held a grimy finger inches from Dalton's nose. "You, Mr

Dalton, are the only one of those bolters never properly accounted for. You left our ring the day before we raided Bothwell. Ran into the bush. We all knew why you'd disappeared. We all knew what you'd done. Did you really think us too foolish to put the pieces together?"

Dalton ran his hand along the shaft of the rifle. "You got the wrong man."

"Have I now?" Howell chuckled and clapped him on the back. "I'll have to beg your pardon then."

That night, laughter rose from the house. A party. The man of the house Bill's birthday.

Dalton paced across the barn.

We all knew what you'd done.

You, Mr Dalton...

There was no anonymity in this land of new beginnings.

He stumbled into the night and peered through the steamy window into the parlour. Guests were crammed around a blazing fire. There was Bill Porter, his bald head shining like a melon, roaring with laughter at what Dalton was sure was one of his own jokes. People were clustered around him, hands full of rum and cigars. Strangers, workers, faces Dalton recognised from the farm beside Annie and Jack's. Grace was hovering by the hearth, watching the Porters' girls toss knucklebones on the rug.

Dalton felt disconnected from the world on the other side of the glass. A world he'd stopped being a part of the night Tom Bodenham had died.

"Let's do this." Greenhill whispering in Pearce's ear. A sound Dalton had never been able to forget.

They'd been walking for sixteen days. Macquarie Harbour lay behind them and who knew what lay ahead. The last of the bread they'd eaten days ago. Dalton's steps were crooked with hunger. His vision was blurred, throat dry.

It wasn't supposed to be like this, was it. They were supposed to have reached the mainland by now in that cursed little boat. Or reached China. He ought to have been drinking ale with some beautiful lass in Kilkenny.

Instead, his stomach was bloated and leeches crawled inside his boots. He didn't have the strength to stop them. The man Greenhill chose to sacrifice wouldn't have the strength to stop him either.

"Tonight," said Greenhill. Dalton was crouched behind a monstrous pine tree. He didn't mean to hide. He was just too weak to stand.

"I can't." Pearce. *Yes, you can.* "Who then?" Pearce asked.

Greenhill whispered, "Dalton. Dalton, the flogger."

So that's your justice then, Greenhill? I take the whip to your back once under orders and you'll cut out my heart?

Did he know Dalton was there? Did he want the flogger to see death coming? Dalton thought of trying to run, turning his back and tearing into the bush. But if he moved, the twigs beneath him would crackle. Ferns would sigh and birds would scatter. Greenhill would see him.

The axe dangled by Greenhill's side, bumping against his calf. Pearce stood opposite, but Greenhill's eyes looked past him, past Dalton. Thoughtful, hateful eyes. Was he tied up on the triangle at Sarah Island, while Dalton heaved fifty strokes of the cat into his spine? Couldn't he hear the overseer beside them, spitting and cursing?

Put your bloody back into it, Dalton, or you'll be next.

Greenhill's eyes panned across the bush, and for a moment Dalton was sure he had been seen.

The night before, he'd sat with Ned Brown and Kennerly, hidden from the others. They'd talked of running. Talked of leaving Greenhill to his nightmarish plans. They'd argued on it.

Kennerly and Brown wanted to go back to the harbour. Face the commandant and his floggers. But there was no going back for Dalton. That hopeless existence at Macquarie Harbour, that wasn't life. He'd rather be dead. Easier to say such a thing though, than face the reality of it. *I'd rather die,* a man could say with all the certainty in the world. But when death was staring him in the face, well that was a whole other story.

Greenhill and Pearce, they turned and spoke. A month from now they'd be circling each other in the night, fighting to be the last man alive.

Dalton stayed where he was, not daring to make the bush crackle or the birds scatter. He stayed as the sun sank, trying to keep his eyes on Greenhill and Pearce as they wove through the purple forest. And suddenly: the crack of iron to bone, hanging on the cold air. Men shouted and cursed at Greenhill.

English dog.

Silence fell over them.

Bodenham. He was only a boy. The youngest of them all. Why him? Did his legs not move as quickly as the rest? Had he cursed at Greenhill under his breath? Looked at him the wrong way over the supper tables one night? Or had he been singled out for his Scottish blood, Pearce reluctant to have the death of a fellow Irishman on his hands?

Had the poor bastard any idea of what was coming? Was there time for thought when he saw Greenhill's axe come towards him? Did his poor, sorry life play out before his eyes? Did he see the stained bulkheads of the convict ship and the blood-splattered triangle on Sarah Island? Or was it just fear and hunger and then eternal darkness?

Afterwards, Dalton went to the creek. Tried to purge himself of all he'd swallowed. Fingers down his throat, retching into the stream. But his body clung to those precious scraps of meat. He splashed his face. The water was icy but he was hot with sweat and fear. Feverish. His slops were thick with dirt and hanging off one shoulder.

He heard a whisper: "That you, Dalton?"

He stumbled, terrified. Freezing water filled his boots. "Get the fuck away from me."

Bodenham would keep the men going for a few days at most. And they'd all stood on the top of that ridge and seen the endless miles of nothing. Someone would be next. If Greenhill had his way, Dalton wouldn't survive the second swing of the axe.

But this was Bill Kennerly, eyes glowing in the light of the moon. Another man behind him. Ned Brown. Last night, they'd talked themselves out of leaving. Convinced themselves there'd be no bloodshed. They were messmates. Brothers in arms. Surely not even Greenhill could go through with such a thing.

But now there was one man less among them. Kennerly squeezed Dalton's shoulders, like he was trying to stop his humanity escaping.

"You're going back then?" asked Dalton. "Back to the harbour?"

"Going anywhere but here. I'd rather die than have this on my conscience. Thought there were nowhere on this earth worse than Sarah Island, but we're all wrong sometimes, aye?"

In every moving shape in the darkness, Dalton saw the arc of Greenhill's axe. In every sound he heard the choke of Bodenham's last breath.

"Kennerly." The footsteps paused. "I'm coming with you."

At daybreak, Brown and Kennerly turned west, back towards Sarah Island. Both men had refused to eat the night before. They'd be on the edge of starvation by the time they reached the harbour. Both would be dead by week's end.

Dalton turned east. Scratched out a life on the edge of survival.

He sank against the outside wall of the house, sweat trickling down his back. What a fool he'd been to think he could erase himself from history. A horror story like theirs would never die. It would be told around campfires for a hundred years or more. Spoken of over market counters, across bars pooled with beer. Told by children hiding under the bedclothes and trying to work themselves into nightmares. No one had forgotten. Eleven years and Howell had known his face at first sight. Had known his story, his name, his crime.

The kitchen door flew open and noise spilled into the yard. A sea of heads and voices. Among them were Edward and the stable-hand with the men Dalton recognised as Annie's neighbours. Two of Edward's younger brothers raced into the wood yard with a cricket bat and ball. Dalton tried to disappear into the shadows.

"What you doing out here, bog-trotter?" drawled Edward. "Our company not good enough for you?"

The faces came towards him. He stepped back. Felt the wall of the house hard against his spine.

"Leave him alone." Grace pushed past Edward. "Are you all right?"

Dalton nodded.

Edward slung an arm around Grace's shoulder. "I want to tell you a story, Miss Ashwell."

Grace glanced sideways at Dalton. "What is it?"

"You'll like this one, I'll warrant." Edward gulped his beer, a trickle escaping out the side of his mouth. "This is the story of Michael Howe, the bolter."

"I ain't interested." She unhooked herself from Edward's arm.

"He lived in the bush for six years like a savage. They caught him at the river just north of Bothwell. Cut off his head and sent it back to

Hobart Town." He grinned. "Governor wanted proof he was dead, see. They can be right bastards, them bolters. Dangerous too."

Grace snorted. "Fine story." She pulled Dalton away from Edward and the others. "Come on. You'll have a drink at least." She led him into the house and poured a glass of brandy from the bottle on the table, pressing it into his hand. "Something's happened," she said. "What?"

Dalton took a drink. What if Howell were to tell her? What if she knew?

"Nothing's happened." He gulped a mouthful and carried his glass back out to the yard. And then a rough hand was on his shoulder, yanking his arm backwards. The glass flew, its contents spilling across the grass.

"That's my pa's brandy," said Edward. "Better it go to waste than be drunk by the likes of you."

Dalton raised his fist. Grace's hand shot out and snatched his wrist.

"Bugger off, Edward," she snapped. "You're pissed as a bloody sailor."

Edward laughed and waved his empty measure at Dalton. "You catch those savages then? Second time this month they've come in and nicked our boots."

"Why would the blacks want your boots?" Grace demanded.

"As if I know how their savage brains work. They're right devils, those black Irish." He gave a liquored-up snort. "That's what we call them round here, you know. The black Irish."

Grace's hand tensed around Dalton's wrist. She glared until Edward gave up and stumbled out to the wood yard to join in the cricket match. She let her hand fall. "He's just trying to stir you up. Don't give him what he wants."

"Stay away from him. He's a bastard."

"Course he is. But his pa is paying us and we was lucky to get any work at all." Her eyes followed the children as they raced after the ball.

"Those kids," said Dalton. "It's not good for you to be around them."

Grace looked at her feet. "I'm fine," she said, though the drink in her blood sent a tremor through her voice. "Porter's kids ain't nothing like Violet."

"Let's leave," he said suddenly.

Grace sighed. "Don't be mad. Just tell me what's happened. Is it

Edward? Does he know something?"

Dalton shook his head. "These people are just scum."

"That they may be, but they're the only way I got of making a life for Nora."

"The candlesticks on the mantel. They're worth a fortune."

Grace glared at him. "No. We ain't thieves." She sighed with weary resignation. "You said you'd try and fit in, Alexander. This don't seem like trying to me."

Grace left the house with a list of medicines to fetch from the apothecary. The wind was icy but the sky a vibrant blue. Her boots crunched on the path, her hair whipping around her cheeks. The days were growing longer and the morning frosts beginning to melt in great bursts of sun. She was craving the spring. Rebirth. A reminder it was possible to start again.

She pulled her cloak tightly around her, savouring the stillness of the walk down the hill into town. After three months in the wilderness, the constant bustle of the house was exhausting. In the two weeks she'd been with the Porters, she'd worked harder than she ever had. Harder even than those first few months with Charlotte Harris when she'd been desperate to prove herself indispensable. She'd been exhausted at the end of every day then too, but it was a mental exhaustion – remembering all the quirks and etiquette of the wealthy. With the Porters, it was purely physical. As the only housemaid, her list of tasks seemed unending – fifteen-hour days of scrubbing, blacking and sweeping. Mostly, she welcomed the busyness, the aches in her body every night. It kept her from counting how many months and years she would need to scrub, black and sweep until she had enough to return to England. Kept her from focusing on all she had lost.

She bought the medicines for Mrs Porter and walked back down the sludge of the high street. Suddenly a little girl darted across the road, blonde plaits streaming out behind her. Grace stopped breathing. She dropped the parcel, the bottles thudding at her feet.

Violet.

CHAPTER NINETEEN

Grace leapt over the bottles and ran. "Violet!"

The girl disappeared around the corner. Grace tore down the side street, slipping, stumbling through the mud.

There, at the bottom of the street. Blonde hair. Brown dress, white pinny.

Violet darted out from between two warehouses and into the filthy grog shop at the end of the alley. Grace rattled the door. Pounded on the window. An older woman with a long nose and narrow eyes poked her head out the door. She reeked of tobacco.

"Ain't nothing for sale today. Coppers are on the prowl. They heard my whisky comes from something other than an honest source. Told 'em they're wrong of course. This is a fine law-abiding establishment. But I'm shutting up til I can get rid of it anyway."

"Did you see a little girl?" Grace asked breathlessly. "In a brown dress?"

"Ain't seen no one."

"She came in here." Grace tried to elbow her way through the door. "Let me in. Please."

"No chance, missy. You could be working for them coppers for all I know."

"I ain't working for no-one. I saw my Violet come in here! Let me through!"

"You're mistaken." The woman threw her weight against the door and it slammed, narrowly missing Grace's fingers. She pounded on the glass but the woman had disappeared. Grace's heart pounded. Was Violet truly alive? Was this woman hiding her? She didn't know whether to cry with happiness or grief.

She crossed the alley and peered up at the tavern. The narrow building was nestled between two small cottages; one with broken windows that looked to be abandoned. Grace slunk down the lane at the side of the building. She rattled the back door. Locked.

The barmaid threw open the door. "Get the hell out of here," she hissed. "We ain't got your girl. Now bugger off before I get my pistol."

Grace hurried back down the alley and hid between two crooked huts, keeping her eyes glued to the tavern.

As it grew dark, handfuls of men sidled up to the front door, to be shooed away by the barmaid. Some drifted away quietly, others hurled abuse, but the doors remained locked. One man pulled a bottle from his coat pocket and held it up to his friends. They howled with delight and stumbled down the road, laughing and passing it between them. Grace held her breath as they passed. She pressed her back against the wall of the hut, trying to hide without losing her view of the tavern.

One of the men caught her eye and grinned, revealing a gap where his front teeth had been. "And here I thought my night was ruined." He dug into his pocket and held out a sixpence.

"I'm sorry," Grace said tensely. "You're mistaken."

"Am I? Ain't that a shame." He pressed his arm against the wall to block her path. He stank of piss and cheap booze. Grace's heart began to race. She tried to duck beneath his arm. He snatched her wrist and dragged her back sharply, digging a hand inside her cloak. Her knee flew into his groin. The man grunted in pain and Grace shoved her way past him, stumbling in the mud. She scrambled to her feet and ran.

Footsteps crunched behind her. Curses and drunken laughter. She kept sprinting towards the lamps of the high street. A rough hand snatched her arm.

"Grace."

She stumbled into Alexander's chest and gulped down her breath. She looked over her shoulder. The men caught sight of her with Alexander and dispersed back down the alley.

"What are you doing here?" she asked breathlessly.

Alexander stared after the men, his eyes black. "I've been looking for you. Mrs Porter said you never came back from town. That's a bad street. Don't go down there again."

"I saw her. I saw Violet."

"What?"

"She's in the tavern. The barmaid has her, I'm sure of it. She's hiding her."

Alexander paused. "Why would she do that?"

"How should I know?"

He took her arm. "Come on now, let's go back to the Porters'."

"Are you mad? I ain't going nowhere! I have to find her!"

He hesitated. "It wasn't her. How could it be?"

"I don't know! But it was!"

Alexander held her shoulders. "Listen to me. Whoever you saw, it wasn't Violet. I'm sure of it."

"How do you know that?"

He dropped his hands and sighed. "Because it doesn't make any sense for her to be here."

"I know what I saw." She wiped her muddy hands on her skirt began to walk towards the alley.

"You need to sleep."

"How could I sleep? Violet is out there. That awful woman's got her. I got to go back and keep watch."

"Then I'll come with you," said Alexander. "You shouldn't be down there alone."

They sat with their backs against a cottage fence, eyes on the darkened tavern. The lamps on the main street did little to light the shadows. Dalton blinked hard to fight off a wave of exhaustion. Beside him, Grace was sitting up on her knees, eyes alert, squinting through the darkness.

He had to tell her the truth about the girl. Owed her the truth. But he couldn't stand to think what it would do to her. There was a fragile peace between them he couldn't bear to overturn.

He knew she needed his innocence. Needed the image of an easy death for Violet. No violence, no suffering. Just a dream-filled sleep, surrounded by coloured birds and a glittering river. An end for Violet that made her sorrow a little easier to carry.

He didn't want Grace to crawl through her days drowning in guilt and regret. There was too much life in her for that. He couldn't bear to watch her fade into the same darkness he woke to each morning. Her pain made him ache. He'd forgotten he was capable of empathy. He felt agonisingly human. A part of him longed for that wordless void he had existed in for the last decade.

When the sky began to lighten, he said, "She's not coming out. Even if she's in there, we'll not find her from here."

Grace stood and whacked at the mud caked to her skirt. "Then we've got to break in."

"We can't do that. You'll lose your job. You don't want that, aye?" He clambered to his feet. "We'll come back tonight when the tavern is open. If she's here, we'll find her then." He caught a flicker of hope in her eyes and hated himself for it. He put a gentle hand to her back. "Come on now. Let's go back to the Porters'."

The moment supper finished, Grace grabbed her cloak and charged from the house. Her eyes were red rimmed with sleeplessness. Her food had gone untouched.

They traipsed into town without speaking. Laughter and yellow light from the grog shop spilled onto the road.

Dalton followed Grace inside. The air was thick and smoky. A fiddler played in the corner, accompanied by laughter and the clink and thud of glasses. Red-lipped women with breasts spilling from cinched corsets sashayed across the room. Dalton looked away, both aroused and oddly intimidated. His every sense felt heightened, overloaded. He fought the urge to run back to the empty street. Instead, he shoved his way towards the bar. He needed a drink.

Grace gripped his arm tightly as though she knew he was contemplating escape. "I've got to get into the rooms above the tavern." She narrowed her eyes at the barmaid. "We'll wait by the counter until that witch is out of the way."

At the bar sat Howell, watching the working girls with interest. Dalton cursed under his breath.

Grace glanced at him. "What?"

"Howell. Porter's government man."

"So what? He's nothing. Ain't even supposed to be here. We ought to report him."

Howell turned, his face breaking into a grin. He slid off his stool and ambled towards them. "Well now. The silent man."

"Leave us be," said Dalton.

Howell clapped him on the back. "No need to be like that. Let's all be civil and have a drink, shall we?"

The barmaid glared as Grace approached. "You again. Thought I told you to bugger off."

Dalton slammed a coin onto the counter. "We're paying customers." The woman eyed him warily before sliding the money into her apron pocket and handing over two glasses of ale. Dalton took a long gulp. Weak and watery. He longed for the numbing effect of Porter's brandy.

Three young men joined them at the bar. They wore holey trousers and stained shirts. Their hands and nails were grimy. "Got good news for you, Howell," said one. He opened the package in his fist to reveal a woolly cloud of tobacco. "New crop's ready for sale."

Howell grinned. "Brilliant. I bet my mate here would like a sample."

The man shoved the tobacco under Dalton's nose. "Fresh picked. Best in the colony. We'll do you a good deal."

Dalton turned away.

Howell gulped his ale. "It's good stuff. Billy over there brought the seeds all the way from Africa. We been growing it out by the creek. Selling it to the toffs. It's made us rich men."

Dalton snorted. "Shame you've not got the freedom to use it."

"That it is." Howell clapped him on the back. "But you see, silent man, I'm inspired by you. You ought to be swinging. And yet here you are, swanning around this bar with a pretty girl on your arm and Porter's money in your pocket. You make me think a life sentence may not always be as long as it seems."

Dalton kept his eyes averted. Howell thumped his arm and nodded towards a blond man on the opposite side of the tavern.

"That there's Jim Berry," he told Dalton. "Serving his sentence in the bloody police force."

Berry was tall and thin, with trousers that reached his ankles. He'd adopted an odd lean against the table while one of the working girls played with the buttons on his coat.

"Happening all the time out here. People started whinging about the bushrangers. Asked them down in Hobart to send us more police. Instead we got Jim Berry." Howell nudged Grace, who was doing her best to ignore the men. "D'you ever hear such a thing, missy? Police force full of bloody lags."

Grace gave Howell a fleeting glance, then turned back to watch the door behind the counter.

Howell laughed. "What you reckon, Mr Dalton? Ever fancy yourself as a copper?"

A shout and clatter of glasses rose from the men at the back of the room. The barmaid cursed and shuffled out from behind the counter. Seizing her chance, Grace leapt from her stool and darted through the door behind the bar. Dalton chased her up a creaking timber staircase to a dim, low-ceilinged hallway.

"Violet!" She rattled and thumped on each of the doors. The steps thudded and Howell appeared behind them.

"What in hell is she doing?" Behind Howell stood one of the working girls from the bar. She was tall and broad shouldered, her curves accentuated by a tight bodice and dirty blue dress. Yellow hair was piled on top of her head, loose pieces clinging to her cheeks and neck. She looked to Grace and Dalton with creased, flinty eyes. "What do you want?"

"My little girl, Violet. Where is she?"

Howell clamped a hand around the top of Grace's arm. "I'll get rid of her, Maryann. The little dishclout can't hold her drink."

"Let go of her," hissed Dalton.

The woman snorted. "Too late for you to start being helpful, Daniel Howell." She turned to Grace. "Only girl in there is Emma. My daughter."

"You're lying. Open the door."

Maryann sighed and pulled a key from inside her bodice. Grace pushed her way into the room. Maryann stepped back to allow Dalton and Howell inside.

The bedsit smelled of tobacco and bodies. A lamp hissed on a crooked table. Blankets were strewn across the mattress in the centre, a crib pushed against one wall.

A little girl was asleep on a pallet by the hearth, her blonde hair in two messy plaits. A rag doll lay at her side. Her face was unmistakably Howell's.

Maryann folded her arms. "That who you saw?"

Grace stared at the girl for a long time. Her eyes glistened. Finally, she cleared her throat. "I'm sorry. I thought she were someone else."

Grace walked back to the Porters' house in silence. She sat on her bed and hugged her knees, without bothering to remove her cloak or boots. The loss of Violet felt raw.

She reached beneath her mattress and pulled out her pouch of money. Six shillings. Wouldn't get her back to Hobart Town, let alone London. She piled the coins into a stack on the mattress. They shimmered in the glow of her lamp.

She missed her girls so desperately. Longed to hold them to her, one little head pressed into each of her shoulders. She'd never hold them both that way again. Violet was lost forever, and each day she felt Nora slipping further away too. Even if by miracle she made it back London, where could she go? And what to future? No man would have a barren woman for a wife. Was she to leave Nora in the hands of her gin-soaked mother while she went out at dawn each morning to work in the factories? Sell her body like the mother of Howell's daughter?

She'd trawled through the same arguments with herself when Harris's child was growing inside her. They'd led her back to the blue house. Without Harris, she had nothing. But the blue house was gone. Her relationship with Harris had rotted and crumbled. How was it possible, she wondered, to have such love for the twins and such hatred for their father?

She'd heard love and hate were two sides of the same coin. Never understood such a thing until James Harris. She'd loved him with a passion that went deeper than her desire for the good life. She had drawn close to him for his wealth and the security it offered, but she knew that even if he were the poorest man on earth, she'd have followed him to the slums and been happy just to wake up beside him.

Once, however fleetingly, he'd loved her too. She was sure of it. If he truly were a poor man, they might have been together for real, without the critical eyes of society on them. It had been a thrill at first; waiting until the house was silent to sneak into his bedroom. Curtseying by day, undressing him by night. But she'd learned quickly that being in love made you want to share. She longed to tell the world she fell asleep with James Harris's lips in her hair. But she would never have what Charlotte had had: that freedom to walk on his arm, to welcome him home with a kiss.

She'd believed that Harris had hated the secrecy as much as she had. Believed he longed for the relative freedom Van Diemen's Land would bring. But with the thrill of the secret ripped away, she saw their relationship for what it truly was. Master and concubine. She'd been no more than a toy to warm the cold sheets left by Charlotte's death.

A knock at the door made her start.

"Grace?"

"Go away, Alexander. What if someone sees you here? What will they think?"

"I don't care."

"Well I do care!" She waited for his footsteps to disappear down the hall. Instead he opened the door and sat beside her on the bed.

"Go away," she said, not looking at him. And then: "What do you want?"

"I'm worried for you."

Grace stared at her coin stack. "You must think me a right fool."

"You're not a fool. You're grieving. And you think her death was your fault." Alexander's voice was husky. "But it wasn't."

"Of course it was. I ought to have been taking better care of her."

He turned to face her. "I'm sorry about your girl, Grace. Truly. I'm sorry."

She lurched suddenly and threw her arms around him. He froze for a moment, taken aback. Then he wrapped his arms around her tightly, pulling her into him.

"Once, Nora, she got out of bed in the night and tried to go out into the street." Her voice was muffled against his neck. "Sleepwalking, you see. I thought, maybe that's what Violet done. Maybe she were sleepwalking and got herself lost."

"Aye. Perhaps."

"She's gone, isn't she."

Alexander nodded.

Grace sat back and wiped her eyes. "I wanted to believe it was her. I wanted to believe so badly."

Alexander glanced at the pile of coins.

"Six shillings," she said bitterly. "I worked myself to the ground and all I got is six shillings. I'll never get back to London without Harris. I never realised how much I relied on him. He stopped paying me when we come here. Said we were as good as man and wife now. 'We share everything,' he told me. Took all my money and put it in his bank account. A hundred pounds I saved, working for him and the girls. And he took every bit of it back. I thought I'd have everything once we were together. I thought I'd never go hungry or cold or wanting again." She swung a hand at the piles and sent silver skimming across the room. "I gave up everything I knew to come out here. Because I were such a fool to think he and I could make a life together." She laughed coldly. "Why am I telling you this?"

"Because there's no one else."

"You're right," said Grace. "There ain't no one else."

Alexander nudged one of the coins with his toe. "What I said about going back to London," he mumbled. "I meant it."

"London?" she repeated. "You? Alexander, I can see how hard this place is for you. How will you survive in a place like London?"

"It's here I can't survive," he said. "Not for much longer." He shifted suddenly and faced her. His eyes were hard and determined. "I can't live in this haunted forest. I can't live carrying the dead. Carrying the guilt. And neither can you." He grabbed her hand and squeezed. "We've got to leave this place. It's the only way I can forget who I am and what I've done. I was a man once, Grace. I want to be again."

She had never heard so many words come out of his mouth at once before. She reached down and ran her fingers over the tasselled ends of his belt.

"Aye," she said. "You were once, weren't you."

She had been the one to plant these ideas of escape in his head. How could she deny him a chance to start again?

She began to gather the coins. "Six shillings," she said. "That's three shillings more than I had a week ago. Six shillings more than I had last month. We work hard. Harder than we ever worked before. Get Porter to put us up to full wages." She sat up on her knees, her heart speeding with fresh enthusiasm. "This is possible, Alexander. It is." She pressed a coin into his palm. "Are you afraid?" she asked. "To go?"

He pocketed the coin. "Aye. But I'm more afraid to stay."

CHAPTER TWENTY

Dalton trudged to the top of the hill with Edward and Howell to rebuild the fences on the western side of the farm. He walked in silence, buzzing with nervous energy. He kept one hand in his pocket, wrapped around Grace's coin.

They needed money. Grace might have convinced herself they could earn enough to get back to London, but he had no such illusions. They had to get away from this place as quickly as possible. Before Howell sought to turn him in. Before Grace was strangled by her grief.

Bronze candlesticks at the back of the Porters' mantel. How much would such a thing fetch?

He looked out across the plains. At the bottom of the hill, he could see the tiny figures of Annie and Jack in their vegetable garden. Far behind, the twisted tree he'd buried their weapons beneath.

"Bog-trotter," called Edward. "You listening to me? I said, you take this corner."

Dalton nodded.

"*Yes sir*," said Edward. "Open your mouth, you useless bastard." He followed Dalton's gaze. Narrowed his eyes at Annie and Jack. "Bloody unnatural. That savage living like one of us." He raised an imaginary rifle and pulled the trigger. "Only his pa's white blood saving him from what we all want to do." He lowered his hands and began to pace, watching the men work.

Dalton clenched his teeth. He focused on the sound his hammer made as he drove the stakes into the earth. *Thud, thud.* He imagined sailing out of this place and leaving Edward Porter to fix his own damn fences.

"What the fuck is this?" Edward snorted. He kicked at the stake Howell was hammering. "Crooked as shit. Do it again."

Howell grimaced. He yanked out the stake and re-hammered it. Again, Edward kicked it to the ground. A light flickered behind Howell's eyes. He swung the hammer, narrowly missing Edward's stomach. Edward charged, head down, into Howell's middle.

Dalton felt his blood heat. He felt an urge to hold Edward's arms and let Howell punch the life out of him. Instead, he grabbed Howell by the hair and pulled him away.

"He's not worth it," he hissed. "The little prick's not worth it."

Howell whirled around and grabbed a fistful of Dalton's coat. It slid from his shoulders, his shirt tearing with a screech. Edward climbed to his feet and wiped a trickle of blood from his nose with the back of his hand. He looked at Dalton and laughed throatily.

"Free settler, you say? Only the worst of the worst got scars like that."

Dalton tugged the torn shirt back up towards his neck. "Your da got scars like that then?"

Edward stepped towards him. Flushed cheeks with that miserable fluff on his chin. All up in Dalton's face, youthful fuck. "Where's your paperwork? Show me your pardon. How we to know you ain't just a bolter?"

"Because bolters don't survive out here."

Edward took a step back, like he'd seen madness in Dalton's eyes. "That's right." A little of the cockiness gone from his voice. "They made it that way. All sea and mountains. The scum that get sent to Macquarie Harbour don't got no chance of ever getting out."

"Aye," said Dalton. "So I'm no bolter then, am I."

Edward wiped his nose again, leaving a smear of blood across one cheek. Finally he turned away from Dalton and glared at Howell.

"You," he said. "If you were dreaming of a pardon, you'd better bloody think again."

They carted Daniel Howell out for a good flogging that afternoon, lining the rest of the household up to watch. A bank of clouds had blown in and fine drizzle was falling.

Edward stood in front of the barn, bullwhip in hand.

Bill Porter marched Howell out from his quarters, a thick hand at the top of the convict's arm. Howell wore nothing but frayed blue trousers and a look of hatred.

"You got no right to flog your own workers, Porter," he spat. "You think I don't know that? I'll have the governor onto you."

Porter laughed. "The governor ain't listening to a piece of shit like you, Howell." He nodded at Edward. "Come on, son. Show this animal who's in charge."

Howell stepped close to his overseer. "You look at me like I ain't worth the time of day. But you got convict blood same as I do. The *hated stain* they call it. The scourge of this colony. You heard that before, I'll warrant. Sure you've come across some gentry who won't come near you. They'll see your criminal blood a mile off. Wouldn't share a shit bucket with an emancipist and his family."

Porter tensed his jaw. Chose silence.

Howell grinned. "I'm right, aren't I."

Porter shoved him against the wall of the barn. He glared at Edward, colour rising in his cheeks. "Do it, boy."

Edward brought the whip down with a loud crack. A line of crimson appeared on Howell's back. Dalton glanced at Grace. She stared at her feet, wincing with each snap of the lash.

He realised Edward was watching him. His eyes were cold, looking past Howell as he brought down the whip. *Bolter,* said those unblinking eyes. *You'll be next.*

Dalton saw his reflection as he walked into the parlour. A cursed thing, he thought, to look into your own eyes at the very moment the crime is committed. For how could you ever hope to pin the blame on another?

He took the candlesticks. Two of them; long and thin. Angels were woven around the bases, their tiny bronze hands reaching skyward.

Dalton shoved them into his pockets. He hurried through the dark house and out into the barn. He placed the candlesticks in the pack with his old clothes.

He'd wake Grace, dig up the weapons. And by dawn this hellhole would be nothing but a bad memory.

"What have you there, silent man?"

He turned. Howell stood in the doorway, a grin plastered across his face.

"Go to hell," said Dalton.

Howell snatched the pack and pulled out the candlesticks. He chuckled. "Funding an escape?"

Dalton said nothing. Howell tossed the pack back in the hay, keeping the candlesticks in his fist.

"You're right to do it. Edward Porter knows what you are. You really think a rat like that's going to keep quiet? The little prick's probably rounding up the police as we speak."

Dalton made a grab for the candlesticks. Howell darted out of reach. Spiderwebs of blood darkened the back of his shirt.

"Edward knows too much," he said. "But then again, so do I."

Dalton clenched his teeth. "What do you want?"

Howell smiled. "Here's how it is. I'm going to run. And you're going to come with me. You know the bush. You know how to survive out there."

Dalton snorted.

"You think I'm joking?"

"A gun," said Dalton blackly. "Smoking pot. Rope for traps. Take those things from Porter and leave me the hell alone. I'm not going anywhere with you."

"Traps? Do I look like a hunter? No mate, I ain't going into that forest on my own. Heard some real awful shit can happen when the food runs out." He looked at Dalton pointedly.

"All the more reason to go alone."

Howell waved the candlesticks in front of Dalton's face. "I could open my mouth right now and have Porter out here. Not sure he'd take it too well to discover you've pinched these. Plenty more I could tell him about you too." Howell glanced over his shoulder at the black plains. "Even you couldn't make it far enough in this darkness without the police finding you."

Dalton stood, breathing heavily through his nose. "Grace comes with us."

"No. She'll slow us down."

"I'll not go without her."

Howell chuckled. "A man like you should know better than to grow attached to someone. A life on the run will always be a lonely one. You'll go. Because if you don't, you'll swing."

Dalton clenched his jaw. "I told you, I'll not go without her."

"Then you'll die with a rope around your neck."

Dalton paced across the barn with his hands behind his head. It wasn't the thought of death he cared about. He'd already lived far longer than he was supposed to. Death would come to everyone. But to stand upon the gallows and have the world know his crimes? To have Grace know his crimes? It was this he couldn't bear.

He rubbed his eyes. "When?" he asked finally.

"What do we need?"

"I told you. Pots and knives. Rope. Gun."

Howell grinned. "You can get us them things, can't you? You're a resourceful man."

Dalton thought of the rifle buried beneath the tree. He hated the thought of leaving Grace here without it. Hated more the idea of going back into the bush with no way to hunt.

Howell clapped him on the shoulder. "You'll get them tonight or I'll tell the world your whole grisly story. We leave at dawn."

CHAPTER TWENTY-ONE

Hobart Town Gazette
Friday 6th August 1824

'It was insisted upon that everyone should partake of Bodenham's remains, lest, in the event of their ultimate success to obtain their liberty, any of them might consider himself innocent of his death and give evidence against the rest.'

"We go north," said Howell. They trudged out of Porter's back paddock with the first threads of sunlight. "I got means out of this place." He jangled the pouch of coins in his pocket. "Tobacco money. You get me the hell off this island, Dalton. But we go up through the wilds, you hear. Disappear into the bush like you and your mates done. Don't want no-one seeing us."

"Aye," said Dalton. "Through the wilds." He began to walk northwest, away from the settled districts. Through the wilds and north would lead them to snow-drenched mountains, impenetrable forests. Over the bones of murdered bolters.

Starting again, it was all an illusion. How could he build a new life when he'd ruined this one so completely?

Perhaps it was best this way. Even if he and Grace ever made it to London, Violet's ghost would always hover between them.

They stopped at the edge of the river. Mist hung over the water.

Howell looked up at the snow-flecked peaks that rose above the cloud. "The rest of your gang still out there somewhere? Living off the land like savages?"

"No," said Dalton. "They're dead."

"It's really true then. What Alexander Pearce said you done."

"Aye," Dalton said finally. "It's true." He took off his clothes and tied them to the end of the rifle, his fingers tight around Grace's coin. He stepped into the water. His chest tightened at the cold.

"They hanged him, you know," said Howell from the bank. "Pearce. Years ago."

Dalton turned in surprise. "Pearce? Hanged?"

"Aye. He escaped the harbour again. Killed the man he bolted with. They found him on the edge of the King River with his mate's liver in his pockets."

Dalton let his feet sink into the muck on the bottom of the river. So he was the last survivor.

You hear that, Greenhill?

It had been Daniel Howell who had relayed the story to him so many years ago, Dalton realised, grimacing at the irony. Pearce had made it to Hobart Town and news of the bolters was travelling into the highlands. Howell leaned close to the fire, his red hair brightened by the flames, a bottle of stolen whisky in his fist.

"Heard the story of what these men done? Can't bring myself to believe a word of it." He waved the bottle at Dalton, who was lying on his side, too weak from hunger to lift his head. "What d'you reckon, silent man? This Pearce fellow talking shit?"

Dalton had smiled into the darkness that night, glad to hear Pearce had taken the axe to Greenhill. The terror had been paralysing when there had still been eight of them left. How bleak those final nights must have been for the last two survivors.

Alone in a lightless forest, each wanting the other dead. Each afraid to close his eyes.

Greenhill had succumbed to sleep first. One swing of the axe and he had become a victim of his own depraved plan. Dalton was satisfied. Pearce would be back at Macquarie Harbour with his back in ribbons, but Robert Greenhill would forever haunt that cursed forest.

Howell stepped into the water and swore at the cold. "And you, Mr Dalton, Pearce told them in Hobart they'd killed you first. At Macquarie Harbour, he claimed you'd gotten lost in the bush. Either way, no one knows you're alive." He grinned. "Except me."

The alleyway was still in the early morning. The windows of the tavern were dark, stray cannikins lying half-buried in the mud. And there was little Emma, crouched beside a puddle, floating leaves across its murky surface. She wore a short-sleeved tunic, her pantalettes sodden with mud. Gooseflesh dappled her arms. Close up, she looked nothing like Violet. Emma's face was much wider, her hair darker. She couldn't have been more than three or four. *What tricks the desperate mind can play*, Grace thought dully.

"Emma? Is your mama about?"

The girl looked up. She moved her lips from side to side, as though debating whether to trust Grace. "She's sleeping."

Wind tunnelled through the alley. Grace slid off her shawl and bundled it around the girl's shoulders. She held out her hand. "Come on. Let's go and see her." Emma's fingers were cold and muddy. Grace squeezed them tightly. How she'd missed the feel of a child's hand in hers. She'd been with Violet and Nora since they were born. Had lifted them from Charlotte's chest when her arms grew limp and her eyes glassy. Grace had been both mother and father to the girls until Harris could bring himself to look at them. Another child's hand in hers felt like a betrayal.

She let Emma lead her down the narrow lane at the side of the tavern and into the hallway of the lodging rooms. Grace knocked softly.

Maryann opened the door. Her blonde hair hung tangled down her back, grey threads at her temples. Her eyes were underlined with shadow. She tugged a tatty pink shawl over her nightshift. "I see you're still hunting down my daughter."

Emma slipped past them and ran into the room. She plucked the rag doll from her sleeping pallet and sat up on her knees, eying the women curiously.

"Emma's father," said Grace. "Howell. Is he here?"

A baby in a crib by the door let out a sudden wail. Maryann ushered Grace inside and grunted as she fished the baby from the cradle. "Daniel? You think he'd come here? Give me a scrap of help? Only time I see him is when he sneaks out for a drink. The children don't even know who he is."

"He's gone," said Grace. "I work at the Porters' with him. He ran away in the night."

Maryann pursed her lips. She snatched a glass from the table and flung it across the room. It exploded against the wall and made the baby screech harder. Emma looked up with wide eyes.

"Bastard," hissed Maryann.

Grace chewed her thumbnail. "He didn't say nothing to you?"

Maryann shook her head. The baby grizzled and pawed at her neck. She dumped him on Emma's sleeping pallet and pressed a sliver of bread into his pudgy fist. "Are you sure?" she asked Grace finally.

She nodded. "He left with Alexander."

"The man you were with. The one with the wild eyes."

"You ain't got no idea where they've gone? Or why?"

Maryann sighed. "Daniel's a no-hoper. Got caught duffing cattle a few years back but earned himself a ticket of leave. Only had six months til his sentence were up. We talked about making a go of it. Land of our own and all. Few sheep or something. Anything so I don't have to do this no more. Then the stupid scab knocked out his overseer. Now he's a lifer. He thought of bolting before. I thought I'd talked him out of it. Don't know what I was thinking pinning my hopes on him. So, no, I got no idea where they are. But I sure ain't surprised."

Hatred for Howell simmered beneath Grace's skin. He'd taken Alexander from her. Left his children without a second thought. "All right," she said finally. "Thank you." She turned to leave.

"You find your girl then?" asked Maryann.

Grace avoided her eyes. "Violet disappeared in the bush a few months ago. When I saw Emma, I just wanted to believe…"

"How does someone just disappear?"

Grace hesitated, taken aback by Maryann's bluntness. "She got up in the night, I suppose. Got herself lost."

"She got up in the night? Wandered into the bush on her own? Is that really what you believe?"

Grace wrapped her arms around herself. "Perhaps."

"And this Alexander. Was he there?"

"Why?" she demanded.

Maryann shrugged.

"He didn't kill her," said Grace, surprising herself with the intensity of her voice.

"You said it. Not me."

She swallowed heavily. "I trust Alexander."

"Well. I trusted Daniel too. And look where that got me."

"Why would he kill Violet?" The words fell out scratchy and half formed. She'd convinced herself of Alexander's innocence. How deep had this doubt been hiding?

Maryann shrugged with infuriating nonchalance. "Perhaps he wanted you all to himself."

Heat washed over her. "No." She felt her carefully cultivated ignorance about to topple. "No, that ain't true." The baby let out a long, high wail. Grace felt the muscles in her neck tighten. She had to leave. Now. She hurried towards the door.

"You looking for a reason for him to disappear?" said Maryann. "Perhaps he was afraid you were going to find him out."

Grace felt anger flare inside her. She shoved Maryann against the wall. "Shut your damn mouth! You ain't got no idea what you're talking about!"

Maryann pushed her away. "Get your bloody hands off me. And stay away from my daughter."

They trudged into the hills until Dalton's eyes were straining in the twilight. He dropped the pack. "Get us some kindling. Lay a fire."

"Here? You reckon we're far enough away from the settlement? They'll not see the smoke?"

Dalton sat. "Can't go any further in the dark. Ground's too steep."

With a thin flame licking the wood, Howell lay back on his elbows and stretched out his legs. He pulled a loaf from the pack and broke off two large pieces. Dalton took the bread and tore the first chunk in half.

"Too much. The food has to last."

Howell chewed slowly. He took one of the candlesticks from the pack and traced a finger over the face of the sculpted angel. "What's it feel like then? To do such a thing?"

Dalton felt his breath coming thick and fast.

You want to know how it feels?

This is how it feels.

Thomas Bodenham was just twenty years old. Arrived at Macquarie Harbour a few months before Dalton. The harbour was not a place where men bonded, but Dalton and Bodenham had shared words over the supper tables many a night. They'd shared their desperation for liberty, shared excitement when they'd fled the harbour. The first night of their escape, they'd talked about the women they'd met in Hobart Town. Two young men with dreams of freedom.

This is how it feels, Daniel Howell, to steal a friend's life for your own survival.

Self-hatred. Revulsion. Terrified by the knowledge that you'll be forever haunted. Afraid to look into the shadows in case there are dead men lurking there. You hide yourself away from the world in the hope that the solitude might steal your memories. But you know that what you've done is buried so deep within you that you'll go back there every time the sun goes down.

"Would you do it again?" asked Howell. "If you had to?"

Never.

Dalton chewed the bread slowly. He knew the land now. How many edible plants must they have passed in those sixteen days after they had left the harbour? How much wattle seed that could be ground into flour? How many men would still be alive if Dalton had known then the things he did now?

"Stop talking about it," he mumbled.

Howell chuckled. "You understand my fascination, mate, surely."

Dalton stared through the trees to the scattered stars. He wondered if Howell knew how to read the sky. Could he tell they were walking in circles?

He lay awake long after Howell began to snore. The crescent moon hung directly above his head. Midnight. He took Grace's shilling from his pocket. He had to get back to her before whatever fragile trust she had in him was shattered forever. Before she drew her own conclusions about his disappearance. Her own conclusions about the girl.

Dalton looked across at Howell. He stood and reached for the gun. Howell moved suddenly and snatched the rifle before Dalton could get a hand to it.

"Don't you try, silent man. You're getting me out of this place."

"Give me my gun."

Howell rolled over, back to Dalton, clutching the rifle to his body. "No, mate. I need a little security."

It said plenty about the village of Hamilton, thought Grace, that there were countless grog shops and no church. She and God had never seen eye to eye, but she felt the need to cram into the inn with the rest of the villagers each Sunday and listen to the reverend spout the dangers of a liquored-up life. It gave her a sense of belonging, she realised. A fragile sense of community to which she could try and belong.

Maryann was waiting outside for her when she left the service that morning. The baby was dangling from her hip and she had a hand clamped around Emma's wrist. She was dressed in a threadbare cloak and the low-cut blue dress she'd obviously been wearing the night before. The lampblack intended for her eyelids had made its way across one cheek.

Grace walked faster. "If you've come to convince me of Alexander's guilt, I ain't interested."

"I ain't come to convince you of anything." Maryann tossed Grace her shawl. "Thought you might want this back."

"Thank you." Grace slowed her pace slightly and let Maryann walk beside her. Emma ran ahead, leaping over puddles and enormous piles of horse dung. Two older women shuffled past them, whispering and shooting dark glares.

Maryann grabbed Grace's arm. "This way." She guided her off the main street and down the track towards the creek. She snorted. "Bloody toffs looking at me like I ain't worth the time of day. Think they know I seen more of their husbands than they have?"

"They know," said Grace. "That's why they're looking at you like you ain't worth the time of day."

Maryann chuckled humourlessly.

Grace watched Emma swing her rag doll in her fist. It was threadbare and misshapen like Violet's Rosie had been.

Rosie was the obstacle in Grace's sleepwalking theory. The doll, like Violet, was gone without a trace. Had she carried it in her sleep? They'd searched for weeks. Every inch of the land, she was sure of it. There had been no Rosie.

Images came to her fleetingly: hands flinging the doll into the river. Into the fire. Whose ashes lay in the fireplace outside Alexander's hut? She forced the thoughts away.

"Daniel left me some money," said Maryann. "Some of what he'd made from that tobacco crop. Found it last night behind the flour pot." She heaved the baby onto her other hip and sighed. "I know we're better off without him. Just wish he'd said goodbye." She touched Grace's elbow. "Listen. I know you don't want to think nothing bad about your Alexander. I went through the same with Daniel. But it got to a point that I couldn't deny it no more."

How could she manage anything but denial? *There's no one else*, Alexander had said. And he was right. She had no one else, so how could she ever think about those dead bolters, or the glassy eyes of the murdered marines? How could she believe Violet's death had been anything but an accident?

She sucked in her breath. "The man I love struck me, then threw me in the madhouse when I tried to leave him."

"Christ," said Maryann. "I thought I were a bad judge of character."

"I left my family on the other side of the world to come out here and make a life with him. Now I have nothing. Alexander is the only person I can trust."

"Alexander left you," said Maryann. She gripped Grace's shoulder with her free hand. "Look. I ain't trying to make trouble. You've been through hell, I can see that. And we're all afraid of being alone. Especially in this place. It's natural to want to cling to someone. But sometimes you got to open your eyes. Or else what happened to your Violet might just happen to you." Maryann tried to catch her glance. "Don't you owe it to her to admit to yourself what really happened?"

Grace swallowed hard. "I don't know what really happened." She looked up to see Emma tottering down the muddy bank into the creek. Grace's heart shot into her throat. She raced towards the water. "Emma! Get out of there!"

Maryann planted a hand on her hip. "Leave her. She's just playing."

Grace splashed into the water and swung Emma into her arms. The girl screeched in shock and kicked against her. Maryann sat the baby on the bank and yanked Emma out of Grace's grip. The doll tumbled to the grass.

"What the hell d'you think you're doing? You've bloody terrified her!"

Grace gulped down her breath. "How could you let her out there? She could have drowned!"

"Drowned?" Maryann set Emma down and rubbed her back. "She weren't in an inch of water! You're off your bloody head, you are!"

"We got a problem here?"

"Oh look," drawled Maryann. "If it ain't Jim Berry, world's crookedest bloody police lag."

He strode towards them, chest puffed out like he'd swallowed a cat. Grace pulled her shawl tight around her shoulders. Her hands were shaking violently.

"Bugger off, Berry," Maryann hissed. "This ain't got nothing to do with you."

"You watch your mouth, Maryann Fairlie."

She unhooked Emma's arms from around her waist. "Why? What you going to do?"

"Could think of plenty nice things to do to a woman like you." Chuckling, Berry stepped close and slid a hand inside her cloak. Maryann yanked away and punched him hard in the nose. Blood spurted down the front of his uniform. He snatched her wrists and wrestled her to the ground. Howls from Emma and the baby.

"Let go of me!" shrieked Maryann, kicking under him. "She's the one you want! The loony won't leave my bloody kids alone!"

Grace stood with her spine pressed against the trunk of a tree. The children sprawled on the grass, red faced and screaming. A second policeman came running towards the creek. Berry yanked Maryann to her feet and wrenched her arms behind her back.

"Hand her over, Berry," said the sergeant. He grabbed hold of Maryann's arm and led her back towards the town. Berry wiped his nose with the back of his hand. He pulled the children from the mud and tucked one under each arm.

Grace watched blankly as they left, the children's cries disappearing beneath the sigh of the creek. She sank to her knees, wet skirts tangling around her legs. Beside her, Emma's doll lay face down in the grass. Grace picked it up and held it to her chest. Tried to slow her speeding heart.

Again, the river.

Howell stopped walking. "You bastard. You've led us back to Hamilton." He wrenched an arm around Dalton's neck and threw him backwards. Arms flying, stumbling, hands in the mud. They scrambled for the weapons. Howell came away with the rifle. Dalton, the axe.

Howell raised the gun. "Think I won't tell anyone who you are?"

"Just try. You're a bolter now too. Open your mouth and you'll be on the scaffold beside me."

Howell paused, breathing heavily through his nose. Dalton swung the axe into the barrel of the gun. Howell's shot flew across the river. Head down, Dalton charged, knocking Howell onto his back. His money pouch spilled into the mud. Dalton threw a wild fist to the side of Howell's head. His cheek split, blood spurting down his face. Dalton punched again, leaving Howell on the edge of consciousness. He grabbed the rifle and rummaged in his pack for the powder and shot. Rammed in the ball. He snatched the money pouch and ran without looking back.

He tore across the plains, past Annie's cottage and over the bridge. Up the hill towards the Porters'. He threw open the kitchen door and charged inside, the rifle in his hand.

The cook swallowed a shriek. She pressed a hand to her heart. "You. What do you want?"

"Where's Grace?"

"She's not here."

"You're lying."

The cook narrowed her eyes. "I never lie. Mrs Porter sent her packing.

Her and that dollymop Maryann Fairlie caused a right scene at the creek this morning."

"What?" Dalton gulped down his breath. "Where'd she go?"

"Couldn't tell you. But you'd best leave too. Mr Porter'll have your head if he catches you here."

He found her sitting at the edge of the creek. Her hands were clasped in her lap and she wore her tattered tartan cloak, the hood pulled up over her choppy curls.

She turned as he approached. "You came back."

"Aye. Of course." He sat beside her. A dirty rag doll lay in her lap. Dalton took the shilling from his pocket and held it out to her. Grace looked at it, but kept her hands tightly clasped. He placed it between them. "Howell knew who I was. He recognised me from the cattle ring. Said he'd turn me in if I didn't help him get away. But I couldn't go without you."

Grace said nothing.

"The Porters let you go?"

She nodded.

"What happened?"

She didn't look at him. "Emma… Maryann's daughter. She ran off and jumped in the river… the creek. I was afraid she'd drown. I jumped in there after her and Maryann went mad. Started screaming at me. She punched that police lag when he came to see what was going on." She sniffed. "Mrs Porter heard about it. Said she didn't want no-one working for her what spent their time with easy women like Maryann." She stared into the water. "Thing is, I don't know why I behaved the way I did. When I saw Emma in the creek, it was like something else took a hold of me. Like something else was making me act. You ever feel that way?"

Dalton nodded faintly. He'd felt that way more times than he could remember. "You think that's what happened to Violet? You think she fell in the river?"

Grace looked at her hands. "You tell me what happened to Violet."

Dalton's stomach tightened.

Finally, she turned to face him. "Am I to believe she just wandered out into the bush on her own? How could she just disappear? How could there be no trace of her?"

Dalton watched the brown water bubble over the rocks. He pulled Howell's pouch from his coat pocket and tossed it into Grace's lap. "Here. Enough for passage to London. And more."

She frowned, opening the pouch. "Where did you get all this?"

"It doesn't matter."

"You stole it? From who?"

"I stole it for you. For us. So we can forget this place."

Grace sucked in her breath and placed the pouch on the ground.

Dalton slid it into his pocket. "We'll go back to Hobart Town. Get Nora. And then we'll be on the first ship back to London. No more Harris. No more asylum. That's what you want, aye?" He put a hand to her shoulder, forcing her to face him. "Grace? Isn't that what you want?" He glimpsed Howell's blood on his knuckles and pulled away. "Would you bloody well speak to me?"

She laughed thinly. "Silence is a real bastard, ain't it."

"She won't go, Dalton. Not with an animal like you."

They turned at the sound of Howell's voice. Grace's eyes fixed on the blood snaking down his cheek. She stood hurriedly, the rag doll tumbling into the water.

Dalton leapt up, clutching the rifle. "Leave us be," he said darkly.

Howell glared. "Give me my fucking money."

Dalton felt Grace's eyes on him.

"Give him the money, Alexander," she said.

He stood motionless, his hand tight around the gun.

Finally, Howell took a step towards Grace. "Ask him about the man they killed."

She looked at Dalton. "What is he talking about?"

Sickness rose in his throat. He reached into his pocket, clasped his fingers over the pouch and held it out to Howell.

No.

He couldn't do it. The money was his ticket out of this place. His ticket to give Grace what she longed for. He shoved the pouch back in his pocket and raised the gun. "Get away from us."

Howell laughed. "You won't shoot me here. You'd hang in a second." He turned to Grace. "Ask him about Tom Bodenham. Ask him what they did to the body."

Dalton stared down the barrel of the rifle. Anything to avoid Grace's eyes. His finger on the trigger. Howell in his line of sight.

"Don't, Alexander. Please." Her voice was husky.

He squeezed the trigger. His warning shot flew over Howell's shoulder.

Howell glared, then laughed coldly. Ran back along the creek and disappeared.

CHAPTER TWENTY-TWO

Confession of Alexander Pearce
As recounted to Lieutenant John Cutherbertson, Commandant of Macquarie Harbour
1824

"'I'll warrant you,' said Greenhill, 'I will eat the first part myself, but you must all lend a hand that we may be equally guilty of the crime.'"

Alexander lowered the gun. "We need to leave." He handed Grace the axe.

"Where are we going?"

He began to walk. His silence told her everything. Back to the forest. To the mountains, the rivers. Back to his world.

They trudged past cattle, past rickety fences, out into the open plains. Grace felt a great weight pressing down on her. She couldn't do this again. Couldn't climb mountains or sleep beneath snow and stars. A pink sky stretched endlessly above her, the plains beneath her feet vast and open. What was she but a speck amongst this desolation? If she were to part ways with Alexander, the emptiness could swallow her and who on this earth would ever know? Her heart thumped at her vulnerability. And so she kept up with his steady footsteps, inching their way towards the foothills.

She said nothing. To speak would mean facing questions she couldn't bear to ask, facing truths she couldn't accept.

They crossed the river, communicating in sparse, wordless gestures: *go, stop, this way.* Grace stumbled out of the water and stood with her arms across her chest, her wet shift tangled around her legs. She crouched on the bank, feeling horribly exposed. Alexander tossed her the pack and she hurriedly pulled out her dress and petticoats.

Her clothes clinging to her wet skin, she stood on the bank and felt her bare feet sink into the mud. Alexander's back was to her as he buttoned his trousers. Giving her the privacy she craved, or needing to hide from her scrutiny?

The foothills rose, then dipped into a slight valley. Night was approaching, the shrieking of the birds fading into stillness. Grace could hear her heart thumping in her ears. She sucked in her breath. There had to be an end to this uncertainty. Suddenly not knowing seemed the most frightening thing of all.

She stopped walking. "Tell me what happened out here. Tell me the truth."

Alexander paused several paces in front of her. She watched his shoulders sink, his head droop. He'd been fighting these questions too, she realised. Fighting to keep the answers inside. He threw down the pack and sat with his knees drawn up. He stared at the earth and shook his head slowly.

Grace stood over him. "Yes," she said.

He hung his head with resignation. His words were low and slow; speaking to the ground as if hoping the earth might swallow his confession. "We'd not eaten in more than a week. There was nothing out there. No animals, no berries, not even a fly. We were at the end of the earth." He covered his eyes. "Greenhill, he'd heard this story of some sailors who got lost at sea. Sacrificed one of their own so the others could survive."

Grace's stomach tightened. *Stop, I can't hear this.* But she couldn't form the words.

"Greenhill wanted it to be me, but in the end they chose Tom Bodenham. Greenhill took to him with the axe we'd been using to cut the pines. Hung his body from a tree and let the blood run out of him. We cut off his head and hacked him up like he was a pig. Put his liver to the fire and shared it among ourselves. Greenhill said it was the only way we'd survive."

Grace bit down on her lip until she tasted blood. She wanted the story she'd concocted the night the marines were killed. Wanted Alexander to have killed those seven men. A simple murder; it was easier to conceive. Easier to give a self-righteous sigh and push away. And the murder of a government man? Weren't they all sent to Macquarie Harbour in the hope they'd die off anyway? But this, this pushed against the boundaries of what it meant to be human.

She stared into the purple sky, trying to cling to the last threads of light. "I don't believe you."

"Yes you do. You don't want to, but you do."

For a long time, neither of them spoke.

"I ran," Alexander said finally. "Before anyone else was killed."

"Stop," Grace mumbled. But his confession seemed to have opened something up inside him. Something he couldn't close down. A need to tell the whole story.

"The soldiers caught Pearce," he said. "He told them everything. After Bodenham, it was Mather. He was praying, Grace. They killed him while he was praying."

And Grace thought not of Mather, but of Alexander raising the rifle as she and Violet hunted for flowers.

Alexander said, "Travers, he was next." And she thought of poison mushrooms mixed with her tea. The thud of soldiers' bodies as they rolled into their graves.

"Greenhill and Pearce, they were the last. Both knew they had to kill the other to survive. Afraid to leave the other's sight." He leapt up suddenly and grabbed at her cloak. "Imagine it. Being too afraid to sleep in case you never woke up."

"Stop!" she cried. "I can't hear no more! Not when I'm trapped with you in this cursed forest again!"

He pressed his hot palms against her cheeks. "I've got the money. We'll get out of the forest. We'll get back to London." He pushed back her hood and dug his hands into her hair. "It's all right, my Grace. You're safe here. It's better this way. Just the two of us. Without the Porters or

Howell or Maryann's little girl."

"Just the two of us?" she repeated. "The two of us without Violet? Alexander?" Her voice grew louder. "The two of us without Violet?"

He stood, breathing heavily, his hands still hard against her cheeks. "Yes," he said finally.

Grace heard a cry from deep in her throat. She stumbled, fighting off a wild sweep of dizziness.

Only two sets of footprints.

The proof had been there since the beginning. She imagined Alexander lifting Violet from her bed. Carrying her into the bush. And then...

With day-to-day tasks, it had been easier to block everything out. Bake the bread and convince herself Violet had just gotten lost in the dark. Wash the clothes, tell herself she'd slipped and fallen. But she couldn't hide from the truth any longer. Shy little Violet, who wouldn't venture as far as the kitchen without her nurse by her side. Timid Violet who wouldn't sleep in the dark unless she were pressed against Grace or Nora. Little Violet who would never, ever have left that hut on her own accord.

Alexander held up a hand, backing away from her. "Let me speak."

"Let you speak?" Her voice was barely more than a whisper. "She was just a little girl." Grace stared at him and saw the beast he had been when she had stumbled to his hut. She had fought with herself then. Trusting the wild man in the woods had seemed a gamble she had had no choice but to take. If only she had taken Violet and kept walking. *If only.* She felt all the compassion she had once felt for him washing away in a flood of hatred. And an odd sense of inevitability.

She lurched for the weapons. Alexander grabbed the rifle before she could get a hand on it. Her wild swing of the axe clipped the side of his head. He stumbled, collapsed at her feet. She grabbed the gun.

"Animal," she spat.

He hovered on the edge of consciousness, waiting to die. Waiting for the shot. But nothing.

Animal. And then silence. He tried to move, but felt a great weight on his chest. Darkness behind his eyes.

An animal? Of course I am.

Even dogs don't eat their own kind.

Imagine it.

Imagine the smell of wood smoke. Eucalyptus. Boiling meat. Hear the pot bubbling, the fire crackling, devils snorting in dams of spilled blood.

No man speaks. They all know that when this pot is done boiling, they'll stop being men. Become beasts.

Imagine you are sitting around that fire, surrounded by men you have come to despise. Imagine hating these men so much you wish you had chosen the hell of Macquarie Harbour over their company. Can you hear the men breathe? There is one man less than the night before. You are watching when someone dips a stick into the pot and brings out the slab of meat. It is passed around. Grey. Tough. Each man pulls off a portion. Passes it on.

Who is the first to put it on their tongue? The first to swallow it down? And where do these bolters go from here? They can never be normal men again now. Not after this.

One day, my Grace, you'll see it was better for you to be freed of your Violet. You'll see everything I did was for you. How could I let anything come between us, mo shíorghra? How could I let anything take you away from me when you are the only thing that makes me human?

PART THREE

HOBART TOWN

CHAPTER TWENTY-THREE

Bathurst Free Press
Wednesday 28th Jan 1857
Derived from the *Hobart Town Gazette*, 1824

"When the first horror was over, a consultation followed. Some would have died rather than live by cannibalism; but it was fiercely contended … that all might share the guilt."

Dalton felt a sharp kick in the shoulder. He opened his eyes. Grace was standing over him, gripping the rifle. His wrists and ankles were bound with his bootlaces. He squinted in the pale dawn. There was a coldness to her. Like she was made of stone.

Dalton sat, his head pounding. He lifted his bound wrists and touched a swelling above his ear.

"The gun is loaded," said Grace.

He nodded slowly.

"Take me to Violet. Show me what you done with her."

He hesitated.

"Of course. Silence. Silence is easy, ain't it? Silence and lies."

Dalton glanced at the rifle. "You mean to kill me, Grace?"

"Take me to Violet."

He nodded. "Let me stand."

Grace reached into the pack and pulled out his whittling knife. She sliced the laces at his wrists and ankles. Dalton stood slowly. A wave of nausea swept over him as he bent to thread the remains of the laces back through his boots.

"Where is she?" Grace asked.

"At the top of the escarpment. Near the soldiers' grave. Back over the mountains."

Tears escaped down her cheeks and she brushed them away furiously. "Take me."

Dalton reached for the axe. Grace cocked the trigger.

"We need it to get through the bush," he told her. "Cut ourselves a path. You know that."

She took a step back, allowing him to take the axe.

"We'll not get over the mountains without food," he said. "We need to hunt."

"We'll go back towards the settlements. There are kangaroos." She shoved him in the shoulder with the gun. "Walk."

They paced up the gradual incline of the plains. The river lay ahead. Dalton stopped. A few hours earlier, he had watched Grace climb from the water and pull on her dress. That blue dress of Annie's, he was sure of it. Now her skirts were brown, her petticoats dry. Her hair, her skin, dry, like she'd been brought across in a boat.

"Grace? Where have you been?"

She dug the gun into his spine. "Move."

Dalton turned. She'd never trust him again. What did he care if she pulled the trigger?

"I been to the police," she said finally.

Panic shot through him. "Police?" And he realised they were all around him. Men hidden in the dip of the earth, waiting for her to deliver him into their clutches. He looked into her eyes and ran.

Marines swooped like a flock of red birds. Grace crouched, pressed her eyes against her knees. Couldn't bring herself to watch.

The night before, she had walked into the Hamilton police station.

Government man, she had said. And *bolter*. Eyes lit up and guns were loaded. And then, the worst of them.

Cannibal.

And that was it. The police had Alexander pegged for the murder of Grace's girl, for those four words were all the evidence in the world.

"My girl, Violet Harris," she said. "And two British marines."

Soldiers were brought in from the surrounding settlements.

"Miss Ashwell," they said, "where can we find the bodies?"

Five days' walk. By the Styx River. An unmarked grave at the water's edge, beneath the pine tree covered with rings of moss.

And: "Miss Ashwell, where can we find Alexander Dalton?"

"I will lead you," she said. "Follow me."

The police reported back. Disappeared into the bush like a ghost. Men sent after him, they said. Heading towards the river, looking for the graves.

Grace sat at the constable's desk. She felt hot and breathless. Surely any second she'd be discovered as a runaway. They'd throw her into the police wagon and back to New Norfolk she'd go. "Can I leave?"

The constable peered over his glasses. "You may. We'll let you know if we find anything. You'd best stay nearby. You work for Bill Porter, you said?"

"Aye," she lied. "For Bill Porter."

The sun was dull and low. Grace hooked closed her cloak and trudged down the middle of the road. She crossed the bridge to the farmland, traipsing through the wet grass to Annie and Jack's cottage. Annie was sitting in a chair beside her vegetable patch with a pipe in her hand. She wore black riding boots over a pair of mud-splattered drawers, her skirts hitched up above her knees. Her pale hair hung in pieces over her face. She puffed a cloud of smoke at Grace.

"Heard you and your friend been causing a stir."

"He ain't no friend of mine." She felt the loss of Alexander as though he had died. In a way, he had. Of course, the Alexander she had known – the one who had helped her hunt for Violet and had pledged to take her back to London – had only ever been an illusion, cobbled together by her own desperation. Hatred bubbled inside her.

"You'll be wanting somewhere to stay, I suppose."

Grace sniffed. "I ain't got nowhere else to go. I'm sorry. I don't know what to do. I—"

Annie breathed out a long line of smoke. "Well. There's a bed here, though I can't guarantee it's a safe one."

"What's happened?"

"Nothing." Annie stood and ushered her inside. "Come on, girl. You look as though you need a drink." She kicked off her boots and poured two glasses of whisky. Handed one to Grace. "Drink up. Bed's yours for as long as need it."

Grace tried for a smile of thanks but tears spilled down her cheeks.

"Stop that," Annie said sharply. "What good did weeping ever do anyone?"

Grace pushed away her tears. She ached for her mother. "I trusted him," she coughed. "We'd made plans to get home."

Annie gripped Grace's shoulders with surprising ferocity. "This new world is a tough place. A woman's got to make her own life. Can't be relying on no man if we're to survive out here. 'Specially not a wild one like that Alexander."

Grace nodded and gulped her whisky. She knew Annie was right. This was no place for the woman in silk she'd once dreamt of being. And it was no place to trust men who kept secrets. Because the secrets woven into this land were horrifying. "He wasn't the man I thought he was. He was a beast."

"He loved you," said Annie. "Beast or no. I could tell. What's he done that's got you speaking of him like this?"

"Love," Grace spat. "A man like that don't know love. Not anymore. I doubt he ever did." She tried to continue, but her throat tightened and the tears threatened to return.

Annie emptied her glass. "You'll tell me in your own time, aye?"

Jack opened the door, arms loaded with hoes and rakes. He dropped the tools beside the hearth. "Don't want nothing left out there," he said. "Those bastards'll take whatever they can get their hands on." He squeezed Annie's shoulder. "Any trouble here?"

She shook her head and smiled wryly at Grace. "Just her."

"What's happened?" Grace asked again.

"The Porters had some cattle killed," Jack said darkly. "Bodies gutted in the paddock and the flesh cut out. Blaming us, of course. They've been trying to get their own back." He nodded at the windows. The glass had been broken, Grace realised. Been patched with rags and nails.

"Howell," she said.

"What?"

"The cattle. It was Howell, Porter's government man. I'm sure of it. He's run away. Needed the food."

Annie refilled her glass. "Porter knows it weren't us. We've got our own bloody cattle. He just wants someone to blame. Makes him feel powerful." She snorted. "Helps him forget he's nought but a lag."

"Why don't you leave?" asked Grace. "Find somewhere new and start again."

"You know what this land is like." Annie lifted her head to look through the window, but the murky rags blocked her view. "It's no place to be roaming without nowhere to go."

The path from the river to the traps had been taken over by ferns. A wallaby carcass dangled from the rope, besieged by flies. Had been there for weeks, Dalton assumed. He hacked at the rope and flung the meat into the bush. Reset the trap and paced slowly towards his hut.

Was he mad to have returned?

He had run west from Hamilton. Crossed rivers and climbed mountains until he was sure the marines hadn't followed. On the fourth night, he lay awake until light began to filter through the trees. He sat and untied the pouch containing Howell's money, stacking the coins into silver columns. At the top of the pile he sat the shilling Grace had given him. The money would get him off this island and out of the haunted forest. But it would put oceans between him and Grace.

Dalton had heard Pearce had tried to hang himself while wandering alone in these woods. *Now where's the sense in that?*, Dalton had thought. After he'd gotten through the rest of the group. After taking the axe to Greenhill before Greenhill had taken the axe to him. For Pearce to take his own life after using so many men to ensure his survival, it hardly seemed a fair thing.

Dalton saw it now, fleetingly, the attraction of ending it all. Ending the pain in his legs, his chest, his heart. But he was the last man standing. His will to survive had always been stronger than his will to die, even when he had felt there'd been little left to live for.

He swallowed the end of the bread. The last of the food, but he knew this land now. Knew its secrets. He tucked the coins into the pouch and shoved it into his pocket. He grabbed the axe.

How are you going to hunt with that?

The voice in his head was Greenhill's.

There's only one kind of animal you can hunt with an axe.

"Go to hell," Dalton said aloud. He looked about him. The highest mountains were capped with snow. The Derwent glittered in the pink light. He knew the voice in his head was right. A man couldn't hunt with an axe. Cross the peaks and he would find his hut, his traps. An easier life, surely, than rummaging for berries and digging tubers with his bare hands. Dare he go back? It had been weeks since he'd killed the marines.

He began to walk, silencing Greenhill's voice with his own rhythmic footsteps.

He stood in the clearing, shards of his woodpile beneath his feet. The roof of the hut lay on the ground to his left, the splintered table to his right. The walls hacked at, the door torn off. His boots crunched over the dried ferns of the sleeping pallets. Flour was scattered everywhere. The locker upturned and empty. Cannikins gone. Shelf torn from the wall. The life he had spent eleven years building from nothing had been obliterated. Axed and pissed on. All that was left standing were the two stools.

He sat on one, because he could think of nothing better to do. He nudged a pile of dried ferns with his toe. Beneath it, a sprig of black hair – his beard.

Wooden faces peered up at him from beneath the fallen shelf. Frozen expressions, still eyes. None of them seemed surprised to see him. Grace's was the only one he had carved from life. He slid it into his pocket. He longed for her then like he'd longed for nothing else. Longed to hear her lullabies and see her skirts hung about the hut, and hell, how he longed to speak to another living person. He couldn't go back to silence. He'd wandered through the bush, Gaelic rolling off his tongue. Sometimes to himself, sometimes to the invisible men.

He needed her there to answer back. To say, *you're being a right fool, Alexander, there ain't no one there but your own shadow.*

He hacked at the broken table until it was kindling, then lay it in the clearing where his fire pit had once been. Green shoots were pushing through the blackened earth. He lit the fire and stared, mesmerised, at the flames.

The forest crackled and he glanced over his shoulder in a vain burst of hope. The phantom men had appeared from nowhere, so why not Grace? This was a forest full of mystery, after all.

He ran his fingers over the carving in his pocket. Then, one by one, he gathered the wooden men from the ruins of his hut. Tossed them into the flames.

Bodenham, the first to die.

Kennerly and Brown, whose last view of earth was the grey shroud of Macquarie Harbour.

Mather, Travers, sacrificed in vain.

Pearce, hanged for his crimes in Hobart Town.

Greenhill. *Burn in hell.*

He watched the figures until they were ash. If only he could burn Alexander Dalton away like this too. See the man he used to be disappear in a puff of smoke. He'd tried hard, but the past had found him. The past would always find him.

He couldn't bear for Grace to live the same way. He wanted her to have London. She'd never leave with him, of course. Not now. But he'd stolen the money from Howell so she might see home again. He pulled the pouch from his pocket. After all he'd done, perhaps this might go some way to helping him sleep at night.

Where to find her? She'd go for the girl; of this he was certain. Would return to Hobart Town, fleetingly at least. Perhaps he'd find her there, perhaps not. Perhaps he'd threaten that bastard Harris into giving him some clue.

Yes. He felt determined. A strange sensation after existing in a void for so many years.

He stood. The light was beginning to fade and the fire had burned itself out. His stomach groaned loudly. Tonight he would eat, rest. In the morning he would go and find London for Grace.

He trudged towards the traps. Flattened ferns. Were they human footprints in the mud? He froze.

Voices. The slosh of shovels.

He took a step backwards, seeking out the patches of moss so he might not make a sound. Another step. Another. He brushed past a tree fern and the leaves sighed noisily. The voices fell silent. The digging stopped. Dalton began to run. He heard footsteps after him. A rifle exploded into the sky. He kept running. And then from in front of him, the sly bastards, two police officers burst from the bush, thrusting their rifles at his chest.

CHAPTER TWENTY-FOUR

Dalton stood on the edge of the grave, hands tied in front of him. He watched two officers dig, searching for the dead by lantern light. Their sergeant stood at Dalton's side, a rifle swinging against his hip.

No-one spoke. Above their heads, an owl cooed rhythmically. The river sighed beneath the hiss of the shovels. An acrid stench rose suddenly from the wet soil and the officers recoiled. They hauled the mud-caked bodies from the earth. Their features were sunken and twisted. One of the men reached into the grave and pulled out a dirty bundle. Grace's shawl.

The sergeant pressed a hand to his nose. "Where's the girl?"

Dalton said nothing.

"Tell us where she is."

"And make your job easier? Why would I do that?"

"So we can bloody well get out of here."

"And you can have me on the scaffold?"

The sergeant sighed. "What did you do with her?"

"Nothing."

The constables hauled themselves from the hole. Their legs were caked in mud.

"You told Grace Ashwell you buried the girl by the marines' grave."

"Aye, well. Now I'm telling you I didn't." He smiled at the sergeant. "You can choose to believe me or not. But the night will only get darker. I'm sure none of us want to be out here on the graves of murdered men."

The police sat around the fire they had built a few yards from the grave. Close, they huddled, the orange glow of the flames flickering on their cheeks. Clinging to the light. The exhumed bodies lay on the grave's edge, covered in old grey blankets. Dalton sat a foot away, hands bound. He felt the thickness of the dark. The bush seemed restless.

The police passed around a loaf and canteen of water. One of the constables handed Dalton a scrap of bread.

"Ought to let you starve," spat the sergeant. "Save the hangman the trouble."

Dalton brought his bound hands to his lips. "You're hoping I'll tell you where the girl is." He chewed slowly. A throaty screech rose from the bushes and the constable flinched.

"Let's go, sir," he said. "This bog-jumping scab ain't going to tell us a thing."

"Can't go anywhere in this darkness," said the sergeant. "We'll stay here the night."

The constable glanced over his shoulder at the bodies by the water's edge.

Dalton caught his eye and smiled slightly. "The Styx River. The boundary between the living and the dead."

"I don't believe in ghosts," the constable said edgily.

"Nor do I. But this forest, it makes you see things that aren't there."

"Shut your mouth." The constable shuffled closer to the fire. After a moment, he looked back at Dalton. "What do you mean, things that ain't there?"

Dalton rolled onto his side and closed his eyes. "Dead men," he said. "Little girls."

At dawn, the sergeant roused them, yanking Dalton to his feet. Fine rain was falling and the mountains lay hidden behind a thick bank of cloud.

"I need you to untie me," said Dalton. "I can't climb without my hands."

"You can and you will."

"Where will I go? I got two men behind me with guns up my arse. If you don't untie me, it'll take us far longer to get over the mountains."

The sergeant scratched his beard. "Do it. Keep the guns on him at all times."

Up they went, into the foothills, into the mountains. The black rock was streaked with snow. Clouds hung in silver threads. At the top of the ridge, the wind howled and stung Dalton's ears. The ground twisted and dropped away into a dramatic downward slope. Peaks Dalton had navigated in the past. Terrain he knew. The policemen were forced to lower their guns and climb with their hands.

Dalton took his chance. He hurled himself down the incline, his back scraping against the rocks. A shout from the police. Bullets whizzed above his head. He ran until sweat poured down his back. The foliage grew thicker. Vast banks of fern he could hide between. He lay on his back, breathing hard, hidden in a sea of glistening green.

Grace woke abruptly at a slam of the front door. She could see the faint glow of candlelight flickering in the kitchen.

"Jesus, Jack," Annie said loudly. "What happened to your face?"

A chuckle. "Edward Porter thought to shoot his mouth off at me. He'll not be trying that again." His words were brassy with drink.

"Bloody fool."

Grace heard heavy footsteps.

"So what? I'm just supposed to take it?"

"You can't go round swinging your fists!" cried Annie. "The Porters are too powerful. They've got those crooked coppers on their side. They'll have you strung up if you don't bloody watch yourself."

Grace sat up suddenly at a flare of orange light. She pushed aside the curtain. Behind the house, a great wall of flame was tearing through the wheat field. She charged into the kitchen, tugging on her boots.

"They're burning your crops," she said breathlessly. Jack's eyes flashed. He snatched the rifle and charged into the paddock, firing wildly into the flickering light.

"Water," said Grace. "From the creek."

Annie shook her head. "It's too late."

They watched in silence as the flames roared through the wheat field and lit the night with plumes of orange smoke. The fire crackled and faded, leaving a field of glowing ash and the earthy smell of burning.

Annie marched inside and sat at the table. Her cheeks were flushed and smeared with soot.

Jack pressed a hand against the back of her neck. In the lamplight, Grace could see a faint swelling beneath his eye.

"We've got to leave, Annie," he said. "I'm sorry. I know we're giving them what they want, but our pride's not worth risking our lives for."

Grace hovered by the hearth, feeling an intruder.

"Our pride?" Annie repeated. "What about our farm? Our house?"

"Our farm that's burnt to ash? Our house full of broken glass?"

Annie rubbed her eyes with resignation. "Where will we go?"

"Hobart Town," Grace said suddenly.

They turned to her. "What?" said Jack.

"Take me to Hobart Town. I've got to get my Nora away from her father." She grabbed Annie's wrist. "He's a wealthy man. Keeps a hundred pounds or more in the house. He don't trust the bank manager because he went to school with him in London and caught him cheating on his finals. So he always keeps a stash at home. Get me to Hobart Town and I'll bring you that money. I'll take what I need to get back to England and you can have the rest. Go somewhere you'll be safe."

"Fine plan," said Jack. "But we've no horses. How are we to get to Hobart Town?"

Annie began to laugh. She popped the lid from the whisky bottle and filled three cannikins. "I'm sure the Porters have some damn fine horses."

The river murmured and sighed. Grace knelt on the bank, the damp earth soaking through her skirts. The hush of the water calmed her a little. She needed Nora. And, yes, she needed to show Harris he wouldn't get away with locking her up like an animal. But she also needed this stillness. Needed to accept that Violet was gone.

She knew it now, deep within herself. There was to be no more searching, or hoping. The time for miracles had passed.

Her fingers tightened around the stalks of the flowers in her fist. Pink powder-puffs of sunshine wattle that had erupted over the tree behind

Annie's vegetable garden. The first of the spring. Violet would have liked the pink. She would have twisted it into her hair, poked a stem behind Grace's ear.

She tossed the rosy globes into the water, one by one. Hoped with all her heart Violet was in Heaven with her mother, not haunting the forest with a gang of dead convicts. Deep, breathtaking pain welled inside her. Violet's body was out there. Hidden in the forest among those blood-covered soldiers. Grace felt a desperate need to see her, even for a second. To hold her and say *I'm sorry*. To beg forgiveness for her terrible judgement, her most costly of mistakes.

She let her tears fall. A release. It was almost a relief to stop hoping. A relief to take a step towards acceptance.

She hugged her knees. What was she becoming? *We ain't thieves*, she'd told Alexander. And yet, when night fell, she would follow Annie and Jack up the hill and raid the Porters' stables. Ride to Hobart Town and steal from the man she'd loved. Take his daughter to the other side of the world.

What dreadful things we are capable of, she thought. *What lengths we will go to for survival.*

"Grace!"

She turned to see Annie trudging towards the river.

"Get back to the house and pack your things. We're to leave at dusk."

Grace nodded. She stood and flung the last of the flowers into the river. They swirled in the current. Disappeared below the surface.

Dalton found the house by following Grace's stories. Tales she'd told by the fire in the clearing.

A house on the edge of the settlement. Northwest. Stone fence. A tunnel of trees.

He'd tried four other farms and found nothing but old men and earth-stained convicts. But this one, this yellow monstrosity with the forest at its edges, this was it. He felt sure of it.

Two looming storeys, stables, shacks for his convict slaves. A patchwork of neat paddocks stretched out into the haze. Who did this toff think he was, claiming so much of this land for his own?

Dalton waited out the daylight behind the stables. Come the dark, he'd go looking. Put Howell's money in Grace's hands and send her home.

They rose from the valley and looked down on the river as it widened and poured into the sea. The lights of Hobart Town opened out before them.

Grace shifted in the saddle. "To the northwest," she said. "You can reach Harris's house without going through town."

They turned onto a narrow dirt path that snaked through the farmland. Jack held a lamp out in front of them and the three stolen horses paced in its orange glow. Lamps flickered in the windows of the sparsely spread properties.

"Which house is it?" asked Jack.

Grace hesitated. The darkness was disorienting. The land felt strange and foreign. "Keep going," she said. And the path disappeared into a sea of black scrub.

Jack pulled his horse to a stop. "We must have passed it."

Grace tried to sift through her memories. Had they made a wrong turn? No, this forest was familiar. It fringed Harris's land. That thick bank of gums with their branches twisted around each other. A tunnel of trees. They'd kept away from it in those first weeks, wary of its alien shadows and tangled arms. Violet had been afraid of it. *Monsters in there*, Nora had said.

Grace pointed to a faint glimmer in the blackness. "It's that one. That's Harris's house. Where the tunnel of trees comes out. That's where Nora is."

They paced down the narrow track and followed an off-shooting path to a low stone fence. The house rose square and symmetrical at the front of the property, lit by a flickering lamp above the front porch. A long, straight path led to the door. The house looked nothing like Grace remembered. But was that surprising? The last time she'd been here, she'd been dizzy with laudanum and had been frantic to get the girls out before Harris came home. She climbed from the horse and stared up at the lightless windows. "I'll bring you the money. Wait outside."

Jack slid from his horse and handed the reins to Annie. "I'd best come with you. In case there's trouble."

Annie pulled a pistol from her belt and handed it to Grace. "Take this. Just in case."

Hesitantly, Grace wrapped her hand around the gun. She slid it into the waistband of her skirt and led Jack around the enormous sandstone walls. Two storeys of black windows stared down at them. Grace trailed her fingers along the wall to keep her bearings in the dark. She rattled the kitchen door. Locked. She tried the windows. One was open a crack. She clambered through into the dark kitchen. Jack hauled himself over the windowsill.

Up the stairs. Grace held her breath. Her eyes adjusting to the dark, she opened the first door. An enormous curtained bed stood in the centre of the room, a washstand and dressing table against one wall. Grace crept towards the bed. Harris lay asleep on his side, his nightshirt open across his chest. A twist of fair hair lay across his forehead. Grace felt a startling urge to reach out and touch it. Nora was curled up against his stomach. Grace's throat tightened. Frozen, she stared at them both; Harris's breath making Nora's hair flutter with each exhalation. She touched Nora's cheek, then let her hand drift until it found Harris's chin. His skin was warm. She could feel the beginnings of a beard. Her heart lurched with buried love.

For a fleeting moment, she was sitting beside him on the piano bench, their knees pressed together as she picked out each chord. She was strutting through the blue house in silk petticoats, falling asleep cocooned in his arms. Then: the creak and thud of her cell door, icy water, straps at her wrists. *Yes*, she thought, *wash the good memories away*.

"Hurry now." Jack's voice made her start. "Grab the girl and let's get out of here."

Grace slid a hand beneath Nora's sleeping body. The bed creaked. Harris opened his eyes and his breath left him.

"Gracie."

CHAPTER TWENTY-FIVE

"Gracie," Harris said again, his voice stronger. Deciding perhaps, that she was more than a dream. "My God, Gracie, I was so afraid you—" He lit a candle and leapt from the bed. Grace stumbled backwards, clattering into the dressing table. Jack stepped between them.

"Who in hell are you?" Harris's eyes flashed.

Jack raised his pistol. "Give her the girl."

"What?" Harris sought out her eyes. "Grace?"

Her heart thudded. She gripped the corner of the table. Knocked over a bottle of scent. Hers, she realised. She had kept it on her nightstand in the corner of her attic room.

"The girl," said Jack.

Harris glared at him. "You'll have to kill me first."

"I'd never hurt her," said Grace. "You know that. Give her to me."

Jack cocked the trigger.

Harris clenched his jaw. He scooped Nora from the bed and placed her in Grace's arms, gripping her wrist in desperation. "What are you doing?" he whispered.

Grace turned away. She was shocked at Nora's size. She was far heavier than Violet had been. Taller perhaps? Her legs seemed far longer. Was such a thing possible?

"Your money." Jack's voice sounded distant.

Harris glared, but pulled open the drawer of his nightstand without a word.

Jack looked over his shoulder at Grace. "Take the girl. Get on the horse and wait for me down the road. I'll see he doesn't follow us."

"Don't hurt him. Please." The words fell out of her mouth on their own accord.

"I'll not hurt him if he does as I say."

Grace nodded tensely. She held Harris's glance for a moment, then rushed down the stairs.

The darkness was thick. Grace felt her way through the entrance hall and out into the night. Annie's lantern flickered faintly at the edge of the property, surrounded by a pool of black.

A movement in the shadows? She clutched Nora and set out towards the horses. She was grabbed suddenly from behind. A hand over her mouth to muffle her scream.

"Don't say a word." Alexander's voice was close to her ear. "I'm not here to hurt you."

Her fear gave way to hatred. She slid a hand inside her cloak. "I've a gun in my hand," she hissed. "Let go of me or I'll shoot you in the stomach."

He released his grip. Grace pulled the pistol from her skirt and held it out in front of her. She could see little of Alexander's face. Just shadows and eyes.

"How did you find me?"

"A tunnel of trees beside the northwestern farms. One end leads to the forest. The other to Harris's land." His glance fell to the sleeping girl slung across Grace's shoulder.

"Don't you even bloody look at her," she spat.

Alexander raised his palm. "Don't shoot. I've just come to give you this." He held the coin pouch out to her. "Use it to get home."

"I ain't taking nothing from you."

She heard Jack's footsteps behind her. "Grace!" he whispered. "Come on. Now."

"Get out of my way," she hissed at Alexander. "I got to go."

"No. Wait." Alexander held the pouch close to the end of the pistol. "Take it."

She tried to push past him. Heard faint voices and hooves. The light

457

vanished. Jack and Annie had gone, Grace realised sickly. Taken Harris's money and left her alone with these men. She stumbled back into the entrance hall, needing the security of the house over the open land.

"Please," said Alexander, following her inside. "Let me do this one decent thing." He tossed the pouch towards her. It clattered noisily on the floorboards.

"And help you clear your conscience? Never." She kicked it away. Stray coins shot across the floor. "You ought to be out there with those dead men, spending every minute thinking about the things you've done. Thinking about what a monster you are." She shook her head. "No. Why should you get to live when Violet don't?" Her voice began to rise. "I wish you'd died when you were supposed to. I wish those men had killed you and torn you to pieces like you did to Bodenham." Her fist tightened around the gun, her arm aching under Nora's weight.

Alexander met her eyes. "Are you going to shoot me to my face?"

"Why shouldn't I? Did you look into Violet's eyes when you killed her? Did you see her face when you tossed her in the river?" Her finger trembled on the trigger. "Tell me, Alexander. Did you?"

"Gracie, put the gun down."

She whirled around. She hadn't realised Harris was behind her. He set his candle on the side table, his eyes darting between Grace and Alexander. He lifted Nora from Grace's arms and laid her gently on the chaise. Grace swallowed hard. She had to tell him. In spite of all he'd done, he needed to know what had happened to his daughter.

"He killed Violet, James." A tremor in her voice. "She's gone. I wanted to believe she'd just run into the forest and gotten lost, but he... I... He took Violet in the night and he killed her." She looked at Harris, not moving her aim from Alexander's chest. His face was unreadable. "James? Did you hear what I said? Violet is gone."

She saw a tremble in his jaw. He stared darkly at Alexander. "Whoever the hell you are," he said, "get out of my house this instant."

"What?" Grace demanded. "You want to let him go? The man who killed your daughter?"

Harris didn't look at her. "Go!" He pushed Grace's arm, shoving the gun aside. Alexander ran. She yanked free of Harris's grip and snapped the trigger.

CHAPTER TWENTY-SIX

She fired again. This time, the hollow snap of an empty barrel. The front door slammed. Harris snatched the pistol and tossed it across the room. He grabbed her tightly.

"Let go of me!" Grace thrashed against him. "How could you let him escape?" She turned in Harris's arms to face him. His cheeks were flushed in the candlelight. Hair hung over one brown eye. She could feel heat rising from his body.

"Why did you let him escape, James?" Her voice wavered, terrified of the answer.

On the breeze came the glassy twitter of wind chimes. A sound from the blue house. A sound from the past.

And suddenly she was breathing the smoky London air. Cold stung the tip of her nose.

Two girls in matching blue coats, fur trims, high collars. Quilted bonnets over their ears. Nora clung to Grace's left hand, Violet to her right.

The river was high and hungry. Tents were lined up at the water's edge; stripes of red, white, gold. Strings of tiny lanterns glittered against the midday gloom. People shoved their way along the riverfront, laughing, talking all at once. Inside the tents were bearded ladies, tattooed men, two girls joined at the hip.

Violet tugged Grace's gloved fingers. "My head hurts," she said. "I want to go home."

"We've not seen the mermaid lady yet," said Nora. Violet's cloudy eyes brightened. And so Grace let Nora lead them into the last tent.

The mermaid was a young woman with legs fused like a tail. She wore a dress of silver and blue. Grace felt sorry for her, but the woman's smile reached her eyes. Her hair was long and golden, flowing loose over her bare shoulders. The girls stared, entranced.

Harris clutched her cheeks in his hot palms. "Grace, you need to listen to me."

But she was not listening. She was in the sideshow booth beside the mermaid. Opposite her sat the bear man, covered in hair from head to toe. Grace stared into the wildness of his brown fur and searched out his eyes. He stared back. Perhaps a smile. Impossible to tell.

She turned suddenly. The girls were gone. She felt hot with dread. So unlike them to run away. She shoved aside the flap of the tent and raced into the crowd. People were queuing at the ticket booth, others huddled at the river's edge, waiting for a waterman. Grace glimpsed the two blue coats several yards ahead of her. They were swept up in the sea of people elbowing their way toward the pier.

"Violet!" she called. "Nora!"

One of the girls slipped through the crowd towards Grace. Her face was stained with tears.

"The bear man," she was sobbing. "I don't like the bear man."

Grace grabbed a fistful of the blue coat before the crowd could swallow her again.

A shriek. People crammed onto the pier. Grace shoved her way through. Women were screaming, waving at the filthy brown river. The waterman tore off his coat and dived beneath the surface, searching for the second blue coat, the second fur trim.

The girl left on the riverbank was screaming and crying, pulling on Grace's skirts, hysterical. Grace realised she didn't even know which one had fallen. She pushed back the bonnet of the child at her skirts. She had Nora. The river had Violet.

Grace felt her legs give way beneath her. Harris dropped to the floor beside her and clutched her hands. "Gracie, this man, he didn't kill Violet. Violet died eighteen months ago at the sideshow at Bankside."

She opened her mouth to speak. Couldn't form the words. "No," she managed finally. "You're lying."

But then she was home in Covent Garden, she and Harris screaming at each other, breathless with grief.

What were you doing taking her out? What in hell were you thinking?

And, God, she was curled up in Harris's bed, her head pounding when she heard the police come to the door, telling him his daughter's body had been found at Saint Katharine docks at the low tide.

Her breath began to race. Cold sweat prickled her skin and she thought for moment she'd be sick. She leapt to her feet and raced upstairs to the girls' room. Ribbons hung from the ceiling like threads of cloud. The walls were draped in fabric, the breeze making them ripple like sea. Dolls peered out of the darkness with unblinking eyes.

One bed.

The room asymmetrical, incomplete. Grace threw open the wardrobe. One coat. One pair of boots. One quilted bonnet. "Where are her things? Where are Violet's things?" She felt Harris's hands around the tops of her arms. "She was here," she managed. "In the forest. And here in Hobart Town. I held her hand as we walked down the gangway. I put both of them to sleep at the end of our bed in the lodging house." Her voice began to rise. "I was up all night with her those first few weeks because she was afraid of the forest."

Harris nodded. "She's been with you since the voyage, hasn't she? That's when you began to see her again." He pushed her damp curls off her forehead. "Doctor Barnes, he says she came back to you because you feel responsible for her death. He says you let yourself believe she was real because it was the only way you could cope with losing her."

"No." Grace shook her head. "No, no, no. That ain't what happened. He killed her. He's a monster. He's done such terrible things. Inhuman things."

Harris squeezed her hands. "We buried her at Saint Mary's beside her mother. It rained that day. I know you remember it. The day we left London, Nora didn't want to go without Violet. You told her they were twin sisters and they would always carry a part of each other with them."

"No. I never said that." She remembered that morning with such clarity. Buttoning Nora into her dress, tying her bootlaces. She remembered the clatter of hooves on stone, the rotten smell of the river. Nora on one side of her in the carriage to the docks, her forehead pressed against the glass. "Goodbye blue house," she was saying. "Goodbye market, goodbye church…"

Where was Violet?

Grace tried to sift through her memories. "Violet was sitting next to you in the coach." But she could hear the waver in her voice. Felt the solidity of her world dissolve to nothing.

No Grace, I never saw the girl. I'm sorry. I saw you sitting on my chopping log singing to the empty night and I saw you curl around your cloak as though it were her body, but I never saw your Violet.

I can imagine the way you'd look at me. Don't be like that. Perhaps I ought to have told you from the start; that you lost her that day because she was never really there. That your mind let her go because you were finally ready.

But who am I to bring your madness to the light? Would you have believed a word that came from me? The man who sees his murdered mates when he looks behind the shadows? The man who builds an extra stool to convince himself he won't die alone?

CHAPTER TWENTY-SEVEN

Hobart Town Gazette
Friday 25th June, 1824

"The circumstances which were understood to have accompanied the ... crime had long been considered with extreme horror. Reports had associated the prisoner with cannibals; and ... our eyes glanced in fearfulness at the being who stood before a retributive judge, laden with the weight of human blood and believed to have banqueted on human flesh! We heard His Majesty's Attorney General ... entreat the jury to dismiss from their minds all previous impressions against the prisoner; as however justly their hearts must execrate the fell enormities imputed to him, they should duteously judge him, not by rumours, but by indubitable evidence."

She lay on her back, staring at the dancing ribbons. Left to right, left to right. The coloured walls moved like sea.

Her thoughts were slow and cloying. She felt Harris's hands in her hair and at once she was back in the blue house, curled up in his arms and tasting his breath. And from Covent Garden to the wild snarls of the Derwent Valley. She felt the wind in her ears, rain on her skin. Saw curls of smoke twirl upwards, disappearing into a silver-black sky.

The thought yanked her back to reality.

She had pulled the trigger.

She leapt to her feet and rushed dizzily down the staircase. She heard

Harris behind her, calling her name. She snatched the candle from the hallstand. At her feet, was Howell's money pouch. The pistol lay in the corner of the room.

Heart thumping, she held the candle up to the wall, running her hand across the surface, searching for a bullet hole. Nothing.

A sound of horror came from her throat. At her feet: a splatter of blood. Sickness rising, she followed the ruby trail out the door. Across the porch. And then nothing. She stumbled down the path and stood at the edge of the stone fence. The land opened out before her, orange in the dawn. She walked towards the silhouetted trees.

"Alexander?" Her voice sounded out of place among the jagged birdsong. She crouched at the edge of the forest, hiding her eyes against her knees.

She'd needed to escape her guilt. Pin the blame on another. And who better than a man who had done the unthinkable?

Her accusation had been all too easy to believe.

Guilty of murdering a girl he had never even seen.

She felt Harris's hand on her shoulder. "Come inside, Gracie, please. You need to rest."

She shook her head. "I got to find him."

"No. Nora's gone long enough without you. You've got to be there when she wakes."

Nora clutched Grace's hand and launched into a whirlwind tour of the house. A bedroom full of rainbow ribbons. Dining room with an enormous pine table. Two guest bedrooms with canopied beds, Harris's study, kitchen and laundry, sitting room with textured gold wallpaper that glittered in the morning sun. He'd transplanted the luxury of their life in London. Built walls against the wilderness. Grace peered through the sitting room window. The edge of the forest was visible, but it felt distant. A land on the other side of the glass.

"Papa said we can get a piano. So we can sing our songs again." Nora pulled her from room to room, her bare feet pattering on the floorboards. "It's much bigger than the blue house. And much prettier too. Don't you think?" She grinned. She was every inch her sister. Every inch that little white face that had appeared between the reeds of the river. But older,

Grace realised. Her baby-blonde hair beginning to darken. A front tooth missing. The Violet of her visions had been frozen in time; the fragile four-year-old she'd been when she'd died. But here was Nora, almost six and a half, long-legged and tanned. Cheeks flushed with sea air.

Grace smoothed Nora's flyaway hair and kissed her forehead. "Yes, mopsy," she said. "It's much prettier."

That morning, she'd opened the wardrobe and found her neatly pressed dresses hanging beside Harris's waistcoats and shirts. On the clothes, she could still smell the smoke and rose air of the blue house. Here was everything she'd brought from London, waiting patiently for her return. A belief she'd come home.

Nora led her through the kitchen where a teenaged girl in an apron and mobcap was slicing ham for breakfast. She bobbed a curtsey and eyed Grace curiously.

"This is the cellar," Nora announced, heaving against a heavy door beside the range. "Papa built it to store the wheat. There's ghosts and monsters in there."

Grace steered her away from the door. "Don't go looking for ghosts and monsters, mopsy."

"Nora knows she's not allowed down there, doesn't she?" Harris's voice boomed into the kitchen.

Nora huffed dramatically. "Yes Papa."

He herded her out of the kitchen. "Why don't we show Nanny Grace the farm instead?"

They walked past lush green paddocks dotted with sheep, past the wheat growing in neat arrows. Magpies carolled above their heads. The farm smelled of damp earth and animals. And there, behind it all, was the clean eucalyptus scent of the bush.

Harris squeezed Grace's hand. "The crop is growing well. Better than I could have hoped in its first year."

"You're a farmer," she said. "Just like you said you'd be."

Harris smiled. "It helped to keep my mind off things," he admitted. "Losing yourself in physical work helps you forget yourself a while."

Nora clambered onto the paddock fence and leant over to touch one of the sheep. Grace waited for Harris to scold her – *that's not the way young ladies behave* – but instead he smiled faintly. He had grown a little rough around the edges, she noticed. Marching about unshaven, his hair curling past his collar, rolled-up sleeves and no coat or hat. The thought made her smile.

"I was so afraid you'd never see all this." Harris stopped walking. "Gracie, I know I haven't always treated you right and I'm sorry for it. More than you could know."

Grace watched Nora edge her way along the fence. For a long time, she said nothing. "You're ashamed of me," she said finally. "The Wintermans…"

"Ashamed? No, Gracie." He turned her to face him. "You weren't well. I didn't want those people judging you… I…" He pressed his lips against hers. "I love you. And as soon as you're ready, I'm going to make you my wife for real."

Grace felt her thoughts knock together. Unravelling. Untangling. She let Harris hold her. Felt her desire for him creep towards the surface.

"I shouldn't have taken Violet out that day," she said. "She was complaining her head hurt. I took my eyes off them for a second. They never ran away before."

Harris turned to face her. There was kindness in his eyes. Sadness. "It wasn't your fault. It was a terrible accident. That's all. Please, Gracie, you have to believe that."

She couldn't look at him. "I'm so sorry, James. For Violet. For running away. For bringing those men here. I'm so sorry for everything."

He said nothing, just combed his fingers through her hair, caressing her jagged curls with the same tenderness he had when they'd reached her waist.

"Violet is dead," she said after a moment.

"Yes."

"She drowned in the river. In London."

Harris nodded.

"Violet never came to Hobart Town with us."

"No. It was just the three of us."

"She was with me, James. She was so real. I could see her, hear her. I carried her on my back. Plaited her hair." How could she trust her eyes now? Her ears? Her hands? She ran her fingers over the smooth fence posts. Over the fabric of her skirt. Over the coarse skin on Harris's knuckles. There was solidity to everything. It wasn't enough. How was she to know where reality ended and dreaming began?

Harris pressed his forehead against hers. "I was a fool to leave so soon after her death. I know that now. I just thought it would be the best thing for all of us."

She'd felt his hot breath against her skin like this, those terrible sleepless nights after Violet had died. Nights when he would climb to her attic room and slide into her bed. He'd said barely a word about his daughter, the way he had never spoken of Charlotte. But that one night, his blood hot with brandy and his cheeks wet with tears, he'd pulled her towards him. *I don't blame you*, he'd said. And: *I love you, Grace*.

"She came back to you on the ship, didn't she?" he asked. "That's when you began to see her again."

Yes. On the ship.

They'd been at sea, how long? Perhaps a fortnight, but already the days had begun to blur. After three days confined below decks, the sea had calmed enough for them to venture out. Grace held Nora's hand as they climbed the ladder from their cabin to the deck. They stood in the sunlight, letting sea spray arch over their heads.

Nora gripped the gunwale, giggling and shrieking. Grace felt numb.

She had not let herself feel anything. Violet's death, Harris's impulsive proposal, a voyage away from all she knew. Blocking it out was the only way she could survive. This ship, this eternal sea, the *great adventure* Harris wouldn't stop speaking of; it was all an illusion. A dream from which she'd one day surely wake.

Nora turned to Grace, her cheeks glittering. "I'm all wet, Nanny Grace!"

They'd been sweltering in the same clothes since London, much of their luggage packed into the hold. Grace had kept them clean as best she could, sponging their salty clothes each evening and draping them over the bunks to dry. She took Nora into their cabin and pulled out the small trunk they had stowed beneath the bunk. She found Nora's fresh dress and helped her out of her wet clothes. Grace took her back onto deck with Harris and returned to the cabin to find her own dry things.

She rifled through the chest. A clean shirt and coat. Petticoat and drawers. And then, a flash of pink silk. Grace pushed the clothes aside curiously, peering at the unknown item. Whatever it was, Harris must have packed it himself. She lifted out the rose-coloured bundle. A pink shawl that had belonged to Charlotte. Wrapped inside was Violet's rag doll.

Grace stared at the doll. It peered back at her with its one bewildered eye, its hair still in the lopsided plait Violet had made the morning of the sideshow. Grace felt a great surge of grief well up inside her. She hadn't known Harris was even aware of the doll's existence.

In that chest was everything he was unable to say. All the sorrow he was unable to express. Grace saw then that Van Diemen's Land wasn't about adventure. It was about escape. A journey to the other side of the world in hope it might dull the pain of so much loss. Fifteen hundred acres so Harris might never again walk among the ghosts of his wife and daughter.

All her fault. The girls were her responsibility and she had failed them. Failed Charlotte and Nora and Harris. Most of all, she had failed Violet. The guilt was an unbearable, physical weight. She couldn't think, couldn't speak. Just took the doll to her bunk and stayed there until she slept. In the morning, the girls came to find her. Two of them, hand in hand.

Get up, Nanny Grace. Come and see the mermaids.

Grace looked back at the house. The sandstone glowed gold in the sun. Each brick was flecked with the marks of the government man who had moulded it. Arrows, patterned scoring. A signature design for each convict so their labours might always be remembered.

She'd been convinced she'd visited this house. Convinced she'd crept inside and plucked Violet from her bed. But of course, it could never have been. When last she had been on this land, they had been living in a tent amongst nothing but foundations. Harris had taken her to New Norfolk so their new life might not be built on illusions.

"Tell me about the journey," Alexander had said one night as they sat by the fire in the clearing. "From the asylum back to Hobart Town to get the girl. How did you find your way in the dark? Why did no one see you?"

"I don't want to talk about it."

She had lain awake that night and tried to sift through her memories.

Days and nights of hills and mountains and tangled trees. She didn't want to talk about the journey, she realised, because she remembered nothing of it.

Castor oil and laudanum, she had told herself. *That's why I don't remember.*

But now she saw the truth. She remembered nothing of the journey because it had never happened. She had run from the asylum straight into the forest and passed out from the drugs. When she had woken, Violet had been sleeping beside her.

Is that really what happened, Grace?

She'd taken Alexander's words as an accusation. But now she saw with clarity. He'd just been trying to blow away the smoke in front of her eyes.

CHAPTER TWENTY-EIGHT

In the morning, she searched the city. Futile, she knew, but how could she just stand still and hope?

Harris walked beside her as she charged out of the farmland and onto Campbell Street. Horses pulled coaches up and down the hill, sprays of brown earth flying from beneath their hooves. Outside the penitentiary, a gang of workers were being led into the city, arms laden with shovels and picks. Chains clattered around their ankles. They turned to watch Grace as she passed. She crossed the street and hurried away.

She wove through the streets towards the battery, calling Alexander's name. She stopped at the bottom of the hill and looked out over the harbour. The sea glittered in the morning light. Whaling ships dotted the anchorage and people swarmed the wharf. Carts rolled between the docks and the markets. Rhythmic hammering came from the convicts building the warehouses in Salamanca Place.

Hobart Town felt different. Pulsing and vibrant, as though a cloud Grace hadn't been aware of had suddenly been lifted. Around her were sailors, convicts, soldiers. The city was noisy and smelled of the sea.

How vivid her memories of this place were; her boots crunching on the cobbles, Violet's hand in hers. But there was a new haziness to these recollections, as though Violet knew she didn't belong in the memories. As though she knew Grace had walked unaccompanied down the gangway of the *Duckenfield*. Slept alone on that bed of ferns. Whispered bedtime stories to empty shadows.

Grace followed the docks, squinting in the sun. A great ship lay at anchor off Hunter Island.

Enchantress, the signs at the ticket office announced. *Hobart Town to London.*

Imminent departure.

They walked wearily back to the house. Lost in her thoughts, Grace barely noticed the silence until Harris said, "Police."

She stopped walking. Her chest tightened.

Harris strode up the front path. The two officers slid from their horses and looped the reins around the posts of the verandah.

"Good afternoon, sir," said one. "We're looking for Grace Ashwell."

"I have told Doctor Barnes I do not wish to return my wife to the asylum at this time," said Harris. "Thank you for your concern, gentlemen, but it's unnecessary. She's recovering well." He glanced over his shoulder at her. "Go inside, Gracie. Everything's all right."

"I'm afraid we need to speak to her regarding another matter," said the sergeant. "The murder of two British marines and the escape of the convict Alexander Dalton." He turned to Grace. "A word, Miss Ashwell, if you please."

"This is mistake, surely," said Harris. "A murder?"

"Is there somewhere we can speak in private?" asked the sergeant.

Grace's heart pounded. "Of course. In the dining room—" She led the men inside and looked about her, flustered. "Where's the dining room, James?"

Harris took her arm, holding her back. "You'll not speak to her anywhere! My wife was not long ago a patient at New Norfolk asylum. She is no state to be interrogated by you!"

"Indeed. An escapee of New Norfolk, I believe."

"It's all right, James," said Grace. "I want to speak to them. It's all a mistake, ain't it? Like you said. Best to be cleared up nice and quick. Now please, where's the dining room?"

Harris led them resignedly down the hall. "I insist you let me stay with her. She is not of sound mind. She cannot be held responsible for her actions."

"Very well." The sergeant gestured to the chairs around the dining table. "Sit. Please."

Grace strode up to him. "The things I said to the police in Hamilton, they were all lies. I didn't know what I was saying. I— He never did any of them, I swear it. I—"

The sergeant cleared his throat and Grace fell silent. He nodded to the chair. "Sit, Miss Ashwell. You'll speak when spoken to."

She sat stiffly. "It's Mrs Harris." She reached beneath the table for Harris's hand. "You don't need to be here," she murmured.

"Of course I do."

Grace said nothing. She felt hot and sick, her skin damp beneath her bodice. She looked back at the officers.

"The Richmond Police apprehended a couple for bushranging yesterday on the road to Launceston," the sergeant began. "They gave us your name in exchange for a lesser sentence. Told us about your time in the Hamilton settlement and said you knew how to find Alexander Dalton."

Grace felt hot with anger. "They're lying."

"You sent the police after Dalton, did you not? You witnessed him kill two British marines. And you had reason to believe him responsible for the disappearance of Violet Harris."

"I was wrong. He didn't have nothing to do with that, you understand me?" She shook Harris's wrist. "Tell them, James. Tell them what happened to Violet."

"She's telling the truth." Harris's voice was husky. "My daughter died in England a year and a half ago."

The sergeant gave him a fleeting glance. "My sympathies." He walked slowly towards Grace. "Six days ago, members of the Clyde Field Police unearthed the bodies of two marines on the south bank of the Styx River. They were following the directions you provided them with on the twelfth of September this year."

Heat flooded her. With the marines' bodies found, Alexander was as good as hanged.

"These same policemen then apprehended Dalton, but he escaped into the bush."

Grace felt the sergeant's eyes on her, but refused to look at him. She stared past him, eyes fixed on the garish floral walls. What god-awful taste in wallpaper James Harris had, she thought dully. "The man you caught," she said, "the one you think is Alexander Dalton, he never killed no-one. He was just a free settler who liked his own space. I heard of those bolters from blasted Molly Finton at the asylum. She told me about the convict, Alexander Dalton, who disappeared in the bush all those years ago. But I'm telling you, the man I were with in Hamilton, that weren't him. The madness in me made a monster of an innocent man."

The policemen exchanged glances. Grace felt her story tangling. She drew in her breath. "They found a shawl buried with the marines. Grey wool with a hole in one corner."

The sergeant nodded.

"That's my shawl. The marines that got killed were sent to find me and put me back in the asylum."

She cannot be held responsible for her actions.

She looked the sergeant in the eye. "I was the one that killed them. I weren't of sound mind."

"What?" demanded Harris. "*What?*"

The sergeant chuckled. "One of the marines died from a blow to the head," he said. "An attack like that was not delivered by a woman your size. It was delivered by a man with military training, like Alexander Dalton."

"Let me speak to her." Harris pulled her to her feet. "I told you she's not fit to be interviewed."

"Mr Harris— "

"James," Grace hissed. "Please."

The sergeant stood, blocking the door. "It may also interest you to know we found traces of dirt inside the nose and mouth of one of the victims. He was still alive when he was buried. Were you aware of that?"

Grace's stomach turned. She remembered the heat of the blood soaking through the shawl. Remembered the dull thuds as the bodies rolled into their graves.

"Alexander Dalton is one of the most troublesome convicts we've had in this colony, Mrs Harris. If you ask me, you're lucky to have come away from this ordeal with your life. Are you aware of the horrific crime Dalton and his fellow escapees committed eleven years ago?"

Grace said nothing.

"I don't know what in God's name would possess you to protect him like this, but I can assure you that if you stand before a jury and claim to have murdered these soldiers, there's not a man in the colony who will believe you. Perhaps you were not of sound mind when these men were killed, but your husband's decision not to return you to New Norfolk suggests to me that you now are. Therefore you will be held fully accountable for any statements you make today." He hovered over her. "Perjury in a double murder trial will get you a sentence at the Female Factory if you're lucky. The hangman if you're not. Although there's always the chance the judge may see a lifetime of incarceration at New Norfolk as the most suitable sentence."

Grace clenched her jaw. The sergeant stepped aside and let Harris pull her into the hallway.

"This is who you're so desperate to find?" he hissed. "This is who was in my home?" He stood close, his voice low and taut. "You told me you'd been in Hamilton with the couple that brought you to Hobart Town. And now I hear you've been out in the wilderness with this madman? And that men have been murdered?"

She turned away from his furious eyes. "I knew what you'd think if I told you."

"What I'd think? Grace, I've no idea what to think. Why in God's name are you protecting this animal?"

"He saved my life, James. Several times over. And I sent the police after him for Violet's murder."

"He deserves to be hanged!"

"I can't just turn him in after all he did for me!"

"It's too late. You've already turned him in. And if he truly killed these soldiers, you were right to do it. Lying for him now can't save him. It will only bring you both down."

Tears spilled suddenly down Grace's cheeks. "It can save him. It can. If I'm found guilty of these murders, I can't be punished."

"The only thing they're going to find you guilty of is perjury. Nora and I have just got you back. Are we to lose you again because you hold yourself responsible for the actions of some degraded convict? If this is what you believe is right, then I fear I've brought you home too soon. Perhaps I ought to send you back to New Norfolk."

"No." She wiped away her tears with the back of her hand. "I carry Violet's death with me every minute. I couldn't bear to carry Alexander's as well. I can use this madness to save him. Let a little good come from all that's happened."

For a moment, Harris said nothing. He stood close, his breath fast and hot against her nose. "I understand," he said, his anger fading slightly. "Truly. But you won't escape your guilt this way. You'll escape it by being a good mother to Nora. By letting us finally start our life out here. Don't we deserve that? After all we've been through?"

She looked up at him. His face had narrowed, the lines around his eyes become more pronounced. Threads of grey had appeared at his temples. Hobart Town had been nothing of the fresh start he had hoped it would be; anyone could see that by looking at his face.

Grace blinked away a fresh rush of tears. "I've got to try and save him."

"No." Harris's voice hardened. "You don't. A man like this ought to be shot on sight. Your duty is not to him. It's to Nora and me." He grasped her shoulders. "I love you, Grace. Nora loves you. I don't want to have to put you back in the asylum. But I won't hesitate to do what I think is best for you. And what's best for my daughter."

Grace swallowed hard. She nodded. *Understood.*

She wiped her eyes and walked back into the dining room. Sat at the table opposite the policemen.

"I hope your husband has talked a little sense into you," said the sergeant. He leant across the table. "Who killed the marines, Mrs Harris?"

She stared into her clasped hands. "He did. Alexander Dalton."

"Would you be willing to state this in a court of law?"

"Yes."

"Good." The sergeant folded his arms across his thick chest. "Now, where can we find him?"

How to find a man who'd hidden from the world for more than a decade? She'd been looking in the wrong place, she saw that now. She'd have to bury herself in that tunnel of trees she'd once been afraid of. Enter the forest on the fringe of Harris's land. Return to the wilds where she'd found him the first time.

"You can't," Grace told the sergeant. "He's too good at hiding."

CHAPTER TWENTY-NINE

They've been walking for sixteen days. Macquarie Harbour lies behind them and who knows what lies ahead. The last of the bread they'd eaten days ago. Dalton's steps are crooked with hunger. His vision is blurred, his throat dry.

"Dalton," Greenhill whispers. "Dalton, the flogger."

What if it were to end here? What if he is the sacrifice? There would be no guilt, no hiding. A better end, surely.

Dalton stands, looking Greenhill in the eye. "Do it," he says.

The axe comes towards him slowly. Why so slow? What's wrong with time?

No. If it ends here, he will never climb the mountains and see the valleys unfold below him. Never stand beneath an electric black and gold sky. He will never feel Grace's heart thud beneath his fingertips, or hold her in the night. And Dalton realises he'd go through all that guilt and hiding a hundred times over so he might know how it feels to come back to life.

He lurches away from Greenhill's axe. Feels a shock of pain as the blade clips his shoulder.

Dalton heard himself cry out. The pain at the top of his arm, it was different now. Sharper, hotter.

And the light. That was different too. Flickering lamplight, not purple dusk.

Grace. Why was Grace here? There was blood on her cheek. What was she doing amongst all this carnage? He couldn't make sense of it. He reached out, sure she'd vanish if he touched her. Her skin was hot beneath

476

his finger.

"I told him to kill me," he said. "But then I thought of you."

"You're delirious," she said. "Try not to move. I got the ball out. Lie still and let me sew it up." She crouched over his shoulder, needle in hand. She frowned in concentration, lamplight flickering on her cheeks.

Dalton swallowed a grunt of pain. He felt lines of blood run across his bare chest. "Greenhill. He was here. But you made him leave." Relief washed over him. The men were in their graves. And the blood on his hands belonged only to him.

Grace cut the thread carefully. She rinsed her hands from a canteen of water and wrapped a length of cloth around his upper arm. Her cheeks were pale. "I watched the surgeon stitch a cut on Violet's head once," she said. "I done the best I can." She dampened a second cloth and wiped it across Dalton's chest.

He tried to sit. She held a hand against his other shoulder.

"Stay down. I think I made it worse."

Dalton grabbed a fistful of her chemise and drew her towards him until her face was inches from his.

She swallowed hard. "Violet... I let her drown... in London. I know you... I don't understand, Alexander. Why let me believe you killed her?"

"You found out what we did to Bodenham. You were going to leave me. But I knew you'd stay if you thought I could show you where Violet was buried."

She sat. "Christ. Do you have any idea of the trouble—"

Dalton said to the sky, "And I thought you'd stop blaming yourself if you believed I was responsible."

Grace closed her eyes. "Alexander..."

"I don't want you to carry that guilt every day," he said. "It will destroy you."

"So you thought you'd carry it for me?" She shuffled on the earth and lay beside him. "That was really bloody stupid."

"Aye," said Dalton. "I know."

"But it was also very kind." She turned her head to face him. "Can you ever forgive me?"

He smiled. She'd searched for him. She knew what he'd done to Bodenham and still she'd come. Trying to fix her own mistakes, yes, but the fact she cared enough to ask his forgiveness brought him a step closer to his own absolution. He touched the coil of hair that hung across her cheek. She flinched and pulled the coin pouch from her bag.

"The *Enchantress* leaves tomorrow for London. You need to be on it. The police will find you here. You got to go, you understand me?"

"Come with me. You and the girl. Like we planned."

She looked away. "You're better off without me, Alexander. Look at all I've done to you. You're lying here in pain. The police know you're alive. They want you on the scaffold."

"It was my fault. All of it."

Grace said nothing. She busied herself wrapping the scissors and tweezers in the remains of his shirt. "I'm not going back to London," she said finally. "I'm sorry."

Dalton felt suddenly cold. Sick. "Is it because of him? Harris? That bastard who locked you up?"

"He was right to do it!" she cried. "You know that! You knew that all along! And you let me go on planning my miserable revenge! Did you never think to tell me the truth?"

"Tell you?" He laughed coldly. "In what world would you have believed such a thing from a madman like me?"

She sighed. "You're no madman."

Dalton sat, dizziness coursing through him. Pain radiated down his arm, across his chest. It seared through his head, tangling his thoughts. "Christ," he hissed. "What in hell have you done to me?" He clenched his teeth. "You trying to finish the job?"

"I'm sorry. I'm sorry. I knew I couldn't get help. I—" She fumbled in her bag and pulled out a bottle. "Drink this. It'll help a little." She held the flask to his lips and drizzled brandy down his throat. He felt warmth rise in his chest. The pain remained hot and sharp. Grace pressed a hunk of bread into his hand. "Eat. You're weak."

He chewed slowly, not taking his eyes off her. "He know you're here then? Creeping around the bush at night?"

She looked away. "Of course not."

"So you'll give up home for a man you speak to in lies."

"I've told him no lies." She picked at the blood beneath her fingernails. "He's sleeping."

Dalton glared at her. "He lays a hand on you. He takes away your chance to be a mother. All those things you said he's done. Were they real?"

"Yes. But I know he'd never set out to hurt me. And I know he'd never hurt his girls. Violet weren't even there!" She sighed. "He's no angel. But I'm not neither. And, Alexander, you of all people should know the value of forgiveness."

"Forgiveness? I'd kill him for what he did to you. I'd make him suffer like he made you suffer. And then I'd kill him."

Grace swallowed hard. "You don't mean that. I know you don't. You wouldn't do that to me." She met his eyes challengingly, waiting for his anger to fade. Or perhaps explode. "Why do you despise a man who wants nothing but the best for me?"

For a moment, Dalton didn't answer. Finally, he said, "I hate him because you love him."

Grace let out her breath. "Well. At least now we're getting somewhere." She stood and brushed the leaves from her skirt. Held out her hand. "Stand up."

"What?"

"You can't stay out here. Not in this state. I'm taking you back to the house. And tomorrow I'm going to take you to the harbour. See you get on that ship."

Dalton began to laugh, slowly, without humour. "You want to take me back to your house? You want to lead me straight to him?" He stood slowly, shakily. "As you wish, my Grace."

Her jaw tightened. She slid his battered coat over his shoulders. "I can't leave you here. Not after all you've done for me." She picked up the lantern and the shadows shifted. "Please don't make me regret it."

Grace shouldered open the door of the cellar and helped Alexander down the stairs. She left him sitting up against the wall and hurried through the dark house, gathering up food and blankets. She returned with her arms full and lit a candle. In the orange light, she could see blood splashed across her skirt and chemise. She pulled off her soiled clothing and tossed it beside Alexander's bloodied shirt. She crouched at his side in her petticoats. "I've brought you food and water. A little brandy. You need anything else?"

Alexander said nothing.

Grace tensed at his silence. She wrapped the blanket around his shoulders. "I need to trust you. Please. If you truly care for me, you'll stay down here and not let no one see you."

"He'd never forgive you for keeping me down here."

"No." Grace stood. "He would never forgive me."

She climbed the stairs, heart thumping. Glanced back over her shoulder. "There's good in you, Alexander. I know it. Please don't let the darkness win."

She pulled the cellar door closed. Stupidity, she knew. But how could she leave him at the mercy of the forest?

She crept up the staircase, her neck and shoulders aching with tension. Nora's bedroom door hung open, the ribbons motionless in the still night. A girl sat in the middle of the room, clutching a rag doll to her chest. Grace tiptoed towards her.

The scarred forehead.

Grace's breath left her. "Violet?"

The girl turned and smiled. "Yes, Nanny Grace?"

Grace's eyes overflowed with sudden tears. "I thought you were dead. The sideshow..."

"I liked the sideshow," said Violet.

Tears dripped from Grace's chin. She knelt on the rug, afraid to touch Violet in case she disappeared forever. "You disappeared. Why did you disappear, angel? Was it because of Alexander? Did he scare you?"

"I thought you wanted me to leave. You said you wouldn't carry me anymore."

Grace stifled a sob and pulled Violet into her. Clung tightly in case she should ever slide away from her again.

"Grace?" Harris's voice in the doorway made her start. "What are you doing?"

"Violet," she whispered. "Violet, angel, it's Papa."

Harris knelt beside them.

"James, it's Violet. See?"

Harris sucked in his breath. He lifted the lamp to the little face on Grace's shoulder. Now she was sleeping. Now the scar on her forehead was gone.

"It's Nora, Grace. You know that. Violet is gone." A tremor in his voice. He lifted his daughter from Grace's arms and laid her back on the bed. Grace stayed on the floor, staring at the rug.

She had seen that scar. Heard that little voice.

She felt suddenly cold. She stood and wiped her eyes with the back of her hand. "Yes," she said, forcing a steadiness into her voice. "Nora. Of course." She heard the clunk and groan of the New Norfolk water pipes. She stumbled to her feet. "I was dreaming, that's all. I was sleepwalking or something. James... I— "

Harris kissed her forehead with unnerving kindness. "I dream of her sometimes too."

But he wouldn't look her in the eyes.

CHAPTER THIRTY

The cellar door creaked as it opened. Dalton squinted. A silhouetted figure stood at the top of the stairs. A girl.

"Are you a ghost?" She gripped the bannister and edged towards him. "I told them there was ghosts down here! And monsters."

"Aren't you afraid of ghosts?" asked Dalton.

She shook her head. "I'm not afraid of anything." She peered at him with wide blue eyes, a spellbound smile in the corner of her lips. A messy blonde plait hung down her back, loose pieces clinging to her cheeks.

So this was the face Grace had seen in the river. The face that haunted her. It was like looking into her mind.

"Is it morning?" he asked.

The girl nodded.

"Where's Grace? Tell her to come and see me."

Nora shook her head. "I'm not supposed to be down here. And besides, she can't."

"Why not?"

"Because she's going away again."

Dalton stood, clutching at the wall to keep his balance. Pain shot through his shoulder and made his stomach turn. "Away where?"

"To the place."

Dalton felt his breathing quicken. "Why?"

Nora shrugged. "Papa said."

He reached into the pocket of his coat and handed her the carving of Grace. She peered at it curiously.

"Do you like it?"

She nodded.

He took it back and slid it inside his pocket. "I'll make you one of your sister."

"My sister is in Heaven," she said.

"I need you to bring me some things. A piece of wood. And a knife. Can you do that?"

A nod.

"Good." Dalton stepped towards her and she shuffled backwards. "Go on now. Quickly. Before someone catches you here."

"I'm sorry, Gracie," said Harris, pacing across the parlour. "Believe me, this is as hard for me as it is for you."

Grace sat on the couch and chewed her thumbnail. "I doubt that."

Harris knelt in front of her. "This is for the best. You know that as well as I do. I wanted you home with me so badly I refused to see you were still unwell." He brought her hand to his lips and kissed it. She pulled away quickly before he saw the bloodstains from the previous night she'd not managed to remove.

"Violet is gone," she said. "I know that. Please don't send me back to that place."

Harris sat beside her on the couch and sighed. "You can't spend your life seeing ghosts. Please, Grace. Just go and get your things."

The maid was dragging a trunk out of the bedroom. She smiled awkwardly at Grace and bobbed a curtsey. "You need help with anything, Mrs Harris?"

Grace shook her head stiffly.

"All right, ma'am." The trunk thudded as the girl dragged it down the stairs.

Grace opened the wardrobe and gathered up two of Harris's clean shirts. Waistcoat, scarf and a heavy woollen overcoat she hadn't seen him wear since London. Gloves, neck cloth, scissors. If she was to be locked back up, she'd at least make sure Alexander got away.

She ran downstairs with the clothes in her arms and tried to slip through the parlour.

Harris stood up suddenly. "What are you doing with my clothes?"

She tried to edge past him. "I'm sorry, James. I'll explain everything, I swear it. Just not now. I can't."

He rubbed his eyes. "Go and get in the carriage." He took the bundle and placed it on the side table. Grace hid her hands hurriedly in the folds of her skirts. Harris frowned. He took her hand and turned it over in his. Faint brown blood was streaked across her palm.

Harris looked up slowly. "Grace?"

"Don't go with him."

She whirled around. Alexander walked slowly towards them, a kitchen knife in his fist. His greatcoat was buttoned loosely over his bare chest. "Come with me."

Harris face darkened. "Jessie!"

The maid hurried inside. Her eyes widened in shock at the sight of Alexander.

"Get my pistol," said Harris. "From my desk drawer."

Jessie thundered up the stairs. Grace took a step towards Alexander, holding out her hand for the knife. She stopped abruptly.

A girl in the corner of her eye.

She glanced out the window. Beside the chopping log sat Violet, Rosie in her lap, building a bed of leaves as she had done in the forest. Grace felt heat flood her.

The maid returned breathlessly and Harris snatched the gun. "Go for the police, Jessie. Now." He glared at Alexander. "Grace? You would risk your life for this monster?"

"He ain't no monster."

"The police sergeant told me about this dog, Grace. He's done more than kill those marines. He's done things no right-minded human would ever consider."

Grace stood protectively in front of Alexander.

Harris let out a humourless chuckle. "You know. You know what he has done and still you're trying to save him."

She met his eyes. "I'm still trying to save him. Because if he's hanged it will be my fault. And I ain't living with any more death on my conscience."

"How dare you think of this bastard's death in the same way as my daughter's! You'll be doing the world a service by seeing him hanged."

Anger bubbled inside her. "He saved my life. Ain't that worth nothing to you?"

"And what about the lives he's taken?"

"There's good in him. I know it. He's a decent man."

"A man? How can you see a scrap of humanity in a beast that's done what he has?"

Grace's voice began to rise. "How can we ever know we wouldn't have done the same? I know what damned, desperate things a person will do to survive. How do you know where you'd draw the line?"

Harris stared, his eyes on her like she was a stranger. Outside the window, Violet made the doll dance on her knees. Grace looked away hurriedly. Perhaps New Norfolk was where she belonged, washing away this ghost girl in a flood of icy water.

Harris turned to Alexander. "Get out. You may have fooled my wife into thinking you're a decent man but I have no such illusions."

"She's not your wife."

Harris raised the gun.

Alexander smiled crookedly. "I'm just a wild animal you got to shoot, aren't I?"

"You expect anything less than to be shot like an animal after the things you've done? You don't deserve to be treated like a human."

"Grace treats me like a human."

"Grace is delusional. But she'll soon see you for the beast you are."

Alexander's eyes shifted. "Tell him he's wrong. Tell him, Grace."

"Don't shoot him, James," she said huskily. "He's leaving. He's going to get on that ship and leave before it's too late. Ain't that right, Alexander?"

Harris stood with the gun poised. "Against her better judgement, Grace seems to care for you greatly. Out of respect for her, I'm not going to shoot you like I ought to. But you leave my house this instant. Get on that ship and leave our lives."

"Grace?" said Alexander. "Is this what you want?"

"Give me the knife," she said. Alexander hesitated, then pressed it into her palm. She looked at Harris. "And the gun."

He didn't move.

"Please, James. You told me you weren't going to shoot him." She held out her hand. Harris clenched his jaw, then passed her the pistol. "Thank you." She placed the weapons on the table. Nudged the pile of clothes towards Alexander. "Tidy yourself."

Alexander opened his mouth to speak, but said nothing. He slid off his coat and eased himself into the clean shirt, stifling a grunt of pain. He looped the neck cloth awkwardly with one hand. Grace stepped forward and tied it carefully at his throat. She took Harris's gold-threaded waistcoat from the table and slid it over Alexander's shoulders. Buttoned it down his chest. She smelled brandy on his breath. The bush on his skin. She could feel Harris's eyes burning into the back of her. She picked up the scissors and trimmed Alexander's beard until it lay close against his chin. The scissors squeaked and clicked noisily in the silence. Black hair fluttered to the floor. Grace slid the gloves into the pocket of the clean greatcoat, along with a flask of brandy from the side table. She handed the coat to Alexander.

"You got to leave us now," she said. "Please." She stepped back, feeling Harris's hand circle her upper arm. Alexander hesitated. Then slowly, without a word, he turned and began to walk towards the door. Grace stared at him until he disappeared.

Harris stood silent for a moment. He began to pace, his boots clicking across the floorboards.

Grace leant her hot forehead against the window. She felt a deep ache for the loss of Alexander, for the loss of Harris that would surely come. She closed and opened her eyes, willing Violet to disappear. There she stayed on the grass beside the chopping block, blanketing the doll in leaves. Grace looked away.

Silence hung between them.

"I always considered my girls very lucky to have you as a mother," Harris said finally. "I always believed they could do no better than to be raised by you. This defiance you have, this determination, I always thought it a positive trait. But I suppose we can see now where your loyalties lie." His voice began to rise. "For you to harbour that monster while my daughter slept upstairs!" He swung a wild arm across the table and sent a vase crashing to the floor.

Grace said nothing. How could she find any miserable justification?

Harris rubbed his eyes and looked back out the window. "Where's Nora?"

"Nora?"

He opened the window and shouted into the garden. That look on his face, Grace had seen it before. Seen that panic, that desperation, the day she'd come back from the sideshow. With the police and without Violet.

Rosie lay abandoned beside the chopping block, the leaves scattered by the swirling wind.

"She was right there," he said. "Playing with Violet's doll."

CHAPTER THIRTY-ONE

"Where is it?" the girl demanded.

"What?"

"The wooden doll of Violet. You said I could have it if I came with you and didn't make noise."

Dalton hesitated. He looked up as Grace approached, her yellow dress bright against the shadowy forest. She shoved aside the hungry undergrowth.

"Nora!" she cried. "Get here now!" She snatched the girl's wrist and glared at Dalton. "Stay away from her!"

"She came to me."

"Like hell she did."

"I had to see you."

"Christ, Alexander, the police are on their way here. Don't you understand that?"

"I can't go without you."

"Well you'd best find a way. You ain't a dead man no more. I've caused you nothing but trouble. You're far better off without me."

"No." He clutched at her collar. "You brought me back to life. I'm so grateful you found me. I thought I'd survived, but all I was doing was waiting to die." She was laced into an embroidered gown, her hair pinned back neatly. Where was his Grace with muddy feet and smoked meat in her fist?

He yanked out the comb holding up her hair, trying to bring her back to him. Her hair fluttered around her cheeks. He could see the faint scar on her chin, could feel her heart thudding beneath his fingers.

Her, with her messy curls and tartan cloak, she'd reminded him there was a scrap of humanity left inside him. Reminded him that even though he'd done things no one dared speak of, there was a part of him that was still a man. How could he give her up?

"You woke me," he said. "Without you, I'd still be lying in that hut grunting at the shadows."

"I tied the noose for you, Alexander! How do you think the marines found those bodies? Because I told them where to dig! I may have brought you back to life, but I did it in the worst possible way!"

"So you'll stay in this Godforsaken prison and let him lock you up? Never see London again?" He shook the money pouch in front of her face. "A way home, Grace. Today." She closed her eyes.

Yes, my Grace. A way home.

Distant voices. Movement in the bush. She turned suddenly.

"Christ," she hissed. "Harris will find us here. He has the gun. You got to leave, Alexander. This second. Get on that ship before it's too late."

She began to march through the bush, clutching Nora's hand. Dalton lurched after her and pulled her back to him. "Did you ever ask yourself why Violet left when she did?"

Grace let out her breath. Squeezed her eyes closed. "She left because I was ready." Her voice caught in her throat.

"She left because you were free of *him*!" Dalton hissed. "Because it was just you and I out there and the rest of the world fell away. You know I'll never judge you for what you did. But he'll wake every morning and look at your face and remember how you let his daughter drown."

Grace's eyes flashed. "Damn you to hell." Her glance fell suddenly to the clearing. A glassy, vacant expression passed across her face. Dalton felt a smile in the corner of his lips.

Well now…

"You still see her."

"No." A tremble in her voice. "No. She's dead."

He followed Grace's line of sight. "Where is she? What is she doing?"

"Nothing. She ain't doing anything." She blinked back tears. He stood close to her.

"I see them too. The dead. In my hut. In the forest. I see Bodenham, who I used for my own survival. And I see Greenhill, the one who made us do it. They're a reminder of what we've done. I tried to take it away for you, but I know now that was foolish. It will always be inside you. Harris will never understand. But I do. We need each other, my Grace."

She glanced over her shoulder as the voices grew louder.

"Nora!" Harris was calling. "Nora, where are you, my love?" And: "Show yourself Dalton, you dog."

He grabbed Grace's chin and turned her to face him. "You want to spend your life rotting amongst the lunatics? Have your senses washed away under those water pipes?"

A warning shot exploded into the sky. Grace clamped a hand over Nora's mouth. She glanced at Dalton. "Harris has the carriage ready. If we take it, we can get to the docks in time. But we got to go now."

Sullivan's Cove was bustling. Coaches crowded Davey Street and streams of passengers hauled trunks and duffel bags towards the docks. The sky had darkened. Black clouds drooped over the harbour.

"Leave the carriage here," said Grace. "We've got to hurry."

She slid from the coach and lifted Nora out after her. Alexander climbed down from the box seat. In Harris's clothing, he could almost pass for a gentleman. Grace felt underdressed beside him in her dirt-streaked dress, her hair unpinned, no bonnet or cloak. She touched his elbow. "How do you feel?"

His cheeks were pale beneath his beard. "Tomorrow I'll wake and see something other than this cursed outpost of the world." He smiled faintly. "I've never felt better."

"There's a flask of brandy in your pocket," said Grace. "It'll ease the pain. But you got to wait til we're on the ship. You got to have your wits about you til then. You can't hold the stuff no more. Do you have the money?"

Alexander nodded.

"Go. Three tickets. I'll get the luggage." She hauled the trunk Jessie had packed out of the carriage. It thumped noisily against the cobbles.

She gripped its handle with one hand and Nora with the other. Began to walk toward the checkpoint. The wind swirled and whipped her hair against her cheeks.

"Nanny Grace? What are we doing?"

She forced a smile. "We're having a great adventure, mopsy." She glanced edgily over her shoulder. No sign of Harris. How long until he found the carriage gone? Enough time for the ship to cast off her moorings and slide through the heads?

Alexander handed their tickets to the guard. Out before them was the rocky outcrop of Hunter Island where the ships lay at anchor. On the right of the island, a dark-wooded whaling vessel with try pots lined up across the deck. On the left, the bustling migrant ship *Enchantress*. And behind, fifteen thousand miles of ocean that would sweep them back to England.

Grace stepped onto the stone causeway that wove through the shallows towards the island. Water licked at the edge of the walkway, washing over her boots with each swell. She'd walked this narrow path, hemmed by sea, almost a year ago. Traipsing into Hobart Town with Harris and Nora. She'd been disoriented and scared. Now she saw things with clarity. Her fear replaced by determination.

They reached the tiny island and walked up the gangway of the migrant ship. The sailor at the gunwale heaved Grace's trunk onto the deck. People swarmed; sailors in white slops, passengers with bags slung across their shoulders. Laughter and nervous chatter. Shouted instructions to the crew.

Grace glanced sideways at Alexander. When had he last been among so many people? His shoulders were hunched, eyes at his feet. She touched his arm in a gesture of solidarity.

They were herded down a narrow staircase into the steerage passage. Men to the left. Women and children to the right.

"Go," Grace told Alexander. "Before Harris comes looking." Passengers pushed past them, chatting, laughing. "We'll find each other once we're at sea."

Alexander nodded. He turned and walked slowly down the passage.

"Nanny Grace?" Nora tugged her hand. "Are we going back to England?"

Grace's throat tightened. "No, mopsy. But Alexander is." She ushered Nora towards the staircase. "Quick now. We got to get off the ship." A woman with two children in her arms shoved past her. All these people would soon see London. They'd go to church at Saint Mary's. Buy fruit from Leadenhall. Walk down Maiden Lane and see the blue house filled with a new family. Grace felt an ache of longing. She pushed it away. She needed to look forward. Escape the past.

"Grace?"

She turned in dread at the sound of Alexander's voice.

"What are you doing?"

She stepped off the staircase. "I'm sorry," she coughed. "It was the only way."

Alexander's eyes darkened. "He's going to send you back to the asylum. He's going to put you under those water pipes until you scream."

"Perhaps. But perhaps that's what I need. I don't want to spend my life seeing the dead." She touched Alexander's cheek. "I'm sorry I lied to you. But you got the chance to start again. You got to take it."

He gave a faint nod. His fingers found hers and she squeezed gently. His hand moved up to her wrist. And then he was pushing her backwards, backwards until her spine was hard against the bulkhead. He forced an arm across her chest.

She tried to pull away. "Alexander, let go of me."

His grip tightened. Grace glanced over his shoulder. The passage was bustling. Cry out and men would come running. But so would the police.

"Harris will have found the carriage gone," she hissed. "He knows about this voyage. He's going to come for Nora. And he's going to bring the police. You've got to let us go."

"I can't." His fingers clenched her wrist and she swallowed a cry of pain. "Without you there's just emptiness and death. But you keep those dead men away."

The ship groaned loudly. Shouted instructions to the crew filtered below deck.

"You were willing to take the blame for Violet. You were willing to make such a great sacrifice for me. Why are you doing this now? After so much selflessness?"

His lips were close to her ear. "Because selflessness brought me nothing but a bullet in the shoulder. It's not human nature to be selfless. You know that. We can try, but deep down, there's that animal need for self-preservation. That need to put ourselves first."

"Then put yourself first!" cried Grace. "Let me go and save your own bloody life!" The anchor groaned beneath her feet. A flurry of children raced back to the deck, trailed by their mothers.

Grace's breathing quickened. "Nora," she said. "You got to get off the ship. Run. Tell them you got to get off."

Nora began to cry.

"Go, Nora. Now."

She pulled Grace's skirt. "I want you to come too."

Grace met Alexander's eyes. She sucked in her breath and shoved against his injured shoulder. Alexander cried out, his arm falling from across her chest.

"Run, Nora. I'm right behind you." Grace looked back at Alexander. "I'm sorry. I'm so sorry." She backed away from him and ran up the staircase. Heard footsteps behind her. She kept running. Alexander chased her up the stairs. Across the deck. Back onto the island. Grace stopped at the bottom of the gangway and collided with the whalers who were loading supplies onto their ship. She fell to her knees, gasping for breath.

"I'm sorry," said Alexander. "I can't do this without you." Sweat glistened on his forehead. The shoulder of his coat was black with blood.

Grace climbed to her feet. "Hell," she said. "You bloody fool." She reached into his pocket and pulled out the flask of brandy. "Drink this. It will help the pain." She held it to his lips, a hand behind his head stopping him from pulling away. A long drink. A big dose. She kept pouring it down his throat until he began to cough. She tossed aside the flask and gripped his arms. Began to walk, forcing him backwards. He stumbled dizzily.

"Do you really want to look at me every day and know I was wishing I were somewhere else?" She stepped onto the gangway, guiding him carefully. "Wishing I were with another man?" One step. Two steps. She looked into his eyes. "Let me go. Be the good man I know you can be." Another step and his boots thudded onto the deck. He stumbled to his knees and gripped the gunwale. Grace knelt on the gangway and clutched his head in her hands. Tears slid down her face. "There'll not a be a day I don't think of you." She held her lips against his bristly cheek. "Goodbye, Alexander."

He looked up at her with cloudy eyes. Nodded slowly, defeatedly. "Goodbye, my Grace."

She turned and walked down the gangway, unable to look back. She grabbed Nora's hand and hurried towards the wharf.

And then the clattering of footsteps. Shouting voices. Marines poured onto the island and shoved Grace aside. Guns out, they charged up the gangway and onto the *Enchantress*.

Grace heard a cry from deep in her throat. Her legs gave way and she sank to the ground, her dusty skirts pooling around her. Nora scrambled onto the wharf. Harris snatched her into his arms; clung to her in a desperate embrace. His face was lined and shadowed with weariness. He ran a hand through Nora's tangled blonde hair. Kissed the side of her head once, twice, three times. He looked over his daughter's shoulder at Grace.

I'm sorry, said his eyes. And: *what choice did I have?*

CHAPTER THIRTY-TWO

Grace packed her things. Took her earnings from Harris and hauled her rose-scented dresses to the Female Factory.

"You got experience with children then?" the matron asked, leaning back in her chair and wiping beads of sweat from her forehead.

Grace nodded. "Yes ma'am."

The matron sniffed loudly. "You want to work in this hell hole, the job's yours." And like that, she became an attendant in the factory's overflowing nursery.

The building was hidden in a valley at the southern end of town. The women woke, worked and slept in the constant shadow of the mountain. The place was damp and grey. Immune to the approaching summer.

Here, there was no Violet. She wouldn't come to a place like this. Here, reality was clear and cold.

Separated too early from their convict mothers, the babies were sickly, weak and needy. The hours were endless and exhausting, but kept Grace's mind from dwelling on all it had lost. She felt needed, worthwhile, like she might do these wretched children some good and begin to atone for her mistakes.

She found Maryann Fairlie in the laundry.

"You." Maryann tossed the sheet she was scrubbing back into the tub and looked up and down at Grace's uniform. "You're here by choice? What's the matter with you?"

"Just want to be of use." Grace drew in her breath. "Are you all right?

You and the children? Healthy?"

Maryann nodded faintly. "Daniel. Did they find him?"

Grace wound her finger around the corner of her apron. "Last I saw he was headed into the bush."

"Stupid scab," said Maryann. "Don't he know there's nothing out there? A man can't survive in that place. Not alone." She plunged her arms back into the tub and began to scrub at the sheet with a new ferocity. Suds cascaded down her legs. Finally, she turned back to Grace. "And your Alexander?"

Grace looked down. "Alexander's gone."

"Well," Maryann said brassily, "if you ask me, it's good riddance to the both of them." But her eyes met Grace's in a moment of unspoken grief. She turned back to her washing. "I'm being assigned. Housekeeper to some toff in Campbell Town. Emma and her brother are being kept here at the factory. They'll be sent to the orphanage when they're old enough."

"I'm sorry," Grace mumbled.

Maryann put a soapy hand out and grabbed her wrist. "You'll take care of them, won't you? You'll make sure they're all right?"

"Of course."

"And you'll tell them about me? Only the good things. Don't tell them what I done to end up here. Just tell them I love them."

Grace nodded. "Every day."

She'd been at the factory a week when the matron found her in the nursery. She took the baby from Grace's arms. "You got a visitor."

Harris was waiting outside the front gates. He wore a frock coat and silk scarf and looked very much the man who had plucked her from the mop fair so many years ago. Grace drew in her breath and stepped through the gates.

They stood without speaking for a long time, the silence loaded with regret and unspoken apologies. Finally, Harris cleared his throat.

"There's a piano at home, Gracie. I hoped you might like to play it."

She managed a faint smile. "'Home, Sweet Home.'"

Harris took a step towards her and tucked a strand of hair beneath her cap. "What are you doing working in this dreadful place?"

"I need a purpose. Something to put my mind to."

The guard at the entrance eyed them curiously. Harris took her arm and led her away from the gates. He stepped close and touched her cheek. "Come home and put your mind to being my wife. To being Nora's mother."

"You want me around Nora?"

"She needs you. So do I." He smiled. "You're part of my great adventure. Come home with me now and I'll see you never need work another day in your life."

"I want to work," said Grace. "It's all I know. I can't just sit on my arse and watch the grass grow."

Harris grinned.

"I'm needed here in a way I ain't needed in that house. You got Jessie doing all the chores. Nora's off at school. And James, all those empty rooms you built, they'll never be filled with children."

Something passed over Harris's eyes. And in that second, Grace saw he too carried his own deep guilt and regret. He took her hand.

"Grace…" He swallowed hard, then met her eyes hopefully. "So perhaps you'll come back to the house with me tonight. And when you're due to work with these children, I'll have Samuel bring you back in the carriage. What do you say?"

CHAPTER THIRTY-THREE

He'd seen the marines coming.

So the gallows would find him at last. With blurred vision, he watched Grace disappear down the path towards the docks. *A fitting end*, he thought. She that had brought him back to life would also bring about his death.

He crawled across the deck on his knees. Tried to stand, but the brandy she had poured down his throat tangled his thoughts and weakened his legs. The ship felt unfamiliar. Distorted.

Here came the marines, their footsteps like drums. Dalton's heart raced. He readied himself. The soldiers charged onto the ship on the other side of the island.

Dalton looked about him. And he understood.

This was no migrant ship. A face peered down at him; the brown, sea-hardened face of the whaling captain.

Grace had seen the marines coming too, he realised. Backed him up the whaler's gangway and given him the chance to disappear.

Dalton heard the marines shouting to the crew of the *Enchantress*. He dug into his pocket and pulled out Howell's pouch, still half full with coins. He tossed it at the whaling captain's feet.

"Hide me."

The whaler picked up the pouch and peered inside. He pulled Dalton to his feet and shoved him into the forecastle.

When the captain opened the hatch, they were at sea. Dalton stepped out into the grey light. Hobart Town was disappearing. Fading into the shadow of the mountains and being pulled slowly over the horizon.

New Zealand, the whalers had told him. *Tahiti*. Strange names, foreign places.

The sky opened. Down fell great marbles of rain that made the deck slick and black. Thunder rolled and jagged light ripped through the clouds.

Dalton gripped the gunwale and turned his face to the sky. He closed his eyes. Imagined the feel of her hands on his cheeks, the blade of his whittling knife sliding through his beard. With each roll of the ship, the distance between them grew. He felt an ache deep inside him.

But then he opened his eyes. Van Diemen's Land had vanished behind a sea of cloud. Dalton felt a great weight dissolve from his chest. A heaviness that had been there so long he had ceased to be aware of it. He felt his breathing deepen. Felt the memories of seven dead men begin to lose their sharpness.

The haunted forest had released him.

Around him were men who knew nothing of his past. Ahead of him, an endless ocean on which Alexander Dalton and his crimes might finally be forgotten. A great wave of gratitude swept over him.

So, my Grace, he thought, *you couldn't save your Violet, but you have saved a man who had been beyond redemption.*

Remember this. And find something close to absolution.

HISTORICAL NOTE

When Alexander Pearce was captured in 1823 and confessed to the murder and cannibalism of his fellow escapees, there were few in the colony who believed him. Pearce's confession was seen as an attempt to cover for his mates, who most believed were living as bushrangers. Pearce was sent back to Macquarie Harbour where he escaped again, this time with young convict Thomas Cox. When they reached the Gordon River, Pearce discovered Cox was unable to swim, and killed him with a swing of the axe. Pearce then gave himself up at the King River (near present-day Strahan) and was discovered to be carrying human flesh in his pocket. Pearce was taken back to Hobart Town for execution and his tales of cannibalism began to be taken seriously.

There are several inconsistencies in the confessions of Pearce, mostly concerning Alexander Dalton. In his confession at Macquarie Harbour in 1824, Pearce claimed there had been four murder victims: Thomas Bodenham, John Mather, Matthew Travers, and finally, Robert Greenhill, whom Pearce had killed single-handedly to avoid his own murder. According to Pearce, the remaining three escapees – William Kennerly, Ned Brown and Dalton – fled the group in fear for their lives with an intent to return to Macquarie Harbour.

Kennerly and Brown returned alone to the harbour and were either unable or unwilling to shed any light on why Dalton was no longer with them. They died of starvation soon after arriving.

But in Pearce's confession to the Rev. Thomas Knopwood in Hobart Town, the details of the story had changed. It was Dalton, Pearce claimed, not Bodenham, who had been Greenhill's first victim, chosen as the sacrifice as he had been given the role of a flogger at Sarah Island.

What could have accounted for such glaring discrepancies in Pearce's confessions? Had the details been blurred by time and immense mental and physical stress? Or did Pearce feel the need to confess his involvement in a fifth murder before his impending execution? Either way, it seems impossible we will ever know the true fate of Alexander Dalton.

What we do know is that Dalton, a twenty-three-year-old soldier from Kilkenny, Ireland, was transported to Van Diemen's Land (Tasmania) in 1820, after being sentenced at Gibraltar Court Martial. In this era, no records were kept of convicts' initial crimes – to avoid judgement in the colonies from overseers and fellow prisoners – but as Dalton received a sentence of fourteen years' transportation, we can surmise he committed a crime such as robbery, forgery or assault. Such crimes were often punishable by death, with many convicts – possibly including Dalton – having their sentence transmuted from hanging to transportation.

On his arrival in Van Diemen's Land, Dalton committed a series of misdemeanours, including perjuring against his fellow convict Michael Flannagan in 1822. It was for this crime that Dalton was sent to Sarah Island Penitentiary at Macquarie Harbour, which would forever be known as one of the most brutal of Australia's penal settlements.

Grace, Harris, and all other characters are purely fictitious.

PLAYING

THE

GHOST

CHAPTER ONE

Australia, 1857

An accident, they say. Some poor fool trying to blast his way to glory by digging with black powder instead of a shovel. But we can all hear the whispers beneath. Those whispers that poor old Fred Buckley did this to himself. Tossed the explosives into his mining claim and leapt in there after them. Another failed attempt at fortune on the goldfields.

And now here we all are in the graveyard, gathered around the small wooden box containing all that's left of the man. I haven't seen inside myself, of course, but word is it contains a few brass buttons and a boot that was miraculously blown clear of the explosion.

I only met Buckley once or twice, but my husband Tom knew him well, their claims not far from each other's on the western edge of the Forest Creek gold diggings. The morning of Buckley's death, Tom said, he was heading out to start work when the explosion ripped through the air and made the ground move like sea.

The vicar murmurs a prayer, and down that sorry little box goes into the ground. Buckley had no wife or children, so there are no tears at his grave, just curiosity, and a fairly ceaseless torrent of murmuring.

We traipse back down the hill after the burial, clouds of dust blooming beneath our boots.

"Well," says Leo Evans, "if you're going to do away with yourself, that's a damn spectacular way to do it."

"Aye," Ollie Cooper agrees. "Something with a bit of drama to it."

"Let's go to Martha's," says a leather-faced digger who's just introduced himself to us as Clyde. "Was poor old Fred's favourite place for a drink."

Martha's is a canvas-walled grog shop on the edge of the diggings, a remnant of the days when this place was nothing but a few holes in the ground, and outlawed drink was sold in the shadows. These days, the town's made of more solid stuff than canvas, but Martha's hasn't lost its pull over the locals.

"Lucy?" Tom asks me. "Do you want to go home?"

"No." I can't bear the thought of another stilted night in our cottage, where Tom and I make strained small talk before falling asleep with our backs to each other. "You knew Mr Buckley well. We ought to drink to him."

We pile into the carts and traps waiting outside the cemetery and rattle back towards Forest Creek. The sun is lying low over the hills, bathing the scarred landscape in shadow. Trees have been cut away in the scramble for gold, and the earth is a bleak forest of windlasses and tents. The evening shriek of birdsong is beginning in the sparse bushland that remains beyond the diggings. A silhouette of parrots swoops past the wagon.

Tom offers me a hand to help me out of the cart. I haven't been to the tent village on the edge of the diggings since we moved into town a few months ago. But one glance at the place, one inhalation of that earth-and-ash scent brings back memory after memory: cooking bread in coals out the front of our tent, walls flapping like sails in the night. The constant rattle of mining cradles, of shovels, of footsteps, of men. Knuckles and fingernails thick with dirt. And the flies, the flies, the flies.

When Tom hands me a tin cup filled with Martha's most vicious moonshine, I gulp it down quickly. I don't want these memories lingering.

The grog shop tent is crowded and noisy, pipe smoke rising into the pitched roof and making the hot air near unbreathable. Men spill into the street, a few patched-skirted women among them. Most of the diggers who didn't attend the burial have finished work for the evening, and the crowd is growing. Conversation turns to who found takings today, before circling back to Fred Buckley.

"It was no suicide," announces Arthur Wallace, who always knows everything about everything. "I heard he just sold five pounds' worth." He brings a fat cigar to his lips. "Why would the man have done away with himself if he'd just found a haul?"

"A haul isn't everything," I say to my cup. I feel Tom's eyes on me, but he doesn't speak.

"Maybe he didn't do away with himself then," says Leo, ignoring my comment. "Maybe someone done it for him."

A fresh murmur ripples through the crowd, more drink-laden thrill than horror at the thought of there being a murderer among us.

"If someone did take him out, you could hardly blame them." Martha, the landlady, speaks up from behind the barrels and wood planks that serve as the bar. "He were fond of swinging his fists, that Fred Buckley. Maybe he had a go at someone who didn't half appreciate it."

"Let's ask him," Clyde booms suddenly, waving his hand with the drink in it and spilling ale over his round belly. "You know, like them girls in America done, with the knocking on the walls. Talked to the dead and all, they did. Asked them all sorts of questions. Knock once for no, knock twice for yes, and all that."

I rush another gulp of liquor. I suppose it was only a matter of time until we got here. Because ask any man on the street and they'll tell you the dead are all around us. There's something about this land, they say, as they toss back ales and speak in whispers. If you listen real hard and the wind blows the right way, you can hear the ghosts of the blackfellas drumming away, keeping watch over the mountains and creeks and the rusty open plains. These are the spirits, they say, that were here long before our ships arrived; those that carved the hills and rivers, and make this land seem to ripple in the dark. And then there are the ghosts we brought out on the ships with us: the banshees and the will-o'-the wisps, and that headless horseman that turned out to be a dressmaker's mannequin someone pinched from the dust yard. The infamous Green Lady who walks Barker Street, despite there being no castle within ten thousand miles. Holding on to these stories makes home feel not quite so far away.

I don't believe in spooks. Never have. Before me and Tom came out from England, I spent five years scrubbing dishes at Hartwell Manor in Horley, a place so full of creaks and groans and ghost stories it was a wonder anyone ever got a wink of sleep. But while the other girls loved working themselves into a frenzy at every screech of the floorboards, I found the draughts and the shadows and the tricks of the light. I couldn't see the fun in having the dead living alongside you.

"What's he going to knock with?" demands Leo. "His hands got blown off."

"A ghost don't need hands," Clyde says matter-of-factly. "They knock with their soul."

I snort into my cup, earning a sideways glance from Tom.

"So what do we do then?" Leo scratches his matted beard. "Go back to his grave and just ask him some questions?"

"No point going to his grave," says Clyde. "He ain't there, is he. Just a few buttons and a shoe. Best off going to his claim. Where he died."

He heads for the door, causing a string of other men to follow.

"Let's go home," says Tom, tossing back the last of his liquor.

"No, I want to watch." There's something oddly enthralling about all this. While I didn't go in for ghost stories at Hartwell Manor, it feels strangely appealing to go along with them now. As though it might take me away from the bleakness of what my day-to-day life has become. Juxtaposed against all that deadness, maybe I'll remember what it is to feel alive.

I can practically see the indecision move across Tom's face. Stupidity, yes, but lately he agrees to anything that falls into the category of *making Lucy happy*. With an enormous sigh so there can be no doubt he's doing this under duress, he nods. Takes a firm grip on my arm and joins the procession across the diggings.

"Do you think there's really a chance Buckley was murdered?" I ask as we weave through the claims. Holes yawn in the earth, signposted by tents at their edges. Smoke curls up from the campfires and disappears into the stars.

I try to keep my voice light. If Tom knew the men's talk has worked its way beneath my skin, he'd be whisking me back home before you could say *knock twice for yes*.

"It was an accident, Luce," he says. "That's all. Black powder's bloody unpredictable. Why do you think the most of us stay away from the stuff?"

But it is not a huge stretch to imagine we might be living beside a murderer. After all, the fact that we're among thieves cannot be denied.

In a place where greed and desperation are this rife, petty thieving is a part of life. Gold nuggets and coins stolen from tents while men sleep. Pockets picked. Goods taken from shop shelves by men with light fingers. Barely a day goes by without a robbery being reported. The troopers have made a few half-hearted arrests – Chinamen and Irish usually – but none of them ever stick.

"Well," says Tom, when I remind him of this, "petty thieving is one thing. Murder is something else. And I promise you there's nothing to worry about."

"I'm not worried," I say. But I'm not sure if that's true. My emotions feel clouded these days, as though I can't quite catch hold of them long enough to read them.

We reach Fred Buckley's claim. Or rather, what's left of it. One by one, we climb over the rope set up by the police to mark the site of the incident. The side of the pit has been blown out in the blast, mounds of earth now filling the shaft. Blackened pieces of the windlass lie not far from the hole. It's only a matter of time before some brassy sods are down there prospecting. If they haven't been already.

We cluster around the ragged edge of the claim, Leo and Clyde shoving their way to the front. I realise I'm the only woman who's bothered making the trek out here.

"Fred!" Clyde bellows. "Can you hear me? Who done this to you? Did you do away with yourself? Knock once for no, twice for yes."

"On the windlass, Fred," Leo adds. "Knock on the windlass."

Everyone falls silent. Waiting. Even I can't pull my eyes from the broken windlass lying by Clyde's feet.

Nothing.

"Were you murdered, Fred?" calls Leo, his face furrowed with such seriousness I'd laugh if I wasn't standing where some poor bastard was just blasted to pieces.

Still no knocking. In the forest behind us, an owl shrieks.

"Fred? You there, man?"

"This is madness." Tom's hand wrenches around my arm, and we're marching away suddenly from Buckley's claim.

"Tom. You're hurting me."

"Sorry." He lets his hand fall. "Watch yourself. The—"

"The claims are hard to see in the dark. Yes, I know."

We walk back towards our cottage in near silence, the newly erected streetlamps throwing yellow light onto the road. Trees tower on either side of us, their white trunks ghostly in the semi-darkness.

"Madness," Tom says again. And then, "Poor Fred. How could those bastards be so disrespectful?"

I give a short smile. "I think Fred's past caring if he's disrespected."

"You think?"

I don't answer. We fall back into our usual silence until we reach the cottage. It sits lightless on the corner of a new row of houses, close to where the town of Castlemaine gives way to the bush. Tom slides the key into the lock.

And then, *crack, crack, crack* – the emptying of the guns, in perfect synchronicity with the turning of the key. Every night this comes; this sudden violent outburst from the diggings that hem the town. And every night it manages to scare me. Nothing to be afraid of, Tom has assured me. Guns emptied in the night to prevent the ammunition becoming damp. There are those who say the emptying of the guns is not a measure of maintenance but a warning to would-be thieves. Stay away from my tent. Hear what I've got in store for you if you try and cross me.

To me, hundreds of weapons roaring together each night is a reminder of how fragile this life is. How easily it could be any one of us lying in the earth, with Clyde trying to get us to knock on the damn windlass. A reminder of how many ways there are to die here.

The last echoes of gunfire are swallowed by the night, the burn of powder faint on the air. And just as I do every evening when the pistols are emptied into this eternal sky, I imagine myself screaming.

CHAPTER TWO

"To those of my own sex who desire to emigrate to Australia, I say do by all means, if you can go under suitable protection, possess good health, are not fastidious or 'fine-ladylike,' can milk cows, churn butter, cook a good damper, and mix a pudding. ... But to those who cannot wait upon themselves, and whose fair fingers are unused to the exertion of doing anything useful, my advice is, for your own sakes remain at home."

Ellen Clacy
A Lady's Visit to the Gold Diggings of Australia
1852

I'm up at dawn, boiling pots of tea and porridge before Tom heads out to the diggings. The kitchen is sweltering with firelight and steam, and carries the faint stale smell of the laundry I've to do today. Our little stone cottage is neatly divided in two; one half the bedroom, the other, the living quarters. The kitchen is crammed with a fireplace and dining table; shelves lined with cups and plates, and pots hanging along the walls.

I take the pot of porridge from the hook above the fire and fill two bowls, kicking muddy boots out from under my feet.

Tom comes in from the bedroom, his shirt half untucked and his vest hanging open. His fair hair is in dire need of a brush. The lines in his forehead always look more pronounced in the mornings.

He lifts the teapot from the middle of the table and fills a cup, sleepy-eyed. "I think I dreamt about Fred Buckley."

I give him a short smile. After the long trudge home from Forest Creek, I fell into far too deep a sleep to dream.

With the cooking done, I toss a bowl of water into the fireplace to put out the flames. Open the window to let the steam curl out of it. Hot summer air blows in in its place.

Tom takes a gulp of tea. "I got a good feeling today, Luce. This might be the one." His smile looks as forced as his enthusiasm. I don't answer. I've run out of appropriate responses.

When Tom bought his mining license three years ago and was given his first claim, it seemed like such a glamorous thing. Here he was in charge of this little piece of the colony of Victoria – never mind that it was just a few feet across. We went to stand on it together, smiling at each other as our boots sank into the mud. I imagined all the gold hidden beneath our feet, ready to be brought up into the light. That little piece of earth, we were both so certain, would see us live a life of luxury until the day we died.

And down into the earth Tom went, sure it would only be a matter of time before he brought up things that glittered. And yes, he brought gold back to that lopsided tent we called home; tiny fragments wrapped in handkerchiefs, tucked into his pockets. In those early days, when they first divided up the land, the earth practically shone. They said if you walked Moonlight Flat with grease on your boots, the gold would stick to the soles.

The first time Tom came home with that tiny suggestion of treasure, we sat at the table and stared at the flecks shimmering in his handkerchief. It felt like a beginning; the start of a golden future in which we would rise above our station and be something we could never have dreamt of being in England. We'd have wealth and luxury, and a life of sipping tea on some grand balcony; me and Tom and the child inside me, conceived in that tiny ship's cabin, with nothing around us but sea.

But there was never more than specks and scraps. And while the men in the surrounding claims pulled nuggets the size of walnuts from the mud of Forest Creek, my husband's land never gave up more than gold dust. He worked from first light until sunset or even later, digging and cradling by lamplight. But finding gold, we both came to realise, was as much about luck as it was about skill and dedication.

Now, almost three years after our arrival in Australia, Tom is working a claim with Leo, a Cornishman he met at Murphy's Hotel. This time, he says, things will be different. No more scraps. Just nuggets the size of walnuts.

With Leo's tin mining expertise, they shored the walls of the claim and burrowed far deeper into the earth than Tom went the first time. Constructed a windlass from a felled tree to bring loads up from the shaft.

But I've stopped waiting for Tom to bring home that nugget. Have come to the conclusion that this is not how our lives are supposed to go. When will he come to the same realisation? Perhaps he already has.

Tom is out the door with the rising sun. I take the breakfast dishes to the trough to wash them, then check on the laundry fluttering on the line at the back of the cottage. It's dried slightly stiff in the hot wind. I pull each shirt, each sheet, each nightshirt from the line and place them in neatly marked bundles, ready to be collected by their owners.

Far too many men on the diggings, I learnt early on, have no thought of how to use a washboard. And in the absence of their wives, their mothers, their housekeepers, a woman can make a good penny washing clothes.

One, two, three bundles of clothing collected and paid for as the day wears on. I pull out the small wooden box hidden beneath our bed. It's empty apart from a few tiny gold pieces, barely enough to make a single sovereign. I toss in the coins, ready for banking later in the week, then tuck the box back under the mattress. I grab my bonnet and head to the Sunday School building for my theatre rehearsal.

The theatre troupe, well that was Tom's idea. A means of distraction. A way to make new friends and move past my grief. I wasn't sure my grief was something I was supposed to move past. But when the young and dashing Will Browning strutted into Castlemaine in his top hat and announced the opening of his new amateur theatre troupe, Tom was adamant I attend.

"You love the theatre," he insisted, though my only experience of such a thing was a church Christmas play when I was nine. Dressed in my most beatific white nightgown, I'd dithered behind the other angels and said my one line – *"Fear not, for we bring you tidings of great joy"* – in such an inaudible voice that one of the other girls had to repeat it.

Nevertheless, I trudged along to the first meeting of Mr Browning's little troupe, determined to despise it.

Somewhat infuriatingly, I did not despise it. For two hours, I sat through a bungled reading of *Macbeth* and prompted the actors with their lines, and had more fun than I'd had in what felt like forever. I came home and offered Tom a begrudging smile. Couldn't help but admit there *was* something I rather loved about the theatre, even though the thought of actually stepping onto stage terrified me.

The ridiculousness of that is not lost on me.

The group had its first performance last month – a half-baked pantomime, performed in the middle of Barker Street and attended mostly by people who wandered out of the tavern and accidentally found themselves in the audience. I stood in the front row and hissed out forgotten lines to those few actors who weren't performing open-book. Did a stellar job of packing the costumes away afterwards.

Beside the hastily constructed Sunday School building, the half-built church emerges from the earth like rock stacks rising from the ocean. Rough wooden scaffolding hides much of the construction, but I see the beginnings of a spire straining towards the sky.

I let myself into the Sunday School, a box of a building with desks crammed in rows and the perpetual smell of chalk and children. Most of the group is already here. They've pulled chairs up around the larger table at the front of the room and are chattering loudly. I weave through the rows of desks and shuffle a chair onto the corner of the table. Edith Markham, with her steel-grey hair and matching face, sets a glass of lukewarm lemonade in front of me.

There are five or six of us who usually turn up to rehearsals, the number swelling or dwindling depending on what play we're reading, and if it's raining too hard to go to the diggings. Edith and I are staunch regulars, and so is the painfully dazzling Clara Snow, the only one of the group with any theatre experience whatsoever.

Well, unless you count my one line in the Christmas play. Which I don't.

Today, Ollie Cooper is here, as is the prime know-it-all, Arthur Wallace. Ollie is a good friend of Tom's, and I know he only comes here for a laugh, while Mr Wallace seems to harbour secret dreams of being the next William Don. Wallace is a wealthy Londoner who pushes papers in the Gold Commissioner's camp; Ollie among the mass of Irishmen come out to escape the Great Hunger.

"Hear about them fossickers last night?" he asks no one in particular. "Out on Moonlight Flat. Some lads come out of their tents and seen lamplight in their claims. Thieves were out of there before they could catch them."

Hardly surprising, given half the settlement was knee deep in moonshine last night, trying to hear Fred Buckley's ghost bashing away on the windlass. There were likely more than a few unguarded claims around the diggings.

"It's those damn Chinese," Mr Wallace snorts, crossing one leg over the other. "Can't be trusted."

"A little predictable, don't you think?" Clara Snow swans into the room, letting the door thump closed behind her. "Anything goes wrong in this place and it's poor old Johnny Chinaman to blame." She takes a chair from behind one of the desks and carries it to the table, lemon perfume wafting in her wake. I shuffle over to make room for her.

Wallace's cheeks turn red in annoyance. "And with good reason. Thieving's been twice as bad since they turned up."

Clara takes off her bonnet and settles into her chair. She pours herself a glass from the jug of lemonade on the table. "Why would they go to the trouble of stealing from the white man? They find more in a day than the most of you find in a week. They must be far more methodical than you lot who just going around swinging your shovels."

Wallace gives her a thin smile. "I must say, Miss Snow, you have quite an opinion on the matter for a woman of your inclination."

Clara's eyes flash, but whatever fierce words she's about to fling out are cut off as Will Browning charges through the door, apologising for his lateness. In his neat frock coat and silver cravat, he somehow manages to look impossibly dashing, despite being so pink and flustered I suspect he may have run here. He slides his armful of bound booklets onto the table ceremoniously. I feel myself straighten in my chair.

Today, well, what an important day it is in the life of the Castlemaine Amateur Theatre Group. The unveiling of Will Browning's new play. An original work written just for us. The ridiculousness of that is not lost on me either.

According to Clara, Mr Browning was a semi-professional dramatist in London, bursting onto the theatre scene at the age of just eighteen, with a play that was wildly successful. Almost a decade has passed since, and judging by the calibre of actor he is now writing for, I can only assume his career has taken something of a wrong turn. Nonetheless, there's a thrill to having been written a piece by a man who once walked the London stage.

As I discover when Mr Browning passes the booklets around the table for us to read, it's not just the men at Fred Buckley's claim who have their heads firmly lodged in the land of the dead.

"*The Lady of Fyvie,*" Clara reads.

"Ah, the Green Lady of Fyvie Castle, I presume." Mr Wallace chuckles as he turns the pages, his animosity at Clara momentarily forgotten. "My dear old granny used to tell me ghost stories about her when I was a lad. Used to scare me half to death."

Clara flicks Mr Browning a smile. "You've certainly managed to find a topic that's all the rage."

I've heard this story too; this folktale he's based his new play on. The woman murdered by her husband in a Scottish castle, who somewhat predictably proceeded to haunt the place for all eternity.

"Been listening in on a few conversations at the tavern, have you, Will?" Ollie chuckles. "There's been talk of sightings of the Green Lady for months now."

Mr Browning sits in the chair left empty for him at the head of the table. He takes off his top hat and sets it beside him. "Indeed." His brown eyes shine boyishly. "I believe one sighting even made it into the papers."

Edith clucks as she turns the pages. "What's this world coming to?"

I open my copy of the script, a small smile on my lips. I think of stealing my older brother's Penny Bloods and hiding in the wardrobe to read them.

We've brought our myths and legends with us to this place; stories to remind us of home, to keep us linked to what we know. The Green Lady walking the streets of Castlemaine is a fragile thread tying us back to our homeland.

I skim through the first few pages. The play has all the mystery and horror of a Penny Blood; Lord Fyvie and his new bride haunted to near madness by the ghostly Green Lady, the vengeful spirit of the Lord's first wife.

The role of Lady Fyvie will obviously go to Clara, the only one of us with anything even resembling the ability to act. The story goes that she was sent over as a convict; spent a few years sewing shirts at the female factory in Hobart before dazzling her overseer into submission and winning her ticket of leave. I have no idea if that's true and am far too terrified of the woman to ask her. The story also goes that in England, Clara was a burlesque performer, thrilling audiences around London with ballad operas and breeches roles. Though I'm simultaneously fascinated and repulsed by the idea, I'm far too scared to ask about that too. I can't imagine what a woman like her is doing in Castlemaine.

The role of Lady Fyvie in Will Browning's new play is hardly Drury Lane, but when he invites Clara to take the lead, she gives him a suitably coy smile and says, "I'd be honoured."

He turns to me. "Mrs Earnshaw, I thought perhaps you might like to read the role of the Green Lady."

My stomach loops. I don't *read* anything. That's not why I'm here. The horror is unthinkable.

"Oh no," I say quickly. "I couldn't. I—"

Mr Browning falters. "You do have your letters, don't you? I'm sorry, I thought—"

"Yes," I say, then wish I hadn't. I've just blown the perfect way out. "But I..."

"Just a reading," he assures me. "You'd be helping me get a sense of the character. Determine whether her lines need work."

I chew my lip. It's mortifying. I'm not here to perform. I'm the line-prompter. The floor-sweeper. The tea-refiller. But I can see the stupidity of joining a theatre troupe and refusing to even read out a few lines. And so, I nod. Besides, the Green Lady is dead. How many lines can she possibly have?

Mr Browning flashes me a bright smile. "Wonderful." He assigns the rest of the parts before opening his manuscript to the first page.

Clara hurls herself into the read as though she were back in the theatre in London, while I tiptoe through my lines in a miniscule voice.

"A little louder, please, Mrs Earnshaw," says Browning, "if you wouldn't mind."

"Well done, Lucy," Edith Markham says dutifully as we make our way out of the Sunday School two hours later. A pleasantly cool breeze rustles the trees, cicadas wailing somewhere in the half-built church. "Shall I see you home?" she asks, tucking a worn carpet bag into the crook of her arm.

The two of us have the kind of friendship that comes from there being few better options. Edith and her husband came out from Manchester, long before Hargraves found those first flecks of gold and the place went madder than a sack of badgers. They'd been full of the same dreams of a new life Tom and I once shared – a life of adventure and success and enough money to bathe in. Twenty years later, Edith is a widow to smallpox, and her sense of adventure seems to have been thoroughly trampled out of her. Nonetheless, when the world flocked to Victoria to dig treasures from the earth, she carted a few of her children down here and opened a general store in her eldest son's name. Now she's a necessity for all the new arrivals; her shelves lined with shovels and gold pans, billies and bed rolls, ropes and coats and pistols and shot.

Edith is stiff and achingly sensible, a trait she claims has allowed her to get so far in such a challenging place. And yes, a trait I have to admire. But it is not a trait that allows for a close friendship.

"I can see myself home," I tell her. "I've to stop at the market on the way."

We make neat goodbyes and I turn in the direction of the grocer. The sound of footsteps stops me. Will Browning is striding from the school, a copy of the script held against his chest and his frock coat open casually. How different he is to so many of the other men here; wool and silk in place of stained corduroy; clean shaven, with not a grimy, earth-caked fingernail in sight. So polished he almost looks out of place. I can count on one hand the number of times we've spoken directly to each other. Usually it ends with me garbling out a flustered response, and then agonising over it for hours afterwards.

He jogs to catch up to me, making my heart quicken inexplicably.

"Thank you for coming, Mrs Earnshaw. And thank you for your reading."

I nod mutely.

"What did you think of the play?" he asks, with something oddly resembling shyness.

"I enjoyed it," I say, finding my voice. "Very much." The play is well written – at least it seems that way to my untrained eye – and the story is thrilling. I enjoyed reading the Green Lady's part far more than I expected I would.

Mr Browning's face lights. I'm surprised by it. I imagined him far too self-assured to be bothered by the opinion of some dough-faced washerwoman.

"You created a haunting atmosphere," I tell him solemnly.

A haunting atmosphere? I curse myself. Just when did I become so afternoonified?

"I'm glad to hear that. It was something I was striving for."

I carry on. And on. "Well, you certainly managed it. Like that part when we learn how the Green Lady died. And when the Lord and Lady see her for the first time, well I thought I was going to jump right out of my skin. I really did, even though I was reading the part myself and I…"

Stop talking, Lucy.

My cheeks get hot.

He gives me a kind smile. "Good. I hope it will have the same effect on the audience."

I pause, mercifully, for a breath. "The people here will love it, I'm sure."

"Do you think so?"

"Oh yes. Last night they were out at the claim of Fred Buckley, who blew himself up. Trying to speak to his ghost, if you can believe it."

Mr Browning digs his free hand into the pocket of his coat. "Yes, I heard about that poor fellow. Bloody awful, wasn't it."

I nod.

"Did they do it?" he asks suddenly.

I blink. "Pardon?"

"Those men who went to Buckley's claim. Did they speak to his ghost?"

"Oh." I give a short laugh. "No, of course not."

"I see." He holds my gaze for a moment with his rich coffee eyes. "Thank you for your kind words, Mrs Earnshaw. It means a lot. And thank you again for the reading."

And I wander dazedly off to the market in entirely the wrong direction.

CHAPTER THREE

"The Chinese here, who have lately arrived in crowds still continue their national costume in a great measure, and their national custom of carrying everything on their necks on a long pole. ... At the end of [the] pole they suspend weights, astonishing considering their slight physical structure. ... They go for scores of miles with ponderous burdens ... their very legs seeming to stagger and their bodies to waver under their loads."

William Howitt
Ballarat
16th May 1854

"Have you heard about these latest thefts?" I ask Tom at supper that night.

He takes an enormous bite of bread and dusts the crumbs from his beard. "There was some night fossicking out on Moonlight Flat. Gold dug directly from the claims." He is still wearing the shirt he was digging in today. I can smell him from across the table.

"You and Leo had any trouble?"

"No. Do you not think I would tell you if I had?"

I hold back a snort. Tom rarely tells me anything that happens on the diggings. Most gossip I hear from Edith, or the men in the theatre group. "I know you don't like to worry me."

He tears off another piece of bread and dunks it in his mutton stew.

"Well. We've had no trouble, in any case."

I've decided I'm not worried. Merely asked out of curiosity. The thefts feel like a distant thing. A thing that's always in the background; something that has little bearing on my life. So many things feel like that these days. Like I'm standing on the outside looking in. Observing life from the wrong side of the curtain.

We eat in silence for several minutes, our wooden spoons tapping against the sides of the bowls. The lamp hisses steadily.

"How was the theatre?" Tom asks eventually.

"Mr Browning has finished his new play," I say. "I read one of the parts."

Tom's face lights. "That's wonderful."

"Just a reading. I'm not actually going to perform it."

"Why not?"

"The stage, Tom?" I say. "Women like me don't go on stage."

"Women like you? What do you mean, women like you?"

I look down, embarrassed. Women who hate being looked at. Women who hate opening their mouths in case something stupid falls out, like *you created a haunting atmosphere*. I know Tom doesn't need me to explain. I'm irritated by his question.

"I think you should consider it," he says around another mouthful. "I really do. It would be good for you."

His words grate inside me. So often, he tells me what I ought to do, what would be good for me. I've come to resent it. It feels as though Tom knows the way through this grief and I don't. It doesn't feel fair that he has navigated a way out, while I'm still foundering.

"Well," I say, sharper than I intended, "I've not been offered the role in any case. So it's neither here nor there, is it."

A knock at the door interrupts. I look at Tom. "Are you expecting someone?"

"It's Leo and Ollie, here for a drink. Remember?"

"No. I don't remember."

Tom shovels down the last of his stew. "I told you yesterday they were coming."

"You didn't," I say stiffly.

He gets to his feet, tossing the dirty bowl into the trough. "Well.

They're here now. You've a cottage now, Luce. You ought to expect a few guests."

We're among the few people I know who live within solid walls. This is not a place of solidity. People come and people go; diggers usually, but sometimes the shopkeepers or even the troopers, going wherever the trail of new gold leads them. I heard that when those first nuggets were found in the valleys, all but three police officers abandoned Melbourne for the diggings.

But my husband promised me some kind of permanence here; at least more stability than those mud-caked miners who move on to the newest diggings the moment the reports come in. It was part of his spiel when he first presented the idea of Australia to me. Back then, I didn't need much convincing. I would have gone working on the railroads if Tom had suggested it.

We met on the grounds of Hartwell Manor, that sprawling estate in Horley, a three-hour ride from London. Tom was one of an endless battalion of farmhands, and there was me in the kitchen. Every day at noon I'd trot out to the fields with lunch for the workers, hoping for a smile from the burly blond-haired farmer whose cheeks were always pink with sun. For months we exchanged nervous pleasantries, thought up, at least on my part, hours in advance.

Tom, at thirty-five, was almost fifteen years my senior, and the other girls in the kitchen tried to nudge me in other directions. *Billy Harper ain't married yet, you know;* or, *That new coachman is real handsome.* There had to be something wrong with Tom Earnshaw, they argued, for him to have got to such an age without finding himself a wife.

"Too soft spoken if you ask me," said the scullery maid.

And from the other kitchen hand: "I heard he's got no money."

But to me, Tom was perfect. He was hardworking, never got mad with drink, and knew the names of all the horses. Each afternoon, when I'd hand him his sandwiches, he'd give me a smile that made me feel like the only soul on the planet.

We spent most of the estate's May Day celebration in each other's company, hiding under trees to shelter from the drizzle, and passing a bottle of mead between us. Our small talk about the manor evolved into discussions about our lives, our hopes, our fears, and our dreams – of which, I realised, I had few. Tom spoke of a longing to see the world, to earn his fortune and be his own man. But my life felt too narrow and fenced in to dream.

And then, because my cheeks were hot with alcohol and the mead was swirling around in my brain, I asked, "Why've you not married yet, Tom Earnshaw?"

Beneath his sandy beard, his lips parted in surprise, but his smile was warm. "Well," he said, "what point is there in marrying until you've found the right person?" And that look that said a thousand words warmed me at my core. That was how it always was with Tom; so many things went unspoken.

Our courtship gathered speed, as though we were making up for all the time we'd wasted nattering about the weather over bread rolls and cheese. Barely a month after May Day, Tom sat me down in the manor garden and spoke of his plans. A meagre inheritance left by his father. Enough for passage on the seas to the colony named for our queen. A small house on our arrival.

"Gold's just been discovered there," he told me. "They say it's right there for the taking. If we get in quick, we'll make a bloody fortune."

And well, I knew nothing of gold mining, or the colony of Victoria, at the bottom of that vast land we'd stuffed with our prisoners. But I knew I loved Tom Earnshaw. I would follow him wherever he led me.

We gave our notice at the manor that afternoon. Two weeks later, there was a wedding ring on my finger, and we were tucked onto a migrant ship, with England dissolving into a wall of cloud. Unsteadying as it felt to be leaving all I knew, there was no sense of sadness. My life in England had been punctuated by loss; my parents within weeks of each other some four years earlier, and my brother the previous Easter. For years, my life had revolved around washing dishes for Lord and Lady Hartwell. Now the manor was a memory and Tom was my everything.

Even on the days when we were tossed by the ocean and could do nothing but cling to the raised edges of our bunk, I felt secure with his arms around me. The days of the voyage blurred, and I remember little but the sensations. Rough hands tracing every inch of me; his coarse beard against my skin, whispering, sighing, and the groaning of the ship. Tom and I discovering each other in the half light of our cabin, tasting sea spray on each other's skin. I felt utterly consumed by him, existing only in the present moment. The land we were journeying to was completely unknown to me, so how could I even begin to imagine the life that lay ahead? All I had to go on was Tom's vision for our future.

I trusted every word of that vision until our first night on the Castlemaine diggings. Beneath a flimsy sheet of canvas, we curled up on a damp sleeping mat and listened to the miners empty their weapons into the sky. Rain pattered steadily into the puddle forming in the doorway, the mud creeping towards our bed like a living creature. What kind of barbaric place was this? Was this really where we would raise our child?

My stomach rolled and rolled; whether with dread or impending motherhood, I couldn't be certain – at that moment, they felt one and the same. This was the gravest of mistakes; I sensed it then with such weight I could hardly breathe.

"This is just for now," Tom promised, breath warm against my nose. "We'll have a real place to live soon. A cottage of our own. Build it just the way we like." He shuffled across the sleeping mat, pulling me into his arms. We were still wrapped in our coats to keep out the damp. He held his lips to mine. And in that kiss, I could sense his own fears, his own uncertainty. "We're going to be real happy here, just you wait. You, me and the little one." I heard his voice waver.

Tom put his name to a plot of land not long after they went up for sale. The tents of the diggings were slowly turning into the town of Castlemaine. It was land we could barely afford, but always one to keep his promises, he scraped together the pennies and set about giving us that life of permanence.

But before the cottage was more than a hole in the ground, camp fever swept through the diggings, taking our daughter Elsie just weeks after her first birthday.

Now we have our permanence. Our walls that don't blow in the night. A locked door to keep out the thieves. The cottage feels far more solid than the foundations my life is teetering on.

I drop my spoon into my half-eaten bowl of stew. "We can't have guests. Just look at the place." I wave at the unwashed stew pot and the flour I've managed to coat the kitchen in. "It's a right mess."

Tom chuckles. "Ollie and Leo won't even notice. You ought to see the tent Leo's living in. Wouldn't keep a pig in it."

I drop my bowl into the trough. "It's near enough to a pigsty in here. And you don't smell much better than one."

Tom peels off his shirt as he goes to the bedroom for fresh clothes. "Calm down, Luce. What does it matter if the place is tidy?"

"It matters to me." I scrub angrily at the plates, water splattering down the front of my skirts.

But Tom is out of the bedroom, tugging on a fresh shirt and throwing open the door. Leo and Ollie waltz into the cottage while I bluster around the kitchen, trying to deal with the flour. I untie my apron and turn to greet the two men.

"I'm sorry about the mess," I say.

Leo flaps a hand in response. He's made a half-hearted attempt to wash himself, gems of clean skin visible between the grime of the diggings and a storm cloud of a beard. He thrusts a bottle into Tom's hands. "Here. Gin from the homeland. A stock of it just came in at the Cumberland."

The men settle themselves at the kitchen table, while I try to surreptitiously wipe a glob of stew from beside Ollie's elbow.

I take a long breath, determined not to let my guests see my annoyance. There were two things my mother taught me about being a wife before she passed. The first was to always put on an agreeable face. The second was to clean the damn house before guests showed up. For not the first time, I wish Leo or Ollie had a wife with them. Someone I could relate to a little. But here on the diggings, the men outnumber the women five to one. We're a novelty – I know that's part of why I cling to Edith like a limpet.

Tom yanks the cork from the bottle and fills a cup for each of us. I perch on the edge of a chair, folding my hands tightly in my lap.

"Lovely to see you both," I say, in an acting display Will Browning would be proud of.

Ollie turns to Leo. "How goes things with the Tipperary boys?" He winks. "They still calling you out for the cheating bastard you are?"

The feud between the Irish and the Cornish has been going on the entire time Tom and I have been on the goldfields. Ask any Irishman and they'll tell you the Cornish use their tin mining skills to drive deep into the earth and dig beneath other men's claims. While Ollie's banter is friendly, I know Leo has had more than one bitter run-in with the Tipperary boys who work the top end of Forest Creek.

He chuckles. "Still talking out their arses. The bastards are just jealous that some of us know how to dig a real shaft."

My eyes dart between the men. I've never had any doubt about Leo's honesty. After all, if he and Tom were driving into other claims, surely they'd have more to show for it than a cradle full of mud.

"Come on now," says Tom, "let's not talk business around Lucy." He gives me a strained smile. "Tell us more about your theatre rehearsal, sweetheart. Tell us how bloody awful Ollie was."

Ollie chuckles, tossing fair hair from his eyes with feigned indignance. "You bastards'll be blown away by my talent. Won't never have seen nothing like it. Lord of Fyvie Castle, I am. Got lines and everything." He nudges me. "Go on, tell them how gifted I am."

I can't help a laugh.

"You want to hear about the mining, don't you, Mrs Earnshaw?" Leo cuts in before I can speak. "That's where all your riches is going to come from. As long as we can keep the thieves out."

"The money in this place is in feeding the masses, not sifting through the ground like badgers," says Ollie, who makes his living at his butcher's shack on the edge of Forest Creek.

"Bull," says Leo. "A good day in the claim and you'll make more than you'd earn in a lifetime hacking up sheep carcasses."

"Least until you end up blown to pieces like poor old Fred Buckley." Ollie leans forward, grey eyes shining. "So what d'you think? He do away with himself? Or someone do it for him?"

"He wasn't murdered," says Tom. "That's enough of that talk."

Leo refills his glass. "I say if we want to put an end to these thefts, we just have the coppers wait outside Johnny Chinaman's camp for a few nights. I bet they'd see a few things."

The men mumble between themselves, evidently all in agreement.

"Where else is all their gold coming from?" Leo continues, though no one is arguing otherwise. "We was mining that land at Moonlight Flat for years before they showed up. Took everything out. Now they turn up, mine the same land and find more? Tell me what's going on there."

"They say they have more luck because they work more methodically,"

I venture.

Tom's glance pulls towards me, annoyance in his eyes.

"Who says that?" Leo demands.

I don't reply. I ought to have known the wisdom of Clara Snow would not be well received in this circle. I look down, sorry to have spoken.

"I don't know why you're on their side," Ollie says to me. "You know they're making money doing people's washing. Some lad at the tavern last night said he took his laundry up to their camp cos they was only charging him sixpence." He jabs a meaty finger in my direction. "You'll be out of a job soon, just you watch."

I turn my cup around in my hands. I didn't mean to take anyone's side.

I was as rattled as anyone when the Chinese appeared a few months after our arrival. They marched into town in single file, long black hair in queues down to their waists, pointed hats upon their heads. They looked like no one and nothing I had ever seen before. All I could do was stare.

I was glad when they set up their camp on Clinkers Hill, away from the main settlement. Glad when they kept to themselves. The thought of sharing the town with people so unfamiliar was terrifying. Because what is more unsettling than the unknown? Isn't that what fear is made of?

Back in Horley, there was no one that was not entirely like ourselves. We were a uniform mass of pale skin and colourless hair; stories of the same people and the same places told in the same neat version of English. No one who wasn't born and bred in Surrey, except for the occasional traveller seeking London, who wandered into town and left as quickly as they came.

But this place, it's so different. Men pour into the diggings from places I've never even heard of, bringing with them their cultures, their languages, their greed, and desperation. Walk down the main street of Castlemaine and you hear a chaos of accents, of stories, beliefs. Selkies in the seas, and knockers in mines; trolls and dwarves that hide in the woods.

"They're digging round mines," Leo continues. "To keep the spirits out. Damn unnatural if you ask me."

I rub my eyes. This from the man who tried to coax Fred Buckley's ghost into conversation.

"Government ought to hike up that tax they're charging them," says Ollie. "That'll keep the bastards out."

I stand abruptly. "Excuse me. I'm not feeling well. I think I'll go to bed."

Tom's eyes meet mine. But he doesn't speak. Doesn't argue. Doesn't insist I stay. I can't tell if I'm annoyed or relieved.

On my way home from the market later that week, I pass the vast expanse of Castlemaine Hall. With its high, pitched roof and grand stone façade, the building always draws my attention. Its owner, Councillor Hitchcock, built it to house his auctioneering business, and now rents it out for everything from public meetings to performances by the professional troupes that tour the goldfields – using the slightly hopeful name of Castlemaine's Theatre Royal.

"Good evening, Mrs Earnshaw." I whirl around at the familiar voice. Will Browning is striding out from the back of the hall, dressed in a dark frock coat and top hat. His smile is warm. "What brings you here?"

"Oh." My cheeks flush. "Nothing, I was just… passing." I shift my basket from one arm to the other.

He nods towards the theatre. "I've just come from a meeting with Mr Hitchcock. He's agreed to us using the hall for the performance and rehearsals."

"Really? How wonderful." I'd expected we'd be prancing around in the street outside the tavern again.

Mr Browning glances over his shoulder, then looks back at me. "May I walk you home?"

A pink dusk has fallen suddenly, shadows lying long over the street. Time for the Green Lady to emerge. Or for the thieves who roam the diggings to emerge, in any case.

"I'd like that," I say. "Thank you."

"Your husband won't mind?"

I pause. In all honesty, I spoke without the thought of Tom entering my mind. "He won't," I say. "He doesn't like me walking the streets alone at night. I didn't mean to be out so late." I don't know if I'm speaking the truth. Don't know what Tom's reaction would be if he saw me alone with Will Browning. And truly, I don't wish to find out.

We begin to walk, Mr Browning with his hands dug into the pockets of his frock coat, and me with my basket hugged to my chest. Cockatoos bawl as they swoop through the dusk.

Browning nods to the street behind Murphy's Hotel. "Apparently the Green Lady was seen over there on two separate occasions."

I nod. I've heard people speak of the ghost sightings, of course. Like any good piece of gossip, one flows into the next.

"Interesting that that's just behind the tavern," I say.

Mr Browning chuckles. "You're a non-believer."

I don't answer at once. It's true, I suppose, though the label feels cold. "And you?" I ask. "Are you one of these so-called spiritualists?"

His smile is tinged with embarrassment. "I confess I may have spent a night or two in a London séance parlour."

"And? What did you see?"

"Some trickery, I'm sure. Theatrics for the sake of making a little coin. Nonetheless, I do believe it would be foolish to close our minds off entirely to the possibility of communicating with the dead."

Foolish, perhaps. But I've learnt that a person can't just squeeze their beliefs to fit their desires. I could wish with all my heart that stepping inside a séance parlour might deliver me a message from my lost daughter. But that doesn't mean I believe it will happen.

I raise my eyebrows. "You think these men really saw the Green Lady behind the tavern? And do you think this is the same Green Lady that's come all the way from Fyvie Castle?"

Mr Browning laughs. "Of course not. On both accounts. But I do think there's much we can take from these supposed sightings. They tell us much more about the living than the dead."

"People are homesick," I say. "Seeing these familiar ghosts here is a link back to where we come from."

"Yes!" His eyes light. "Indeed. And I believe ghosts represent that which is yet to be understood. The things we fear because we cannot make sense of them. So is it any wonder that in a place as unfamiliar as this, we might see such manifestations of our collective terror? After all, this land can be downright frightening at times."

I blink, feeling suddenly overwhelmed. No one has ever discussed anything so intellectual with me before. Up until Will Browning, my life was all, *wash those pans, would you, Lucy;* and *mind where that horse has dropped one…*

He's right – there is something frightening about this land; the way it stretches and stretches and seems to disappear into the sky. The way the clouds feel so impossibly high, and the dark so impenetrable it could hide the devil himself.

I choose my words carefully, afraid of upturning the intellect and revealing myself as a grand idiot. "This place is so raw and confronting. It's not an easy life. Sometimes people need to escape to another world for a time."

He looks at me with interest. "They do. Certainly."

I offer him a shy smile. "Maybe your play will help them do that."

"I hope so."

I glance sideways at him as we walk. A sudden seriousness seems to have fallen over him, giving his brown eyes an almost sombre expression. In this moment, he looks flawed and human, and I don't feel quite so overawed by him.

"Why are you here?" I blurt. I feel my face flush, grand idiot style. "I mean, what could possibly have drawn a man like you to a place like this?"

He walks for several paces with his eyes down. Watching your feet is a habit you learn quick here, or you'll topple headfirst into someone's claim.

"Well," he says finally, "I'm here for the same reason as so many others. I'm hoping to find a little success. Although in my case, it's success in the theatres, rather than on the diggings."

I nod, urging him to continue.

"I came to realise I was not going to have the career I hoped for in London."

"I heard your first play was extremely successful."

"Well, yes, it was. But with that came enormous expectations. From both myself and the public. Expectations I'm afraid I was unable to live up to. After a number of failures, I began to suspect my reputation had suffered irreparable damage. And they say this is the place to come for a new start, whether you're a prospector or not. I thought perhaps I'd start small here on the goldfields. Provide some much-needed entertainment. Gain a few reviews and something of a following before I try my luck in

Melbourne."

"I see." I'm surprised at his openness. At his willingness to share such things with someone like me.

He smiles, his solemnity evaporating. "I enjoyed your reading very much. Perhaps you might consider performing the role?"

My chest jolts. Oh no, there is not a chance. No way in hell am I getting on that stage.

"I couldn't," I say.

"Why not?"

I falter. *Why not?* My usual line of self-critical thought has tangled with Will Browning's eyes on me.

"Won't there be auditions?" I ask, clawing desperately at the prospect. "Surely there's got to be auditions?"

Mr Browning chuckles gently. "And who do you imagine might audition? Truth be told, I wrote the part for you. I rather hoped it might convince you to take the stage. I can tell just from the way you prompt the actors that you have something of a talent."

The thumping in my chest intensifies. What in hell am I to say to that? And even more horrifying, how can I possibly turn the part down now? I feel frustratingly cornered, though oddly, I'm far more flattered than angry. And in a flustered mix of delight and dread, I find myself agreeing.

He smiles; a gentle, warming thing that seems to reach deep inside me. "Excellent." We walk in silence for several paces, my heart knocking hard. "Do you know the Commercial Hotel?" Mr Browning asks suddenly.

"Of course."

Everyone knows the Commercial. It was one of the first public houses to emerge in this place that was made of brick, rather than the liquor-filled tents that surround the diggings and operate as sly grog shops. But in the two and half years since the hotel's doors opened, I've never done more than peek through the window. The Commercial is a place for gentlemen and merchants, and miners who have found that elusive fortune. It's not a place for people like me.

"I gather there on Friday evenings with friends," says Mr Browning. "Likeminded friends. I'd very much like you to meet them. I think you might enjoy their views on the world." He buries his hands in his pockets. "You ought to bring your husband, of course."

I smile wryly to myself. The only thing more out of place than me at the Commercial would be Tom at the Commercial. He's a grog shop man, a back table at Murphy's Hotel. I can't imagine him sitting among men like Will Browning and discussing the manifestations of the colony's collective terrors.

He shakes his head. "I'm sorry. It was out of place of me to ask."

"No," I say hurriedly. "It wasn't. I just... I'm not sure it's my husband's scene." I'm caught off guard by how much I don't want to talk about Tom.

"Well," says Mr Browning after a moment, "you could always come alone. If you wish."

My mouth opens and then closes again, without any words coming out. "You wouldn't be offended?" I ask, colour flooding my cheeks. I can hardly believe I'm considering something so indecent.

Mr Browning just gives a cool smile, his eyes meeting mine. "Of course not. After all, rules are made to be broken. You'd be very welcome. With your husband or without."

CHAPTER FOUR

"It appears that some individuals ... have laid a wager with a mischievous and foolhardy companion ... that he durst not take upon himself the task of visiting many of the villages near London in the three different disguises of a ghost, a bear, and a devil; and moreover, that he will not dare to enter gentlemen's gardens for the purpose of alarming the inmates of the house. The wager has, however, been accepted, and the unmanly villain has succeeded in depriving seven ladies of their senses."

The Morning Chronicle
London
9th January 1838

I step into the Commercial Hotel, my heart thundering.

I told Tom I was going to a rehearsal. He was so pleased I've agreed to perform that he didn't even question my going out alone in the evening.

Word will get back to him eventually, I suppose. Though I don't see anyone I recognise inside the hotel, I'm sure there are a few familiar faces I've missed. Familiar faces with a love for gossip who might tell my husband I've been gallivanting about the place like a wild thing.

But I'm too exhilarated to care. I need more of that kind of conversation I had with Will Browning the night he walked me home. Conversation that sparked my thoughts like they've never been before. I want to be taken to new places; places that aren't quite so bleak and suffocating as the life I've stumbled into.

The Commercial is richly decorated with dark wooden panelling, gold trim lining the bar and balustrades. Lamps are dotted along the walls, casting a warm glow over the place. The men and women sitting at the tables are dressed in bright, lavish colours, a distant cry from the mud-coloured mutedness of the prospectors I usually associate with. The place is a chaos of laughter and voices, and the constant clinking of glasses.

I'm not sure I've ever been more nervous. The day I stepped off England's shore and felt the ship quake beneath me, perhaps. But this is certainly a close second.

In the sixteen months since Elsie died, my days have felt interminably empty. Time seems to stretch out around me, vast and unfillable. I can't seem to remember how I passed my days before I became a mother.

This week though, as I've lost myself in Fyvie Castle and the Green Lady, the emptiness has not felt quite so deep. Mr Browning's belief in me has given me a scrap of belief in myself, and my initial horror at taking the part in the play has given way to something bordering on enthusiasm. I finished the laundry and housework in record time this morning and spent the rest of the day learning my lines.

Beyond the nerves, as I make my way further into the hotel, is a long-ago feeling I recognise as excitement. I am wearing my blue wool visiting dress with all three of my petticoats beneath it, and the ribbon-trimmed bonnet I usually save for church. I shuffled out of the cottage with my hands pressed to my sides, so Tom wouldn't notice the extra flounce of my skirts. Even so, when I pass two men dressed in fine embroidered waistcoats, I feel like I've crawled out from under a bridge.

A sign on the wall coaxes me towards the room for unaccompanied ladies. Through the doorway, I glimpse a sea of feathers and coloured skirts, hear a peal of high laughter. I keep walking.

Rules are made to be broken.

I glance around, sure it will only be moments before someone bundles me back out to the street. Or into the unaccompanied ladies' room at the very least. The barkeep catches my eye for a second and I feel my cheeks heat.

What am I doing here? I'm not this person.

Flustered, I turn on my heel, ready to jot this down as a mistake. And then I hear someone call my name.

Will Browning sits facing the door, several people around him at the table. He waves me over enthusiastically. I try to swallow, my mouth ridiculously dry.

"I'm so pleased you could make it." He pulls out the chair beside him and gestures for me to sit.

I realise, with no small amount of relief, that I'm not the only woman Mr Browning has invited to this… whatever this is. Not the only woman who's dared to shun the unaccompanied ladies' room. Sitting between Browning and two young men I don't recognise, is Clara Snow. She is dressed in striking mauve taffeta, with a black trim at her waist and collar. Her dark curls are piled high on her head, several loose pieces falling onto her shoulders. Shadow on her eyelids and scarlet salve on her lips. She is head-turningly bold, and almost painfully beautiful.

"Clara," I say, giving her a shy smile.

There is a flicker of recognition in her eyes. "Oh yes. You're from the theatre group…" She hesitates, then glances up at Browning for assistance.

"Lucy," I supply. "Lucy Earnshaw."

"Of course. Yes. Lucy."

Mr Browning gestures to the two young men beside him; one tall and slender, the other with round glasses and thinning hair. The three men are dressed so similarly they may as well be in costume – a fashion plate of silk shirt sleeves and bright, double-breasted waistcoats. "These are my dear friends Charles and Matthew. Visiting us from Melbourne for a few weeks. They're keen to see what all the fuss is about. Gentlemen; Mrs Lucy Earnshaw."

I hold out my hand to the men and murmur a greeting, dazed by Browning's introduction. Am I really to call them by their given names? My mother would be horrified.

Mr Browning lifts the wine bottle from the centre of the table and fills the glass that has clearly been put there for me. I breathe in the heady smell of cigar smoke and allow a little of the tension in my shoulders to dissolve. For a strange, dizzying moment, anything feels possible.

"You're a Castlemaine resident then, Mrs Earnshaw?" asks Charles, the taller of Browning's two friends. He leans back in his chair and brings a cigar to his mouth. "Tell me, what do you think of the place?"

No, I don't want to speak of myself, or of this dirt-encrusted town. I want to hear the stories of these people and their lives and their travels; want some glimpse of the outside world to take back to the cottage and cradle.

I garble some flat response about the diggings that makes it clear I have little of interest to say. "And you?" I ask. "Have you been in Australia long?"

"Barely a fortnight," Charles tells me. "Came over with that mad sea captain who says he can make the journey in two months."

"Captain 'Hell or Melbourne Forbes'," Matthew puts in with a chuckle. "Sixty days to the colonies – or die trying!"

I sip my wine. "And did he do it?"

"In fifty-eight days." Matthew pushes his glasses higher up his nose. "Though I don't think my nerves will ever be the same again. Or my insides, for that matter."

My mind goes fleetingly to my own journey on the oceans. Though the days melted into one another, I know we were at sea for far longer than two months. Not that I minded much, intertwined with my new husband. Those days feel impossibly distant.

"Charles and Matthew attended a séance in Melbourne," Mr Browning tells me, with a glimmer in his eyes that, I've noticed, appears whenever our conversation heads in the direction of the supernatural. "The great Madame Moulin. She has quite a following in London. It seems spiritualism is beginning to find its way across the seas."

"Only a matter of time, wasn't it," says Matthew. "Where England goes, the colonies follow close behind."

A smile flickers on Clara's red lips. "What did you think of the great Madame? Do you believe she's able to speak with the dead?"

Charles blows a line of smoke into the faint cloud above the table. "I believe in the great art of deception. Praying on women in widow's weeds and calling up dead Johns and Marys. I hear the crazy old bat hollowed out the walls in her parlour and hid people behind the wallpaper to make ghostly noises."

Matthew laughs. "She's making, what, five, ten pounds a night? Nothing crazy about her."

"That's how they do it?" I ask. "They hide people in the walls?"

"Among other things," says Browning. "Hidden wires and the like."

"It's all electricity," Charles cuts in.

"Electricity?"

He nods. "All those bells ringing mysteriously, and words appearing on slates, they're simply the result of a natural force. One we don't yet fully understand."

Mr Browning smiles at me conspiratorially. "I hope we haven't destroyed the illusion."

"Not at all." Because as I sit here immersed in spiritualism's scams, I feel a spark of old enchantment. For a second, I'm a girl hiding in the wardrobe, scared and thrilled by her brother's Penny Bloods, with her life stretching out in front of her, full of possibilities. And that requires more than just a small amount of magic. "It's fascinating," I say. And dizzyingly refreshing to be speaking about something other than Tom and Leo's empty claim.

"Mrs Earnshaw had some interesting insights into the sightings of the Green Lady," Browning tells the table. "A symptom of homesickness." He turns to me with an encouraging smile. "Tell them."

I take a gulp of wine for courage. "Well, yes. The ghost sightings, they remind us of the home we've left behind. One we'll likely never return to. People convince themselves they're seeing these spirits because they want a little of the familiar."

I'm relieved by the murmurs of agreement.

"You're right, I'm sure," says Matthew, refilling his glass. "Why else would people claim to have seen the Green Lady all the way out here?"

What a strange thing that people like this might be sitting here among their wine bottles, nodding along to something that came from me. And for a second, amid all this talk of ghosts and trickery, and amid these voices of strangers, I see outside the shell my life has become. And I'm peering into a world in which it might be possible to live again, instead of just survive.

I feel myself smile. Feel myself sit a little straighter in my chair. Feel a long-forgotten shine behind my eyes.

I'm suddenly aware of Will Browning's gaze on me. A passing, sideways glance, but one that simmers against my skin. Clara sips her wine, peering between us over the rim of the glass.

"Speaking of the Green Lady," she says, "will you be performing with us, Lucy?"

"Yes," I say, clinging to that hint of boldness I've just managed to unearth. "Yes, I'm looking forward to it." I realise it's the truth.

Clara gives an approving nod.

"Can we expect a bit of ghost hoaxing then, Will?" asks Matthew. "To stir up a bit of publicity for the new play?"

Browning smiles crookedly. "In a place as small as this? I wouldn't dare."

"Ghost hoaxing?" I repeat. "What do you mean?"

Matthew grinds his cigar into the ashtray in the middle of the table. "Will here has been known to play the ghost," he tells me. "He calls it an act of publicity." He chuckles. "I call it being a public nuisance."

I frown. "Play the ghost? You mean dressing the part and scaring passers-by?"

"Like Springheeled Jack himself," says Matthew.

I know of Springheeled Jack, of course, the devilish ghost that leapt from the darkness across England to terrify those who crossed his path. These days, we all know he was nothing more than a string of different flesh-and-blood men donning a costume and creeping about the night, to satisfy their need to create havoc.

"I thought ghost hoaxers were all troublemakers." The words fall out before I can stop them, bringing a round of gentle laughter from the table.

"He's a troublemaker, all right," says Charles. "The dreaded Phantom of Fitzrovia." He adopts a theatrical voice. "Come out from the shadows to terrorise the living."

Clara laughs loudly.

I look at Mr Browning with a surprised smile. I imagined him far too put together to do such a thing. But the thought intrigues me. "The Phantom of Fitzrovia?" I repeat on a laugh.

He chuckles. "To be fair, that name was not my doing."

"Why did you do it?" I ask.

He turns the stem of his wine glass around between his fingers, and stares into the crimson liquid. "Well," he begins after a moment, "as you know, I enjoy writing about the supernatural. And I hoped talk of the sightings would heighten enthusiasm for the play I was working on. But it was also for the exhilaration. For the thrill of being someone you're not. Escaping your reality for a time." He sips his wine and gives an unenthused chuckle. "It all sounds rather mad when I say it out loud."

"That's Will for you," laughs Charles. "The public nuisance with the greater goal of fostering interest in the arts."

Mr Browning laughs too, a thin sound, with little humour. His brown eyes lock onto mine. "Haven't you ever wanted to be a troublemaker, Mrs Earnshaw? Even for a night?"

I allow myself a small smile. But speaking is too dangerous. My heart is speeding, and it feels as though anything might escape my lips.

"In any case," Browning's voice levels as he turns back to Matthew, "there'll be no hoaxing here. In a small settlement like this it's far too dangerous. Anyone could recognise you."

"Not if you do it well enough," says Matthew.

"It would be quite something, Will," Clara puts in. "People have been wandering out of Murphy's in their cups for months and telling stories of seeing the Green Lady. Imagine if there was actually a sighting. By someone who wasn't half-shot."

"Quite something indeed." But I can tell he's unconvinced.

I look around the table, feeling a smile. It's as though I'm part of a delicious secret. Us against the world.

Mr Browning catches my eye and smiles. I notice the faintest hint of a dimple in his cheek.

Clara stands abruptly. "I'm going to the retiring room, Lucy," she declares, and it takes me far too long to realise it's an invitation to join her.

I stand beside Clara while she peers into the mirror and dabs scarlet salve against her lips. I look at my reflection. Look into my own eyes. Into the grief and the worry and the tiredness that has been there for so long I can barely remember being without it. I look closer to Tom's age than my own.

Clara holds the pot of lip salve out to me. I've not gone near makeup since the queen pronounced it the domain of actresses and whores. But I feel violently plain standing next to Clara, with her red lips and felonious curls. My hair is neatly parted and pulled back within an inch of its life, trying so hard to be blonde, but only managing something like the colour of half-cooked toast.

I reach for a miniscule dob of lip salve. I'm an actress now, after all. The queen would approve. Even if my husband wouldn't.

"Will is quite taken with you," Clara says, as casually as if we were discussing the weather. "I can tell."

A blaze goes through me. "I'm married," I say.

Clara slips the lip salve back into her reticule. "Yes."

I peer sideways at her, trying to find the meaning behind her response. What in hell am I to do with this information? I know what I ought to do, of course – tuck it away into some forgotten part of my brain, never to be thought of again. But I also know how little chance there is of that happening.

"Don't look so terrified," says Clara. "Will's a good man. And he knows you've a husband. He'd never do anything untoward. I can just tell he enjoys your company."

I hover by the mirror, suddenly afraid to return to the table. And perhaps even more afraid to stay in the parlour with Clara. I feel as though I've just leapt inadvertently off a cliff and am tumbling towards something I can't quite make out the shape of.

CHAPTER FIVE

"It was a sight! Mounds of earth lying beside holes presented the dismal appearance of a graveyard, [men] washing dirt in tubs, carrying its colour on their skin, hair, hats, trousers, and boots, miserable-looking low tents their places of refuge. ... The whole scene to a new chum was one of unspeakable squalor..."

James Robertson
New arrival on the goldfields
1852

I kneel over the washtub on the square of grass behind the cottage, scrubbing sweat stains from the shirt of a stranger.

With my hands pruning in the washtub and ants crawling up my ankle, it feels as though the previous night never happened. At least it would feel that way if it weren't for the remnants of the wine still thumping around in my brain.

I arrived home close to midnight to find Tom sprawled across the bed and snoring. When I woke, sun was blazing through the curtains and my husband was gone. The first morning in almost four years of marriage I was not awake to see him off.

I hang up the shirts, then follow the aroma of baking bread into the kitchen. I pull the loaf from the oven and set it on the table beside an unwashed pan of bacon grease.

When the loaf has cooled a little, I hack off a couple of slices and wrap them in a cloth, setting out towards Tom's claim.

I can't stop thinking about playing the ghost. About how it might feel to be utterly unrecognisable; to hide from the world in plain sight. I've always been a hider. Always one to avoid attention, and yet is it possible that some part of me also craves it? Longs to be seen, to be heard, to be more than I am?

To find that momentary escape from reality.

Hollow walls and ringing bells and electrical currents making shapes of ghosts. My thoughts are circling around and around the idea and refuse to let it go.

The moment I get to the diggings, I can tell something isn't right. Men are charging between each other's claims, locked in red-faced conversation. The eternal rattle of mining cradles has been replaced by angry voices.

Bunching my skirts into my fists, I make my way through the maze of pits. Some are neatly dug, walls shored firmly with a windlass above. Others are little more than holes in the ground. In the hot morning, dust rises from the claims in clouds, the river a thread through parched brown earth. The sky is fiercely blue.

I find Tom hunched over the windlass, winding the handle with his sleeves rolled to his elbows. His sweat-soaked shirt clings to his back and shoulders. He unhooks the bucket of earth and gives me a strained smile.

"Has something happened?" I ask. "Everyone seems worked up."

"The thieves came out to Forest Creek last night," he tells me. "At least three people reckon their claims have been dug into." He tips the bucket of earth into the cradle.

Leo's grimy head emerges from the depths of the claim. He leaps up the ladder and squints in the sunlight. "This is the worst possible time for this to happen. We're close to a big find. I can feel it."

Tom nods.

I wave a wild hand, battling away an onslaught of flies. How much time do Tom and Leo spend convincing each other that today is the day?

A murmur ripples through the diggings as two policemen appear, the Gold Commissioner on horseback beside them.

"Here we go." Leo takes off his straw hat and uses his wrist to wipe his forehead. "About bloody time. For all the good these bastards are likely to do. What's a place coming to when we're trusting lags to uphold the law?"

It's no secret that Constable Stone, the taller, stockier of the troopers, was sent out here as a convict. Though his sentence is behind him, so they say, the convict stain follows a man for life. Everyone knows who came out by choice, and who was sent here at Her Majesty's pleasure.

Stone nods at Tom as he passes. The two met in the boxing ring last month and I can still see hints of Tom's right hook on the side of the trooper's jaw. He tips his hat at me.

"Mrs Earnshaw."

Following my husband's lead, I turn away in silence.

Stone and the other policeman go to a claim a few hundred yards away that I guess belongs to the fellow who sent for them.

The thieves must have come close to Tom and Leo's claim last night. Why does that make me so uncomfortable? It's not like they would have found anything.

I suddenly remember the bread. "Here." I hold it out to Tom. "It's still warm."

He smiles; a true smile this time. "Thank you. I'm starved." He unwraps the cloth and takes a bite. Hands the other piece to Leo. "You were late last night," he says to me, his mouth still half full. "Was it a good rehearsal?"

Remorse twists my stomach, and I can do little more than nod. "I'm sorry I wasn't awake to make you breakfast."

"I can find my way around a kitchen when I need to. You know I'm glad you're doing this little show." Tom glances at the troopers, then back at me. "You ought to get back to town. There's no need for you to get involved in all this mess."

Three days later, I venture onto the stage beneath the beamed roof of the Theatre Royal. Last year, Lola Montez danced right here with her legs on display, twirling her skirts in her infamous Spider Dance. Left half the colony cheering and the other half in fits of outrage. Had men throwing gold nuggets at her feet. There's something oddly thrilling about performing on the same stage.

Edith, who's requested only a small part in the play, watches from the front row, ready to prompt us with forgotten lines. The rest of us flit around the stage at Browning's prompting; Ollie Cooper and Clara as the Lord and Lady, and Arthur Wallace as their footman. And then, of course, there's the ghost.

I am acutely aware of Browning. Acutely aware of the way his eyes follow me around the stage. I'm being foolish, of course. What kind of half-baked dramatist would he be if he wasn't watching his actresses closely? But I am painfully deliberate in not looking his way. Allowing myself to believe what Clara said – that Will Browning might be taken with me – is a thing I cannot go near.

Nonetheless, I'm excited about my role in the play. Excited to be more than just a shadow, hidden at the back of the theatre with a teacup in my hand. I have only a handful of lines in the opening scenes, my role largely involving hiding in the shadows and looking suitably terrifying. But I've spent hours this week memorising everything up to the end of Act One. Reading the script has become something of an addiction. Losing myself in the world of the play, I've discovered, makes the oppressive walls of the cottage retract, and the silence around our supper table feel far less hollow.

Arthur Wallace charges onto stage and announces Lord Fyvie's arrival in a display of overacting that makes Ollie snort with laughter.

Clara rolls her eyes.

"Perhaps a little less gusto, Arthur," says Browning. "After all, Lady Fyvie is expecting her husband's return. There's no need to announce it as one would the outbreak of war. Let's take the scene from the top, if you please. Mrs Earnshaw, perhaps we might try it with you standing stage left so the footman passes you when he arrives."

I hurry across the stage with my head down.

We stumble through the Lord's arrival again, Ollie squinting at his script in an attempt to find his place.

"You have your back to the audience," Clara tells Mr Wallace as he prances through his next lines. "They'll not hear a word you're saying."

Wallace ignores her.

"Did you not hear me?" Clara demands. "Or are you just pretending not to?"

"I heard you, Miss Snow," says Wallace. "But I don't remember you being in charge of this production."

Browning clears his throat and hurriedly calls a break. Ollie tosses his script on the floor and heads for the tray of Edith's biscuits, while I fling myself between Wallace and Clara in an attempt to diffuse the tension. "Some tea?" I ask, whisking her off the stage before she has a chance to protest.

Mr Wallace paces back and forth repeating, "'My Lady, your husband has returned.'" Clara looks over her shoulder and gives him a glare I'm surprised doesn't turn him to ash.

I fill two teacups from the pot Edith has set up on a small table beside the stage, leaving Clara to stew in the front row of seating.

"We've two rather strong personalities to contend with, don't we," Mr Browning murmurs, appearing at my side.

My heart jolts at his sudden closeness. I stir the tea with exceptional vigour. "We do," I manage. "Yes."

Arthur Wallace was one of the men who made a scene over Lola Montez's Spider Dance, though I suspect he secretly enjoyed it. No doubt he has a similar disdain for a former burlesque star like Clara.

"See if you can't calm her down a little," says Browning, filling a cup of his own. "I'll take care of Arthur." He gives me a conspiratorial smile that I struggle to return. "Hopefully we can make it through the performance without blood being spilled."

I nod hurriedly and disappear with the two cups in hand. I pass one to Clara, taking a seat beside her. "Don't let Mr Wallace bother you," I say. "I suspect he just doesn't like being told what to do by a woman."

"No," she says icily. "I don't suppose he does."

I give her a sympathetic smile. "This must feel like quite some comedown after performing on stage in London."

She nods at Ollie, whose mouth is rammed with biscuits. "What's someone like him doing here anyway? This is all a joke to him."

"You're right," I say. "He's a friend of my husband's. I know he's only here for a laugh."

She gives a wry smile. "Never would have guessed."

"Why not try and find paid work on the stage?" I ask. "There's all sorts of acts touring the goldfields now. And think how many people were here to see Lola Montez perform."

Clara gives an unenthused chuckle. "Can you imagine how the men in this town would react if they saw me doing the Spider Dance? Arthur Wallace would chase me into the bush with a pitchfork." She sips her tea. "I tried finding work on the stage when I first got here. But the theatre world's too small. Everyone knows everyone. No one wants to hire a lag." She gives a wry smile. "Especially a woman past thirty whose career's been somewhat... interrupted."

I've never heard her speak of her transportation before, and it catches me by surprise. A part of me believed it a myth, made up by men like Arthur Wallace in an attempt to shame her. Clara Snow, with her taffeta gowns and red lips, is not what I imagined an ex-convict to look like.

I realise with horror that my eyes have drifted to Mr Browning as he chats with Wallace – presumably telling him not to speak with his back to the audience. I focus intently on the contents of my teacup.

"It was good of you to join us on Friday," Clara says.

"It was?" I'd not imagined my presence, or lack of it, would have any bearing whatsoever on the life of Clara Snow. She looks at me quizzically and I scramble to redeem myself. "It was a very interesting night," I say, feeling the thump of my heart strike up again. Before Clara can speak of other Will Browning-related things, I add, "I enjoyed hearing about the ghost hoaxing."

Her lips tilt upwards. "The hoaxing. Yes. It wouldn't be the worst idea. It'd certainty stir up interest in this play if we got people talking about seeing the Green Lady." She smiles wryly. "Although after this rehearsal, I'm not so sure stirring up interest in the play is such a good idea."

I laugh a little. Although I do think she may be right.

"Of course, you ought to be the one to do it," she continues, "given you're playing the Green Lady."

"Me? No, I couldn't..." I trail off. Because isn't this what a part of me has wanted since I first heard Browning speak of playing the ghost? Isn't this what I've been angling for? However subtly and unconsciously.

Perhaps I do want to be a troublemaker.

"Maybe you should tell that to Mr Browning," I say, stunning myself with my boldness.

"Maybe you should be the one to tell him. Might have a little more bearing." She sips her tea. "I asked him about you, you know. He thinks you're rather lovely. And that you have a lot of interesting things to say about the supernatural." She chuckles. "The surest way to a man's heart."

My fingers tighten around my teacup. "Why are you telling me this?"

She shrugs. "Just thought you might like to know." After a moment of silence, she looks sideways at me. "Sorry. I know you're a married woman."

Yes, I am a married woman. One who has never questioned her love for her husband. But this new world of theatre and magic that Will Browning is pulling me towards is far too alluring to turn away from.

When we flounder to the end of the first act, Browning claps his hands together. "Thank you, everyone. That's enough for today."

Clara plants her hand on her hip. "You can't leave things there. That was a complete disaster."

"Sorry love," Ollie sings. "It's four o'clock and the tavern waits for no man."

Clara snorts. "Get out of here and learn your lines then." She drops her voice. "Or learn to read at least." She watches him leave, then turns to Browning. "Get rid of him, Will. He's not taking it seriously."

"Yes, well. I'm afraid this is not the professional outfit you're used to, Clara." Browning gathers up his notes from the table and slides them inside his script. "We'll go over the last few scenes again on Saturday."

Clara huffs dramatically and strides from the stage. As I make to follow her, Mr Browning calls my name. I look back, heart thumping. He steps towards me.

"You seem rather distant today," he says, voice low. His forehead is crumpled with concern. "Did I say something to offend you on Friday night? If I did, I apologise."

"No," I rush. "Not at all. I suppose I'm just…" I dare to look up at him, and the intensity of his gaze steals my breath. "A little uncertain about all of this."

His face lightens, and I'm surprised at his palpable relief. If he's sensed the hidden meaning beneath my words, he doesn't show it.

"You've a talent," he says. "Truly. There's no need to be nervous. All you need is confidence." A little of the tension in my shoulders eases. His words warm me like wine.

Unbidden, something flickers inside me. Something distant, almost forgotten; something I dimly remember from the early days of my marriage. That feeling of being drawn to a man; of wanting skin against skin, the warmth of another's breath. And – perhaps I'm imagining it – that feeling of a man's eyes drinking me in. I'm mistaken, surely. Clara is mistaken. What single thing is there about me that might make Will Browning look at me in such a way?

"Thank you," I say, and it's a weighted phrase. Because it's not just his kind words I'm thankful for, it's this world of newness he's leading me into, and everything forgotten he's waking within me.

As if sensing the gravity of my words, he gives a faint, wordless nod, a tiny smile attached. I'm rushing off the stage before either of us can speak again.

Clara is waiting for me outside the hall. "You have somewhere to be?" she asks.

"No." I tie my bonnet beneath my chin, trying to steady myself.

"Good. We need to keep rehearsing. Come on."

She grabs my arm, and before I know what's happening, I'm being swept out into the street in her wake.

"Can we rehearse at your house?" she asks.

"My house?" I think of the hastily painted sign on the fence, advertising my laundry services. If Clara Snow sees it, I might just die of shame. But I don't want to turn her down either. I nod. "This way."

"Bloody Browning," she says as we walk. The road has just been watered to keep down the dust and the wet earth sighs beneath our boots. "He's too soft. How's he expect to make something of himself if he's letting people like Ollie Cooper make a joke of everything he's worked for?"

"Did you know him?" I ask curiously. "In London?"

"A little. We moved in the same circles. I worked on one of his early plays at the Haymarket before I got hauled out here. Could hardly believe it when I saw him strutting around the Commercial."

"What was he like?"

"Passionate," she says. "And talented. But he could never quite live up to the success of his first play. They had him pegged as one of the great playwrights of the nineteenth century. Expected everything that came from him to be gold. But his second and third plays were lacking. It was as though he couldn't quite find the magic of his first piece. The reviewers tore him to pieces. Said his first play was just a stroke of luck. Some even went so far as to suggest the work hadn't been his own."

"That's awful."

Clara shrugs. "That's the theatre for you."

"What about the ghost hoaxing?" I ask. "Were you involved in that?"

"The hoaxing? No. Will got into all that after I was gone."

I watch my feet as I walk. "It's so interesting," I say. "The way no one knew it was him."

Clara smiles crookedly. "I suppose shock can blind us to what's right in front of us."

I herd her quickly past the laundry sign and unlock the front door. Realise with horror that I've forgotten to clean the bacon pan. The smell of cold grease turns the air. I charge past Clara and grab the pan, tossing it into the trough. "Sorry about the mess," I babble. "I'll just do a quick wash—"

Clara takes my arm as I blunder past with the bucket. "Lucy. It's no matter." She holds my script out to me. "Scene six."

I put down the bucket and take the script. Force myself to concentrate. Though this is just an amateur play, I want to do a good job. I want something I can be proud of. And perhaps there's a part of me that wants Will Browning to be proud of me too.

I toss the script on the table and act through the scene from memory.

"You're good, Lucy," says Clara, after we've run it several more times. "There's no need to be so nervous." She takes a seat at the table. Her eyes drift around the kitchen, taking in the blackened bricks above the fireplace, the faded gingham curtains pulled back from the windows. "Why did you come out here?" she asks curiously.

I sit opposite, turning the pages of the script without reading. "My husband said he was going to find our fortune." An all-too-common tale. I'm almost embarrassed to tell it.

"And you're still waiting?"

I find a wry smile. I know our ash-streaked cottage speaks for itself.

"Well. I'm making my own luck," says Clara. "Going to make my own fortune. I've got myself land on Hargraves Street. I'm going to open a dressmaker's parlour."

"That's why you came to Castlemaine? To start your own business?"

She nods. "I've been working as a seamstress since I came up from Hobart. Small, private jobs and the like. Thought I could make a go of running my own place. The land's a little cheaper here than in Melbourne. And there's plenty of folks on the goldfields ready to spend their new fortune before they ride off into the sunset."

I smile. I like the idea of making your own luck, instead of hoping blindly for the earth to give up its secrets.

"Some of the men have been making trouble for me though," she says. "Men like Arthur Wallace. They don't like to see my kind have success. Not an outspoken woman with the convict stain. I think this place is too upside down for their liking. Anyone can make something of themselves, even if they've got a prison sentence behind them. Men like Wallace, who are used to being on top, it makes them nervous. Makes them question how powerful they really are."

I frown, playing with the corner of my script. "What are they doing to you?"

"Nothing I can't handle. Little comments when I pass them in the street. That sort of thing. Someone even tried to oppose my purchase of the land. Don't know for sure that it was Wallace, but I know he's capable of it." She snorts. "Have you seen the way he struts around with the Commissioner like he has a pole up his arse?"

"Maybe that's why his acting's so bad."

Clara laughs. "Do you want to see some of the pieces I made?" she asks suddenly. "I'd be interested in what you think of them."

"Of course."

She gets to her feet, and soon I'm trailing her across town again. She stops outside the boarding house on the edge of the settlement. I look up at the narrow, wood-panelled building in surprise. Edith once told me the place was full of no-good dollymops, and since then I've gone out of my way to avoid it.

"You live here?" I ask.

"For now. I'll move to the room behind the shop as soon as it's finished." She looks at me pointedly. "Is there a problem?"

"No," I garble. "Of course not."

I follow her inside, and onto a creaking wooden staircase. Soft laughter floats up from a room below. A young woman passes us on the stairs, dressed in threadbare brown skirts. Her lips are painted red, her eyes dark with lampblack. I smell a fog of liquor on her skin. I find myself stepping away from her instinctively. Does someone as glamorous as Clara really live in such a place? I imagined her in a suite at the Commercial Hotel, where I know Browning lives.

She pushes open a door off the corridor. Five or six narrow beds are lined up across the room, an older woman dozing on one of them. The room smells of bodies and woodsmoke that lingers in the walls. Though the building can be no more than a few years old, the light blue paint around the doorframe is already beginning to peel, the washstand in the corner chipped and discoloured.

Clara goes to the bed in the centre of the room and drags a small wooden chest out from under it. She fishes a key out from inside her stays and unlocks the trunk. She reaches in and lifts out the bodice of a steel-grey day dress. Hands it to me. "What do you think?"

I hold it out to inspect it. Fine embroidered flowers decorate the collar in silver thread, a row of tiny white buttons down the centre. The stitching is tiny and impeccably neat. "You made this?"

She nods. "Ready-to-wear pieces are all the rage these days. And if people see things they like in my window, they're more likely to come to me with commissions."

"It's beautiful," I say. "Really."

"Learned a few skills when they had me locked up at the female factory. Turns out I'm quite something with a needle and thread in my hand." She chuckles to herself. "Who knew?"

I try to imagine Clara in convict slops, her dark curls tied back and her lips free of salve. The image doesn't seem to fit.

She laughs a little. "Thieving," she says.

I blink. "What?"

"You wanted to ask me what I did to get sent over. I could tell."

"Oh." I feel my cheeks turn pink. "I…"

"Had a gentleman caller who tried to take more than I was willing to give. So I pinched his pocket watch when he got too close. An act of revenge I didn't think through so well. Coppers came to the theatre and arrested me before a show one night."

"That's dreadful," I say. "I'm sorry."

She shrugs. "Wasn't my finest hour."

The woman on the bed sighs loudly, making a show of flinging herself onto her side and pulling her pillow over her ears.

I run a finger over the neat stitching on the hem of the bodice. "Is it true you charmed your overseer into giving you your ticket of leave?"

Clara raises her eyebrows, a smile on the edge of her lips. "Is that what people are saying? Why not? Makes a good story." She kneels beside the trunk and pulls out a gown, smoothing its violet skirts over her knees. "My overseer at the female factory was a flat-faced matron with a temper like a hurricane. Believe me, no one was charming her. I served my time. Nothing more dazzling than that. Now I'm a free woman. And I plan to make the most of it."

The woman on the bed lets out another dramatic sigh and gets up, shooting us a glare as she tromps towards the door. I watch after her as she disappears down the hall.

"The women here," I begin, "do they... I mean, are they..."

"Whores?" Clara says brusquely. "Yes, some of them. Do you have a problem with that?" Sharpness in her words, and I see it then. See that, for a woman stripped of everything and transported to the colonies, mere sewing jobs would not be enough to afford a shopfront on Hargraves Street. When I look closely, and glimpse beneath her polished surface, I see the tarring on her boots, the criss-crossed mending on her skirts. And I see what Clara was forced to do to make her own way in the world.

I'm suddenly ashamed of the revulsion I felt when I walked past the woman in the stairwell. Ashamed of looking down on her. Ashamed of the self-righteous glances I threw the working girls who strutted through the diggings at night. Because what choice did any of them have?

I realise then how utterly tiny my life is. What a strange thing that my world might feel so small and sheltered when I've crossed oceans and traversed the globe. Even on the other side of the planet, I'm still the same righteous woman who feels the need to scrub her parlour before visitors arrive. Sometimes that woman is so rigid and dreary she makes me want to scream.

"Of course I've no problem with it," I say quickly. "I'm sure it wasn't a matter of choice."

"No." Clara takes the bodice from my hand and folds it, before setting it back in the trunk. She locks the lid and slides the chest back beneath the bed without speaking again. Have I offended her?

"I'd best go," I say stiltedly. "I've got supper to make."

Clara flashes me a smile and I feel my shoulders sink in relief. "I'll walk you back. Maybe I can show you the shop on the way."

"Here she is," Tom calls as I let myself into the cottage. "My little star."

I find him sitting in the kitchen, his long legs stretched out in front of him. An open bottle of liquor is on the table, a half-empty glass beside it.

"You're not usually one to drink alone." I take off my bonnet and hang it beside the door.

"Just something to take the edge off the day."

"Have there been more thefts?" I ask.

"No thefts. Just a long day is all." He smiles up at me. "But enough of that. Tell me about your play."

I realise with a bolt of panic that I left my script on the kitchen table when I went to the boarding house with Clara. Has Tom peeked inside it? The thought makes me oddly uncomfortable. As though I don't want him prying into this world he isn't a part of.

"It's a good play," I say. "Mr Browning is very talented. I think everyone will enjoy it."

Tom takes my hand. The gesture feels oddly foreign, and I feel my body stiffen. "And you? Are you enjoying it?"

"I am," I say. "Much more than I expected."

"Good. I'm proud of you, Luce. I know it was a difficult thing for you to agree to."

I looked down at our intertwined fingers. "Sometimes I can barely believe I'm doing such a thing. I hate people looking at me." Our conversation feels oddly pleasant, oddly easy. And that in itself stirs up wariness within me. Pleasant and easy is not something we do.

Tom reaches up and tucks a stray strand of hair behind my ear. "I don't know why," he says. "You're a beauty."

"Don't be mad. I'm no such thing." I turn away, suddenly embarrassed.

He wraps his arm around my waist, finding the curve of my hips. "I'm not being mad." His familiar scent surrounds me; whisky and earth and the carbolic soap we keep in the washbin. His closeness fills me with both comfort and dread.

I can barely remember the last time Tom and I were together. Since Elsie's death, there has been an invisible barrier between us in the bed.

In the first days and weeks, we held each other in the night – those long, silent nights not broken by the wails of a baby. Slowly, we reached an unspoken agreement that neither of us could handle the pain of losing another child. And so we would not take the chance of bringing another child into the world.

But in the past year, that unspoken agreement has become something deeper. These days, our conversations rarely do more than scratch the surface. Our reluctance to talk about our daughter has become a reluctance to talk about anything of meaning. I'm left to constantly guess what Tom is thinking, feeling. Left to wonder if there are traces of Elsie in his thoughts, or if his hunt for gold consumes all else. A part of me desperately wants for us to speak of our child; to remember the good times, and shoulder each other's sadness. But there's a fear in me of these conversations. A fear that it will be too painful, that I might say things I regret, that somehow it's easier to keep Elsie tucked away in my memory than to speak of the anger and grief that's festering inside me. And though I'm certain Tom will never speak unprompted about our daughter, there's a still a part of me that's fearful whenever he opens his mouth. These days, when I'm in my husband's presence, there's a knot in my stomach I can't find a way to unravel.

I swallow heavily, shifting my weight. "I ought to make supper."

"Supper can wait." Tom keeps his arm tight around me. His other hand slides over the side of my ribcage and squeezes against my corset.

"Tom," I murmur. "You're drunk."

"Drunk? Hardly. I've had one glass."

And I see it then – the liquor was not to ease the stresses of the day. It was to give him the courage to lie with his wife.

Emboldened by the whisky, Tom is persistent, a hand working beneath my skirts to squeeze my thigh. A sharp exhalation escapes me, and I stumble backwards involuntarily. Tom lets his hand fall.

"I'm sorry," I hear myself say.

Tom gets to his feet, grabbing his glass and tossing back the last of the liquor. Then he strides into the bedroom without speaking.

For several moments, I don't move. Just stare into the lamp, watching a draught catch hold of the flame. Tears prick my eyes, blurring the orange light. I blink them away quickly. I've had far too many tears. I don't want to cry any more.

Instead, I sit at the table and open my script. A slight tremor in my hands, I turn the pages to the scene Clara and I were rehearsing this afternoon.

I read through the lines several times. A confrontation between Lady Fyvie and the ghost.

"'I have been here longer than you know,'" I murmur. My voice sounds hollow in the empty kitchen. Out of place. What a strange thing, I think distantly, that my voice might sound so displaced in my own damn house. But it's not my voice, is it. It's the voice of the Green Lady; this watery tone I've adopted to play a part. A voice full of someone else's pain.

I repeat the line, louder this time. More confident. It seems to heighten the silence.

And: "'Beware of the man you married,'" I say, well aware of the irony. The poor devoted Green Lady, betrayed by the husband she loved so dearly. Starved to death in the charter room of Fyvie Castle for failing to provide an heir.

Here I am reading her lines with my half of the marriage bed cold and my thoughts swirling around another man. I feel the guilt twist violently inside me as I read, "'He is a cold and heartless beast.'"

CHAPTER SIX

"There are distinct signs that ghosts, which we thought were laughed out of existence by the robust common sense of the eighteenth century, are creeping back into the world, revisiting again the glimpses of the moon, in these rather sickly times of the moribund nineteenth century."

The *Argus*
Melbourne
March 1884

"I thought we might go to the ball tomorrow night," says Tom. He's standing with his back up against the wall of the cottage while I crouch over the tub of laundry on the grass behind the house.

"We don't have to do that. I know you don't like dancing."

"I want to go," he says. "Everyone will be there. And it's about time we attended one."

His words sting. We've missed both the annual goldfields balls in our time in Castlemaine, buried in grief as we were last year, and tied up with a newborn the year before. There's something brutal about being able to attend this one.

I pull a shirt from the washtub and feed it through the wringer.

Tom stands watching patiently, waiting for me to speak. I sling the shirt over the washing line, then gather the courage to face him.

We've barely said two words to each other in the days since he attempted to take me to bed. Sometimes, like right now, I miss my husband intensely. How is that possible, I wonder, when he's standing not a yard away? The loneliness feels painfully deep.

I nod. "All right. Let's go to the ball."

"Good." He gives me a smile that doesn't reach his eyes, then turns and disappears back inside the cottage.

The following night, I'm sitting in front of the mirror on my side table, trying to wrangle my hair into something other than its usual lifeless bun. I tell myself the extra effort is because it's the first goldfields ball Tom and I will have made it to, and definitely not because Will Browning is going to be there. I squint at my reflection. My cheeks are turning golden brown, after having caught the sun. I wish I had a little powder to cover them.

The floor creaks loudly and Tom appears behind me in the mirror. He's dressed in a clean shirt and waistcoat, a neckcloth knotted at his throat. Clean-shaven for the first time in what feels like a decade. He looks younger without his scruffy beard. I feel a sudden urge to touch his smooth cheek. But something holds me back.

"You look lovely, Lucy."

He puts tentative hands to my shoulders, as though his thick fingers are trying to remember the shape of me. The feel of him makes sudden tears gather in my throat. Tears of happiness or sadness, I can't tell.

There are moments of this. Moments where there is no past or future, there is just him and me, existing. But they've become so rare, so fleeting. Him, fixated on a future in which he finds the gold he craves. Me, stuck in the past, wondering if there was something I might have done differently to keep Elsie with us. Things that have become much too painful to talk about. Silence and small talk are far easier.

I stand up, turning to face him. I grip the hem of his waistcoat, as though I might prevent the moment from slipping away. "Do you really want to go tonight? You hate dancing."

He chuckles lightly. "I do. But I just want—"

"Me to be happy," I finish. "I know." I let my hands fall, that familiar tug of unease returning. What is so wrong with sadness? Isn't that the right thing for a woman to feel after she's buried her child?

Except I realise then, with a quake that goes through my whole body, that it isn't sadness I'm feeling. The grief that has pressed down on me every bleak, lightless day since Elsie's death, I've stopped feeling that with such bone-breaking intensity. Somehow, in the wake of the play, and my night at the Commercial, and yes, in the wake of Will Browning, my pain has eased enough for me to breathe.

I swallow a gasp at the realisation. I am a horrible person.

Tom frowns. "Have you changed your mind about going?"

I hesitate. It would be safer, of course, to stay home. Far less temptation.

But I can't bear another stilted, silent night in the cottage with our unspoken grief hanging so thick in the air.

I force a smile. "No," I say. "We should go. Can't have you shaving for nothing."

As we make our way to Castlemaine Hall, I glance out towards the glow of campfires that mark the edge of the diggings.

"Are you not worried about the night fossickers?" I ask. "With so many people away at the ball, it seems like a fine time for thieves to strike."

Tom doesn't answer at once. "Maybe it is. But how often do I get the chance to take my wife dancing? Besides, we've barely found more than gold dust in weeks." He chuckles humourlessly. "If fossickers find anything down there, good luck to them."

My chest squeezes. It's the first time I've heard anything but optimism come out of Tom's mouth, at least as far as the diggings are concerned. Is he starting to lose hope? Maybe it's best that he does. At least then we could acknowledge this adventure as a failure and move on to the next part of our lives.

Admitting he had failed on the diggings would crush him. When we first came out here, he didn't for a second consider the possibility of failure. That he'd dig his way to wealth and success was just a given.

I slip my hand around his elbow and give it a gentle squeeze. It's a pitying gesture, but what does that matter? These days, anything that makes me feel close to my husband is precious. I can barely remember the last time I wanted to be near him. But maybe we really can find a way to move forward. Find a way back to each other.

The wail of bagpipes tumbles out into the street, and we follow the sound into the hall. I'm pleasantly surprised at what I find. The walls are hung with blue and white calico, which looks in the lamplight to ripple like water. Chairs and small wooden tables dot the edges of the hall, a bunch of bright yellow flowers in the centre of each. The stage where I walk as the Green Lady is tonight filled with fiddlers and pipers and everyone else who thought to throw an instrument in their luggage. People mill by the edges of the room; others leap around wildly to the music. Men are clustered around the handful of women, vying for a chance to dance with them. Those who know they have no hope dance with rolled-up swags instead. One look at their clothing tells you who's found success, and who's still slumming it in tents the calibre of pigsties.

Leo and Ollie wave us over. They're sitting at a table close to the door, tin cups in front of them.

"Give me a dance, Mrs Earnshaw," Ollie demands, on his feet before I've even made it to the table. "I've been waiting an hour for the company of a lady."

Tom slides an arm around my waist. "Will you at least let her sit down first?"

"Johnny Chinaman's having a party tonight too," Ollie says, as Tom pulls out a chair for me. "Sold half my meat to them this morning. Saw their camp all lit up on my way past tonight too. They was thrashing away on drums and everything."

"Good," says Leo. "It'll keep them away from here."

Tom goes to sit, but I press a hand to his arm to stop him. "Fetch us a drink?"

"Oh. Yes. Of course. Ale?"

"Stronger."

Off he goes to the bar, leaving Ollie and Leo to harp on about the Chinese. When he returns with a cup of gin for me, I swallow it down quickly. Feel a satisfying buzz in my brain.

My eyes drift to the other side of the hall, where Will Browning is sitting with Charles, Matthew and Clara. A burst of laughter rises from their table.

Mr Browning looks across the room and catches my eye. I turn away quickly. I can't let myself so much as look at him, not when my husband feels closer than he has in months.

I turn to Tom. "Will you dance with me?"

"In a while. You know me. Need a few drinks to work up the courage."

I smile stiffly. Tom has never been one for parties, and I can tell he's uncomfortable. Still, he was the one who insisted we come. I hoped he might make a little more of an effort.

"Coppers've showed up," Leo reports, nodding towards the bar. Constable Stone and two of the officers are standing in the corner, drinks in hand.

Tom takes another gulp of ale.

Leo snorts. "Little wonder they've no idea who's robbing us blind if they're spending their nights gallivanting around the ballroom."

The band bursts into a frantic jig and Ollie leaps from his chair. "You gonna dance with her or not, Tom?"

Tom glances at me, then gestures for Ollie to take me out to the dancefloor.

"Miserable old bastard, aren't he," Ollie chuckles, as he takes my hands in his. "One of the few lads who's got a lady with him and he won't even dance with her."

"Tom's not much of a dancer," I say.

"So I hear," Ollie replies, though he's not exactly setting the boards alight himself.

After the jig with Ollie and a reluctant set with Clyde, I excuse myself and head back to the table. "Now?" I ask Tom. My legs are getting tired, and I want at least one dance with my own husband before I'm farmed off to entertain all the other single men.

Tom glances up at me fleetingly. "In a minute, Luce." He turns back to Leo. "But it's all a matter of progress. They want to find more gold, then they…"

I grit my teeth and head for the bar, dumping enough coins on the table for a fresh cup of gin.

Clara sashays towards me in her shimmering violet-black skirts. She nods towards the side of the stage, where Arthur Wallace is in conversation with a group of other men. His thick grey brows are furrowed as he nods along to the speaker.

"Did you hear? Arthur's pulled out of the play. Will's going to take his part."

"Really? Why?"

"Says he doesn't have the time. But I think we all know that's bull. He just doesn't like being told how to act by a government woman. Especially one who's seen him with all his bits out."

I choke on my drink. "You and Wallace... I mean, he was your...?"

"My punter," says Clara. "It's all right, Lucy. I don't mind if you speak about it."

My cheeks heat at her directness and I swallow an ocean of gin.

"Was a cheap bastard too. Used his tent at the Commissioner's camp instead of paying for a room." She shrugs airily. "Mind you, I suppose I can't blame him. It just doesn't make good sense to rent a room for the night if one only needs it for two minutes."

A laugh escapes me and my eyes drift to Mr Wallace. Suddenly his animosity towards Clara makes much more sense.

"Made me promise him my silence every time I left too," she says. "I doubt he'd have bothered if he knew how many men here were doing the same thing."

"No wonder he doesn't like you telling him how to act."

Clara waves to the barkeep and orders a glass of wine. She turns to look back at Wallace as she brings it to her lips. "I learned a lot about men like him when I was working the streets. They just want things to be how they were in England. Everyone in their place, their class. They don't like that a lag can make something of themselves. When they see noblemen digging alongside ex-convicts, their poor little brains just implode. They can't make sense of it."

I nod.

"I think Wallace saw me as some creature of the night who ceased to exist in the daylight. Couldn't handle it when he realised we were to live in the same society." She presses her shoulders back. "Anyway. Wallace and the others of his kind will be mad as hops when their wives are coming to me to have their dresses made. Just think of the stories I could tell them."

I grin. "You wouldn't."

"Course not. But they don't know that, do they."

"Come on then, Luce," Tom bellows suddenly, lurching towards me and grabbing my hand. "Let's have a dance." I can smell the ale on his breath.

I wrangle him onto the dancefloor, desperate to get him away from Clara. I don't want these two parts of my life to become entangled. And maybe I'm a little embarrassed of the lumbering boor I'm married to.

Tom slides his fingers through mine. Looks me in the eyes and smiles. For a moment, I see him; the man I fell in love with. That gentle farmhand with dreams not tarnished by the goldfields. Something tightens in my chest and I let him pull me close. But before we can negotiate the steps of the Gallopede, Leo comes charging up to us.

"Clyde says he's just seen the Green Lady. Out behind Murphy's."

I look to the doorway. Clyde's telling a story to a gathering crowd, waving his arms animatedly. I dart a glance to Browning's table. I half expect one of them to be missing, dressed up outside Murphy's in a ghost hoaxer's costume. But Browning, along with Charles and Matthew, is at their table watching Clyde with amused eyes. Clara is still at the bar with her wine glass in hand.

Tom and Leo head for the door. With little else to do, I follow, and am swept up in the crowd. The Gallopede loses momentum as half the fiddlers climb off the stage to see what all the fuss is about. Clyde leads the throng of people towards the alley behind the tavern.

A part of me understands. If you can't catch a thief, why not catch a ghost?

"She was right over there by the window," Clyde's saying, a stumble in his step. "I swear it."

The men charge into the alley, peering behind bins, shouting *'Where are you, woman?'* and other phrases similarly unhelpful for catching a ghost.

Bitterness sears through me as I watch Tom among the men, chasing after shadows. I know I didn't imagine that precious closeness between us. But it's gone all too quickly.

As I look to the half-lit window at the back of the tavern, I see it. That pale sheath of curtain trapped beneath the window frame. With lamplight behind it, it seems in motion, almost breathing.

The Green Lady.

Do the men not see it? Or are they just choosing not to? Perhaps it's more fun to indulge in fantasy for a time, than to face the harshness of this life we've chosen.

"A manifestation of collective terrors," says a voice from behind me.

I turn to look over my shoulder, flashing Browning a quick smile.

"You see it, don't you?" he asks.

"The curtain? It's so obvious I'm surprised everyone doesn't see it."

I think of what Clara said: *Shock can blind us to what's right in front of us.* This colony, these men, they're so ready to be fooled.

From deep in the alley, Tom glances over his shoulder at me, as though ensuring I haven't been spirited off into the otherworld.

"Forgive me," says Browning. "I ought to leave you. I—"

I grab his wrist to prevent him stepping away. See the flash of surprise in his eyes at the contact. And I say, "I want to play the ghost."

CHAPTER SEVEN

"Residents of the quiet township of Rosaville ... have been startled during the past week by the nightly appearance of a ghost. The nocturnal visitor assumed the form of a young girl, draped in what appeared to be a white shroud. ... [One resident] of a more practical turn of mind looked upon the matter as a hoax. ... He therefore laid in wait, and when the nocturnal visitant appeared ... his arms encircled the form of a young girl who was enveloped in a sheet, instead of a disembodied spirit. The practical joker was conveyed home and cautioned against repeating her folly."

The Express and Telegraph
Adelaide
19th August 1880

I let my hand fall from Mr Browning's wrist. "I want to play the ghost," I say again, softer. "Look." I gesture at the men, who are hammering on the back windows of Murphy's Hotel. "They're longing to see the Green Lady. So why not give them what they want?" My thoughts begin to catch up to my outburst. "Just think of how much interest it would create in your play. Get people talking about the Green Lady and they'll be lining up to see the show."

But it's not about the play. Not really. Yes, I want Mr Browning to have success, but this is something I long to do for myself.

My entire life I have followed the rules. And where has that got me? I want to do the unthinkable. Be someone else.

I want to be a troublemaker.

Mr Browning's face is creased with a frown. I can tell he was not expecting this from me. And why would he? I was barely expecting it from myself. He shakes his head. "I really don't think..." He looks up as Clara makes her way towards us, without having relinquished her wine glass. "Ah, Clara. Tell Mrs Earnshaw that playing the ghost is a terrible idea."

Clara's eyes shine. "Playing the ghost? I think that's a wonderful idea. This town is desperate to see the Green Lady. Let's give them what they want." She winks at me. "You can wear the costume I'm making for the play." She drains her wine, then turns to Browning. "I'll promise I'll make her look simply dazzling."

He swallows visibly and I feel my cheeks heat.

"Don't pretend you're not excited at the prospect," Clara says, pointing a long finger in his direction. "Phantom of Fitzrovia."

I hide a smile.

"That was different." He turns to me. "Once they see you on stage, they'll know you were the one behind the hoaxing."

"Good." My response is thoughtless, but I realise at once that I'm speaking the truth. Because I'm coming to see I don't want to be hidden anymore. Don't want to be so silent and submissive. There is so much grief and anger and frustration in me that I need to let a little of it out. Otherwise it might swallow me whole.

"We can do it with or without him, Lucy," Clara says easily. "I've nearly finished your costume. And he'll be ever so grateful when the masses are lining up to see his play."

I eye Mr Browning, hoping for a smile of agreement. But he shakes his head, arms folded across his chest. "It's a bad idea."

I hold his gaze challengingly. His lips part, but he says nothing.

"What's going on here, Luce?" I whirl around to see Tom marching towards us.

"Oh," I rush, "these are... from the theatre group..." My mouth feels too dry. "Mr Browning and Miss Snow."

Tom's eyes move between them warily.

"A pleasure to meet you, Mr Earnshaw," says Browning, shaking Tom's hand with a cool smile. He looks at the men outside Murphy's, then back at my husband. "Did you find the Green Lady?"

Tom gives a strained chuckle. Rubs his square jaw. "No, I uh… I'm not quite sure I believe in all that." His hand curls protectively around the back of my neck. "It's getting late, Lucy. Let's go home." His voice leaves no room for debate.

I nod obediently, murmuring hurried goodbyes.

"I wouldn't rush to be so sceptical, Mr Earnshaw," Clara calls as we make our way out of the alley, Tom holding tight to my arm. "Perhaps the Green Lady will show herself again soon."

Three nights after the ball, and I've arranged to meet Clara at the Commercial to deceive the superstitious people of Castlemaine. I plan to rattle out my well-worn lie – tell Tom I'm going to a theatre rehearsal. Not entirely untrue, I reason. After all, I'm about to play the Green Lady.

When Tom returns to the cottage late in the evening, he's flustered and angry. He paces back and forth across the kitchen as I serve up the stew that's been congealing on the hook since dusk.

More night fossicking at Forest Creek, he tells me. More claims robbed while people slept.

"Coppers have any word of who's responsible?" I ask, battering away the flies that have arrived in droves through the open window. The heat in the kitchen is thick and heavy.

Tom slides a chair up to the table. "We don't need to speak of it."

"You can talk to me about this," I say, tugging irritably at my damp stays. "I'm not going to fall to pieces at the slightest sign of trouble."

He hesitates, stirring and stirring his stew. Finally, he says, "There's been no arrests. Coppers are a pack of useless bastards. Talk among the men is it may be bolters. Bushrangers."

The muscles in my neck tighten. I've heard of the bushrangers, of course. Escaped convicts who hide in the Black Forest between Castlemaine and Melbourne, terrorising the coaches on their way to and from the goldfields. I don't like the thought of them straying into our settlement.

"Bushrangers?" I try to keep my voice from rattling. "Do you think maybe they were responsible for… what happened to Fred Buckley?"

"What happened to Fred Buckley was an accident," Tom says firmly. He puts his spoon down. "Listen to me, Lucy. Whoever's behind these thefts, it's gold they're after. Nothing more. They'd have had no need to take out poor old Buckley. Much as I don't want to speak ill of the dead, he shouldn't have been messing round with black powder."

I nod. Tom's explanation is the most likely, I suppose, no matter what my racing imagination tries to tell me. "There were no thefts the night of the ball, were there?" I ask. "Even though half the claims must have been unguarded."

Tom shakes his head. "Not that I know of."

"Do you think that just a coincidence?"

"I don't know," he admits. "Maybe not. All I know is I don't want them in my claim. I know what I said about them being welcome to whatever they could find there, but…"

"I know," I say. "You didn't mean it."

"I've worked too hard, Luce. I'm not about to let anyone get their hands to whatever's down there." He meets my eyes. "Leo and I have decided we need to take turns sleeping out there. Keep an eye on things. I told him I'd go out there tonight. I'm sorry."

"Don't be sorry."

"Of course. You'll be off galivanting around the stage anyway." He stirs his stew. "You're friends with that Clara Snow woman now are you?" It sounds like an accusation.

"Do you have a problem with that?"

"Leo says she used to work the streets."

I hold his gaze. "Yes. To earn money to open her dressmaking parlour."

Tom blinks at my directness. "I'm sure you can find more suitable people to be friends with. Why don't you pay Meg a visit?"

Meg was my closest friend when we lived at Forest Creek. But after an agonising spring in which we both buried children, the friendship became too tainted to hold on to. We've not spoken in almost a year.

"Tom," I say, sharper than I intended, "you were the one who pushed me to join the theatre group. You were the one who pushed me to perform. And now you don't want me to be friends with these people?"

Tom sticks his spoon in his mouth. "I've laid out far too logical an argument for him to dismantle. After a moment, he nods resignedly. "Mrs Markham will see you back?"

I can't meet his eyes, my self-righteousness dying in the wake of my lies. "I'll be sure not to walk home alone."

I'm a jittery mess as I make my way towards the hotel. Though the population of Castlemaine is swelling by the day, there are still far too many familiar faces for me to disappear into anonymity. But the thudding of my heart makes me feel alive. Excited. And this is not a feeling I'm willing to give up.

The main bar is busy, the air thick with pipe smoke and jumbled conversation. I hear Clara call my name. Turn to see her sitting alone at a table by the window, a glass of clear liquid in front of her. She has not even bothered to sit in the ladies' area. A table of men sits opposite her, shooting her glares and murmuring between themselves. She gestures to me to join her. Emboldened by her presence, I march past the men and up to her table.

"Do you have the dress?" I ask.

"Upstairs in Will's room."

My heart quickens. "In Will's room? I thought he didn't want to be involved."

She flaps a hand dismissively. "He'll come around. He was the one who told me to use his room. Said it was safer than using the retiring parlour. Less chance of getting caught." She tosses back the last of her drink and slides from her chair, looping her arm through mine. She flashes the men a defiant smile – "Gentlemen" – then we sweep through the bar and up the staircase that leads to the lodgings.

We reach a narrow, lamplit corridor with doors on either side. The noise of the bar has become a muffled chatter. Clara knocks on what I assume is Mr Browning's door, and I feel a fresh flicker of nerves.

He answers at once. Leans against the doorframe as his eyes bore into me. "You're really going to do this then?"

I swallow. "I am. Yes."

"Very well." He takes his frock coat from the hook beside the door and slides it on. "The room is yours." He looks at Clara. "I'll be downstairs. Let me know when you're done."

He is off down the hall without another word, and I find myself staring after him. Feel a tug between my ribs at the brusqueness of his words.

Clara puts a hand to my shoulder, ushering me inside, clearly unfazed by his coldness. Browning's room is small and neat, with curtains drawn across a large window and a canopied bed in the centre. His rosewater scent infuses the space with his presence. I can picture him hunched over that little table in the corner, scrawling down the words to the play, ink splattering over the page and his dark hair spilling across his eye.

"Do you think he's angry?" I ask.

Clara pulls an array of salves and powders from her reticule and sets them on the table. "Don't worry yourself over it. He'll be thanking you when he fills the Theatre Royal."

I feel a knot in my stomach. As much as I want the thrill of playing the ghost, Browning's resistance cuts me. I can't make sense of why he's so against it. I'm only doing something he himself has done before.

Clara points to the dress lying across the bed. "What do you think?"

I take a step closer to inspect it. Its wide skirts and sleeves shimmer in the lamplight, a single line of beading along the neckline. I run a tentative finger along it. "It's stunning."

"I'm pleased with how it turned out," she says. "As far as history tells us, it's quite close to what Lilias Drummond, Lord Fyvie's first wife, would have worn when she was alive." She smiles crookedly. "And afterwards too, if you believe the stories."

She gestures for me to sit in the chair beside the dressing table. I feel like a blank canvas, ready to be done with whatever she pleases.

I close my eyes. Feel brushes and powder glide over my cheeks. Lampblack swept over my eyelids.

"Did you learn this from your time in the theatre?" I ask.

"I did. It's been a while. But it seems I remember more than I thought." She works in silence for several minutes, then takes a step back. I open my eyes. Clara tilts her head to inspect her work. "Perfect."

"Can I see?"

"Not yet." She presses the lids back onto the powders and slips them into her reticule. "Take off your dress. The Green Lady's gown laces at the back. I'll help you get into it."

I unbutton my bodice and step out of my skirts, letting them settle on the floor around me. The green gown sighs like sea as Clara sweeps it from the bed. She lifts it over my head and it falls cloudlike over my body. After the cloying weight of my pleated calico skirts, the silky gown makes me feel almost weightless. Clara guides the narrow ribbons through their eyelets on the back of the dress. My breath roars in my ears, heart fast with anticipation. With the Green Lady's gown flowing against my body, the excitement in me is building. Pushing out whatever doubts Mr Browning's coldness dredged up.

"Can I look now?" I ask.

"You can."

I turn to face the mirror above the dressing table. The face staring back at me steals my breath. Clara has turned my skin pale and otherworldly, highlighting my eyes in deep lampblack shadows. Against the whiteness of my skin, my mousy hair looks almost raven dark, lips the palest pink. The Green Lady has just enough realism to make men stop and question. Enough ghost about her to keep them awake at night. Beneath her wraithlike pallor, she is beautiful.

It cannot be Lucy Earnshaw, because Lucy Earnshaw would never do a thing like this, never in a thousand lifetimes. Tonight, I am someone else. Some*thing* else. I am utterly unrecognisable, even to myself. And how liberating that is.

"And now?" I ask, surprised when my own voice comes out of those unfamiliar lips.

Clara grins. "Now you play the ghost." She opens the door and peers out into the corridor. Gestures to me to follow. "We'll take the back way," she says. "It comes out beside the stables. From there you can—" The stairs creak loudly. "Inside." She shoves me back in the direction of the room.

Before I can get anywhere close to the door, a figure appears at the top of the staircase. Will Browning. He stops in surprise at the sight of me.

"Lucy. You look… unrecognisable."

Clara plants a hand on her hip. "Thought you wanted nothing to do with all this."

"Well." His eyes meet mine, before he looks back at Clara. "I thought if Lucy was determined to go out there tonight, I ought to be the one to go with her." He scratches his neck. "For safety and all."

Clara gives a snort of laughter. "Safety. I see."

Browning ignores her. "What do you say?" he asks me. The intensity of his gaze makes something heat in my chest. And when, I think with an ache, was the last time I felt that way while looking into my husband's eyes?

I push the thought of Tom away. Tonight, I am the Green Lady. And I can put Lucy's troubles aside.

"I'd like that," I manage. I glance at Clara. "For safety and all."

"Good." Before Clara can respond, Will has scooped up my arm and is leading me down the passage. Flames dance within the lamps and make the walls seem alive.

After several paces of stilted silence, he gives me a begrudging half-smile. "Two weeks ago, I practically had to beg you to perform the Green Lady. Now look at you."

The staircase creaks beneath our feet. "You're not angry?"

"That would be rather hypocritical of me, don't you think?"

I don't answer. Don't want to upset the delicate truce we're balancing on.

He guides me to the back entrance of the Commercial and holds open the door for me. I peek out to check the alley is empty. The earthy smell of horses and hay floats out from the stables beside us. Though it's less than an hour from midnight, the wind is still warm, carrying the steady wail of cicadas. At the end of the lane, a wider street unfolds. A carriage rattles past, making a dog bark loudly. I draw in a breath and press myself against the wall of the hotel.

Will's eyes move over me. "I must admit, you do look rather otherwordly. And rather beautiful."

I swallow, heart knocking hard. And I realise at once that I have no thought of what I'm doing. How on earth do you go about playing the ghost?

"What do I do?" I blurt. The moment the words are out, I regret them. Because I'm sure Will is looking for any excuse to bundle me back upstairs and get me away from this madness. But he says:

"That's up to you. Although I've found it works best to be discreet. A fleeting glimpse can be the most powerful thing of all. It's often what most sends our imaginations racing."

"And it works?" I ask hesitantly. "I'll not be recognised?"

"It works," says Will. "Because people want it to work. They want to see ghosts. They want that bit of magic in their lives."

I smile faintly. I want that too. I remind myself that I barely recognised my own reflection. A fleeting glimpse of the Green Lady and no one will know who she truly is.

I see a small smile on Will's lips too. He understands, I realise. He understands this need to be someone new. To make trouble. To seek magic.

"Will you wait here?" I ask.

"Of course."

"For safety."

He grins, the dimple appearing in his cheek. "For safety."

I take slow, steady steps towards the main street, my heart pounding in my ears. I will hover at the end of the alleyway, I decide. Tempt passers-by with a peep at the Green Lady before she disappears, leaving them with more questions than answers. Mysterious. Fleeting. Appearing in shadows, like Springheeled Jack.

I peer out at the street beyond me. There is the bank, the dispensary, the cobbler's. A street I must have walked a hundred times or more. And yet tonight it feels different. Feels as though I'm seeing it through someone else's eyes.

I stand with one shoulder pressed to the wall of the alley, letting the wind breathe into the folds of my dress. Streetlamps flicker, making the shadows move.

For a long time, no one notices me. A well-dressed couple strides past with their heads down; a man rides by on horseback. Others howl with laughter as they stumble from the tavern, with not so much as a glance in my direction. I'm too hidden. Always, I'm too hidden.

I feel as though I truly am a ghost; like I'm balanced on the edge of existence, viewing the world without taking part in it. The sensation is suddenly unmooring. Because isn't that how I've lived my life since my daughter died? As though I'm existing without really living? As though I'm doing nothing more than waiting for my own death?

I don't want that anymore. Can't bear another day of it. This is not what playing the ghost was supposed to be about.

I step out of the alley.

Several yards away, a young woman stops walking. I feel my heart quicken. The woman is a stranger, and yet I'm suddenly terrified I will be seen for what I am; a living, breathing human.

What does it matter that I'm wearing this old-fashioned gown, that my face is made up beyond recognition? Surely people will just see a misguided woman standing in the shadows, trying to escape reality.

I fight the urge to turn and run. To call the whole thing a mistake.

I think of the curtain shifting in the back of the tavern; enough to convince Clyde he saw the Green Lady. I think of the men at Buckley's claim, desperate to speak with his ghost. And I hold my ground. Because perhaps it's our curiosity, or our desperate need for proof that death isn't the end, but there's just something about us that makes us want to see a ghost.

I continue to stare. To watch. Motionless.

The woman's eyes widen.

Yes, these people want to see spirits. Perhaps this generation's obsession with the other side has begun to twist our thinking. And instead of rationality, our minds leap straight to the fantastical.

Two knocks for yes; well of course that's a spirit trying to speak.

And an eerie figure in a Renaissance dress? No question that she's a ghost, brought out on our ships to terrorise the living.

I look past the young woman with a vacant, dead stare. I am burning with curiosity, with impatience, waiting to see what she does next. How does one behave when they see the walking dead?

There is no screaming, no running, just an almost imperceptible intake of breath. She edges backwards, as though afraid I might give chase.

But no, the Green Lady does not chase. The Green Lady does not engage. This motionless, unblinking stare, I know instinctively, will be the most unnerving. Most likely to have the woman racing home to tell this story in a breathless, half-whisper.

She turns and hurries away, leaving me to slip back into the alley. "Did you see her?" I hear her say to people I cannot see. "Tell me you saw her."

But no one else is to see the Green Lady tonight. Let them wonder, let them talk. I glide back to the hotel where Browning is waiting.

"Well?" His eyes catch the shine of the lanterns above the stables.

Without a thought, I throw my arms around him. Exhilarated. Alive. Realising at once the indecency of what I've done, I pull back. His hands linger against the side of my ribs for a moment before releasing me.

I can't hold back an enormous smile, well aware of how foolish my grin must look, dressed as the dead. "There'll be talk, I'm sure," I say. "A woman saw me. Just for a second. Enough to give her a good scare."

He gives a short chuckle. "Well done." He's standing close to me; too close, yes I know that. But I'm hovering on the border of another world, and I can't find the need to step away. Right now, I'm someone else, and my guilt will not find me.

Somewhere distant, the diggers' guns are emptied into the sky. Tonight, I barely react as the gunfire splits the night. Tonight, it feels like nothing more than an echo.

Browning is the one who finally shifts, putting a little more space between us. He clears his throat, hands in his pockets. "Well. I'm glad you got that out of your system."

And though I say nothing to upturn the fragile peace between us, I know this won't be the last time the Green Lady walks the streets of Castlemaine.

CHAPTER EIGHT

Dysentery...[is] now stalking abroad through the diggings. ... Death follows death in quick succession."

The *Argus*
Melbourne
March 1852

It's morning and Tom's side of the bed is empty. No doubt he's still out guarding the claim. I'm glad of it. Glad I didn't wake up eye to sin-filled eye with him.

I crossed no line, I tell myself. Kept Will Browning at a safe distance. Mostly. But at the back of my mind, I know the truth – he was the one mindful of keeping his distance. And that distance was anything but safe.

I think of Tom camped out by the claim, sleeping under an impossibly vast sky, with nothing but a sleeping mat and his old worn coat. The thought of his discomfort, his anxiety, make my guilt come to life. He was out protecting our land last night, while I was busy creating a public nuisance, and fawning over some dashing young playwright. There is fear for Tom there too – are there truly bushrangers in the forest outside Castlemaine? Sneaking onto the diggings at night and rifling through the claims? I hate the thought of Tom being in their line of fire. Can't shake off that irrational dread that Fred Buckley's death was not an accident – and that perhaps my husband might meet the same fate. I know if Tom caught someone robbing his claim, he would confront them. Finding success means too much to him not to do so.

I climb out of bed and splash my face at the washbin, collecting up the cloth I used last night to wipe away the remnants of the Green Lady. Straight into the laundry it will go, so I might scrub away my secrets. But I find myself squeezing it between my fingers. Find my eyes closing and my thoughts gliding back to Will Browning. The feel of his fingers grazing my ribs. His gaze burning into mine. I open my eyes hurriedly, trying to anchor myself in reality.

I dress and hurry out to the kitchen, flinging the cloth into a bag of laundry.

I fry up some bacon and slap it between two pieces of yesterday's bread, then trudge out to Forest Creek.

When I arrive at the claim, I find Leo at the windlass, Tom's sleeping mat rolled up on the side of the hole. Leo unhooks the bucket and nods in greeting, hollering down into the shaft to announce my arrival.

I tense as Tom's mud-streaked face appears over the edge of the claim. I feel as though everything I've done is visible in my eyes. He climbs the last few rungs of the ladder and dusts the loose earth from his knees.

"Did you have any trouble last night?" I ask, struggling to keep my voice level.

Tom waves a fly away from his face. His eyes are underlined in shadows of exhaustion. "Didn't see nothing."

"I reckon he was sleeping all night," Leo grins. "Snoring away while them bolters had the pick of the place." He upends the bucket of earth into the cradle and I see tiny flecks of gold glitter within the soil. Once upon a time, those golden flashes felt like magic. But I've long learned they're not enough to change a life.

Tom chuckles. "It's your turn tonight, you bastard."

I hand him the sandwich, catching a glimpse of the revolver tucked into the pocket of his trousers. "How long are you planning on doing this?" I ask. "Guarding the claim at night?"

He unwraps the bread and takes a bite. "As long as we need to," he says, mouth half full. "I'm sorry, Luce. I hate leaving you alone at night. I wouldn't do it if it weren't so important."

"It's all right. I understand." I can't look at him.

"You keep the door locked?"

"Of course."

"Good." He hands me back the cloth I wrapped the sandwich in. "I won't be home too late. I'm bloody exhausted. Thanks for breakfast."

I mumble a quick goodbye, then escape the diggings before my guilt swallows me whole.

I'm halfway to Pennyweight Flat before I realise I'm going to visit Elsie.

The cemetery is ringed by trees, a stillness over the place that feels immune to the distant echo of shovels and cradles.

Most of the children's graves are sparsely marked; small wooden crosses, or piles of rocks, weather-worn dolls and toy soldiers standing at attention. In the valley beyond the cemetery, the diggings of Moonlight Flat scar the landscape. With row upon row of neatly dug shafts, it looks for all the world like another graveyard.

I sit on the earth beside the tiny circle of stones that marks the place my daughter lies. The late morning is hot and still, insects hissing in the long grass that hems the cemetery.

In the first few weeks after Elsie's death, Tom and I always visited her grave together. An unspoken agreement that we needed each other to keep from falling. That this was not something we could do alone.

I can't place exactly when that changed. Can't remember the first time I visited the cemetery alone. I only know it's become far more comforting this way.

Tom and I have never spoken about Elsie's death, not really. Before the camp fever upended our own lives, the outbreak was all we talked about. Each night, Tom returned home with another story about who had fallen ill, and what they'd been doing before the pains and fever took root. We traced their movements like detectives, avoiding the shops and markets and taverns where we knew the sick had been. Soon, there were too many places to be able to avoid them all.

We slept with Elsie in the bed between us, and I refused to let her crawl on the earthen floor of our tent. When I unwittingly passed a man vomiting in the creek, I took off my dress and petticoats before stepping into our tent. Burned them in a bonfire in front of the door, standing there in broad daylight in nothing but my shift.

In the face of so much death, I felt utterly powerless. Tom and I prayed ourselves into exhaustion, the weight of the situation pressing down on us from all sides. The tears of loss and physical pain that drifted across the diggings were sounds I learned, out of necessity, to ignore. Barely a day went by without us hearing of another death.

By the time the sickness reached our little family, it almost felt inevitable. But I told myself Elsie's fever was just warmth from the fire. The speckled rash spreading over her skin was insect bites, or prickly heat, or my frenzied imagination. Reality was far too brutal to accept.

After she was gone, Tom and I stopped speaking of camp fever. Stopped making plans, or thinking of the future, or burning our clothing when we'd been near the sick. It was easier to sit by the fire in silence, fingers intertwined. Every possible topic of conversation felt so trivial, so wasteful. My grief was a gaping abyss; Tom's fingers between my own the only thing stopping me from falling away entirely. I took the chalk and brandy potion I'd given Elsie and flung it into the fire. Waited for the fever to take me too.

All too quickly, Tom was back at the claim, and I was left with an empty tent and an anger taking root beside my grief. Though I tried my best not to, there was more than a small part of me that blamed Tom for our loss. Blamed him for bringing us to this place. Blamed him for wooing me back in Horley, for infecting me with his blind optimism and for fooling me into coming here. Why did we go searching for riches when we already had everything we needed? How different it would have been if we'd raised our child on the immaculate grounds of Hartwell Manor. If she'd been born within solid walls, instead of in a windblown tent, with mosquitoes in the doorway and rain puddles at the foot of the bed. If she'd been baptised in a church, instead of a clearing beside the creek.

My anger at Tom never feels more acute than when I'm here at the cemetery. Is that why I came here today, I wonder distantly? Because I need to feel that anger? Because that rage will dilute my guilt over the ghost hoaxing a little? The guilt over these thoughts of Will Browning that refuse to lie down.

I stand up, dusting the earth from my skirts. I can't stay here with my daughter if I'm to let my thoughts stray away from my family. Sending a silent goodbye to Elsie, I trudge back down the hill towards town.

Tom is home early the next evening. "No need to cook tonight," he tells me. "Meg and Richard are having us for supper."

I stiffen. "No Tom, I can't."

"I already told them we'd be there."

"Well, tell them something's come up."

Tom sighs. "I don't understand this, Luce. You and Meg were the best of friends."

He understands it. I know he does. I've told him my reasons for pulling away from Meg on more than one occasion. This is not a case of him not understanding. It's a case of him not wanting to discuss what needs to be discussed.

But he's clearly made up his mind. I know there's to be no arguing. And so I take off my apron and trail him out the door.

I met Meg the day we arrived on the goldfields, and we became friends almost instantly. A handful of years older than me, and a currency lass born and raised in the colonies, she became the guide I so desperately needed. New wife, new immigrant, mother-to-be. In their tiny tent next to ours, she lived crammed in with her husband and four children, but seemed to sail through the experience with grace. She taught me to cook damper, and to pickle the mutton so nothing went to waste. Showed me how to turn the flour bags into baby clothes, and how to make a veil out of poplin to keep the swirling dust from my eyes. I would hardly have survived that first year if it weren't for Meg and her seemingly endless supply of knowledge.

When the camp fever barrelled through, it took two of Meg's sons a few weeks after it took Elsie. Our first instincts were to lean on each other, and on the other lost women who had buried their children on Pennyweight Flat. We found some fragile sense of comfort huddled in the corners of each other's tents, stumbling through our losses with cups of smoke-scented tea. All our stories were so similar; fear and denial, and the fever taking its young victims so quickly it was as though our legs had been kicked out from beneath us. A small blessing, we told each other over and over, that our children had suffered just days, instead of weeks or months. A tiny, hollow blessing.

But then those mothers, with their lukewarm tea and their suffocating sadness, they began to blame themselves. *Should have burned the clothes, should have given him more water, could have moved away…*

I stepped away from those tentative friendships, forged in tragedy. I couldn't handle the heaviness, the reminders that came with them. I tried to keep hold of my friendship with Meg. I knew that without her in my life, the loneliness would strangle me. But enter her tent and I was back in those bleak days of our shared grief. Any small glimmers of light I'd begun to see were immediately extinguished. And I made the choice to step away.

I miss her, sometimes deeply. We carried each other through both the births and deaths of our children, and I assumed, once, that that would bind us together for life. But being around Meg draws me back into a time I can't bear to face. When we finally moved away from the tent beside theirs, I allowed myself to cry with relief.

And now here we are, following the creek to the camp in which we lived for more than two years; among them, the worst months of my life. My stomach is knotted and I feel uncomfortably hot, despite the cool wind whipping up the dust.

The sun is beginning to sink, silhouetting trees with blinding orange light. The creek is still alive with men and the clatter and sigh of the cradles.

Tom gives me a smile that feels too broad. "I'm glad you're here," he tells me.

I wonder then if this evening is his doing; did he coax Meg and Richard into inviting us tonight? Is this about his disapproval of my friendship with Clara? Or another attempt at showing me the way to be happy?

I press my lips into a thin white line and sidestep a mound of horse dung.

Meg and Richard's son and daughter are tossing a ball to each other in front of the tent, bounding after dropped catches like hares. A campfire smoulders in front of the door, meat-scented steam rising from the pot that sits on the embers. In spite of myself, my eyes drift to the place our neighbouring tent once stood. A wattle and daub shack is in its place now, smoke puffing steadily out a crooked stone chimney.

At the sound of our footsteps, Richard emerges from their tent and tosses out greetings, a blank-faced baby tucked into his elbow. I'm reminded suddenly of how Elsie looked in Tom's arms; so fragile and doll-like against his wide brown hands. I turn away quickly.

Out comes Meg, offering us a warm smile. Her eyes are bright and she's less painfully thin than last time I saw her. Straw-coloured tendrils of hair escape from beneath her cloth bonnet and blow across her cheeks. She pulls me into her arms, then steps back and gives my hands a squeeze. "How are you, Lucy?" There is no animosity in her voice; no anger at the way I cut her out of my life so completely. I am grateful.

"I'm… I'm well," I say, and I realise it's the truth. At least, it's beginning to be.

"I'm glad." She bends to stir the stew pot, then turns back to me. "Supper's not far off. But maybe a drink first?"

"I'd like that."

"Good. Jack!" she hollers at her son. "Come away from the creek! Get those clothes wet and you ain't got no more." She shakes her head in resignation and puts a hand to my shoulder, leading me inside. The men stay by the campfire, chatting between themselves. Meg uncorks a bottle and fills two cups, kicking at a mouse that darts beneath the table. "Here. Let's enjoy the peace while it lasts."

I sit, taking a small sip from the cup. I recognise the scent of Meg's homemade dandelion wine. The taste is at once both sweet and sour, and almost sickeningly familiar. I set the cup back down in front of me.

"How's the cottage?" Meg asks.

"The cottage is fine." I draw in a breath. "I'm sorry I haven't—"

She puts a hand to my wrist, cutting me off. "Don't apologise, Lucy. Please. There's no need." Her eyes meet mine and I see the deep understanding beneath them. "I'm just glad you're here."

I give a short smile, unsure if I can say the same. "I've missed you," I say instead.

"I've missed you too." She sips her wine. "Tom still working with that tin miner?"

"Leo. Yes."

"Any luck?"

"Enough to keep food on the table. Not much else."

"Well. You know how quickly fortunes can change out here."

It feels like a conversation we've had a thousand times. Everything feels like yesterday. Feels as though it has been minutes since I last sat in this chair, drank this wine, rather than a year. And there it is, that underlying pull of dread, inches beneath the surface. This is what has kept me away from my closest friend for so long. I feel it threatening to rise and consume me.

Because there, in that corner, is where Meg's two little boys once slept. Over there is where Elsie got into the potatoes while my back was turned and flung them across the tent like bowling balls. And there's the half-drunk bottle of chalk and brandy on the shelf, a tincture we learned the hard way does little to fight camp fever.

How can Meg and Richard continue to live in a place so haunted by memories?

We cram around the table for a supper of mutton stew, the children's creek-soaked boots tipped over by the door, and the baby asleep in a crib beside the washstand.

I try to find the comfort in this; in being around old friends. Old friends who know what we've been through. But this tent, so cluttered with chatter and life, it doesn't feel like what Tom and I have. Once we leave the chaos of Meg and Richard's home, all we will go back to is emptiness.

"Did you hear about that ghost sighting a couple of days ago?" asks Meg, making me straighten in my chair.

"A ghost sighting?" I repeat.

"Apparently it was a woman in an old-fashioned dress," says Meg. "Just standing there behind the tavern or something. Jenny from the grocer's was talking about it the other morning."

I try not to let the smile show on my face.

"Lucy is starring in a ghosty play," Tom announces.

I look at him in surprise. "How do you know it's a ghosty play?"

"Seen your little book lying on the table," he reminds me. "*The Lady of Fyvie*, by Will Browning."

"Oh yes," grins Meg, "Will Browning. That's that fancy fellow who started up the theatre troupe. I didn't know you were a part of that, Lucy."

She leans towards me conspiratorially. "I've seen that Mr Browning about the place. Don't you think he's just ever so handsome?"

I garble something that's not really anything, relieved when the baby interrupts with a shriek.

"Sorry," says Meg, going to the cradle. "I hoped he might sleep through supper."

"He never sleeps through anything," announces Meg's daughter, Alice.

I feel Tom trying to catch my eye. Keep my eyes on my plate. Tension gathers in my shoulders. I take another mouthful of wine, but it makes me feel worse.

"Did you read any of it?" I ask him under the baby's squalling. "The play?" I don't want him knowing I'm playing the part of the Green Lady. Not yet, at least. It feels safer to keep it a secret.

Will people make the connection when I step onto stage dressed as a ghost? I know it likely. Once I reveal myself, the mystery will be gone, and the hoaxing will have to end. But this knowledge only makes me more eager to play the ghost again.

"Didn't read any of it," Tom says. "Just the cover. Why?"

I shake my head dismissively.

I try to let that piece of knowledge settle me. Try to focus on the thrill of the Green Lady being spoken of, rather than the dread this tent is dredging up within me.

"Good for you, Lucy," says Richard. "Very brave of you getting on stage like that. We'll all have to come and watch."

Tom makes a show of squeezing my hand.

"I heard there's a woman up in town holding séances in her cottage," says Meg, plugging the baby's mouth with a knotted cloth pacifier. "Jenny said her sister went up there and they tried that spirit rapping."

"The mediums sometimes hollow out the walls," I say. "Hide people in there to make the rapping sounds."

Tom raises his eyebrows. "How on earth do you know that?"

I shrug. "Just heard it somewhere." I take another mouthful of dandelion wine, swallowing down the memories that arrive with it. But I can't get them down quick enough. There we all are, sitting around the shared campfire in front of our tents, wrapped in blankets and swatting away flies among the shrieks and laughter of three lost children.

And there is the time when Tom was everything and more to me; a time when we'd fall asleep each night with hands and legs intertwined, the feel of his heart beating beneath my fingers somehow assuring me we'd survive.

"Stop it, Jack!" Alice wails at her brother, the sound making me jump. "Ma, he's kicking me!"

I get to my feet almost instinctively. Mumble something about relieving myself and lurch out into the open air.

Meg's tent is stifling. Pulling me back down to a hell I've only just managed to poke my head out of. And before I can make sense of what I'm doing, I begin to walk. Away from the tent. Away from the diggings.

I'm beginning to see my methods of coping could use a little improvement.

I stride back into town, glancing constantly over my shoulder to see if I've been followed. No sign of Tom. How long will it take them to discover I've run off like a petulant child? I can't manage more than a small tug of shame.

I've walked with no purpose beyond escaping, and I have little thought of where I should go. I can't bear the idea of going home. The memories Tom and I have created there are hardly more pleasant than the memories trapped in Meg and Richard's tent.

I stop momentarily outside the boarding house. Consider going upstairs to hunt down Clara. No. She is busy preparing for the opening of her shop, spending long nights with a needle and thread in hand. I've already interrupted her once this week to have her magic me into the Green Lady. Not that she needed much convincing.

I keep walking. There is the Commercial. And yes, I'm fairly sure that somewhere in my mind, I knew all along that this was where I was going to end up.

I look down at my flat, mud-streaked skirts. Try to bash the creases out of them. I can still smell woodsmoke on my skin. But I don't care. Not tonight. I walk into the tavern without a second thought.

The bar is quiet, and I feel something sink inside me when I see no sign of Will. My eyes drift to the staircase that leads to the lodgings before I hurriedly look away. I might have eradicated my nerves over stepping into the Commercial but waltzing up to a man's room is still far beyond me.

I take myself to the unaccompanied ladies' room. Sit in the corner, sipping from a glass of whisky. The room is quiet and softly lit, and a gentle piano melody floats in from the main bar. As the liquor slides down my throat, I feel a little of the tension inside me drift away. There is a newness to this place Meg's tent doesn't have. The Commercial, somewhere I've only just discovered the courage to enter, makes me think of the future, instead of the past. And there's a newness, too, to the woman I am when I'm here. She is not the most decent of women, I see that all too clearly. I see my mistreatment of Tom and Meg, and the childish rebellion of ghost hoaxing all laid out in front of me. But my time in Castlemaine has taught me that so much of life is mere survival. And right now, this person is who I need to be to survive.

So there's been talk of the Green Lady sighting. I've rattled the place, just as I hoped. Meek, invisible Lucy has made people talk. At least, the woman I pretended to be has.

Laughter floats out from the billiards room across the hall. Familiar laughter. I pick up my glass and go to investigate.

Charles and Matthew are dancing around the billiards table with cues in their hands. Charles looks up as I hover in the doorway.

"Evening, Mrs Earnshaw."

I smile. "It's Lucy."

"Come in, come in, Lucy." Matthew ushers me through the door. From his brassy voice and the half-filled glasses on the edge of the billiards table, I can tell they've been in their cups for hours. "Don't be shy. Here." He shoves the cue into my hand. "You may as well take my shot. Charlie's already wiping the floor with me."

I smile, holding the cue back out to him. "I don't know how to play."

Charles grins. "Neither does he."

"Come stand here." With a hand to my shoulder, Matthew positions me at the corner of the table. "This ball in this pocket. Take your time. Line it up."

I set my glass on the edge of the table beside Matthew's and copy the position I've seen the billiards players assume. My cue barely makes contact with the ball, which dribbles across the table for a few sorry inches. I grin. "I told you I didn't know how to play."

Matthew takes the cue back and executes a shot that is marginally better than mine. "Were you looking for Will? He's upstairs writing."

"Oh no," I say hurriedly. "I was just… passing." My cheeks blaze in embarrassment, but the two men barely react. And then, because I can't help myself, I drop my voice and say, "I went out playing the ghost this week. Got people talking."

Charles grins at me. "Didn't think you had it in you."

"A woman saw me in street," I tell them excitedly. "She ran away, all terrified. And the other morning, Jenny from the grocer's was talking about it…"

The men chuckle at my enthusiasm, and instead of being embarrassed, I'm glad to have entertained them.

"So," says Matthew, "when will we be seeing the Green Lady again?"

"I don't know," I admit. "Will wasn't all that happy about it. I don't think he wants me to do it again. And we need to use his room to get ready."

Charles snorts. "Miserable sod's probably just wishing it were him out there causing trouble."

I smile.

"You know Will's not the only one with a private room," Matthew tells me with a wink. "Why don't you and Clara come by tomorrow night? I'll clear out and let you use my room. You can give this town their ghost again."

The darkness is thick when I let myself back into the cottage. In the muted glow of the lamp, I make out the inky bulk of my husband sitting at the table. One side of his face is lit with candlelight, the other bathed in shadow. For a rigid moment, we eye each other without speaking.

"Where in hell did you go?" he says finally. "I've been looking everywhere for you."

I almost laugh at that. I was hardly hidden away, whacking billiard balls around the table in one of the town's biggest public houses. Tom clearly did not even think to look for me at the Commercial. I'm infinitely relieved, of course, that he chose not to.

"I'm sorry," I murmur.

"You've been drinking. I can smell it on you."

I don't answer.

Tom's voice sparks suddenly. "How could you do that to Meg, when she—"

"I told you I couldn't go out there," I hiss. "I told you it was too much. But you always seem to know what's best for me, don't you. You always seem to know better."

Tom sighs heavily. He slumps back in his chair and picks at something underneath his fingernail. I grip the edge of the table, listening to the lamp hiss in the stillness. My head is beginning to ache.

"It's been more than a year, Lucy," Tom says finally.

My heart jumps because this is as close as he's come in months to speaking of our loss. *More than a year since what?*, I want to push. I want to hear him speak of our daughter. I can't remember the last time I heard him say Elsie's name. But he falls silent.

"And so?" I say bitterly. "I ought to just forget?"

Tom looks out the window into the dark garden. He rubs his stubble, not looking at me. "You ought to…" Another sigh. "Richard and Meg, they've carried on. Their new son…"

I stare him down. "And is that what you want, Tom? A new son?"

He exhales sharply. "Of course it is."

"Fine." I take off my bonnet and fling it onto the chair. "Fine. I'm here, aren't I? Do as you wish."

I stride into the bedroom and crawl onto the bed in my skirts and boots. Stare into the darkness. Tom enters the room and I feel the bed shift as he sits on the edge. His breathing is loud and rhythmic. Indecision? Isn't this what he wanted? His wife compliant and willing? Ready to give him that precious new son?

He turns suddenly, lurches, lowering himself over me. He grips a fistful of my skirts and yanks them to my waist. His hand finds the laces of my drawers, and he fumbles for a moment with the knot. His hot fingers reach beneath the waistband and I swallow my sharp inhalation. Resist the urge to pull away.

Tom releases me suddenly. He rolls over, back to me. "Go to sleep," he mumbles, letting the silence settle heavily around us.

CHAPTER NINE

"Night at the diggings is the characteristic time; murder here – murder there – revolvers cracking – blunderbusses bombing ... one man groaning with a broken leg – another shouting because he couldn't find his way to his hole, and a third equally vociferous because he has tumbled into one – this man swearing – another praying – a party of bacchanals chanting various ditties to different time and tune, or rather minus both."

Ellen Clacy
A Lady's Visit to the Gold Diggings of Australia
1852

Forest Creek, I say when I get to Matthew's room the next night. This is where I want the Green Lady to be seen. It's the diggings I want to terrorise. For this is the place the holds the heart of my grief, the place that has Tom in its grip, the place where my daughter was stolen from me. I want to burn it to the ground.

I waited until Tom was snoring lightly to slip out of bed and dress, before making my way to the Commercial. He has always been a heavy sleeper, and I know I'll be able to creep back into the cottage in the early hours, leaving him oblivious to my adventures.

It's almost eleven, and Matthew's room is hung with cigar smoke. He and Charles are halfway through a bottle of whisky; opposite each other in matching armchairs, glasses in one hand and cigars in the other.

I sit beside the unlit fireplace while Clara and her makeup brushes turn me into a Scottish wraith. The delicate folds of the Green Lady's dress sigh against my body.

"Forest Creek?" Clara repeats. "That's miles away."

"*A* mile," I say. Maybe a little more, but she won't debate the issue. I can't imagine she's spent much time in the diggings. "People are already speaking of the first sighting," I remind her. "It'd really get them talking if the Green Lady was seen out among the mining claims. Imagine how mysterious she'd look out there."

Matthew eyes me with a grin. "You've created a monster, Clara. A *monster.*" He howls with laughter. Charles, after a second of deliberation, decides to join in.

"Keep your bloody voices down," Clara hisses. "You noisy bastards want to give the game away?"

"Where's Will?" Charles asks, still chuckling mindlessly. He grinds his cigar into an ashtray on the tea table. "Didn't think he'd be one to miss a little hoaxing."

Clara dusts powder over my cheeks. "Lucy says he's being funny about the whole thing."

"He's working tonight anyway," Matthew tells us. "Writing his new play."

Clara raises her dark eyebrows as she presses the lid back onto the jar of powder. "Can't imagine him getting any work done with you two carrying on in the next room."

Charles lurches to his feet and pounds a fist against the wall. "Will! Come on out, you prickly bastard! Don't pretend you don't love a good scare."

"Don't," I murmur, too softly to be heard. But while I know Will won't be pleased I'm playing the ghost again, I can't deny there's a part of me that's desperate to see him. When the door clicks open and he pokes his head inside the room, my stomach turns over in response.

He shakes his head at Charles. "What in hell—" His eyes fall to me. "Ah." He takes in the wide sweep of the Green Lady's gown. "I thought you were done with all this."

I hold his gaze. "I didn't say that."

"The Green Lady will be seen on the diggings tonight," Clara announces, swanning past him as she unpins my hair. It tumbles over my shoulders.

"The diggings?" he repeats. "Lucy, that's madness."

But the Green Lady makes me bold. "I wasn't asking for your permission."

Will opens his mouth, but says nothing, silenced by my sudden audacity. I don't miss the smile Clara tries to hide behind her hand.

"It's dangerous," Will says finally. "Walking among all those holes in the ground."

"Stay to the outside of the tents and you won't fall. I lived out there for more than two years."

But the danger, it's there all right. Because even though Tom is fast asleep in bed tonight, Leo is out at their claim with his eyes open for thieves. Bushrangers, bolters. And perhaps a ghost or two. Talented as Clara is with a makeup brush, I doubt the disguise will fool my husband's close friend.

But I want that danger. I want that thrill. It's part of what drew me to hoaxing in the first place. Even the thought of there being bushrangers out in the forest is not enough to deter me. Because this rush of fear and exhilaration makes me feel alive.

Will looks at me for a moment without speaking. If he's going to be angry, so be it. Acceding to him, giving in, and being what he wants me to be – where can that lead? Nowhere, while I wear Tom's ring on my finger. But playing the ghost; that leads me to a place that's dizzying in its excitement. A place where my pain and frustration is blissfully distant.

"Let's go, Lucy," Clara cuts in. "It's already past eleven."

Will's eyes dart to Charles and Matthew, then he looks back at Clara and me. "The two of you are going out there alone?"

"Can hardly take these animals with us," Clara says, waving a hand in the direction of the men. "We'll be fishing them out of the mining claims."

"You're not going out to the diggings alone," Will says firmly. "Let me get my coat."

Clara bubbles with laughter. "Honestly, Will, you're so predictable." She takes a fresh glass from the shelf and fills it, perching on the arm of Matthew's chair. "Enjoy yourselves."

I get hesitantly to my feet. "You're not coming with us?"

"All the way to the diggings?" She brings her glass to her lips. "Wouldn't dream of it."

Will strides from the room without another word, leaving me to follow dazedly. For a fleeting moment, I felt in control, but in the wake of Browning's anger and Clara's total orchestration of the situation, I feel like I'm being pulled along in riptide. But I have neither the will nor the inclination to protest a walk out to the diggings alone with Browning. My heart is thundering at the prospect.

He disappears into his own room for a moment, returning with a sack jacket and a large black greatcoat, along with a lamp he has taken from the table. "Put this on," he says stiffly, handing me the coat. I slip it over my shoulders and follow him out of the hotel.

I keep my head down and my collar pulled up as we make our way out of town. Even in the darkness, heat is pressing down on the land, but I wrap myself in Browning's greatcoat, letting the sleeves fall over my hands. His rosewater scent clings to the wool and I draw in a long breath to drink it in.

The lamp in his hand does little to cut through the night as we leave the streetlamps behind. Sparse clouds drift in front of the moon. The horizon is glowing with the campfires of the diggings, but they're too far away to offer much light. The bush on either side of us rustles and sighs, alive with unseen animals.

We walk close together, our shoulders brushing against each other's. I glance his way, but his eyes are fixed to the path ahead, jaw set firmly.

"Are we going to walk in silence all the way there?" I ask finally.

He eyes me. "I don't think you should be doing this."

"I know you don't. But you volunteered to come out here, remember?"

"Well. I could hardly let you and Clara go alone. What kind of man would that make me?"

"Is that why you don't want me to play the ghost?" I ask. "Because you think it dangerous?"

"It is dangerous."

I say nothing. Our footsteps crunch loudly on the dry dirt road. Will lets out a sigh. But then he says, "Charles tells me you're a better billiards player than Matthew."

I eye him. "Apparently that's not difficult."

He gives a short chuckle. Looks down at his feet. "I'm sorry I missed you," he says after a moment. "I would have come down if I'd known you were there."

I feel a smile on the edge of my lips. Feel a little of the tension drain from my shoulders. "Can I take that to mean you forgive me for going hoaxing?"

He returns my smile tentatively. "Let's not get carried away."

I pull his coat tighter around me. "They said you've been writing?"

"Yes. A new play."

"About the supernatural?"

"Not this time. My time here has inspired me to write something a little more realist. Something a little more challenging. An exploration of how we're shaped by the natural world around us."

I look ahead to the firelit plain of the diggings where the trees have been torn from the earth. "I would have thought rather the natural world is shaped by us."

Will hums in thought, shifting the lantern from one hand to the other. "Yes, in a way. But don't you think the harshness of this land strengthens us? Makes us capable of more than we would otherwise have been?"

I almost laugh at the searing truth of his words. Look at me, in the Green Lady's dress, walking shoulder to shoulder with a man who is not my husband. Here in this new life of mine, I'm certainly capable of more than I once was.

I've been shaped, I suppose, by the world I'm in. After all, it's this town, this land, these infested, sun-bleached goldfields that were supposed to give us everything that I blame for all I've lost.

"You're right," I say, and I'm glad for the cordiality we seem to have rediscovered.

From out of the dark comes music; an undulating vocal melody, sung in Irish beside the diggers' campfire. Though I don't understand its meaning, the sadness is inescapable. I can feel it in my chest.

I first heard the Irish keening days after we arrived on the goldfields. A funeral of sorts, Meg explained. A way for the Irish to honour their dead.

"Do you hear it?" I ask softly. "The keening?"

"Yes. It's very beautiful. Very haunting."

And it's this I will focus on tonight; the otherworldly atmosphere the singing creates. Not the memories that come with it. How many nights did I lie in our tent, listening to the Irish mourn their dead through song? Those plaintive voices became the sound of my own grief.

But not tonight. The Green Lady's costume shields me from those memories. Tonight, the keening just creates a world in which people are willing to believe in ghosts.

It's not just the Green Lady's costume that shields me from the memories, I realise as I walk. It's Will Browning's presence, and the way he drags my mind out of the past. When I'm with him, I'm so intrigued by the present that I don't feel so trapped by what has come before.

"It must have been a challenging life out here," he says.

"In some ways." I keep my voice light in an attempt to scramble past the subject.

"Do you miss England?" he asks.

"Sometimes. In parts." I miss not knowing the hollow ache of losing a child. But I don't miss scrubbing dishes at Hartwell Manor, or winters so grey you can feel it in your bones. And nothing in England ever thrilled me as much as sneaking out here to the diggings with Will Browning, about to play the ghost. "And you?" I ask.

As he opens his mouth to speak, an owl lets out a hoarse shriek that sounds like someone's just been done in.

He smiles wryly. "I miss not fearing for my life whenever I go for a stroll."

I laugh. "It's just an owl. We used to hear them all the time from our tent. I'd rather be strolling out here than walking through London at night. All those dark little streets and alleys. Bet there's far worse things than owls hiding in there."

He grins. "Why do you think people believed in Springheeled Jack for so long?"

"*Mysteries of London* was my favourite Penny Blood," I tell him. "I was reading it right up until we came out here."

He raises his eyebrows. "Didn't pick you as a Penny Blood reader."

"I used to steal them from my older brother when I was a girl. I'd read them before bed and scare myself silly."

He laughs. "I loved them too. Although I have to say, *Mysteries* went downhill somewhat after they changed authors. You haven't missed much."

I smile to myself, imagining Will as a boy, hiding under the covers to read Penny Bloods, just as I used to do. Perhaps we're not from such different worlds after all.

"Are you angry with me?" I dare to ask.

He gives a half-shrug. "It's like you said, you don't need my blessing."

"That doesn't really answer my question."

"I just don't want to see you get into trouble," he says. "But if this is something you need to do…"

Something you need to do.

What does Will Browning imagine it is that made me need to play the ghost? I've told him nothing about Elsie. Nothing about the grief that was pulling me below the surface until I found the Green Lady. I don't want him to look at me with pity. But perhaps I've already said too much.

His eyes on me feel suddenly piercing, and I have to look away. "It's nice to be someone else for a while," I say, not wanting to go further.

"Even if she's dead?"

I laugh a little. "Yes, even if she'd dead."

His hand brushes against mine as we walk, and for a fleeting second, our fingers intertwine. So brief I can't tell if I imagined it. I feel my body pull instinctively towards him. Feel a tug deep inside me of something I distantly recognise as desire.

How dare you?, says that faraway part of me that is still Lucy. But the part of me that is someone else is winning. Whatever this woman does, it doesn't seem to matter. When the sun comes up, it will all be relegated back to the world of myth and fairy tale.

A loud argument crashes through the melody of the keening. The shouting is coming from somewhere near the creek. I strain my ears, but I can't make out the words.

"Is it always like this?" Will asks. "Are the miners always so angry?"

"People are on edge," I say. "There's been a lot of thefts lately."

"Thefts? Among the miners?"

"No one's sure. Word is it could be bushrangers."

He frowns. "I think we ought to leave."

"No." The word is out before I can even think about it. My tone leaves no room for argument.

Will nods faintly. I can tell he has witnessed something behind my eyes. Something darker than he was expecting.

He puts down the lamp and takes a step closer to me. Folds my hand in both of his. I see a new seriousness in his eyes. "Be careful, Lucy, won't you. If anything were to happen to you…" He swallows. "I would feel horribly responsible."

I nod. "I'll be careful."

I go to step away, but he keeps my hand in his for another moment. Gives my fingers a gentle squeeze. A bolt of energy tightens my shoulders.

I didn't believe it. Not really. Didn't believe that a man like Will Browning might be drawn to a woman like me. Didn't believe he could find a single thing among my stumbling sadness that might make him look at me twice. But in the way his thumb glides over my knuckles; in the way he looks at me as though he's staring into my soul, I know that Will sees more in me than I see in myself. At once, I'm terrified; I'm flattered; I'm grateful. And I want to take this nervous excitement that is charging through my body, and use it to play the ghost.

I slip the coat from my shoulders and hand it to him without a word. I breathe deep and force myself to move slowly. A ghost among the wilderness. I keep myself close to the thick white trunks on the edge of the diggings, giving stray eyes nothing but a hint of a flowing green skirt.

No one is close, but I see clusters of men around the campfires in the barren plains among the claims. I think of all those nights I spent in our little tent out here, falling asleep to the distant laughter of men at their fires. Listening to them curse and chatter in the strange, wide accent of the currency lads. Soothing Elsie's tears each night she was torn from sleep by the emptying of the guns.

I tried, in those first two years. I tried so hard. Tried to share Tom's enthusiasm, his drive, his belief that this was the right thing to do. I told myself it was only a matter of time before he came home with those nuggets in his pocket, and we'd have the riches we craved.

I was ignoring reality long before I pulled on the Green Lady's gown.

I continue my walk around the rim of the diggings, past campfires surrounded by miners; past men on sleeping mats, their hands folded over their pistols. Careful to keep my distance from Tom and Leo's claim. Careful to stay away from Meg and Richard's tent.

No one looks up as I pass. No one pauses in conversation or turns at the crackle of twigs. My footsteps are too careful, too silent, and the moonlight is not falling the right way to light the mint-coloured folds of my dress.

I make out the figure of a man up ahead, back to me as he pisses against a tree. He'll see me, I realise, when he turns around. What will he make of me?

I take a step closer, partially hiding myself behind the silky trunk of a gum tree. I position myself for full effect, the ethereal fabric of my skirts whipping against the bark.

Patience.

As the man turns back towards the camp, he stops walking. And he sees a ghost.

"Christ Almighty," I hear him hiss. He stumbles backwards, shoulder bumping against a tree in his shock. And then he is off into the dark, without looking at me again.

Before my image can be scrutinised, I grab my skirts in my fist and run into the blackness that enfolds me.

I dodge tents and trees with little more than instinct. When I am surrounded by silence, I stop running, gasping down my breath. I feel oddly exhilarated. Strangely buoyed by the knowledge of how easily I could have plummeted into an open claim. A laugh escapes me – what a dramatic end that would have been to the story of the Green Lady.

I turn in a circle, trying to get my bearings. The campfires behind me tell me I've run farther away from town, out towards where the forest thickens. I walk back in the direction of the camp. I feel as though I'm hovering somewhere between this world and the next.

The diggings are quieter now, many of the campfires reduced to embers and much of the chatter silenced. The tents dotted around the claims are dark.

On the edge of my vision, I see a flicker of light. A pinprick of white moving along the ground. So fleeting and fragile it flits in and out of my sight.

I think of the night fossickers; the men who creep out to the goldfields in the dark and dig up other people's claims by lamplight. Night fossickers were seen on Moonlight Flat the night of Fred Buckley's burial, and on several occasions since. Is this what I'm seeing?

I creep towards the lamplight and peek out from behind a tent. I need to watch. I know how rattled Tom is over these thefts. If there's a chance I can catch a glimpse of who is responsible, I have to try.

My heart thunders. Am I watching a bushranger at work? Perhaps even Fred Buckley's killer? My palms prickle with sweat.

A broad figure emerges from the earth, a lamp in hand. And as he hauls himself from the claim, the light flickers over his features.

I swallow my gasp.

Though he is dressed in black rather than his trooper's uniform, I have no trouble recognising Constable Stone.

I grip my skirts in my fist as I turn this discovery around in my head. Maybe Stone is out here in an official capacity. As part of an investigation.

Maybe not.

I take an involuntary step backwards, earth crunching beneath my boots. Stone looks up suddenly. And his eyes meet mine. Is that recognition in his gaze? Surely not. I barely know the man, and my disguise is a good one. But his eyes seem to pierce me. And as though I'm the one who has seen a ghost, I turn and race out across the diggings, back to where Browning is waiting.

When we get back to the hotel, I hurry upstairs to change, wiping off my makeup with the cloth beside the washbin. I shake off Will's insistence to walk me home and rush back to the cottage.

A part of me is desperate to tell Tom what I saw. But how could I explain what I was doing out on the diggings? Tom can never know I was ghost hoaxing in the company of another man.

I slide the key into the lock and creep inside, pulling off my dusty boots.

As I push open the bedroom door, my heart jolts. The bed is empty. Tom was asleep when I left, so he must know I've been out of the house. Has he gone out to find me?

I throw off my dress and yank the pins out of my hair. I ruffle it up, in what I hope makes it look as though I've been asleep for hours.

How long has Tom been gone? Does he know I've been out for most of the night? Or did he wake just minutes ago and notice me missing? I have no way of knowing.

With my shawl wrapped around my shoulders, I open the front door and peer out into the street.

"Tom?" My voice disappears into the night and a shiver goes through me. I know there are plenty of indecent things going on in that darkness. After all, I'm a part of them.

I go to the gate and peer into the street. Everything is still, and I can hear insects flitting around the streetlights, frogs clicking in the creek. I start at the sound of footsteps, letting out my breath at the sight of Tom emerging from the shadows. He hurries towards me.

"Lucy. Where the hell were you?"

"I… I couldn't sleep. I just went for some air. When I came back to bed, you were gone." I hold my breath, waiting for him to dispute the matter.

"Some air?" he repeats.

"Yes."

His eyes flicker over me. Does he believe me? Strangely, I can't tell. I have always been able to read him.

"You shouldn't be out this time of night," he says. "Especially not now. With all that's going on."

"I'm sorry. I didn't mean to worry you."

Tom opens his mouth, but he decides against speaking. "It's very late," he says finally. "Let's get back to bed."

"'Perhaps the Green Lady will forever walk,'" Ollie croons, staring into the distance with what I assume is supposed to be a look of deep contemplation.

We've made it to the end of rehearsal and, somehow, miraculously, the play. All without Will Browning speaking directly to me. With just three other performers in the show, I'm certain this level of snubbing takes a special kind of talent.

Maybe I'm mistaken. Maybe my new theatrical self has become too precious for her own damn good. Nonetheless, my heart is thudding when I make my way towards him as the others file off the stage.

At the sight of me, he folds his arms across his chest. "Well done, Mrs Earnshaw," he says stiffly. "You acted well today."

I blink, words dying in my throat at his brusqueness. What happened to that comfortable chatter we found on the way to Forest Creek?

"Thank you," I spit out, but there's not an ounce of gratitude in my words. I march off stage and grab my bonnet, clenching my jaw in anger. I can't help another glance back in his direction, but he's poring over his script like he's never seen anything so exciting in his whole damn life. Rage shoots through me. Am I truly so dispensable? So easy to push aside? Or is this coldness my punishment for defying him by playing the ghost?

"What happened out at Forest Creek last night?" Clara asks as we walk to the door. "Why's Will so wound up?"

I snort. "Damned if I know."

She gives me a wry smile. "These fickle theatre types are trouble. You ought to stay away from them."

Though I know she's half-joking, she's also right. I should stay away. After all, why in hell should I care if Browning is being cold to me? What I really ought to be thinking about is what I'll make for supper tonight. With not much growing in the garden beyond potatoes, it'll likely be Irish stew again.

Yes, good. This is much safer. Onions, potatoes, a little smoked meat...

"I heard some chatter about the Green Lady at the market this morning," says Clara, voice low. My thoughts about the stew disintegrate. "A ghost peering out among the mining claims. You've certainly got people talking."

"Good," I snap. Because much of my need to play the ghost is built on anger and frustration. And Will Browning is digging a hell of a lot of both up inside me right now.

I can't resist another glance over my shoulder as we leave. Will has disappeared backstage, but I can hear his footsteps clomping around on the floorboards.

Clara pushes open the door, orange dusk flooding inside. "You'll come to the shop sometime this week? Help me set things up?"

I nod. "Yes, on Thursday."

"Perfect. Shall I see you home?"

I shake my head. "I can make my own way."

I watch as she disappears back towards the boarding house. And I stand outside the theatre, caught in indecision. Because what I really want is not to return to the cottage and make another damn pot of Irish stew. It's to march back inside the theatre and demand to know why in hell Will Browning is being such a bastard. The intensity of the thought shocks me. I don't *march* anywhere, and I certainly don't *demand* anything. But maybe I should.

I shove open the door before I can change my mind. Stride back down the aisle.

Will is carrying a small tin of paint onto the stage, large swathes of painted cloth spread out at his feet. His eyes meet mine for the first time today, and somehow, infuriatingly, it drains away my resolve. Suddenly I'm tearing through my thoughts, trying to determine what I might have done wrong to make him act so distantly. What might have turned our night at Forest Creek into two hours of stilted silence.

"You're back," he says. His eyes give nothing away.

I make my way towards him, the click of my boots echoing in the empty space. The ghost light paints a frayed gold circle in the centre of the stage.

"What's this about then?" I ask, my voice far less assertive than I hoped it would be. "I thought we were all right."

He holds my gaze for a moment. "We," he repeats finally. "There is no 'we', Lucy."

I grit my teeth. "You know what I meant."

He sets down the pot of paint and looks at me with faintly apologetic eyes. "Would you like to help me?"

I open my mouth, caught off guard. "Help you with what?"

"Painting the set."

"You're doing that yourself?"

He kneels beside the paint tin and pries it open with the end of a pencil. "Just one of the challenges of starting at the bottom again. No one to do these things for me."

I hover at the foot of the stairs that lead up to the stage. Fold my arms across my chest. "I don't know anything about painting."

"Nor do I. I'm banking on the fact that no one in this town does either." He holds out a paintbrush, a wordless peace offering with the faintest of smiles.

I take my bonnet back off and put it on the floor in the corner of the stage. I take the brush, my fingers grazing his.

"Here," he says, pointing to the large sheet of calico at our feet. A neat stone wall has been outlined across it. "You can paint the bricks. I've outlined them already. They just need filling in."

I kneel beside the cloth, dipping the brush into the pot of sand-coloured paint he sets beside me.

"I had no idea you were making all this," I say, in spite of myself.

"I made Clara buy me this fabric when she put in her last order. I'm afraid it won't look quite as solid and professional as I'd like, but it ought to create something of an atmosphere at the very least." He kneels beside me, painting carefully around the hanging hooks at the top of the fabric.

"Am I painting the walls of Fyvie Castle?" I ask, tracing the outline of a turret.

"You are." He dips his brush into a pot of water. "I visited the castle as a child. And I always remembered the turrets. They felt like something straight out of a fairy tale. I made up a story about a prince who could turn into a dragon." He smiles to himself. "My imagination always was a little peculiar."

And how is it that we're back here, in this compatible comfort, talking about dragons and fairy tales and castles with turrets? I don't know, but I'm glad of it. I need this, I realise. I need this easy, warm conversation. Need conversation that makes me think, makes me someone I never used to be. I need to feel that light inside me that comes from looking forward instead of back.

And I need someone to look at me the way Will Browning does.

"If you want me to stop hoaxing, I will." The words are hard to get out. Because there's an exhilaration to playing the Green Lady, whether out on the diggings, or on the stage of the Theatre Royal. A blissful thing to be taken from my real life for a time. It doesn't matter that it's into this story of betrayal and despair. Because funnelling my own gloom into the

Green Lady eases it from my body. Makes me feel a lightness I can barely remember feeling. When I'm lost in the world of Fyvie Castle, I don't think of Constable Stone crawling from the claim. I don't think of Tom either, or that questioning look in his eyes.

But I don't want all that if it means losing this unnameable thing that's simmering between Will and me.

For several long moments, he doesn't speak, just runs his paintbrush over a wild twist of ivy. "You shouldn't stop on account of me," he says finally. "I know playing the ghost has its way of… making you forget your troubles."

A splodge of water plops off my brush and makes the painted bricks look rain-washed. "Why are you so against it?" I ask. "It's not just because you think it dangerous, is it. There's more to it than that."

Will lets out a soft sigh. His gaze is fixed to the darkened auditorium, to the rows of empty seats. "I suppose it reminds me of a time in my life I'd rather forget."

Something tugs inside me. "The failure of your plays."

He nods. "When my first piece was a success, I thought I'd made it. But I couldn't seem to replicate the quality of it again. And the more bad work I produced, the more the reviewers crucified me. It took away the love I had for the theatre. Took away my passion for what I do. I felt a great anger at that. At the critics. And at society as a whole for rejecting my work." When his eyes meet mine, he looks suddenly young and vulnerable. "I suppose playing the ghost was a reaction to that. A way of rebelling against society. And escaping the harshness of reality for a time." He rinses his brush and sits back on his heels, his arm grazing mine. "It's foolish," he says. "I know."

"Well," I say, "it may be foolish. But I understand."

"You do." It is not a question.

Perhaps it's not my grief he can see. Perhaps it's my attraction to him that is simmering beneath my skin. I've not done much to hide it. Perhaps he does not imagine it's grief I'm escaping, but rather, my marriage.

Perhaps he is right.

I sit back too, and my shoulder presses against his. Will Browning is utterly magnetic, and I can't manage to put space between us.

"When I saw you go out there to play the Green Lady, it just reminded me of that time in my life when I felt the need to go hoaxing. Reminded me of everything I hoped to forget by coming to Australia."

"Then I won't do it again," I say firmly. "I can't bear the thought of making you feel that way. And I don't want this coldness between us each time I play the ghost."

"No, Lucy." He puts a hand out suddenly, gripping my forearm. "If you need to do it, you should. I apologise for my coldness. Truth be told, it had less to do with the ghost hoaxing, and more to do with the fact that…" He swallows visibly. "That I enjoy your company far more than I ought to." He gives a humourless laugh. "I know I may have a strange way of showing it. But last night, when I was out there with you, I felt…" He clears his throat, his words dying away. "Well, what I felt is neither here nor there. You belong to another man. I just thought it best to keep my distance."

I can't look at him. Who knows where that might lead? My heart is thundering so loudly I'm sure he can hear it. Finally, I murmur, "I enjoy your company far more than I ought to as well."

My words hang in the silence, above the pearly glow of the ghost light and the painted walls of Fyvie Castle. I'm frozen in place, knuckles white around the paintbrush, too afraid to move, to speak.

Will jumps suddenly to his feet, dragging the cloth to the edge of the stage to dry. The biting smell of wet paint wafts into the air. "The pieces I did yesterday are dry," he says, a little too brightly. "Shall we hang them up and see how they look?"

He disappears backstage before I can respond and returns with several folded-up pieces of cloth. When he opens them out, I see they're painted with the same bricks and narrow windows as the section we have just finished.

He passes me the cloth and goes backstage again, returning with a ladder. He climbs to the top and I pass up a corner of the fabric, allowing him to hang it from the rail at the back of the stage. When one wall of Fyvie Castle has been erected, he moves the ladder to the other side and we repeat the process.

I stand at the front of the stage, turning in a slow half circle, a smile on the edge of my lips. Shadows shift on the makeshift walls, transporting me to Scotland, and the cloud-drenched world of Fyvie Castle. Motes of dust sparkle in the lamplight. I know this is as close to home as I'm ever likely to get again. But right now, it's enough.

I want to ask Will whether *The Lady of Fyvie* has helped him rediscover his lost passion for the theatre. Whether it's possible to come back from a despair so deep it threatened to swallow you whole. But I don't want to break the silence. It feels almost otherworldly.

I sense his presence behind me. And I take a step in his direction.

I understand what kind of person this makes me. I understand the crushing shame I ought to feel. But I want it; deeply, desperately. I want closeness, intimacy, to feel another's skin against my own. Want someone to take me out of my own head and look at me with lust in their eyes. I want all those things Tom and I have lost.

He is close. I can feel his breath flutter the hair at the back of my neck, as though he is daring himself to touch – or trying to prevent himself from doing so. My heart is loud in my ears.

And then his hand moves against my shoulder, wrapping around the curve of me. Seeing his paint-splattered, imperfect fingers against my body gives me the courage to turn and face him. To look up and meet his eyes.

He presses a palm to my cheek. "Tell me to stop and I shall."

No.

There will be consequences, of course. There always are. But perhaps these are consequences I'm willing to accept. A fair trade.

I lean forward to meet him, my lips to his. A kiss that thaws me from an eternal freeze. My mind is blissfully blank. All I'm aware of is the sensation of being alive.

When Will pulls away, I hear a murmur of disappointment escape me.

He leans his forehead against mine and tucks a strand of hair behind my ear. "Lucy, I…"

I take a step back, and that action is enough to silence him.

I can't ask him to be this man. Can't ask him to dive into this; a thing which can never be. Not out in the daylight. Dizzying and blissful as my lips on his felt, we can only ever exist in that place beyond reality.

I run down the steps and off the stage. Leave without another word.

CHAPTER TEN

I rush from the theatre and the rippling walls of Fyvie Castle. Weave between streetlamps so I might avoid their scrutiny. I dart off the road as a carriage rattles past.

And I stop abruptly at the sight of my husband walking towards me.

"What are you doing here?" I ask.

Tom's hands are dug in the pockets of his coat, collar turned up against the wind. "I came to walk you home from your rehearsal. I wasn't sure what time it finished. I suppose I'm a little late."

I wrap my arms around myself, unable to look at him. It feels like he knows, he knows, he knows.

How could he know?

"Is this because you don't like me being friends with Clara?" I ask stiffly. "Because she already left. I—"

"I just thought it might be a nice thing for me to walk my wife home. I know I've been out at the claim a lot." After a moment of silence, he sighs. "I'm trying, Lucy. I'm really bloody trying."

Guilt cuts me and I take a step closer to him, looping my hand around his arm. "I know you are. I'm sorry."

It's sure as hell more than I can say for myself.

"How was your rehearsal?" Tom asks as we walk.

"Fine."

"Good."

And at this moment, I'm infinitely grateful for the pattern of small talk we've fallen into. Small talk, I realise, is an easy thing to hide behind.

Somewhere far away, thunder rattles the sky.

"Weather's turning," says Tom.

"Mm." I notice a dribble of paint on my skirts and shift my arm to cover it.

At the top of our street, Tom stops walking. "Is that…"

I freeze. Constable Stone is on our doorstep, a large cloth bag at his feet. Tom strides down the street and I hurry after him, dread knotting my stomach.

"What the hell do you want?" Tom hisses at the trooper. I'm taken aback by the venom in his words.

Stone looks past him and gives me a thin smile. "Mrs Earnshaw."

"Constable." My voice is tiny.

He nods toward the sack. "I've laundry that needs doing."

Not once in three years has Constable Stone ever come to me for his laundry. I know it no coincidence he has appeared tonight.

"Don't be ridiculous," says Tom. "It's late. Come back in the morning."

Stone's eyes meet mine.

"It's all right, Tom." I grab the bag. "One shilling."

"Lucy," Tom snaps, but Stone is already pressing the coins into my hand. I pull out my key, fumbling as I shove it into the lock. "I'll deliver it to you when it's done."

"Good. You can bring it to the police station." He takes the bag of laundry from my hand. "I'll carry it inside for you."

He saw me playing the ghost. More than that, he knows I saw him climbing out of that claim. Of these things, I have no doubt. What I do not know, is what he will do with this information.

This is not a visit for the sake of his laundry, of that much I'm certain. Is this little house call to warn me against telling anyone what I saw? Or to let me know that I've been caught?

I know there are ghost hoaxers in England who faced the courts, but surely I won't suffer the same fate. Those English hoaxers were arrested for assault, for breaking and entering, but I've not broken any laws. All I've done is stir up a little gossip and create a bit of a scare. Still, I know the people of Castlemaine will have something to say about it if they discover what I've been doing. If I'm to keep hoaxing until the play, I need to keep the Green Lady's identity a secret.

Stone's message is clear enough: if I open my mouth, he will open his. And neither of us want that.

He looks me in the eye, the faintest hint of a smile on his lips. Yes, message received. But there is something else in his gaze; a searching look, as though he's trying to determine what led me to do what I did. As though catching Tom Earnshaw's mousy little wife playing the ghost among the claims at midnight is a thing that requires an explanation. I suppose it is. But it is not an explanation I'm about to give.

Tom presses his palm flat to Stone's chest to prevent him from entering our cottage. "Leave it," he says tersely. "I'll carry it in."

"Very well." A smile on the edge of Stone's lips. He drops the sack, and it thuds softly on the doorstep. "If that's what you want."

Thunder rolls again, closer this time. I can smell the rain on the air. He turns and marches down the front path and I realise I'm barely breathing.

"Listen to that rain," Tom says the next morning. "I guess you'll not be doing Stone's laundry today."

I watch from beneath the blankets as he climbs out of bed and pulls on his trousers.

"I'm going to take it back to him," he says. "Tell him to wash his own damn clothes and stay the hell away from us."

I sit up, taken aback by his fervour. "You don't have to do that."

Tom tucks in his shirt. "He's a corrupt bastard, Luce. I don't want you anywhere near him."

I wonder if my husband has any idea of the extent of Stone's corruption. "Tom." I reach for his forearm. "Please. It's just a little laundry. I'll do it tomorrow and be done with it. Besides, we could use the money." I look at him pleadingly.

He sighs. "Fine. But if he comes here again, you tell him you're not available."

I nod wordlessly, not sure it's a promise I can keep.

Tom pulls back one curtain and shoves open the window. The cool change has blown in overnight and the bedroom fills with rain-scented air. Water streams down the glass. He curses under his breath. "No going out in this. Claim'll be half underwater."

"Maybe it'll clear," I say, clinging to the possibility. "You know what the rain's like in this place. Pouring one minute, dry the next."

I can't bear thought of being trapped in the cottage with Tom all day. Especially now my head is so full of Will, and all that passed between us last night. I was awake hours before dawn, trying to find the guilt I know I ought to feel. Told myself I ought to step away from the play, and never go near Will Browning again. My new rebellious side refused to listen.

Tom hovers at the window for another moment, then climbs back into bed. I lie frozen beside him, arms held across my chest. When he shifts on the mattress, I flinch.

"Don't worry, Luce," he says dryly. "I wouldn't dare."

The coldness in his voice makes my chest ache.

After just minutes, he is out of bed again. I follow him into the kitchen and light the fire. Set a pot of porridge simmering on the stove. Rain thunders against the windows, punctuating our silence.

The day stretches out bleakly before us. There is painfully little space between the two of us as I boil the tea and make the porridge. As Tom goes from window to window, watching the rain. By the time I serve up the food, it feels as though the walls of the cottage are closing in on me. Making it hard to breathe.

"I'm going to the market," I say, after a few spoonfuls of porridge.

Tom doesn't look up from his bowl. "It's pouring rain."

"Yes, well. We still need to eat." I take my cloak from the hook beside the door. "I'll be back soon."

Tom looks up at me for a long second, and I see an unspoken apology in his eyes. As though he knows I'm leaving to avoid being around him. But he doesn't open his mouth. Doesn't attempt to find the words to make me stay.

The barrage of rain has turned the unpaved streets to swamp, and I pick my way between shop awnings, water rolling steadily off the brim of my bonnet. The boggy roads are barely accessible, and the town feels oddly empty without the constant rhythm of horse hooves and wheels.

608

When I return to the cottage, my skirts are soaked, and half the main street is caked to my boots. I shoulder open the door, lugging in the basket I'd filled with food we didn't really need. I'd just craved the space the market would provide.

Tom leaps from his chair and takes the basket, carrying it into the kitchen and setting it on the floor. The contents of the money box are spread out over the table; coins stacked in neat columns, a few scraps of gold beside them, ready to be weighed and banked.

"You're soaked," he says. "Come and get dry."

I shrug off my cloak and hang it back on the hook. Kick off my muddy boots.

"I made tea," Tom tells me. "Should still be hot." He lifts the kettle from the hook and refills the pot while I unpack the basket, my wet stockings leaving footprints on the floorboards.

Tom sets my tea on the table for me, then sits and brings his own half-drunk cup to his lips. "Looks as though the rain's set in. Real waste of a day."

My gaze drifts to the small knots of gold on the table, vividly lustrous against the rough-hewn wood. My chest squeezes. "Tom," I say carefully, "you know it's not your fault, don't you? That you've not found a big haul yet?" I hold my breath, half expecting him to fly into a rage, or veer wildly away from the subject. Instead, he just puts down his teacup and sighs.

"I know," he says. "I do. I just... I just wish things were different."

I put my hand to his forearm, feeling its broadness. *I wish that too.* It doesn't need to be said.

A violent shiver goes through me, and I pull my hand away.

"Take that dress off," says Tom. "You'll catch a chill. It's cold today."

I go to the bedroom, unbuttoning my wet dress and petticoats and hanging them over a chair to dry. I slip my flannel robe on over my shift and drawers.

My script is poking out from under the bed. The sight of it brings that powerful desire to lose myself in the world of the play and all it has come to represent. I force the urge away. Pad back out to the kitchen and sit at the table beside Tom.

Maybe this is what we need; to be held prisoner in our little cottage for a time. Maybe then we'll find a way to have those conversations we ought to have had months ago. Conversations where we speak our daughter's name and let the other peek inside our head for a moment. Those conversations that might somehow lead us back to each other. But is that really what I want? I can't tell anymore. And that doubt is more than a little terrifying.

Tom scoops the coins and gold pieces back into the box and sits it on the shelf behind him. He reaches into the drawer beneath the cupboards and pulls out a pack of cards. He begins to deal. "You remember how to play All Fours, don't you?"

I smile. "Of course." Tom taught me to play on the voyage, and we passed endless hours of ocean with cards in our hands. Our games were slow and chatter-filled, and half the time we'd end up rolling around beneath the blankets before we declared a winner.

I look across the table, trying to see him as I did back then. Trying to remember what it felt like to be so besotted with Tom Earnshaw that I had to toss down my cards and fling myself into his arms mid-game.

That little crease of Tom's brow as he looks down at his cards, the way he scratches the place his beard meets his neck; I remember that. Remember watching him so closely I might memorise every detail of him. And though I remember that attraction, that need to feel his skin against my own, I can't quite recall how to feel it.

Rain drums against the glass as we pore over the cards. The earthy smell of the burned-out fire is thick in the air.

"You let me win," I say, counting up the points.

"I wouldn't do that."

"You always let me win when we played on the ship."

He chuckles lightly. "Well. I had other things on my mind back then. Today you just outplayed me." He scoops up the cards and begins to shuffle them. "Another round?"

I nod.

A knock at the door interrupts us. Tom gets to his feet, and I tug my robe tighter around my body.

My shoulders tighten at the sound of Constable Stone's voice. What is he doing here? Is he after his laundry? Surely not. Nothing will dry in this weather. There must be another reason for his visit. I get to my feet. If Stone is here to see me, I need to interject in the men's conversation somehow. There's far too much he could tell my husband.

But then I hear a second voice. Stone is not alone, and the realisation goes some way to easing my panic. Surely he'll not speak of that night in the presence of another trooper. Stone is a former convict. If he were found guilty of night fossicking, he'd be hauled out to Port Arthur, or somewhere equally as hideous.

"We can speak outside," Tom says, and the door closes neatly behind them. I strain my ears to catch a thread of their conversation. But their words are muffled by distance, and the faint patter of the easing downpour.

"What did they want?" I demand, the moment Tom comes back inside. Rain has darkened the shoulders of his faded blue vest.

"It's all right." He puts a hand to my shoulder. "They just had some questions about Leo and these driving accusations the Tipperary boys are making against him. Thought there might be some connection between that and the night fossicking."

My heart quickens. If Stone is pointing the finger at Leo for his own crimes, there's no way I can stay silent about what I saw. "Surely they don't think Leo's involved?"

"I doubt it. They're just clutching at straws if you ask me. I told them Leo never had nothing to do with any driving. Couldn't imagine anyone less likely to be a thief." He takes his coat from the hook beside the door and slips it on. "I'd best let him know the coppers were asking after him. Warn him to keep out of trouble."

"Please, Tom," I say suddenly. "Stay."

My own words surprise me. I can't remember the last time I craved my husband's company. But I want him here now. Want to sit at the table with him and play All Fours. Our strange, unexpected compatibility feels precious. Fleeting.

His lips part, as though he's surprised by my request. "I can't," he says after a moment. "I'm sorry. If it were me the coppers were asking after, I'd want Leo to tell me right away."

"Of course." My voice is thin.

Tom hovers in front of me for a moment, as though caught in indecision. "I'll be back as soon as I can."

I feel a hollowness inside me as the door thumps shut. Clinging to these moments of happiness with Tom feels like trying to catch hold of the wind.

CHAPTER ELEVEN

"What do you think?" Clara leads me into her dressmaker's parlour. The building has just been completed, sunlight spilling through large windows and lighting the chaos of chests, fabric rolls and wooden mannequins. A large oak table is pushed up against one wall, supporting a tower of boxes.

I look around incredulously. "Where on earth were you keeping all this while you were living at the boarding house?"

"Some under the bed. Some in Will's room at the Commercial. Even hid some things in here once it had a roof. Don't think the builders even noticed. Mind you, most of this fabric didn't arrive til yesterday."

I peer through the door at the back of the parlour. It leads into small living quarters; a fireplace in one corner, a sleeping mat in the other. A small table sits in the centre of the room, a crimson and white bodice and skirt laid over a chair beside it.

"The place looks wonderful," I tell Clara. "I'm so happy for you."

"The outfit on the chair," she calls, teetering towards the back room with a box in her arms. "Try it on. I need to see how it looks on a real person."

I run a finger over the vividly coloured fabric. I've never worn anything so vibrant. Everything I own these days either started life as, or has ended up, the colour of mud.

She dumps the box in a corner of the living quarters and picks up a wide hooped underskirt that's leaning against the wall. She holds it out to me. "Wear it with the crinoline cage."

I eye the cage warily. I'm not the kind of woman who wears hoop skirts. I'm not even sure how I might get into the thing. "Really?" I ask. "I'm not sure I…"

Clara rolls her eyes impatiently. "Honestly, Lucy, don't be so mopesy. Everyone's wearing them these days. This one's just come in, all the way from London."

I take the cage, suddenly embarrassed by the dowdy flatness of my own skirts. Tom has always been adamant that I dress for safety rather than fashion – we both know women who near burnt themselves to a crisp strolling through the campfires of the diggings in wide, fashionable skirts.

But there are no campfires here in Clara's parlour. My husband is not here either. And perhaps with a little concentration, I can manage to wrangle myself into a hoop skirt.

I take the clothes into the corner of the living quarters and dress myself carefully, stepping into the cage and fastening it at my waist. Then I attempt the crimson skirts and bodice.

Buoyed by the crinoline, the skirts swell around me in a bell-like shape I've never dared to wear. I catch a glimpse of myself in the mirror that leans against one wall. Against the deep red, my skin looks fashionably pale, and my blue eyes seem brighter than I remember. I smile at my reflection.

Clara comes in, hand on her hip as she inspects the dress, a frown of concentration crinkling her nose. She tugs the bodice down towards my hips. "It's not sitting right." She rifles through a box, emerging with a pincushion. Then she comes to stand behind me, pinching and pinning the pleats at my waist.

The front door clicks open. "Anyone here?"

At the sound of Will's voice, something flips in my chest.

"In here," Clara calls. She moves around to face me. "Will's bringing Charles and Matthew to help me shift that dreadful table." She frowns at my expression, making me suspect I've done quite a terrible job of looking unflapped. "There's no problem is there?"

"No," I garble. "Of course not."

I've told Clara nothing of what passed between Will and me at the theatre. I think perhaps I'm wary of her questions. Questions with answers that are too confronting to say out loud.

He appears in the doorway of the living quarters, Charles and Matthew in tow. The three of them are dressed casually in rolled-up shirtsleeves and simple linen waistcoats, yet still manage to look like they've just danced out of the pleasure gardens.

"Lucy," Will says in surprise. "You look beautiful. I mean… the dress, Clara," he stumbles. "You've quite a talent."

Clara almost manages to hold back a laugh. "The table's in the front room. It needs to go in the other corner. I tried to move it myself, but I could barely shift it an inch."

"What happened to the window frame?" Matthew asks, joining Will in the doorway. "Why is it covered in white paint?"

Clara shakes her head. "Just a little trouble from the locals."

I frown. "What happened?" I didn't notice the paint on the way in.

"Someone painted a few choice words on the window frame," she tells me. "The white paint was all I could find to cover it. I'll have to fix it later."

"Those bastards," says Will. "Do you know who—"

"It's fine, Will," Clara cuts in. "Just help me with the table. You can put the boxes in the corner."

"As you wish." His eyes meet mine for a second, then he quickly looks away.

I hear a dull thud as one of the boxes hits the floor.

"Careful!" barks Clara.

"How goes the ghost hoaxing, Lucy?" Charles calls over his shoulder as he heads into the front room. "You giving the good people of Castlemaine a decent scare?"

I think of Constable Stone crawling from the claim. Think of the vandals at work on Clara's window frame. "They deserve a good scare."

Charles laughs.

I lean forward, trying to catch Will's reaction. I hadn't intended on bringing up hoaxing again – at least not within two minutes of his arrival.

Clara jabs me in the side. "Stand still."

I'm statuesque as she steps back again to inspect the adjustments she's made. I hear the men mutter and curse as they heave the table across the outer room.

"That's sitting better now," says Clara. "You can change back if you like. Just be careful with the pins when you take it off."

I open my mouth to tell her there's no way in hell I'm changing my clothes out in the open now Will is here, but she's already charging out into the parlour, berating the men over where they've put the table. I scramble out of the crimson skirts and back into my own clothes so fast I'm surprised I don't get vertigo.

"I'm glad we got to see this shop of yours finished before we went back to Melbourne," I hear Matthew tell Clara. "You certain you don't want to come with us, Will? Haven't you had enough of this outpost yet?"

My stomach plunges, but Will says, "I'm happy where I am for the moment. Besides, I told you, I'll be down in Melbourne for a few days next week. Get my dose of the place then."

"You're going to Melbourne, Will?" asks Clara. "No, that's too close to the window! I already told you, it needs to go in the corner."

I hear one of the men groan.

"I'm going to see George Howard's new play at Astley's Amphitheatre," Will says. "They're using both the ring and the stage. It's supposed to be quite the spectacle."

Clara snorts. "George Howard? The man's a bastard. Wouldn't even give me an audition."

"You'd much rather be working for me anyway," Will teases her.

"Indeed. It's always been my dream to act alongside greats like Ollie Cooper."

He laughs. "Well, you've already scared Arthur off. I'm sure with a little focus you can get rid of Ollie too."

I fasten the last of my buttons and catch a glimpse of myself in the mirror. Out of the crimson gown, I look decidedly plain and colourless. But when I step out into the parlour, Will is deliberate in looking my way. And suddenly I'm back on the stage at the Theatre Royal with the castle blowing around us and his lips against mine. I shake the thought away hurriedly.

A thing that can never be.

"Lucy," Clara calls, snapping me out of my haze. "The blue gown I showed you last week. It's in the chest over by the window. It needs to go on the mannequin."

I scurry obediently to the chest, glad for something to do. I find the gown and unfold it carefully, sliding it over the wooden bust of the mannequin at the front of the shop. Realising I've forgotten the underskirts, I go back to the chest to fetch them, and when I try to tie them beneath the gown, I somehow manage to entrap myself in reams of blue and white fabric.

"It's not right," I hear Clara say. "Maybe the table was better where it was. Move it back. Come on, Charlie. Quickly."

"Save me," Will murmurs, appearing at my side.

I emerge from the skirts and offer him a grin. "She just wants everything to be perfect."

"She's terrifying." He lifts the blue skirts, allowing me to straighten the petticoats.

"When will you go to Melbourne?" I ask as I work.

"I thought to leave on Monday. Perhaps see the performance on Tuesday afternoon."

"I've heard Astley's Amphitheatre is quite something."

"It is. And the performance of *Joan of Arc* I plan to see has been getting fabulous reviews. They say the staging is breathtaking."

"It sounds wonderful."

For a moment, Will doesn't speak. He glances over at the others before looking back at me. "You could…" He falters. "You could always come with me." His voice is barely a whisper. "You'd have your own private room, of course. I wouldn't…"

My mouth opens and closes, caught off guard by his invitation. I can barely believe I've heard him correctly.

For a moment, I allow myself to imagine what it would feel like to accept. But no, I can't follow this thought too far. It will lead me to places I can absolutely, positively never go.

Places like Astley's Amphitheatre with Will Browning.

Impossible, of course. For so many reasons, not least the scraps in our coin box. I shake my head. "I don't have the money."

"Don't worry about that. I…" He looks down for a moment, then back up at me shyly. "I'd like you to come, Lucy. Very much." He swallows. "Perhaps you might think about it?"

And though I try my hardest not to, I think about it. I think about it when I'm whacking filthy shirts against my washboard. Think about it when I'm lying frozen in bed beside Tom. And I'm thinking about as I stand in Clara's parlour a few days later, waiting for her to put the finishing touches on the crimson skirts.

"It looks good on you," she says. "I want you to wear it in Melbourne."

"How did you—"

"Oh please. I have ears. And eyes. I can see the way you and Will look at each other."

I flush. I'd convinced myself I had been discreet. Kept my feelings to myself. Kept what happened at the theatre well hidden. "There's nothing between Will and me," I say.

"Is that so?" Clara kneels at my feet to stitch up the hem.

I trace a finger over the delicate embroidery along the neckline. "He did invite me to Melbourne," I say finally. "But it's not as if I can go."

"Why not?"

I don't know why I'm still shocked at her bluntness. But even though there's a part of me that wants to, I just can't see the world as Clara Snow does. Can't just leap inside a carriage with a man who's not my husband and clatter off into the sunset.

Clara pulls out a pin and digs it into her apron. "You deserve to be happy, Lucy," she says. "We all do. Every one of us that ended up out here."

I've said nothing to Clara about the sadness that follows me like a shadow. How much of my pain do my eyes give away?

"I think maybe you were as reluctant to come here as I was," she says.

I swallow heavily. "That's not true."

"Well," she says finally, "you deserve to be happy in any case."

I was happy once; I remember it like a fading dream. I was happy with Tom, dizzy in his company. We lost that happiness when we lost Elsie and have never been able to find it again.

But when I'm around Will, when my mind is full of new ideas and new possibilities, I catch fleeting glimpses of a future in which I'm not tied to my grief. A future in which I might find a way to be happy again.

"I can't go with Will," I say. "I'm a married woman."

Clara stops stitching for a moment and looks up to meet my eyes. "Do you love your husband, Lucy?"

The question is like a blow to the chest.

And so is my hesitation.

I think of the warmth I felt when Tom and I sat together playing cards by the fire. But was that happiness based on nothing but a memory? Was I trying to catch hold of joy that has long passed? Once, I loved him with such intensity it almost scared me. A love I thought would see us through anything. And while it's turned out to be a love that has buckled under the strain of loss, I'm far too scared to cut myself loose from it completely. While I'm anchored to my grief, I'm also anchored to Tom, and the security that comes with being a wife in this strange land. "Yes," I say finally. "I do love my husband. Of course I do."

Clara doesn't answer at once. She steps back, then walks in a slow circle around me, inspecting the hem of the dress. Then she goes to the cupboard and returns with a small jar filled with dried leaves.

"I want you to take this."

I frown. "What is it?"

"Thunder god vine. From the apothecary at the Chinese camp. Stops an unwanted child."

My eyes widen. "What are you talking about? Why are you giving me this?"

"I just thought that if you do decide to go with Will, it's best if you—"

"I'm not going with Will!" I cry. "And I'm certainly not… I certainly don't need this!" I feel my cheeks blazing. With anger or shame, or something else entirely, I can't tell. "I love my husband," I gush. "I do. And I would never…"

"All right," says Clara. "I'm sorry. I didn't mean to offend you."

"Well, you did." Without bothering to remove the crimson gown, I grab my own clothes from the floor and charge out of Clara's shop.

It's not til I get back the cottage that I realise I've brought the jar of thunder god vine home with me. I shove it into the back of the cupboard, catching a glimpse of my reflection in the window. In spite of my anger at Clara, I have to admit the gown is stunning. Like nothing I've ever worn in my life. For a fleeting moment, I imagine walking the streets of Melbourne on Will's arm, these fine skirts swelling around me. I shove the thought away. I can't allow it to take shape any further than it already has.

The door flies open and Tom charges into the house, leaving a trail of muddy footprints behind him. He disappears into the bedroom.

"Tom?" I call. "Are you all right?"

He grunts in response.

I hurry into the bedroom, steering my hooped skirts past the side table. Tom has pulled the washcloth from the basin and holds it to his eye as he paces back and forth across the room. I can see flecks of dried blood on his knuckles.

"What happened?" I ask.

"Nothing. It's fine."

"Were you in a fight?" In all the years I've known Tom, I've never once seen him be aggressive. "With who?"

He sighs heavily. Puts the cloth back in the basin to dampen it. I can see a bruise beginning to swell beneath his eye. The skin below his temple has split, leaving a rusty streak down his cheek.

"Jesus, Tom. Sit down. Let me clean you up."

Reluctantly, he sits on the edge of the bed. I dip the cloth back in the basin and sponge the blood from his cheek.

"Who did this?" I ask.

Tom hesitates. Is he truly going to be closed up about this? But then he says, "Clyde."

"You got into a fight with Clyde? Who started it?"

"Really, Lucy? Do you need to ask that?"

Yes, I do. Because I've never known my husband to come home with bloodied fists before. Have rarely known him to even raise his voice. What are the goldfields turning him into?

I lower the cloth so we can look eye to eye. His swollen by Clyde's fists, and mine full of guilt. After all, the secrets I'm keeping are far greater than why Clyde smacked my husband in the eye. But truth-telling is becoming more complicated by the day.

"He's been going around interrogating us all," Tom says finally.

"Asking us what we seen, what we heard, like we're all guilty men."

"And so you started a fight with him?"

"He swung the first punch," says Tom. "I just gave him a bit of a shove. Told him I didn't appreciate him making accusations."

I think of Constable Stone climbing from the claim by lamplight. "No, I'm sure you didn't." I wrestle my skirts aside as I bend to wash out the cloth.

"What on earth are you wearing?" Tom asks with a dull chuckle.

"Clara made it. She thought I might like it."

He begins to unlace his boots. "This isn't the place for a dress like that. You'll go up in smoke if you're not careful. Besides, it's not really you, is it. Take it off."

I clench my teeth. "I'd like to go to Melbourne for a few days," I blurt. "With the theatre."

Tom looks up. "Melbourne?"

"Yes. To see a play at Astley's Amphitheatre. There's a play on about Joan of Arc that uses both the stage and the ring. We're going to use the theatre's funds to pay for the trip."

"The theatre's funds?" Tom repeats.

"Mr Browning says if we see real actors and actresses perform, it will help our own performances." I realise I'm talking too quickly.

"Does he now?" Tom uses one boot to kick off the other. I can practically see his thoughts churning. Can tell he hates the idea. And yet he was the one to nudge me in the direction of Will and the theatre troupe in the first place.

"I'm not sure that's appropriate," he says finally.

"In England, perhaps," I say. "But things are different here."

"Not so different."

I wring out the bloodstained cloth.

"You're a married woman," says Tom. "You shouldn't be gallivanting about the colony without your husband."

I hold his gaze. "Come with me then," I dare him.

Tom gives a snort of laughter, as though taking me to the theatre is the most insane idea he's ever heard in his life. "Who will be going?"

"Everyone," I say, wincing inwardly at the lie. "Clara and Mrs Markham and Arthur Wallace…"

I am the worst of people; I see this with such clarity that I'm on the verge of taking it all back and admitting to my lies. This is not who I want to be; this I know with certainty. And yet I can't deny the excitement that floods me when Tom finally nods in agreement.

CHAPTER TWELVE

Will and I are in the stagecoach at dawn. The sun is a faint glow behind the cloud bank, but there's a fragrant thickness to the air that promises heat. The coach is full, and there are one or two familiar faces among the passengers. Men and women I've passed at the market, seen in church services.

I pretend Will and I are nothing more than acquaintances. Nods of greeting, *good morning, Mr Browning,* and we take up seats on opposites sides of the coach.

Though the day has barely begun, I can hear the rattle of mining cradles as we pass Forest Creek. How many mornings have I been woken by that sound? That rhythmic scrape and thud that's as familiar to me as breath.

I look out over the scarred landscape, dotted with tree stumps and holes in the earth. At the hint of mountains behind the morning haze. We wind past the blue shadow of the hills and past plains golden in the sunrise. Kangaroos make tiny silhouettes, flying away across the paddocks as the carriage rattles past.

The further we get from Castlemaine, the more the tension in my shoulders begins to melt away, replaced with nervous excitement. As I peer out the opposite window at the wide, rusty landscape, my eye catches Will's and he flashes a quick smile.

The Black Forest creeps up on the carriage like fog; a few trees breaking the monotony of the plains, then more, until we are surrounded by bush and the soft daylight has drained away.

I've passed through the Black Forest before, on our first journey to the goldfields. The place unnerved me then, and that was before I heard all the stories of the bushrangers who hide in the caves, attacking gold-laden carriages on the way back from the diggings. Though Captain Melville has supposedly cleared out of the forest to wreak havoc on the coast, there's no shortage of stories from people who've experienced a holdup here.

A restless energy hangs in the coach as we rattle down the narrow dirt road, people murmuring under their breath, ladies clutching their reticules a little tighter. The horses' hooves beat a steady rhythm that rattles alongside my heart. I press my forehead to the window, eyes darting, trying to catch hold of the shadows flitting between the trees.

I'm glad when the branches of the Black Forest part and sunlight spills over the coach. I catch a glimpse of searing blue sky and release the breath I'm holding.

By the time we reach Melbourne, I'm exhausted, my eyes heavy from the early start, and my bones rattled by hours in the coach. When I make my way to the door of the carriage, Will is waiting for me at the steps. Offers me his hand to help me climb down.

Melbourne is all sound and colour. Carriages pass below domes and spires that look transplanted from England, bright painted signs above doors announcing the barbers, the tailors, the dispensaries. The lamplighter moves through the purple dusk, climbing his ladder and coaxing the streetlights to life.

Will nods at the three-storey building beside the Cobb and Co terminus. A grand archway welcomes us to the Albion Hotel, decorative balustrades hemming semi-circular balconies. Men in top hats and frock coats spill from the adjoining bar.

"I stayed here the night I arrived in the colony," Will tells me. "I think you'll like it. It's rather beautiful inside. And there's fine views from upstairs."

I follow him into the hotel foyer, terrified of catching sight of anyone I know. The thought is laughable of course; I don't know anyone in Melbourne, nor do I know anyone who spends their time in places like the Albion. Besides, what do I have to hide? I'm just a woman travelling to town to see a show at Astley's Amphitheatre.

Maybe if I tell myself that enough, it will somehow become true.

My eyes shift around the foyer, taking in the rich polished oak of the woodwork, the delicate lace curtains fringing the arched windows. A different world from the leaky lodging house Tom and I stayed in on our first night in Australia. We told ourselves that when we next returned to town, we'd be staying in places like the Albion. The irony brings a wry smile to my lips.

Will moves away from the front desk and comes towards me with a smile on his face. He holds out a key. "Here. I've got us both rooms on the top floor. Overlooking the river."

I shoot a hurried glance to the man behind the counter. Is he watching me? Judging? But his eyes are turned downwards as he writes in his ledger. I'm sure this town of new wealth has seen far madder things than me.

And up the stairs I go behind Will, gripping the bannister like it's a life raft.

When we reach the top floor, he stops at a room on the corner. "This is yours," he says. "I'm two doors down. Room three-one-four."

I grip the key in my clammy palms. "Thank you," I manage. "For all of this."

"Of course." He hovers awkwardly for a moment, and I can tell neither of us have any thought of how this is to proceed. Are we to pretend this is just a thing of private rooms, and separate seats on the coach? Am I to pretend my heart's not speeding beneath his gaze; and that surely, surely, he can sense it?

"I thought to go down to the supper room," he says. "Have a little food. Will you join me?"

But with his closeness, with this sudden upturning of everything I've so far been, my stomach is cartwheeling. I can't tell if it's excitement or dread. All I know is I can't bear the thought of food. Nor can I face, right now, the possibility of where this thing might lead. And exactly what it might mean.

"I think I'd rather just go to bed," I say. "If you wouldn't mind? I'm exhausted."

"Of course." Is that relief in his eyes? Does he feel the weight of this too? He pecks my cheek. "Good night, Lucy. Sleep well."

And before I can reply, he is gone.

In my palatial bed, I barely sleep. I tell myself it's my nagging conscience keeping me awake, and not the thought of Will in bed a few doors down the hall. Because I most certainly am not the kind of woman kept awake by thoughts of men who are not her husband.

Nor am I the kind of woman who wears crimson and crinoline cages. But here is my reflection, fastening the row of tiny buttons up my chest with Clara's cherry-red gown exploding around me. I'm wearing the simple white day bodice she made to match the skirts, and with my skin safely covered to my wrists and neck, it feels like a far less daunting outfit to wear to breakfast than the eye-catching eveningwear she pinned me into at the shop.

When I arrive downstairs, I find Will sitting at a table by the window, a notebook open in front of him. He is scrawling in it furiously. A stray piece of hair falls over his eye and he tucks it thoughtlessly behind his ear, without the pen leaving the page. For a moment, I just stand watching him, not wanting to interrupt. Wanting a silent moment to take him in. I can't believe I'm in his company.

Alone, in his company. I feel oddly outside myself.

Will looks up. At the sight of me, his face brightens.

"Good morning." I feel his eyes taking me in. "You look lovely."

I lower my gaze shyly. "Clara's dress."

"Ah. Yes. It's stunning."

I hover, uncertain if we ought to be seen sitting together, but Will pulls out the chair beside him, answering my silent question. I perch tentatively on the edge with as much grace as I can muster. Before we left, Clara put me through a vigorous training regime in which I practiced hoicking up the back of the crinoline cage to wrangle myself onto a chair. I'm terrified of giving the breakfast room an eyeful of my underwear.

"You're writing?" I ask Will.

"Yes. I always find a change of scenery is good for motivation." He closes the notebook. "But I'll have plenty of time to do that later. How did you sleep?"

A waiter appears at the table, filling my cup with coffee.

"I slept well," I lie. Telling the truth will get us into questions like 'What kept you awake?' and no way in hell am I going there.

"I'm glad to hear it." He plugs the cork into his ink pot. "And your room? Is it to your liking?"

Are we really having a conversation so mundane and simple? And why does it not feel completely wrong? Because the strangest part of all this is that somehow, as we sit here drinking coffee and speaking of the views from our bedroom windows, Will and I have managed to find a sense of comfort. The unease I felt in the hallway last night has vanished with the sun. Somehow, so subtly I can barely place it, being around him has become easy.

Will Browning is the man I could once barely speak to. But as I sit here with him, in a scene that belongs in someone else's life, I feel an unexpected sense of peace. A peace that even my raging conscience can't disrupt. Escaping my life for a time – and yes, escaping my marriage – feels like the air I have been craving for far longer than I've dared to acknowledge.

"I understand you not wanting to be seen with me in the coach," Will says as we walk into the theatre that afternoon. There is a smile on his face. "But do you think we might sit together for the show?"

I am awed by Astley's Amphitheatre; by the huge circus-like ring that unfolds before us; by the curtained archway hiding a stage I suspect is enormous; the chandelier glittering from a mile-high roof. I point everything out to Will like an overexcited child. Tiers and tiers of velvet-lined seats. Benches so close to the ring they must make you feel a part of the show. And would you just look at all these people?

I suspect Will might be regretting his request to sit to beside me.

He chuckles gently at my enthusiasm. "Did you never go to Astley's in London? It served as a model for this place."

I give a short laugh. "I'm from Horley, remember? I've been to London twice in my life. And the only time I ever went to the theatre back home was when our church put on its Christmas play."

"Oh yes," he chuckles. "The angel in the nightgown. Where you got your start in this fine industry."

I burst out laughing. Mercifully, I'd forgotten I told him all about the

Christmas play after a little too much wine at the Commercial that first night. I can't believe he remembers.

We take our seats on the second level. They have a fine view of both the stage and the ring. A hush falls over the audience as the great chandelier above our heads dims and the curtain rises.

The show is like nothing I've ever seen. Armies and horses engulf the ring and make me feel a part of the battle, while the actress playing Joan of Arc is breathtaking. It's all smoke and light and music coming from an orchestra hidden in the wings.

And yet I find my gaze drifting to the man beside me. His eyes are fixed on the stage, lips parted slightly. His gloved hand rests on his knee, inches from mine, as though tempting me to take it.

My thoughts pull towards Tom like a compass towards the north. The man I promised to love until I died. But these memories I have of him, of us, they are founded on something that no longer exists. And now all that's in their place is guilt and regret and that horrible suffocating silence. Conditions in which a person cannot survive.

I reach over and cover Will's hand with my own. Though his eyes remain fixed to the stage, I don't miss the small smile that appears on the edge of his lips. And when his fingers slide between mine and give an almost imperceptible squeeze, I can think of nothing but the coiled desire inside me, threatening to tear itself free.

"Quite something, don't you think?" Will murmurs in my ear as we stand with the rest of the audience to applaud the performers.

"Amazing, truly."

"And to think this is all happening so far from England. Whoever thought we'd make a civilised land of this outpost?"

"Strange what a little gold in the earth will do."

The curtain falls and the applause peters out. Will puts a light hand to my back as we funnel towards the doors with the rest of the crowd. "One day soon," he says, "it'll be my work performed here at Astley's. Just you wait and see."

I look over my shoulder to catch his eye. "I have no doubt."

I feel his fingers move against my back, an almost imperceptible movement.

"How is the new play coming along?" I ask, as the corridor widens and we're able to walk side by side.

"I believe in it," he says. "More than I've believed in anything I've written for a long time." His voice thickens. "This is the work that's going to reinvent my career, Lucy. I feel sure of it."

I take his arm instinctively and press myself closer to his body. I feel stirred by his enthusiasm, his ambition. This is who Will Browning is, I see then; he pours passion into everything he does, even a play written for arguably the world's most dreadful amateur theatre troupe. Little wonder he took it so hard when his career stalled. How brutal that criticism, those accusations of fraud must have been for him. Enough to drive him to rebel against society. Enough to drive him to play the ghost.

But it isn't just in ghost hoaxing that Will Browning seeks to rebel, I see then. It's in every aspect of the way he lives his life.

With your husband or without.

Rules are made to be broken.

I don't mind being a part of his rebellion. After all, he is part of mine.

But Will's rebellion, I soon learn, goes only so far. Because after a meal in the Albion's supper room, he walks me upstairs and stops outside my door. For a long moment, he holds his lips against the edge of mine, his fingers curling around my ribs. Then he murmurs a goodnight. Disappears into his room without another word.

From this, I understand two things. The first is that Will Browning will not come to my room tonight. The second is that if I can somehow find the courage to go to his, my advances will not be rejected.

I stand with my back to the door. Close my eyes and tighten my fist around the key. The urge to go to him is overwhelming. I try to find the self-loathing I know should accompany my desire. But I can't quite make myself feel it.

I am supposed to feel like a terrible person. But I just feel human. So desperate for happiness I can hardly breathe.

In two days' time, I will go back to that grease- and ash-scented cottage in Castlemaine. I will sit around the table with Tom and serve the same mutton stew I serve every Thursday. I will listen to him talk about how tomorrow will be the day that he will find a nugget and everything will change. In his eyes I will see the same strain and tension I know he sees in mine, and I will drown under the weight of it.

This moment here, now; it feels like my only chance to take in the air I need to survive.

I think of Elsie. This woman I am becoming is not who I wanted her mother to be. But Elsie is gone. She won't see. She will never see. Perhaps this was about her once – perhaps in so many ways it still is. But right now, it is about me. And it is about Will. And about taking the chance to live before I die.

There's an inevitability to this, I tell myself as I step out of my room. Of course there is. Did I not toss the jar of thunder god vine in my luggage? Pretend it a last-minute impulse, when I knew it anything but?

Will doesn't look surprised to see me. He stands in the doorway, still dressed in his shirt and waistcoat. I step forward and begin to open the buttons at his chest.

His hand catches mine. "Are you certain?"

And I nod because I can't bear to look again, or to analyse, or even think. I rise on my toes and press my lips to his.

Just for now, I'll simply let myself exist.

CHAPTER THIRTEEN

The night blurs. Hands and undone laces; lips finding places that have not been found in so many cold and lifeless months. Will lavishes me, pushes me, makes me bold; and I sense, in his wordless gasps, and the racing heart I feel when I drag my hands over his chest, that impossibly, I'm doing the same for him.

The pleasure is shocking, and almost-new. The air I need. And I'm unable to get enough.

After a few short hours of sleep, I feel the morning sun against my cheek, and for a moment, I'm afraid to open my eyes.

How will this look in the harsh light of day? With my eyes closed and Will's warm shape beside me, I can find no regret. But I can't stay here forever.

When I finally open my eyes, the room is hot with late-morning sun. In the hazy pink light, it's easy to convince myself I'm still dreaming. Easy to tell myself this is all a fairy tale, and that nothing I do here matters. Easy to roll back against Will's body and feel my skin against his, feel the weight of his arm as he pulls me into his chest.

I let myself exist in that fairy tale for the rest of the day; as we sit at the breakfast table with our knees touching. As we walk hand in hand along the river, and through gardens alight with colour. As we explore the neat grid of a city that gold has drawn on the map. In this fairy tale, there is no past and no future, and I'm so close to joy it's almost frightening.

"I've had a wonderful few days," Will says that night. "Being here with you." We are in a palatial dining hall at the top end of town, not far from

Astley's Amphitheatre. It's a place of marble stairs and white tablecloths, and velvet chairs so lavish I'm almost embarrassed to sit on them. The kind of place Tom and I dreamt of frequenting once he pulled our riches from the earth. The kind of place I never truly imagined myself going. But this grand dining hall, like the wine in front of me and the roast pigeon on my plate, are all things I've come to accept as pieces of the fairy tale. Pieces I know will inevitably give way to the mutton stew and mining cradles of reality.

"Champagne! More champagne!" bellows a man a few tables over, waving broadly to get the attention of both the waiter and the entire restaurant. He's new wealth, that rare success story – I can tell by both the pristine, barely worn clothes he and his wife are wearing, and by the excited curses he drops when the new bottle of champagne is brought to his table. Curses that flow like water from the mouths of the men on the diggings.

"Good for him," says Will, laughing lightly. He turns his wine glass around by the stem. "After the play," he says carefully, "I may move down here. Try my hand at bigger things."

Something sinks inside me. I look out the window and watch a coach roll past. I can't pretend to be surprised by this, of course. A man like Will is far more at home walking the streets of Melbourne than traipsing through the mud of the gold diggings. And he was clear about his ambitions at Astley's yesterday. But I can't help the sudden pain that lodges in my throat. With Will gone, Castlemaine will be a bleaker place. I keep my eyes averted for a moment too long.

His hand covers mine. He has removed his gloves, and his skin is warm against my own. "Lucy," he says. "Look at me."

I do.

"You could always come with me."

I smile, though I pull my eyes away instinctively. How can he dare to speak of such things? It brings this far too close to reality.

"Would that please you?" he asks.

"You know it would." My voice is almost a whisper.

"Then perhaps—"

"No," I say. "You can't talk of these things. I'm married."

"But not happily."

The knot in my throat tightens. At his boldness. At his truth. "What does that matter?"

"What do you mean, what does that matter?" He squeezes my fingers. "Happiness is everything. It's all that should matter."

"To you, perhaps. Your life has been all... well, it's been all theatres and hotels and places like this. But that's not what my life has been."

"I don't think my life has been quite as easy as you think," Will says gently. "I've had my share of challenges. Believe me. But that's exactly why I believe we should strive for happiness above all else."

I feel oddly irritated. Because this enormous proposition has not only thrown me completely off balance, it has also reminded me of the world that lies outside this blissful bubble we've created over the past two days. A world in which I have sworn myself to Tom Earnshaw for as long as we both should live.

"Do you feel no guilt?" I ask softly, gently. "At asking me these things? All the while knowing I have a husband back in Castlemaine?"

He lets out a humourless laugh. "Guilt?" he repeats. "Lucy, sometimes all I feel is guilt. I know this is wrong."

"And yet?" I ask, because I can sense that coming. That *and yet*; that reason why we both ought to push through our guilt and seek the happiness we crave. That happiness we cannot find within the confines of an orderly, moral life.

I'm not the kind of woman who...

How many times have I told myself this lie? Told myself I'm not the kind of woman who does these immoral things? But this is exactly who I am. Telling myself otherwise doesn't make it any less true.

But I can't shake the exhilaration, the happiness I feel when I'm with Will; that same rush that comes from playing the ghost. Upturning the way things are supposed to be.

Being a troublemaker.

Will looks across the room for a moment, eyes drifting over the digger who's refilling his glass of champagne. "Would you start again, Lucy? If you could?"

But what's the point of thinking *if you could*? Because I can't, can I. None of us can.

I shake my head, unable to look at him. "I can't."

"But what if you could?"

I let his words hang between us for a long time. A part of me desperately wants to agree to his request. Take me away, to this place where I'm happy. But I know I can't outrun the past, or the sadness that comes with it. We are shaped by what has come before. Wherever I go, I will take my memories. I know that if I were to make a life with Will, I could not hide my loss from him forever. As much as I wish it to be otherwise, I know my grief goes a long way towards defining me. But it's a part of myself I never want him to see. I don't want his pity.

"A marriage is for life," I say, staring into my half-empty wine glass.

"It doesn't have to be. And I think perhaps a part of you knows that. Why else would you be here with me?"

I dare to face him then. Because I know he's right. Deep down, a life without Tom is exactly what I have been seeking.

But walking away from a marriage is not something decent women do. At least, not in the life I know. The only women I have ever known to leave their marriages were those terrified wives who raced through the diggings and hid in each other's tents to escape their violent husbands. Or those sorry women put up by their men for sale. But Tom has never laid a hand on me. And he's not the kind of man who would take his wife to market. I'm far more responsible than him for the disintegration of our marriage.

But I am coming to realise that the life I know is one that encompasses the smallest fragment of all there is to experience. And perhaps if I were to peek into this vast array of possibilities, I would see a world in which I could truly move on. These past few days have made me feel far more alive than any other day I've crawled through since I lost my daughter. Maybe I can't live by the rules anymore.

Will lifts my hand and brings it to his lips. "I know it's a lot," he says. "But just think about it. There's no need to make a decision now."

Knocked off kilter by Will's proposition, I drown myself in wine, and when we emerge into the street an hour later, the edges of reality feel blurred and malleable. A policeman rides past on horseback, and the clops of hooves echo inside my body.

As we meander back in the direction of the Albion, a broadsheet plastered to a brick wall catches my eye.

Madame Moulin, Revelations of a Spirit Medium. A list of dates is printed beneath, tonight among them.

I snatch Will's arm. "Oh look! Madame Moulin's séance! Isn't that who Charles and Matthew saw?" I point at the broadsheet, bouncing quite drunkenly on my toes. "Her next sitting is at ten. Let's go and visit her."

He chuckles. "I don't think that's a good idea."

"Why not?"

"Because her séance parlour's on Lonsdale Street. That's far too close to the… less savoury parts of town."

"Less savoury parts of town?" I raise my eyebrows. "Do you truly think I've not been in worse places on the diggings? Come on, Will," I push. "You adore all this spiritualist business." I squeeze his arm. "Please?"

He shakes his head and sighs, though there's a smile on his lips. He glances at his pocket watch. "We'd best hurry then," he says finally. "It's almost ten." He offers his arm and we begin to walk briskly through the lamplit streets. "Why are you so interested in spiritualism all of a sudden?" he asks. "You and your rational brain."

Me and my rational brain. Why am I so interested? I'm not quite sure. I only know that the night feels like an adventure, and I don't want it to end. Besides, my rational brain has become somewhat scrambled by all the wine I've scarfed since Will so politely invited me to leave my husband.

Madame Moulin's séance parlour is in an unassuming townhouse in a residential part of the city. Will and I arrive breathless a few minutes after ten. A young man dressed entirely in black stands guard at the door.

"Have you reserved a place?" he asks us in a deep, theatrical voice.

"I'm afraid not," says Will. "Is there any way you might find room for us?"

The man makes a show of counting the tickets in his hand, then says, "Two shillings each."

Will hands him the money and he steps aside, allowing us to enter.

We follow the dull smoulder of light down a passage and into the parlour. A long oval table sits in the middle of the room, a single candle sighing in the centre. Dark drapes block the window, and an odd smoky fragrance thickens the hot air. There are seven or eight others inside, already seated around the table. Two couples among them; one close to my age, and the other several years older. The rest of the crowd is made up of elderly women wearing dark shapeless dresses and veils. Have these people come in hope of receiving a message from a lost loved one? Or are they, like me, just here for the spectacle? A thing of curiosity? Either way, these ladies in widows' weeds make an easy target for Madame Moulin. One of the women shuffles onto the chair beside her, allowing Will and me to sit together. Will gives her a nod of thanks.

I take my seat, glancing around the parlour. I think of what Charles told me about people hiding in hollowed-out walls. I squint into the darkness, searching for any hint of movement behind the wallpaper, but the single candle flickering in the centre of the table leaves most of the room in shadow.

Slow footsteps click down an unseen hall and here is Madame Moulin, a predictable cliché of dark skirts and silver hair. She sweeps into the room and takes a seat at the head of the table.

"Welcome. Tonight, we seek to uncover the mysteries of the other side." Her accent is unplaceably odd – I guess it European of some kind. I also guess it to be fake. I exchange humoured glances with Will.

Eyes darkened with lampblack peer across the table, inspecting each of us in turn. "Please place your hands on the table." We all do so obediently. "Close your eyes." Madame Moulin takes a long, dramatic breath. "I now call forth the spirits."

Silence settles over the room, so intense I can hear the candle sighing. I open my eyes, peering curiously around the table. Will winks at me and nudges my knee with his.

"There is a spirit with us now," says the madame suddenly. Cue a chorus of gasps and murmurs. "The name is John. Who here has come to speak with John?"

"John? My husband, John?" an older woman speaks up.

I roll my eyes. Madame Moulin's séance is just as Charles described it.

"Are you willing to speak with us, John? One rap for no, two raps for yes."

Two raps, of course, coming from the wall behind the madame.

Poor John's wife barely swallows a wail. My gaze drifts past Madame Moulin, straining into the darkness in an attempt to see the wall. Is the wallpaper moving, breathing, as if there is someone behind it? I can't be sure. The dark is too thick.

"Tell us, John," says Madame Moulin, "are you suffering?"

One rap. No.

"And do you miss your dear wife?"

I can barely hold back a snort at the madame's inane questions.

Two raps and his wife is in tears, no doubt with a sizeable gratuity for the medium as soon as this charade is done.

A bell rings from the darkness above our heads, bringing gasps from the sitters. And with my eyes open, I catch it; that faint shift of the madame's skirts. The slight movement of her thigh to pull on that unseen thread.

Madame Moulin is no more real than the Green Lady.

This feels like a joke. A mockery to all those of us who have lost our loved ones. Is this what I'm doing when I go out playing the ghost? Making a mockery of those who believe? Playing on their fears to satisfy my own need to rebel?

Shouldn't I know better?

Perhaps. But I also know it's because of Elsie's death that I need to play the Green Lady.

Madame Moulin's eyes turn upwards to the bell. "There are more spirits with us here tonight." She draws in a deep breath and closes her eyes again, keeping her chin tilted upwards. Begins to sway back and forth. The silence is almost tangible, broken only by the squeak of Madame Moulin's chair. Candlelight flickers on faces, casting shadows beneath eyes. I see fingers curl against the tabletop, but otherwise, the attendees are frozen. Subjects in a death photograph.

The madame reaches for the slate and chalk sitting in front of her on the table. Eyes still closed, she holds the tip of the chalk to the slate. It begins to move between her fingers.

At first, nothing appears on the slate but a chain of loops and curled, meaningless figures. And then, with excruciating slowness, there are letters.

I am here.

And in the corner of the slate, in a strange childlike hand: *Mama.*

On the other side of the table, a young woman cries out. The word knifes me, and I close my eyes, forcing away tears.

"Ask the spirit their name," the woman sobs.

The anger that tears through me is hot and fierce. Anger at Madame Moulin for preying on these people in mourning. Angry at these wailing women for falling for her tricks. Most of all, I'm angry at myself. Because I'm watching that young woman stare at the slate, and I can see her hoping with every inch of her being that her lost child's name will appear there in front of her. And yet I can't make myself believe.

I want to, desperately. Want that possibility that perhaps, against all reason, my daughter is in this room with us. That she might be just inches away, through a veil so thin I can almost reach her. But all I can see is trickery, and a world in which Elsie is gone forever.

I make suddenly to stand. Will's hand covers mine.

"What are you doing?" he murmurs.

"I want to leave." The room feels hot and airless and full of lies, and I suddenly want to be anywhere else.

Madame Moulin's eyes spring open. "There must be no breaking the circle," she says sharply. "Doing so will invite the spirits to take hold of you."

I clatter to my feet, stumbling out of the smoky parlour. The doorman looks at me in surprise as I blow past him.

"All right, ma'am?" he asks, in a broad London drawl that's completely different from the persona he affected when we first arrived.

I don't answer. I just hurry down the street, in a desperate attempt to escape the séance parlour.

I hear Will's footsteps behind me. Feel a pull of dread. Because how am I to get by now without telling him of all I have lost? And how can I share Elsie with him when I can't even share her with her father?

But there are no questions. He just wraps his arms around me, pulling me close. I catch his rosewater scent, laced with the fragrant smoke of the séance parlour. I am so grateful for his silence, his lack of questions. There is an unspoken understanding between us that, deep down, we are strangers, each with our own secrets and pain.

And right now, that is enough.

CHAPTER FOURTEEN

"The police are making efforts to clear Little Lonsdale Street of the dens which at present disgrace it."

The *Australian Star*
30th December 1889

"Are you all right?" Will asks finally.

I step back from his embrace. "Yes. I'm sorry. I didn't mean to embarrass you. Or… break the circle."

He chuckles. "I'll take my chance against the spirits taking hold of me."

"It's a scam," I say bitterly. "A joke."

"Yes. A very elaborate one."

"I thought you were open-minded about these things," I say.

"I am. But I'm not a fool. Madame Moulin's séance was clearly full of theatrics." He reaches an arm around my shoulder, pulling me close. "Let's get back to the hotel."

"No. Not yet." I don't want to go to bed with the dead at the front of my thoughts. These past few days have been such a blissful escape, and I need that to continue. I don't want to be pulled beneath the surface by Madame Moulin and her hollowed-out walls. I need something to take my mind off the letters that appeared on that slate.

I start walking, with little thought of where I'm going. There are no carriages on this street, and the men gathered outside a building on the corner are without the top hats and silk of the people we have been surrounded by for most of the evening. The trails of light from the lamp on the main street are all that illuminate the shadows.

Will jogs to keep up with me. He takes my arm, forcing me to a halt. "Lucy, stop. You're upset, I can tell. Let's just go back."

"I'm not upset."

His look clearly says he doesn't believe me. "I'm sorry for the things I said. For suggesting you leave your husband. I can tell it's rattled you."

"I don't want you to be sorry," I say. "I'm rattled because... because I'm thinking of it."

"You are?" I hear the spark of hope in his voice.

"Yes. And I'm not ready for our night to be over."

"All right," he agrees. "But this is a terrible part of town. Let's head back towards the Albion."

I peer across the road at a narrow doorway. I watch two Chinamen enter, followed by a group of white men. It's a strange sight; I've never seen the Chinese miners mingling with our kind in Castlemaine.

"What is that place?" I ask Will.

He examines the building, then shakes his head. "Never mind. Come on. Let's go back."

I raise my eyebrows. Keep my feet planted on the ground.

"It's an opium den, I imagine," he says finally. "They've become quite the rage since the Chinese brought the stuff over. All underground, of course. Seems as though the police are turning a blind eye to what's going on in this part of town."

Full of curiosity, I dart across the road and step inside before Will can stop me. He calls my name. Hurries after me.

The den is candlelit and full of shadows. A thick fug of smoke stings my eyes. Men lounge on divans and benches covered in straw matting, bringing long pipes to their lips. I notice a few women among them. There's a dull hum of chatter in the hot floral air. I glance at Will. I half expect him to demand we return to the hotel, but there's a look of interest in his eyes.

"Have you tried it?" I ask him. "Opium?"

He laughs. "Where do you think all that rubbish about Lady Fyvie's visions came from?"

"What's it like?"

"You've not taken laudanum before?"

"Well, yes, but not for… pleasure."

He hesitates for a moment. "Then I really don't think you need to—"

"Mr Browning," I say with mock sharpness, "it's far too late for decorum. You've already swept me away from my husband under false pretences. You've watched me play the ghost. Do you really think me so innocent?"

The words sound like more like Clara's than my own. If that colourless kitchen hand from Horley saw me now, she wouldn't recognise herself.

Will's hand finds the bare curve of my neck. "No, Lucy," he murmurs, close to my ear. "I've no illusions of your innocence."

My body sears with both shame and desire, but before I can speak, Will has a hand to my shoulder and is ushering me further into the den. He pays the Chinaman behind the bar, who gestures for us to sit on a narrow divan in the corner of the room.

Will and I sit close together, our legs pressed against each other's and our hats and gloves strewn in a careless pile beside us. The man appears with a long bamboo pipe in one hand and an oil lamp in the other, a candle flickering inside it. He sets them on the small table in front of us.

Will nods his thanks. With practised ease, he heats a dark knot of opium paste over the lamp, then places it in the bowl of the pipe. Leans back to take a long, slow draw. He blows a line of sweet-smelling smoke into an arc above his head. "I find it quite relaxing," he tells me. "Good for the creativity."

"I want to try it."

He hands me the pipe. "Not too much," he warns.

My throat burns as I inhale, but a warmth comes over me almost immediately. I feel the edges of the world unravel a little, and my anger at Madame Moulin fade. I lean against Will, feeling his arm wrap around my shoulder. Enjoying his solidity, his aliveness.

I open my eyes, picking out shapes in the shifting shadows of the den. The patrons are slow-moving, and the hum of voices is almost musical. Tonight, with the edges of reality softened, I am not so afraid of the Chinese men floating past me. Tonight, we feel like one and the same.

"Do you really believe there are people who can speak to the dead?" I ask Will. In the back of my mind, I see Madame Moulin's chalk meandering along the slate.

I am here.

Mama…

His fingers trace slow circles over my bare forearm. "Perhaps. I know most mediums are just performers. It's all trickery and theatre for the sake of those in mourning. But can we truly claim to know so much about the universe that we can definitively declare it's impossible to speak to the dead? What about men like Andrew Jackson Davis? Some of his revelations are so eye opening I believe there's every chance they come from the spirit world, as he claims. And several men of the cloth have claimed it to be a true phenomenon. After all, does the Bible not speak of ghosts?"

But I've stopped listening. Because through the sea of smoke-hazed figures is a face I never imagined I would see again.

Impossible.

Fred Buckley died six weeks ago when black powder exploded in his claim. We saw his remains buried in the cemetery on Campbell's Hill. And I listened to Clyde try to coax his ghost into rapping on the broken windlass. Two knocks for yes.

And yet there he is, walking past the bar and looking as real as Will and me. His long chin and fire-coloured hair leave me in no doubt. Fred Buckley has a face that's hard to forget.

He turns a corner and disappears. Instinct takes over and I scramble to my feet. Charge after him. I hear Will call my name, but I don't look back. I chase Fred Buckley down a dark, narrow passage. What I will do if I catch him, I have no thought, but I need to know if I saw what I think I did. Need to find that hazy line between reality and fantasy.

I break into a second smoke-filled parlour at the back of the den. Buckley is about to sit on a divan in the corner when I reach out and grab his arm, making him whirl around in shock.

"You're Fred Buckley," I say.

He chuckles at my look of horror. "Afraid you've seen a ghost?"

"You died in Castlemaine," I say. "I attended your burial." And then my thoughts catch up with me from the smoke-frayed world they've been

642

languishing in. "You're not a ghost."

He barks a short laugh. "No missy, I ain't." He sinks back on the divan and waves to an approaching server to put his pipe and lamp on the table in front of him.

"You faked your own death?" All too easy, I realise then, to throw black powder down into a claim. No one would question the lack of a body. "Why?"

Buckley lifts the pipe and leans forward to hold the opium over the lamp. Candlelight flickers beneath his eyes. "Leave me alone, woman. It's none of your business."

"Please. Tell me why you did it." Beyond the opium haze, my mind is beginning to race. All is not well on those diggings. I need to know what caused Buckley to stage his own demise. Did it have something to do with the thefts? With Constable Stone and the night fossicking? Or am I just jumping to conclusions?

"What's it to you?"

I suck in my breath. "I'm Tom Earnshaw's wife," I say, eyes pulling downwards with shame. "I'm worried for him."

Buckley's eyes flicker with recognition. And more than a little surprise. "Is Tom here?"

My face heats. "No," I say. "He's... He's not here."

Buckley just nods. What does he care about my infidelity?

"Did it have something to do with the police?" I press. "With Constable Stone?"

"Constable Stone," he snorts. "He's nothing."

"He's corrupt," I say.

"Of course he is. They say he beat a man half to death to get sent out here."

"Is he the reason you did what you did?"

Buckley shakes his head dismissively. "Just stay away from the police, Mrs Earnshaw. That's all you need to know."

"Stay away from the police? What do you mean? All of them? I—" Dizziness presses down on me suddenly and I stumble forward, bumping into the edge of the divan.

"Steady on there," says Buckley with a dull chuckle. He takes my elbow to steady me. "Why don't you head on back to whoever it is you're here with and leave me in peace?"

I feel the evening's bedlam of wine and opium lurching up inside me. I fly to the door at the back of the parlour. Stumble into a narrow lane and retch, surprised when nothing comes out. I lean against the brick wall, resting my head against my arms. I try to pull Clara's crimson skirts closer to my body. She won't be impressed if I bring them home smelling like whatever the hell is in that bucket beside the door.

I swallow hard as the stench turns my stomach again. Fred Buckley's words are thumping around in my brain.

Stay away from the police.

He's mistaken, surely. Misguided. Or trying to cover for his own crimes. The Castlemaine troopers are decent men.

But I realise I have nothing with which to back up that belief. Really, I know nothing of the Castlemaine police; not their names, barely their faces. Not beyond Constable Stone at least. But the men in uniform; aren't they the ones we're supposed to trust?

I feel a hand on my arm and dare to look, half expecting Will. Instead, it's Fred Buckley standing over me with a cup in his hand.

"All right?" he asks. He hands me the cup and I bring it gratefully to my lips before realising it's full of liquor. I groan and shove it back against his chest.

I straighten and look sheepishly at Buckley. "Thank you for coming after me."

He shrugs. "Well. Could get yourself in all sorts of trouble if you're not careful. I'm sure Tom wouldn't like you being alone out here." He eyes my plunging red neckline. "Especially dressed like that."

My cheeks flush and I fold my arms instinctively across my body. "The police are the ones behind the thefts?"

"I don't know why it surprises you. Greed is what keeps the goldfields alive."

I look at him squarely. "I need to know why you did what you did."

"Why?"

I close my eyes for a moment. Breathe deep to steady myself. "I caught Constable Stone night fossicking a few weeks ago," I say. "He knows I saw him. He's made threats… of sorts. And I need to know what I've gotten myself involved in."

Buckley's eyes take me in and he gives a single, short chuckle. "Didn't know Tom was married to such a menace."

I grit my teeth. When I don't answer, Buckley sighs.

"I made a stupid mistake. Got into a fight with one of the other diggers. Beat him up real bad. The troopers threw me in the cells. I thought for sure I were going to end up breaking rocks at Port Arthur. But the officers made me an offer. Said they'd let me go free if I went to work for them."

"Work for them?" I repeat. "Night fossicking?"

"At first. Then other things."

"What things?"

Buckley hesitates. "They're running a racket in the Black Forest," he says after a moment. "They send men out to hold up the coaches to and from the goldfields. A cut of the takings goes to the coachmen in exchange for their silence. And to keep them from firing a shot."

No. This is too much. "We passed through the Black Forest on the way here," I say. "Didn't have a single problem."

"Lucky you." He snorts. "It's happening, Mrs Earnshaw. Believe me. I were one of the poor bastards the troopers sent out there. Hold-ups once a month, all prearranged to make sure the right men are driving the coaches."

"The right men?" I repeat. "You mean the ones willing to stay quiet?"

He nods. "First Monday of the month, Castlemaine to Melbourne. Third Friday for the return journey." He smiles wryly. "No one notices the regularity because the hold-ups ain't hardly ever reported. Coachmen are paid to keep their mouth shut, and the passengers, well they just want the whole thing over and done. They know once their treasures are in the hands of bushrangers, they ain't getting them back again."

But my thoughts are caught on *third Friday for the return journey.*

The third Friday of the month is in two days' time.

We're due to take the coach back to Castlemaine tomorrow – Thursday. Can I convince Will to stay another night? I need to know if Buckley is telling the truth. Need to know the kind of place I'm living in, and just what I've entangled myself with.

"They gave you a cut of the takings too?" I ask.

"A few scraps. Most just goes into the officers' pockets. I only did it to stay out of the penal colonies. They're doing the same thing to that poor bastard Stone. Forcing him to get his hands dirty and giving him pennies in return."

For several moments, I say nothing, my mind struggling to make sense of all he has told me.

"And you couldn't get out?" I ask finally. "That's why you did what you did?"

Buckley nods. "I'd just finished my sentence before I went out to the diggings. I didn't want to live a life of crime no more. I knew if the Gold Commissioner ever learned of the racket going on under his nose, we'd be in no end of trouble. The officers'd likely get a slap on the wrist, but lags like me and Stone, we'd be off to the hangman. I tried to leave one night, but the coppers must have got word I was leaving. They caught me on the road out. Said they'd kill me if I left. I suppose they was worried about who I might tell. So I set off some black powder in my claim. Made it look like I done myself in. I—"

"Lucy!"

I whirl around at the sound of Will's voice. His hand slides around my arm. "What the hell are you doing out here?" His eyes fall to Buckley. "Who is this?"

"It's no one," I say hurriedly, turning from Buckley and ushering Will away. "I just wasn't feeling well." I feel a hand on my other arm, yanking me back.

"Mrs Earnshaw," Buckley says, his voice low, "you can't tell a soul what I just told you. Any of them coppers find out what you know, you won't see another day."

"What is he talking about?" Will demands.

I shake free of Buckley's grip. "I have to tell Tom," I say, my voice rattling. "He needs to know he can't trust—"

"No, you don't," Buckley snaps. "You just tell your husband to keep his head down and stay the hell away from the police."

CHAPTER FIFTEEN

My encounter with the all-too-unghostly Fred Buckley is enough to make me flee the opium den. The smell of the sea hangs on the wind and I lift my face to the sky. Try to order my thoughts.

Will appears behind me with our hats in his arms. He hands me my bonnet and gloves. "What was that about?"

"It's nothing," I say. "Just take me back to the hotel. Please."

He asks again when we're back in his room, my opium-scented gown flung over a chair in the corner. He stands close to me, lamplight painting shadows on his bare chest.

"That man knew about the thefts on the gold diggings," I tell him. I don't want to go into any more detail. The thefts are on one side of my life. Will Browning is on the other.

"You're worried for your husband," he says.

"Yes," I admit. "But that doesn't mean I…"

"I know," he says gently. "It's all right. I understand."

The silence seems to thicken, to tense. I don't want thoughts of Tom intruding into this room.

I shuffle closer to Will. Tug at my laces, releasing my corset.

In the darkness I feel his lips against my own, but my thoughts are wandering, wandering, to Buckley, to Tom, to crooked troopers and the Black Forest racket.

"What do you think about staying one more night?" I blurt.

"Don't you need to get back?"

"Not urgently. I'll just tell my husband the coach was delayed. I've had such a wonderful time. I don't want it to end."

It's not a lie, I tell myself. Two days in Melbourne with Will have left me feeling lighter than I remember feeling in forever. But I need to know if Buckley is telling the truth.

"Well," he says, "we've to be back in Castlemaine by Saturday for rehearsal. But I don't see why we couldn't manage one more night."

By Friday morning, my nerves have caught up with me. Am I really doing this? Knowingly climbing onto a coach that in all likelihood is to be set upon by bushrangers?

It's too late for regret. Before we left the hotel this morning, I slipped off my wedding ring and tucked it into the bottom of my case. Made sure I have a few coins in my pocket to hand over to the highwaymen.

"Are you all right?" Will asks as we wait at the terminus for the coach. "You're quiet this morning."

I pace in impatient circles. Manage a smile. "A lot on my mind is all."

He nods, pressing my hand between both of his. I let myself enjoy that fleeting feel of him. By the end of the day, we'll be back in Castlemaine, and I will go back to being Tom's wife.

At least for now.

The coach rattles up to the terminus, pulled by two large brown horses. Will helps me into the coach and I take the seat beside him. Things have gone too far for false propriety. There are no familiar faces in the carriage, and besides, if we really are about to be set upon by bushrangers, I want him beside me.

As the coach pulls away from the terminus, my pulse begins to thunder. Is this the most foolish thing I have ever done? There have been so many contenders over the past few weeks it's difficult to say.

I glance at the chain of Will's gold watch hanging from his pocket. "Perhaps you ought to hide that," I say. "Just in case."

He gives me a quizzical smile but unhooks the watch all the same.

I sit stiltedly beside the window, toes tapping nervously. The neat chaos of Melbourne vanishes over the horizon. Ahead, blue-grey mountains are half hidden by cloud.

I close my eyes and try to breathe.

Like it or not, I'm involved in this tangled mess of thieving that is going on in Castlemaine. Perhaps I ought to go to Constable Stone and speak openly. Promise him my silence. If Buckley is telling the truth, and those who claim to uphold the law in Castlemaine are doing anything but, surely the town is not a safe place to be. I fear for Tom, sleeping out in the open with his revolver in hand. If he and Leo continue guarding their claim at night, how long will it be until they catch a glimpse of a thief? Catch a glimpse of the truth?

And this truth – if that is really what it is – is a dangerous truth to know. The miners have had more clout since the uprising in Ballarat a few years ago, but it's still the men in uniform who hold the power. A miner who knows too much could be taken care of with minimal fuss.

And so could his wife.

Here is the forest. Muted sunlight struggles through the branches, painting long shadows over the road. Light rain has begun to fall, speckling the windows and blurring my view of the trees that lie beyond. The horses continue their steady rhythm, drawing us deeper into the forest. I realise I'm holding my breath.

The coach careens to a sudden stop, bringing a cry of shock from several of the passengers. I grip the edge of the seat to avoid being thrown forward.

"What's happening?" another woman asks shakily.

But I do not need to be told.

Horses appear on either side of the carriage, ridden by men in tatty, colourless coats and trousers. They both wear wide-brimmed hats pulled down low over their foreheads, neckcloths tied over their mouths and noses to hide their faces. Each has a pistol in their hand. One fires a shot into the sky, making the passengers gasp. Birds shriek and vanish. Will slides his hand into mine.

One of the highwaymen leaps from his horse, his boots crunching loudly on the road. The door of the coach clicks open and he's inside in a single, swift movement. With the pistol still between his fingers, he reaches into his coat and produces a small cloth sack. He strides through the carriage, directing the nose of the gun at a gold ring on one lady's finger. She slides it off tearfully and tosses it in the sack. The highwayman steps slowly through the carriage. A hat pin. A watch. A gold necklace.

Before he reaches me, I fumble in my pocket for the coin pouch. I've played this moment over and over in my head; walked into it headfirst, but I'm still hot with fear. I shove the pouch into the bushranger's sack, rigid in my seat.

Almost as quickly as they appeared, the highwaymen are gone. Around us, the forest is still, the clatter of hooves fading and becoming silence. For several moments, the only sound is the heavy breathing of the passengers, and the muffled sobbing coming from the woman who gave up the ring. Faint rain patters against the glass.

"Are you all right?" Will murmurs.

"I'm fine."

But it's a grand lie. The highwaymen appeared at the exact time Fred Buckley said they would. Coincidence? Hardly.

And that means there is every chance his other tales are also true.

The coach begins to move again, pulling us back towards Castlemaine. And the knot in my stomach grows a little tighter.

CHAPTER SIXTEEN

"The nuisances caused by the Celestials are becoming so serious that unless some measures are adopted to check their increase, a very pretty quarrel will happen … and result in something unpleasant. The Chinese are congregating around Forest Creek in great numbers, disgusting by their filthy habits the decent diggers among whom they happen to squat…"

Mount Alexander Mail
Castlemaine
13th October 1854

"A hold-up?" says Tom. "Oh Lucy, that's awful."

I arrived home to an orange dusk, just minutes before Tom returned from the diggings. At the sight of me in the kitchen, a day late, he pulled me into his arms, catching me by surprise.

I'm glad the news of the hold-up has taken his focus off my late return. Glad he hasn't stopped to poke holes in my garbled story of the coach's delay.

He unlaces his boots and kicks them under the table. "Did they hurt you?"

"No." I dump a handful of limp carrots into the soup pot. "And they only took a few coins. I hid my wedding ring in the bottom of my case before I got in the coach."

"Smart girl. You must have been terrified."

I stir the soup, not answering. I feel as though I'm seeing the town with fresh eyes. Seeing the dark current beneath the surface. Maybe I can't be surprised. As Fred Buckley said, this is a place grown on greed. Everyone came here hoping for a better life. And for those of us who have been unable to find it, it's only a short step to immorality and crime.

Tom smiles at me as I set his soup bowl in front of him. He's washed his hands and face for supper, changed into a clean shirt. The bruise beneath his eye has lightened to a faint shadow.

"How was the theatre?" he asks.

"Wonderful," I say, unwilling to go into more detail.

Tom tears the end off the loaf of bread. "I saw that woman from your theatre group at the dispensary. Clara."

The kitchen feels suddenly cloying. "Yes?"

"She didn't go to Melbourne with you?"

"No. She decided to stay. Make sure everything was ready for the opening of her shop." The lie comes to me too easily.

"I see."

Does he believe me? I can't tell.

There is nothing but warmth in his voice. But perhaps he's testing me. Perhaps I'm not the only one who's learnt a few acting skills over these past bitter months.

"Have there been more thefts?" I ask.

"A couple of tents were robbed out by Pennyweight. Nothing major. Clyde reckons he saw that Chinaman Ah Tam out at Forest Creek, sniffing around in other men's claims."

I shift uncomfortably. "Is he certain?"

"You'd have to ask him that," says Tom.

"Have you been guarding the claim?"

"Every second night. Alternating with Leo."

I stir my soup, my appetite gone. "You ought to give them what they want," I blurt. "The thieves. If they want to raid your claim, just let them." My voice wavers.

Tom frowns. "Why in hell would I do that?"

I grit my teeth. How desperately I want to tell him of Fred Buckley and all I have learnt. But Buckley's warning rings in my ears. *Any of them coppers find out what you know, you won't see another day.* There's so much I need Tom to hear. But so much I can't speak of. It would just put him in danger.

"These thieves," I say instead, "who knows how violent they are? Who knows what they're capable of? If they want to dig in your claim, you should just let them do it."

Tom gives a thin smile and turns back to his soup. "Don't worry, Luce. There's nothing in my claim but mud anyway."

I go to Clara's shop the next morning. The place is far more orderly than it was last time I saw it, with mannequins arranged in the windows and the reams of fabric lined up neatly in one corner. A broadsheet advertising her wares is plastered to one window, and the white patch on the front door has been painted over in a handsome grey-green.

I find her sitting at the table in the corner of the shop, sketching the beginnings of a new design. I hold out the gown and hoop skirt.

"Here. Thank you for lending them to me."

Clara nods, barely looking up from the page. "Just put them on the chair over there."

I set the skirts down and hover beside the table. "How have your first few days of business been?"

"A decent start," she says. "I've commissions from two of the ladies I used to sew for."

"That's wonderful." I shift my weight, making the floor creak noisily.

Finally, she looks up. "Is there something else you need, Lucy?"

"When you've the time," I begin awkwardly, "will you take me to the Chinese camp? Show me where to get the thunder god vine?" My voice is impossibly small.

Clara smiles to herself, tapping her pencil against her chin. "You had a good time in Melbourne then?"

I nod faintly. I can't go into more detail. Can't speak of what Will asked me to do. Speaking of it makes it far too real.

"Good." Clara eyes me, but when it becomes clear I'm not going to offer any more information, she lets the matter slide. She puts down her pencil. "Let's go now. I've a client coming for measurements in an hour."

Off we go in the direction of Clinkers Hill, where the Chinese miners have made their camp, away from the settlements of the white men.

I've heard stories about the mysterious tonics and potions to come out of the Chinese apothecary, cures much more outlandish than the fish oil and earthworms on the shelves of the dispensary in town. Before Clara had tucked the bottle of thunder god vine into my hand, I'd always brushed their concoctions aside, put it down to a quirk of their culture. Even when Elsie fell ill, venturing to the Chinese camp for a cure had not even crossed my mind. What kind of person would feed their child something that came from this unknown race?

But I do not have the same fear for myself. Moments before I crept into Will's hotel room, I tossed back the thunder god vine without a second thought.

Through the warren of tight huts, I see the dark heads of the Chinese moving through the streets. Though they have swapped their pointed hats for woollen caps more like our own, their unfamiliarity is unnerving. I feel wildly out of place.

"Let's just go back," I say suddenly. "I'll… I'll just take the risk."

Clara frowns. "What are you so afraid of?"

I hesitate. I can't place it. But it has something to do with that terror wrought by strangeness, by the unfamiliar. That same terror that has us transplanting myths of haunted castles across the seas to unknown lands.

There's been talk of the Chinamen luring unsuspecting ladies to their tents. Talk of them having the power to wipe a woman's senses clean. But the rational part of me knows this is little more than gossip. It also knows that this is not what's causing me to be afraid. This is just fear of the foreign.

Clara loops her arm through mine and keeps walking. "You're being stupid," she says, and that's the end of the matter.

I try to conjure up the apathy towards the Chinese I felt swanning through their opium den on Little Lonsdale Street. It's much harder to do without lungs full of smoke and a head full of wine.

The Chinese apothecary is a primitive, windblown place, like the tented shopfronts that lined Forest Creek when Tom and I first arrived. A rickety shelf teeters at the back of the tent, a makeshift wooden counter in front. An older man stands behind it, threads of grey streaking his long queue.

I stare at my feet, far too overcome with fear and shame to make eye contact with anything other than the floor.

"Good morning," says Clara.

I glance up curiously to see the man nod in response.

"Thunder god vine," Clara tells him.

He nods again. Disappears behind a flap at the back of the tent. I hear him murmuring to someone on the other side.

The man returns with a small jar. He puts it on the counter and holds up one finger.

Clara nudges me. "One shilling."

I fumble in my purse and dump the money on the counter. I slip the jar into my reticule, nod my thanks and rush from the shop.

In my hurry to escape, I narrowly miss colliding with a Chinese woman and her child. I stumble, caught off guard by the sight of them. I'd not realised any women and children had made the journey out here with their countrymen. Certainly, I've never seen them in town.

"I'm sorry," I murmur, holding up my hand in a gesture of apology.

The woman nods, bowing her head. Then she looks up, her eyes meeting mine. I feel a sudden, unexpected moment of connection; as an Englishwoman, I feel like a novelty among all the men here on the diggings – I can hardly imagine how it must feel for her.

She steps inside the apothecary, passing Clara in the doorway.

I whirl around at the sound of footsteps, wild voices. One of the Chinese diggers thunders past, pursued by a group of white men. The Chinaman skids on the loose earth as he rounds the corner, falling to his knees. One of the men leaps on top of him, pinning him to the ground.

"Bloody thief," the Englishman hisses. "Stay the hell away from our claims." He brings back his fist, pounding the Chinaman's nose. Blood spurts onto the footprinted earth.

This man is innocent. I know it. He's being punished for the crimes of Stone and the other troopers.

Open my mouth and my secrets will spill. But how can I allow this?

Before I can change my mind, I race towards the men. "Stop!"

The attacker turns to give me a fleeting glance. The rest don't even acknowledge me.

The Chinaman groans as a boot flies into his side.

And then, more footsteps; more men approaching. Tom is among them. At the sight of me, he stops in surprise.

"What in hell are you doing here?"

I'm breathless. "They're attacking the wrong man."

"How do you know that?"

The Chinaman is coiled, pleading, shielding his face from the men's wild kicks.

"Do something!" I cry, pushing past Tom's question. "They're going to kill him!"

Before he can reply, the police arrive on horseback, firing a shot into the sky. Like frightened dogs, the men scatter, leaving the Chinese digger curled up on the ground. Two of his countrymen hurry to his side, helping him to his feet. They rush him into a nearby tent, a stream of blood running down his face and blackening the collar of his shirt.

The police horses canter up the hill towards us.

"Why are you here?" I ask Tom, my voice low. "Did you come to attack that man?"

Hurt flashes across his eyes. "Is that what you think of me now?"

I falter. I don't want to believe Tom has it in him to attack another man. But I think of the night he came home swollen-eyed, with Clyde's blood staining his knuckles.

"Leo told me a group had come here to confront Ah Tam," he tells me. "I came along to—"

"To watch?"

"To hear what he had to say for himself. I didn't expect them to just jump him like this."

I let out my breath. I can't tell if my husband is naïve or a liar.

"Lucy?" says Clara. "Are you all right?"

"She's fine," Tom cuts in tersely.

I give her a strained smile. "I'm all right. Thank you. You ought to get back. You don't want to be late for your meeting."

Clara hesitates for a moment, then nods, turning and disappearing between the huts. Hot wind blows up the hill, whirlpooling the dust.

Suddenly I want nothing more than to escape the Chinese camp, with

Ah Tam's blood black on the ground. I start to walk, Tom jogging to catch up to me.

For several long seconds, we walk in silence, our footsteps crunching rhythmically.

"How do you know they were attacking the wrong man?" asks Tom.

I watch at my feet as I walk.

Telling him everything Fred Buckley told me is too dangerous. But I have to give him something.

I stop walking, tugging him into a narrow alley behind the marketplace. The stench of boiling meat floats out from a cookshop and makes my stomach roll.

"I saw Constable Stone night fossicking at Forest Creek. Three weeks ago."

For a moment, Tom says nothing. "Stone," he repeats.

I nod.

"How do you know he wasn't just on duty?"

"He wasn't wearing his uniform."

"That doesn't necessarily mean—"

"He's involved in this, Tom," I push. "I know it. I saw him climbing out of another man's claim in the middle of the night. Alone. You have to believe me. The Chinese miners are innocent. Tell the other men not to go after them again."

For several moments, Tom just stares at me, his face unreadable. We are standing toe to toe, and I can feel the heat rising from his body. Can see the dark flecks in his blue eyes. And the coldness.

"What in hell were you doing out at Forest Creek in the middle of the night?" he asks finally. There's a strain to his voice, as though his control is about to tear loose.

"I came out there to find you. You were guarding the claim that night." A lie, yes, but how could he know this? "You left your coat and I was afraid you might get cold in the night..." My words are thin with guilt.

"You never brought my coat to the claim."

"I know. After I saw Stone fossicking, I got scared and ran."

He rubs his square jaw. Tries to take a step back from me, but his spine meets the wall of the hut he stands in front of. "Why didn't you tell me this earlier?"

And the answer to that, well, that comes easily when I think of Constable Stone on my doorstep with threats in his eyes. When I think of Fred Buckley hurling black powder into his claim to escape the troopers' clutches.

"I was afraid. Afraid of what he might do if he found out I'd told anyone."

Of all the lies I've just spouted, it's this truth that brings the look of doubt to Tom's eyes. I can see it all – the anger, the hurt, the questions. But he doesn't voice any of it. Instead, he just nods stiffly.

"Stone," he says again.

"I'm telling the truth, Tom. You have to believe me."

"Why would I not believe you?" The words are spoken so simply, but I can hear everything that lies beneath them. My late-night rehearsals and midnight walks for air, and *I saw that woman from your theatre group at the dispensary.*

He starts to walk. Impulsively, I follow.

I glance sideways at him. His eyes are storm clouds, face furrowed in a deep frown.

"Tom," I say. "You can't tell anyone what I just told you. Promise me. It's very important."

He doesn't answer. Doesn't promise. Instead, he says, "Why were you at the Chinese camp?"

"I went to their apothecary. Clara said they could give me something for… headaches." My fingers tighten around my reticule, tracing the shape of the jar inside.

"You were visiting someone, weren't you," Tom says suddenly. "Out at Forest Creek. The night you saw Stone fossicking. You were visiting another man."

I feel his words like a physical blow. Hear my involuntary inhalation.

"I came to bring you your coat," I manage.

Tom breathes heavily through his nose. "Were you visiting the same man you went to Melbourne with?"

Heat courses through me. "I went to Melbourne with the theatre group."

But I can hear the waver in my voice. And I know my husband can hear it too.

CHAPTER SEVENTEEN

Tom does not come home for supper. The stew I've cooked sits congealing on the range. I stare mindlessly at the pot, letting flies gather around the rim. My throat is thick with tears.

I try to tell myself this is what I wanted. For Tom to discover my secrets. In fleeting moments since I returned to Castlemaine, I've even imagined him being the one to cast me out of the house. Then I could disappear off to the salons of Melbourne with Will, the decision made for me.

But Tom's absence leaves a deep coldness inside me. How much does he know? How many conclusions has he drawn?

I turn the pages of my script and recite my lines. But it brings me none of the usual joy. The Green Lady fails to pull me from reality like she has always done.

Craving company, I leave the house and head for Clara's shop.

Though it's getting late, I can see through the window that she's still working, stitching buttons onto a waistcoat on one of her mannequins. Her dark hair hangs in a long plait down her back, a frown of concentration creasing the bridge of her nose. At the sight of her entrenched in her work, I turn to leave. I can't bother her with troubles I've brought on myself.

As I reach the corner, I hear the front door click open. She steps out into the street, calling me back.

"You're busy," I say. "I didn't mean to disturb you."

"It's all right, I could use a break. Come in. I'll make us some tea."

I follow her back into the shop. She carries the lamp into the living quarters and sets it on the tiny table. Stokes the fire and hangs the kettle above the flames.

The back room is chaos. Petticoats are strewn over the unmade bed, swathes of fabric draped over chairs. A half-drunk cup of cold tea sits in front of me at the table, among a pile of hairpins, scissors, and a copy of yesterday's *Mount Alexander Mail.*

"How was the meeting with your client?" I ask.

"Fine." She takes the dirty teacup and rinses it in the trough. "Has your husband found out you were with Will?"

"Is it so obvious?" I play with a splintered edge on the table. "He doesn't know it was Will. He just suspects I've been with another man."

"How did he find out?"

I rub my eyes. "I told him you were coming to Melbourne with me. And then he saw you at the dispensary."

"Oh hell," says Clara. "I'm sorry, Lucy. I—"

"Don't be foolish. It's not your fault. And I told him I was out on the claims one night and he thinks I was out visiting."

"Why in hell did you tell him that?"

"It's a long story. That man they attacked at Clinker's Hill today…" I fade out, not wanting to revisit the whole sorry mess.

"Maybe it's for the best," says Clara. "You and Tom are unhappy, that much is obvious. Maybe you'd both be better off finding your own way."

The thought brings sudden tears to my eyes. "A marriage is for life," I say, for not the first time.

Clara shakes her head. "Open your eyes, girl. Whatever precious little bubble you existed in in England, it's gone now. Things are different here. People are not so stuck in their ways. Not so worried about what society thinks of them. Look." She flips through the newspaper lying on the table and scans the page. "Here. *'To my wife Margaret Owens, having gone away with Peter Worthington, I declare myself no longer responsible for your debts and financial upkeep.'*"

I frown. "That's dreadful."

"Is it? Sounds to me like Margaret Owens and her husband might be far happier without each other."

Perhaps she's right. But the thought of Tom posting such a message fills me with unfathomable shame and sadness.

My tears spill suddenly, and I swipe at them with the back of my hand. Clara lifts the kettle and fills the teapot, placing a cup in front of me on the table. She presses a hand to my shoulder for a second.

"Let's go back to the front room," she says. "It's too hot back here." With the lamp in one hand and her teacup in the other, she leads me back out to the parlour. "What do you think of this?" she asks, handing me a sketch of a pin-striped gown. "Too garish?"

"Not at all," I say. "In Melbourne, the women were wearing—"

My words are lost beneath a sudden crash, and I feel glass graze my cheek. A large rock thumps against a mannequin, knocking it to the floor amongst shattered pieces of the window. I stumble backwards, tea spilling down the front of my dress.

Clara tears through the front door. "You bastards!" she yells into the street. "Come back here and show your damn faces!"

She comes back inside and slams the door.

"Did you see who it was?"

She shakes her head. Closes her eyes for a moment and leans against the door. Her jaw trembles, then she clamps it closed.

"Are you all right?" I ask gently.

She opens her eyes. Nods. Then she kneels carefully among the glass, shifting the mannequin and its waistcoat away from a pool of spilled tea.

I kneel beside her and touch her wrist. "I'm sorry," I say. "We'll fix this."

"Of course we will," she says, picking at the glass shards with hard eyes. Earth-scented wind gusts through the broken window and blows our hair back from our faces. My hand tightens around her wrist. "Don't let these men stop you."

I expect some sharp retort from Clara – *no, of course I won't* – but her lips are pressed into a thin white line. She reaches for another piece of glass, cursing as a shard slices into her finger. A bead of blood appears on her pale skin. I stand carefully, holding out my hand to help her to her feet. "Come on," I say. "I'll help you clean this up."

"Are you coming to the hunt?" asks Tom.

Every few months, the diggers shoulder their weapons and charge out to the bushland to blast possums from the trees. First man with a hit gets his drinks paid for all night.

Tom stands by the door with his revolver in hand, looking at me expectantly. I'm not sure what game we're playing. Am I to pretend there are no secrets between us? Or am I to demand that we throw things out in the open? Tell my husband everything and let whatever is to come of it come?

No. I can't do that to Will. Can't throw him in the path of Tom's wrath. Nor can I face the confrontation of it. After a year of small talk, the thought of having a real conversation with my husband terrifies me.

Pretending feels like the only way forward. Pretending everything is fine. And pretending I don't think running through the dark with rifles and chasing some poor creature up a tree isn't the stupidest thing I've ever heard.

"Of course I'll come," I say, taking my bonnet from the hook.

I follow Tom out of the cottage and through town towards the scrub on the edge of Moonlight Flat. The streets are busy, loud. Men stride past, laughing and chattering, bottles in one hand and rifles in the other. A thin crescent moon hangs among an explosion of stars, silently watching the chaos below.

I can feel tension pouring from Tom's body. "Slow down a little," I say, jogging to catch up with him.

He stops charging. Still doesn't speak.

"I wonder if Leo will win again this time," I say, trying for lightness.

Tom grunts noncommittally. He shifts his revolver to his other hand, widening the space between us.

A crowd has gathered among the trees, shining lamps up into the branches. An unseen creature rustles the silver leaves.

"Careful, man," someone calls, "ain't you heard there's ghosts out here?"

A roar of laughter.

A shot echoes into the sky. Tom hurries after the crowd as they chase the animal further into the bush. I let myself fall behind.

A group of men have their rifles raised towards the dark silhouette of a tree. I hope the poor creature manages to outrun them. I also hope Tom won't raise his weapon, but just watch proceedings as he did the last time we came to one of these debacles. I don't like the sight of my husband with a weapon in his hand.

Last time we were here, we stood on the edge of the cluster, arm in arm, buffering each other against our fresh loss. We had gone to watch the hunt in hope it might distract us. And yes, for a few hours, it did. Because standing there arm in arm with Tom, with the rest of the settlement cheering and howling around us, it felt like us against the world. How have we taken such a wrong turn?

Tonight, Tom is not just watching proceedings. Not that I expected him to. He lifts his revolver and fires, barely even aiming.

"Take your time, Tom," I say. "That was a terrible shot. You'll hurt someone."

He holds the weapon out to me. "You want to try?" Bitterness in his words.

I wrap my arms around myself. "Of course not."

He turns back to the trees. Fires again. This time his shot is so wild it brings laughter from the men standing beside him.

"All right, Earnshaw, that's enough," Clyde barks. "You ought to listen to your wife. She's right, you'll have someone's head off." He waves at Ollie, who's standing to Tom's left. "You're up, Cooper."

Tom steps back, shifting the revolver from one hand to the other. I watch as Ollie carefully lines up his shot and pulls the trigger. He curses as the possum darts away again. Laughter ripples through the crowd.

"That creature's too smart for you all," I say to Tom, forcing a smile.

He doesn't look at me.

"Are you ignoring me?"

"I'm not ignoring you. I'm hunting."

I wrap my arms around myself. "Speak to me then."

"About what, Lucy? What would you like to speak about?" He looks at me fleetingly, before turning back to the hunt.

My throat tightens, and I blink back tears. "Speak about anything," I cough. "Anything at all."

He turns to me then, and the coldness in his eyes makes him look like a stranger. "Anything? How about we talk about whose bed you've been rolling around in?"

Dread sears through me. Eyes pull towards us, before hurriedly turning away.

"Jesus, Tom," I hiss, pulling him backwards, away from the crowd. "Keep your damn voice down."

"Am I embarrassing you?" he says loudly. "Isn't this what you wanted, Luce? For me to talk to you?"

Rage shoots through me. "You're a bastard." In an instant, my guilt is gone. I can't bear to be around him for another second. What was I thinking, coming out here with him tonight? Trying to save something that cannot be saved. Something I don't even want to be saved. My hatred for Tom is suddenly blinding.

I whirl around and begin to charge back towards town. He snatches my arm.

"Where are you going?"

"Anywhere!" I cry. "Anywhere away from you!"

Tom lowers his voice. "I don't want you running around out there on your own."

I shove him away. "I don't care what you want! Stay the hell away from me." I've never spoken to my husband like this before. Would never have dared. But what do I care now? It's only a matter of time before he's posting a message in the newspaper to let the world know he's washed his hands of me.

I'm running down the dark ribbon of the road before I'm fully aware of what I'm doing. I'm beginning to make a habit of running away.

I wait for Tom's footsteps behind me, but they don't come.

When I reach the edge of town, I stop to catch my breath. I hear drunken shouts coming from the hunt, gunshots piercing the sky.

The hatred inside me builds, threatening to consume me. Hatred for this place, with its hollow earth and desperate men, and all those lost children buried on the hill. I snatch a stone from the side of the road and fling it wildly to let a little of the rage loose from my body. It strikes a drinking trough with a violent, satisfying clang.

I run to Clara's shop and pound on the door. Squint impatiently through the window that's not boarded up. I can see faint lamplight coming from the back room.

"I need the Green Lady's dress," I say when she answers.

"What in hell, Lucy?" She ushers me inside, locking the door behind us. "Are you all right?"

"Where's the dress?" I gulp down my breath. "I'm going to play the ghost."

Clara puts her hands to my shoulders. "You can't go out hoaxing in this state," she says. "Why don't you come and sit down? Tell me what happened."

I shake my head. I've already done far too much talking tonight. I need to disappear into a world where reality is a little more distant. "Where's the dress?"

"It's in the back," Clara says after a moment. "I'll get it for you. Just stay here."

She returns a moment later with a half-filled glass of gin. She nods to the chair beside her work table. "Here. Sit down and drink this. Might relax you a bit."

"Where's the dress?" I ask again.

"I said I'd get it for you. Just sit down."

I sit, finally accepting the glass. Pulling off my bonnet, I take a sip, listening to Clara's footsteps disappear into the living quarters. The liquor burns as it slides down my throat.

I can't go home yet, not after the way I spoke to Tom. Nor do I want to. I can't bear the thought of crawling into bed beside him. What would happen if I disappeared for the night? Would he tear the town apart looking for me? Or would he leave me to my own devices? Wash his hands of his unfaithful wife?

I realise the shop has fallen quiet. I call Clara's name, but there's no response. I get to my feet and peer into the back room. It's dark, except for the muted glow coming from the remains of the fire. Has she gone out the back door? I barely heard a sound.

The door bursts open suddenly, and she flies back inside, Will in tow.

No, no, I don't want him here. Around Will, I have always hidden the most damaged parts of myself. And I am acutely aware they're on glaring display right now.

But when he pulls me into his arms, his touch is so filled with care and affection that it makes my throat seize with pain.

"Tell me what's wrong," he says, impossibly gently.

"Nothing's wrong. I want to play the ghost." My voice is muffled against his chest.

"I don't think that's a good idea."

I slide out of his arms. "Don't you?" I say tautly. I look back at Clara. "Is that why you fetched him? So he could tell me what to do?"

"Of course not," she says, "I—"

"Have you seen the men out on their stupid possum hunt?" I demand, uninterested in their response. "Running around like children and scaring the life out of these poor sorry creatures? Maybe they need to be given a bit of a fright themselves."

I rub my eyes, trying to calm myself. Like it or not, if I'm to go out hoaxing, I'll have to get past these two gatekeepers first. And to do that, I'll have to show them I can keep myself together.

"I need that escape," I admit. "I need to forget everything for a time."

Will nods faintly. I can tell he knows he's played a role in my internal chaos. That his offer to build a new life with me has rocked me at my foundations. And I can see the wordless apology in his eyes. I don't want him to feel regret. Because right now, his offer of a new life is the only thing keeping me afloat.

"Yes," I say suddenly.

He steps back, hands still around my forearms. "Yes, what?"

"I want to go to Melbourne with you. I want everything we spoke about."

He catches Clara's eye for a moment, and she disappears into the shop. Maybe she's finally going for the damn dress.

Will runs his thumb over my cheek, smooth as silk compared to Tom's rough skin. "Nothing would make me happier," he says, "but you're in a state, Lucy. I'm not sure you've thought this through."

I exhale sharply. It feels like I've done nothing but think. Nonetheless, I understand Will's reluctance. I suppose I was something of a walking disaster when I came charging into the shop. "It's what I want," I say, levelling my voice. "But if it makes you happy, I'll think it through some more tonight."

Will holds his lips to my forehead. "Good." And then a firm kiss against my lips. I hear myself murmur against him, my fingers making a tight fist around the hem of his jacket. He tucks a strand of hair behind my ear. And just when I expect him to talk me out of going hoaxing tonight, he gives me an empathetic smile. "Shall we find out where Clara's keeping that dress?"

I step out into the street, reams of green skirts flowing behind me. Lilias Drummond, the poor Green Lady, betrayed by her unfaithful husband and doomed to wander the halls of Fyvie Castle forever. I wonder, as I glide past the stables of the Commercial, whether Lilias Drummond really existed. Was she once as earthly and human as me? Or is she like so many of the stories told in this place; nothing but a myth? A way of making sense of the world; of our fears, our regrets, the darker sides of ourselves we hide beneath the surface?

The street is a little busier than when I raced to Clara's shop in disarray. Apparently people are growing bored with the hunt, though I can still hear plenty of pistol shots coming from Moonlight Flat. Still hear plenty of drunken, boyish laughter. For a second, I wonder what Tom is doing. I push the thought away quickly. When I'm the Green Lady, there's no room in my head for Tom, or for Will, or even for Elsie. That is part of the allure; this blissful emptiness, as playing the ghost consumes me.

I have an eerie glide down to a fine art. Tiny, slow steps that look for all the world as though I'm floating along the street. As always, I keep to the alleys, to the narrow lanes. Let those walking the main thoroughfares catch no more than a glimpse of me.

The woman who sees me tonight belongs at Madame Moulin's séance table. Hunched shoulders and darting eyes, her small body swamped in widow's weeds. At the sight of me gliding down the alley, she lets out a sharp cry, a hand pressed to her chest. She turns and stumbles back in the direction of the main street, and I instinctively hide myself in the narrow gap between two houses.

The woman is crying now, dreadful searing wails. Though I can't see her, the nearness of the sound makes me certain she is still in the alley. Footsteps thump towards her.

"Ma?" says a young man's voice. "What's happened? What on earth are you doing down here?"

The woman replies only in sobs.

"Has someone hurt you, Ma? Who's there?"

I hold my breath.

Between the woman's wails, I make out, "The lady."

"Which lady?" asks her son. "Who?"

I glance over my shoulder. I can't disappear this way. The only way out is back through the alley.

"Come on, Ma," I hear finally. "Let's get you home." The crying gets gradually softer. Finally, it disappears.

I close my eyes, trying to slow my heart.

Though there's a thrill to being seen, I can't help but feel guilty at the woman's distress. Perhaps the Green Lady has been out for long enough tonight.

I slip out from between the houses and head in the opposite direction to where the woman disappeared. Back towards Clara's parlour.

And out I float into a lane behind the shop, rounding the corner and coming face to face with one of the possum hunters. I stop abruptly. I did not expect anyone to be here, and I try not to let my surprise show on my face.

He stares at me for a long second, eyes wide and lips parted. The terror on his face makes me feel powerful.

And next, well, does it happen as though in slow motion, or does it all happen at once? I don't know. Hand in his pocket. Pistol in his hand.

And that terror in his face, that fearful instinct; it makes him fire.

The sound is deafening, distorted, my brain registering the noise at the same time it grasps the blaze above my hipbone. I look down to see a bloom of crimson creeping over the pale green bodice of my dress.

And then I am falling, the man cursing, stumbling; my earthly, flowing blood bringing far more horror to his face than the sight of the Green Lady.

CHAPTER EIGHTEEN

"For God's sake bring me a light, for we have caught Springheeled Jack here in the lane."

The Times
London
22nd February 1838

The shooter's face swims in and out of my vision.

"I didn't... I thought..." He is dithering, hand-wringing, face white with panic.

"Get out of here." Will shoves him away. Kneels at my side. He's asking me questions, whipping off his neckcloth and pressing it to my hip. His words all seem jumbled. All I can make sense of is the roar of pain in my side.

I hear Clara's voice too: "I'll go for the surgeon."

And then I'm in Will's arms, being carried away from the glare of the streetlamps and through the back door of Clara's shop. I close my eyes, feeling every jolt in my body. Will lays me gently on the bed and smooths my hair from my forehead. Kneels at my side with words I'm sure are supposed to be calming, but the panic in his voice betrays him.

The door cracks open as Clara charges through it. "Surgeon's on his way." She reaches into her reticule for a small bottle and hands it to Will.

"Give her this. It's laudanum. For the pain."

He pulls out the cork and holds the bottle to my lips. I gulp down a few drops, a trickle running out the side of my mouth. For a second, I wish desperately for Tom.

"Am I going to die?" I ask.

"Of course not." I hear the waver in Will's words. He strokes my hair with an unsteady hand. I close my eyes, desperate for the laudanum to have a scrap of an effect.

"There are police in the lane," says Clara. "We ought to tell them what happened."

Panic grips me. I don't want those corrupt troopers anywhere near me. Who knows what they're capable of? "No. No police." I try to sit, but pain rips through my body, making me cry out. "Please."

Clara and Will exchange glances. I can see their unasked questions. And I sure as hell am not about to answer them now.

Without releasing the pressure on my hip, Will wipes a damp cloth over my cheeks and forehead. To calm me, I think at first. Or is it? As he dips the cloth back in the washbin and continues to scrub at my skin, I realise he is cleaning my face of makeup. Washing away the Green Lady. Hiding any hint of what I've been doing.

And then there's another person in the room. A man leaning over me. Mr Hamilton, the settlement's surgeon.

"What happened?" he asks.

"Possum hunt," I manage.

Will presses a gentle hand to my shoulder to still me. "An accidental shooting," he tells the surgeon.

Hamilton lets out a grunt that says he knows we're lying. The hunt is taking place all the way out on Moonlight Flat. Too far from Clara's shop for my story to be believable.

Scissors slice through the fabric over my hip, freeing me from the Green Lady's gown. Blood trickles down my side.

I close my eyes against the violent tilting of the world. Fragments of the surgeon's verdict reach me through my haze.

Hit above the hip, clean entry.

And then there are hands on my shoulders, holding me to the bed. A cloth held over my mouth and nose, damp, with a sickly-sweet smell. The chloroform struggles to drag me down, the burning in my side refusing to let me slide into unconsciousness. I'm hovering, somehow, on the edge of two worlds. A place of haunted castles and ringing bells, and Elsie's name appearing in chalk on a slate. I'm in an opium dream I can't break free from, charging through the Black Forest and hearing myself scream. I see men in the earth and piles of gold I can't quite reach, and an empty wooden box going down, down into Fred Buckley's grave. And then, mercifully, the dark swallows me and I'm aware of nothing more.

When I open my eyes, Will is sitting on the edge of the bed, my hand between both of his. His jaw is tight, his eyes dark with worry.

"Is it over?" I ask. I'm scared to move.

He nods. "How do you feel?"

My hip is pulsing and I can feel tight strapping around my middle. I dare to glance down. Blooms of crimson still blot the sheets, the stained dress of the Green Lady in pieces around my body. I try to tug the blanket upwards to hide myself. Will eases the covers up to my shoulders and gently smooths my hair. "Mr Hamilton says you ought to make a full recovery. He took the ball out cleanly." He holds my hand to his lips. "I'm so sorry, Lucy. I should never have let you go out there tonight. I should never have let you play the ghost in the first place. I always knew it was a bad idea…"

His words make rage flare inside me. It was my decision to go out there tonight. I didn't go seeking his permission. But I'm too exhausted for anger. "It wasn't your fault," I croak. My mouth feels impossibly dry. Before I can ask for water, a violent rush of sickness tears up from inside me. Will gets to me with the chamber pot just in time. I empty my stomach into the pot, then roll onto my back again, wincing at the pain.

"I'm sorry," I groan, swamped in embarrassment.

"There's no need to be sorry." He presses a cup of water to my lips. "Here, drink this. Mr Hamilton said the chloroform will make you a little nauseous for a while."

"How long have I been out?"

"Less than an hour." Will tugs at his collar, as though caught in hesitation. "Shall I fetch your husband?" His voice is thin.

"No," I say hurriedly. "Just take me home."

"I can't do that. Mr Hamilton said you're not to be moved for at least two days."

"I can't stay here for two days," I hiss. "I have to get home. Tom will…" I try to sit up, pain knifing my side and making my head spin. I feel Will's hand slide behind me, lowering me back down to the mattress.

"Lucy," Clara speaks up from the other side of the room. I didn't realise she was there. "You told me Tom already knows you've been unfaithful. What difference does it make if you stay here?"

"Your husband knows you've been unfaithful?" Will shakes his head. "I'm sorry. I… That's not important right now." But I see his jaw tighten.

Tears well up behind my eyes. "He suspects. But he can't know any of this. He can't know I've been playing the ghost. He'd be so ashamed. I couldn't do that to him." I turn my head on the pillow as my tears spill, feeling the need to hide. How can I let Will see how much my betrayal of Tom is breaking me?

"You don't think he'll notice when he sees the bullet wound in your side?" he asks, trying to bite back his sharpness.

"I'll think of something to tell him."

Clara lets out her breath. "Lucy, that's ridiculous. You—"

"It's not your problem," I snap. I wipe my eyes, regretting my outburst. "I'm sorry, I… Please. Just help me get home."

Reluctantly agreeing to help me in case I try and get home myself, Clara and Will ease me back into my shift and dress and help me to my feet. I lean on them heavily for several moments, the lamplit shop tilting around me. Finally, I dare to take a step, grateful when my legs hold beneath me.

We step out into the lane behind the shop. At the end of the alley, I see the main street filled with people. The tavern is overflowing, one man standing with an ale in one hand and the body of a possum in the other. My eyes dart across the crowd, but I don't see Tom.

By the time we reach the cottage, the pain is far too consuming for me to care who the hell sees me. Tom included. My fingers dig into Will's arm as I try to keep upright. The noise from the main street has become muted, and my breathing is thunder in my ears.

"The house is dark," says Clara. "I don't think your husband is home." She reaches into my reticule for the key and unlocks the door.

The house is black and airless. Will fumbles through the dark and lights a lamp in the kitchen, before Clara guides me into the bedroom.

Will hovers in the doorway. I understand his reluctance to enter. Tom's shirt on the chair, Tom's scarf on the hook, Tom's shaving mirror on the washstand. Even in his absence, my husband inhabits this room. Clara helps me out of my dress, then eases me onto the bed and pulls the blanket to my chest. She hands me the bottle of laudanum. "Take another drop. It will help you sleep."

I bring the bottle to my lips.

"That's enough." She pulls it away quickly. Looks over her shoulder at Will. "You ought to leave. In case her husband returns."

He looks down at me, indecision darkening his face. I see the worry and the affection he has for me, and I hate that I've brought him here, to stand in my husband's bedroom.

Finally, he nods. He comes to the bed and bends to kiss my forehead. "Take care, Lucy," he says huskily. His footsteps echo across the room and out of the cottage. I feel a dull ache in my chest.

"You should go too," I tell Clara, eyes closed against the drumming in my hip.

"Don't be mad. I'm not leaving you on your own."

"I'm all right. I promise. I just want to sleep." When she doesn't respond, I say, "Please. This will be easier to explain to Tom if I'm alone."

Clara hovers by my bedside in indecision. "Fine," she huffs. "Fine. If that's really what you want. I'll come by and check on you in the morning."

Despite the laudanum in my blood, and the remnants of the chloroform, the pain keeps me awake for most of the night. I hear Tom clatter through the front door sometime in the early morning and it takes all my willpower to stifle the groan when he flops onto the mattress beside me. He is snoring in minutes, the smell of ale and sweat rising from his skin.

By the time dawn filters through the curtains, I'm exhausted enough to drop into a broken, and painfully short-lived sleep.

Tom hauls himself out of bed, making the mattress lurch. "Lying in this morning, Luce?" His voice is full of bitterness. "You have a busy night last night then?" He yanks back the bedclothes. "Up you get. Those clothes ain't going to wash themselves."

I try to sit, gritting my teeth against the wall of pain. Tom turns and frowns down at me.

"Lucy?" The anger is gone from his face. "Are you hurt?"

"Hurt? Of course not." I try to keep my voice light. "Cramps, that's all."

Tom nods faintly, but I see the doubt in his eyes. "Is there anything I can do?"

"No. I'll be fine. Really." I sit slowly, trying to keep the grimace from my face. "I'll get you some breakfast."

Tom puts a hand on my arm to stop me. "I can feed myself. You stay in bed. You look as though you need it."

Too exhausted to argue, I nod. Ease myself back onto the mattress as Tom makes his way to the kitchen. Some distant part of me is glad for the pain. It prevents me from thinking too hard about the vicious fight I had with him last night. And what in hell he would do if he discovered the bullet wound in my side.

Somewhere in my hazy thoughts, I wonder whether people are talking about the shooting. Sightings of the Green Lady always generate gossip, so I know there's every chance this will too. My only hope is that the man who shot me is keeping himself hidden. I have no idea whether there were any other witnesses. I was not aware of any other people in the alley. But the gunshot brought Will and Clara running. It's unlikely the incident went by unnoticed.

But for now, I can't think that far ahead. For now, I just have to hide a gunshot wound from my husband.

Tom pokes his head back into the bedroom. "I can stay here today," he says, "if—"

"No," I reply, too quickly. My secrets are far too close to the surface. We'd never get through the day without them spilling over. "I'm fine," I say. "You go the diggings."

"Are you sure?"

"Of course."

Tom hesitates a moment longer, then turns without another word and disappears out of the house.

Later in the morning, there's a knock at the door. I've been lying in bed for hours, unable to get anywhere even close to sleep.

"I'm not working today," I croak.

"Lucy? It's me." Clara. I take fresh swig of laudanum and get shakily to my feet. I pull my flannel robe on over my shift and shuffle to the door.

"You look like hell," she says when I answer.

"Thank you. I feel it."

"Is Tom here?"

I grip the doorframe to keep my balance. "No. He's gone to the diggings."

"Did he suspect anything?"

I let out a humourless laugh. "I'm sure he did. But I think he's learned better than to ask questions."

Clara puts a gentle hand to my shoulder and ushers me inside. "Come and sit down. Shall I make us some tea?"

I nod. My mouth is parched and I'm lightheaded from the laudanum I've been tossing back like it's barley water. Leaning heavily on Clara, I settle into a chair at the table, directing her to the teacups on the shelf.

"Will came to see me this morning," she says, crouching to light the fire. She hangs the kettle on the hook. "He's very worried about you. He wanted to come and see you. I told him that wasn't a good idea."

I'm grateful. The last thing I need is Will Browning appearing on my doorstep and crossing paths with Tom. My eyes fill suddenly with tears, and I blink them away. What right do I have for tears? I brought all this on myself.

Clara stands over me, watching as I wipe my eyes. "Shall I send Mr Hamilton over?"

"Yes," I say dryly. "Tell him I want another hit of chloroform."

"Take the laudanum I gave you."

"Will you fetch it for me? From the nightstand."

Clara disappears into the bedroom and returns with the tiny bottle. "Have you taken any this morning?"

I shake my head. Tell myself those couple of mouthfuls I've had don't count.

She sits the bottle on the table beside me. "Just a few drops," she warns. "Or a ball in the side will be the least of your troubles."

I nod obediently.

She fills the pot from the cannister of tea Tom has left on the table and pours the boiling water in. Hands me a steaming cup.

I pull the stopper from the laudanum bottle and ease a few drops into my tea, aware of Clara's watchful eyes on me.

She sits beside me, turning her cup around in her hands. "Will asked you to move to Melbourne with him? He asked you to leave your husband?"

I nod.

"And you're going to go?"

I remember it now; the promise I made to Will last night when I was fired up with rage at Tom. Full of a desperate need to play the ghost and upturn the world. Is it still what I want in the harshness of morning? My thoughts are too clouded to tell.

"Will cares about you very much," says Clara. And this I know, even with my drug-addled brain.

"I care about him too. I care about him so much it's frightening."

"Why did you do it?" asks Clara. "Lie with Will? And play the ghost? Is it because you married the wrong man?"

I squeeze my eyes closed. Admitting I married the wrong man feels far too brutal. I tighten my grip on my teacup. "I lost my daughter," I say finally. "A year and a half ago, in the camp fever outbreak. And since then, I can't seem to find my bearings. I needed a way to escape the grief."

The words feel strange on my tongue. I can't remember the last time I spoke of Elsie. For so many months, she has existed only within my memories.

Clara lets out her breath. "I'm so sorry, Lucy."

I stare out the window. Behind the cottage, the fronds of my little vegetable garden bend in the wind. "I know it's no excuse. Hundreds of other people lost their children in that outbreak. And none of them are running around playing the ghost. Or crawling into bed with men who aren't their husbands."

"How do you know what all those people are doing?" Clara asks gently. "You don't see into their lives every day."

"I see my husband every day," I say. "And he's not falling apart. He's getting up and going out to his claim and trying to find our fortune." I hear the bitterness in my voice. The anger. And for a second, I do not feel bad for lying to Tom. Do not feel bad for going to Will's bed. Because it feels as though Tom needs to be punished for the way he glided past our daughter's death. His life has gone on just as it did before Elsie died. And for that, I feel a tangled mix of jealousy and rage.

"Playing the ghost," I say, "it felt like a way of getting back at this place. Punishing it for all it's taken from me."

And is Will a way of getting back at Tom? For bringing us out here? And for not caring enough about losing our child? Perhaps somewhere in the back of my mind, he was once. But it goes far deeper than that now. Will Browning has awoken something in me that had been long dormant. Something I'm not sure I have the strength to give up.

I stay at the table for what feels like hours, turning my empty teacup around and around between my hands. It's far too hot in the fire-warmed kitchen and I wish I'd asked Clara to open the windows before she left. A headache thumps steadily behind my eyes.

"Mrs Earnshaw?" Constable Stone's commanding voice is accompanied by a loud knock. I stumble to my feet, clutching the wall for balance as I hobble to the door.

Stone is alone. At the sight of me, he gives a brisk nod. He doesn't look at all surprised to see me in my robe in the middle of the day, my hair hanging limp and tangled down my back. I can barely muster a greeting.

"Last night two women claimed they witnessed a man shoot the Green Lady in the alley behind Hargraves Street. The shooter has been taken into police custody."

"And you're here to ask after my wellbeing?" There's a coldness to my voice, but I see a flicker in Stone's eyes that looks oddly like compassion.

"Does that surprise you?" he asks evenly.

"It does," I say. "I know you're not the most honest of men."

"But not entirely without morality."

"I find that hard to believe." If he is to speak openly about the night we caught each other out at Forest Creek, I will do the same. "You're letting other men take the blame for your night fossicking. A poor Chinaman was nearly beaten to death."

"Well. I can't control the way the colony feels about outsiders."

But of course, I have spoken out of place. Stone has little control over anything. My anger is misplaced. No doubt he was sent out to Forest Creek that night by his superiors. What did they threaten him with? I'm sure those corrupt officers above him could make life hell for a trooper with the convict stain.

"I could easily have killed you," he says coolly, "the night you saw me at Forest Creek. But I chose not to."

I let out a mildly hysterical laugh. "Why are you telling me this?"

"To show you I do have a little morality. To convince you that I do in fact have your best interests at heart."

"Is this an official police visit?" I ask doubtfully.

"No," he admits. "No one else in the police force knows who the Green Lady really is."

I swallow. "I'm not going to tell anyone I saw you fossicking. I swear it."

Does he know I'm lying? I've already told my husband.

Stone gives a faint nod. "I'm not here to threaten you, Mrs Earnshaw. I really am here to ask after your wellbeing. And to find out whether you plan to lay charges against the shooter."

"Of course I don't."

"I see."

"What will happen to him?" I ask finally. "You said he's in the cells."

"Well," says Stone, "he won't be charged if no victim comes forward. There's no evidence that a crime took place."

"No victim is going to come forward." I make to close the door, but Stone holds out a broad hand, preventing it from closing. "Are you certain you're all right? You really don't look well."

The concern in his eyes catches me off guard. Convict, corrupt trooper, yes, but I see a glimmer of decency behind Stone's eyes. Has that always been there? I've never looked this closely before. Perhaps he's like so many of us here; our morality hidden behind desperation.

Yes, he could easily have killed me that night. Put a bullet in my chest and carried me out to the bush to be lost among the wilderness.

I squeeze my eyes closed, swamped by sudden dizziness.

Stone dives forward, gripping my arm to stop me from falling. "Maybe you ought to sit down."

I follow his gaze. Blood has soaked through my shift, flecking the front of my robe. And before I can speak, before I can sit, I feel myself swallowed by dark.

CHAPTER NINETEEN

I wake up in bed. Tom is on a chair at my bedside, a deep frown crumpling his forehead. I shift at the sight of him, and pain grips my body.

He presses a hand to my shoulder. "Lie still."

My heart races. How much does he know?

I close my eyes against the afternoon light streaming through the gap in the curtains. "What are you doing here?" I ask. It feels like a foolish question.

"Constable Stone found me on the diggings. Said he came here to bring you his laundry and you collapsed at the door."

I close my eyes for a moment, grateful for Stone's discretion. And, I suppose, for hauling me off my doorstep.

Tom holds up the empty laudanum bottle. "I found this on the table. Did you take it all? No wonder you've been out for hours." He lifts a cup from the side table and slides a hand behind my head to lift it. "Drink some water." He drizzles the liquid down my throat, and I gulp at it thirstily.

I dare to glance down. The blankets are curled around my legs, and I see the ink-dark blood staining my shift.

"I sent for Mr Hamilton," Tom says, voice low. "He changed the dressing of the wound."

I turn my head on the pillow.

For long moments, there is silence. I can't bear to look at Tom. I know he's waiting for me to speak. Waiting for me to cobble together some kind of explanation. He lets out a small sigh.

"What happened?" he asks finally.

I say nothing.

"Lucy. Please. Did someone hurt you?"

The worry in his voice fills my throat with tears.

"Was it the man you…?"

I close my eyes. "No."

The silence is thick and heavy. Haunting.

I dare to glance up at Tom. He is leaning close, his blue eyes dark with worry. He clears his throat. "I know we don't… That we've not spoken much lately. And that… there are things in your life I don't know about." He lets out a breath. "I don't care about any of that now. I just need you to tell me what happened to you. Please."

I want more than anything to tell him the truth. To tell him I took a bullet in the street. But how can I do that without revealing everything else I've been a part of? Besides, if he learns of the shooting, he'll go straight for the police. And there's no way I can let that happen. I don't want my husband anywhere near those crooked troopers.

My tears escape, and I turn my head on the pillow, unable to look him in the eye. I know I owe him at least an attempt at an explanation, but where do I even start?

Tom's chair squeaks noisily and I dare to face him. I realise he has a fresh nightshift laid across his knees. His fist tightens around it. "I thought you might want a change of clothes."

I glance down at the blood staining my hip. Nod slightly.

He eases his hand beneath my shoulders, helping me sit. He grasps tentatively at the hem of my stained nightshift and then stops, as though suddenly uncertain. I suppose I can't blame him. I've barely let him close to me in months. Instinctively, I put a hand over his.

Tom," I say, "it's all right."

He swallows visibly, easing the shift up over my head. His rough fingers graze the side of my ribs, and I hear my sharp inhalation.

"Am I hurting you?"

"No." It was the feel of him that caused my breath to leave me. The strange newness of his skin so gentle against mine. Suddenly, I miss him deeply. And I'm achingly glad he's here.

He pulls my clean shift over my head and eases me back onto the mattress. "All right?"

I nod, throat stabbing with unspoken words. He brushes his hand across my forehead, through my hair.

"I'm sorry," I cough. "I'm so sorry."

Tom gives the faintest of nods. His lips part, and I hold my breath, each of us waiting for the other to speak. "Get some rest," he murmurs at last.

I close my eyes, wait for him to leave. Wait for the creak of the floorboards, the dull thud of the door. But there is nothing. Just his steady breathing, the creak of his chair and his constant, wordless presence.

For almost a fortnight, as I lie in bed, Tom asks no more questions. He refuses to go to the diggings, instead staying home and haunting my bedside. Neither of us speak of the night of the shooting, and though there is now another huge addition to the pile of *things we don't talk about*, we manage to fill the days with chatter that is almost civil. Almost warm. He tells me about Leo's latest run-in with the Tipperary boys, and the new lemonade stand that's popped up near his claim. I tell him of Clara's shop, and the trouble she's had with her former clients. Our conversations would almost be easy if it weren't for the poisonous topics we have to constantly veer away from.

I wonder if, outside, people are talking. Did others witness the shooting of the Green Lady? There's a chance of it, I know, and I'm glad Tom is here, away from the gossip of the town.

When I'm able to manoeuvre around the cottage without leaning on my husband or the wall, I send him back to the claim.

"Are you certain?" he asks, hands on my shoulders.

"I'm fine. Go."

When Tom leaves, my first instinct is to open my script. Somewhere, at the back of my mind, is the knowledge that the performance of *The Lady of Fyvie* is planned for tomorrow. I have no thought of whether it's still to take place. Though Clara has been at my door several times during the past week, asking after my recovery, we never touched on the play in front of Tom.

I skim through the words of the script. I know my lines as though they're a part of me, and I feel physically strong enough to appear on stage. But the prospect of the play is tinged with bitterness now. And maybe a little fear. My hand moves across my body, finding that place above my hip where reality came crashing into the Green Lady's world.

In the afternoon, I build up the courage to step out of my cottage.

After Tom has sat at my bedside for two weeks in the face of my silence, visiting Will feels like the worst of betrayals. But how can I stay away? When Will last saw me, he watched the surgeon pull a bullet from my side. I can imagine his worry. Perhaps his guilt.

I can't bear to hurt either of them.

I pass Clara's shop on my way to the Commercial. And I stop in horror. The mannequins from the window display are strewn over the floor, their fine gowns and waistcoats in shreds. Reams of fabric have been unrolled across the floor, long jagged tears down the middle. Design sketches and broadsheets have been ripped from the walls and windows.

I rush through the door, calling Clara's name. She's sitting on the floor in the back room, huddled against the wall with her knees pulled to her chest. She looks up at the sight of me, hurriedly wiping away tears. Hair is coming loose from the tangled knot at her neck, curls clinging to her wet cheeks. Her eyes are red and swollen. I've never seen her like this; so broken and defeated.

"What happened?" I ask. "Are you hurt?"

She shakes her head. I lower myself carefully onto the ground beside her. Cover her hand with mine.

"They broke in while I was at the bank this morning," she says after moments of silence. She coughs back tears. "They've destroyed months of work. In broad daylight, if you can believe it."

"I'm so sorry," I murmur.

Clara turns her face away, pressing a palm to her eyes.

"Do you have any thought of who it was?" I ask gently. "Mr Wallace…" I fade out. Though I know Arthur Wallace and Clara have never seen eye to eye, he doesn't seem the kind of man to break into her shop and destroy her work.

Clara gets to her feet and goes to the drawer of her nightstand. She pulls out a handful of folded pages. "It's not just Arthur Wallace," she says, tossing the pages towards me. "These are from men whose wives have commissioned me. Men who were once punters of mine. They make their feelings quite clear."

I open the letters, one after the other. They're full of thinly veiled threats, and words like *disgrace* and *whore. Dressmaking is a domain for the upper classes; I'll not have my wife seen in such company; women like you bring a bad name to this town.*

Two of the letters are unsigned, others marked with names I vaguely recognise. Men who, like Arthur Wallace, hold positions of power within the town.

"I'm unwelcome here, they say," Clara snorts. "Don't remember them saying such things when they were panting all over me with their arses in the air. A whore is most welcome til she starts making something of herself. Starts showing her face in the daylight." She sits beside me again and taps a long finger against one of the pages. "This fine chap," she says bitterly, "refused to pay his wife's credit. Left me five pounds out of pocket." She leans her head against the wall. "Don't know which one of them did this. Or who they sent to do it for them. But it hardly matters."

"Have you been to the police?" I ask.

She nods. "They said they'd be by shortly. Not that I'm expecting them to do much. Can't hardly see the coppers going round questioning men like Arthur Wallace over an attack on some lag, can you?"

I don't answer. Just reach an arm around her and hold her tightly. "What will you do?" I ask.

She rubs her eyes. "Close my doors for a while. I've no choice. I've barely anything left to sell. And even if new commissions came in, I'd have no fabric to make them with until I can get another order from Melbourne." She takes the letters from me and puts them on the table. I wonder if she kept them because she foresaw something like this.

"I thought I could start again," she says, her eyes fixed to the letter at the top of the pile. "I really did. I thought once my sentence was over, I could put the past behind me." There's something new to her voice; at least, something she's always kept hidden from me. Vulnerability, grief. I see the cracks in that shield she puts up with her sharp tongue. "These men," she coughs, "do they really think I chose to make my living the way I did? Do they not think I was dying of shame every time I so much as looked at their faces?" She sighs heavily. "I thought it was all for a purpose. Thought it would get me what I wanted. But look at this place." She waves a hand at the devastated parlour. "Look at all I've got to show for myself. And here I thought I could start again."

I don't speak, sure I'll never find the right words.

Maybe there's no such thing as putting the past behind us. No such thing as starting again. Without our pasts, we'd be different people.

Maybe that's what Clara is seeking.

Maybe that's what I've been seeking too.

The front door clicks open and she gets quickly to her feet, glancing in the mirror and trying to scrub the tearstains from her face. She looks into the front room. "Troopers are here. For whatever good they'll do."

Troopers.

My stomach lurches at the mere thought of their presence.

Clara holds out a hand, helping me stand. "There's no need for you to stay," she says.

I hesitate. Half of me wants nothing more than to put as much distance between me and the troopers as possible. The other half can't bear to leave Clara alone with them.

I tell myself she's in no danger. It's only the men involved in their thieving racket who end up in pits full of black powder. Or who pretend to, at least.

Clara heads out to meet the troopers, while I stand dithering in the doorway, a hand pressed to my aching hip.

I eye the two policemen. Their bearded faces are vaguely familiar, but I've no idea of their names. No idea whether they're part of this racket. They follow Clara around the shop, listening as she describes her return from the bank to find the back door broken and the place in disarray.

While the police are picking their way through the chaos of the window display, Clara joins me in the doorway. "There's really no need for you to be here. I can manage." She lowers her voice. "Have you been to see Will?"

"Not yet. I was on my way…"

"Go. He's been very worried for you."

685

I nod, eyes down. "And the performance?" I dare to ask. "Is it to go ahead?"

"I'd say that depends on you."

I draw in a breath. "Shall I come by in the morning? Help you clean the place?"

Clara gives a short smile. "I'd like that."

I pull her into a quick embrace, then hurry towards the front door.

The officer looks up as I pass. "Leaving, Mrs Earnshaw?"

My heart speeds. "How do you know my name?"

He looks amused at my question. "It's our job to know everyone in this settlement."

Is there something behind his eyes? Something I can't quite catch hold of? Perhaps just my imagination. Nonetheless, it makes me dart from the shop like my skirts are burning.

CHAPTER TWENTY

I'm still jittery when I arrive at the Commercial. Jittery when I climb the stairs to Will's room. I knock lightly. He opens the door, letting out his breath at the sight of me.

"Lucy. I'm so glad to see you. How are you feeling?"

I try for a smile. "I'll live."

He steps aside, gesturing for me to enter. He closes the door behind us. Keeps his distance.

"I wanted to come and see you," he says. "More than anything."

"I know. Thank you. And I'm glad you chose to stay away. It's best that way."

"I'm sure." His smile doesn't reach his eyes.

I don't know where the two of us stand. Can't make sense of the chaos in my brain. The warmth I've felt towards my husband these past days has been undeniable, but I know how this will go: one day soon, the warmth will give way to silence and the cold will creep back in. I know this with every piece of myself; and yet if there's even a scrap of a chance I might be wrong, how can I turn away?

But I can't deny the joy that Will has made me feel. Perhaps it's wrong to seek a happiness that might never come, when I have a chance at it right in front of me.

Either way, I know I must make a choice. I know how lucky I am that neither Tom nor Will have turned away from me yet. I know it's what I deserve. And I know, if I stay trapped in indecision, one day soon they'll both wash their hands of me, and I'll find myself alone.

Will folds his hands behind his back, but he stands close, eyes on mine. "There's been talk," he says, "of the shooting. Gossip. A man firing at the Green Lady."

I nod. In spite of his stiltedness, there's a kind of relief to being around someone who knows everything that happened that night. Despite the truce that appeared between me and Tom these past two weeks, I was constantly aware of my secrets. They hung between us, draining the air.

Will says, "I think we ought to cancel the play."

"Is that what you want?" A part of me hopes that two weeks without my attendance at rehearsals – or Ollie's complete inability to learn his lines – might have convinced Will otherwise. Convinced him it's a bad idea to put *The Lady of Fyvie* on the stage.

But I can't be surprised when he says, "Of course that's not what I want. The play is important to me."

I nod.

"But so is your safety," he says quickly. "The moment you step onto stage dressed as the Green Lady, people will find out you're the one who's been deceiving them."

"Yes. They will. I've known that from the beginning. The shooting doesn't change anything." I'll hide myself away for a few days and let the story lose momentum. Soon there'll be another possum hunt, or someone will run off with their kitchen maid and the Green Lady will be forgotten.

But it's not the townspeople finding out that scares me. It's Tom finding out. I feel instinctively that if he were to learn what I've been doing, if I were to bring this deep shame to him, it would be the end.

'I declare myself no longer responsible for your debts and financial upkeep…'

The thought begins to break me, and I look up at Will for strength. I know how much the play means to him. I know how hard he has been working to build a name for himself again. I want to see his work performed at Astley's, and all across the colony. And I know *The Lady of Fyvie* is a stepping-stone to help him get there. If I walk away, all the work he's put into it will be for nothing. For all the trouble it might bring me to step onto stage and reveal myself as the Green Lady, I have no intention of letting Will Browning down.

It's getting dark when I leave the Commercial. Fine rain has begun to fall, casting a yellow haze around the streetlamps. I hear a distant burst of gunfire. A single pop, not the nightly emptying of weapons. No one reacts. A carriage rolls and women pass in chatter. A boy jogs past with a dog at his heels.

When did we all become so desensitised to such a thing? When did the sound of gunfire become a mere inconvenience?

But the screeches that come minutes later, they're impossible to ignore. A woman's howl, tightening my shoulders with dread.

People hurry in the direction of the scream. Others step from the taverns, squinting into the fading sunlight.

The body is lying on the road to Melbourne. People are clustered around the figure, and I shove my way to the front of the crowd.

A dark shadow of blood is growing on the man's chest. Still strapped to his shoulders is a large pack and swag. It's clear he was attempting to leave Castlemaine.

I can't pull my eyes from the body. Shot on the road out of town. Was he, like Fred Buckley, involved in this racket run by the troopers? Was he trying to escape, just like Buckley had been? Was he shot down by the police themselves?

Perhaps I'm jumping to conclusions. Seeing things that aren't there. Perhaps the man was killed in a squabble over gold. It's far from unlikely. But the alternative gnaws inside me.

I try to push away the dread that is building inside me. But when I look up to see troopers approaching, fear strikes me between the ribs. There are five of them marching towards the crowd – no, six. Among them are the two men who attended the break-in at Clara's.

Leaving, Mrs Earnshaw?

And yes; leaving, leaving, leaving. Leaving this place and never looking back. The thought swings at me with sudden, violent intensity. Though I'd not spoken a word to them before today, the troopers know who I am. Has Stone told them I caught him night fossicking? I'm painfully aware I know too much. And even more aware of how easily I could be removed from the situation.

The terror is suddenly consuming. I can't stay here another day.

I hurry to the cottage. Though the darkness is thickening, Tom is not yet home. I light the lamp and pull our trunks out from beneath the bed. I stop suddenly. One trunk or two? After everything I've done, will my husband flee with me? Do I want him to? I have no thought of either. There's every chance I'll have to find the courage to leave this place alone.

I leave Tom's trunk at the foot of the bed and toss mine open on the mattress. Pull my clothes from the cupboard. I shove them into the trunk, not even bothering to fold them.

My mind is full of Will. Will's play, Will's kiss, Will's offer of a new life. Leave Castlemaine tonight and I'll be leaving that behind forever. The thought aches. I promised him I would not let him down. But I'm too scared to stay.

"What are you doing?" I spin around to find Tom in the doorway, arms folded across his chest. "You're leaving? With who?" His voice is ice.

I shake my head hurriedly. "No. It's not like that. I… It's not safe here." I grab a stray shift from beneath the bed and shove it into the trunk. "A man was murdered on the road out of town tonight."

"I heard." Tom reaches for my arm, forcing me into stillness. "Stop, Lucy. Look at me." He turns me to face him. "What are you not telling me?"

I want him to hear everything. Fred Buckley, corrupt troopers, and the Black Forest racket. I want to tell him how it may all be connected to the dead man on the road. But I can't risk putting him in the line of the troopers' pistol fire.

Buckley's warning was clear: to keep my husband safe, he can't know any more than he already does.

"I don't want to be here anymore, Tom," I say instead. "I don't want to live in a place where men are murdered in the streets."

Something flickers in his eyes. "We can't leave."

"We can go to the other goldfields," I say desperately. "Ballarat or Bendigo. Or up to the mountains even. Perhaps you'll have more luck there. Please."

"We're not leaving." Tom runs his hand through his hair.

"Why not?"

"Because this house is all we have in the world. Run away from it and we won't have a thing to our name." He lets out his breath, as though irritated by my questioning. "Besides, I'm so damn close to that haul. Do you know how many hours of my life I've put into it?"

A cold laugh escapes me. Yes, I know every damn second of it. A thousand days of promises and wishes, and desperately hoping things will change. "You've been so close for the past three years! Do you truly believe things will be different now?"

"I have to believe it," he hisses. "Otherwise what has all this been for?"

"We failed, Tom," I say. "Why can't you just accept that?"

He shakes his head. "No."

My anger rises. "We failed. You found nothing, and we lost our daughter, and I—" I stop abruptly.

"And you *what?*" Tom presses. "What did you do? Go to another man's bed? And what else? What have you got yourself involved in that's making you so damn terrified?" He begins to pace, back and forth across the tiny space. "Do you think this man on the road was killed by the same man who shot you?"

A murmur of shock escapes me.

"I know it's a gunshot wound, Lucy," he says sharply. "Mr Hamilton told me he took the ball out of you at Clara Snow's shop." Before I can speak, Tom says, "Did you really expect him to say nothing? I'm your husband. I have every right to know." His hands clench. "Can you imagine how it feels to have you keep something like that from me?" He pounds a fist suddenly against the wall and I back up against the bed in shock. He's carried this knowledge for a fortnight, I see now. Carried it in silence.

Somehow, that only makes me more furious.

"Yes," I hiss. "It's a gunshot wound. I was shot in the street when I was playing the ghost."

"Playing the ghost?" he repeats. "What in hell does that even mean?"

We need this, I tell myself. Need these secrets to come out. If we are to have any hope of being happy again, it's the only way.

"Hoaxing," I say. "Playing a part. Making people think they're seeing a ghost. Because that's what's people want to see."

Tom stares at me, not speaking.

I drop my voice. "I just needed to be someone else for a time. I needed an escape."

His boots thump against the floorboards as he paces. His eyes are down, as though he can't bring himself to look at me.

"The man who shot me, it was an accident. He'd just come from the possum hunt, and I caught him by surprise." I perch on the edge of the bed, knotting my fingers together. "I told the police I didn't want the man charged. It had nothing to do with the murder tonight."

Tom stares out the window into the dark street, his back to me.

"Are you not even going to speak?" I ask finally.

"And say what? What should I say when you tell me you've been out pretending to be a dead woman because your life is so unbearable? And that you were shot in the street and you thought to hide it from me?"

"Anything!" I cry. "I don't care what you say! Anything but this silence we've been living in for the past eighteen months!"

Instead of speaking, Tom looks back at me. *Eighteen months.*

No doubt he can see how closely my behaviour is tied to Elsie's death. He turns away, jaw clenched, as though trying to keep his rage inside.

But I want his anger. I want to be confronted. I want to know what's inside his head.

"It was Will Browning," I say, rounding on him to look him in the eye. "From the theatre. He's the man I went to Melbourne with. We spoke of making a life together—"

I stop talking suddenly because I see my words have had the desired effect. I see the anger flaring in Tom's eyes, see the tremor in his locked jaw.

I brace myself for his fury. Never once has he struck me, but never before have I given him a reason like this. He takes a step backwards. I come at him, shoving hard against his chest.

He grabs my wrists, holding me at a distance. "What are you doing?" he demands through gritted teeth.

"I'm trying to get a rise out of you. I want to see that you're angry."

He laughs icily. And he strides past me, through the back door of the cottage. I race after him onto the grass behind the house.

"If you know what's good for you, you'll stay away from me, Lucy," he says, marching back and forth with his hands behind his head.

"No." I want these threats. I want this rage. "I want to see you have some damn emotion inside you."

Tom stops pacing. "What are you talking about?"

I glare at him, aware that tears are rushing down my cheeks. I have no idea how long I've been crying. "It was as though losing Elsie didn't even affect you."

He stares back at me; lips parted, but silent.

"You just went on as though nothing had happened. The day after we buried her, you were back out at the claim. Carrying on as though everything was normal. And you just stopped speaking of her. As though she'd never existed."

"I thought..." Tom's voice is strangled. "I thought that was the best way to get through it."

"If she'd been a son? Would you have felt different?"

He makes a noise in his throat but doesn't speak for a long time. Wind flies across the yard, blowing his ragged hair across his cheek. "I was trying to hold myself together for you," he says finally. His voice is low and taut. "Because I thought that was what you needed. Do you really think I wasn't falling apart?" He stares out into the darkness, refusing to look my way. "I took her crib to the fire while you were asleep so you didn't have to see it. I went up to Pennyweight Flat alone to choose where she was to be buried. And you think I wasn't falling apart?" That faint waver in his voice, am I imagining it? It sends fresh tears down my cheeks.

I wipe my eyes with the back of my hand, feeling grief tear open inside me again. "I didn't want you to hold yourself together, Tom. I wanted you to fall apart with me. I wanted to see that Elsie's death broke you as much as it did me."

He rubs a hand over his face. "I can't believe you would doubt that." His voice is thin and cold, and as strained as I have ever heard it. Deliberately hollow, as though even now, he has no emotion to give. Or at least none he's willing to let me see.

And so perhaps, even now, I do doubt it. It's easier to keep telling myself that Tom is the cold, emotionless man I convinced myself he was. Because if he really is this achingly decent man who buried his grief so he might carry mine, what kind of person does that make me? It's more than I can bear to think about.

"That's what you've been thinking all this time?" he asks. "That my daughter's death meant nothing to me?"

I don't answer. I know I don't need to.

And how is it that we are only speaking of these things now? How might things have been different if we had found a way to be open with each other in those days of burning cradles and burial sites? How might it have been if we'd done those things together?

But we didn't. We've lived through almost a year and a half of coldness, and now the walls we've built around ourselves are so high we can't find a way over them.

I glance at Tom, who is leaning against the outside of the cottage, the moon lighting one side of his face. If our daughter had lived, I know she would have grown up to look like her father. I saw it in Elsie's mop of sandy hair, in her broad cheeks, her vivid deep-sea-blue eyes.

I wipe my tears and step back into the cottage. Look down at the packed trunk I've laid across the bed. We're not leaving, that much I understand. At least, we're not leaving together.

"Put your clothes away, Lucy," Tom says from the doorway. "We're not going anywhere. This house is all we have in the world. We're not just walking away from it."

"But—"

"You're not going anywhere," he barks again. "I forbid it."

He walks from the bedroom without another word.

Something yanks me from a broken sleep. I sit up, trying to find my bearings in the dark. The other side of the bed is empty, but I can hear Tom snoring softly in a kitchen chair. After all we discussed a few hours ago, I'm surprised either of us have managed to find sleep.

There it is; the creak and click of the gate. Footsteps approaching the house.

I slip out of bed, grabbing my shawl from the end of the bed and tiptoeing to the front door. It's madness, of course, creeping about like this when a man has just been murdered. But whoever is coming to our door, I feel instinctively it's my misdeeds that have brought them here.

Constable Stone ensuring I'm keeping my mouth shut. Or perhaps even Will. I don't want Tom entangled in my messes any further than he has to be.

My first guess turns out to be correct. Stone is hovering on the doorstep, fist raised, as though he were about to knock.

I step outside, pulling the door closed behind me.

"It's not a good time for a woman to be out at night, Mrs Earnshaw," he says.

"I'm not letting you inside," I hiss. "So if you wish to speak to me, we speak out here." I fold my arms across my chest. "I promised you my silence. And I told you I'm not going to come forward about the shooting. So I think it's time you stayed away from my house."

Stone's mouth opens, as though he's taken aback by my boldness. I'm a little shocked by it too. "I'm not afraid of you," I tell him. "Not anymore. I know you're not the one pulling the strings." I've said too much, of course.

His eyes flash. "Whatever you think you know, you would do well to keep your mouth shut. You understand me?" His voice is thin; half-warning, half-threat, and it sends a shiver through me.

I manage a nod.

"Where's your husband?" Stone asks.

"This has nothing to do with him," I say. "Leave him out of it."

Before Stone can reply, the front door cracks against the wall and Tom blusters through it. "Get away from her, Stone," he hisses.

Stone takes a step back and Tom ushers me back inside. I don't want his protection. I don't feel as though I deserve it. I got myself into this mess and I don't want to drag my husband into it any further. I've already hurt him enough. Constable Stone and the troopers are my problem.

But Tom seems intent on getting involved.

"Stay the hell away from my house," I hear him say through the closed door.

I can't hear Stone's response, but I know his words, at least, can't hurt me anymore. I've told Tom everything. Laid the whole truth out for it to destroy me.

After a few moments, he steps back inside. I'm hovering just inside the door, arms wrapped around myself. "Are you all right?" he asks.

"I'm fine." I go to the window and peek through the curtains. See the dark figure of the constable disappearing down the street. "Stone has been paying me visits since the night I saw him fossicking," I say. "But I don't know why he came here tonight. Maybe he thinks I hold him responsible for the murder of the man on the road. Perhaps he's worried I might tell someone."

Tom frowns. "And do you? Hold him responsible?"

"I don't know. I don't think he's a killer." Stone is nothing but a pawn to the officers; I know this now. But of course, I cannot tell Tom.

"Do you think the murder is connected to the thefts on the diggings?" he asks.

"Maybe."

I reach for the matchbox and light the lamp. I guess it still a few hours from dawn, but I'm not going to sleep any more tonight. I sink into a chair at the table. "In the morning," I say, "I can… leave you if you wish. You deserve to be free of me."

Tom sits. Folds his hands on the table in front of him. He stares into the flame flickering inside the lamp. "Is that what you want?"

After a moment, I shake my head.

Tom slides his chair around the table so it's close to mine. A fragile peace has settled over us, and a part of me is afraid to speak in case I upturn it. But I can manage no more silence.

"I'm sorry," I say. "For everything." The words don't feel like enough, not even close. But I have to start somewhere.

Tom's eyes are on his clasped hands. "So am I."

"What do you have to be sorry for?"

He draws in a breath. "I know you wanted to speak about her. About Elsie. I know that would have made things easier for you. But I couldn't. I just couldn't, Luce. I'm sorry. It was too much." He stares into the lamp for a long time, the firelight making his eyes shine. "And I'm sorry I brought us out here."

Tentatively, I slide my hand around his elbow, relieved when he doesn't pull away. "I chose to come," I remind him. "I chose to marry you."

I rest my head against the broad plane of his shoulder. It feels like a miracle that he is sitting here with me, after all I've confessed. Perhaps he and I are too broken to ever be fixed, but right now, it almost feels possible.

I feel the weight of his head against mine.

"Why are you being like this?" I ask.

"Like what?"

"Understanding."

He doesn't answer at once. "Because I've missed you, Lucy," he says finally. "So much. Besides, haven't we gone through enough?"

CHAPTER TWENTY-ONE

"The peculiar shrinking which ghost stories excite in children's and some mature minds is due to the … combination they present of the familiar and the unknown."

Northern *Argus*
Rockhampton
24th July 1865

I must have dozed off at the table because I'm next aware of dawn lightening the kitchen and the cold shaking me from sleep. I shift uncomfortably in my chair, aware of a dull ache in my hip.

Tom is crouching in front of the grate, holding a match to fresh pile of kindling. "Good morning," he says.

"Good morning." The cold has stretched the distance between us again, but perhaps something has shifted.

"All right?" Tom asks, and I nod. Last night's fear has faded with the morning. While I'm still desperate to leave Castlemaine, I can see that tearing into the darkness with no money and no place to go is not the right way to do so.

As we move about the cottage in our well-trodden morning routine, there are faint smiles, eye contact. We don't make such a show of stepping aside to allow the other to pass. While the wall between us still stands tall, its foundations have been rattled.

But this is the day of Will Browning's play, and I know I have no choice but to speak of it.

"The play is tonight," I say throatily, as Tom makes for the door after breakfast. "If you're to forbid me from going, I ought to let Mr Browning know."

I stare at my feet. I don't want to put Will between us again. But I also know I owe him more than to just to walk away from the play. Especially after I threw him in the path of Tom's rage by admitting whose bed I've been visiting.

"I'm not going to forbid you from going," Tom says shortly.

"Thank you," I murmur. "I... It wouldn't be fair to the others if I didn't go, and—"

"Then go." Tom pulls on his boots and laces them without looking at me. "I'm not going to stop you."

A broadsheet is attached to the door of the theatre.
One night only – The Lady of Fyvie
An exciting new work by Mr William Browning
And there at the bottom, for everyone to ponder:
Lucy Earnshaw as the Green Lady
It doesn't matter. Not now. Tom knows it all. And somehow, that knowledge has led us to a peace I can't quite understand. I know enough to suspect this peace will not be long lasting, but at least now my secrets can't hurt me.

When I slip through the side door of the theatre, an anticipatory stillness has settled over the place. I glimpse the stage as I pass through to the dressing rooms. Long shadows lie across empty seats. A hot draught blows in, making the calico walls of the castle move.

Inside the dressing room, I find Clara sitting in front of the mirror, running a comb through her hair. Her eyes are dark with theatrical lampblack, and with her cascading curls and the hard look she gives her reflection, I am almost back to being afraid of her.

But when she sees me, she turns, and the expression on her face lightens a little. She nods to a pale green gown on a coat hanger over the door.

"Your costume. Just one of my old dresses, I'm afraid. I didn't have the time to make anything new."

My mind goes suddenly to the blood-dark folds of the Green Lady's gown. To the violent, blazing pain of a bullet in the hip. Scissors cutting the dress away from my body.

And at the thought of playing this part again, I'm suddenly alive with panic. It's only fear of the past, I tell myself. And after tonight, I never need think of the Green Lady again.

To Clara, I say, "Thank you. I'm sorry you had to go to the trouble of finding me something else."

"You're lucky I found anything. Those bastards that ransacked the shop didn't leave much for me to work with."

I sit at the dressing table beside her. "What happened with the troopers yesterday?"

She snorts. "Nothing of any use. I showed them the letters but they said there's no proof of any connection. This whole place is a bloody gentleman's club."

"You've no idea," I mumble.

She catches my eye in the mirror. "You don't have to do this, you know. Play the Green Lady again. Will will understand."

"I want to."

Clara sees through my lies, of course. How could she not? But she doesn't say more. Doesn't try to talk me out of it. She just stands behind me with a comb in hand and begins to turn me back into a ghost.

The lights are lowered and a hush settles over the audience. We have hung crude curtains to operate as wings and I wait behind them beside Edith, as Clara and Ollie take their opening positions, act through the opening scene. Will stands in the wings opposite. He holds his breath as Ollie stumbles through his lines. But I feel his eyes flickering to me.

Out I go. Out onto stage with my name on the broadsheet and guilt in my eyes. My gaze moves over the audience. I'm stunned by the size of the crowd. When our little troupe last performed, we managed to wrangle an audience of ten from outside Murphy's tavern. But almost every seat in the place is full. The Green Lady sightings have done just as I once hoped – they've drawn people in to hear her story.

With the theatre near full, the air is stifling and thick with breath. I recognise face after shadowed face; there's Meg and Richard, their children between them. There's Leo, Clyde, faces from church, the diggings, the market. And there, standing by the door at the back of the theatre, is Tom.

My first instinct is one of panic. He's here to confront Will, surely. And yes, we deserve no better, I see that with clarity. But – I send him a silent plea – please not here, with half the settlement watching.

He is leaning against the wall with his arms folded across his chest, and as I catch his eye in desperation, his face lightens into the faintest of smiles.

He's not here for Will, I realise. He's here for me.

Tears of gratitude prick my eyes. I don't deserve for him to be here. I deserve an announcement in the papers in which he throws me aside. But despite every lie, every second of stilted silence, every time I climbed into Will Browning's bed, there is Tom.

I don't care that I'm breaking character. I smile back at him.

Then I force myself to focus. Force myself to wade through the Green Lady's lines.

I have been here longer than you know…

Lines I've spoken so often they have become second nature, but here on stage with the audience before me, and every piece of my life so uncertain, I'm grappling to find the right words.

Tom slips silently out of the theatre. I understand, of course. Understand that his being here was a knife to the ribs. I am infinitely grateful he made an appearance at all.

More so, I'm grateful he disappeared before Will stepped on stage. I'm well aware of Tom's new willingness to swing his fists.

"'Beware the man you married,'" I say to Lady Fyvie. And I hear the crowd murmur.

Yes, it was me. The Green Lady who walked the alleys of Castlemaine, who haunted the forest on the edge of the diggings. Whose blood was spilled in the lane behind the dress shop.

I push through the shame. Remind myself it will all be over soon.

Harsh whispers, growing steadily louder. Clara raises her voice slightly to make herself heard. A group of men get up from their seats and head for the door. Ollie falters mid-line. His eyes dart between Clara and me; curious, uncertain.

"Just keep going," Clara murmurs to me as she passes.

For several long moments, I'm alone on stage. Alone with the murmurs and the restless crowd. I search my memory for my next line, relieved when I manage to prise it up from the chaos inside me.

When I speak my next line, my voice is lost beneath the hum of the crowd. And just as I have rehearsed a hundred times, I turn my face from the audience, hiding them from my sight. I kneel in the back corner of the stage, my head down. Try to ignore the sound of footsteps moving between the aisles.

And then Will is on stage with me. No, this isn't right. This isn't his entrance. But he's rushing towards me, frantic, a hand around my arm yanking me to my feet.

"Get off the stage," he hisses.

And I see them; six – seven – wild-faced men charging the stairs onto the stage. Will whips me behind the curtain before the men can get a hand to me, and I rush down the passage towards the dressing room. I hear Edith behind me, demanding the men stay on their side of the curtain. Will slams the dressing room door behind us.

"What about the others?" I ask breathlessly. "You can't leave them out there."

Will turns the key in the lock. "You're the one they're after, Lucy."

Fists pound on the door. "Where is she?" an angry male voice demands. "Where's that prowler who's been playing the ghost? Scared my ma half to death, you did! She hasn't got out of bed since!"

The knot of regret tightens inside me, and I take a step towards the door. Will grabs my arm, pulling me back. "What are you doing?"

"I need to tell him I'm sorry. I never meant to hurt anyone."

His hand tightens around my wrist. "Going out there is not going to fix anything. Not while they're angry like this. It's just going to put you in danger."

More wild thuds at the door.

I squeeze my eyes closed. And I feel it all crumbling; that fantasy I created in which I could escape reality. That fantasy in which Will Browning would take me away from everything that caused me pain. There's no magic that can change the past or make me forget. It's all just trickery and illusion. Hidden wires and hollow walls.

A woman in costume trying make herself believe.

"I just wanted to escape," I cough. "Just for a little while."

Will puts a hand to my arm, turning me to face him. "From what?" His eyes meet mine, imploring. "Escape from what, Lucy? Why did you play the ghost?"

I shake my head. Because Elsie, she's not for Will's ears. Losing her was a thing Tom and I should have carried together. I want to speak of my daughter, yes, but I want to do so with her father. Not another man.

Will nods almost imperceptibly. A nod of understanding. But also one of sadness. Because he knows, I can tell, that I will never truly let him in.

He hurries to the window and pulls back the curtain. It's narrow and high, but I'm sure I can fit through. I take off the Green Lady's gown and throw on my own colourless skirts.

Will hesitates. "Perhaps I ought to come with you."

I shake my head, ignoring the knot in my throat. "No. You need to stay here. Make sure everyone else is safe." My voice catches.

He nods wordlessly. And he takes the cloth from the washstand, wiping the pale makeup of the Green Lady from my skin for the last time. His thumb brushes my cheek. At once there is everything and nothing to say.

I see it now; that magical, painless world Will led me into – that can never be reality. I've been through far too much for that. All the theatre in the world can't change what has already been.

Nor do I want it to.

Neither of us speak. This is the end; that much is clear.

People will talk of this night, of course. They will talk about me, the Green Lady of Castlemaine, and the way the people came for her. And perhaps when they do that, they will talk about Will's play too. Perhaps his name will be spoken around the colony; first as gossip, then later in theatre circles. Maybe by the crowds that file into Astley's Amphitheatre and cheer beneath that glittering chandelier.

I hope it desperately. I hope the Green Lady will help people remember his name. Hope my disgrace will give him back his career.

I kiss the edge of his lips for a long, still moment, and for a few seconds, the shouting at the door feels distant.

"Thank you," I murmur. "For everything."

He nods faintly.

I drag a stool to the window. Will offers me his hand to help me climb onto it. Ignoring the dull ache in my hip, I push on the jamb. Hot, fragrant air gusts through, blowing my loose hair back from my face.

"Be careful, Lucy," Will says finally. His fingers slide through mine as I gather my skirts and ease myself over the window frame.

I can't look back at him as I lower myself down onto the street.

CHAPTER TWENTY-TWO

I hurry to the cottage with my head down and my bonnet pulled low. The men are still inside the theatre and I'm able to slip unnoticed into the dark alleys behind the hall.

I rush towards the cottage. Try not to think of Will. Of all I've turned away from. All I've left behind.

I feel, somewhere deep, that I have made the right choice. Feel, in that same depth, my love for Tom. The desire I have to mend things between us.

Because he's the one tied inescapably to both my past and my future. He's the one I wanted most when I lay on the street with my blood running into the earth. And he's the one I'm thinking of now, as I hear shouted voices echo in the night. My need to get to him is overwhelming.

The cottage is lightless, curtains drawn over the windows.

Where is Tom? I expected him to be home. Needed him to be. He's out at one of the taverns, I tell myself. Tossing back liquor to drown the sight of me on stage in Will Browning's play.

Not far away, I can hear the angry voices of the townspeople. How long will it take them to realise I'm no longer at the theatre? How long will it take them to come after me?

I fumble in my pocket for my key and clatter the door open.

And I'm greeted with a revolver, pointing between my eyes.

A scream escapes me, the sound dying in my throat at the sight of my husband on the other end of the gun.

He lets out his breath. Lets the revolver fall. "Jesus, Luce. I thought you were someone else."

"I used my key…" I'm hardly breathing.

"I know. I'm sorry. I—" He grips my wrist and pulls me into the bedroom. Confusion and fear pour into me and I shake free of him. A single candle flickers on the nightstand, and in its rusty glow, I can see the cupboard has been emptied, its doors hanging open. Two bundled packs sit at the foot of the bed. My thoughts charge.

"What's happening?"

Tom stands with his back pressed to the closed bedroom door, fingers wrapped around the revolver. "Isn't this what you wanted? For us to leave?"

"Is this because of the men at the theatre?" I ask. "Because they haven't followed me. They—"

"What men at the theatre?"

I take a step back. Away from my husband. Away from his gun. "Tom? What's happening? You're scaring me."

He pulls back the curtain to peek outside, then turns back to me. Nods at the pack closest to the door. "Look inside."

I creep forward and unbuckle the pack. Tucked between Tom's shirts is a large coin pouch. I pull it out. It feels firm, heavy in my hand. My breath leaves me when I see the mass of coins inside. I look up at Tom with wide eyes.

"Leo and I found a nugget today. A big one. We took it to the bank this afternoon and split the money."

"You found…" My words fade. This was all Tom wanted. So why are we hidden away in near darkness? Why does he have a revolver in his hand? No part of this makes sense.

A violent thump on the door. And then another.

"Open the damn door, Earnshaw. I know you're there."

Constable Stone.

Is he here for me? Have the troopers sent him? Do they know of all the things Fred Buckley told me? I wish for my ignorance; wish I'd let Buckley disappear into opium smoke, nothing but a ghost.

Tom's knuckles whiten around the revolver. "Don't move," he murmurs. He steps out into the kitchen, closing the bedroom door silently behind him.

Another violent knock against the front door. And the sudden splintering of glass. Stone's footsteps thump in through the window.

I peer through the keyhole. See the two men facing each other on opposite sides of the table.

"Give me the money, Earnshaw. You and I had an arrangement."

Tom's voice is steel. "This was not part of it."

I have no time or space to make sense of these words. Because I see the pistol in Stone's hand, barrel to barrel with my husband's weapon. And just as there's no space for thinking, there's also no space for chance.

I tiptoe to the bed. Take the candlestick, a heavy makeshift weapon. I blow at the flame and the light vanishes, leaving me in a darkness thick with sound.

I edge towards the door on silent feet, skirting the inky shape of the pack full of coins. I understand, in all my confusion, that it's this Stone has come for. But nothing makes sense on either side of that knowledge.

"Get the hell out of here, Stone," Tom is saying.

"Do you really want to push me? You know I could have you in the cells for all you've done."

And maybe it's the horror of finding out what these words really mean that has me blowing through the bedroom door and swinging the candlestick into the back of Stone's head. He crumples forward against the table, then slides onto the floor. I hear a murmur of shock, and I can't tell if it comes from Tom or me.

I stare at my husband through the darkness, hand trembling around the weight of the candleholder. "What arrangement?"

He bends to pick up Stone's weapon. "Get your pack, Lucy. We need to leave."

I'm frozen in place. "What arrangement?"

Tom moves through the shadows towards me, and instinctively, I shuffle back, gripping the candleholder.

"We can't stay in the house," he says impatiently. "We have to get away from Stone while he's down." He glances at the motionless body. "Unless he's…"

Dread squeezes my chest. A thin line of blood snakes down past Stone's ear – but have I truly struck him hard enough to kill him? I reach a trembling hand down and touch his neck. Sigh with relief when I feel a steady pulse beneath my fingers. I have not become a killer.

"Get your pack," Tom says again. "I'll tell you everything. But not here."

My fear is fraying the edges of reality and I'm not sure how to react. Fear of Stone and the angry townspeople; and yes, perhaps, my fear of Tom. I shake that thought away before it comes too close. I can't fear my husband because where would that leave me?

But if I am not to fear him, I need answers. An explanation. And I need them now.

"I'm not going anywhere. Not until you tell me what's going on."

Tom glances desperately at the door, then at the constable's motionless body. Finally, he looks back at me. Rubs his eyes. "I've been working with Stone."

"Working with him? What do you mean?"

"Night fossicking. Thieving."

I stare at him. No, this isn't right. The pieces don't sit where they're supposed to. My husband isn't a thief. And when I caught Stone fossicking at Forest Creek, he was alone. Tom was home in bed.

No. The cottage was empty when I returned. I believed Tom had left the house to look for me. Had he been out there with Stone? Did we pass each other unseen while I was playing the ghost?

My stomach knots.

The night of Fred Buckley's burial; the night claims were raided at Moonlight Flat. I'd slept so deeply then I'd not have noticed if Tom slipped out of bed and...

I feel suddenly unmoored as the pieces fall into place. And they make sense, I realise. They make perfect, horrifying sense. Stone's visits to our cottage. Visits I believed centred around my witnessing his theft. They were not about me at all. He had come to speak to Tom.

Did Clyde suspect his involvement? Was that why they fought that day? Tom's anxiety over the thefts, I see with sickening clarity, was not because he feared his claim would be robbed. It was because he feared he might be caught.

Or perhaps he feared I would find out the truth.

I think of the look of pity Stone gave me when he came to the cottage after the shooting. Was it pity over all I didn't know?

My stomach turns over and over, and I take a step backwards, my spine pressing hard against the wall. My fingers grapple behind me, searching in vain for something to cling to. I stare up at my husband, so many questions knotting in my mind.

His eyes find mine. "Say something, Lucy."

But before I can find words, Stone's boot scrapes against the floorboards. Tom inhales sharply and grabs my hand. "We need to leave."

As he throws open the front door, a storm of angry voices flies into the hut. It's that drunken, wild chaos that engulfs this place on the nights of the possum hunts, or when someone strikes it rich and pulls the whole town into their celebrations. But tonight, I'm all too aware the chaos is my doing. Those men have marched from the theatre and whipped the streets up into madness. No doubt told everyone in earshot who was behind the Green Lady.

"A man at the theatre," I splutter. "His mother... I frightened her... playing the ghost. The men want me punished."

A groan comes from Stone, his fingers scratching the floorboards. Tom darts into the bedroom and grabs the coin pouch from the top of the pack. Then he snatches my hand again and pulls me out into the yard.

He leads me towards the tall wooden fence at the back of our property. "Reach for the top," he hisses. "I'll lift you over."

But before I can move, I hear Stone calling Tom's name. Inside the cottage, chairs scrape against the floorboards. The glass of the lamp shatters and the bedroom door thumps against the wall.

Tom pulls me down to hide behind the woodpile. Silently, he brings the revolver out of his pocket. He cocks the trigger and the click echoes in the darkness.

The back door opens with a creak and I press a hand over my mouth to silence my ragged breathing. I hear Stone's footsteps sighing against the dry grass. In the faint moonlight, Tom's knuckles tighten around the revolver.

I see now that I have underestimated Stone. He may be a pawn, but that has made him desperate. And I know the kind of madness desperation can drag you towards.

I feel my body tremble as Stone's footsteps cross the yard. Hear my pulse thundering in my ears. It's a fear of the mob. It's a fear of Stone. And it's a fear of the things my husband has done. And why.

The footsteps disappear. I hear the front door click closed.

Tom lets out his breath. "I think he's gone."

But the thought brings me no relief. Because Constable Stone has left our cottage with blood snaking down his neck. Is he going to the other troopers? Will he tell them of my attack? At best, the assault of a police officer will lead me to the cells. At worst, to the hangman.

Tom stands from behind the woodpile and peeks tentatively into the house. He looks back at me and nods. I stand, catching his arm before he steps back inside. I pull on his wrist, forcing him to look at me. "You were working with him. Why?"

He scrubs a hand over his moonlit face, and for a moment, I think he will refuse to speak. Then he says, "He caught me thieving from a tent one night. A few weeks after Elsie died. He told me he'd not arrest me if I gave him a cut of what I'd stolen."

I try to swallow, but my mouth is dry. "A few weeks after Elsie died? You've been doing this all this time?"

He nods faintly. "After that one time, Stone wanted more. He told me I was valuable to him. I knew which claims were unguarded. Which men were camped out there with their pistols loaded. I told him I wasn't interested. That that one time he'd caught me had been a mistake. But he said he'd arrest me if I didn't help him."

I let out my breath. All those nights I believed Tom out protecting his claim against thieves. All those nights I was sneaking around guarding my secrets, he had been keeping secrets himself. Not guarding his claim against thieves. Thieving to fill Stone's pockets.

"Stone found me on my way to the theatre tonight," says Tom. "Said he heard I found a nugget. Guess Leo couldn't keep his mouth shut. I told Stone I hadn't found a thing. He let me go, and I thought he believed me. But then he turned up at the cottage."

"Wanting money."

He nods. "He claimed we had a deal. I'd give him a cut and he'd keep me out of the lockup. But I'd only agreed to give him a cut of stolen goods. Nothing I found myself."

"Why?" I ask shakily. "That first time. Why did you do it, Tom? You're not a thief. You've never been that kind of man."

He sighs heavily. "I was desperate, Luce. I brought us out here and promised you the world, and couldn't find more than scraps. And every day I'd think of our child, and how I'd given her a home she couldn't survive in. Just once, I wanted to bring you something more than gold dust. Just once. I know it could never make up for what we lost, but…"

I swallow hard. Let my tears slide off my chin.

Tentatively, he touches my hand. "I'm sorry, Lucy. More than you could know. I'm sorry for all of it."

But what I feel is not anger. It's relief. Relief that I was not the only one so marooned by loss that I would throw my life upside down. Relief that Tom mourned our daughter as deeply as I did. Relief that I was not the only one to break.

I throw my arms around his neck, holding him close. I don't want to let go. Because this is how it ought to have been from the moment we buried our child on Pennyweight Flat; us together, leaning on one another. Because apart, we foundered and flailed and tore ourselves to pieces.

I brush my lips lightly against his; a tentative, testing thing. Tom's fingers dig into my hair to prevent me from pulling away. His kiss is fierce, possessive, and my body comes alive at the memory. Somehow, through his crimes, I have found my husband again.

"We'll go inside and get the packs," he says, his lips close to mine. "Then we'll get out this way. Over the fence. Where the mob won't find you. And then we're going to leave this place. Tonight."

But as I cling to him, fingers digging hard into his arms, that fleeting relief I felt slips away. Because I think of Fred Buckley, a living ghost in opium smoke. I think of the empty box we gathered around at the cemetery on Campbell's Hill. And I think of the body found on the road, with all his worldly goods tied to his back. Tom may be coerced by Constable Stone, but Stone's strings are being pulled from far above. By men who do not allow those caught in their net to slink away carrying their secrets.

And here we are, planning to leave Castlemaine with a pack full of gold.

I pull back, gripping Tom's forearms.

"You've no idea what you've gotten yourself into."

CHAPTER TWENTY-THREE

"This isn't just about Stone," I say. I'm pacing, pacing, dry grass crunching beneath my boots. Forgotten laundry flutters in the hot wind.

"What are you talking about?"

"He's being forced into this. The officers are forcing him to go out thieving and give them a cut of everything he takes. Everything *you* take. It's not just Stone that's corrupt, Tom. It's half the damn police in this town. Or all of them. I don't know. I—" I gulp down my breath as my words threaten to run away. "The officers are running the racket. There are other men just like you. Men they arrested for petty crimes who are being forced to do their bidding. Stone is under their control, just like you are."

Tom's lips part. "How do you know this?"

I blurt out everything; about finding Fred Buckley in the opium den, and all he told me about the troopers' racket. I see Tom's jaw tighten. See the look of faint disbelief in his eyes.

"The man who was murdered last night..." he begins.

"I think was being coerced by the police, just like you and Buckley. He had his pack on his back. He was clearly trying to leave. To escape the troopers."

"Men leave this place all the time. He was probably leaving for other goldfields—"

"So late at night?" I demand.

Tom falls silent. "Men like me and Buckley," he says finally, "we're just penniless diggers. Why would the troopers go to such lengths to stop us from leaving?"

"You said yourself – you're valuable to them. You know what's happening on the diggings. You know who's out guarding their claims. Besides," I swallow hard, "you know the police here are corrupt. They're not just going to let you walk away. Who knows who you might tell?"

I think about the officer at Clara's shop who knew my name. Did he know me because I'm Tom's wife? Is that why Stone recognised me so easily when I was playing the ghost? Have they been watching us? My stomach rolls at the thought.

"We have to assume the police know Stone is coercing you," I say. "And Stone knew you found gold today. So we have to assume the other troopers know that too."

"And you think they'll know I'm planning to escape tonight?"

"Maybe. I don't think it's a risk we can take."

Tom closes his eyes for a moment. His jaw ticks, shoulders rigid with tension. He puts his hands behind his head and begins to pace across the yard. Kicks at a log that's rolled loose from the woodpile and curses under his breath. "You ought to have gone with him. Browning. You ought to have taken what he was offering you."

His words strike me. "No." I see that more clearly than I ever have. That life of theatre and breakfast rooms and roast pigeon on gold-rimmed plates, that is not what I want. I want to escape in the night with my criminal of a husband. "No. I love you."

I stand on tiptoe and reach my arms around his neck. He holds me at the waist and presses his head to my shoulder. "Neither of us have done very well, have we."

I allow myself the briefest laugh. "No." My words are muffled by his hair. "We've not done very well at all."

Fists pound the front door, making me swallow down my smile. My chest tightens.

Tom takes the revolver from his pocket and strides into the house. Men's voices are flooding in through the broken window. Too angry, too jumbled to make out their words. But their meaning is all too clear. They want the Green Lady punished.

"Get the hell away from my house," Tom bellows through the locked door.

I fumble in the darkness for the matchbox, broken glass crunching under my boots. "The window." The words escape on my breath. The men outside have found the broken pane. One of them leaps up, cat-like, his boots crunching against the window frame. Tom shoves him backwards. Fires a warning shot over the man's shoulder.

I drop the matchbox and push in front of Tom. "I'm sorry," I plead. "I never meant to do anyone harm." My stomach rolls at the size of the crowd. The handful of men who came after me at the theatre has become a heaving throng of faces; some laughing, some jeering, some flashing with anger like the man trying to climb through the window. The son of the woman I frightened in the alley.

He gives a cold laugh. "Sorry?" He looks between the other men. "She's sorry, she says."

"Let me see your mother," I say, desperate. Desperate for him to leave, to take this crowd with him, to get the hell away from our window before Tom puts a bullet in his chest.

"You ain't getting nowhere near my mother," the man snaps. "But I'm sure the rest of town would enjoy a public shaming. They do like a spectacle."

What his shaming will entail, I can't imagine. But I see that, if the town's eyes are on me – if the *troopers'* eyes are on me – perhaps they will not be on my husband. Perhaps he can escape. Perhaps—

Tom scoops me into him with one steely arm, the revolver pointed between the man's eyes. "Leave," he says firmly.

"You can get away," I argue. "The troopers—"

"Don't be mad." His voice leaves no room for argument.

But I say, "I deserve it, Tom. All of it."

"You can't go out there." His voice is low. "You can't let anyone see you. Especially not the troopers. If Stone told them you struck him…"

He doesn't need to finish. The cells or the hangman. Then the town will really have their spectacle.

Tom's arm tightens around me for a moment, then he turns to the mob. "Get the hell out of here." He gestures with the revolver. "Believe me, I've nothing to lose by using this." I hear his voice strain on the last words. And I look up to catch a glimpse of dark blue uniforms through the broken glass.

Police.

Are they here to prevent Tom from leaving? Or to punish me for my attack on Constable Stone? Either way, it doesn't matter. We can't let them find us.

Tom and I rush through the back door. I hear broken glass crunch as the men from the theatre haul themselves through the window, but I don't turn to look. We scramble for the fence, trampling the vegetable plot beneath our feet.

I hear the troopers calling Tom's name. And we run.

CHAPTER TWENTY-FOUR

We are in a back alley, another alley, and then out onto the main street. I stop running, knowing it will draw attention. Head down, my hand gripping Tom's, we walk; past the dispensary, past the bank. Directionless, but too afraid to stop moving. At any moment we could turn a corner and find one of the troopers, or one of the men from the theatre.

Instinctively, wordlessly, we find the darkest, least-inhabited streets and alleys. I'm walking the same route I took when I played the ghost.

We pass the road that leads out of town to the north. The urge to take it, to leave Castlemaine behind us, is almost overwhelming. But the troopers were waiting for Buckley on the road out of town. They were waiting for the man who was killed yesterday. And if they've heard about Tom's success in the claim today, there is every chance they'll be waiting for him too.

"We'll go out to the diggings," Tom says, his voice close to my ear. "Hide ourselves in the bush outside the claims."

I think of that dark mile of road that leads to Forest Creek, lonely at this time of night. I'm afraid to walk it with so many people after us. But stay in Castlemaine and we're rats in a trap.

Tom puts a hand to my shoulder, ushering me back down the street we've just come from. We'll make our way to the edge of town, and out towards the diggings.

As we reach the end of the street, I see them, flashes of blue – two troopers striding in our direction. Instinctively, I run. Run with no thought of where I'm going. And it's not until I pass the boarding house that I realise Tom is no longer behind me.

I whirl around, panicked. Hiss his name. There are men behind me now, a dark shadow of uncountable bodies. The old woman's son is at the front of the throng. He and another man grab me; one at each of my arms.

They drag me back towards town and I swallow my screams. Fight my urge to call for Tom. I can't draw attention. Not to him. And not to myself. I can't let the troopers find us.

The men drag me into Murphy's Hotel. I glimpse the alley where the Green Lady was first sighted, sparking Will to write his play. And I think fleetingly of the men gathering there the night of the ball, seeing a ghost in the fluttering curtains.

Murphy's is crowded. Men shove up against the bar, their drunken voices a tangle of sound. The air is thick with pipe smoke, the floorboards strewn with earth.

"Here she is," shouts the man, his grip vice-like on my arm. "Your Green Lady."

At once, all eyes are on me. I scan the crowd, desperate for an ally.

A barrage of voices is at me, words I can barely make out. Some are angry, some are wild. Other men just laugh, enjoying this spectacle of the Green Lady's demise.

My captor uses his foot to drag a stool towards him. "Stand up here," he hisses. "Let them see you."

"I'm sorry. No. Please." But there's little I can do as they lift me onto the stool. The wound in my hip groans in protest.

"You're soft in the head, Lucy Earnshaw," shouts one man, and I think he may be right.

From high on the stool, I see Clara slipping into the tavern. At the sight of me, trapped in the jeering crowd, her mouth opens in horror. She tries to push her way towards me, but the men shove her back violently. I see an older man shout at her with venom in his eyes, but his words are lost beneath the noise of a crowd turning wild. She mouths something to me, something I can't make out, then she darts back out the door again, leaving me alone with the mob.

She will get help, I tell myself, but the thought brings me little peace.

Because if she brings help, it will be in the form of the troopers, and I'll be thrown in the cells for my assault on Constable Stone.

I see sudden movement in the corner of my eye and I pitch forward as something strikes me above the ear. Glass explodes against the wall, and in the same second, I feel the burn of it. One of the men catches me before I tumble off the stool. I feel a thin trail of blood run down my cheek.

"That's enough, Bobby," I hear someone call across the tavern. "You've had your fun. Let her go."

The man, Bobby, snorts, and shoves me off the stool. I pitch forward onto my knees, pain rattling through me.

Hands pull at my hair, yanking my head back. Drinks are poured over me, soaking my clothes and hair. I feel thrown objects strike me, unseen as I cover my head to shield myself. I let out a cry as someone kicks at my arms.

I'm an outlet for them, I realise suddenly. Their despair, their exhaustion, their frustration; each of these men is like my husband – so desperate for the earth to give up that treasure that might change their lives. And just like Tom, none of them have found it. Instead, they've been stolen from, been betrayed by their troopers and been haunted by a woman who had nowhere else to stow her grief. In a twisted way, as my heart hammers with fear, I understand their anger. This is not rage at me. It's rage at this brutal, blazing life they chose because they thought it would lead to happiness. It's rage at their empty claims and their aching bodies and their children buried on Pennyweight Flat. I'm just a place to put that anger. And this childish game I played, in an attempt to escape it all; I see now that perhaps I might just die for it.

I smell the smoke first. Acrid and tarnished, wafting under the doors of the tavern.

Is my frightened mind just imagining it?

No, because now people are starting to talk. Starting to flood to the windows. Starting to grow bored of me.

I stay for a moment on my hands and knees. Unplaceable pain pulses through my body and sounds are distorted in my ears. Can I make it to the door without anyone noticing? Doubtful.

But then someone is pulling me to my feet.

"This way," Clara says, dragging me with her as she races for the door. Her presence bolsters my courage, and I rush out of the tavern on shaky legs.

Outside, the air is thick and smoky. I rub my stinging eyes and feel the blood smear along my cheek.

"A fire…" I begin.

"Yes," says Clara. "I know."

And I see it then. See, through the curtain of smoke, that it's Clara's shop the flames are pouring out of.

I can't hold back a shout of despair. Of wild, consuming anger. "The bastards!" I cry. "Who…? What happened?"

"It doesn't matter. Those dogs in the tavern are distracted now. You're safe."

And the possibility swings at me. I snatch her arm, wide-eyed, hoping desperately that I'm wrong.

Those dogs in the tavern are distracted now.

This fire in her shop; it was all her doing. And she has done it for me.

A spectacle of her own creation.

"Clara, no. How could you?"

"You were in danger, Lucy. Who knows how far those men were going to go?"

"The shop was your dream."

"The shop was a target," she says bitterly. "If I'm going to make something of myself, I need to go somewhere no one knows my past. Somewhere no one knows the things I had to do to get here." She stares ahead, the firelight making her dark eyes glitter. I feel the heat against my cheek. "It's no stretch to believe someone would want to burn this place to the ground. I'll collect the insurance money and try again in Melbourne. Somewhere I won't draw quite so much attention."

I don't speak, because what can be said? It's far too late to change her mind.

The doors to Murphy's Hotel have been thrown open, and people are spilling into the street, most with glasses still in hand. Horses are rattling down the road, pulling the fire pump behind them. A group of children runs excitedly beside the cart.

Clara gives my wrist a squeeze. "Go back to your cottage. Hide yourself away for a while. The mob will forget about you soon enough."

But of course, I can't go back. Can't hide away. I need to find Tom. And somehow, we need to leave Castlemaine.

There they are in their neat blue uniforms; the town's troopers, some marching towards the burning building, others working the fire pump. And I see that Clara has done more than distract the men from their ghost hunt. She has also drawn the attention of the police. Perhaps the roads out of town are not being guarded tonight.

Clara watches as a mannequin in the window is swallowed by flames. A roar comes from the front of the shop sending sparks shooting above the roof line. In the copper light of the fire, I see a tear slide down her cheek. She pushes it away quickly.

"Well," she says, too brightly, "now I've just to convince them I'm heartbroken about my loss. It's a good thing I'm a fine actress." We both pretend there is no waver in her voice.

I enfold her hand in mine. "I have to leave Castlemaine," I tell her. "Tonight."

"What? Why? Because of Will? And Tom?"

"No." Tom will be waiting for me at the diggings, I tell myself. Waiting by the claim for me to find him. And then we'll disappear into the bush like we planned. And maybe, with the troopers gathered at the fire pump, maybe we'll have a chance to escape. "Best you don't know the reason," I tell Clara, thinking of Fred Buckley's warning.

I pull her into my arms. Hold her tightly. Hope I convey the ocean of gratitude I feel towards her. I take a step back, meeting her eyes. I have no thought of whether I will see her again. No thought of what shape my life will take once I run towards the diggings. But the life Tom and I have made here needs to be destroyed.

"Be safe," says Clara. And away I rush, into the dark, sweaty and smoke-stained and bleeding.

CHAPTER TWENTY-FIVE

Tom is not at the claim.

I should have known he wouldn't be here; if Stone were to come searching for him, this is one of the first places he would look.

I stand for a moment beside the shaft, staring down into the inky earth. I imagine Tom pulling a nugget from the mud, imagine it glittering within the cradle.

Not far away, the night is lit with campfires, and the laughter of the men around them feels strangely calming after the chaos in town. I can still see the silver column of smoke rising from Clara's shop.

In spite of the heat, the sight of it chills me. Makes me desperate to find Tom, and to leave these diggings behind. When I leave this place, it will be for the unknown. But that doesn't make me want to stay.

I start to walk, ignoring the groans and aches of my battered body. I feel, instinctively, that I know where to find my husband.

The cemetery is almost lightless. A thin moonglow struggles through the trees, catching the motionless stares of the wooden dolls guarding the graves. I shiver in the silence. I have never been here at night before.

But I am not alone. Tom is crouched beside that tiny, unmarked circle of stones I have come to know all too well. His eyes are cast downward, but he has a distant look about him. I can't tell if his thoughts are in the present or the past.

For a moment, I just stand there and watch him. A ghost in the moonlight. But as I shift my weight, the ground beneath me crackles, and he turns. Rushes towards me.

"Where have you been? I thought you ran ahead, and when you weren't at the house, I thought maybe you might come here—" He stops, eyes pulling towards the dried blood on my cheek. At the liquor-scented hair clumped against my neck. "You've been hurt."

I shake my head. "It's nothing." What happened to me doesn't matter. Not anymore. "The troopers. They're in town. A fire…" I can't bring myself to say more. Clara's sacrifice stings too much.

"All of them?" Tom asks.

"I don't know. But we have to take a chance. If we keep away from the roads…" The journey ahead is overwhelming. A night of picking our way through the darkness, hoping we remain unseen.

Tom puts his hands to my shoulders, follows their curves with his fingers. "When the sun comes up, we'll find the Melbourne road. It's always busy. Someone will take us into town."

The confidence in his voice, whether forced or not, goes some way to easing my fears.

"And then?" I ask.

"And then, whatever we want, Luce."

I don't let that future take shape in my mind. Not yet. When we're out of this settlement, when the buildings of Melbourne are cutting the sky, then I'll let myself think of what might come next. Right now, it feels too far away.

I take Tom's hand, and in our clumsy, wordless way, we walk back to Elsie's grave. I kneel beside it and run a hand over the smooth, weather-worn stones. Tom crouches beside me.

"When was the last time you were here?" I ask.

"I don't come here," he says. "Ever. Not since I stopped coming with you." He clears his throat. "I don't think of her as being here. I can't. It's not how I want to remember her."

I wrap both my arms around one of his and rest my cheek against his broad shoulder.

I don't want to think of Elsie as being here either, not anymore. We are to leave this place forever, and I need to believe we will carry our daughter with us.

As I kneel there pressed against Tom, I wonder what Elsie would think of us; her foolish, flawed parents. Neither of us have handled our grief with grace, but perhaps if we learn to lean on each other, we might find our way back to decency.

Just as I must believe we can make it through that dark forest and emerge onto the Melbourne road at dawn, I must believe we can forgive and move forward.

"Are we terrible people?" I ask.

"Yes," says Tom. "The most dreadful. The very worst." But there's a smile on his lips and light in his eyes. I kiss my fingers and touch Elsie's grave. Tears blur my vision, but they're not entirely tears of grief. There's hope in there too, and things I can't quite find a name for. And then we stand together and walk into the dark, in the hope it might lead us to a place far less haunted.

HISTORICAL NOTE

The legend of Springheeled Jack entered English folklore in the 1830s. According to stories, he was a terrifying entity with clawed hands and glowing eyes, and the ability to leap to enormous heights. Sightings of the creature, which were later proven to be the work of ghost hoaxers, were recorded across London, the Midlands, and as far north as Scotland. Springheeled Jack featured in several Penny Dreadful stories (also known as Penny Bloods) from the mid-19th century onwards.

But it took some time for the practice of ghost hoaxing to reach the Australian colonies. "Playing the ghost" became popular in the goldfields of Victoria from the late 1860s, and continued into the early 20th century. As it was important for the story that playing the ghost was as yet a little-known pastime, Lucy and co – ghost-hoaxing in Castlemaine of 1857 – are somewhat ahead of their time.

The goldfields, thanks to its vast mix of cultures and superstitions – and the extraordinarily high death rate – provided a fertile breeding ground for belief in the supernatural. The spiritualism movement gained momentum across the colony, while ghost hoaxing was hugely popular in the "golden triangle" of Ballarat, Bendigo and Castlemaine. As the years progressed, ghost hoaxers would dress themselves in increasingly elaborate costumes, often involving highly toxic phosphorescent paint. While some hoaxers simply slipped away unpunished, others faced fines, jail time, or beatings at the hands of the public. A number of ghost hoaxers were even sent into the care of the nearby Ararat Lunatic Asylum.

Theatre was another important part of life on the diggings, with few acts more memorable than Lola Montez's spider dance, performed across the goldfields of both California and Victoria. Appearing on stage in risqué knee-length skirts, Lola's act involved repeatedly touching her legs as though trying to get a spider out from within her skirts – incensing half the audience and enchanting the other. Today, theatres still stand on the sites of both Astley's Amphitheatre in Melbourne and Castlemaine's Theatre Royal, although there is little remaining of either original building. Astley's Amphitheatre was rebuilt in 1886 as the iconic Princess Theatre – and is now home to one of Australia's most enduring ghost stories…

ABOUT THE AUTHOR

Johanna Craven is an Australian-born author, composer, pianist and terrible folk fiddler. She currently divides her time between London and Melbourne. Her more questionable hobbies include ghost hunting, meditative dance and pretending to be a competitor on *The Amazing Race* when travelling.

Find out more at www.johannacraven.com.

Printed in Great Britain
by Amazon